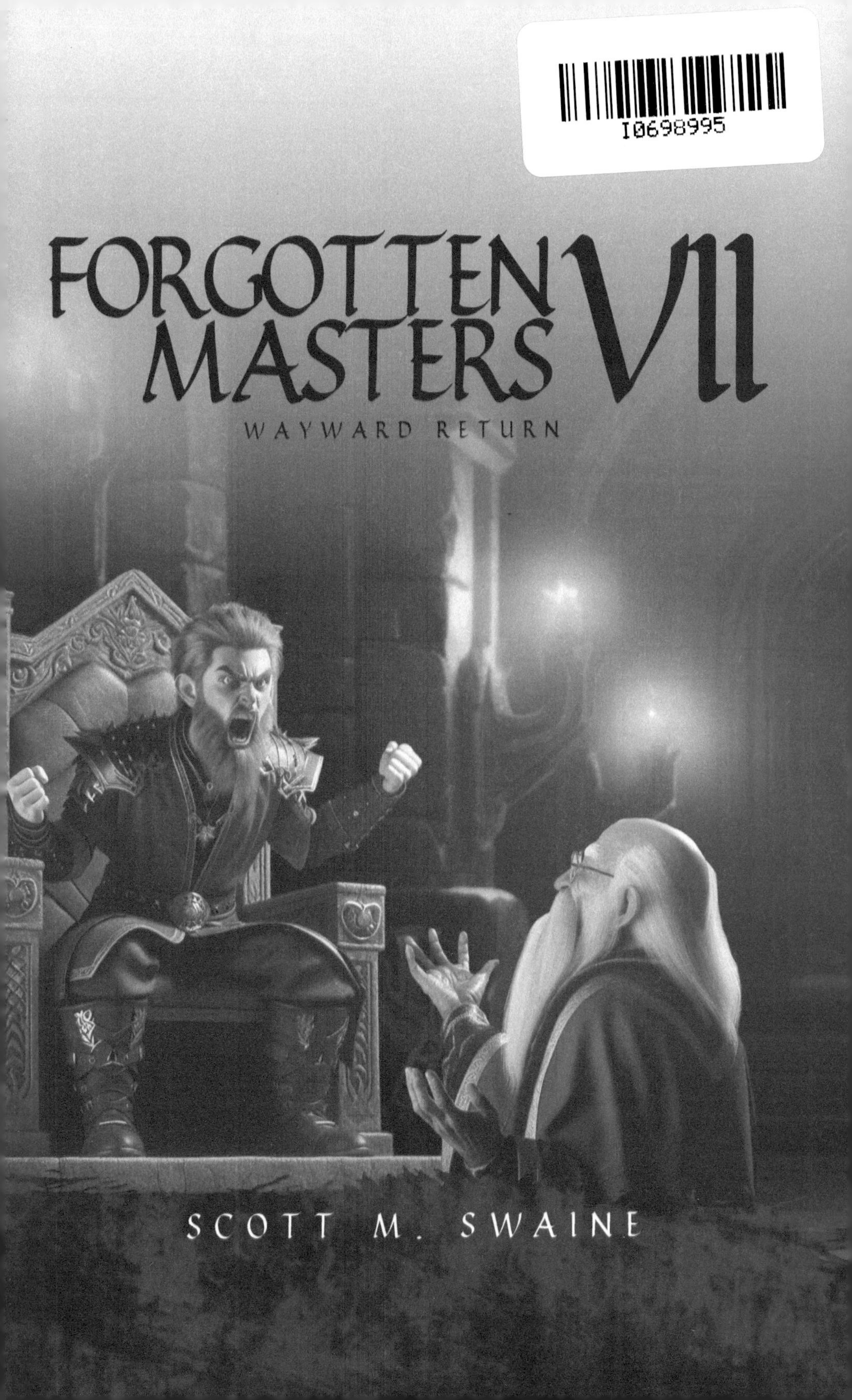

FORGOTTEN MASTERS VII

WAYWARD RETURN

SCOTT M. SWAINE

Primix Publishing
East Brunswick Office Evolution
1 Tower Center Boulevard, Ste 1510
East Brunswick, NJ 08816
www.primixpublishing.com
Phone: 1-800-538-5788

This is a work of fiction. Names, characters, places, and incidents either are the product of the author's imagination or are used fictitiously, and any resemblance to any persons, living or dead, is entirely coincidental.

Published by Primix Publishing: 12/11/2024

ISBN: 979-8-89194-154-0(sc)
ISBN: 979-8-89194-259-2(hc)
ISBN: 979-8-89194-155-7(e)

Library of Congress Control Number: 2024907437

Because of the dynamic nature of the Internet, any web addresses or links contained in this book may have changed since publication and may no longer be valid. The views expressed in this work are solely those of the author and do not necessarily reflect the views of the publisher, and the publisher hereby disclaims any responsibility for them.

CONTENTS

Chapter 1

ACQUISITION

In a conference room, inside the guildhall of the Order of Tyr, the military body serving the Kingdom of Tae'Eladar, Lord Thaelyn was hosting a meeting between his people and a small group of foreign military officers. This strange body of visitors might normally be the last thing you would expect to see around here. Not only are they foreign to this world, but they were generally considered the enemy in a quasi-wartime engagement between the two sides…even though the other side was completely unaware of it.

Fleet Commander Lajivi Kriv'tik, and his two officers, Lieutenant Ayene Ti'van and Lieutenant Ganaal Az'krun, three members of a recently captured Suuden-Aryku military mining base, were meeting with Thaelyn and his military advisor, General Gabarleine, along with two others of the same racial species, but a different faction, the Daanen-Aryku. One was High Commander Kailen Nazég, who had been working alongside Thaelyn during the course of this war since they first met on another world that was under siege at the time. The other was his younger sister, but now an officer in Thaelyn's military, Lieutenant Kaliya Nazég.

"Commander!" Ayene asserts as she argues with her superior. "I swear to you, all my life, I listened to the Marshal and his promises, and the Council and their instructions that we should help Sargeras with his problems, and now you're telling me it was all a lie? In all the nether-space!" she shrieks. "If I was ready to quit the military before this, I think you can consider my resignation signed, sealed, and delivered!"

"Ayene, calm down a moment," he soothes. "It probably couldn't be helped, especially if you consider he's been directing our lives for much longer than simply the time he 'officially' arrived on Azgarén."

"Officially? How do you define 'officially'? It was just under ten millennia ago when he and Sargeras arrived on Azgarén with this story of insurgents. The Council essentially gave our entire society over to them, polluting our bodies with these horrible parasites," she glances down at the seed entity that was infecting her back. "And these damnable chips of his," she thumps a finger to the right side of her head where she recently had an interface unit attached. "And now, here we are, sitting at the table with those same people he once claimed to be the ones who stole something from Sargeras, but in fact, it's the MARSHAL who is the criminal here, and on multiple levels, not the least of which is modifying our species. And then we have Sargeras, the last surviving member of a dead race of...gods?" she winces.

"Lieutenant," Thaelyn interjects calmly. "I can fully understand your distress. There are many who would likely feel as you do, but Darumon is developing a rather substantial reputation for his misinformation and propaganda. No doubt, he has been using it on your people for a very long period of time. This seems to be a common practice for him, and likely as a means of getting you to do any work for him."

"Yeah, getting us to do any work, like drugging a bunch of dwarves to do slave labor, and literally working them to death. And then, building a super doomsday weapon for him to kill off these other gods. And let us not forget Ytani and his tail-swinging mania, thinking himself to be nearly a god with that nether-wild skill of his. I'm truly fascinated, as well as repulsed over THAT story! The infamous Tav'ageen Anomaly, the alien parasitic scourge that was causing such a fantastic panic attack that it frightened the horns off nearly every citizen in the world. Suddenly, they forgot we were a long-time space faring race with hundreds of millennia of technology to our credit, and instead chose to take the advice of a superior alien mind to use the WORST invention we ever came up with…the nefarious An'gamu Seed. Unbelievable!"

Thaelyn raised his brow at the extended rant. He glances briefly at the General, then Kailen and Kaliya, and finally Commander Kriv'tik.

"Commander, when I look at this, and compare to the Med-tech as we were in our original meeting, and the reactions she was having, is this common in your species over there?"

"Your Lordship," he chuckles. "Our people are all under the influence of the Suppressor chip, so you're not going to see much in the way of emotions at all. But I can recall from my youth, before all this happened, yeah, our women do sometimes carry a lot of passion," he smiles gently as he glances back at Ayene.

"Yeah," she relents. "We sometimes do have loud reactions and vivid tempers. My apologies, Your Lordship. I guess we're lucky our men have a lot of patience with us. But still, I think I'm justified on at least some of this. After all, look at me!" she directs at her disfigured body for the seed entity. "I hate this thing with a passion, and I'm sure I'm not alone. I did not want it, but at my second centennial, it was pushed at me as part of that insane Council mandate. I'm sure it was no different with that chip when I was a girl at four decades."

"Four decades?" Kailen wonders.

"Yes, Commander Nazég, this is the OTHER hideous mandate we have to live under. It's supposed to be to counter that alien parasite thing that was allegedly targeting those early children. And then we have that military bug. I was working in law enforcement and civil security before this, part of the city offices in C.P. Then, one day, I see a flier from Central Command looking for recruits for a high-security project directly in the service of the Marshal, and I thought to myself, wow! Here is a chance for me to serve a really important role in something. Instead, I got a new slave chip stuck in my brain, and I'm assigned to a mining base where we drug and enslave the local population to do our work. And worse is to have that young kid demanding us to raise our tails whenever he gets the urge."

"And I can see you have quite a potent attitude on these matters," Thaelyn notes. "Well, we should not let this go to waste. If these issues are so disturbing for you, I would invite you to join our efforts. Such ambition as this can be useful to see a job done."

"Me?" she winces. "I mean…well, you would actually hire me, even after all this screaming?"

"Lieutenant, I am one who likes a good challenge on occasion, and you look like a fine one. And we Celestials are known not to throw people away. Instead, we choose to teach and guide you, and help you find a better purpose for yourself."

"In all the nether-space, if that doesn't twist the horns, to go work for the enemy. Well, I don't want to say no, especially after all you people have been telling us about those two. But I think I need a little time to settle myself. I'm still trying to recover from HER," she points assertively at Kaliya, "breaking into my room, throwing something at me that immobilized my body, and then telling me she's part of a military law enforcement thing, and we were all basically under arrest. Yeah, that's a fine hello."

"Hey," Kaliya retorts playfully. "At least I took the time to talk. I could've simply grabbed you, slapped a stun on you, then hauled you away by the hooves."

"Yeah, I suppose I should be thankful for that much. But I'm still trying to figure out how you did it. What was that thing you hit me with? I couldn't move a muscle, and you were across the room from me."

"It's…magic!" she smiles and flutters her fingers.

"Uh huh… Well, next time, maybe you can just knock."

"Lieutenant," Thaelyn resumes. "We have a situation here that needs to be approached very carefully. Darumon and Sargeras are enemies to just about everything out there, and Darumon has demonstrated this on multiple occasions, some of these in a rather obscene manner. We are always open to find new friends and allies, especially if they can serve a role to bring us closer to our goals, and your people would be very valuable in this regard to help us help the rest of your world. So, if you truly want to serve a valuable role of any kind, I might encourage you to consider ours. Perhaps we could join forces together on a few smaller ventures until you feel more at ease. We do things differently here, as compared to what you might be familiar with back home. And as I said to the Commander during our initial meeting, we would recommend some education and adjustment to our methods, so we can find a productive union together as we move forward."

"All right, I can understand this. I'm not against the idea, and I do want to see that…thing removed from our home, along with his…master…ugh…" she grimaces. "To think of why he pushed these seeds at us, as if I wasn't disgusted enough over them in the first place. And then, how he continued to push them at us, even to go so far as to tell us to destroy our native environment as further justification. I simply cannot believe how far he went, and then the Council on top of things to let it happen."

"I'd like to take a close look at that Council of yours," Kaliya muses. "I want to know what sort of people we have over there running the place."

"Good luck to that. All I know of them these days is they spend all their time in their chambers deliberating something, presumably Darumon's great wisdom he supposedly gave them. But if that's not what he's really here for…"

"Yeah, what ARE they doing in there, unless they're hiding, and only come out when he wants them to pass some new mandate or something."

"Very well then," Thaelyn concludes. "Let us bring ourselves into a form of agreement where we can collaborate for a common cause. It is clear to each of us that you on Azgarén were heavily victimized by those creatures. I will offer my help to see them removed, and perhaps even to assist in whatever is within my power to correct the damage left behind."

"No offence, Your Lordship," Ayene accedes. "But from what I'm seeing of this place, um…" she glances around the room, which gave the impression of a neat, but otherwise primitive, by comparison, social culture. "Do you actually think you can correct for the magnitude of damage he caused us? We have a massive level of environmental decay in our world, and then we have these chips and seeds. I suppose the chips we can take care of ourselves, with a bit of surgical restoration, but the seeds…" she frowns deeply as she again examines her body.

"What I think I can say, Lieutenant, is not to underestimate our abilities based on how you see the world around you. Our methods stem from a very different foundation of knowledge base. While I will admit, we may not have, in this world, quite the level of technological achievement as yours, at least not in the modern day, we do have a few things that can compensate. And our people are quite ingenious and very progressive. We will find our answers, and do so as expediently as possible."

"All right, fine, I guess I can't ask for anything more than that. And I will thank you deeply for even this much."

"Very good. Now, our first objective should be to find you a place of temporary residence. Our world, when considering our native architectural designs, is not exactly appropriate to accommodate people of such generous proportions as yours," he smiles delicately.

"Yeah," she glances up at the low ceiling for her native height. "I don't recall ever suffering from claustrophobia, but if I stay in here much longer, I'm afraid I might. Do you have any alternatives?"

"There are a few possibilities ahead of us, but I need to investigate my options first. Meanwhile, all I can do is ask for you to be patient and take a few deep breaths, maybe also go for an occasional walk, and enjoy the sights. We will see to it as best we can."

✦

A group of dwarves had been busy in recent times excavating a region of their underground home that collapsed due to the heavy bombardment of the outside world by the Suuden-Aryku military. This was part of Darumon's efforts to clean out any resistance to his illegal mining activity in their world.

"Hold there, lads! What be this now, ay?" shouts one of the dwarven miners.

"I might be a-thinkin' it nay be any simple stone fallen from the roof," asserts another.

"Aye! Methinks we found the door, thanks be t' the All-Father. Clear the way; give us t' see what we have here."

The dwarves working their way through the upper town district of Glimmerheim had been hard at work digging through the rubble that collapsed from the roof of the cavern just inside the doors. They finally punched through to find a small section of the front doors, and now they were clearing away the dirt and small stone debris to gain better access to it. As more of the fallen material was removed, they could see the doors more completely. They represented a massive feature set into the wall, ornately carved with old dwarven rune craft and gold accenting, though much of it was dirty, and some was damaged due to the collapse.

They continued removing the dirt and rocks, but it soon became apparent there was a problem. The damage to the surrounding rocks had caused the doors to twist and break away from their hinges, turning them awkwardly within the fractured shards of the old framework.

"This nay be a good sign, lads," the foreman states. "We'll need t' pull them down if we want t' be a-goin' outside."

"Aye, but I can see through the cracks, an' we nay be even close t' that. There be even more rubble beyond."

"What in the name of the Dwarffather happened t' the mountain?" shouts another worker. "It looks as if the whole side came down on us."

"Mayhap it did, Brothers," infers the foreman. "So, we need t' be a-diggin' our way through if we hope t' know the truth out there."

The dwarves continued their work, clearing out the loose debris and throwing hooks and chains around the door fragment. Some brought in hammers and adamantium chisels to cut through the broken hinges. A long string of workers then gathered up on the tow line to pull down one of the doors. It creaked as loose material broke away from the surrounding wall and upper framework.

"Carefully, lads," cautions the foreman. "We don'na want t' bring down the rest of it on our heads."

They heaved on the lines, and the door began to topple slowly, dislodging even more debris from the frame and finally crashing to the ground. It made a resounding boom which echoed through the cavern, shaking dirt loose from the wall and exposing a curious opening just behind leading into a neatly carved tunnel.

"What be that there?" calls one of the workers.

"Easy lads, take care," the foreman warns. "That nay be a natural burrow."

They carefully moved around for a better look at the strange cavity cut into the dirt and rock outside the door. It seemed to form a large dome-like antechamber, with a side passage leading into the distance. Several of them crept forward to examine the bizarre material forming the walls. It appeared as stone, but it was continuous and smooth.

"This nay be any stone I ever did see afore!" calls one worker. "Nay a chisel or pick mark on it. It looks like one solid block, carved out smooth."

The foreman steps in closer to make an inspection. He could see light shining through from a nearby lantern.

"This here belongs t' someone, an' nay any of us!"

As he stood there trying to interpret what he was looking at, an elderly voice echoes through the opening.

"Hello! Be there anyone about?"

The dwarves inside the doorway all glance around at each other, silently asking themselves if this might be friend or foe calling through the opening. The foreman tenderly offers a response.

"Ye out there!" he shouts. "Who ye be a-hollerin'?"

"Oi! Be there folks still alive in there? Great All-Father! We've been a-sittin' out here for a good long while, scratchin' our backsides an' wonderin' if anyone still be a-livin' in the old city. Ye have half the mountain come down on ye out here, an' there nay be a way inside. We cut part of it away, only t' come up on yer doors. But the doors be stuck tight, an' with more rubble on the inside. We thought all was lost."

An aged man in tattered clothing strolls confidently into view of the door. The meeting was engineered by Thaelyn's people as part of a larger plan to introduce the people of Glimmerheim to the truth of their world outside, as opposed to the wild stories their local Thane had been dishing out when Darumon's occupation began. The outside excavation had stopped, once they found the door, to allow the people inside to make the final step. As he came into view, the other dwarves watched him cautiously.

"Me name be Belrum Strongfoot. Mayhap ye'll let me come through?"

"Aye, I s'pose," affirms the foreman. "But what be this ye say about the mountain? It came down on us? How?"

"Oi, that be a long waggle of a tale, t' be sure. We have a camp out here we set up, those of us who still be alive, waitin' t' see if there be anyone diggin' through from the other side. But nay a soul ever came out this way."

"Nay a soul?"

"Aye, lad! How d' ye burrow yer way through a stuck door an' half the mountain, ay?"

"Well, aye," he chuckles weakly. "I s'pose that nay would make any sense. But tell me, Brother, what be the tale of the outside? Ye say, those of ye who still be alive. Be this because of the war?"

"War? What war? I nay be a-knowin' of any war in me lifetime. I be but a poor farmer's son, me'self. We used t' have land out in the old Sungold Fields, but that was yay long ago in me father's days, an' his afore him, when the land was still able t' grow anythin'. Nay anymore, though," he hangs his head solemnly.

The foreman stared at the elderly man, especially his clothes, which clearly betrayed a destitute condition. He then glanced at the other miners for their opinions.

Belrum was working off a script as part of his play to cautiously reveal certain precise details to the people in the city, since they had no idea who Darumon was, or any of his hidden exploits.

"But, friend Belrum, we have tales in here of a war with point-ears. What be the word on this with ye an' the others outside? Did they lay so much waste t' the land that now ye look like this?" he waves at the man's obvious poor attire.

"This?" he glances at his ragged apparel. "This nay be for anythin' like a war. An' point-ears, ye say? Oi, friend, that yay be a long while ago. This be a tale me father's father once told me as a wee babe! But it nay be a good one."

"Yer father's father!" the foreman shouts. "What about YE then? By the looks of yer clothes, ye look like ye came out of a war, yerself!"

"Mayhap so, but nay anythin' with sickly point-ears. Brother, everythin' out there be dead, with nay but a few of us still clingin' t' life by a thread. The land be a-dryin' up, such that nothin' can grow by now. Every city an' town was blasted t' the All-Father way back, well afore me own time. An' it was nay because of any sickly point-ears. Their tale ended barely a hand or two of years after it started. It was the pummelin', lad! That be what brought us down."

"Pummelin'?" the foreman wheezes. "What sort of pummelin'?"

"The kind that brought yer mountain down on ye," he thumbs outside the doors. "It came from the sky. We nay be a-knowin' how or why, but it laid everythin' t' waste out there. If ye still have a city down here, it may be the only one left by now."

The foreman drew back in shock at the depiction. He could barely envision the scene being described to him.

"But what about the men an' bricks we send out?" ushers one of the miners.

"Men an' bricks?" Belrum muses. "I nay be a-knowin' about any bricks. What kind d' ye mean?"

"Adamant, man! Only the finest fare we can make up for the war said t' be outside!"

"What?" he chuckles faintly. "Lad, I don'na know where ye get yer tales, but methinks bein' buried under the mountain closed ye off t' the real tales up here. But, aye, I d' recall seein' some men once. They were also haulin' up Adamant bricks in a mine t' the south of here. Some of us figure they must be from the city…there nay be anythin' else out there t' send men t' work. Although, how they got out there, I nay be a-knowin', what with yer doors bein' buried as they were."

"That other door," whispers another miner. "Back there in the room, the one goin' up."

"Aye," a third one grumbles. "An' the Thane with his wild tellin'!"

"Lads," Belrum continues. "Another thing. I don'na know who sent them or why, but they look t' be under some sort of a spell, we don'na know what kind. They nay speak a word, an' work without end haulin' up bricks day an' night. An' we once saw who picks up the bricks."

"Ye did?" the foreman ponders. "It be said in here there should be warriors out there pickin' them up. But ye say there nay be a war at all?"

"Aye, lad. These be a tall folk. An' they come an' go in a flyin' ship of some sort."

✦✦✦✦✦

Elder Vankkar and Elder Girhani, of the Daanen-Aryku Council, had arrived in the city of Rolsklinde, which was found on a world called Therinë, by special summons to meet with Thaelyn. It was the day after Thaelyn's interview with Commander Kriv'tik, and a decision had to be made on the disposition of the Suuden-Aryku defectors. But neither of the two Elders could be told directly about the raid on the Suuden-Aryku outpost, as it was still being kept a close military secret, for security's sake in case Darumon came to investigate what they were doing. Nevertheless, Thaelyn knew he had to come to some form of settlement on a few matters of politics, and this ultimately reflected on his future needs for these, and perhaps other defectors he might acquire.

"Your Lordship," Elder Vankkar bids politely. "I have not had much opportunity to meet with you personally. We had that one brief occasion for Kaliya's ceremony, but I have been trying to keep my distance due to your issues of security for this war."

"Indeed, this is an unfortunate affair," he responds. "If only for the unpredictability of Darumon and his antics."

"Still, since we have this opportunity, I think it would be appropriate for us to offer our deepest thanks for all you've done to help our people. I don't think we've ever encountered any other race during our long journey that did nearly as much for us as you have."

"Why thank you, Elder Vankkar, and I do hope we can share many more moments in the future together."

"And as for me," Elder Girhani adds. "I think I speak for both of us, and many others, that we are so very thankful to you for rescuing our children and providing us with the services of your society to regain some of our former prestige."

"Good friends, it is to my own honor that I offer this to you, to uphold my beliefs and the teachings of my people. I can do no less."

"We were somewhat surprised by your summons," Elder Vankkar confesses. "As I said, we have been trying to keep our distance due to your need for security."

"Yes, but on this occasion, I have a need to speak with you on matters of a more political nature, which is outside our concerns for the uncertainties of war. Would you wish to join me in the conference room where we can find better comfort?"

Thaelyn leads the two Daanen'kai Elders to a conference room on one side of the WIC building. They each take up seating and settle themselves for their conversation.

"This matter concerns our situation on Ruuki uy'Daan," Thaelyn begins. "Up until now, we have had a garrison in place to hold our position while we plan our future movements in our war effort. But it occurs to me that we need to make a more official proclamation as to the political sovereignty where that world is concerned."

"Yes, we have deliberated on this a few times, as well," Elder Vankkar suggests. "What position do you hold on it, if I may ask?"

"The world in question was originally home to the orcish

population. But since they have been relocated off-world, for their safety as well as ours, and in the absence of any other form of indigenous sentient life, by some definitions that world now falls into a category of neutral territory, available for colonization by another party, if desired."

"While I understand the designation, it doesn't settle well in my mind. It feels like we're stealing something."

"I understand, and I suppose I feel the same, but I must approach this from a technical, and perhaps also a tactical standpoint, and this is essentially where we are. As such, we must then reference your former home. Even though it is largely still in a state of disrepair, you once made your presence there, and I would still consider this to be your territory."

"I suspected you might suggest this," he sighs. "But at the same time, I do not have any strong desires to return there, and I believe many others feel the same at this time. We have been making good progress on building new homes here on Therinë. With your permission, and the hospitality of our new neighbors, perhaps with just a modest amount of land to build on, I think we would be very happy to remain here."

"Perhaps, but some of your younger population still seems to hold a certain association to their birthplace. Even your own daughter, to my understanding, feels this way."

"That may be true, but we lost too many people on that world. It holds a lot of bad memories for many of us. I know some people have made efforts to return to their old homes to see about recovering any surviving family mementos, but this is all we have left by now."

"The ghosts of your families haunt you, I suppose, and I cannot argue this, from the stories I have heard. But your society has lived a very nomadic lifestyle. Could this be becoming a habit by now?" he smiles.

"You may be right about that," he chuckles. "My hope is we might finally have a lasting home this time, but I've seen too many pass under me to be so easily convinced."

"Yes, it is most unfortunate that you had to suffer so many of those occasions. Then what is your position with Ruuki uy'Daan as a whole? That one city may bring old memories, but you still have the rest of that world."

"Your Lordship," Elder Girhani proposes. "Santari and I, as well as Master Velen, and many others, I'm sure, including Commander Nazég, believe we would rather relinquish our claim to that world. We should have plenty of space here, with your gracious consent, to rebuild our society. There are enough resources, and we feel there should be no problem for us to negotiate with you for trade if we have any special needs arise. If you can find a use for Ruuki uy'Daan, we feel it would likely serve better value to you than to us."

"Do you also recall my offer of a union, if that should ever suit your desires?"

"Yes," she grins. "And I already know there are many who would likely take you up on that offer. In fact, I'm beginning to wonder about my own position on the Council, if we should one day lose any kind of population to govern over."

"Well, you would be welcome amongst us, and you might even find great comfort along the way. But this is a choice that you must feel is appropriate. In the meantime, as to Ruuki uy'Daan, if this is your decision, then it might seem as though I am inheriting another world. Such a curious affair..." he sighs.

"Curious, Your Lordship?" she asks. "Why would you use that term here?"

"Our society, as I am sure you must know, is still in an early stage of development, and travel to other worlds was not something I would anticipate for quite some time to come. When I first engaged in this war, it was to protect my people on Tae'Eladar from the orcs. Then we arrived here to find more of our own kind, apparently immigrants from Tae'Eladar at some forgotten moment in history, and of course you. I suppose I can accept the inclusion of one more world, but two? This is surprising."

"Yes, I see what you mean by that. In fact, one might wonder if the term kingdom would even be appropriate under these conditions. It might be due for an upgrade to a higher standing," she grins.

"Oh, speak not too loudly, dear lady," he laughs. "For there are those about who may take the notion seriously..."

<hr>

Word had been spreading like wildfire through the streets of Glimmerheim. Belrum and his fellows from outside had delivered their message to the workers and others inside the city, and now the citizens were calling out for an explanation by the Thane as to his actions and causes.

On the steps of the Thane's Hall, the Chancellor tried to appease the people with a few carefully chosen words and promises to get to the bottom of it the next time the Thane made his appearance.

"An' what be the tale with him on the men an' bricks goin' up, Chancellor?" shouts one angry citizen. "For as long as any of us can remember, he be a-tellin' us they be t' serve up fare for the war!"

"Aye!" calls another one. "But the word from outside tells there nay has been a war for centuries! Instead, all the world was blasted by somethin' big an' powerful from the sky just after the point-ears stopped floppin' on t' the ground through their portals."

"What was the tale about those men, anyway?" yells one more protester. "They were sent out from the feast, but sent t' work in mines, nay t' forge anythin' for the warriors? An' where be all the cities he said were a-burnin'? The tale now tells they be nay more than big holes in the ground from all the blastin'!"

"An' the men workin' in the mines," shouts the first one again. "They be under some sort of spell where they nay even know if a man lays a hard one t' the jaw. An' then he said there be some strange new folk rompin' 'round an' pickin' up our bricks!"

"Good people, please!" cries the Chancellor. "I hear ye an' I feel for ye. These tales be as much a sorrow t' me own ears as they be t' yers. I can'na tell ye anythin' right now because the Thane nay be inside today. He don'na come out till he feels it t' be time, an' I can'na change that. But I'll be a-bringin' this up t' him the next time he calls for me, ye can be sure of it! An' I'll d' me best t' get the answers ye need. There be a lot of holes in these tales, an' we all need t' know the truth of it. I'll ask ye t' go back t' yer work now an' try t' d' your best t' keep this fine city of ours t' its good name."

The Chancellor offers a polite wave to send the people on their way while he struggles to pass through the crowd back to his office down the lane. When he enters through the door, he finds he has a visitor waiting for him inside. He looks back through the door again and closes it to offer privacy.

"Aye lass, what d' ye have for me today?" he asks.

Eiki had been watching from a distance as the mob stood in front of the Thane's Hall protesting the new revelations brought in from outside. Her mission today was to meet with the Chancellor with new instructions.

"Chancellor, me friends outside delivered new word today," she declares. "We have another task now, an' this be an important one, but also a hard one. I fear I have t' lay it on yer shoulders, since ye'll be the one t' deliver it."

"This job of mine be a-gettin' harder each day. What be it this time?"

"Mayhap ye'll like it this time, as it will be the last time ye'll have t' listen t' that wailin' wild man ever again. As ye know, they took that base over our heads a few days ago, so there will nay be another Suuden-Aryku at our back door. But this nay be the end of it, an' we still need t' be a-watchin' if that leader of theirs comes sniffin' up our backsides."

"Aye, an' I don'na know if I care t' see the result of that."

"Right ye be, but now we need t' be a-bringin' down the Thane, or whatever he be on the real side of it."

"Did I hear it said that he be another of the Suuden-Aryku?"

"Aye, 'tis true that, but a special sort who can change his shape t' look like a dwarf. But I nay be a-knowin' the exact time for it. Me friends will pass the word, an' I'll pass it t' ye. They say he may pop in one more time t' check on the mines for our last word of the veins runnin' out. If he does, ye'll let him know the veins are growin' mighty thin, with mayhap one or more runnin' out by now. This will put a wee bit of a sweat on his brow, for sure!"

"Aye now!" he chuckles. "But I nay be a-wantin' t' hear his yowlin' for that part."

"Mayhap, but at least this time, ye'll know it be WE who be a-playin' the game, nay him by now."

"Aye, this here be a good thing."

"But this here be our plan. Ye an' I both know he be the same one t' be a-tellin' us these tales since the beginnin', but we need t' be a-makin' him admit t' it somehow, or else t' foul up his stories so grandly, that it nay make any true sense t' a thinkin' man. Then, ye can bring it out in the open t' the people. This will tie him in t' all the tales outside an' the people will lose faith in him. We need this afore the folk up top can finish with him."

"An' how long for that?"

"They say he tends t' make a quick showin' in his Hall t' rage at ye now an' then, an' a final one afore his folk pick up the bricks the same day. They think this will come 'round in a few days' time. So, he'll call for ye, rage at ye for the usual fare, but this time ye'll turn on him with these new tales, givin' up a good show an' askin' why they nay be t' fittin' together right, confoundin' him with his own wild tellin', an' leadin' him t' give ye what ye need t' bring him out of his cover. Can ye d' this?"

The Chancellor sighs heavily, but offers a modest grin.

"Aye, lass… Mayhap I can think of a few good tales t' spin his way. He nay be a good leader, I can tell ye that, an' his favor t' ragin' makes him easy t' rouse up. If I can get him burnin' hot enough, mayhap I can get him t' lose his way with his words."

"Aye an' good. Ye know, if it helps any," she considers briefly. "Aye, this might prime the pot for ye. Ye've got all this rousin' outside. Mayhap we can use it if we can get a few shouts risin' up when he's in his Hall one time. If we can arrange a protest goin' 'round in circles out front, the noise will echo inside there. Then, ye can speak of the people gettin' restless over such things as, oh, how he ne'er once asked how we be a-farin' down here for food an' such. Ye know, for so many wearin' rags by now, an' with bellies only half full. An', oh! Here be a fine one. Ye know how Adamant be a precious thing t' us, such that for all the tradin' he was s'posed t' be a-makin' up top, how we ought t' be a-livin' a good life down here."

"Aye! There ye have a fine one."

"An' of course, the men an' bricks goin' up t' serve anythin', an' how this war has been a-ragin' for so long, but Adamant should run longer than this if it be forged by a proper smith for a proper weapon. What be they a-fightin' with, or be they simply rebuildin' all those burnt cities with our bricks? This fool nay even seems t' know what Adamant be about," she giggles. "Mayhap we should give him a few words for it, just t' let him know how much of a fool he be t' try foolin' our folk who know better."

"Oh, Eiki," he smiles gently. "Ye be a darlin' with yer words. Aye, if I see him afore this runs out, I'll give him a wee bit."

"Good, an' I'll pass the word for the timin' when they get ready for the final run."

✦✦✦✦✦

It was the beginning of the week, and Thaelyn and his officers were gathering in a conference room inside the guildhall. It was time for a much-anticipated meeting with Adalon regarding Darumon's weapon, among other things. As the members arrived, they were joined by Commander Kriv'tik and his two Lieutenants, as they once asked to participate in this affair for their own information. As they all assembled, the Commander approached for a few words.

"Your Lordship," he begins. "I realize we have a language barrier here, so if someone could offer a few translations to help my team understand what is being said..."

"Naturally, Commander," Thaelyn nods. "And this is not the first time for us when dealing with so many foreign associates. Perhaps one of the Daanen-Aryku can help."

"Good. I am very interested to know how you might proceed with that weapon. It worries me for the potential danger it holds."

"You are not the only one. Adalon called on us some time ago to prepare this meeting, and I am sure we are all very interested in what she has to say about it."

They gathered their attendance in the conference room, which in this case was a large room with high ceilings. The Suuden-Aryku and Daanen-Aryku members would feel more at ease in this room, being able to stand up fully in a two-story design. They were joined by Aerlie, the General, Kaliya, Kailen and Ankhia, Padriyl, Chief Technician Lapäli, and Professor Cogswoggle. As the Commander and his people entered the room, they gawked at the wide variety of people and races represented.

"In all the nether-space, Commander," Ayene whispers. "How many different societies live on this one world?"

They all took up space at the large conference table and settled in.

"I would like to bring this meeting into order," Thaelyn announces. "For the benefit of our guests, at least for now, we will use their language. Commander Kriv'tik, Lieutenant Ti'van, and Lieutenant Az'krun, this is my wife and Queen, Lady Aerlie," he begins directing around the room. "You already know the General, as well as Kaliya and our own High Commander. Next is Med-tech Ankhia Tad'vaal, with a temper comparable to the young Lieutenant here," he winks at Ayene. "Lieutenant Padriyl Lapäli, Chief Technician Tanjhira Lapäli, and our own Professor Cogswoggle."

"Am I developing a reputation here?" Ayene offers with a tender smile.

"If you are," Ankhia muses. "It can't be a good one, if it involves me," she smiles back.

"Yeah, but seriously, you have so many varied races represented here. How did this happen?"

"Other than for the Daanen-Aryku," Thaelyn asserts. "The rest are either the result of the Sarrukh seeding our world with the human population, meaning such as the General here, or the rest being immigrants from other places. The Gnomes and the Elves," he points to the Professor and to Aerlie as examples, "both came from a world we refer to in our history as Feyri. The elves involve multiple clans, each with different features, where Aerlie and hers are rather unique for their wings."

"And you tend to…um…intermingle?"

"Indeed, this can occur on occasion with certain members," he smiles. "Humans and elves, for example…"

"How interesting. I'm trying to imagine what sort of offspring you might have."

"Aerlie and I have not gone as far as that yet, but others have, and we give them the name of half-elves. They carry features attributing to both sides."

"Um…" Ankhia poses. "It would seem we're alone so far…so, what do we talk about until Adalon comes along?"

"I suppose, since we have the Commander here, we could spend a moment to talk about what we can do for them, such as for accommodations. We understand our native architecture does not provide proper comfort to your proportions, but then we are not accustomed to those who stand taller than our usual ceiling height. But Ruuki uy'Daan makes a good alternative for us, since the housing, some of which was previously refurbished by the refugees there, can give us a starting point. I will be assigning work crews to finish the process, and perhaps the Commander and his people can offer a hand here and there as needed."

"What will you have us do to offer our service to you?" he asks.

"For the immediate term, establishing a foundation would be useful. I think working to build a colony setting would be more productive than a mining base to build a weapon. We can treat you as a foreign body we can interact with for trade, in order to establish a functioning economy, and to provide goods to support you. If we should ever find an opportunity to…liberate…any more people, having this functioning base would be valuable to give them space for themselves."

"This is reasonable."

"There is some industry that could be useful, and I think to expedite a few of our operations, we should involve a bit of our native technology to jump us ahead a bit. For instance, I am aware they have a fusion reactor over there, although currently in an inoperable condition. But if we can refurbish it, we should be able to provide you with sufficient power for the rest."

"We'll need fuel for that. We have a reactor in our base, and we had regular shipments of fuel coming in for it. Would you redirect this to Ruuki uy'Daan?"

"This may be one solution, but we are still using that base, so the existing reactor will require it as well. Rather, this is one of those avenues where we may need to provide our own solution."

"Uh oh…" Kaliya grins. "Watch out people. I hear the sound of many horns dropping," she giggles.

Thaelyn halts his statement briefly to raise his brow at her before continuing.

"Right. Well, overall, I think it might be necessary to pursue this direction, since it fits so nicely with our manners."

"Why am I starting to feel my horns sag," the Commander wonders. "Regardless of her statement."

"We have a technology to construct fuel cells using hydrogen as a fuel input. This is a form of hybrid technology for us here, where part of it would follow your classic physical sciences, and the other part our arcanic studies. We use a special generator device to create hydrogen as needed from the flows and feed this directly into the fuel cell. This provides what is essentially a perpetual feed without the need for external supplies."

"What?!" Ayene screeches. "I may not be a physics professor, but that shouldn't be possible!"

"Ooh look!" the Professor giggles. "A girlish rant. I'm so happy."

"Yes, Professor," Thaelyn smiles. "If you wish to hear more of those, I think you are following the wrong female."

"Oh, please," Tanjhira begs. "He's bad enough chasing after just one of us."

"Anyway, if to ramp this up sufficiently, I think we can supply a reactor. And then, from there, it is just a matter of maintenance."

"This I need to see," Ayene muses. "A perpetual supply resulting in free and unlimited energy."

"This sounds a lot like setting up a new base of operations," the Commander suggests. "But if we have to refurbish a half-destroyed city, can you provide us with anything to help get us going?"

"Keeping in mind our technology differs from yours in multiple ways," Thaelyn advises. "So, you will need time to acclimatize yourselves. Along the way, I would highly recommend you take courses in our language to make things easier. These courses are freely available in our academies here. One primary goal would be a hub station for our Gateway network, which functions much like your conveyors, but here for personal travel."

"A conveyor for personal travel?" Ayene muses. "Amazing. How do you use it?"

"We use these as a form of public transit here. Typically, the destination pointer, which in our modern day cycles on a rotating schedule, aligns with the endpoint, and you simply step through. This is most often for intracity or intercity use here within our planetary sphere. Lately, when speaking of our recent acquisition of Therinë, we are using a passenger vehicle, which in our case is one of our newer motorized examples, to carry people across, since you now have a tunnel to pass through, and it is a bit awkward for the casual traveler to do this so exposed and on foot."

"A motorized vehicle.... Are we speaking of something on wheels here?"

"Indeed, which should offer a rather curious mode of travel experience."

"Curious indeed! Interplanetary travel on wheels!"

"Our military might find cause to go by foot, if we find ourselves travelling to a tactical destination, but I would prefer our civilian population to use a more cultured method. This is a recent development for us, and in the absence of true space travel, this is the best we can offer for now, at least until our technology can catch up to the demands."

"So, this basically means, due to this war you are thrust into, you had to jump ahead of yourself a bit."

"Indeed, and I suspect we are not finished yet. Anyway, our hub stations usually sell tokens for intercity travel, but we also have local intracity nodes which tend to go as a public service."

"Fascinating, to travel from city to city by conveyor. Instantaneous transport..."

"And not just people," Kaliya adds. "But cargo and a mail service, too. Who needs ground transport anymore, except maybe for local transit?"

"In your case," Thaelyn continues. "It will likely only hold a limited number of destinations because we have an issue of security to deal with concerning the Daanen-Aryku Elder Council."

"Why is that?"

"Lieutenant," Ankhia explains. "We came to learn that Darumon was apparently riding along with us on our long journey and impersonating one of our Council Elders. This meant he was a major security threat, giving away our location to your delightful military so they could come along and blast us just for sitting on a planet trying to live our lives."

"Yeah, and I can see what he means by your temper. Welcome to the club," she smiles.

"I'm sorry, but we lost so many people along the way, it's tragic beyond measure. But we became concerned, during our time on Therinë, and after His Lordship realized this issue, that he could try returning to spy on us, if he should hold any interest in seeing what we're doing over here. This places our Council at risk as an information leak. So, we had to ask them to step down and stay out of our military affairs while we plan our return. They currently have no idea what we're doing or how close we are to returning home. They still think we're stuck on Therinë, or perhaps Ruuki uy'Daan, if you consider Kaliya's efforts. And they don't know about you."

"Got it, so keep away from them."

"Now, back to the city," Thaelyn resumes. "We have obvious concerns for the basic needs, like food and such, which will be attended to as needed. We are thinking of redirecting your supply deliveries from the base to you on Ruuki uy'Daan, as this might be more familiar than our own selections. But ultimately, I might suggest you try discovering some of our native foodstuffs, because eventually, I suspect once that base is gone, so too will be your native foods."

"Right."

"What about medical needs?" Lieutenant Az'krun asks. "What if any of us should become ill or take injury?"

"We have two options available for this," Aerlie offers. "Our medical profession is partly based on a scientific study, much like yours, and partly as the priesthood. Our priests perform part of our medical service here. As they conduct their worship, they can earn blessings of one kind or another from the Estelar which they can then apply as their healing service. Your surgery, for instance, was partly conducted by our people as well as Ankhia's. If it involves any sort of common injury or minor illness, a simple laying on of hands can take care of that instantly."

"That doesn't even sound realistic, but I'll take your word for it, if only for the interface being removed and the patch left behind being healed over already."

"Yes, we have already been in study of your anatomy, so cuts, abrasions, broken bones, these are easy for us. We also have a number of remedies based on our alchemy studies to provide curative solutions for illnesses of one kind or another. Although, I will admit, your biology, where infection and disease are concerned, might require us to expand our libraries a bit. This could easily relate in one way or another to your own pharmaceutical industry, although the formulas would be different. But if it involves anything especially technical, we always have Ankhia. I'm sure she can help from her side."

"Eventually," Thaelyn accedes. "We will establish some markets for you to choose from, but with such a low population count, it is more likely you will need to travel here, or maybe Rolsklinde, for most of your shopping needs."

"Shopping..." Ayene considers. "I'm sure we use a very different form of currency back home, and technically, I'm flat broke right now."

"Not to worry, we will put you to work with good employment

and good pay. And I suspect some of our own people will eventually migrate over there to take up some of the space. This will surely expand on the setting."

"Lieutenant," Aerlie begins. "How do you feel after your initial consultation with your Commander?"

"Very unsettled about many things," she concedes. "To learn that all my life I've been following the instruction of a monster that came to us simply to use us for whatever master plan he has in mind, is not only a shock, but very disappointing for what I hoped to accomplish in my life."

"I understand. I am sure you and others will probably feel this way, and this might create some traumas for you. I am studied in psychology, among other things, and I would be very happy to offer you consultation, if you need it, to help you adjust."

"I thank you. Maybe someday I'll take you up on that. One thing that intrigues me, and I'm still trying to figure this one out, is how that young velvet-horn over there," she glares playfully at Kaliya, "so expertly took us all captive. Granted, most were asleep, but her efficiency at infiltrating the base and taking even those people who were awake and on watch is a little scary. I had a chance to debrief a few of them, and they tell me something literally popped into view out of nowhere, and before they had time even to turn and look at it, they were on the ground."

"Yes, our magic is a powerful tool. So, be careful if you should ever call it mysticism," she smiles warmly.

"Lieutenant Nazég, I recall you speaking to me briefly before I guess you put me to sleep. I vaguely recall you waving a hand over my face, so I have no idea what you used on that occasion."

"A priest sleep chant," Kaliya replies. "It's one of those things we can order up from our worship of the Estelar."

"Oh wow…so you carried the power of a god with you in there? I'm going to stay away from you from now on," she chuckles. "But then, what did you do that caused me to freeze in my hoof steps? I couldn't move a muscle, and it frightened the wits out of me."

"I'm sorry, but you were packing a weapon and looked very

nervous. It was the quickest and easiest way to contain the situation. It's part of our magical studies here. I threw a Spell of Holding at you, which basically locks you in place until I can gain control of the situation."

"Magic…" she muses. "All right, but how does that work?"

"We were speaking to the Commander about it briefly during our interrogation. We have an energy layer here called the Dynamistic Flows. Such beings as the Estelar, and even Sargeras and his kind, would need this as a support layer. But beings like us can also learn to use it. It's a form of organic energy that follows the will of the mind. We need to take special training, and it involves a lot of practice and discipline to do it right."

"Like that time you blew up the mage training field?" Kailen chuckles.

Kaliya glares at him and playfully jabs an elbow into his side as she continues.

"Yeah, like that. My father and his science faction, which speaks of metaphysics, would be perfect for this study, as it describes invoking an alteration of our reality using the power of the mind. We imagine an outcome of some sort, according to some very precise studies, and this energy follows our direction to create this effect. As such, we can literally control the natural elements around us with our minds."

"This defies everything I thought I knew about science," Ayene reflects.

"Same for me, and our faction is the one that should be inventing this stuff! But then, I started studying it here, and now I'm a fairly advanced player in the field."

"Maybe one day I could take a look at it. I recall you also appeared out of thin air. How did you do that?"

"An invisibility cloak, another trick we can play."

"That makes you a little dangerous," she grins cautiously.

"Only a little?" she flashes her own. "Combine that with our stun strike, and you're going down before you know what hit you, very literally."

"And you were all dressed in black, like a shadow, which was also very eerie, but I suppose reasonable if you are running a covert operation. But what got to me most was you were so slim, as compared to us, and well…" she glances at her figure and the seed entity. "This created a surreal image that probably hit me harder than anything else. It was abnormal."

"Looks who's talking," Ankhia mutters softly. "Not that I wish to offend, but you took this thing without even arguing it, apparently."

"I did argue, but it's virtually pointless. It's a mandate by the Council. We don't really have a choice in it."

"Lieutenant…or can I just call you Ayene? Many of us are on a first-name basis around here for how we had to huddle together for our mutual survival."

"All right, fine by me. The Commander and I sometimes do this."

"Good, but Ayene, with respect, don't you have free minds and free opinions in that society? Can't you just say no?"

"No…" she chuckles at her own response. "I mean, not the sort of 'no' that I can say it at all, but that I can't say it to the Council. No one ever says no to the Council."

"Grace of the cu'Nar, have you all turned into robots over there, bowing down to them every time they call for it? And you talk about Ytani."

"Yes, I would agree. The All-Powerful Council of Elders, that our entire society seems to follow almost like they were a god entity."

"You know," Kaliya surmises. "That sounds like a good analogy. Especially if you look at the history of it. You can't protest or debate the issue? Is there no other authority you can appeal to, like a legal counsel or a court?"

"Not that I ever saw. I hold a law degree from my university studies, but not even that helps me. We just go in for our second centennial and make an appointment for it. It's just like with the Suppressor chip we receive on schedule at our fourth decade."

"Children?" Ankhia winces. "They stuff this inside your head as a child?"

"Yes, this is when they deem it to be the greatest threat to discover these symptoms, and therefore the need to cover it up."

"I don't believe it!"

"Well, if it means anything, I think most of us hate both of them. I was beautiful up until my second centennial, but all that changed after I got this," she points at her seed entity.

"All right, I'll back off. I'm just upset that so many people who claim themselves to be so sophisticated by so many means would stoop so low as to kiss under the tail of not only the Council and all their nonsense, but an alien creature and all his fantasies…and for what…a false promise of great wisdom?"

"It didn't apparently seem false at the time, but then I wasn't there."

"I might say that statement is subjective," Kaliya mutters.

"Oh, Kaliya?" Thaelyn wonders. "How would you describe this?"

"First and foremost, who is talking. The gluttonous Council? Yes! They were probably drooling over it. All those people kissing under their tails? Probably the same. But for anyone who still held that sophisticated mind, they might first ask for proof that he had it at all to make the offer. After all, we're not a religious society. We shouldn't be taking things…on faith," she smirks.

"Very clever, Kaliya," Aerlie nods.

"What if I could offer to help you?" Ankhia suggests.

"Help with what? Learning how not to kiss under someone's tail? I think I already got that lesson by now."

"No, that thing," she points at the seed entity.

Ayene follows Ankhia's direction, but the suggestion seemed empty in her mind.

"Uh-uh, Med-tech…" she shakes her head. "You can't help me with this. This is permanent. You can't just simply cut it off or lure it away with a piece of meat. If you try, it kills me. I might hate this thing with a passion, but I want to stay alive a little longer."

"No one ever tried to research a way to remove it?" she winces. "I mean, seriously, in all this time, and for all the other nonsense, like your industry polluting the place, and Darumon with all his talk of an evacuation, even AFTER he gave you what was effectively a solution to that Anomaly, and further to say this thing was supposed to be temporary…above everything else…you didn't even once think of trying to discontinue it or to remove those that were already there?"

"Well, um…"

"How long did it take for him to pollute Azgarén? How long did you have to wait for this miracle cure to the Anomaly, and how long until you people ever realized you're not going anywhere? And be careful…" she wags a finger at Ayene. "If any of your answers are, 'We didn't consider this…', I don't want to hear it!"

Ankhia huffs and folds her arms as Ayene considers if she wants to reply at all.

The Professor anxiously leaned on the table as he watched the show.

"This is more fun than a night at the theater," he beams in delight. "But if I may offer a few words. From what we know of Darumon and his manners, he likely did create a rather complex situation, and a lot of rhetoric to dilute their ambitions to solve these problems. If we look back on Therinë, he held a tight layer of control over what people think, where none of them really knew what the other side was doing. They are told the world is at war, but no one is fighting. The orcs may make occasional hits on the Night Elves, but this is the nature of orcs. The Suuden-Aryku hit the Daanen-Aryku, but this is Darumon playing his games. All this might be enough to remind them there are bad things out there, along with the stories of the Flame Elves, and so we have the concept of war. The human city never gets hit, but they do have those implants making trouble for them."

"Implants?" Ayene wonders.

"Yes, your Marshal Darumon, when he was playing the Governor of Rolsklinde, called upon your medical industry, it would seem, to apply what the Daanen-Aryku call Belvik Spores into medical implants and used this to falsify a type of plague. And then he had the local priesthood claiming a holy cause to fight their oppressors by using a blessing of their gods to protect them from this same plague. In reality, they were secretly inserting these implants, and the Spores were designed to destroy brain tissue."

"Ew!" she screeches. "That monster! That's at least as bad, or worse than anything he ever did to us."

"And they were never permitted to question it, even after four hundred years of this blessing not showing any true results. They still died from it. The people were so deluded to believe what they were told, because they were made to think their authority figures held supreme power to make these decisions, and you simply don't argue it."

"And so, we have the Council back home, and everyone bowing down to them, because they can do no wrong...ever! In all the nether-space, I'm sorry to be a part of that society now."

"I don't blame you, Ayene," Ankhia shakes her head. "In a lot of ways, we were doing the same with our own Council, at least until we began to realize these same failures. But to think he can actually do this in the first place."

"Indeed," Thaelyn nods. "He must hold a very rigid control mechanism to restrict the interchange of knowledge. He invokes this panic, and probably keeps it that way, telling everyone it is only temporary, and given their lethargic manners to begin with, they might go centuries before ever thinking with their right minds of why they are waiting so long for it, but not before he refreshes the idea with something else."

"And this is probably because he bred it into us for our ridiculously long lifespans."

"You know," Ayene muses. "You people use that term a lot, and you use it in multiple directions of context."

"Yes, Ayene, it's both a good thing and a bad thing, depending on how you apply it. But anyway, back to your problem with that thing crawling up your back. I'm not talking about simply cutting it off. I know how to kill those things, despite any of YOU not thinking with your horns turned the right way for it."

Ayene glared at her for the seemingly ludicrous suggestion.

"Kill it? How do you kill something like this?" she urges. "To simply try would also kill the host. No offence, Med-tech, but WE invented it. The ARC back home owns the patents on it, and not even THEY know how to kill it. It's not made to be killed. It's made to attach itself to you and stay there until YOU die."

Kaliya chuckles as she listens to the tirade.

"Are these more of the same who are told how…any day now…you'll be leaving home, so don't waste your time thinking about anything else?" she snickers.

Ayene glares at the perky young officer, but the wording certainly did hit a mark.

"Who is this ARC, by the way?" Ankhia asks. "I've heard that name a few times by now."

Ayene sighs before replying.

"It's a large medical research laboratory and manufacturing facility on the outskirts of C.P. called the Ark'ravan Research Center, or ARC for short. They make all sorts of medical tools, analysis equipment, pharmaceuticals, and other things, including these seeds," she thumbs at her back. "They're also a large global distributor to a lot of clinics and medical labs."

"That sounds like a megacorporation entity," Aerlie reflects.

"Yeah, you could call it that. Everyone back home knows the name ARC."

"And so," Ankhia continues. "They made this horrid little parasite, but never once tried suggesting a way to reverse the process? These are scientists, I suppose, at least for the medical faction, right?"

"Yes, but don't ask me why they never tried it…or maybe they did but were unsuccessful. All I can say for sure is it's a government mandate, so I guess researching a counteragent just isn't going to happen unless you have government support for it."

"Who actually runs your medical industry, your government or someone who actually cares about the health of the people?"

"Ankhia, the science factions don't do anything UNLESS they get a grant, or some other instruction by the Council. Remember, they're a god entity."

"Naturally, I should've thought about that before."

"I think that's your answer," Kaliya offers. "If Darumon is involved, I might say they were denied even to try. He WANTS these things, so why would he authorize their removal if he's the one who invented them in the first place."

"Yeah, good point," Ankhia affirms. "So, it's more likely they are being denied the opportunity."

"Denied the opportunity?" Ayene wheezes. "So, there may actually be a way, but that villainous beast won't let us have it? Ooh!" she screams.

"And therefore, since I'm not governed by your heretical Council or Darumon, I used one of his little death toys as my own weapon, and I found a way to remove them safely."

"You did?" she whines. "But using what? And where did you get a test subject to try it on?"

"Oh, that…yes," she coughs subtly. "Your wonderful benefactor, with all his superior wisdom and desires to uplift your society, weaponized those things once and used them as a terrorist device on our people on Ruuki uy'Daan."

Ayene was stunned briefly. She turned stiffly to gaze at the Commander and Lieutenant Az'krun, neither of whom could look her in the eyes, as they too were dazed by the suggestion. She began whimpering, which escalated to a wail, and finally a boisterous shriek as she grabbed her horns and doubled over on the table.

"What has he done to us!" she shouts. "How many atrocities can one creature commit?"

"This one is apparently capable of a lot," Ankhia relents as she reaches over to lay a hand on Ayene's shoulder. "He is known, to us at least, to have used several death toys so far, or at least this is how we might describe them. And by the sound of it, he's using this ARC of yours as his design and production team. We intercepted one of his special deliveries on Therinë, and it had the ARC logo on it."

"All right, so you're saying the ARC is a puppet organization under him, like everything else. How typical! It's no wonder no one researches anything. Unless he needs it for himself, he simply doesn't order it."

"And this further reinforces the idea that he wants us to have this," Commander Kriv'tik admits. "Regardless of our personal feelings on the matter."

"And all simply to support his master," Lieutenant Az'krun adds. "That's his primary purpose in life, aside from taking his revenge."

Ankhia continues, "That seed entity we had on Ruuki uy'Daan might not be a death toy exactly, but it sure could ruin your day. And then in Rolsklinde, he had those implants with the custom Belvik Spores, killing them in a rather disgusting manner."

"I swear!" Ayene asserts. "How does someone even imagine something like this?"

"Don't ask me. He also ordered a supply of a pharmaceutical called a Kajik'tav Serum, which according to our own records is for a rare lung disorder, and was going to feed it to a bunch of students that were making too much noise for his liking."

"Wonderful, what would that have done to them?"

"Killed them, of course. But not a simple death. My estimation here is it was in a severe overdose form. The normal dose for one of us was a fraction of the size he ordered, and he was hoping to give it to humans."

"Uh huh, and they're a fraction of our size," she considers as she glances at the General for an example. "So, we're speaking of many times an acceptable dose, as well as an alien species that might not react to it nicely in the first place."

"Right, and so, my analysis tells me this would likely invoke a severe constriction of the lungs resulting in a painful suffocation death."

"Sounds lovely. And for what reason? They just made a little too much noise over something?"

"Basically."

"All right, so the message here is you do NOT want to make noise, even if you DO want to argue something. He kills you for it. What about this other thing, the seed and your solution to it?"

"I took his Belvik Spores that eat neural tissue and reprogrammed them for the seed. It seems the seed has a rather unique genetic coding which is easily targeted by the Spore to attack and destroy it."

Ayene felt the blood rushing out of her face, as well as the air from her lungs. And although she wanted to scream, she had nothing left to do it with. She glanced at the Commander and the other Lieutenant, both of whom returned blank stares.

"Belvik Spores," Lieutenant Az'krun mutters. "Those darling little beauties."

"And it actually worked?" Ayene wheezes.

"Within acceptable parameters," Ankhia nods. "I was able to program it to the coding of this weaponized example, and we processed several hundred victims of his abuse. It attacked from the inside at the cellular level, digesting it bit by bit, and essentially bypassing this reflex reaction."

Now Ayene fell to the table and hid her face, silently weeping.

"I would give anything for this," she whimpers.

Ankhia felt badly for the girl, so she reached an arm around to give the girl a comforting hug.

"I should probably admit, my solution worked for the one on Ruuki uy'Daan, but my studies of the one you people use has a different set of coding, so I would need to rework it. But in theory, I feel it should follow the same principle."

"How do you reprogram it? And where did you get the Spores? From those implants? This is all ARC again, I think."

"Yes, we have a large supply from Rolsklinde after we removed them from the city's population. But I'll admit, we don't have the means to produce them here."

"Then you need to go back to the ARC. I wonder if we can convince them to side with us somehow."

"That would be a good idea, if only to get them to STOP producing Darumon's death toys. But I would need to make a careful study of the original seed core. I used an example I found in some old ammo the orcs used, which was unspent."

"Orcs? Those creatures on Ruuki uy'Daan? Why did they have them?"

"Your people equipped them with rifles firing some marvelously advanced rocket-propelled projectiles at our people."

"Oh! Marvelously advanced, were they? Wow, Darumon doesn't spare any expense on this stuff!" she huffs sarcastically.

"Yeah. Kaliya found the specimens we needed, and I did my study. I would probably want to follow the same pattern here, as I feel it would give me the best results. I was using a cloned replicant as my test platform to demonstrate the procedure, infecting it with the core, then studying and testing my solution, before moving to a live subject."

"That sounds like an interesting, if also a complex procedure you developed. My apologies, Ankhia, for yelling at you. This is what happens when you spend your life listening to people who tell you they know what's best. But you need an unspent core for it?"

"This is how I did it last time, so I feel it's best to repeat the process. I needed to study the bio monitors to see how it was responding during the procedure."

"I see, and for this you probably need to visit the place that makes them. All right, this is something to look forward to. Thank you."

The conversation carried a few more topics to ease the tensions until the appointed time, when a tall figure sauntered into the room.

Kailen and the other Daanen-Aryku, with the exception of Kaliya, who had met her before, and Ayene and her fellows all gazed in wonder at the slender shape of the tall female in silver hues and catlike eyes.

"In all the nether-space," Ayene whispers. "Look at that one."

Adalon entered the room and made her way up to the conference table. The table was large and sat many chairs around it, although she was not interested in sitting. Instead, she arrived at the head of the table in an open area where one might give presentations, perhaps using a whiteboard on the wall.

"Adalon," Thaelyn announces. "We are very pleased to see you again."

"Indeed... And ssso am I. I sssee we have guesssts."

"Yes, the Commander and his officers expressed an interest in sharing our details for that weapon, so I felt it might be reasonable to include them. Although, they do not speak our language, so we might need someone to offer interpretation."

"It will not... Be necessssary. I can ssspeak... Their language..."

"Adalon," Kaliya wonders. "You can speak our language?"

"In my time... I have learned... Many thingsss. Thisss will not... Be a burden..."

She now prepares herself for a proper introduction, this time speaking the formal Suuden'kai language, which was the same for the Daanen-Aryku members.

"To those of you... Who do not know me... I am called... Adalon the ssSilver..."

"Is that Silver part actually necessary?" Ayene mumbles timidly.

"Indeed, it is. My kind are known... As Draconicsss... And we tend to identify... Oursselves... By our colorsss... As each holdsss... Different mannersss... And qualitiesss... In clossse asssociation... To our appearance..."

"All right, maybe someone can explain that to me later."

"I recall when Kaliya met with you once," Kailen reflects. "She described you as a type of saurian who stood as tall as a five-story office building."

"Huh?" Ayene blurts. "Commander Nazég...an office building?"

"He is correct..." Adalon replies. "Thisss form... Is a manifessstation... Avatar... We might sssometimes use... When we have a need... To interact... With sssuch beingsss... As yoursselves. It makesss the occasion... A little easier. Esssspecially... If we have a need... To enter inssside... Sssuch placesss as thisss..." she directs to the room around them.

"All right, suddenly, I think I don't really need to know the secrets of the universe."

"As to our businesss. We have two... Primary concernsss... We musssst contend with. The firssst being... Darumon'sss weapon. The sssecond being... The Dynamissstic Harvesssster..."

"A Dynamistic Harvester... What's that?"

"There are sssome sssocieties... Very advanced... Sssuch that they know... How to collect... And processss... The dynamisssstic flowsss… Directly… Without the need… To draw from a natural sssource. In our effortsss… To approach your home… We will need thisss… As our own methodsss… And technologiesss… Demand thisss application…"

"That hissing is going to put me to sleep soon," Ayene mumbles playfully.

"Therefore… We mussst borrow… From thisss knowledge… And create our own… Example. But thisss carriesss… A ssstipulation…"

"A stipulation?" Thaelyn wonders.

"Thisss representsss… A form of knowledge… Well above… Where thisss world is found… Presently. Therefore… We will permit oursselves… Thisss occasion… But only thisss occasion. Afterwardsss… It mussst be sssecured… Until the people… Are more appropriately… Elevated… To receive it naturally…"

"Ah, yes, of course."

"You must live according to some very strict rules around here," Ayene mentions.

"We do…" Adalon affirms. "And for good reason. The Child Racesss… Mussst learn… And grow… At their own rate. They might desire more… But to give thisss to them… Can cause great sssuffering. Perhapsss alssso… To corrupt them… To pervert them… And possssibly even… To cause them… To dessstroy themssselves…"

"Ouch. All right, I get it. And I suppose I have to admit, we already did this."

"You have indeed. But now we mussst… Correct thisss…"

"Adalon," Thaelyn inquires. "Where do we find this technology, and does it come preassembled, or is it something we will need to meet halfway on…knowing how you tend to do things," he grins.

"On thisss occasion… I will be generousss. But you will need… To perform… Sssome of the work. The Daanen-Aryku… And our own Professssor… Mussst work together… To sssolve thisss problem… As it involvesss… Asssspects of both. But I will provide for you… The initial designsss…"

Adalon now steps to one side and turns slightly to the space near her, where she then brings a hand up to her temple. The rest of the group studies her.

"Is she telepathic?" Kaliya mumbles softly.

The elegant female hovered this way for a bare moment, until the room began to glow with a surreal light.

"Powers behold," Thaelyn jerks forward in his chair. "Something is coming."

"Good or bad…" Ayene whines.

A brilliant column of light erupted into the room, penetrating through the building into the space adjacent to Adalon at the head of the room. A remarkably tall figure emerged out of it. Her form exceeded even that of the Suuden-Aryku or Daanen-Aryku. She was dressed in noble armor and displayed a radiant pair of large wings on her back.

Thaelyn and his people instantly stood up and bowed. Kaliya followed immediately after, then with Kailen and his people, and Ayene and hers.

"Dame Seraph," Thaelyn issues. "Good greetings to you."

"That's a seraph?" Kaliya whispers urgently. "Cu'Nar's Grace, my lessons didn't do them enough justice."

The majestic female stepped forward to make her introduction.

"I greet thee, Thaelyn, as I do thy guests. My name is Thaliel, chief headmistress of the seraphim attendants to Maker Kuroku."

"Great cu'Nar!" Kaliya gasps. "You work for her?"

"I do. Thou hast spent much time contemplating her mysteries, and thou hast come to many conclusions. But the Maker must keep her secrets until this ordeal with the Ancient One is fully resolved. Until that time, she hath given instruction to provide unto thee this gift to assist thee in the immediate performance of thy duty."

Ayene and the others gaped at the extraordinary glamour of the visitor's presentation and poise, as well as the formulation of her diction. Then Thaliel turned to reach into a side bag she was carrying and pulled out a large square-cut crystal that filled her palm. It radiated with light, and she set it down on the table for the others to study. She then waved a hand over it to bring up a holographic virtual image that floated in the air above. Except for Thaelyn and Aerlie, who held their previous experiences as Celestials, the rest of the group, especially the Daanen-Aryku and Suuden-Aryku members, gawked at the otherworldly device.

"Where is the power source for that thing?" the Chief Technician mumbles.

"Forget the power source," Ayene leans forward. "What is it and how is it creating a data display without a projector of any kind?"

"This artifact," Thaliel advises, "is a component of wisdom maintained by the Great Powers. It is known as a concept prism, and it represents a recording device to store and retrieve information for later dissemination. Within this device, thou wilt find the design schematics of a Dynamistic Harvester compatible with thine approximate degree of technological prestige."

"This looks like a lot of fun," the Professor giggles. "I can hardly wait to open it up with the lovely Tanjhira here and take a peek."

Ayene stares at the two of them.

"Is there something going on between you two that we should know about…or maybe I don't want to know about it," she grins.

"He's been like this ever since we first met," the Chief Technician relents. "It's apparently natural for them, so this is fair warning."

"Dame Thaliel," Thaelyn begins. "May I ask where this originally came from if it was designed to be compatible with our local capacity?"

"Unfortunately, I am not permitted to reveal this at the present moment, other than to say it originates from a society that once passed through a similar era."

"I see, very well, and so this is a donation to our cause. Good, we shall examine this carefully."

"I have a guess," Kaliya smirks. "It's probably the same people who gave us that ship, if she's playing consistent with things."

Thaliel remained silent, and simply smiled pleasantly at Kaliya for her input.

"Next would be the weapon, I suppose," Thaelyn resumes. "Adalon?"

"We mussst dissspose… Of the weapon… But at the sssame time…

We do not wish… To invoke… Sssuch cataclysmic devassstation… By sssimply detonating it… Where it sssits. Therefore… We have come… To the conclusion… That we should remove it… To sssuch a location… That it will not bring… Any noteworthy harm… To anything… In the sssurrounding region…"

"Is there no way to simply diffuse it?" Commander Kriv'tik asks.

"There is… But the methodsss require… Sssome elaborate technologiesss… To decompresss the energiesss. And we do not have thisss… Immediately available. Therefore… We mussst use… The more direct method…"

"And for this, how do we proceed?" Thaelyn wonders. "It is my interpretation this material is extremely volatile and dangerous to handle."

Adalon nods and turns once again to Thaliel.

"The Maker did once consult with Primus, and together they have determined a means to deliver this unto a destination focus within an ancient conglomerate body of a barren Prime domain that is long in a state of decay. The means will involve the application of a mecha-arcanic door assigned to a delivery endpoint just beyond the event horizon of a massive gravastar."

"A gravastar!" the Chief Technician blurts. "Grace of the cu'Nar, yeah, if you want to get rid of something bad, that'll do it!" she chuckles.

"Indeed!" she smiles. "This example is located far from any thriving Child cultures, and therefore should not invoke any hazards. However, the installation of the device will demand the involvement of the modrons to provide support, and for this, they will need transport. We are aware of a large transport vessel acquired from thy previous activities within the Prime domain thou dost give name of Therinë."

"Oh great!" Kaliya chuckles. "And do you want Marelle to fly it again?"

"If she wouldst be willing…" Thaliel grins.

"I was joking…but I guess you're not," she laughs. "All right, but last I heard, it had a lot of racks and trays inside. Should I assume we need to clean it out first?"

"This would indeed be desirable," she nods, "as the modrons and their devices will require the space."

"All right, we'll pass the word. How long before we need this?"

"Our scheduling must occur before the timing of thy need to dispose of the deviant Suuden'kai still located within the outpost. But we might also suggest, the sooner, the better, to secure our position."

"Got it."

"And I would offer... A final sssuggestion..." Adalon adds. "We will leave... One unit... Of the Agent... Affixed to a timed... Explosssive. I wish to leave... A messssage... For Darumon to find..."

"A message?" Thaelyn inquires.

"He will know of it... When he sssees it. The blassst radiusss... Of thisss one unit... Will ssspeak for itssself."

"Uh oh..." Kaliya moans. "Let me guess...someone stole his weapon, and this is a message saying they know what it is, right?"

"You are very clever... Tall One..."

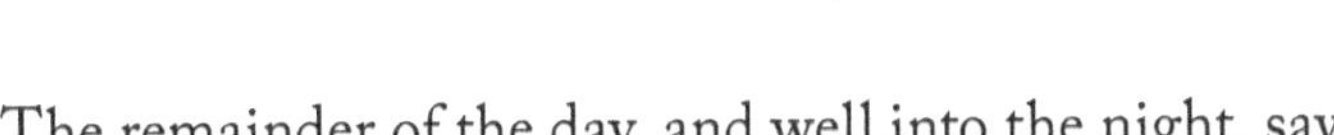

The remainder of the day, and well into the night, saw the cleaning out of the large cargo transport once discovered in front of the mine north of Rolsklinde. This is the same one that Marelle, Relissa, and Padriyl took their joyride in as they commandeered it away from the Suuden-Aryku troopers who were picking up the local stores of adamantium.

A small army of modrons had also arrived. These curious living machines represented a variety of shapes and sizes, and they were importing the components for their own brand of portal device. Once the transport had been stripped bare, they began to load up and pack their hardware, along with a crew to assemble the parts onsite.

Kaliya was tasked to oversee the operation from her side,

and Ayene was just arriving to see if she could join on behalf of Commander Kriv'tik.

"Lieutenant," Ayene calls. "My Commander has asked that I accompany you to assist in this operation, or at least to play the role of an observer so I can file a report later."

"Did Thaelyn have anything to say about this? Technically, this is our operation, so he's the one in command here."

"Yes, the two of them conferred on this, and I was given the assignment."

"All right, fine by me. So far, we're still loading up, but we're almost there."

"Who is the pilot, in this case?"

"Over there..." she points. "Marelle?" she calls out.

Marelle was also overseeing the packing of materials inside the vessel when Kaliya called her name. She turned and made a brisk strut over to join in.

"Yes Ma'am!" she stands at attention.

"Marelle, are you doing that again?" Kaliya grins. "Didn't I say last time that you don't need to play this game with me? We're friends, remember?"

"Yes, well, this is kind of an official duty, so I need to remember my practice."

"Uh huh, about that... I think I recall you also held the rank of Lieutenant."

"Well, yes, but that was back when I was in the Guard."

"All right, whatever, this is Lieutenant Ayene Ti'van."

"Good greetings to you, Lieutenant."

Ayene observed the interaction with growing curiosity. But as Marelle offered her greeting, she felt the need to return her own.

"And a pleasant greeting to you, as well... Um, so the two of you are friends?"

"Yeah, we've known each other for a few years now in the academy. We originally met through a mutual friend we have named Relissa, and my brother, Haran."

"Ah, then it sounds like you're a fairly close-knit group. We were like that, at least somewhat, in our base. Living and working in such close quarters for so long can really bring you together with your fellow staff members."

"Ayene…" Kaliya begins. "Or do you prefer I address you by your rank? Like Ankhia said, we tend to go on a first name basis around here."

"That's fine, I can accept that. I would usually address Lajivi by his rank, maybe because I have so much conditioning inside me, but he would sometimes use my name instead. It actually felt a little comforting in that environment, a bit like a family."

"Did you have any close friends in your base?"

"It's difficult to develop strong friendships while under the effect of the Suppressor chip, but I had a few close associations…one of those was Hena," she lowers her head.

Kaliya studied her a moment, and she quickly came to a conclusion.

"I'm going to make a wild guess here and say she was that last one to visit Ytani, right?"

"Yes. Ensign Hena Ka'zheen. She volunteered for this occasion. We were isolated in that base, and not permitted any real contact with Azgarén due to our situation of security for the mining operation. No one knows what we're doing out there. For instance, my communication with my parents was monitored to prevent any accidental, or intentional, release of critical details. I could say hello, I'm fine, and I'm just working my job, but without saying what my job actually was or where I was located. In fact, I doubt anyone on Azgarén even knew we found a new universe out there."

"I believe the Commander said that once. And, oh! I can hear the horns flying already if that should ever leak out on the news wires."

"Yes, I'm sure it would cause the sensation of the millennium," she chuckles ironically.

"Well, maybe we could develop a few friendships here, since I suspect we might be working together for the foreseeable future. Would you like that?"

Ayene considered the prospect as she glanced at the two people in front of her. She began to curl a tiny smile at the idea.

"Yes, I would indeed enjoy that, especially now that my Suppressor chip is removed, and I can actually enjoy something now."

"Excellent. Anyway, Marelle has some…" she coughs gently, "…experience in flying this thing, so we should be in good hands."

"Um, one moment. When you say she has some…" she coughs subtly, "…experience, how do you mean the…" she coughs again for emphasis, "…experience aspect of it?"

Kaliya grins mischievously and diverts to Marelle to give the explanation.

"Yeah," she begins avidly. "You see, we found it up near the mines Darumon was operating on Therinë, and our objective was to disrupt that operation. Originally, we were going to leave a mess to suggest a surprise raid by orcs. But then I had the idea to suggest the orcs actually took it."

"This would be to distract Darumon, I suppose, with these orcs turning against him?"

"Yeah, and then I would fly it back to our base as a wartime acquisition."

"Oh! Well, that might explain it. Then, I suppose you must be a rather well-trained pilot. Had you ever flown anything like this before?"

"No, not before this, this one was new."

"Interesting, then you must also be adaptive to make the adjustment. What sort of aircraft had you flown previously?"

"Previously, I was a city guardsman in Rolsklinde, Civil Watch office."

Ayene's expression dropped as she stared at the jovial auburn-haired young lady.

"Civil Watch? What does that do?"

"Well, according to our Governor, which was actually Darumon, our only real purpose was to keep the drunks off the streets."

"Oh, how delightful. Then, this is to say, you had no previous flying experience at all?" she wonders tenuously.

"Nope, we don't have aircraft. So, we don't have a clue what flying is about, other than watching birds. Our society didn't even have electricity."

"Didn't have electricity?" she shouts. "Then how in all the nether-space could you even conceive of such a thing as flight?"

"Well, I rode on a gryphon once."

"A what?"

"It's an animal, in this case a flying mount."

"Wait! I can understand the concept of a mount, but a flying one? And you rode it… But IT was doing the flying, not you, in this case."

"Well yeah, technically, but it sure was fun…once you got used to the idea that it's a long way down if you fall off."

"F-f-fall off…" she stutters as her face turns pale. "But how did you manage to fly this thing?" she thumbs at the transport.

"Oh, I had Relissa helping me in the copilot's seat."

"Ah! There we go, so SHE must know something."

"Actually, no… She's training as a ranger."

"What's a ranger?"

"Someone who talks to squirrels."

"Huh? What's a squirrel?"

"They're cute little furry critters she likes to keep in her pockets."

Now Ayene was turning white, as much as any blue-skinned Suuden'kai could.

"Do they fly?" she asks timidly.

"No, not in this case."

"Oh, good. Remind me to keep my distance from her."

"But as a consolation, we also had Padriyl with us."

"Wait, who is that?"

"Oh, sorry, you might know him as Lieutenant Lapäli."

"Ah! NOW we're getting somewhere. So, HE was flying the thing."

"No, I was in the pilot seat. He was in the navigator's seat."

"Oh no…" she moans and lays a hand on her forehead. "Why was he in the navigator's seat?"

"Well, he doesn't actually have any training as a pilot, so he took the closest thing he could associate with, which was the navigation console, hoping he could figure out where we're supposed to be going."

"Hoping…" she blurts nervously. "And did you actually arrive there?"

"Well, eventually. We took the thing out for a little spin first."

"A spin…" she wheezes. "What kind of a spin?"

"We flew out west of our location a bit, gained some altitude, and pumped up the throttle to see what it could do."

Ayene was now in a panic. Her face contorted as she tried to imagine this scene.

"And you're still alive?" she screeches.

"Yeah! So, now I'm in training to learn how to fly."

"OH!" she shrieks. "I see it…NOW you're learning how to fly… AFTER the fact," she covers her face and turns away to recover herself. "Are you at least trained enough to fly it without the help of people who talk to animals this time?"

"Oh, not a problem. And you can be sure, with me in the pilot seat on this mission, we're sure to come home safe."

"Oh, great! Um, why should I be so confident?"

"Because Adalon once said I have a fated encounter coming up one day, so it's a sure bet I'll live long enough to see it."

Ayene was just about to turn tail and run away at this moment for the insane reasoning in practice around her.

"And you people are supposed to be chasing a godlike creature in a completely different universe?"

"Well, someone needs to do it," she grins harmlessly. "But I'll tell you what. If it makes you feel any better, you can sit in the copilot's seat with me."

"Um, I was actually thinking of sitting this one out. I'll just write my report that you took off, flew out of visual range, and I didn't actually see that huge fireball rising up over the hillside."

"Oh, come on. I'm in training as a combat pilot right now. My flying skills are actually very good. We use a different configuration in our design, but I can still associate. In fact, my flight instructor… what's left of him…thinks I'm doing very well so far."

"Wait, I think you said what's left of him. Why?"

"Well, he's had to regrow his horns several times by now, but you people just don't know how to fly a good combat role. I'm basically inventing it on our side."

"I…think…I need…to go now…"

"Ayene," Kaliya smiles calmly. "Relax. We simply do things a little differently here."

"Kaliya, different, I can accept. But there should still be the aspect of sanity involved somewhere."

"Yes, but at the same time, our people were never a militaristic society, regardless of what Darumon tried making of you back home. These other races actually have better skills and sharper reflexes in this area, and a LOT of daring to defy the odds. We just weren't made for it, which is probably why Darumon stuck those chips inside your head so he could get you to do any work."

"Maybe you're right," she sighs. "But this example here, um…" she glances at Marelle one more time. "Kaliya, what about you? You're in training too, right? How do you manage?"

"With people like her?" she points at Marelle. "I lost my horns more times than I can count, until eventually I grew a much sturdier set that can tolerate things better. Also, I grew up in a battle zone. My life was miserable from half a century up. Learning to fight was a necessity. Then Thaelyn came along and showed me how to tame all my anger and frustration. He taught me how to refocus myself on the higher virtues and philosophies of life. We don't fight because we like it; we fight because we need to, in order to protect those who cannot protect themselves. We serve a righteous cause to uphold the truth, to serve justice, to protect the innocent, and to encourage admiration and respect for all things around us. But along the way, we also make friends and enjoy a few laughs. It's all a part of the adventure of living, and the people of Tae'Eladar developed a virtual utopia from his teachings."

"A utopia…" she muses softly.

Ayene stared at them, passing between Kaliya and Marelle, and within her, she began to feel a small fire igniting. Her own ambition to serve a greater purpose was renewing itself, and she began to smile.

"All right, Marelle, if you need a copilot, I'll give it a try. Let's just try not to run any joyrides today."

"Sounds good enough to me," she affirms.

The loading process of the transport was nearly complete. Kaliya checked the time.

"We're going to run this as another nighttime mission," she announces. "Ytani should be in bed for it, so he shouldn't notice anything. Sunset on Morndindor will be coming up soon, so we need to get this baby moving."

"Um, Kaliya," Ayene wonders. "Last I checked, we're still here in this research center of yours on Tae'Eladar."

"Yeah, the Bahlaie Center..."

"Right, so just to help keep what's left of my horns from falling off, how do you expect to move this to Morndindor?"

"We'll use rune transport, which is an application of our magic to send it through a portal event."

"This thing?" she waves her hands at the huge vessel.

"Yeah, we can do it, believe it or not. We did this when we brought it here, and I have a rune to a location near Captain Hagmaert's camp over there. After that, we'll follow along through the normal portal links."

They continued to wait as the last of the equipment was secured and the lead modron came forward with his report.

"Prime entity," it announces in a monotonal machine voice. "Our preparatory procedure is now complete. We await further instructions to define the fulfillment of our purpose."

"Good. We will need to relocate this thing. Stand by. Marelle, close that door while I charge up the rune."

Marelle rushes over to hit a control on the outside of the transport to close the large loading ramp. Kaliya then pulls out her rune and begins to enchant it. Ayene studies her carefully as she begins to see the strange energies circling around the odd stone-like object. She feels compelled to step back.

"All right, this is a big one," Kaliya asserts. "So we need a little extra push. Stand back..."

She steps forward to the large vessel and makes ready to touch the rune to the side. She applies extra focus into her enchantment as she raises the stone up and finally makes contact with the hull. The energies race through the bulk of the vessel, causing it to glow brightly and enveloping it in a huge ball of light that pulls it out of the local sphere of space with a thundering crackle.

Ayene jumped at the sight of the large vessel vanishing away due to such a tiny thing like the rune stone. She found herself marveling at the sheer power of this thing called magic, and what it was apparently capable of.

"All right everyone..." Kaliya continues. "Marelle, you lead, Ayene you follow. Friend modrons, we are now travelling to another Prime domain where we will reunite with the transport and proceed from there. But we must consider the time of day in that place and move only at night when our actions are less noticeable. Do you understand?"

"Acknowledged."

The procession now followed Marelle as she led them through a series of gateways from the Bahlaie Research Center to a nearby military hub station, which led to a local city hub, continuing ultimately through to Rolsklinde, then the dedicated portals to Ruuki uy'Daan and Morndindor, arriving in the outpost with Captain Hagmaert.

"Are you the one responsible for dropping that heap out there?" he gripes mockingly.

"Yes Sir," Kaliya responds. "We have all this empty space, so we thought we might offer a bit of decoration."

"Well, the least you could've done is to brighten it up with some festive banners or a bit of garland."

"Ah, but that's a separate shipment."

They all shared a laugh as they sat down for a chat, waiting for the sun to eventually set and nighttime to arrive.

Chapter 2

DEMISE OF VANITY

It was late in the day and Ytani had been considering a visitation inside the dwarven city below to check on the supplies from the mining operation. Silently, he was concerned over what he might learn of the dwindling mineral veins. The mining had been slowing down recently, apparently due to the veins running out. This could interfere with the operation as a whole. As for the people, he generally regarded them as imbecilic and primitive, where he could just barely tolerate interacting with them for all the arguing he had to lay down to get them to provide for his needs. Still, the deed needed to be done. He had a quota to fill for the local metal.

He was just settling into his favorite chair to make his meditation practice to release his spirit projection outside his body. He calmed himself and descended into a sleeplike trance, then began lifting his projection out of his body into the space nearby. He checked his image to ensure it was normal, as was a common practice by now, before folding his projection to the Thane's private chamber in the city down below.

Inside the room, he altered his form to that of a native dwarf. He only used one image for his projection, as he had no need for anything else, and therefore all he ever learned was the one image.

He then checked his clothing drawers for a selection of attire, even though he didn't actually wear it physically. He just needed a color arrangement to simulate for his projection, something that was known to be in his wardrobe, in case anyone ever paid attention to it. After choosing his dress style, he modified his image to match, before unlocking the door and stepping outside, then proceeding down the hall to his royal throne as the Thane of Glimmerheim. There he sent a messenger to find the Chancellor.

The Chancellor was in his office when the messenger came in. He didn't have any prior instructions that today was the day for the pick-up event, since the scheduling was still a couple of days away, so he took it as a follow-up visit relating to the mines running out instead. He prepared himself for his visit and rushed out of the office to the Thane's Hall.

Along the way, he called up a group of people in the streets, passing along a few whispers for them to form up a protest group, so the Thane, who was expected to be in the Hall at this time, could hear their displeasures. It didn't take long for the people to gather up in a crowd and begin shouting. The Chancellor then proceeded into the Hall proper for his meeting.

"Ah, good Thane," he announces obsequiously. "Good greetin's t' ye!"

The Thane sat in his chair, feeling his oats like he usually did on these occasions, at least until he began to overhear the ruckus outside the front doors.

"What be that noise out there!" he shouts.

"What? Oh, that…" the Chancellor feigns. "Aye. It be just a few folk in the streets a-makin' a wee bit of rousin'. Ye know, they be a-growin' a mite anxious for this nasty war. Ye should be expectin' this, ye know, it be a-takin' so long for the warriors up top t' bring it under control."

"Aye, they be a-workin' hard for it, don'na ye worry about that! So long as we keep up with the bricks!"

"Aye! Right ye be. Ye're in here early this time, good Thane. Be ye feelin' a bit restless, like all the rest?"

"Uh, aye! Just a wee bit. I be a-thinkin' of the mines down there runnin' out an' thought I'd best be a-checkin' t' make sure the miners be a-diggin' up hard an' fast!"

"Oh, aye! I was just checkin' down there this morn. I've been a-receivin' notes now an' then about their progress. One of the old veins has run out an' another be a-lookin' mighty thin by now. They think it may follow soon. But the miners are searchin' every old tunnel for more."

"Huh? Searchin' every OLD tunnel! What about diggin' a few new ones? The point-ears be a-ragin' out there! We can'na be a-spendin' our time searchin' old tunnels, we need t' be a-diggin' new ones!"

"I know this, good Thane, an' I told our miners t' see if there be any space down there t' dig somethin' new that don'na collapse the city in t' a well, an' this be why they have t' go searchin' the old tunnels, t' see about any good space for fresh diggin'."

"Argh!" he roars. "I knew this would happen one day! All right, fine! Tell them t' search until there nay be anyplace left t' search. What about diggin' out the side, instead of down? How about diggin' deeper in t' the mountain? Anythin' t' get us cookin' up more bricks!" he shrieks.

"Aye, this here be a good one. An' mayhap t' dig up. We ne'er tried that afore!"

"Up?" he hesitates as he glances upward while visualizing the base above. "Uh…up may be nay such a good idea. I mean, uh, well, we don'na want a lot of rocks fallin' on our heads, ye know."

"Oh, but I nay be a-thinkin' we should worry about that. We dwarves know how t' dig such that we nay have t' worry about rocks fallin' on us!" he chuckles confidently.

"Uh huh. Fine, but nay too far. After all, we don'na want to punch through the roof. Ye know, there be point-ears out there."

"Oh, that! Aye, good Thane. So, I'll get t' this just as soon as we can clear the streets of the folks outside who be a-protestin'. Once we can get them t' go back home, I'll get the miners back t' work!"

"What?!" he screams. "Protestin' in the streets! What are they protestin' out there? I swear, Chancellor, this nay be what I want t' hear right now."

"Aye, I s'pose. I think it was a-comin' for a long time. What with us bein' locked away down here inside the mountain, the food nay be as good as some would like, an' we're also seein' the wool for clothmakin' runnin' a bit thin that some folk are havin' a hard time with fresh clothes."

"What?" he shouts. "What d' ye mean, food an' clothes! I thought we had that workin' for us once already."

"Oh, good Thane, I be a-thinkin' it may have been once upon a tale. But things change over time, if ye don'na check on it now an' then…nay that ye ever did for all your woes about bricks. But surely, as any Thane should know, ye need t' keep on top of it, even WITH yer woes about the war."

The Thane gaped at the Chancellor for his statement, which was cleverly disguised as an innocent insinuation. For all his groaning over demanding the ingots, he forgot to conduct any other management duties…not that he cared as much to begin with.

"But anyway," the Chancellor continues. "The folk outside be a wee bit wantin' for the finer fare once recalled from all the farms an' herdin' above. Oh, good Thane, if ye could only recall the tales of the fine goods they must have for sale up there. An' this brings us back to the bricks."

"Aye, bricks!" he demands. "We need those bricks for the war! The warriors need them t' hold up the lines! Every city be a-burnin' without them!"

"Aye t' that, good Thane, but for all the Adamant we've sent up by now, we should be a-livin' the good life down here. Oh, t' think of the wealth of Adamant sent up…an' nay a tinkle of it comin' back t' us in our trades."

"Huh? What are ye blabberin' about now? This here be for the WAR, ye fool!"

"Right ye be!" the Chancellor admits casually. "But it be said ye were TRADIN' it for somethin', nay simply givin' it away. Nay a soul would d' such a foolhardy thing as that. After all, anyone who knows what Adamant be about would know it be a fine an' precious metal for any form of tradin'. An' all this minin' an' diggin' up our most precious metal, an' then t' see it runnin' out like this," he shakes his head. "It yay be a bit upsettin' for the folk t' see our city wealth runnin' out on them."

"City wealth! What about the war outside?" he screams.

"Ye're right, good Thane. But war or no war, folk still need t' live. An' for all we gave t' them, some have gone t' say we should be a-walkin' on streets paved in gold, an' livin' in homes built from fine gems by now for all we sent up so far."

"Gold?" he wheezes. "An' gems... You actually mean... An' they actually want... Argh!" he screams.

"Aye, I know the feelin' good Thane," the Chancellor patronizes demurely. "After all, for all the mountains we've been a-sendin' up, it be a cryin' shame for how little we got back. An' surely, any proper dwarf would know the true value of Adamant as a trade good. It be a precious metal, more so than gold in some ways. Every dwarf knows this. But then, I think I nay need t' tell this t' ye, ye bein' the Thane as ye be," he chuckles innocently.

"Chancellor!" the Thane rages. "Why should I actually...um, what I mean is, we have a war up there, an' the warriors need bricks! This here be more important than..."

"Paying us for the favor of it?" he interrupts. "Mayhap, if every city be a-burnin' by now. But people still need t' eat. An' they still need clothes on their backs. An' regardless of the war, we still use coin t' make our way in life. An' there were a grand many tales of fine food an' cloth t' be found up there, which we nay have seen in all this time."

"What food an' cloth!" he shouts mindlessly. "It all be a-burnin' by now! This here be why the warriors need bricks t' hold up the lines! Nay t' trade for such nonsense as...um..." he catches himself. "Well, what I mean t' say, it be yay more important t' help the warriors out there. Those point-ears be a-ragin' across the land, d' ye remember?!"

"Aye, good Thane," he responds supportively. "After all, for all the tellin', it be a hard one t' forget. We keep sendin' up our men t' make the fare…men with the skills ye need t' actually MAKE Adamant. Ye know, it nay come easy, an' nay cheap. It nay be the same as, say, iron. Any fool can make that. But Adamant…" he whistles and rolls his eyes.

The Thane glares at his obvious display, thinking the man must be losing his mind. After all, how can anything coming out of this primitive society be so hard if it doesn't even meet up to his own form of technology.

The Chancellor continues, "A good smith might spend much of his life learnin' how t' make it proper, passin' the skills from master t' apprentice. This nay be somethin' t' shake a stick at. An' most of all, ye simply don'na throw it away. Neither d' ye let it go without proper payment for yer services."

"Don'na throw it away…" he mumbles privately.

Now the Thane was faced with a new dilemma that he apparently didn't consider before…skilled labor. He reflected briefly on a recent argument with the base commander about his skilled staff members. And since he already knew the Suuden-Aryku had no idea of how to make this stuff, therefore this imperative need for local labor, this obviously implied that same local labor to hold important skills. But his clear lack of knowing, or caring, about the delicacies involved, simply led him to another mindless outburst.

"I swear t' ye, Chancellor! Fine, it be a metal. All we need are bricks, nay any fine art. The point-ears…"

"But, good Thane," he interrupts again. "Any good dwarf would know, Adamant nay be any simple metal, nay even t' make bricks. Ye first need t' know how t' actually mine it. It takes years, even t' learn this much, because ye can'na simply dig it out of the rocks. It takes special handlin'."

"Special handlin'?" he mutters distantly.

"Aye! An' then ye need t' know how t' refine the ore. This also takes special handlin'. Ye don'na learn this from a book in school. Ye need t' work it proper, an' it can take many a year t' get it right, even t' know how t' make the right fires for it, because we're nay speakin' of simply burnin' wood here, especially as we're deep below ground with nay any wood t' burn. But surely, as the good Thane ye be, ye already know this," he smiles confidently.

The Thane suddenly found himself with yet another paradox. To forge something, you need heat, and to make heat, you need fire, and to make fire, you need something that burns. But if you're underground and surrounded on all sides by noncombustible rocks…

The Chancellor continues, "An' so, good Thane, it be a simple thing that for all the miners be a-strugglin' t' make for ye, they'd like t' see their lives made finer for it."

"Argh!" he screeches. "Grand, are we speakin' of a strike now?"

"Well, it nay be as much as that, methinks. They be just a wee bit riled for how little be a-comin' back t' them. An' then there be the other thing…" he pauses conspicuously as he thumps a finger to his chin.

The Thane glared at him, wondering what new calamity was waiting outside.

"What?" he demands. "What other thing?"

"Well, a piece of it be the smiths have been a-growin' tired of makin' up bricks for a war that nay be a-slowin' down. Surely, Thane, ye would know what a good piece of Adamant be good for, ay? Of course ye do, as every good dwarf knows it be the finest metal ye can use t' make weapons an' armor for a war. There nay be anythin' better for fightin' back yer foes. Aye, a sturdy warrior bearin' up a fine Adamant axe an' armor yay be hard t' kill, an' truly nasty t' anyone who yay be foolish enough t' stand in front of him."

"Huh?" the Thane blurts mindlessly. "What d' ye mean, nay anythin' better? The warriors up top need more bricks t' keep up the war, d' ye hear me?!"

"Aye, good Thane. But the point here be that those warriors, who KNOW what Adamant be good for, should've killed those nasty point-ears nearly as soon as they showed their gnarly faces. An' worse…Oi!" he animates with his hands. "For as much as we've already sent up, I would think half the world would be a-wearin' it by now. This would be enough t' kill them, their fathers, their brothers, an' all their cousins, an' anythin' else too foul t' look at, long ago."

"Uh..." the Thane hesitates.

The Chancellor continues unabated, "An' it lasts a long while, too! I know a few tales of weapons that get handed down from father t' son, t' his son, an' t' his son, an' it yay be just as strong as ever."

"Ye must be kiddin' me..." the Thane emits uncertainly.

"The same for armor," the Chancellor continues as if he didn't hear the statement. "Whole families may pass it down an' see it used again an' again, one battle after another. It simply don'na ever quit. An' we dwarves should know, as we've been a-workin' this for thousands of years, since the early days of our kind."

"Thousands...?" he mumbles.

"An' so, any good dwarf who knows how t' fight, nay be usin' bricks...nay unless yer rebuildin' all those burnt cities with it," he chuckles. "This here be part of the rousin' outside. The war should be US ragin' across the land, nay anythin' else. But I should be on with me'self..."

The Chancellor turns and begins walking away, still rambling for the Thane to hear.

"I nay be t' thinkin' ye need a history lesson from me. After all, ye be the Thane, an' ye should know fine an' good how strong Adamant be that just ONE dwarf with an Adamant axe can cut through a whole army of foes. Ye nay need any more than that. An' a warrior dressed up good an' proper in Adamant armor would be nigh invincible t' anyone holdin' anythin' less than more Adamant. An' those point-ears can'na be as good as we dwarves at forgin' up our most precious metal. Nay t' that, I say!" he echoes as he leaves the room.

The Thane sat there glaring vacantly at the Chancellor as he departed the scene. He continued to sit there in a now empty room, pondering his thoughts openly.

"What in all the nether-space is that idiot rambling about? As if these puny dirt-shovelers might know anything about anything our own technology couldn't identify."

He considers these words for several long moments.

"Well, except for this, as our tech can NOT identify it, which is why we need them. But seriously, this stuff sounds almost magical. And that's simply ridiculous. One warrior can hold up to an army of foes... Ha! On the other side of it, this could explain why they constantly argue the need for more of it. Those stories of demanding more are falling on people who think they already did enough to win this war. I may need to change the stories a little to counter this."

He gets up from his chair and meanders back to his room.

"And I always did wonder how they make the stuff down here, being underground without anything to burn in those forges of theirs. It must be chemical or something. But special handling? Well, if it's chemical, it might take something special. But it's a metal! Just put a little ore in a furnace, turn up the heat, and boom, you have metal, right?"

He continues down the hall, still mumbling to himself.

"Then again, if the mines run out, it might not even matter. This city will be useless, except for pulling out mining teams. Hmm, skilled labor. It takes forever to learn how to do it?" he huffs. "In all the nether-space, can they actually be so slow to figure it out? Step One: dig here. Step Two: pull out ore. Step Three: drop it in a furnace. Skilled labor? Skilled to learn how to walk from the mine to the forge, maybe. Anyway, as for them, I might need to change the stories for that, also. In fact, I may need to take up the Commander's idea of a new survey, simply to keep the processor working."

He enters his private chamber, where he closes and locks the door. He examines the neatly refreshed furnishings from the chambermaids who visited during his outing, and proceeds to mess up the bed to give it a used look. Then he pulls out that set of clothes he was looking at earlier, and tosses them into a heap on the floor, again to give a used look. He pauses to study the scene while still in thought.

"Yeah, surveys. After all, if I want to keep this operation running, we'll need more mines. Hmm..." he begins to curl a malignant grin.

He then flashes out of the room back to his house up in the

mining base, where he reunited his spirit projection with his natural body.

Several hours had passed for Kaliya and her team in Captain Hagmaert's camp. Now, nighttime was falling. Scouts had returned with reports that Ytani appeared to have returned from a recent visit to the city and was now retiring to bed.

"I wonder how the recent play went," Kaliya muses.

"This is the one where we make up the story of the mines running out, right?" Marelle asks.

"That, and protests of people who are angry for all their precious metal being spent on a never-ending war. And further is a hint that the city is running down as the result of...bad management," she grins.

"If Ytani behaves in his usual way," Ayene offers. "I think he will either reject the whole idea, since he doesn't give anyone enough credit to know anything, or else he'll try covering for it somehow with a new story. Or maybe both."

"Maybe so. All right, everyone, this is it. Modrons, we are on the move."

Marelle hurries over to open the loading ramp and the modrons climb in and take up space to secure themselves. She and Ayene move forward to the pilot's cabin while Kaliya closes the door and files in behind to sit in the navigator's seat."

"Am I the one who'll be trying to find our way now?" she teases.

"Actually," Ayene offers. "This shouldn't be too bad. I've flown around out here enough times; I can do it blindfolded."

Marelle powers up and they lift off. She applies the thrust and carries them over the nearby hillside.

"We need to be careful not to be seen in the valley just outside Glimmerheim," Kaliya notes. "They have access to the outside by now, and we don't want to frighten anyone down there that might be walking around."

"Don't you have control of them by now?" Ayene asks.

"Partially, up to the point that they know Ytani's stories aren't fully correct, but not to the point where they know about us yet. We're trying to break it to them in pieces, and keeping certain parts out in case Darumon tries sticking his nose in things."

"Ah, right. But this sounds like a complex bit of intrigue."

They continued along behind a row of hills parallel to the large valley south of the city, until they eventually arrived at the range of broad mountains. Marelle turns to align them towards the base and carries them a few more miles until they arrive in view of it.

"Ayene," Marelle begins. "Maybe you should call them to let them know we're coming in, and to make sure the conveyor is pointing the right direction."

"Understood."

She engages the local com-link and makes the call.

"Morndindor base, this is Lieutenant Ti'van in H-T One, are you receiving?"

"H-T One, this is Morndindor base, what is your status?"

"We are inbound and requesting confirmation of routing for the conveyor to Madzurki. Acknowledge."

"Affirmative, the conveyor is available. Proceed when ready."

"Understood. H-T One out."

Marelle piloted the heavy transport down into the ravine where the base was found and lined up with the conveyor. She proceeded ahead slowly until she penetrated the containment field, and finally the rift itself.

As before, she found herself travelling through the long conduit, attempting to follow the slipstream as it gently twisted and turned. Ayene was a veteran at this form of travel, but she held back on the controls and watched as Marelle carefully guided the huge vessel towards its destination. They arrived back through the dimensional membrane into the vicinity of the processor.

"Petrith should be down there already with the instructor," Kaliya notes. "Call him up for us."

Ayene once again engages the com-link.

"This is H-T One calling Madzurki processor. Is anyone receiving?"

"This is the Madzurki Exotic Mineral Emporium…Petrith Girhani speaking, Chief of Marketing. How can I help you today?"

Ayene glared at the com-station, and then peered around at her cohorts.

"Do you know this guy?"

"Yeah," Kaliya affirms. "He's my boyfriend."

"I should've guessed," she returns to the link. "Um, we're just passing through to…um…look over your inventory of sales products. Do we have any specials today?"

"Oh, indeed we do. We're having a clearance right now, so if you hurry, you can pick up some great bargains."

"Thank you, can you set the conveyor for us?"

"No sooner said than done. Have a nice day."

Ayene felt a perky grin spreading over her face as she cut the link. Soon, they took notice of the conveyor outside reconfiguring.

"We don't do things this way on Azgarén."

"We're not on Azgarén," Kaliya offers.

Marelle turns them around and proceeds through to the next destination.

"All right," Ayene mentions as they arrive at Ooduan. "This thing is huge, and that flight hanger isn't quite designed for it. So, I'm going to suggest we turn around and pull in backwards…very carefully. It'll be a tight squeeze, but if we can twist in sideways, we might just fit inside the curtain."

Marelle and Ayene now coordinate to maneuver slowly in reverse, lining up and gliding into the hanger gradually, then angling to pull in the rest of it sideways. They lower the landing gear and settle down gently.

"You know, Marelle," she states. "You're actually not so bad. I'd like to see this combat training of yours, though. If it's enough to cause your instructor to lose his horns, I wonder how someone with real patrol piloting skills would see it."

"You're invited to watch, if you like."

They now proceeded to the unloading, opening the door and allowing the modrons to get to work. They brought out all the components for their custom portal device and moved it into the facility, setting it up along the central avenue between the storage sections.

"Just keep in mind," Kaliya cautions. "We need to keep the vibrations of the construction effort to a minimum. This stuff is supposed to be very sensitive."

"Acknowledged..." responds the lead modron.

The construction effort went along quickly, as the components were already partially assembled, so they only needed to be connected. Fuel cells were attached to provide power in this barren environment, and the portal itself was oriented as a horizontal aperture where items could simply be dropped into it.

Ayene assisted in programming the automated retrieval networks to begin delivering the units out of storage one by one, and the modrons carried them in sequence to the portal, dropping them inside to send them on their way.

In a far distant galactic cluster, somewhere on the edge of the observable universe, a long series of flashes were erupting as the cubical containers suddenly arrived out of nowhere and were almost instantly devoured by a massive black hole. The local space was being torn apart by the blast effects, but the black hole simply absorbed it, as it did everything else.

The Modrons were making these runs from each of the warehouses, gently picking up the cubes and carefully walking them to the portal, then dropping them inside.

"Friend modron," Kaliya asserts. "We have instructions to keep one unit available. I have a special container in the vessel and a timing device for an explosive. My instructions are to use this as a demonstration for Darumon."

"Acknowledged. Prepare the destination container and we will deliver the unit into position."

Kaliya returns quickly to the transport and brings out a large rectangular metal box reinforced for use in a zero-atmosphere environment.

"This is the container," she affirms. "But I also need to bring this outside the flight hanger, where it is out of reach from anyone tampering with it. Do you have a suggestion for this?"

"Where is the intended coordinate objective for delivery of the container?"

Kaliya glanced outside the atmosphere curtain and selected a spot off to one side, still within view, but out of the way of any potential traffic, and too far to reach by any physical means. She directs the modron, and together they carefully assemble the bomb with the timer. The modron then takes the container and strolls outside with it.

"Are those things able to simply walk around out there?" Ayene wonders.

"Well, they're not organic, and I guess as machine entities, they're not as limited as we are to the atmospheric pressures. But I do hope the little guy makes it back."

They watched as the modron travelled along the tarmac outside the curtain and carefully deposited his cargo, then returned back inside to rejoin the others.

As the remainder of the cubical containers was disposed, Ayene and Kaliya found themselves engaged in conversation over her next mission.

"The plan goes like this," Kaliya reflects. "Ytani is going to call for his next payment, so we'll play on that last argument with the Commander of using either your least valuable staff member, or some random and completely innocent civilian."

"Wow, when you put it in such terms as those, I feel for those civilians."

"Yeah, but this civilian won't be quite so innocent, to say nothing of random."

"Kaliya, did I hear it said you will be projected during this time?"

"Yes, so there's no real worry for my safety. I'm going to put on a show to swing my tail at him, but I'm going to play hard to get, and if he wants me, he has to show me a few thrills first, like all his wonderful goodies."

"Goodies? What goodies?"

"In this case, these things we just tossed into a gravastar. My purpose is to lure him here, and then set off that bomb out there."

"Are YOU able to walk around out there?"

"I won't be corporeal, so I don't think it'll matter."

"Maybe you should test it first. All right, so we'll say you draw him here…but how do you keep him here long enough to set off your bomb?"

"We're thinking of having Marelle fly 'my' shuttle, along with her instructor…or maybe you would do it?" she grins.

"Me? Do I need to know how to talk to animals for this job?"

"I don't think so. The controls don't speak squirrel in this case," she giggles. "Then, when we show up in our little follow-the-leader game, she takes off and we steal his along the way."

"All right, but can I offer an alternative, just in case?"

"Sure, what kind?"

"Ytani is argumentative. The Commander had a good plan when he tried to have him go out on this survey mission."

"Right, we saw that in our spy video, but Ytani didn't buy it."

"Both agree we might need this if to continue the supply of the metal, but Ytani wants his girls to play with, and doesn't like going too far out of the way for it. Also, with so many past arguments between the two of them, and him becoming increasingly agitated that he isn't getting what he wants, and therefore to make his threats, I'm wondering how eager he might be to follow you willingly all the way to a place none of us wants to visit."

"All right, point made. Do you have a suggestion on how to ensure we get a result?"

"One obvious suggestion is to point the Morndindor conveyor away from Azgarén. If he can't call on his army of dwarves, he'll call on the Marshal instead, but without the means to go there, he can't do it."

"We've already got that covered, but he could still project and go there."

"Oops, he can?"

"Any recalled memory image will do. If he's been there before, he can go there again. So, we need to keep him corporeal."

"Been there before," Ayene muses. "But this would require him to have actually BEEN there before. He was a child when he first arrived here, remember, and I doubt anyone back home knew about it."

"You're right. So he might not even know where to go, other than maybe passing through to…what? The tarmac outside the control center, maybe?"

"Maybe, which could be bad enough, and then walk inside from there."

"But let's also consider his skill level. If he only knows how to imitate a dwarf and go into the city, how much does he know about anything else? My information says he uses only one image…in all this time. He doesn't even consider the aging process of the locals, or changing from one generation to another to simulate the passing of individuals."

"That's not very wise, if he's trying to make them believe he's one of them."

"And then, recall what I said about Darumon. He only teaches you enough to do your immediate job."

"Granted, so this could also be a factor. Either way, this could complicate things. But if he wants his playthings, he should be corporeal so he can actually enjoy it, right?"

"Yeah, that's usually how it goes."

"Anyway, my thoughts are if he does try to go there…using his shuttle, that is…and the conveyor is pointing at Madzurki, he'll go there instead. Then, he'll likely turn around and try going home. But if you use that strange boyfriend of yours," she grins cautiously, "and keep him to the official statements, he could redirect him here. But now, we have to keep him here."

"Yes, this could be a problem," Kaliya muses. "At this point, he'll probably grumble about the conveyor and turn around again."

"And this is where you need to act fast. Come with me, I want to show you something."

Ayene leads the two of them up to the control booth where she brings them to the conveyor controls.

"Do you know how to shut down a conveyor?"

"Not personally."

"All right, watch closely and pay attention. You have the status readouts and the diagnostic displays," she directs to a series of panels. "They show such things as power output, rift generator operating conditions, conduit stability, containment field integrity, and so on. There is a shutdown procedure if you want to bring it down for any reason. First you need to disengage the rift generator. This panel here," she points at a display with a set of icons on it. "Hit this icon to begin a shutdown sequence. You'll need to tap on a confirmation button along the way. Then the containment field, this other icon over here, which will become available only after the rift generator goes offline, as a safety protocol."

"Are these interfaces touch responsive, or conductive? In projected mode, I can't do conductive."

"Oh, um, touch, I believe. I don't think we use the conductive type very often. I think this also goes as a safety in case something conductive comes in contact with it, and then BAM, you have several things going off simultaneously, and you need to spend the rest of the day trying to repair the damage."

"Oops. All right, but the next question is whether Ytani knows how to turn it back on."

"Would you even give him that much time?"

"Probably not," Kaliya grins.

◆◆◆◆◆

"The mines below are running out completely this time?" the projected Suuden'kai Commander asks.

"It would seem that way," Ytani reports. "I paid a little visit last night to check on things, and I've been trying to think of solutions to it. It would also seem they're starting to complain about the length of the war…well, more so than usual…and, get this, they had some sort of protest going on outside in the street."

"I suppose the complaints might be expected, if to say they would desire their war to be finished by now. These people might demand faster results than our own interpretation. But a protest? For what reason?"

Ytani was reporting to the base Commander on his last visit inside the dwarven city. So far, he was unaware that Kaliya and her team had abducted the real base crew and replaced them with her team in projected form. The projected teammates were simulating the operating crew, and this often required a bit of acting talent to meet the needs.

"For one thing," Ytani recalls. "They're starting to run low of basic needs, like food and clothing. I thought we had this solved once, but I guess their population is starting to use it up too fast."

"This is reasonable. If the population count is rising, they will require more resources."

"Also, they're complaining about the lack of trade value with anything outside. They're apparently unhappy about us stealing all their metal, not that it matters. And those little dirt-shovelers seem to hold the opinion that this metal makes up a primary component of their city's economic wealth."

"I suppose this could hold merit. This metal does give the appearance of a precious resource, by the mining output we have measured."

"Maybe…as if I cared," he huffs indignantly.

"Ytani, you may wish to reconsider that attitude, because if they feel they are being cheated, it could affect their output."

"Commander, I'll say it again, this is what superior firepower is used for. Anyway, because of it running out, they're angry that their net worth has run out. Furthermore, and this is a good laugh, they're upset that my…trade…with the outside world isn't bringing in any of those fine luxury items we blasted once," he chuckles.

"This is also reasonable if you think of it. After all, they still think there is a world out there, and no doubt they once did enjoy those items."

"Commander, I swear. Once again, ask me if I care," he growls.

"I think I do not need to ask this, Ytani. But at the same time, it is reasonable to suggest you should understand this to begin with. You also have luxury goods in your home. Now imagine if none of that existed, or was taken away, due to YOUR lack of worth to obtain it by legitimate means. And when I say legitimate means, this is to say you perform a work effort that is recognized by some authority that would then pay you for your labors. And the pay would be appropriate to the complexity of your labors to earn it."

"Commander…!" he begins angrily.

"Ytani, this is how life works, and it STILL works this way back home, regardless of your attitude relating to the Marshal, and what he does or does not control. You are impersonating their leader. And as a leader of a society, it becomes your responsibility to understand how to manage that society successfully. It works the same way for us and our own Council."

"Uh huh, sure, whatever…" he shrugs it off indifferently. "As for ME and MY pay, I get free living here, so I don't care about working for it. All I need to do around here is deliver the metal, which again is FREE. And my pay is also FREE. And I do so love the 'free' aspect of it."

"Indeed, you do," the Commander spook concedes grudgingly.

"Next is what the Chancellor was ranting about. I don't know if he was just rambling on a history lesson, or suggesting a public complaint over my management practices, but he dared to suggest this metal is actually better than anything WE might know about for its usefulness. He said the war should've been done and gone long ago because anyone using this stuff should be able to singlehandedly win a battle against a full army of point-ears…as if he has any idea who those point-ears might actually be and what they're capable of."

"I suppose this might hold merit, if we consider we do not have a full definition of the properties of this metal, even when we do have it in our hands to study it. And if we required local labor to do our work, it stands to reason THEY should know what it is capable of, and perhaps even more so than we might."

"Commander, now hear this. Does the term 'superior technology' mean anything to you?"

"Yes, Ytani, it does, up to the point where that same superior technology fails to explain this metal. Then it falls to some definition OUTSIDE that superior technology, and therefore OUR ability to define it. This might also fall within the explanation of us being in a completely different universe, and whatever unique properties this universe might hold to create something our superior technology might not otherwise provide definitions for back home. Therefore, a NATIVE society might hold knowledge we do NOT hold, and again, your attitude against them may seem irrelevant, if you, yourself, never once bothered to take the time to understand this to learn the difference."

Ytani went silent for a moment as he considered this idea.

"Furthermore," the Commander spook continues. "Do we have an accurate definition of these point-ears to explain a measurable comparison?"

"How in all the nether-space should I know what a real point-ear is. This is a myth we created for this excuse of a war. But this does bring up a good point, and that being I'll need to modify the story to create something...measurable. If they're protesting in the streets, supply or no supply, this could shut down the whole operation, including pulling out teams for any external mines."

Ytani pauses to consider these prospects.

"What was the last stockpile count at the depot?" he asks.

"We show just over eighty-six percent."

"Dammit! So close! All right, I'll keep on this to see if those little runts actually manage to find any more down there. He mentioned the city being so riddled with holes by now, it could fall into a pit. That wouldn't serve us much to pull out more people. So, I might need to have them shut down their local operations and simply use them as a feed to the other mine. We may find ourselves doing surveys after all."

He cuts the link.

The base Commander turns to his local officers, all of whom were projected agents working for Kaliya.

"Too bad he won't be around that long to give it a try."

"Yes…" responds one of the teammates. "But you made a good effort at trying to clue him in on what this stuff is good for, or at least that it might hold value beyond his idea of 'superior technology', as measured back home."

"Maybe, but his poor educational level is revealing itself that he didn't finish ANY schooling back home, not even enough to hint that there could be more out there to learn. He's not taking into consideration new discoveries that even OUR level of tech might find new and fascinating to study. He seems to think we already know everything there is to know, so who cares about the rest."

"Sounds like a junior school student to me. I heard he came here at only seven decades."

✦

"'Ere now, girl, what's this fancy get-up you're sporting now?" Relissa razzes. "You look like you're setting up to flash your delicates at every guy on the street!"

"Sorry, I'm just trying out new clothes for my next mission," Kaliya responds.

"Jiggers, and they let you go outside in that?" she reflects as she candidly peeks around Kaliya's example outfit.

Kaliya was in her dorm room, and Relissa was visiting to check on her. It was nearing the end of the week and she was preparing for her mission to Morndindor later in the evening to close up the final details relating to Ytani. At this time, she was in her projected form and standing in front of her mirror imagining different sets of clothing to use for her disguise, some of which were rather revealing.

"I wonder what the current fashion is on Azgarén these days?" she muses.

"Probably military blue, if you go by what the Suuden-Aryku tend to wear."

"Yeah, but I have to wonder about the civilians. Those people we found in the processor didn't seem too bad, and Ayene is turning out to be a nice person, now that she's rediscovering herself."

"I haven't met her yet. But Marelle told me a bit about your run out there to get rid of that bugaboo of a weapon. Poor girl, she got a real hard initiation on that one," she snickers.

Kaliya tries another projected illusion to change her clothes. Relissa studies her, glancing around at different angles.

"Do you have anything underneath that?" she asks tentatively.

"Hmm, interesting point, do you think I should go without?"

"Hey now, I'm the wrong person to ask that. But what do Daanen'kai boys think about it?" she smirks.

"I suppose I could ask Petrith, but if it doesn't involve soap, it might not be enough," she chuckles.

"That poor guy," Relissa shakes her head.

"More important is what a Suuden'kai boy would think, especially if he likes abusing women."

"Under those conditions, I guess he probably wouldn't care how little you're wearing. He'll tear it off anyway."

"True, but the idea is not to let him tear it off, simply to get him to follow me to my target. And for that, I need to be very appealing."

"Appealing is one thing, but do you think there's such a thing like trying too hard?"

"You're probably right. I want it to look good, but not necessarily like I'm trying to be so provocative that it might seem suspicious."

"What sort of reaction are you expecting out of him?"

"According to Ayene, almost anything is possible. But one thing is for sure, he'll most likely want to drag me back to his torture chamber and have his way with me."

"Jiggers, girl! When you put it like that, I wonder how much of you will be coming home."

"It's not really how much of me, it's how much of him, and we can't allow any."

"Aye, I know. So, what if he doesn't play nice with you?"

"I'm thinking of all sorts of things right now, Relissa. Will he follow me? Will he not follow me. Will he drool over me so much that he softens up to my demands, or will he just want to grab me, and to all the nether-space with the rest."

"Well, all I can say is, I might not be Suuden'kai, but you've got enough to turn just about anyone's head already. And if it works on him, good luck with it."

Kaliya changes to one more fashion style, and Relissa once again checks her figure.

"Criminy, girl, you're really not wearing anything under that!" she yips as she notices Kaliya's features protruding beneath her exceedingly short mini skirt.

Kaliya shows off a broad smirk as she feels the power of her sexuality.

"Now wait a minute!" Relissa gripes teasingly. "You wipe that snigger off your face and lower this hemline."

"Oh Relissa, haven't you ever worn anything sexy in your life? I can try new clothes and not even pay money for it."

"Aye, and in projected form, you can get yourself in trouble for it without actually getting yourself in trouble. Bring this down just a bit. We don't want to let out all our secrets at first sighting."

She adjusts her image to bring the skirt down until it's suitably modest while still suggestive.

"I still think that's a bit high," Relissa remarks. "But at least your bum's not hanging out now. Where did you get this idea, anyway?"

"There are certain fashions we used to have back home on Ruuki uy'Daan, maybe not quite as small as this, but close to it on a few occasions. My mother wouldn't let me wear any when I was little because first, I was too young, and second, well, I was her little girl, and she was finicky about my presentation. Still, I did try to wear clothes that would show off a little sometimes."

"I'll bet you had a lot of boys chasing after you, too."

"I didn't do it quite as much as Suli, but I had a few moments, and it made me feel good."

"Must be something about your culture over there. We Night Elves don't usually go out in such tiny bits…" she comments as she makes another pass for a fresh review. "But I suppose it does give a girl a few ideas," she finishes with a timid smile.

"Yours is probably much more conservative. What if I add some leggings to it?" Kaliya wonders.

She tries a few ideas for leg coverings, eventually settling on a stocking design partially covering the thighs and lower legs.

"What's normal for you in this area?" Relissa asks.

"When I was little, I would sometimes wear a knee-length dress and full leggings down to the ankles. But those are little girl clothes, and I'm not a little girl anymore."

"So, you're cutting the dress in half and ripping out the top part of the leggings? Jiggers, you big girls don't hold back, do you," she giggles.

"Nope, not if we want the boys to take notice. Haven't you ever done anything like this?"

"Nah, I never had the chance," Relissa relents.

"Why not? You're certainly cute enough."

"Thanks, but you're forgetting I wasn't very popular as a tyke. With all my groaning about elven traditions and the war grinding my nerves, I didn't make many friends."

"What about now? You're doing much better after joining up here."

"Aye, but I've also had my mind too deep in my studies to do much else. Maybe later, after my first century, I'll see what kind of mischief I can get into."

"Need any lessons? I got a bag-full of ideas from Suli the other day."

"I'll bet you did, from what I'm seeing here. Maybe I'll make a visit sometime."

◆◆◆

"Reporting for duty, my Lord," Marelle presents herself in a formal salute.

"Good, Cadet. Rest at ease," Thaelyn responds.

Marelle had arrived in the strategy room in the WIC building, there to meet with Petrith and Ayene. It was late afternoon, and they were preparing for their part in the upcoming mission.

"Here is the plan," he continues. "According to a meeting I shared not long ago between Kaliya and the Lieutenant here," he directs at Ayene. "Ytani may or may not cooperate politely. On the one hand, if she is successful in bringing him to Ooduan, you will serve as the decoy shuttle for our young female concubine in her little game. After he lands, you must confiscate his shuttle and depart promptly."

"All right, this seems fairly straightforward."

"On the other hand, if he does not follow our lead, he might become suspicious of our efforts that the Commander is once again trying to play a stall tactic, or some other detour around his demands."

"This sounds bad."

"If this is the case, he might try escaping to Azgarén in the hopes of lodging a complaint with Darumon. So we will need to redirect him forcefully to Ooduan using the conveyors. Kaliya tells us the Lieutenant demonstrated a shutdown procedure she could use on this occasion to buy time to trap him."

"All right, that's not so bad."

"Therefore, if this becomes our direction, we will not have you go there at all, keeping you out of the equation as Kaliya will be detonating the bomb at this point."

"Ouch. THAT is bad."

"Of course, there are other variables that could occur along the way, so stay alert. Your aircraft has been delivered by rune transport just outside the outpost on Morndindor. The reasons here are the same as with the large transport we used earlier for the modrons and their actions."

"Got it, so I'll need to fly up there manually again."

"And none of your little joyrides," Ayene adds playfully.

"Indeed!" Thaelyn affirms. "And as before, we will send

Petrith by rune into the base proper to wait for you. We will also involve the Lieutenant on this occasion, since it would seem you are becoming something of a team lately, and she does seem a very capable individual."

Ayene smiled at the compliment.

"I like her," Marelle smiles and glances at Ayene. "She's a little stiff from being so long under that emotion chip, but I'm sure we can soften her up."

"Just so long as you leave something of her to do her work," he grins. "She will be your sidekick pilot if we should have the opportunity to move forward."

"Good, we did well together last time."

"Now, as before, you will need to deliver Petrith to the Madzurki facility so he can take up his position. However, we have an issue of timing to consider here. This must be done before you can make ready for the mission proper. We are considering Ytani's next visitation down below, and your timing must coincide with that, so he does not take any special notice of our actions in the base. Then you must be ready for his return and whatever course we might find ourselves taking from there."

"Sounds like a tight fit."

"It will be, and for this you need to be away quickly to reach your mark before sunrise, local time."

"Then I'd better hurry," she grins.

"Simply try not to crash into any mountains, will you?" he smiles playfully.

"My Lord! When was the last time I plowed into a mountain?"

"I am simply trying to avoid the first time."

"By the way, speaking of blowing things up, what are we going to do with the processor?"

"We will be relocating that atomic device Darumon was going to use on the mines to the north, and use it here instead, but not yet. We may still have a need to keep it in case anyone asks to make an inspection tour."

"Well, I was thinking of something. Since we're going to be

testing some of our new technologies one of these days, and we might want to test it in an environment devoid of the flows, could we use that?"

"This is an interesting point, and with a conveyor present, it provides easy access in and out, in case the other forms do not function for us. I will consider this. But for now, you must be on your way."

Marelle salutes again and heads out the door with Ayene and Petrith in tow. The three of them navigate through the connecting portal gates to Ruuki uy'Daan, and then Morndindor to the outpost.

"Captain," she shouts. "These two need transport up to the base."

"Right away, Lieutenant," he responds.

"I'm not technically a Lieutenant, remember? I sort of lost that when I left my old service."

"Oh, is that so. Well then, you'd better get your greenhorn backside over here to pick up your new stripes."

"What?" she gasps unexpectedly.

She steps over to the captain's hut as he ducks inside to pick up a box that was delivered to his desk earlier in the day. He comes back out and opens it up for her. Inside was a Lieutenant's badge.

Marelle felt a welling up of emotion inside her as he pulled it out and pinned it to her lapel. He then stepped back and offered an honorary salute. She pulls up to attention and returns with her own, barely able to constrain her tears.

"We certainly can't have our cadets running loose on a battlefield without some form of decoration," he asserts.

"Absolutely, Sir!"

"Just don't let it go to your head. You've got serious work in front of you."

"Understood, and thank you."

He dismisses her and she makes a brisk trot out to her ship.

The aircraft was the same one she had been using for her training exercises at the Bahlaie Center, where they had been training new pilots and researching their new technologies. She climbs inside and shuts the door, then settles into her seat. She powers on the craft according to a ritual practice she was well familiar with by this time and waits for the diagnostics to finish. When all systems were checked, she applied the flux field, hit the switch for the landing gear, and engaged the throttle, taking off and turning to the north to find the base. She would follow the same path as before with the heavy transport, keeping out of sight of anyone on the ground.

Kaliya had settled herself on her fashion attire. She was still in projected form, having spent much of the late afternoon on it, and now it was going into early evening. She had everything she felt she needed to begin her work, so she offered a goodbye to Relissa, who was still groaning over the risqué nature of the clothing, and folded her image to the WIC building for a final review of her mission.

"My Lord, I'm ready," she declares as she arrives in the room.

Kailen was standing near the table as she made her appearance. He studied her intriguingly.

"Kaliya," he mentions. "If Mother were to see you like this, well, I'm sure she would have something to say about it."

"Kailen, I'm four centuries, not four decades. I'm legal age and able to make my own choices in life. And right now, I'm choosing to dress up like a second centennial flirt looking to get her tail tagged for the first time."

"That's for sure!" he chuckles.

"Dear Powers," Thaelyn moans. "Clearly, I need to study your culture more if I am ever to understand your society."

He walks around to examine Kaliya's projected image from different sides. He folds his arms and taps a finger on his chin.

"Young lady, I must agree… If you were my daughter, I would be very concerned over where you might end up this eve. My only hope, in such a case, is that you find enjoyment from it. However, as to this mission, such a display as this should invoke that Ytani to follow you to the ends of the universe, I should think."

"All I need is two jumps through a conveyor, that'll be fine for my purpose. Do you have any last-minute instructions?"

"We have a scout projecting inside the Thane's Hall at this moment waiting for him to appear for his presentation. Marelle has her instructions and is currently on her way. You will go to the control booth and wait for the scout to return, informing you of Ytani's appearance, and then later his departure. We will expect him to make a call on his return, and our projected Commander Kriv'tik has his role to play that leads to yours. This is where your mission begins. Good luck to you, Lieutenant."

She salutes and brings her mind to focus on the control booth of the mining base, folding out of the local space and projecting forward to her post.

✦✦✦✦✦

Marelle was travelling quickly on course with her objective. She did not have a nav point on her screen in this case, since the local region was uncharted in her guidance system, but she reflected on her previous run with Ayene and the sights they passed along the way. She eventually came upon the broad range of mountains and banked around in the direction of the base. The terrain was slightly more familiar to her this time, and she found her mark fairly easily. But before dropping into the base itself, she slowed to a halt and dipped into a neighboring canyon just out of view of Ytani's house, but still able to see a portion of the roadway. She then opened her com-link.

"This is..." she smiles mischievously, "Sparrow-hawk calling Foxhole. I'm in position."

"Sparrow-hawk, this is Foxhole," the voice on the com-link replies back. "Acknowledged. We are awaiting confirmation of the play. Standby."

Marelle felt empowered to be part of this new operation. In her mind, this is how the game should've been played from the beginning. The use of disguises, espionage, codenames, and tactical planning... this is how you win a war, not sitting behind a desk taking names and dropping drunkards into a prison cell overnight. But for now, she had to hold her position hovering above the landscape until her cue was given.

Kaliya was inside the control booth when the call came in from Marelle. She stood and supervised the operation, waiting for her turn and mulling over how it might play out. She also felt a surge of enthusiasm over the recent events. Now they were fighting back, and delivering justice wherever needed. They held control of this base, and needed to play it right to conceal their actions. Ytani had to be isolated so he couldn't report home, therefore the base com-system was reconfigured to disable his link to Azgarén, and the conveyor was pointing the wrong direction for him to escape.

In the house on the far end, Ytani was finishing up his morning ritual of a meal and a quick sprucing up for the day. He stepped into his kitchen dining nook to look outside the window. All seemed normal from his perspective.

"They should be leaving soon to pick up the metal again," he snickers quietly. "And I'll get another playmate out of it. Oh, I love this job...well, maybe not the job itself, it's so boring, but the payment...free sex without conditions. Where are you going to find that back home?"

He strolled across the room to his favorite chair, which was positioned between his desk and an entertainment system. He sat down and relaxed, mulling over his mundane duty to bully the people of the city below, and perpetually annoyed by the Chancellor's obsequious manners.

"And all I have to do is scream at some runt about delivering goods at my hooves, completely free of charge...well, other than for that recent protesting. But everything in this job is free of charge. You couldn't ask for anything better. Free food, free living, free pleasures... Of course, that Commander is giving me a hard time lately. Hmm, I wonder how much arguing I'll get out of him today."

He reflected on his previous encounters on the com-link. The arguments, the debate over the survey, and the apparent stall tactics. He recalled the slowing production in the mines within the city, that last meeting with the Chancellor, and the potential delays it could bring if it runs out completely.

"New surveys…yes…" he muses distantly. "But if it runs out completely, and they're already protesting down there, I need a new story to bring it back under control. Hmm, something measurable, is it? If that metal is supposed to be so good, or at least those runts think it is, I should give them something new. What if I say the point-ears have developed something even better? Ah! That's it! Oh, I like that one. Therefore, we need so much, because their legendary super-soldier warriors are being cut down like bugs with an even better metal. I might need a name for it, though. Either way, I want this operation to continue indefinitely…for as long as we have people down there to do the work. And then, I'll get my treats every time I ask for it…my special payment. Oh, how lovely," he grins wickedly.

His mind drifted a moment to his sexual pleasures and his past delights. But it soon came back around to the arguments with the Commander.

"If he even dares to deny me my allowance for this run…"

He now recalled his threats and coercive statements of his alleged dwarven army, or even to bring the attention of the Marshal into it.

"If I call the Marshal, he'll simply put everyone on active and it won't be as much fun. But if I use the dwarves…oh yeah, now we're talking. I would need to rally them up into a riot that their precious metal is going somewhere other than they think. They're already upset for spending so much, so this shouldn't take much effort. I'll just say all those burning cities finally burned and they're right on top of us now, tying it in with the rest. Although I'm not sure how you get point-ears out of something like us. I'll need to change that somehow, since we don't actually have pointed ears."

He pondered the situation for a moment to find a satisfactory excuse.

"Wait, I know…they called in reinforcements. Ooh! I like that. And these reinforcements brought that new super-metal that's cutting everything else out there in half. But then, let's see… I don't simply want to throw away all those women. I could still have fun with them. So, they take everyone prisoner...yeah. After all, these people have been stealing precious goods and all their men down there, so they'll want a little revenge. But not the women! They can have the men, but I'm taking the women for my...um...personal interrogation. Perfect! I, the Thane of Glimmerheim, need easy subjects to torture in order to get information about the surface world. And I'll take my lovely time with it...one by one."

He reflected on his past victims in his bondage room, and how he played with their bodies. They were tied up in his restraining mount, completely helpless, while he applied his pleasure toys, and ultimately himself, until he had his fill of it.

"And that last one," he muses. "Oh, that was good. To see the look in her eyes when I cut that seed parasite. There's no return from that, and she knew it. The look of dread...of finality...I'll bet she didn't make it halfway up the road before it finished her. But the next one...hmm...I think I'll draw it out a little longer. After all, if this is to be her last day, let's make it memorable."

But before he could enjoy his pleasures, he had work to do. He had to quiet his anticipation, close his eyes, and ease himself into his meditation, releasing his consciousness from his physical body into a manifested form outside. This was a process he had been making for centuries by now, and it felt so very familiar.

Ytani projected himself and stepped away from his body, glancing around to check his image before envisioning his typical disguise as the dwarven Thane. It was the only one he ever used. He had no need for others.

He again folded his image into the Thane's bedroom, which is where he always began his work. He checked the room to ensure it met with his approval from the last time he was here. There was the pile of crinkled clothes at the foot of the bed, along with some slippers tossed on top, to simulate his used laundry from his previous visit. He then checked his drawers quickly to decide which set of attire he would use this time for his projection. For this occasion, he selects a set of olive-colored pantaloons and a vest, a white ruffled shirt, and of course his royal robe. He also chooses a set of rust-colored slippers to go along with it.

Having chosen his design, he closes the drawer and reimagines the outfit onto his body. He had no need for the actual clothes, but the image had to match his next set of laundry he would wrinkle up and toss away. This was his pattern after he finished in the throne room.

He walks around to a mirror to check himself quickly before opening the door and stepping out into the hallway. He continues along the corridor to the Great Hall, and there he sits on his throne and sends a servant to call for the Chancellor.

Nestled in a small nook on the shoulder of a statue across the room from the throne is an odd insect sitting next to a camera device. When the Thane takes up his seating on the throne, the insect perks up, and then disappears in a puff.

"Lieutenant," calls a scout appearing in the control booth of the base. "He's in the Hall."

"Good," Kaliya declares. "Get Marelle down here. Petrith, get outside."

"Sparrow-hawk, this is Foxhole," the team agent announces on the com-link. "The spook is staging. You are cleared to land."

"This is Sparrow-hawk…acknowledged," Marelle replies.

She gives her aircraft some thrust to boost her over the hill and swings around to line up with the roadway in the base, landing just in front of the conveyor. She jumps out of her seat to open the door and allow Petrith inside, then returns to her controls.

Petrith climbs inside, closes the door, and takes up seating next to her as she lifts off again and orients with the conveyor.

"You did set that thing correctly, right?" she asks.

"Yeah, no worries. Downtown Capitol Prime on Azgarén."

"Wonderful! What's the weather like over there?"

"Cloudy with a chance of plasma fire."

"Sounds like fun."

She throttles forward and they penetrate the rift.

"Chancellor," announces a messenger entering the office. "The Thane be a-callin' for ye in the Hall."

"Aye t' that, we don'na want t' keep him waitin'!" he responds. "An' this be the right day for it," he mumbles softly.

The Chancellor gets up from his desk and checks himself in a small mirror on the wall, preening his white beard and hair for a suitable appearance. He pulls himself up straight and clears his throat. This had to be a good performance if he were to get what he needed to bring this to a proper close. He then steps out the door and saunters up the lane to the Thane's Hall.

Ytani waited for the Chancellor to arrive. His mood on these occasions was never very high. He actually had grown to hate interacting with these people, with their simple-witted manners and grungy behaviors. This job was entertaining in the beginning, in those early days when he first started, a little like playing a game with a toy city. But as the centuries wore on, it became monotonous, constantly demanding more ingots and hassling over why it was needed.

The extended duration caused him to reinvent many of the original stories, in order to give continued justification as to why the war was still ongoing and why more materials were needed to fight it. The constant bickering over sending up more metal to fight any kind of war had become tedious, a habitual rehashing of alleged invasions, cities under siege, and warriors on the front lines forever fighting intruders that never seemed to stop.

And then the Chancellor arrived.

"Ah, good Thane, how ye be this day?" the Chancellor announces in an uncharacteristically gracious tone. "Did ye have a good sleep?"

"Aye, fine t' that, but now, tell me about the fare below," he charges harshly. "The first thing I want t' hear be about the diggin'. Did they find anythin' new down there?"

"Oh, good Thane, I think ye'll be glad t' hear they be a-diggin' up a storm like ye ne'er did see."

"An' did they find any new Adamant?"

"Well, it yay be a bit soon t' say just how much they be a-findin', but I can assure ye, the diggin' be hard an' true. In fact, I hear tale that they be a-breakin' through t' new ground for us."

"Good! An' what about that protestin' we had out there afore this?"

"Oh, aye! That be a fine one. The folk outside, they were askin' a good many questions about this nasty war. Ye know, these things happen. So, I went out there an' had a nice long talk with them t' try t' settle things. Ehm, good Thane, they did actually bring up a few things which needed t' be made better understood, so I promised them I'd get t' the bottom of it, an' this naturally needs yer fine wisdom on the matter."

"Argh!" he shouts. "Grand! What be this about now? D' I once again need t' remind ye about the point-ears out there?"

"Oh, I think ye don'na need t' remind ME about it. I yay be good an' proper on all yer past tales. But some of THEM may need a wee bit of clearin' up. Ye see, good Thane, they say some of the old tales nay be a-fittin' together in a right way for their proper understandin'.'"

"Uh huh, an' what d' they need this time t' clear them up on things? I swear, Chancellor, for all the times I need t' be a-tellin' these people about the war up there."

"Aye, good Thane, I know the tale. For one thing, they be a-worryin' about all those cities ye say were a-burnin' for so long. Some have come t' think this war has gone so long, an' those nasty point-ears have been a-ragin' so far an' wide, ye might think there nay be anythin' left of the place up there. We may be the only ones still alive down here under the mountain."

"Oh! That!" he gushes unexpectedly. "Um..."

"An' of course," the Chancellor interrupts. "This also leaves us down here as the last an' only city with any forges t' d' any work."

"Aye! Uh, that be the way of it, an' all the more reason t' get those forges cookin' it up as fast as ye can. The war still be a-ragin' up there!" he shouts.

"Aye, good Thane, an' with every city an' every town burned up, this means there nay be any more forges t' make up fare of any kind. An' this naturally brings us back t' the bricks. If nay any of those cities have anythin' left t' forge with, who be a-makin' the fare for the war?"

"Uh, well…"

"An' more!" the Chancellor interrupts again. "We have the warriors themselves, who LIVE in those cities an' towns that be so burned up. There should nay be any more homes for them t' live in! All-Father help us, this here be a bad hole. We have a war a-ragin' all across the land with so many homeless warriors an' nay any proper fare because WE nay be a-makin' it up for them, as we should be, t' give them what they need t' actually fight with!"

"Argh!" he screams. "Be that what they be a-hollerin' about now?"

"Part of it, t' be sure. But it does paint a curious picture of why those point-ears be a-ragin' so much, if the warriors have nay any more homes t' live in an' nay any proper weapons t' fight with."

"Well, I, uh… Only part of it?!" he shrieks. "How much more can they be a-groanin' about out there?"

"Well, mayhap ye can give us this much afore we go in t' the next bit."

The Thane found himself in a paradox, which represented a clear error he created during this time for his constant rewriting of their history, and it was now coming back to him. He had to think fast to cover for it.

"I swear t' ye, Chancellor. Right! So here be the tale. First, uh, the warriors be a-comin' from…CAMPS. Aye! They made a long line of camps t' hold them while they fight the point-ears. An' they moved the forges in t' the camps, so this be where the bricks be a-goin' t' be turned t' the fare they need. It yay be a simple answer, why don'na anyone know this?"

"Aye, that be a grand one t' ask, good Thane. Oh, why we can'na have such a simple thing as t' hear word from above tellin' us these tales. Mayhap it be because the doors be closed an' nay any word can get down here?"

"Aye! That be the way of it, ye fool. The doors were closed t' keep the point-ears out!"

"An' so nay any new tales of the outside can get in here either."

"Huh? What be this about now!" he rages. "I be a-tellin' ye! The point-ears be a-ragin' out there! What more d' ye need from it?"

"Well, for one, a way for YE t' know about it. The folk outside be a-wonderin' where ye get these tales, so mayhap ye can give us a wee word on how ye hear of it, an' no one else?"

"ME?!" he screams. "I be the THANE here!"

"Aye, this here be as clear as can be. But even a Thane needs someone t' pass the word. Ye can'na be pullin' it right out of thin air," he chuckles satirically. "An' t' me proper knowin', ye ne'er come outside, 'cept t' call for bricks. We nay see ye takin' visitors from anywhere. An' again, the doors be closed, which says nay a one, nay even t' speak t' YE, can bring them in."

He now found himself in another paradox...closed doors equate to closed access, even for him.

"Oh, that..." he flusters. "I...uh...well, aye! I have special messengers come in from time t' time...but we have a secret door. Nay anyone be s'posed t' know of it. Ye know...t' keep the point-ears out."

"Ah! Good Thane, that helps grandly. So, ye have this secret door, an' mayhap ye use this for these messengers as well as the bricks goin' out?"

"Um, aye! Right ye be. We use this for the bricks, an'...an' it be right there in the store," he points outside in the direction of the storage drop site. "But don'na ye get any ideas about goin' out there. Remember the rule here. The war be a-ragin', I say!"

"Oh, ye don'na have t' remind me. I recall the tales. Four hundred years it be, an' we dug deep an' closed the doors t' keep it out. But our good Thane has his secret door so we can help by sendin' out bricks an' men t' serve up the fare...while the rest of the land be a-ragin' with EVERY city an' EVERY town burnin' t' the ground. But why be it these nasty point-ears ne'er found us in this hole. Mayhap ye can tell us?"

"I don'na understand where ye're gettin' all this!" he yelps confoundedly. "They can'na get in here for the doors being closed!"

"Which one be that? The main doors that lead in t' our fine city, or this secret one ye say leads outside, with people who CAN find it t' come in here an' give ye these tales, but those point-ears, who be a-ragin' everywhere else, can'na find it? Some folk yay be askin' how much ye need t' pry those doors open? If they be everywhere up there, some folk be a-thinkin' they should've found us by now."

"What? Nay!" he shrieks. "They nay can find us. We be buried under the mountain…an', um, they be bad diggers. Ye don'na know this?"

"Ah, this here be a new one. Be this t' say our doors be buried along with the city? Hmm, I nay recall the doors t' be buried. After all, they were s'posed t' open up t' the outside."

"Argh! Nay! Um, what I mean is, aye! Well, actually nay now. We had a slide come down…more of that war, ye know! Those point-ears brought a big slide down on us. So, there nay be a way inside for that."

"Ah, aye!" he croons. "This can explain it. An' be this the reason for yer secret door?"

"Aye, the secret door t' go 'round it."

"Go 'round, with all those point-ears ragin' all across the land, includin' right in front of our city, even WITH a slide on top of it?"

The Thane was growing tired from all these conflicting details. The obvious tangle of statements was confounding his efforts to bring any level of justification to the stories he was telling.

"But good Thane," the Chancellor begins again. "This also brings up one more thing. Ye said these point-ears were bad diggers, ay?"

"Aye, d' ye need me t' say it again?"

"Nay t' that, just t' bring the mention. But some folks be askin' how such bad diggers can yay be such good fighters, especially against sturdy dwarves in Adamant armor. There was once a tale they be sickly an' weak, d' ye recall this one?"

"Aye, they be bad diggers because they be…um…" he halts abruptly.

The Thane suddenly realized yet another flaw as he started pronouncing this statement. The term sickly and weak would inherently mean bad everything, not just digging.

"Aye, good Thane," the Chancellor continues. "That old tale where it yay be more of a mercy killin'. This be the last word we got from the outside afore the doors were closed."

"Aye! Right, AFORE the doors were closed. After that, um, they grew stronger, an' NOW they be a-ragin' all across the land!"

"Of course, how silly of me nay t' think of this. So, they grew stronger, strong enough t' burn every city an' town, also t' fight off all our warriors bearin' up Adamant armor, mayhap even strong enough t' remove the slide they brought down on top of us, so they can NOW dig us out? Methinks this city, by the old tellin', be a yay grand one, a wee bit hard t' miss if ye be a-walkin' 'round out there."

"It be…it be…um…nay! It be all burned up by now. They nay can see anythin' worth lookin' at."

"Ah, what a shame that be. But yer secret door goes 'round it, ay?"

"Aye! It goes 'round…"

"Goes 'round t' where? We be under a mountain. The only way t' go be t' the south in t' a valley. An' these point-ears, by the tellin' of it, own that by now."

"Argh!" he screeches.

The Thane grabs his head and stomps his feet in frustration. The Chancellor observed and felt a hidden mote of pleasure watching the show. This was payback for all the suffering he had to take from the Thane during all his previous meetings.

"Chancellor!" the Thane screams. "What are ye tryin' t' say here? I be a-tellin' ye there be a war out there with warriors in camps holdin' up a line! They, uh, are holdin' it up right outside here, an' so we have our secret door goin' out there…with the bricks…an' they have their forges…so they can fight the point-ears who be a-ragin' everywhere else!"

"Ah, so that be where they are. Aye, this makes perfect sense. Ye know, for all our men goin' up, some folks were worried they may be a-gettin' lost out there, with all those cities burned by now."

"Nay, they be fine, don'na ye worry about it! They be a-makin' up the fare just outside here."

"Aye, good Thane, that be a grand one. So, um, why have we nay ever seen a note from them in all this time, if they be right outside our doors?"

"What?!" he screeches. "What d' ye mean, a note?! Why d' ye need a note from them?"

"For their wives, ye know. Some of them had wives an' other family who might want t' hear word from their men that they be fine an' good. But t' me knowin', nay a soul ever heard from their men in all this time we be a-sendin' them up t' make the fare."

"I... Ye... Argh! Notes now, be it? I nay be their father t' tell them t' write notes!"

"Aye, this be true enough, an' in four hundred years, ye might think one of them would think of it themselves. Even if the doors be closed AN' buried from a slide, if ye have a secret door that leads just outside here, that nay be far t' walk, an' nay much reason for a man t' forget t' write t' his pretty back home...or for that matter simply t' WALK back inside here t' say hello."

The Thane glares at the man for a long moment as he realized he just backed himself into a corner. If the men were immediately outside, what's to stop them from coming back in to meet with friends and family.

"An' so, good Thane," the Chancellor continues, hoping now to finish things. "We have yer tales of the point-ears a-ragin' across the land for four hundred years, burnin' every city an' town till there be nay anythin' left t' burn, beatin' back our warriors, with nay a home left t' fight for, an' mayhap no food t' eat, as well...we forgot about that."

"Food?" he blurts helplessly.

"Aye, we need t' eat, ye know. If the point-ears were a-burnin' the cities, they were probably also burnin' the farms. I think the last time we spoke, when I mentioned our folk here wantin' for better food an' cloth, ye said there nay be any by now. Such a shame," he shakes his head. "Anyway, now they be backed up against our mountain, fightin' t' their last breath, along with our men workin' hard t' forge up the fare, ay?"

"Aye, um, food. Well, aye, they've got food. Ye nay should be a-worryin' about that. They be a-makin' good enough with, um, new farms. After all, they still be a-fightin' up there, an' this means we still need t' make up bricks for them!"

The Thane was feeling weary by this time, for all the arguments. He was now hoping to finish this so he could return to the calmness of his home.

"Now Chancellor," he continues. "I've had about as much as I can take out of this! They need BRICKS! An' they be a-fightin' a WAR, it don'na matter where! An' it nay be a-lettin' up, d' ye hear me, finally?"

"Right ye be, just outside our doors now, with our good Thane keepin' us safe down here. An' for how long again?" the Chancellor leans forward with a quirky grin.

"Aargh! I swear, Chancellor!" he bellows. "For the last time, this has been a-goin' on for four hundred years since the day I first sat in this chair. What be the matter with ye?! Ye can'na count that high?"

"Oh, but good Thane, aye!" he acquiesces graciously. "I mean, as the Chancellor, countin' be somethin' I d' quite often in that office. An' oh!" he lauds the Thane's youthful figure. "Such a strappin' young lad ye be at that age. I recall me own days..." he nods his head thoughtfully. "Ye must take good care of yerself in that room of yers, aye?" he asks energetically.

"Huh?" the Thane blurts unexpectedly. "Take good care..." he glances at his image. "Well, aye! I mean...aye! Sure! Of course I take care of me'self. After all, I be the Thane here. I need t' take care of me'self...um, why are we even talkin' about this?!" he shouts again.

"Oh, just because ye look so good...fine an' young. An' as someone who knows how t' count, I be a-thinkin', for all the years ye've been a-sittin' in that chair, ye held up well t' it. In fact, ye look younger than the whole time I was a-workin' in me own office."

"I d'? I mean..." he glances at himself briskly again.

The Chancellor continues unabated, 'An' on top of this, as someone who spends most of his days countin' things, he might also take note that..." now he turns serious. "We dwarves don'na live that long!" he growls harshly.

"Uh oh…" the Thane mutters softly.

"Aye!" the Chancelor argues. "Ye call me the fool, but who be the fool here who plays the Thane for four hundred years an' ne'er once recalls that we tend t' grow old after a while? Ye say I don'na know how t' count? How old are ye, good Thane, or whoever ye be on the outside of it, that four hundred years yay be but a wee drop in a pond t' ye? It be quite clear t' me that the one an' only thing ye truly care for be bricks. Nay the lives of the people who make them, an' nay anyone else in this world. A Thane? Nay t' that! What ye be, yay be a foul-mouthed tyrant with nay a proper mind for tellin' tales that make any sense. Ye clearly don'na know what Adamant be about, but any DWARF would know! It be a part of our heritage. An' what more, ye clearly nay have any proper knowin' that an army fightin' for their homes would nay allow themselves t' be pushed up against our mountain when the rest of the world be a-burnin'. There nay be enough space up there for a full world of people t' be a-takin' refuge behind your camps with their forges an' new farms."

The Thane reeled back in his chair at the insinuation, as this suddenly exposed another error. The world population would naturally be much more than what would fit in a single valley. Not that he actually cared, as that world, in reality, was gone by now.

The Chancellor continues, "An' this be without the tellin' that if those point-ears have burned everythin' else, I doubt those last few warriors would have any say t' it by now."

"Um, well…"

"Save it, Thane!" he blasts. "Yer tales yay be as wild as a hill cat. We dwarves know a thing or two about fightin'. But methinks YE don'na have a clue. A proper warrior, in proper armor, an' with a proper weapon, would nay be a-fightin' a war for ONE year, much less four hundred. An' if YE be the one t' tell us t' close our doors, all that long time ago, ye can'na be a dwarf. An' this don'na leave too many other choices! 'Cept that ye can dress up as one. An' further that ye don'na recall t' change it on occasion."

The Thane now feels a spike hit him as the realization sets in. He let go of something he took for granted before this. He got started with only one image for his projection, and forgot to update it on occasion for the timespan involved. And unfortunately, he wasn't paying attention to the local lifespans. After all, this was simply a toy city filled with toy people, and he felt himself to be above that little detail.

Again, the Chancellor continues, "D' ye recall when I said we have people diggin' new holes? Well, Thane, those holes be a-pushin' through the upper city t' find those doors ye told us t' close off. An' we found the mountain came down on us, an' the slide outside. So, this here be the only part of yer tale that holds any truth t' it."

"Yer diggin' outside?" he mumbles.

"Aye! An' ye know what we found? It nay be our warriors just outside fightin' anythin', an' it nay be camps an' new farms. It be a dry waste, burnt an' then some, mayhap all four hundred years ago. But we DID find somethin' ye apparently forgot t' tell us about. We found people still alive out there with the REAL tale, an' it nay involves any point-ears. I don'na know who ye be in your right name, but ye're nay a Thane an' ye're nay a dwarf. The folk outside told us of our men servin' up in a mine under some sort of spell that makes them look like they be asleep on their feet an' minin' up more bricks! An' the ones who be a-pickin' them up nay be dwarves!"

"Uh oh."

"Aye, it be! An' worse, they die after a year or so, an' therefore we have yer feast. Such a fine one, that is! D' ye recall what I said about smiths who know how t' make Adamant? Well, Thane, if ye an' yer kind like usin' others t' d' yer work, it yay be clear ye don'na know how t' d' it yerself. An' ye think we dwarves are the fools t' nay know any better? Ye don'na just dig holes an' cook it in a forge. Adamant nay be as simple as iron. It has properties ye don'na find elsewhere, an' THAT be what ye need skilled talent to cook, nay any simple metal."

"But it looks like a simple metal."

"Did ye ever take a close gander at it? It glows!"

"Aye, I did see that once. But I thought it was a trick of the light, or somethin' bad inside."

"Nay t' that. This here be what makes it so much better. An' then we learned what truly happened t' all our kinfolk outside. Every city was said t' be blasted t' the All-Father, an' it came from the sky. An' those point-ears were only a minor sore on the backside in the first hand or two of years when those tales were actually circlin' 'round."

"They be real?" he mutters.

"Oh, ye don'na even KNOW of them? That be a good laugh. So where did YE get the tale from if ye don'na even know they be real? Be this one of yer secret messengers through that closed an' buried door? They came out of a portal, ONE portal, by the tellin', four hundred years ago, an' they WERE sickly an' weak, an' hard of breathin', barely enough t' stand up t' a babe, much less a warrior. An' then they stopped. An' then the blastin' came down an' destroyed our full world out there. So, ye may want t' tell yer kin up on top of the mountain, beyond yer secret door an' that clean tunnel of yers, that we know of them. An' the last of our Adamant will be put t' real weapons an' armor for our folk t' go up an' show ye what it truly be good for, since ye clearly don'na know for yerself."

The Chancellor strutted determinedly towards the doors, but stopped short to turn back into the room.

"Four centuries, Thane…that be how much of our most precious Adamant ye stole from us. It makes me wonder what ye were a-makin' with it. Since ye don'na know what it be good for, I doubt ye even know how t' forge it proper. An' ye think WE don'na know enough. What a shame, Thane…or whoever ye be. Methinks, wherever ye came from, ye be the one with the lack of knowin' if ye don'na even know what our native metals are. It nay be a wonder yer tales ne'er made any sense t' those of us who know better."

"But ye fell for it anyway, ye fool!"

"Aye, mayhap we did, if only for the true folk that played this nasty game on us. Ye bring shame t' yerself for all yer high knowin' that ye play these games on those of us who nay did get as far. The seat of a Thane be a high one in our culture. We dwarves give it a grand bit of respect, as the one who holds it be worthy of it. But YE disgraced the seat with yer foul manners an' bad temper. A true an' proper dwarven thane be a man with high privilege an' appeal. He comes from a proud family, an' holds himself up for the people t' respect him. I wonder if ye hold any such place amongst yer own, or if ye're just as foul with them, that they may one day turn on ye for similar wrongdoin's."

Ytani quickly reflected on the people up in the mining base, and all the arguments he had previously with the base commander.

"Ye come in," the Chancellor concludes. "Ye fill our heads with all yer guff, ye tell us there be a war out there an' t' close the doors. But methinks if it came t' a true battle, ye'd ne'er win. Who be the fool here, Thane, me an' my kin, or the cowards who don'na even know how t' fight proper?"

Now the Chancellor turns and exits the building, leaving the Thane sitting there alone in a daze.

"Dammit," he curses under his breath. "That blows all our efforts for sure. And worse is they apparently know of the tunnel, which means the base. So, I guess the idea of the uprising might come true after all…just not mine."

He quickly got up and hurried back to his room.

✦✦✦

Marelle had returned from her trip to the production facility to drop off Petrith, and landed on a pad opposite Ytani's house, facing away so he couldn't see inside the pilot's cabin. Ayene joined her, and the two of them now ducked below the window. Kaliya stood ready with her disguise in the control booth. The conveyor was still set to Madzurki, so even if Ytani tried to escape, he couldn't run far. At the same time, the com-link was disabled so he couldn't send any reports. Now it was just a game of wait-and-see.

After a long wait, the scout from the Thane's Hall returned to the booth with his report.

"Lieutenant, he's returning to his room. That Chancellor put him through a good run."

"Thank you. Can you give me a few highlights of what was said?"

"The Chancellor thoroughly shot down all of the Thane's stories, as well as his rebuttals as he attempted to make up new stories and excuses. The warriors are all homeless, with every city destroyed by now. They were lined up in camps just outside the slide that came down in front of their doors, along with new farms and all their forges to keep them supplied as they continued to fight the point-ears that seem to own everything else out there. And best of all, the men they send up seem very absent-minded to write notes, or even to walk back down into the city to say hello."

"Ooh! I like that one."

"He also got the Thane to admit to the four-century aspect of it. And oh! The good part. That…young…Thane looks so damn good for outliving the average dwarven lifespan by twice or more, including the time the Chancellor spent in his office watching the affair."

The group shared a bold laugh together as the scout continued.

"And here is where he sprung his trap to reveal the digging to the outside and the local stories. As well as a threat to use the Thane's secret access door for all his secret news reports no one else was privy to, to demonstrate what adamantium was actually good for."

"I'll bet that kid is steaming mad right now."

"No doubt. The Chancellor chastised him as a bad example of a thane by dwarven cultural standards, and further to accuse him of complete ignorance of what the metal does or how proficient a dwarven warrior might be on the field of battle. Not that I would expect a Suuden'kai kid to understand this to begin with. After that, Ytani ran off to his room mumbling to himself."

"No doubt trying to think up a new set of excuses right now," suggests one of the other teammates.

"I wouldn't be surprised, Navina," Kaliya nods. "And I'll bet part of it involves the Commander and his crew going nether-wild on them to regain containment. So, we'll see what he has to say for himself. We'll try not to demand too much out of him to give him a chance to make his play. Meanwhile, send word quickly to Marelle."

The agent on the com-link sent out a quick message that Ytani was returning. This would prepare Marelle for the final part of the plan. Now they must wait for Ytani's anticipated report, which would normally be expected by the Suuden'kai Commander.

Inside the city, the Thane returned to his room. He rushed inside and closed the door to hide from anyone who might be watching. He stared into the room to see the bed had been made and the laundry picked up, but he no longer cared about that. He had deeper thoughts on his mind.

"Dammit…" he curses again. "So, they actually went outside? And we still have people out there? Unbelievable…"

He delves into his thoughts trying to imagine how this could be.

"They blasted this world thoroughly," he muses. "There shouldn't be anything left out there…but wait. Oh, of course…why didn't I think of this before? These little runts like to dig in any hillside or dust pile they can find. They probably had someone in some tunnel or mine or something out there. But there couldn't be too many of them."

He wandered in circles in his room as he pondered the situation.

"Blasting… He must be talking about the bombardment, so we have that. The men in the mine…someone must've found them, which makes sense, I suppose. If they're looking for survivors, they might eventually discover it. And this naturally leads us back to see who is picking up the ingots. All right, so we're basically exposed now. And then he mentioned the tunnel… Yeah, they know."

He recalls his projection back to his house and returns to his body. Ytani stands up from his chair, circling the room still in thought.

"No more games, I guess. But we still need more metal, and I'm not finished here yet. We'll need military action now. Yeah, that's what we want. And this could also solve the issue of the survey. Yes! This is perfect. I know how to fix this. Ooh, this will be good, and it'll spice things up around here. I should've done this long ago. We'll just take them all prisoner and make proper slaves out of them!" he begins laughing maliciously. "Meanwhile, I want some fun."

He returns to his chair and spins around to his terminal to call up the control booth. Inside the booth, a beeping ring comes in.

"That's got to be him," Kaliya states. "Spook Commander, this is your moment. We'll play him along, but not too aggressively."

One of her team members was projected to imitate the Suuden'kai Commander. Her team had been studying the spy videos to learn how they behave and interact, so he knew his performance. He answers the call.

"Commander Kriv'tik, speaking," he announces in a flat Suuden'kai monotone.

"Commander, as you might have guessed by now, I have returned from my most recent duty."

"What is your report?"

"We are experiencing a little bit of a disturbance among those runts down there, but I have a wonderful idea on how to correct it."

"What sort of disturbance? Does this relate to that protest you mentioned last time?"

"Somewhat. It would seem some of them are getting restless about sitting in that hole while the rest of their world is apparently engaged in this awful war. So, they disobeyed my mandates to stay put and started digging themselves out. Would you believe it, but there are actually survivors out there! Incredible..." he huffs. "But anyway, they apparently shared a few stories, and they know the real world is different from anything I was telling them about, and so they're a little upset."

"When you say a little upset, how upset are we speaking about? Do they know about us?"

"Well, let's put it this way. Those survivors out there, and I'm guessing they were probably hiding in some hole somewhere, must've found our miners at one time, so the story about that is out. He also mentioned seeing who is retrieving the ingots, and unfortunately it wasn't any of their warriors fighting a war."

"This is unacceptable for the security of our operation. Do they know of us up here?"

"I think, if the mention of a tunnel says anything, that answers it. But Commander, not to worry, for I have a wonderful solution to all this..."

Kaliya glared at the Commander projection, and then passed among the other team members, as they continued to listen.

"This actually makes perfect sense to me," Ytani continues. "I wonder why we didn't think of this before…this job is so boring. We're clearly going to need to take thorough control of this situation if we're going to keep the metal flowing. I suppose this also solves that problem of the survey along the way. So, what I'm going to do is have you call in a large military deployment and take over that city properly, as it should've been done a long time ago. We don't need that stupid drug. We'll just beat them until they do what we want." he begins laughing maniacally.

Kaliya and the others stared at the com-link as Ytani continued raving over the speaker.

"And who cares if those mines down below are failing. We'll bring them outside and build a new city. And we'll find all those misbehaving survivors. We'll round them up and put together a REAL slave population," his laughing gets louder. "We'll put them to work in mine after mine, the Marshal will be swimming in the stuff. And I'll be KING over all of it! We'll build an empire out of it!"

His laughing had built up to a roar as his mania finally took over.

"And Commander, if you DARE say one word against it, I'll have him place your entire staff on active… In fact, to the nether-realms with the threats! If he wants his metal, I'm sure he wouldn't hesitate to put EVERYONE on active! And I'll have all of you licking my tail from now on. Girls who don't argue, soldiers who do whatever I say…it'll be a dream come true!"

Kaliya turned to the others in the room and shook her head silently.

"But now, Commander," Ytani asserts. "As for my little treat… I hope you gave serious consideration to my previous statements on your choices. The only thing I want to hear from you is who will be coming to serve my needs. No more arguments!"

"Yes…" he responds flatly, to simulate a mode of displeasure. "I gave consideration to your previous statements. If you will recall, I said my staff are all trained professionals, so if you want this base to continue operating, we need to keep them here. And since this operation is so heavily classified, I doubt Central Command would be willing to throw so many…trained professionals…at something without eventually questioning why we are losing them to such frivolous accidents. We are not supposed to be going out there into that desert to HAVE accidents."

"Commander, should I remind you who owns it?"

"No, Ytani, you do not need to remind me. However, I think even HE would not want all HIS trained professionals lost to such meaningless accidents either. Furthermore, he cannot put everyone on active, as you suggest. He needs at least some of them capable of independent thought to get any OTHER work done. He cannot do it all himself, and I doubt he created our military only to find himself performing all those actions our military is supposed to be performing for him. Remember, he has a final goal, and we are supposed to be helping him with it…voluntarily, not as slaves. There was never any mention in our agreement to kiss HIS tail for the mere pleasure of it."

"Hmm… Maybe…" he mulls privately.

"The other suggestion you made was to bring in a civilian."

"Ah!" he elates. "Commander, are we conspiring together now? Wonderful, what a nice alternative. And when I'm done with her, we can just drop whatever is left out in that desert. Send her on over, I'll be waiting…"

"No."

The link suddenly went silent, and Kaliya and the others waited for a response. It was still open, so they knew he was still there. Then he spoke again, but eerily smoothly.

"Commander… Is that word 'no' to say you are not conspiring? Well, I don't care. I'm still talking to the Marshal about this change of plans, and maybe also a change of staff! Is it to say you might not want to drop her in the desert? I don't care! When I'm done, you can let her rot out there in the street. But if it's to say you're not sending her to my house, I might get a little upset."

"Ytani, she is civilian, and the term 'civilian' is described as NOT part of our military. Therefore, she is NOT under my command to simply give orders. And like most civilians back home, she does not have an authority chip to simply program her into compliance. Therefore, she will be waiting for you outside. If you want her, you will need to attract her yourself. This is outside my authority."

"Outside your authority?!" he screeches. "She's a tail-flipping civilian and you can't teach her how to walk up to my front door? In all the nether-space, Commander, what does it take to get anything done around here?"

"As I said, she does not have an authority chip in her head; therefore, the Marshal does NOT control her as he does the rest of his military servicemen. And I believe this applies to ALL our civilian population back home."

The line goes silent again briefly.

"And this, as opposed to one of your...trained professionals?"

"Yes, Ytani, as those trained professionals take years, sometimes decades of preparation to serve their roles, and this is only AFTER finishing such as junior, senior, and university education courses, which you apparently did not fulfill. Does THAT answer YOUR question, Ytani? You do not throw that sort of education out a window. And I believe even the Marshal would agree...if HE wants anything done around here. Once again, he asked for our help, but that help requires well-educated individuals with the right skills to do the work. Not simply the education, but also the work experience, all of which you seem to be sorely lacking."

"Commander! I am unique with my skills..."

"Yes, Ytani. Unique for this one, and likely the ONLY one operation, to which there is a limit. After all, I believe the Marshal has a quota to fill, and we are currently at eighty-six percent capacity. Once this is done, I imagine he would want to move on, and our operation would come to an end. I wonder how your...unique... skill will serve you once you go back home. I suspect you will need to find a real job and earn real pay for all your future...luxuries."

"We'll see about that, Commander," he begins again, but a little calmer. "I'll simply have a little talk with him to see if we can extend this wonderful arrangement. After all, if he likes this stuff so much, surely, he will want more of it. If this metal is so precious, I can't see how you can ever get enough of it. Meanwhile, next time, I'll expect you to teach them how to make house calls."

The line goes silent.

"That guy is sick!" Kaliya relents. "But I'll also admit, Spook Commander, that was a good argument. It brought up some valid points, all of which he SHOULD be taking note of, but it would seem, like everyone else, he's clueless over what the Marshal is actually doing out there. All right, I'm going."

She folds herself outside in front of the building, facing away from Ytani's house, and taking up a sensual pose, swinging her tail in a smooth tick-tock motion.

Ytani reluctantly rose from his chair and headed for the door. He hated going outside in the native heat and dry air, but on this occasion, he didn't have much choice. He would simply take it out on his pleasure victim later. He exited outside and strolled out onto the roadway in the direction of the command building. But as his eyes focused on his prize, he halted abruptly.

"Huh?" he mutters privately. "Is that…"

He squinted to ensure he saw what he thought he saw.

"That's not right. Who is that girl?"

He continued forward, slowly at first, then picking up speed to close the distance, but then halting several paces away. He gazes at her. She was gorgeous.

Kaliya was standing out in the open, turned away from Ytani's approach. Her hands were femininely clasped behind her. She was wearing a pink mini vest over a white blouse and a matching pink mini skirt extending midway down her thighs. She had stockings from the mid-thigh to the ankles, and gold anklets around her hooves. Her feet were spaced apart with modest suggestion, and her tail swaying in a smooth arc.

Ytani studied her form longingly. He stared at her long slender legs, smooth tail, delicate curves, and trim figure. He moved another step closer, trying to peer around the side, and asking himself how and where this sensual creature came into being.

The people inside the control booth watched as the muscular Suuden'kai male made his advance. He came within proximity of Kaliya, and she made her first move.

She turned slowly to cast a seductive stare over her right shoulder. Ytani stopped in his tracks. He had never seen a face with such fine lines and perfect features. Her skin was clear, her contours were well-defined and feminine, and strangely, just like she didn't have the seed entity, she also didn't have any implants.

"Well now," Kaliya croons. "They told me there was a big strong man here, but they didn't tell me he was so handsome. And look, are you fully natural? How did you manage that?"

"Me?" he gushes and glances at himself. "Yeah, I'm a special case. What about you? How did you get out of it?"

"Which one, the seed or the other nether-bilge they hand out?"

"Nether-bilge?" he chuckles. "I like that."

"We could say my mother disagreed with the idea of the chip, and then argued with them until they finally shut up about it. As for the seed…well, they still think I'm underage for it," she giggles softly.

"Really! Hey, that's a great idea. So, um, where did they actually find you?"

"Well," she turns away demurely. "I saw an ad for a companion and playmate. I was curious. It said something about getting away from things. So, I applied."

"An ad? Wow, he actually did conspire a little. So, what do you think of getting out of this heat and we'll see what kind of fun we can have together?"

"I'd love it! But before we go romping around the kitchen, I'd like to be wooed a little. I absolutely love it when someone shows off. You know, I come from a rather privileged family, the kind that likes nice things. It gets my tail tingling so much; I go wild with it."

"Nice things?" he grins haughtily. "Well, doll, you've come to the right place. I've got a few things I could show off. But I don't keep them outside here. This place is too dusty for it."

"Yeah, I can see that. They said this is a mining operation…"

Kaliya now goes into her act, using Sulíma's figure-eight pacing routine as her starting point.

"But I've always fantasized about something," she continues. "I'm imagining a man who's a wealthy entrepreneur. He has lots of money, whole vaults of precious metals, but so unfortunately, he's all alone in this big place. This is why he's looking for that special someone who can make him happy."

She glances up at him shyly and presses a finger to her lower lip.

"Of course," she resumes. "As a girl who is rather special, I'm not going to give myself to just anyone. You know how it is back home, right? All those people…" she turns to glance inside the booth, "…like them."

"Yeah, I know the feeling. I've had that problem too."

"And so, I've been keeping my tail reserved for only that one man who knows how to treat it right. But I need to be sure I have the right one," she draws her finger off her lip with a sultry stare that drifts away. "We privileged families tend to stick together. We don't associate with just anyone, you know. So, do we know of anyone around here like that?"

"Doll, if you're here, you must already know. I'm your man."

"Then you must be really successful to own all this," she waves conspicuously at the base. "What kind of mining are you doing here? It can't be some simple rock, not all this way out in the middle of nowhere. No, I think you must have something special going on here. Precious metals, perhaps?"

"Um, well…sure, a special rare metal! You're not going to find it just anywhere. In fact, I was just speaking recently to our, um, mining foreman about how rare and valuable it actually is."

"Ooh, I like that. Do you have any you can show me? I'd love to see it. This is the sort of thing that gets my tail tingling most of all…to see a man's wealth shimmering in the light," she emotes theatrically.

"You know…" he chuckles. "I've got something better than shiny metals to show off."

"Oh, come now. How hard can it be? A little peek at your mountains of precious metals. I suppose you must have a vault somewhere. Every rich man should have one of those."

"Um, well, actually this particular one goes to a processor first."

"A processor...hmm... Ah, right," she coos. "And this is where you make your ingots, or maybe jewelry or something else that makes you so fabulously rich, right?" she smiles expectantly.

Kaliya was still walking in the figure-eight pattern and giving off occasional coy glances and flirtatious smirks. Ytani was nearly aching by this time to grab her and haul her back to his house, but he kept his place for the conversation, which was also rather enjoyable.

Inside the control booth, the others watched.

"Cu'Nar's grace, look at her," mutters one male. "Where did she learn that again?"

"I hear she took lessons from Sulíma Tad'vaal," replies another. "The Med-tech's sister."

"Well, whatever the case, I would imagine my body is feeling a rush right now."

"You men!" issues one of the females. "I swear...so I suppose I should probably take some notes on this."

The two of them glanced up at her for the suggestion.

"Well, hey..." she protests. "I might want a little one day."

Kaliya was still performing her act outside.

"Well, if we can't go to the processor, where does it go after that? This is where you put it in your vault, right?"

"Um, well, yes and no," Ytani offers.

"Yes AND no?" she muses intriguingly. "Oh please. Either you have a vault, or you don't, and either it goes into a vault, or it doesn't. Remember, Big Boy...I have a special tail waiting here. So, what are you hiding that you don't want me to see? Are you so afraid I might steal something from you? I'm here for one reason: To find that special man who needs my attention...and my attention is the finest money can buy."

"Well, to be honest, it's not actually money, or jewelry, or whatever in the vault. It's a kind of stuff that goes boom."

"A kind of stuff that goes boom, made from shiny precious metals? This is interesting. How does it look?"

"Um, well, I don't usually go there to study it for long periods. I've only been there a few times, and I prefer to stay out of it."

"Come on…" she croons. "Don't be bashful…"

"Bashful? Oh no, I'm not bashful…"

"Then tell me. Is it really interesting, or very drab? Remember the tail. If you give the right answer, great things can happen."

"Great things…" he ponders desperately. "Well, all right, um, the last time I was in there, I saw them storing these cube-like boxes, transparent so you could see inside."

"Sounds good so far…"

"Right, and they use some kind of gel stuff to hold this thing, and it looks kind of like a crystal with long spiky things sticking out that seem to change as you watch them."

"Wow…that sounds really interesting. But a crystal that has long spiky things that change? How do you get a crystal to change its spiky things?"

"I actually don't know. It's a really weird stuff they make. It's made for the Marshal, so only he really knows what it is."

"Ooh! You work for the Marshal? Wow…" she exalts. "Then you must be very special if he has you doing something like this. In fact, I'll bet you're more important than the richest man back home. And so young! Just think of all the time we could spend together. Hey, can we go see these things? I'd really like to see how these crystal things change like that."

"Well, um, like I said, they go boom if you're not really, REALLY careful, so I tend to stay away from it."

Kaliya was realizing by now that he was faltering, and so this might be the moment for her to try Sulíma's secret weapon. She begins by circling partway, then turning over her shoulder with a sultry look and her mouth slightly agape, and finally running her finger off her tongue, swinging around, and pointing.

"Tail…" she announces in a come-hither tone. "Where else are you going to find something as perfect as this? And all you have to do is show me your secret hoard. We'll take a quick peek, just for fun…but carefully, if it scares you so much, and then this tail will be open for business."

Ytani stared at her nearly drooling. The people inside the booth were also nearly drooling at that last move.

"Oh, that does it for me," moans one of the men. "When she comes back, let's rush her."

"Hey, you!" yips one of the females. "Remember that part about being a paladin?"

"Navina, I'm only kidding. But you have to admit, that could work wonders in a relationship."

"Well, yeah, I suppose it could. I definitely need to take that home to my husband. I might even get another child out of it."

"More than one, I'll bet."

Ytani's body was throbbing by now. He looked over his shoulder in the direction of his house, thinking of his sex toys and bondage gear, but this image of perfection was nearly enough to change his mind about it. He has an opportunity for an exceptionally fine treat, one that might even be worth keeping around, and all he needs to do is make a brief visit to the depot.

The depot. The… Depot… A place that was coincidentally away from his house, and everything else. Isolated. And worse, filled with a lot of highly explosive items. And the last place he would want to be for any reason.

His mind began turning over with all his recent thoughts. First, the arguments with the Commander over the previous occasions, as well as this one. Trained professionals, educational demands, civilians with minds of their own. And you don't throw talent away. But SHE was a civilian. This didn't count the same as a military specialist.

Then came the Chancellor, openly wondering how Ytani's own kind might see him for all his bad behavior. Then back to the Commander and his past stall tactics, as well as that most recent statement about getting a real job after this operation was complete. He was fighting, not conspiring. He had that suggestion of a survey… something that would take time, and also in projected mode, which would surely occupy him away from his pleasures, thereby preventing the Commander from losing any more of his trained professionals. But again, THIS girl was a civilian.

Finally, he began to reflect on where she came from. She responded to an ad? What ad? Where do you post an ad for something like this? And how could it find a girl like this, of all things. Furthermore, the base was classified as top secret. No one knew about it, neither were they ever supposed to know. And the next thing…a privileged family? She didn't have the seed OR the interface. And no one defies the Council, no matter how privileged they may be. The Council demanded everyone to be the same, there were no exceptions. Even the Commander admitted to this in one of his recent arguments.

Therefore, this girl couldn't be so special. If she didn't have the seed, she had to be underage. And if she didn't have any chips, that meant there was something funny about her with her opinionated mind making her own decisions. He thought about his own chip. It was removed once upon a time…a special privilege for his work assignment, care of the Marshal. But THIS girl couldn't be working for the Marshal, and for all the recent complaints against him by the Commander…

This simply meant she was a decoy to lure him outside, especially with this fancy display she was putting on. It was too good.

Ytani rolled his eyes towards the command booth. His mood was turning sour by now. He could see several officers gazing through the window as if they were watching a spectator sport.

Inside, Ayene was studying his reactions.

"Be careful people," she whispers. "I know that look. This isn't turning out right."

Ytani returned to examine Kaliya, who was still standing in front of him, attempting to disarm his growing skepticism with more innocent expressions and sultry eyes. But even she could see his change in posture.

Ytani recalled how the Commander knew of his opinions over the seed entities, and bringing in a girl like this would surely draw his masculine urges to a boiling point. But she was pushing to go to the depot. Why? Simply to look at shiny things? This was on the other side of the conveyor from the processor, and he didn't want to get trapped over there by some swag-tail trick.

Nevertheless, her perfect body was delicious. An underage girl could still be a lot of fun…maybe even more so for her youth. Suddenly, he realized his dream. This might be his ticket away from the repugnancy of the others, to take young girls before they're infected with that horrid parasite. And as he considered these topics, his face transformed again to one of licentious determination.

"You know, doll," he intones with a rude smirk. "I actually think I have a much better idea. In the end, it all comes down to business…MY business. How old did you say you were again? Do your parents know you're here? You say you got out of that awful seed. Yeah, that's a good one. Maybe I'll ask for more like you later. Meanwhile, let's go inside my house and see what we can do about it. Having a cute body like yours will really make my day. Even better, if you don't have that emotion stunting chip, I could get some genuine screams out of you."

Kaliya watched as he mulled his thoughts. She had been studying him for his changing behavior, and she could see in his eyes his mania taking over while he lustfully studied her body. She tried one last time, although it seemed pointless by now. She gazed at him poutingly.

"Does this mean you don't want to show me all your nice things after all?" she asks with feigned despair.

"Nice things? The only nice things I have to show off are all those toys I like to use on girls like you. You'll love it, just like all the others. Although, without the seed, this might take a little longer to finish up, but that's fine by me."

"Uh huh, without anything to cut and make a quick kill. All right, Ytani, you want it the hard way? Fine. But you should know, I'm not underage, and neither am I some cheap tail-swinger you can have your way with. You want me? You'll need to work for it."

"Oh, really! This should be fun."

He tried lunging for her, but she simply jumped back.

"Let's see how well you can fight," she announces. "And I'm talking real combat, not that nonsense they teach on Azgarén."

Kaliya quickly swings a roundhouse kick to the jaw, knocking him sideways. She then turns to the control booth and shouts in Tae'Eladaran to conceal her words from him.

"We have a problem out here! Get Marelle and Ayene in the big transport!"

Ytani was knocked almost to the ground by the unexpected hit. The projected form of Kaliya's body didn't carry the mass of a physical one, so the hit didn't deliver as much of a physical shock force, thereby causing direct injury. But it did carry an inertial force, based on her perceptions of the effect, to knock him off-balance.

He recoiled back and glared at her, now realizing she was indeed a fake, and he tried lunging at her again. But she again evaded to the side.

"You hit like a girl," he scowls.

"Um, excuse me, but I am a girl. On the other hand, would you like me to hit harder? Let's try this…"

Kaliya returned with an elbow jab to his flank, then spun around with a back-fist to the face, followed this time by a two-handed smack, which was further exaggerated with stronger willpower to the force applied. The result nearly lifted him off the ground and sent him flying to the side, landing face down on the roadway.

"Was that any better?" she jests.

She waits for him to climb back onto his hooves before making her next move.

"You like to play with girls, Ytani? Let me show you one who knows how to play rough."

She continued with several more jabs, and a foot sweep to knock him down again.

The others inside the booth rushed out to assist. Now Ytani found himself outnumbered. Several of them grabbed him by the arms and legs and started carrying him along the road.

Marelle and Ayene were both hiding inside the small shuttle, but on receiving their new orders, they hopped out and ran over to the large cargo transport the staff so often used to retrieve the metal. Ayene opened the rear loading ramp while the group lugged the squirming Ytani into the cargo hold.

"We need to restrain him somehow," Kaliya shouts. "Go inside his house and bring his own bondage thing out here."

Some of the team now diverted to the house. They poured through the door and into his exercise room, where the large prisoner restraining mount was found. But the nature of the projected teammates only allowed one of them to actually carry it, as they couldn't interact together with inanimate objects. Therefore, one member grabbed the device and hauled it outside while another grabbed the cuffs and straps to tie him up.

"Who are you?" he screams. "I'll rip you apart, you little skank-tail!"

"Careful of your words, Ytani," she cautions. "I'm a military officer, not some underage kid for you to play with. Did you actually think no one would take notice of murder around here? I think even the Marshal would have something to say about you killing HIS specially trained people who are here to perform HIS operations. After all, don't forget why he made this military, and it wasn't for you to toy with."

"You fool! That's exactly why he put me here! I'm the one who runs things, not any of you! I'll have all of you put on active for this. Then we'll see who has the last say."

"Ytani, you were put here to play an angry dwarf. THAT is your job, nothing more. And these chips can be deactivated, did you know that? And all the base people had theirs done by now. And I don't even have one."

"Then I'll get them turned back on. And as for YOU..."

"Ytani, you're missing something big here," Kaliya explains. "Whether military or civilian, we do have laws, and when you have people who go to a university to learn how to be law enforcers, that means you will PAY for your crimes. And murder is a crime."

"Dammit! How many times do I have to say it, you fool! The Marshal owns everything!"

"Ytani, YOU are the fool here, a deluded little tyrant who never finished junior school. One, the Marshal doesn't throw his people away. He needs them. Two, he wouldn't appreciate YOU throwing them away. HE needs them. And three, like the Commander said, he can't put everyone on active, and those who are working normally will eventually figure it out and give you some of that law they enforce over there. I don't know about the civilian side, but I would imagine military law involves a death penalty for murder. And HE would not get in the way of that...because he NEEDS them to actually work for him. Otherwise, he becomes next, when he interferes with their laws, and they turn their guns on him now."

"Oh? And who makes those laws! The Council! And he does own them!"

"If he really owns them, I imagine they'll be losing their jobs soon. Aside from that, I can say life on Azgarén DOES still have laws. It has universities that teach people about laws. And it has security agencies and law enforcement services to catch criminals. And they also have courts to prosecute those criminals. And if they have all that, not HE nor the Council own it to the point where it ever stopped. And if either he or the Council should TRY to stop it, they'll have a full world of people coming down on them. And this would include all those security and law enforcement agencies, and likely also the military. And I doubt he could turn those chips on fast enough to prevent it. And then you have US, who aren't even a part of it."

"What? Then just who are you?"

"Justice, Ytani...the kind that gets the job done, despite your precious Marshal and his desires for a pet minion species. Oh, you didn't know that, did you? You're a pet minion creature he keeps around just because he doesn't want to bother himself with such a boorish thing as a mining base."

"You idiot, he OWNS the thing, just like he owns everything

else. And I'm his favorite. I'm unique! Once he finds out, you're all in for a huge amount of trouble."

"The same as on Therinë, where he ran away from us? Yeah, sure, Ytani. You know, owning something is not the same as running it. He leaves that to cheap labor, like you. As for trouble, HE is the one in a huge amount of trouble, and by those very same beings he's hiding from right now. So, you can keep your threats to yourself. You have absolutely no idea what you're talking about…much like you have no idea what adamantium is, but those dwarves downstairs sure do."

"What?" he shrieks. "Are YOU the one responsible for that?"

"We're the enemy, Ytani, those so-called insurgents you keep hearing about. And we're here to correct things."

"And these parasite-infested half-horns are actually helping you?"

"Well, yeah, actually," she smirks. "Would you expect them to help you instead, for all your threats. You killed one of them. Some people take exception to that."

The other teammates had been trying to hold him while they attached the straps, but Ytani's struggling was making it difficult.

"Lieutenant," remarks one member. "We can't get a good grip on him to hold him in place."

"Try it like this. It's a conflict of will here, so you need to exaggerate yours to overwhelm his."

The teammates tried this tactic to reimagine a supercharged push to press him down into place for the straps to link with the hooks on the mount. Ytani groaned as he suddenly found his arms and legs wrenched into position and held firm. The team members were now able to lock him down, and Ytani found himself stuck to his own bondage toy.

"All right…" Kaliya orders. "Pilots to your seats, everyone else out! Get this thing out of here. Send word to Petrith, we're coming through. I'll meet you there."

Kaliya leads the team out of the vessel and Ayene closes the door. Kaliya would now fold herself directly to Ooduan while Marelle and

Ayene fly the vessel there. Ayene joins Marelle as they take up their seats in the pilot's cabin.

Ytani tried to struggle out of his straps. His long time working out on his exercise equipment had built up a considerable amount of upper body strength. So, he figured, with a bit of effort, he could probably break free.

Marelle powered up quickly. She hit the flux lever to gain some altitude and threw it in reverse. Ayene braced herself as she felt the vessel lurch backwards. As they aligned with the conveyor, Marelle throttled forward hard.

"In all the nether-space, Marelle," Ayene shudders. "No wonder your instructor is losing his horns."

"I haven't broken anything yet, so stop complaining."

They passed through the rift locus and quickly found themselves hurtling through the conduit.

Ytani was getting desperate to free himself. He could feel one of his wrist cuffs stretching as he strained to pull himself away. He similarly struggled with the other one, spending all his strength to break out of them.

The vessel arrived through the conveyor at Madzurki. Ayene got on the com-link as soon as they were clear.

"Petrith!" she shouts. "Swap us over fast. He's fighting us, and we have him tied up, but not for long."

"Got it..." he responds and hits the conveyor selection choice for Ooduan.

Marelle pulled a fast U-turn, which swung the vessel around hard. Ytani and his mount slid to one side while Ayene grabbed her seat to hold on.

"Are you absolutely sure you never broke anything?" she gripes.

"Well, at least not on any of the simulators."

"Oh great!"

Once she saw the conveyor realign, she throttled up and plunged into it again.

Once more, they were rushing through the conduit. Ytani

continued to tug at his straps, until finally one of them broke. With one arm now free, he reached over to release the other one.

Ayene was trying to keep one eye on him, while simultaneously gasping at Marelle's reckless flying. When she saw him free one arm, she felt a chill.

"He's breaking loose, Marelle!"

"Then get back there and give him a good stomp where it hurts."

"The way you're flying? I can't even stand up like this."

Ytani was still struggling with his other wrist strap when they arrived through the next conveyor. Marelle increased the flux field while diving into the ground. Ayene screamed as she saw the rocky surface approaching, only to halt as the vessel compressed into its flux cushion. Marelle angled towards the flight hanger and throttled up, barely missing the upper frame of the curtain field, then throttling back and turning sharply to slide in sideways.

"Get the door!" she urges.

Ayene springs out of her seat and staggers towards the rear. Ytani tried grabbing her as she passed, snatching her by the ankle. Ayene reached out to a nearby shelving rack for support, and with her free leg, stomped down firmly on his groin. He bellowed in pain, reflexively releasing her leg, and moving his hand to cover his private area. Ayene then leapt away out of reach towards the door. She hit the button to open the loading ramp, but at this time, the vessel was not technically landed, only hovering.

Kaliya had folded into the hanger and was waiting as a bug when the transport arrived. She reimagined her image into its natural form when she saw the door open.

"Kaliya," Ayene shouts. "He's trying to get out of his bonds."

"Just you two wait," he shrieks. "You're not leaving me here!"

"Simply leaving you isn't quite what we had in mind."

He was finally able to release his other arm from the strap. Now it was just the two legs.

"Ayene," Kaliya issues urgently. "Get out here! Grab the bottom part!"

Ayene jumps out of the vessel and spins around. The two of them grabbed the base of the bondage mount and hauled the apparatus out, dropping it to the ground and twirling it partway to one side, away from the ramp.

"All right," Kaliya snaps. "Get back in there and go."

Ayene jumps around to the ramp and climbs back up. Ytani realizes it's now or never, so he scrambles to unhook the remaining straps. Ayene glances back at him one more time.

"Hey, limp-horn," she shouts.

Ytani impulsively looks up at her glaring at him from the top of the ramp.

"This is for Hena, you over-pumped cow!"

Ayene turns around and flips her tail straight up at him, representing a strong obscene act of defiance.

"You little skank-tail!" he growls and returns to fight with his remaining restraints.

She hits the button to close the door as he manages to loosen one leg, then the other.

"Oh no you're not!" he screams.

The door closes just as he manages to get to his feet, and Marelle hits the throttle again, pulling the vessel out of the hanger.

Ytani stood there gaping at the transport departing outside the atmosphere curtain and turning to orient at the conveyor, then to throttle forward and vanish. He then turns to glare at Kaliya. He glances briskly around the empty hanger. There were no other shuttles present.

"It looks like you missed the boat, little girl," he emits harshly.

"I don't need a boat," she returns casually.

Ytani lunged at her once again, but this time she held her position for it. He grabbed her by the arms and jerked her up to him.

"I'm going to have a lot of fun with you," he growls in her face. "First, I'm going to bend you over and give it to you in all your tight little places. And since we're all alone up here, I'm going to spend lots of time with it. And just before I finish up, I'm going to stick your head outside that curtain and see how well you can breathe as I finish you on this side. What do you think of that?"

"Very graphic, for one thing, and perfect for a demented pervert who thinks entirely too much of himself."

"Really! Well, let's just see what you're made of under this cute little dress!"

"Ytani, did it ever occur to you that I might have missed that boat for a reason? Did you see me riding along on that transport? Do you see any other shuttles in here that I might have taken? How do you think I got here? Do you actually pay attention to anything, or is your ego so big, it blinds you to what's right in front of your face?"

"Huh?" he halts as he begins to wonder if something was wrong with this scenario.

"You know," she muses casually. "You spent four centuries complaining about those dwarves not knowing their native metals, when in fact YOU do not know their native metals. And apparently, you never bothered to ask about it, at least as much for your own knowledge, so you could keep your stories straight. You simply assumed you know best, and they do not. That world is in a completely different universe, Ytani. There are a few differences there than what we have back home, and THEY know what they are. This also equates to where we are now, you and me, and what I know, but you must not be paying attention to, all because of your bad attitude."

"Oh, and what is that supposed to be?" he blasts defiantly.

"For one thing, how does someone travel to places not otherwise accessible by conventional means?"

"What do you mean, conventional means?"

"Well, let's take you as the Thane. By conventional means, we might say to walk down there. Did you do that? Here we are, on a moon. How do you arrive on a moon? In a ship, right? Fine, where is my ship?"

He pauses as he reflects on the transport that just left, but he also had to admit, she wasn't on it. He glances outside again before returning to her. He saw her gazing at him with a curiously mischievous grin.

"Ytani," Kaliya giggles. "You're such a silly boy! You must not have a very long attention span. Do you think I would actually sacrifice myself to you?"

At this point, she flashed out of his arms to a position a few paces away.

"I'm not even corporeal," she finishes pertly.

Ytani gawked at the obvious display, glancing at his now-empty hands, and then at her as she smirked at him teasingly.

"How did you do that?"

"Oh, please, Mister I'm-So-Unique," she retorts brashly. "For a guy who's been playing a dwarf for four centuries, I might expect you to recognize your own trick being played out. The only REAL difference here, other than me being a girl and something you regard as a pleasure toy, is I have an imagination. And in the few YEARS, not centuries, but years I could count on my fingers…that I've been playing with this, I've learned more about how it works than is healthy for a person. Didn't you ever try experimenting with it to see where it could take you, or did the Marshal simply tell you it's only good to make a dwarf and nothing else."

He suddenly found himself stunned at the notion of another person with the same skill. But the concept of it being useful for anything beyond simulating a dwarf was absent to him. Kaliya studied him for his extended lapse.

"Yeah, as I thought," she surmises. "The one, the only, Ytani the Egomaniac, who doesn't have a clue what it is he's actually doing. But he sure does think himself to be a god with it. Oh wow, look at me, I can imitate a dwarf…"

At this time, Kaliya chooses to make her own impersonation. She reimagines her shape to that of a common dwarf.

"But is this ALL I can do?" she muses in her dwarven accent. "Hmm, what about this?"

Now she goes into her routine of practice animal shapes. First, she takes the form of a squirrel, then a tiger, then a hawk, finally a tree, and back to normal. Ytani is dumbfounded by the demonstration.

"And that's just a small taste," she continues. "I'm teaching an army of people this skill, Ytani. And we've been learning everything there is to know about it. We've played everything from clumps of dirt to god figures, it's just a matter of the imagination conjuring something up. We can impersonate anyone or anything we see, like the base staff, for instance. Those were MY people in projected form, not the originals. You think you're so special? Uh-uh, by my standards, you're an amateur."

"But…how?" he mutters softly. "Did the Marshal teach you?"

"Darumon is no Marshal, he's a criminal on the run from a governing body. So, your statement of HIM owning anything is wrong. He and Sargeras are refugees from an ancient war where they lost."

"An ancient war?"

"Right. There's another body out there called the Estelar. THEY are the ones who own everything. Do you know the name Moradin?"

"Um, no, why?"

"Maybe the more common name… The All-Father."

"Huh? The All-Father? That nonsense name those runts keep using?"

"Yeah, those runts with their god. He's the leader of a group known as the Morndinsamman, a faction of the Estelar dedicated to the dwarves. The Estelar are responsible for killing off all of Sargeras's people. It's called law enforcement. But you know, you probably made a really big enemy out of him for all your insults to their race. They're his Children…in a philosophical sense. And these…gods…aren't nonsense. They're coming to finish the job now, all thanks to your precious sugar daddy Marshal splashing in a puddle he should've stayed out of."

Kaliya now begins pacing in an arc around Ytani as she begins a more detailed explanation.

"Sargeras is the last of a dead society of beings who treated little things like us as toys. This is why the Estelar exterminated them like bugs. Darumon is simply a servant creature under him, nothing more. He might THINK he owns Azgarén, but only because your dull-horned Council sold the people out to him."

"Why are you saying MY dull-horned Council. What about you? You're one of us, aren't you?"

"Technically, yes, although when I look at what you idiots did over there, I'm ashamed to admit to being part of the same race. I wasn't born on Azgarén. So, I'm not subject to those loose-horns and their nether-wild mandates. That base staff…you asked why they would help me. Well, technically, the REAL base staff was captured several days ago by my military Special Ops team. But overall, yeah, they were tired of the treatment they were getting back home, and especially by you. Even with chips in their heads, people still have opinions. And the Commander was two steps away from taking his own action against you for Ensign Ka'zheen. If it weren't for me intercepting him first, you'd be dead by a pulse pistol."

"He was going to do that?" he shouts. "And what do you think the Marshal would say about it! He put me there to bring up the metal!"

"Ytani, being placed in the role of bringing up the metal is NOT the same as owning the lives of people. The Marshal made a military to fight HIS enemies, not be YOUR playmates. Furthermore, you committed murder, it's that simple. Not only that, but multiple counts of torture and abuse, to say nothing of rape. Ayene tells me she has a university law degree. This says the people of Azgarén do actually have law and justice, and the Marshal does NOT own it, like you think he does. He might control the military with these chips, but murder is still murder. I think if Central knew what you were really doing out here, there would be several hells to pay for it, and you would be on the front line, regardless of the Marshal. The people will demand it, and not even HE could stop that. But it's all moot now."

She pauses as she begins pacing back along her steps.

"We've been chasing him across several worlds so far," she continues. "And we're soon to arrive on Azgarén. I'm here to stop him, and the people I work for are coming to finish him and Sargeras as part of that last battle where they were supposed to be killed anyway. What he wants doesn't matter. What YOU want doesn't matter. This is what we call Law and Justice. And despite what you, he, or your Council might think, WE will bring it!" she asserts firmly.

She glared at him for a response, but he was simply staring back at her in silence.

"Do you actually know what this fantastic skill is called?" she asks. "Did the Marshal give you a name for it?"

"A name?"

"Yeah, it's what people usually give something when they get tired of saying, 'that funny thing someone did one time'..." she smirks cutely.

"Ha ha..." he drones.

"You know, your reactions tell me you didn't get much in the way of a proper education. How much did you actually get before you were relocated to the base?"

"I uh..."

"You were probably pulled out of junior school along the way. Seven decades, was it?"

"Yeah."

"You do realize there is more that should come after that. Did you ever try to finish it, like with a remote feed or something?"

"We didn't get that at the base."

"Naturally, it was so hush-hush."

"And besides, when the Marshal pulled me out, he told me I didn't need any more."

"Uh huh, and I suppose this is where your complete lack of respect OR appreciation of skilled labor comes from, since you never got any. In a proper workplace, you would be completely useless."

"What about this skill of mine? Isn't that useful for something?"

"Ytani, I could answer that in a couple of ways. First, in OUR society, you need at least a senior school education to qualify even for the lowest form of employment. And this is probably not in your best interest, as you might also need government support to fill in for that which you're not capable of providing yourself."

"Why do you say that?"

"Well, typically, people work to make money. And they use that money to buy things, like food, clothes, pay for their homes, and so on. But if you're working at the lowest of the low jobs out there, you might not be making enough to afford everything. Therefore, here's your government aid to fill in for the rest of it. But Ytani, this is not actually what a person WANTS to have, as that government support might come with conditions to GET that higher education so YOU can do it yourself. They don't necessarily like babysitting people who don't like to work."

"Oh."

"And this is where the rest of it comes in. You'll need some amount of college or a university education before you can be useful in any halfway decent job position. And this skill isn't a part of that, especially if no one ever gave you a name for it, which means no one knows what it is. And THAT means, it doesn't hold a role… in OUR society."

"Uh oh."

"Therefore, no, it is not useful, at least not by itself. It could be used as a tool, but you still need to know HOW to use it, and what to use it on. Simply pretending to be a dwarf, if this is all you know how to do, is not going to be useful, as I doubt there are any job roles for dwarves on Azgarén."

"Well, no, probably not."

"I've learned how to use it for all sorts of things, from spying on people to interacting with political and diplomatic talks. I can impersonate someone, like an enemy agent, and go into his own office to give orders to his own people to break things he uses to hurt others. I can go places and use things, like machines or devices, without being noticed, and this may be to arrange something in my favor to help others later. I'm a soldier fighting a war, Ytani, so my roles are mostly to fight my enemies. But I'm also discovering a lot of things it can be used for that aren't necessarily for a military role. And like I said earlier, I'm training an army for this, which will eventually need to serve a government role to teach and administer our people back home, likely replacing the Council and their dull-horned attitudes, and carrying our world into a new Era. THAT sort of role would surely be useful, but it will also take a lot of specialized training to achieve it."

"Yeah, it sounds like it."

"And once again, if no one even knows what this is, except maybe the Marshal, then clearly, he forgot to tell anyone else. How nice of him for all his promises of great wisdom. I guess this one wasn't included. Unfortunately, this brings us to the next part. If he once said you didn't need any more education than that little bit you got previously, this means he probably doesn't HAVE any other job roles for you. You are using a skill he forgot to tell the rest about, and in fact is actually HIDING from them, as he lies to them about it, along with all his other promises."

"Lies!" he surges.

"And you going home for any reason would represent a liability, especially if you start showing off a skill he doesn't want them to know about."

"Um, well...hiding it?"

"Let's take a few examples," Kaliya issues. "Apparently, for all the science factions who crave new knowledge, no one back home was told you people found a new universe. This would represent the sensation of the millennium. But he forgot to tell them. Then, we have the metal, which some of us call adamantium. Ytani, in all this time, did you ever once try to investigate what this stuff actually is, or did you simply figure, because it came out of such a backwards society as theirs, it's of no real concern?"

"Um..."

"I think the answer is probably, you did. YOU don't know what this metal is, meaning to say Azgarén does not know what it is, not simply you, personally. And this is evident that our science back home has no definition for it. So, what right do you have to tell someone he doesn't know his native materials?"

"It's a metal, that's all."

"No, it's not! It's a metal, yes, but if our people could gain one nano-fragment of an idea what to do with it, it would revolutionize most of our industry for its sheer strength alone. Forget even the highest grades of steel, this will cut right through it."

"Huh? You're kidding me!"

"Me? You already rejected the idea from a man who knows it best. Dwarves are masters in this knowledge, despite their lack of technological wherewithal in other areas, and this METAL beats most of it." she shrugs.

She continues her pacing, now turning back again.

"Not everything in life requires electricity to power it, or even spaceships to carry it. You need special skills to make this stuff, which takes time, practice, lots of experience, help from those who know better, and only after decades of hard effort will you begin to realize all the little secrets of how to forge it into something useful. You can't just put it in a fire, smelt the ore into a metal, pour it into a mold, and poof...something useful comes out. You need very special knowledge and skills to keep the unique properties intact that make it so powerful to begin with. Otherwise, you can spoil it. And those properties are specific to what you'll find in that universe, as it's all related. Therefore, we might not know how to use it, but they certainly would."

"But couldn't we learn?"

"We could, if we were to spend enough time there and stop denying such things as all that mystical magical nonsense you refuse to accept. This is exactly what it is. And the way you were spending all their highly skilled labor in those mines, I'm surprised you still have people who know enough even to make the fires in their forges to smelt anything at all, to say nothing of forging it into something."

"Is it something chemical? They don't have wood down there..."

"True, but no. The way I hear it, you have some special minerals you can find in places like those, but the fire, in this case, isn't your traditional combustion fire. It's based on yet another principle our science back home wouldn't be able to explain, but in THAT UNIVERSE this principle gives you a special result. And this result is what you need to work this metal...in that universe. Get it?"

"In that universe...not in ours."

"And therefore, people like us, who come from a different universe, and who do not have the native environmental qualities, would have no idea how to use it. And here you are, telling native people, who DO know what this is, that they don't know what they're talking about."

"All right, fine. But how am I supposed to know anything about this?"

"Well, for one thing, you could ask. If not one of them, for instance if you're trying to impersonate a dwarf who ought to know to begin with, then maybe ask the Marshal, who would surely know, and could maybe give you a few pointers so you could get some of your stories right. Equip an army with this stuff, meaning to say armor for the body and weapons, like swords, and you'll cut through anything that gets in your way that isn't also equipped with the same. And dwarves are also very good at warfare, so whatever it is that gets in the way had better be VERY good at fighting."

"Uh huh, and so they argue about everything."

"Yes, because you are speaking to people who live by these rules. Ours, by the way, do not. If all you know is how to blast things with a pulse rifle, you probably wouldn't know much about fighting with swords. And if you allow someone to come up so close that NOW you are being hit with a sword, that's trouble, especially if you consider those seeds. And dwarves won't hide behind walls for you to shoot rifles at them. They'll rush you in hordes to take you down."

"That sounds bad."

"Now, as for this strange skill... As I said, no one knows what this is back home. And knowing our people as I do, for all the sagging horns, and their pure desire to measure things in numbers, if they were to see you using it, you might start a mass panic, followed by an angry mob chasing you with pitchforks and torches until they hung you from a flagpole. How does that sound for your god syndrome?" she smiles pertly.

"You're losing me."

"The Marshal didn't give you a name for it, and neither to Commander Kriv'tik and his people, who might have a need to know, as this is an important part of their operation to bring up the metal. This means, the Marshal doesn't WANT any of you to know what it is. So let's ask ourselves why. Is it really such a bad thing? Well, that depends on who you ask, but if he's not telling you, it means he has a reason for it, and this reason is also why you don't have that horrid little Suppressor chip in your head. THAT is the reason you can do this, as the chip turns it off."

"It turns it off?"

"It's a cover-up for something we ALL have in us, Ytani. This is the reason everyone has one. He doesn't want ANY of us to know about it. But YOU, he made a special exception for you, I'm sure, because he needs someone to do a job in that city…a job HE doesn't want to do himself. And if he told you not to worry about any more school, this means, this is the one and only thing for you to do for the rest of your life…however long that might be. No more need for school also means no need to worry about jobs back home, as you wouldn't qualify for any of them."

"Uh oh…"

Ytani grimaced as he started to piece together an idea.

Kaliya continues, "Darumon is an example of someone who gives out just barely enough information for a person to do their immediate job. Therefore, you were probably only told you can make a dwarf and nothing else, because he doesn't want you getting any funny ideas about using it beyond that."

"Um…" he reflects on his past history. "He also showed me how to move to that room down there."

"Well, all right, this makes sense. After all, I think it might look funny if you simply walked in. There's not supposed to be a world out there, remember. The point-ears burned it up already. But the simple fact that he even allowed you this much is a miracle. By the way, where are your parents? If you started at only seven decades, I should think they might have something to say about you being out of school, to say nothing about being away from home."

"They, uh…are gone. I heard it was an accident, and then the

Marshal came along and took me in, promising to teach me a secret so I could do some special work for him."

"Oh!" she elates emphatically. "Such a fabulous offer! Tell me, did you have your chip at four decades, like everyone else?"

"Uh, yeah, actually, but after he came in, he took it away."

"Yeah, this makes very good sense to me. After all, who want's that silly old thing with an offer like this!" she giggles satirically. "So, let's see, your parents so unfortunately die from something, and then HE comes along with this fantastic offer to serve in a top-secret military base no one knows about, also producing a very dangerous substance no one knows about, and for reasons no one knows about. Yeah..." she nods. "I would imagine, from the other side of it, you probably disappeared off the scope, right along with your parents."

"Huh? What are you talking about?"

"Ytani! I find it highly unlikely your parents simply died in an accident, and as a result, the Marshal, of all people, gives YOU, an underage juvenile with an incomplete education, the offer of a lifetime as a replacement to a normal life. I believe there is a law about putting children to work in an official duty role. One more violation for the list," she tosses up her hands. "More than likely, if your parents died, you probably went missing. That way, no one asks questions about where you are, including any other members of your family. To them, you don't exist anymore."

She once again turns and begins pacing the other way.

"Wait a minute," he frowns. "What do you mean, I don't exist? I'm right here! Doesn't that mean something?"

"I swear..." she groans softly. "You know, Kailen was right, the Commander has to spell things out for you. Let me try it this way. Listen carefully. One, that base doesn't exist, it's a big secret no one knows about. Two, the people working there don't exist, or at least not WHERE they exist. I would imagine Central Command shows them working somewhere else, NOT at that base. This means, no one knows you are out here, because 'out here'..." she waves her fingers, "...doesn't exist on the records back home. Three, your parents are gone, so they don't argue about you not being at home or in school.

Four, likely, YOU are also…gone…" she air quotes figuratively, "…so no one ELSE asks questions about you being at home or in school. And this is because you are NOT at home OR in school. Instead, you are in a secret base no one knows about, or is supposed to know about. Is this starting to build a picture for you now?"

"Uh, well…"

"Therefore, five, you don't exist. You are wiped from the books back home, likely as part of that same 'accident' that killed your parents, and this is an excuse to bring you to a place that doesn't exist, doing something no one is supposed to know about."

"Wow."

"Darumon taught you this skill, which is the famous Tav'ageen Anomaly, that thing you people presumably went into a panic over trying to get away from it, all because an alien super mind came in and said: RUN!" she screams and waves her hands theatrically. "Then he invents this chip and tells the Council to mandate it in every citizen…no exceptions. This is called a cover-up. Are you with me so far? He knows what it is, and it's NOT an alien parasite trying to kill people. He invented the whole story to force-feed the people his solutions for his own reasons."

She continues pacing. Ytani is glaring at her for the abnormal conversation.

"Now, here you are with knowledge no one is permitted to have. You're put to work in a top-secret base no one knows about. What I mean by this is, if no one is intended to know about it, it doesn't officially exist. No one working there officially works there. Nothing you do there officially happened. And more, you don't have a family asking questions about it. What do these add up to so far? Certainly NOT you trying to claim yourself to be a king of any kind. What it adds up to is once your work is done, it's all forgotten."

"Forgotten?" he winces.

"The Commander tells us he was sent on numerous missions, all forgotten as they are locked behind security blockades. No one knows what they are, and are not allowed to ask about them. This means, Darumon tells people to do stuff, but never talk about it…

ever. He hides it so it is forgotten. And this is his grand crusade against his insurgents everyone is so anxious to listen to, but never hears about. The same would be true for the base. Once your work there is done, it gets erased from the books…it never happened…forgotten."

"Hmm…"

"Ytani, he is here for a reason, and it's not giving toys to people like you. YOU are a toy to HIM. He doesn't like little things like us with fancy skills. But he DOES need some of us to do his work for him…like you. Work that he doesn't want to do himself, or maybe he doesn't want to be SEEN doing, if it exposes him to his enemies."

"Well, yeah…" he flusters. "He wanted the metal."

"Granted, this is the only thing you have right. He wanted the metal. Or perhaps I should say, it's that special stuff inside the metal you need those fancy skills to take out. Not the metal itself. And that stuff, which he's using to make that bomb, is a trace element that can only be found in that universe…or at least a universe like it. Here is where those special skills come in, if you have them raised high enough to do the work right."

"And this is why they're complaining about their men going out and not coming back, and whatever."

"Right. Lose that, and it's gone. Maybe, one day, far in the future, someone could learn it again, but I doubt it would serve YOU, as whatever you have in mind with your military takeover would only take over a bunch of people who no longer remember how to do the work. All their highly trained masters are gone due to that drug of yours killing them. So, don't get your hopes up thinking you can just walk in and shove a gun in their face. This doesn't magically change someone's skill level."

Ytani huffs and crosses his arms as he stands there glaring at her while she continues.

"But these stores over here only hold just so much, and I think this is your quota, right?"

"Yeah. So?"

"So? This is a highly destructive explosive material. And my guess is, he only needs just so much of it. Therefore, once it's full, I doubt he'll want to make more of it. You once told the Commander you would keep the operation going forever, so the Marshal could go swimming in this stuff. This…stuff…Ytani, is a doomsday weapon to kill whole universes. You don't need so much to go swimming in it. You only need enough to do the job, which as it turns out, isn't that much. And what he has here is a LOT. This is a terrorist weapon, and he was hoping to use it on the Estelar. Well, sorry, we're on to him, and the mining base is now closed to business."

"And so, what then? Does he know about this yet?"

"Not yet. And we don't usually go around telling people we're sneaking up on them to kill them. It kind of spoils the surprise. He was doing this to the Estelar, so we'll play the same on him now."

"Oh…"

"And here we come full circle on your usefulness. Once your quota was full, your job is probably at an end. You only need to blow up a universe one time, Ytani. After that, there's nothing left to blow up. So, it goes without saying, your job has a limited lifespan. Therefore, unless Darumon has some other nether-wild idea to blast some world apart and enslave more people, it's unlikely he'll have any more use for you. Unfortunately, if no one knows that base exists, it also means they don't know any of you were ever there. No one was told, and will never BE told. And do you know what that means?"

She pauses to glare at him for a response.

"Um, well, you said forgotten, so I guess we go home, right? Probably not to talk about it, if it's not supposed to exist?"

"All right, this is better. I suppose you are at least partially right. So I'll give you a half point. Here we come back to the issue of education. You were told not to worry about any more of yours. However, those of you with that full and very valuable education, and we are speaking of the military people, because it takes time and money to train and condition them, and you don't go wasting good talent. They might get reassigned. This is what it means to be a part of a military, or anything else that involves the investment of time and resources to educate someone past junior school."

"Uh huh, and so you're telling me I had to go back there to learn more, I guess."

"Technically, you should not have been pulled out in the first place. Typically, you earn your place through hard work and dedication, earning degrees, certifications to perform certain jobs, and so on, all because you spent time training for it. And no, you can't just replace people with any other random person, because they might not hold the same training to do the same job. Furthermore, in a military, or even a civilian role, as you gain higher ranks in your occupation, you become MORE valuable, and even harder to replace with some other random person. But YOUR skill is a little too…weird…to be useful anywhere else. After all, who wants to listen to an angry dwarf back on Azgarén?"

"All right, sure."

"Instead, you were wasting these people as your playthings, and I doubt any military command would tolerate that."

"Well, they did."

"Can you actually be so incompetent to understand this? YOU FALSIFIED YOUR REPORTS!" she shouts. "You lied to them, which is also illegal, so add that onto your list of criminal charges. If they KNEW about it, meaning to say those reports actually told them what you were doing, you would be standing trial right now… Oh wait, you already are," she giggles mindlessly. "And this actually brings up an interesting point. If Central knew what was happening out there, they would surely call for an investigation. And no, your sugar daddy Marshal would NOT be able to stop it. The Commander was only a step away from mutiny. This means, that chip is getting turned off. I also hear the HC is close to his boiling point, too. If the Marshal tried to interfere with the investigation of you at the base by turning chips to active, this would more likely cause a rebellion. The military would finally realize what he's using those chips for, and turn their guns at HIM now."

"You think?"

"It's certainly reasonable to occur at some time. You can't just keep doing this without someone finally breaking from the pressure. And then, they would begin to investigate HIM for all of his crimes, including blasting innocent worlds and enslaving innocent populations. And if you would then go and say the Council would do something, I would probably just extend this rebellion to involve them, hauling them out into the street and arresting all of them for handing our world over to an alien creature. The Marshal does NOT hold any legal authority to do anything on OUR world, and the Council would also be illegal to give him control of our military."

"Really!"

"Yes, and you can ask Lieutenant Ti'van about this, as she holds a university law degree, the sort of thing you need to have to understand these things. A junior school education doesn't do it."

"Thanks…" he muses resentfully.

"As for you, you're a nearly uneducated civilian tail-puller with very poor skills in anything other than screaming. You hold virtually no value to anyone as you are. If you had, say, a university education and expert technical skills, oh yes! You might hold value. But the Tav'ageen Anomaly is in ALL of us. This is why Darumon made everyone take his nether-wild chips. Everyone! Therefore, you become expendable, once your immediate role is complete. The reason you do NOT need more school is because you are not intended to go home at all. If he needs another like you, HE can pick one at random off the street, and teach them in private, as he likely did with you, and then repeat all this. However, since you possess knowledge he wants to cover up…BOOM! Just like your parents."

Ytani frowns morosely as the concept finally settles in. Kaliya felt a tiny mote of sympathy for him, as he began to realize his predicament, but justice still had to be paid.

"The people back home don't know what the Tav'ageen Anomaly really is, and he has no intention of telling them. But here you are using it, and he probably won't let you go home and tell them THAT, either. And since he's well-known for making up lies about every little thing he does, I would imagine, other than a few people at Central, the rest of the world probably thinks the Commander and his people are working elsewhere. And THEY will likely be sworn to secrecy for what they did here, just like what Kriv'tik once told me about so many of his OTHER missions to blow things up while on active, and no one knows about it."

"Wow, he did that? But can't I be sworn to secrecy too?"

"Well, I suppose we might suggest this much, if the Marshal had any idea to actually do it. But here is where you also splashed in the wrong puddles, Ytani. Without your parents teaching you better manners, or anyone to help you finish your schools, so you might know the ways of our people, with or without the Marshal pulling any strings, you killed someone. You also committed torture and rape along the way. All of these are criminal acts. And worse, you showed no remorse, and desired to do it again. This is now worse than criminal, this is pure malevolence."

She pauses to glance around the room while she prepares to wrap up.

"I'm sorry, Ytani. It's not nice, and it's not fair, but at the same time, you had the opportunity to make friends, and even to play with girls for a little bit of fun. But did you treat them nice? Did you treat them with respect? No. Just look at that statement you gave me here a moment ago. This is who you are. Our society holds certain values of morality and ethics. We like to think of ourselves as above such primitive animalistic actions as mauling lesser creatures for fun. But you apparently missed that lesson in those few years of junior school you actually attended. Instead, you turned psychotic on them. We could possibly blame some of it on the Alpha Male syndrome, but you simply went too far."

"A what syndrome?"

"Do you know what the Alpha Male syndrome is? Did anyone tell you about this?"

"Um, no, I don't think so."

"All right, a little lesson on biology. Among our people, a young male, like you, who takes up a weightlifting hobby, like you were doing in your house, builds up more than just muscle. He also builds up a higher-than-average hormone flow in his body. This means, your body produces an excess of those hormones you might feel at puberty which turn on your sex drive. And this is bad. My brother went through this once, but in his case, he took the proper lessons and conditioning to help him deal with it, so he didn't go nether-wild on everyone in the process. You apparently missed this part."

"Uh huh... So, what does that mean for anything else?"

"What it means is you went WAY too far with those girls. And without anyone telling you different, you turned psychotic and started hurting them, even killing them. And STILL, without any controls to put a stop to THIS, you developed this mania, thinking you might want to be some sort of god-king over a destroyed world, turning everyone into slaves because your fantasy-father Darumon will give you the keys to it. And all this if you only provide him with an unlimited flow of the metal, to produce an unlimited amount of this...stuff...he can go swimming in, when you have absolutely no clue why he wants it in the first place. And like everyone else back home, no idea who he is or where he came from, even after all this time fighting his fantasy insurgents."

"I thought I heard he was going after them once. There was something happening on a world called Therinë, I think."

"Yes, this is correct, but unfortunately, according to Kriv'tik, it was cancelled. I'm so terribly sorry, but we finally learned who he was, and a benefactor, he is not."

"Really! Well, all right. So what happens to the rest of it?"

"The mine, and everything associated with it, will be shut down. None of us really wants any of this...stuff. We don't usually go around blowing up universes. It takes all the romance out of evening strolls on the beach gazing at the stars."

"Uh huh, sure. And this is where we go home, I guess, or at least the base people. But what about me? Are you just going to leave me here?"

"Ytani, justice has a way of biting you in the tail, and I'm the law. We have already tried and convicted you of your crimes, and at this point, there's only one thing left to do. But the problem we are faced with comes in multiple parts. If you simply go home, the first thing they'll do is throw you into a prison cell, assuming they don't simply give you the death penalty. I don't know what sorts of laws they have for something like this, but your example is a bad one."

"Uh huh. Sure."

She begins strolling back along her path.

"The Estelar, who actually are gods in relation to people like us, teach us a principle we call the Measure of Balance. It is a complex system of rules and principles, philosophies, and policies. One of these is to say life is precious and not to be violated. You failed this rule when you killed that one girl, and I'm told there were two others that came before. So we might want to consider those, as well. Furthermore is your abuse and torture, and this is made worse by your apparent lust for more. This, by itself, declares your privilege to live as forfeit."

"Uh oh…"

"Yeah, the rules tend to run as absolute principles. But this isn't everything, so far. The next problem is our war against Darumon. He cannot know we are coming for him. And we certainly do not want someone, like you, going up and telling him. Swearing someone to secrecy might be an option, but we are also faced with a third problem, maybe even a fourth. One of these relates to the needs of the greater numbers, like our full world population back home, and anything else that might be alive out there. And one little guy, like you, doesn't compare to that, god complex or otherwise. Darumon, and for that matter, Sargeras, are demons for their potential to destroy life, and this again violates the Measure of Balance, such that they must be brought down at any cost, but preferably one that doesn't destroy whole universes."

"Wow."

"But then we have the Tav'ageen Anomaly, your funny skill no one knows about. And this relates to knowing hidden secrets, and what you can do with them. And Ytani, the Prodigy Gift, as we call it back home, is simply dangerous, if you know how to use it right… or even wrong. And you, Mister Unique, can't be trusted with it."

"But…" he flusters.

"Under normal circumstances, we could possibly just throw you into a prison cell and walk away. But not so in your case. If you were to spend even a fraction of your ego on experimenting with the skill, you might learn new ways of using it, and there goes your god syndrome to a whole new level, as you no longer need to be physical to hurt people. I've been able to kill in this form. This makes you potentially dangerous in a way that is entirely intolerable. A simple prison cell no longer qualifies."

"Oh no… But, um…"

"Therefore, since you took so much pleasure in what you did, the only resolution to this is that final decree. The same as what the Estelar did to the Primordials…Sargeras's people. They had to be eliminated altogether to prevent any more destruction."

Ytani's face suddenly went blank, and he could almost feel the blood rushing out of it. Kaliya turns and strolls nonchalantly out of the hanger and up the lane that ran between the warehouses. Ytani followed her with his eyes, as he began to realize where she was going.

"What are you doing?" he asks tentatively.

"If you recall, Big Boy, I asked to see all your shiny things. Let's take a look, shall we? After all, it's not every day you get to see the most powerful super weapon ever known."

"But wait, are you going to do something? You said it destroys whole universes!"

"This is true, but I should probably also mention what kind of universe it destroys. OUR universe might be safe, within reason. But most others are not. Why? There's a special energy layer to be found in most other universes out there, but unfortunately not in ours. Don't ask me why, we're just unlucky that way. By the way, this is why our science doesn't understand such things as adamantium, and why it's so superior to our own technology. WE don't have this energy layer, so WE don't have the good stuff, but THEY do. Therefore, people like those dwarves you so often berated could actually be above us on a few things."

"Above us? How can they be above us if they don't even have electricity?"

"They don't need it. They're not following the same tech tree as we were forced into for our LACK of this stuff. But here is where this weapon comes in. Blow it up in one of those universes, and boom, there goes the whole envelope, which might involve the whole universe. In ours, well, I'm not exactly sure how big the explosion might be, but from the things I've heard, I would expect it to be a horn-puller. Something on a stellar scale, for sure."

"Stellar!" he yelps.

Kaliya arrives at the first warehouse and steps inside. Ytani tried following, even though he didn't like the idea, but he had to see what she was doing. Projected or not, he didn't want her causing any trouble.

"So, this is the famous vault where the famous Ytani was keeping his famous changing crystals. Hmm, where are they, Ytani? I don't see anything here."

Ytani hesitated before entering the building, but on the mention of something gone missing, he stepped inside to study the transparent wall peering inside the vault.

"Huh? Wait a minute."

He turns to find the terminal and searches for the icon to pull up an inventory count.

"What? Zero!"

He then rushes outside and across to the opposite warehouse, where he engages the next terminal.

"Zero again!" he shouts.

He follows with the remaining two warehouses, checking each of them.

"Zero...and zero? What in all the... Where did everything go? Did you people steal it?"

"Steal it? Like stealing all that metal from those dwarves? Wow, what an irony that would be! You robbed them blind to make this... stuff, and then someone robs YOU blind to take it away from you. Isn't life simply awful," she giggles.

"No more jokes! You said this stuff blows up universes."

"All right, no more jokes. Stealing it? Confiscating it is a better word to use there, and by the authority of those people who KNOW what it is and WANT it taken away from you. It was then disposed of using a custom conveyor device into a massive gravastar on the edge of the universe, as a way of preventing anything else bad happening. The universe is safe for another billion years, thanks to us…well, except for one piece."

"What? What one piece?"

"The one we were told to use as a message to Darumon. You asked if he knew about it yet. Well, he will…in a manner of speaking," she grins brightly. "You see, these things are like really big bombs. And if you set one off…well, like with all bombs, they blow up. Now, if you apply a little mathematics to it, you'll find it creates a blast sphere equivalent to the amount you use in the detonating charge. Are you following me so far? Good. And therefore, if you use only ONE of these, you can probably calculate how much was in the charge by the size of the cloud. So, if Darumon thinks you had almost two thousand of them in here, but he sees a blast cloud only big enough for one unit, he's going to wonder where the rest of it went. And do you know what he'll probably conclude about it?"

"I don't think I want to ask."

"Well, I'll tell you anyway, just because I like to hear myself talk, and there's not a nether-wild thing you can do about it. He'll know…without a doubt, I would imagine…that someone stole it and learned what it was along the way. You see, Ytani, Darumon is as much a liar and a cheat as he is a murderer. He recently attacked a world out there filled with people who don't take no for an answer. These people are closely associated with the Estelar, and now we're coming to find him. But Darumon, bless his infernal heart, likes using distractions to turn people the wrong direction. Look at your stories of point-ears. He used that as a way to distract the dwarves while he set down your base and blasted the rest of their world to oblivion. Well, here we are, doing it to him now while we go to Azgarén to blast HIM to oblivion. How do you like that for your sugar daddy Marshal?" she smiles sweetly.

"But wait, if you're not actually from Azgarén, who are you and where did you come from?"

"Oh!" she slaps her head humorously. "I'm sorry, I missed that part. Yes! My father is your famous traitor to the Council, Velen Nazég. You probably remember the story of how this really huge ship came and took him away to join Darumon's insurgents, right? Well, the REAL story, Ytani, is he was evacuated, as he was probably the only person who might be able to figure out what the Tav'ageen Anomaly truly was. And I think you can probably put it together for yourself how Darumon might feel about that."

"Oops. If he was trying to hide it…"

"Yeah, and another oops as Darumon and his shiny new military chased us all across the galaxy and into a completely new universe before we met with the people who evacuated us. By the way, this was on Therinë, the REAL reason his games over there were cancelled. When he saw who we finally bumped into…" she whistles and rolls her eyes. "Now, we're turning it around and chasing him. Get it? It's actually very easy, within a certain context."

"You were evacuated and carried away to meet with someone," he mumbles uncertainly. "And now you're coming back to get him."

"Very good," she muses fondly.

"But who was it to teach you how to do this…thing?"

"The Tav'ageen thing? I had a trainer amongst these other beings who are half god. That's how high you have to be to understand what it is, which is something of a paradox for us. We have the skill, but you might think we are nowhere near to being godlike," she giggles. "So ironic… And I guess it just goes with our ultra-bizarre evolution…" she begins walking away, "…which probably involved something external interfering with those Eracyodines. But this isn't really important now."

"If you say so…" he begins to follow her. "But then, what are you going to do next? Are you just going to leave me here, or take me away somewhere? You said something about prison…or actually, no prison…and that Measure thing, and um, can't be trusted, um…"

"As for a prison, the people I work for right now don't spend much time building big fancy prisons for people like you. It's a waste of taxpayer money. It's much better to simply create a utopian paradise where people like you never come up in the first place. You have two choices in a case like that…conform or be destroyed.”

“Wow! That sounds serious.”

“Yeah, it goes along with that Measure of Balance and a rather absolutist mentality. The greater needs of the people outweigh the individual whims of a person to commit crimes and such. So, you work to culture and educate them to think in terms of cooperation, not competition.”

“Uh huh.”

“As for you, I’m simply going to leave you here. It seems like such a lovely spot, and with great views!”

Kaliya arrived back in the hanger, where she could gaze through the window up at the gas giant overhead.

“But don’t get used to it,” she continues. “I don’t expect it to last long.”

“Why is that?”

Kaliya now strolls up to the atmosphere curtain to peer outside.

“It relates to that bit of not being trustworthy. And this again relates to the Tav’ageen thing. With or without the Marshal teaching you anything, simply speaking to ME, in this case, has likely opened up a few ideas in your head, assuming you’re actually paying attention to it. And this means, if I ‘simply’ leave you here, you might try projecting yourself somewhere, like back home to Azgarén, maybe to Central Command. You do know where that is, right?”

“Well, yeah, it’s right across on the other side of the conveyor.”

“Good. Now, apply a little imagination, and do with that what you did as a dwarf in the Thane’s Hall. But leave the dwarf part out. They might not know how to handle that one. And the Commander tells me the Marshal has an office over there. What does this say?”

“Um, wow. I can actually do that?”

“Oh please,” she moans and shakes her head. “Dear cu’Nar, give me strength. That, and a few other things, Ytani. Yes. But we can’t allow that, so here is where we will leave you.”

“So I can’t go through that conveyor…” he muses.

“Yes, not that one, not this one,” she glances outside. “Or even to simply travel across the galaxy for it, as you technically don't need a conveyor at this point. Therefore, our problem."

She now gazes out onto the tarmac.

"Do you see that little box over there?" she points.

Ytani cautiously approaches the curtain to look outside. He saw a rectangular box that looked just large enough to fit comfortably within the arms.

"Yeah, so what?"

"That's the one remaining unit of Arcanicium."

"Arca...what?"

"Arcanicium, otherwise known as the Agent of Unmaking. That's the name of the stuff your wonderful Marshal was making. You remember I said we saved one out for his message? Well, there it is, inside that pressure-sealed box, along with a little plastic explosive and a ten-second timer device."

"Uh oh..." he moans nervously.

"Ytani, I want you to recall that last girl you had. Her name was Ensign Hena Ka'zheen. She had a life, no doubt a mother and a father, and maybe other relatives who are now beside themselves with grief over her loss. I'm sure she probably had hopes and dreams for love, a life, family, a future...and you stole it away from her with your excessively perverted lust, your god complex, and those obscene demonic fetishes in your exercise room. I wonder what her final moments were like...the pain she felt, the terror. Do you recall this? You were probably looking at her directly in the face as you cut that seed entity. I want you to think really hard on this, what SHE went through in that final moment. This is your penance."

Kaliya now super-enlarges her fist and draws it back. Ytani gazes at it in awe as she makes ready. She then slams it harshly into his body, sending him flying across the hanger into the far wall. The light lunar gravity made his journey especially graceful as he collided against the wall with a heavy thud, then collapsed to the ground.

"Actions carry consequences, Ytani," she decrees firmly. "The Measure of Balance doesn't tolerate examples like you. Life is precious, and must be respected. But your example is a waste, as was what you made of the base staff. And this is a form of law set down by gods! YOU don't argue with it. Even Darumon is going to learn the true nature of it, but in his case, for all he's done, a simple death penalty just isn't good enough. Now, while you hoist yourself up off the floor, I'm going for a little stroll outside."

Ytani was dazed by the impact. He struggled to pull himself upright.

"Wait!" he groans. "You can't do that! It's empty space out there!"

"Oh, I'm so touched that you care suddenly," she feigns. "Especially after your threat earlier, sticking my head out there as you take the rest of it in here. Ytani, as a projection, I'm not physical, and therefore not subject to those hostile environments that might otherwise kill me. So, in this final moment of YOUR life, I want you to think of hers. This is what happens to people like you. In life, you receive that which you give. Even in the afterlife, although in your case, I doubt it'll be pretty. And unfortunately, out here there's no desert to bury you in. You'll simply be scattered to the stars as tiny quantum particles...if that much," she smirks.

"No!" he shouts.

Ytani manages to rise to his feet and rushes her. He desperately lunges at her, grabbing her by the arms and hoping to restrain her from going out past the curtain. Kaliya simply turns to gaze at him indifferently as she modifies her phased condition to an intangible apparition. Ytani suddenly finds his hands passing right through her seemingly ghostlike image.

"Years, Ytani, not centuries...and barely a handful at that. That's all I spent in study, and I know more about this than is healthy for a person. Even Darumon would be impressed if he actually knew about it."

She now turns and proceeds outside the curtain.

Kaliya passes through the curtain and onto the bare surface of the moon, which was the zero-pressure environment of open space. Ytani glared at her in awe that she could actually go out there and survive. He tries shouting at her. Kaliya turned to look at him, and she could see his lips moving, as if he were yelling something. But outside, with no atmosphere, all she could do was point at her ear and shake her head, then shrug.

She then strutted along the tarmac until she arrived at the box. She glanced back at him, still standing there and apparently screaming at her and waving his arms. She looked down at the timer device and pressed a button. A digital display began to count down from ten. She held up her hands with all ten fingers and followed along… ten, nine, eight, seven…and then imparted a flirtatious wave and a frisky wag of the tail, before vanishing in a puff.

In a lonely star cluster, on the far side of the galaxy, was an orange dwarf star with at least one gas giant circling it. There was nothing especially unique about it, until a blinding flash erupted, blasting the star and everything else nearby completely out of existence. The resulting cloud of shredded space-time would mark the first time such a sight had ever been seen since the ancient and nearly forgotten occasion of the final Celestial War. But thankfully, this would not spread beyond the sphere of the one star system and its surrounding debris cloud.

Kaliya had flashed into the factory control room on Madzurki, where she met with Petrith, Marelle, and Ayene. The two women had landed there in the transport to pick up Petrith, and to observe the conveyor linkage for Ooduan. As they watched, the line entry pointing to the storage depot began flashing with a highlight as a warning for a loss of signal, and finally to gray out reading Inoperative.

"Well, I guess that answers that question," Kaliya retorts.

"Yeah," Petrith muses. "And Ytani?"

"Given what this stuff does to the local fabric of space, I doubt there's enough of him even to go to his Maker."

"Ouch!"

"You took long enough to return back to us," Ayene reflects. "I was starting to wonder about you and what you were doing."

"I had to give him a few parting words," Kaliya shrugs. "This guy was a sorry example. That junior school education, or the lack of one, left him with virtually no real capacity to interpret the situation. He regarded his gift to be so supreme, it could be used anywhere.

Unfortunately, he apparently never once tried experimenting with it to realize what it could be used for, to say nothing of his worth once your top-secret and completely hidden operation came to a close. That statement of never having enough of that...stuff."

"Yeah, he seemed to think it could go on forever, even though we had a clear quota we were aiming for."

"Right, and whatever would follow after that. And then we have the fact that his sugar daddy Marshal was Creation's Most Wanted criminal."

"And what did he have to say about that?"

"Oh, this was hard, Ayene," she frowns. "Much like with your Commander and his idea of a survey, I had to spell it out for him. His parents were apparently lost in a mysterious accident, and with no one else in the family screaming for a lost child, he's probably also listed as MIA or simply dead. But he never thought about this, as the Marshal gave him an offer he couldn't refuse...to play god with a unique skill that doesn't even have a name to it. And that overrides everything else, including our native laws for the legality of the operation. But in the end, as I gave my parting goodbye, and reminded him of Ensign Ka'zheen, he seemed very excited."

"Excited?"

"Oh yes! He was shouting and waving at me through the curtain!" she grins.

Chapter 3

IN SHEEP'S CLOTHING

"Chancellor, I need t' speak with ye," Eiki announces as she enters his office.

The Chancellor had returned from his confrontation with the Thane earlier in the day and was settling into his thoughts about how to present this to the people of the city. He knew it would hit hard, but one way or another it had to come out or else the people may start to riot if they didn't receive any other form of resolution to the stories being told from outside. At the same time, however, he also knew they might cause trouble seeking vengeance for all the false tales and deception.

"Aye lass, come in. I hope ye have a few kind words for this old head."

"Mayhap so, but we also have a wee bit of a spot that needs t' be closed up by now."

"Aye, an' I think I know of what one ye speak. I got the right word from the Thane, mayhap more than one," he chuckles. "He tried t' tell a new fib or two about the warriors an' men bein' right outside our doors fightin' the war an' makin' up the fare. Of course, this nay did fit with the men gone missin', any kind of notes, or simply t' walk back down inside t' see their pretties, t' say nothin' of anythin' else he be a-tryin' t' fool us with. He yay be a poor teller of tales."

"Aye, mayhap, but his tales were a-growin' a mite complicated by now, I s'pose. An' what about the four centuries of tellin' them?"

"Aye, that too. All four of them, he be a-givin' us these tales, ever since he took up the throne in there. But ye an' I know, nay a dwarf can live that long. An' even better, for a young lad, yay less than me own time in this office, he was a fine an' stout one!" he chuckles.

"Oh! I'll bet that went over grandly."

"An' he verily has nay a clue what Adamant be about. An' then were his partin' words. They still be a-ringin' in me ears."

"What words were those?"

"How we all fell for his tales. It be a cryin' shame, what they did t' us. If only for their higher knowin' an' the cheatin' games they played. Though I did give it back t' him about how our culture looks upon the throne of the thane here, an' how he disgraced it with his bad manners. Then t' wonder how his own folk would yay look at him, if he behaves the same with them."

"Aye, that should make him stop an' think a bit, if he yay even bothers with as much. But rest easy, good Chancellor," she soothes. "Our tale may be a sad one here, but we need t' be a-turnin' it 'round. An' ye're right, those Suuden-Aryku did'na have it much better. I hear recently how they too had their woes, an' they be almost as bad as ours. That nasty Thane was as bad on the outside as he was on the inside, treatin' that crew up there as his personal patsies."

"Fine, lass. But now, how d' we bring this out t' the people so they don'na go out lookin' for the ones that did this t' us?"

"Mayhap I can help."

"If that be the way of it, ye have me ear. What be yer plan, Eiki?"

"I got word from a friend, she be one of those who be a-fightin' this Darumon beastie, that the Thane, or rather t' say that tyrant of a man who was a-playin' a role on so many others, yay be dead now. Even better that she laid a few burnin' hells on his shoulders for all he did," she chuckles.

"Really now," he smiles tenderly.

"Aye, so this can give us back a wee bit, even if we nay were there t' see it. But they did him in fine an' proper after he got back from yer little talk."

"Good, an' I thank ye for that, but there still be a few holes t' fill for how t' bring this out t' the people."

"I know this. I've been a-thinkin' about this for a while. More an' more I know there will be questions asked an' the people will nay be a-wantin' t' hear more wild tellin' t' cover for it. An' I mentioned this t' that young lass…she be a right smart one, ye know," she smiles softly. "She agreed, an' offered a few ideas. But we still need t' keep things quiet, mostly because of that Darumon, if he comes by sniffin' 'round."

"Aye, then. What be these ideas ye speak of? Most importantly, how d' we make the people happy an' also keep the secret? That be the one makin' me poor head pound."

"There can be only one way at this time. They all need t' be told t' keep the secret. On the outside, they can know only as much as what ye might learn from those people out there, but nay the bits from our friends."

"Methinks that nay be a-keepin' them all happy."

"If we work it right, we can tell them how the game yay needs t' be played, an' they all need t' know how t' play it. We can give them a few bits t' tide them over, but those bits can nay be spoken out in the open."

"Hmm, aye…" he nods. "But for how long?"

"Until our friends make their final move against our foes, or mayhap if our foes should get the idea they lost this world an' decide t' pull up an' leave us be."

"Fine, an' I guess this mayhap can work for us. But now, what tale d' we give out here?"

"I think we should both go out there. Yer head may be a-poundin' already, but t' have me at yer side mayhap can give ye a wee bit more strength."

The Chancellor mulls it over briefly and agrees this will take more than he can do by himself. The two of them leave his office and stroll out into the street, calling for the people to gather around the Thane's Hall front steps in a public gathering. The word shouts through the streets as more people are brought to the attention of the town meeting. The square in front of the steps fills to capacity as the people come in from all sides, crowding together and waiting to hear a final explanation as to the many conflicting stories circulating around by now.

Eiki and the Chancellor stand up on the stairs, getting ready to give their presentation.

"Good citizens," the Chancellor begins. "The time has come for some troublin' truths t' be told. An' at the same time, we need yer ears t' listen hard, as the tales t' be given here nay be easy t' tell. An' they'll nay be easy t' hear. An' what more, there be secrets t' be kept amongst all the folk here in the city, because the true foes against us be a-playin' a hard game, an' now we need t' play it back at them the same. Ye need t' be a-knowin' the truth, but ye also need t' be a-keepin' it a secret, just the same as our foes be a-keepin' their secrets. This be the way of the real war, a war of secrets, an' movin' in the shadows."

"What?" shouts one citizen in the square. "How d' ye play a war of secrets an' movin' in shadows?"

"People of the city," Eiki announces. "This be the tale, an' this will be the tale ye'll be a-tellin' in the streets an' whisperin' in the taverns an' alleys. First, ye need t' be a-knowin' the true foes nay be point-ears. Those folks only came upon our land for a hand or two of years, an' these be the tales from our kin outside. They be a-knowin' this because they be a-seein' it with their own eyes."

"Aye, an' this yay be one of the things we be askin' here. What was this war the Thane be a-tellin' about?"

"A lie t' take our Adamant."

This announcement stirred up an instant roar of shouts and slurs against the Thane. Eiki knew this would happen, but she allowed them this moment before calling their attention again.

"People, hear me!" she shouts. "This be why we need t' keep our secrets. We were nay ever told, an' nay ever permitted t' know who they were out there. This was a secret they kept from us, an' they expected us t' play the fool for it. That pummelin' ye heard of from our kinfolk outside be what happens t' good people who nay be wanted t' make their rousin' for the tricks played against us."

This quickly silenced the riotous outburst from the crowd, as Eiki prepared to continue.

"There be a foe here, a big one, one who leads the rest, an' he don'na like people complainin' about what he demands out of them. He makes people work, sometimes without the freedom t' ask questions or t' argue with it. If ye d', he kills ye for it, or mayhap play some foul bit on ye that ye lose yer mind t' think at all. So ye need t' know what ye can say in the open while he be about."

"Great All-Father!" moans one observer. "Where did such a foe like THAT come from?"

"Aye, this be a good one, t' be sure!" Eiki shrugs. "This here be the way t' play a war of secrets; now that we know. We may be the last of us in here, 'cept for a few here an' there outside. An' we surely don'na wish t' see any more pummelin'. An' here we now have TWO tales t' tell. One be a tale of what we pretend t' know in case any of them come back t' check on us. The other can be a tale t' help us understand what be really happenin' out there, but nay t' be told on the outside...nay until we can solve the greater woes in our world."

"An' how d' we solve those greater woes if we're s'posed t' play the fool for them?"

"For this, let me finish. This here will be hard t' explain, but ye need t' hear all of it t' know me meanin'. First be the tale we be expected t' know on the outside. Our kinfolk out there carries the real tales of the point-ears, so whatever the Thane was a-tellin' us, it yay be a pack of lies by now. They tell of a mine t' our south filled with what we think t' be the men goin' up t' serve this fare we were always told about. Instead, they be a-minin' up more bricks, same as what we have in here. This be another tale made a lie. An' finally, they say those men were glassy-eyed, an' with nay enough mind t' know day from night. This be t' say, if they ever had the mind t' ask why they be a-minin' up more bricks, someone took it away from them."

This revelation stirred up a rush of gasps and moans through the crowd, along with several grumbles for the offence.

Eiki continues, "What this says so far yay be the real foes, whoever they be by name, be a-stealin' our most precious Adamant, an' this be why the Thane was only askin' for bricks, because it be easier t' carry."

"This here be outrageous!" shouts one angry man. "This would yay be a crime of the highest sort!"

"Aye, I know this! But remember the pummelin' for those who complain about it. We be a-speakin' of a sort of folk with a mighty high knowin' here, the likes of which can travel beyond our world t' the sky an' all the stars above. They have knowin' of things our kind be simply too young for, an' they used this in a cheatin' manner at the demand of this one big foe. HE be the one t' put the blame on, because HE be the one takin' all the Adamant. Nay anyone else… they all be but slaves t' him."

Another rise of moaning and whispers runs through the crowd as Eiki pauses to collect herself.

"At the same time, I think we also need t' take a wee bit of blame for ourselves for ne'er once makin' a proper effort t' check up on things. We took the Thane at his word, even WITH all his holes. We trusted him, bein' the thane of our people, who normally holds a high place among us. But THIS one, he disrespected his place, an' all of us, while we, with our strict culture t' play under his rule, ne'er once demanded him t' explain just how he came t' his own knowin' for the closed doors, an' with nay any of our men writin' word back t' the people for it. Further, the need for bricks, bricks, an' more bricks, t' fight a war that ne'er ended. We dwarves should know better."

Another rush of groaning rumbled through the gathering at this clear and obvious error.

"He kept us locked inside here, denyin' us t' go outside an' look at anythin', tellin' us his frightenin' stories an' makin' us huddle 'neath the sheets. An' yet, ne'er once put guards on our doors for all the precious metal goin' out in what should have been a grand showin' for all those point-ears ragin' across the land t' see it!" she chuckles. "An' here we are, thinkin' ourselves t' be safe. An' we come from a long line of folk who are s'posed t' be of a finer mind t' know war!"

Yet another round of moaning and grumbling resounded in the crowd as they felt this rub for their own failure.

"An' what be worse, did anyone here ever pay attention t' the fact that he nay had a family in all this time? Who was the Thane four hundred years ago? Who came after, an' who be it in that chair today, tellin' so many wild tales? Well, the Chancellor, in this last meetin', got ye the answer. He was the same man, one of THEM with a life that runs yay longer than any of us, an' we ne'er took notice of it. How d' ye like that for people payin' attention t' their leadership!" she chuckles ironically.

"He be the SAME?" shouts a woman off to the side. "But wait now," she argues. "I served as a chambermaid in there. An' I would see him now an' then. He be a dwarf, by the looks of him t' me eyes!"

"Aye, he LOOKED like a dwarf, but he held a special skill t' change his shape on us, an' he apparently only used one during all this time. His mind at impersonatin' a dwarf was about as keen as his mind t' make up tales that made any sense. He nay knew what Adamant be truly about, only that it held value t' him. He nay held any thought that we poor folk knew what we be a-talkin' about when we try t' explain it, only that he with his higher knowin' was above us, an' he don'na care for anythin' after that. He was a foul devil of a man, whatever he be on the outside of it."

"Aye! I'll agree with ye on that much!"

"So far, this here be the tale we can speak of out in the open. We feel this bigger foe, who it be said can also change his shape, can peek in on us t' check on things. If he hears us speakin' the wrong words, he might finish it for us. So our words need t' be only what our folk outside tell us of what they saw, an' mayhap a wee bit of figurin' for how it fits with the Thane an' his wild tellin'. This also includes our folk out there seein' a mighty tall crew pickin' up our bricks, an' this here must point t' those who be a-stealin' from us, but with nay a name t' go with it."

"Aye, an' so far, I hear ye," issues another male protester. "Although me beard be all twisted up from it. But then, what d' we d' t' set things right? We can'na keep it like this!"

"Nay, but we nay can d' anythin' direct. So here we go with the OTHER tale, the one I'll tell ye a wee bit about, t' keep yer beard from tyin' up on ye fully, but this be one ye need t' keep t' yerself."

Eiki paces a few steps in front of the Hall as she tries to compose this next part.

"There be a war out there…a real one. Our world was simply run over for the favor of our Adamant. We have a few names we know of, but I think it would be safer if I keep those out for now, just in case that big foe comes sniffin' 'round. We don'na want any accidents in our words. He comes from a time long behind us, part of an old society now gone t' their maker…assumin' any would take them. There be two of them, actually; a master an' a servant under him. They be foes t' another folk, one where they once fought a war an' lost. An' as ye can probably guess, they nay be right happy for it. But with only the two of them remainin', they want t' take revenge for the rest. It be all they have by now."

"That nay sounds any good for someone," remarks the man. "Though I can nay be sure of who by now, what with our home been run over like it was."

"Aye, 'tis true. This foe nay be a-carin' much for the little folk. Nay unless he can use them for somethin'. He first found a world filled with these people of the high knowin', an' he made a promise t' them t' share even more, but it was a lie t' buy their service…at least until he played his tricks t' put them under his control. He used them t' harm a great many more out there, for one thing or another. An' then one day, he found us."

Eiki now turns and paces the other way as she reflects on a few historical details.

"Ye may recall a few tales from our forefathers. Five hundred years ago, a gnarly group we once called orcs came at us through portals. But they were nay much t' speak of, as our warriors made good work of them. However, this was merely a test t' see how we fight, nay more than that. He owned them, the same as the point-ears. And they were nay more than a distraction t' turn our eyes the other way while he played a very clever trick on us."

She halts her pacing and turns directly to her audience.

"Right above us, on top of the mountain, through that one door in the store over here," she thumbs to her side. "Up a long stair, along a very clean road, an' through a very clean tunnel, ye'll find yer answer t' who be a-stealin' our bricks. They put a military camp up there."

This new bombshell invoked a renewed outburst of rage among the people.

"This here be why the Thane denied us t' go outside," Eiki affirms. "The real doors leading t' the real outside were closed an' buried by the pummelin'. This other one be a back door t' the Thane's crew up there takin' the bricks."

The rumbling in the street rose as this only added insult to the previous statement.

"An' also the men," Eiki submits. "Which were sent out from the feast. But that feast be another lie. Instead, it be a type of poison t' put them under this spell where they nay know up from down."

"A poison?!" shouts a woman.

"An' now, here it gets really hard for us down here, as I know many of us had husbands an' other family sent out for it. Me own was in there once. We had the Thane call for it, again an' again, year after year. Why? Because this poison kills after a while."

Now the gathering erupts violently in an uproar of fury. Screams echo in the streets from the men, while wails and moans sound out from many of the women.

"This here be madness!" shouts one angry man. "I had me a brother sent on the feast once! What sort of devil be it that can call up a feast t' send men t' their deaths in a mine, just so he can steal our Adamant? Be we as low as briar sheep sent t' slaughter?"

"Blame it on that big foe, nay any other," Eiki accedes. "An' aye, t' him, we are. Even those folks up top were a-feelin' the punch for their own woes. They had their own threats on their shoulders. But the Thane…Oi! He loved his place of power. Power over us, an' power over that crew the same!"

"All-Father help us…" he moans.

"Now, this big one, he moved forward an' found another world out there, where he made a bad move. His old foes, the ones he was a-hopin' t' lay his revenge on, most of them forgot about his kind. But one of them was a-watchin', an' waitin' for him t' make this move. When he saw this, he ran off, back t' the place of the high folk. This be where he an' his master be a-hidin'. They think themselves t' be safe there, hidin' in a hole nay a soul knows about. But this one who be a-watchin' knows well enough, an' now we have this new folk givin' chase, but quietly, just like he was a-tryin' t' make for himself."

"An' this here be part of that war of secrets ye spoke of?" asks a man. "He was a-tryin' t' sneak up on them, but ran off when he was found, an' now they be a-tryin' t' sneak up on him now?"

"Aye, but this new folk be a clever crew. They started chasin' him, an' along the way, they found one of the worlds he pummeled. On that world was another mine, the second one from the Thane's feast. It was nay even on OUR world."

The crowd ushers up a series of moans and whispers.

"This here be the one where me own husband was found, along with the crew he got sent out with, an' it was a few years back by now. They rescued them an' helped them away from this poison. After that, they found us here, an' what be left of our home."

"Be this the reason for the one feast stoppin'?" asks a woman.

"Aye, it stopped because that one mine was closed, an' the feast callin' up for it ended. Nay for the war lettin' up, only for one mine lost t' them up there."

"An' be they here now?" inquires another man. "An' then, what say ye t' that camp ye spoke of up top?"

"They own it now, an' the Thane be good an' dead for all his crimes. It went along right after the Chancellor's last meetin'. He an' I, along with a few others, have been a-workin' in secret for a time, along with me husband, an' the folk outside. This new folk found the wreck of a world out there, found the last of our kinfolk, an' started gatherin' them up t' bring away t' better lands. They found us, but had t' move real quiet under the Thane an' his crew. They took that camp up there a while back, but chose t' wait with the Thane so we could have our time with him in here for his last ragin'. An' here, our good Chancellor turned it 'round on him prim an' proper!" she laughs.

The crowd now ushers up a warm cheer and applause, which left the Chancellor feeling a sense of comfort for all his troubles.

Eiki continues, "They brought out the men in the mine t' the south, an' helped them the same, an' now they be a-makin' new plans t' move forward t' finish it."

"Will any of them be a-comin' home?" asks another woman. "Me husband was part of that last feast. I hope he be alright by now."

"They'll be a-comin' home in time, but first we need t' be a-knowin' how t' tell these tales, so if that big one comes 'round, we nay be a-lettin' out what we know beyond what the folk outside might tell us, an' of course the Thane himself for all his yowlin'. These men were ne'er s'posed t' come home."

"Aye, I think I see it. So, if they come home, an' he comes a-lookin', we need t' keep it quiet an' mayhap hide them, ay?"

"Aye, mayhap just t' keep it quiet. I think he would nay be a-knowin' their faces."

"An' for how long?"

"Our friends want him t' turn away from us here t' keep away the pummelin'. They be a-makin' up a few of their own tales now t' send HIS way. They hope t' build up a tale that our mines be a-runnin' out, we be a-rilin' up for the great loss, an' finally, the Thane, for all his bad manners an' wild tellin', finally fouled it up so badly, it fell apart on him."

The crowd resounds with more whispering and murmuring while Eiki makes ready to finish it.

"But now, here be the part where mayhap we can help fight the war. We nay can fight it directly, but we can help our friends an' the fight they make. So, if ye want t' get back at this big one for all the harm he brought t' our folk an' our world, ye can d' it, but just remember t' keep it quiet."

"Aye lass," calls a man. "That would be a fine one. But how; if we nay can go out an' d' it ourselves?"

"As I said, the camp belongin' t' this folk up top now belongs t' our friends. But afore this, our miners who were a-diggin' out the upper town were told nay t' go up while these foes were still there."

"An' this be why we had t' keep the door closed, ay?" suggests another man.

"Aye, but we should still keep it that way until this big one has nay anymore interest t' come 'round. Our friends will take care of things up top if there should be more comin' t' check on us, an' they'll play a game like all be fine an' good in that camp up there, at least until they make ready to go forward."

"D' they have any word on how long this could take?"

"I nay be a-knowin' how they plan this, but these be a right smart folk, an' good at such things as fightin' secret wars. So, I say, let them d' it the way they know best."

"Aye then…but this brings me t' wonder somethin'. If ye say they come from some other world, how d' they move about? Ye say this first group can move across the sky?"

"This be true, when ye have such a high folk as this. Those stars out there might have more worlds like ours. An' if ye have a mighty ship t' travel that high, ye might find a way t' it. But this nay be the only way. If ye recall those old tales of the point-ears, they were said t' come out of portals. This be a kind of knowin' that some folk learn about. For the crew up top, it be a form of study of how things work, such that they can build devices t' d' this. But for these others, they d' the same, but they also learn the ways of magic much more than we tend t' study here. So the devices THEY use tend t' be more of the magical sort."

"Aye, an' there goes what be left of me poor head," he shakes his head and turns away.

"Aye, man, ye're surely nay the only one! But now, as for how we can help. We nay can make any direct moves or words on it, but what we can d' yay be t' open a wee bit of trade. An' methinks this can be a grand thing for all of us down here t' get some fresh wares in the city t' make up for the long while we've been without. The folk outside know the better of it already. I heard from me dear husband, the folk outside who were gathered up, were moved t' this other world where they have better land. This out here be a-dyin' by now for all the heat. But on this other world, ruled by a kind an' generous King, he ordered up a new village t' be built t' hold them over till we can sort things out here."

"He ordered up a new village?" he intones intriguingly. "A whole village for nay more than homeless folk from a dyin' land? All-Father be blessed, he must be a wealthy one."

"Nay just this, but he be a determined one too! I spoke with him once, an' he said the lives of these folk were more important than the cost of a village t' hold them. That yay be the sort of man we be a-speakin' of here. Me beloved husband has been a-livin' with them for a few years now, along with three hundred others from the mine he was a-workin'. So, if ye have any doubts, ye can talk t' them about it."

"An' the trades they be askin' for? What d' we say about that? This yay sounds like it'll make a bit of noise in the streets of these friends we're nay s'posed t' be a-talkin' about."

Eiki holds the conversation for a moment as she tries to think of a good answer to maintain the aura of security, but also to provide a solution to this.

"Ye may be right, but mayhap we can find a way t' keep it quiet. If we can keep it out of the main streets an' lanes, mayhap t' a corner nay as much travelled..." she pauses in contemplation. "Let me ask our friends t' see if they can offer any ideas for this. Meanwhile, if ye think ye can hold up on all the rest, we can push these foes back t' where they come from an' hit their master where it hurts the most."

Kaliya was just arriving in the guildhall courtyard after her classes. It was the last day of the week and after her mission the previous night to deal with Ytani. Relissa, Sulíma, and the gang were in discussion of the events that took place as Marelle told it from her side piloting the ship, and with Ayene in the copilot seat swearing a few of her own lessons in piloting.

"Kali!" Sulíma shouts. "I've been waiting for you to show up. How did it go with Ytani? It sounds like you did it, but I want to hear about your technique," she grins.

"Which part of her technique, Suli?" Petrith winces. "The tail wagging or her martial arts workout? I was talking to a few of those people and hearing about the fight she had."

"Yeah, I'm a little bit disappointed that my trick didn't play out as nicely as I had hoped."

"Suli," Kaliya offers. "Don't worry about your trick. If Ytani could've been any normal boy, he would be a puddle under my hooves by now. I nearly had him drooling over it. But that guy was twisted, so we can't count him as anything remotely normal."

"All right, I feel better then."

"In fact, according to Navina…you remember her, right? Tana's mother… She was saying half my team was getting ready to jump me on my way back."

"Ooh! I like that. I wonder if I can make this work on a group level."

"Oh no!" Túfula moans. "Suli, just how many boys do you need chasing your tail at one time?"

"Well, chasing is one thing, but I'll stay true and let only the one boy take hold of it," she grins at Petrith. "But he'll need to work a little harder if he ever hopes to live up to all those promises he keeps making."

"Hey," he protests. "You play your tricks, I'll play mine."

"Uh oh…" Marelle smirks. "Do we have a little foreplay going on here?"

"When dealing with her, it's mostly foreplay," he smiles.

The group shares a laugh until Túfula resumes the conversation.

"But now, Kali," she wonders. "What happened in the end? As far as I understand it, you had to wrestle him into that large transport, and Marelle and this new girl, Ayene, flew it to the depot site, right?"

"And according to Ayene," Petrith adds. "She nearly took out half the flight hanger on the landing."

"Nearly taking it out isn't the same as actually doing it," Marelle corrects. "That thing was huge, and Ytani was breaking free of his bonds, so I simply didn't have time to make it neat. But I'll have you know; I didn't actually break anything."

"I was watching you, Marelle," Kaliya notes. "I was inside there when you almost...ALMOST...smashed into the wall."

"I swear, no one around here trusts me. You should see me on those simulators. That 'almost' bit is what I'm best at."

"All right, but let's hope we don't have another occasion where we need to test that theory."

"This much I'll agree on. Adalon might say I have something waiting for me, but I would like to actually see it."

"As for Ytani, we dropped him in the hanger, and Marelle and Ayene took off again, leaving us behind."

"But you're projected still, right?" Sulíma asks.

"Right, so I'm quite confident I can handle things. But I'll tell you, that guy was probably the worst dull-horn I've ever seen. His ego was astonishing, thinking he was so special. But in all four centuries he was playing a dwarf, he never once got any ideas to see what else he can do with it."

"But how is that possible?" Túfula considers. "You've created so many fascinating new images, and many of them right when you needed to solve a problem. Why couldn't he do the same?"

"We had a little talk about this. Apparently, the Marshal didn't teach him enough about this Gift for him to realize the full potential. He only got enough out of it to know how to make a dwarf and shout at people. A while back, I was speaking to Ayene, trying to get a little background information on him. She said he was assigned to his job at only seven decades, if you can believe it."

"What? That's underage, to say the least!"

"That might also suggest he missed a lot of school," Haran notes. "And this could easily relate to his poor skills with that base."

"Yeah," Kaliya nods. "And even his bad upbringing…or total lack of one. When I asked about his parents, he said they were both reported as killed in an accident. Uh huh, sure, and he was probably listed as missing as part of that same 'accident', and you can bet Darumon is behind it so he could essentially abduct him and hide him in a top-secret military base no one knew about."

"Very convenient."

"Furthermore, he was told he doesn't NEED any more schooling, as he already had enough to suit him for whatever might be the rest of his life. This might tell you about what sort of life he might have from this moment forward."

"Yes, and especially using a skill no one knows about, or is intended to know about, and where he might find himself after that role is complete."

"Exactly! And he apparently DID have a chip at four decades, like everyone else, but Darumon ordered it removed so he could use his skill."

"Oh…" Túfula huffs. "That must've been fun."

"Yeah, he got an offer for this fabulous job, along with the removal of his torture device. You can't beat that!" she giggles. "Even worse is when I tried to explain the level of intrigue here. I literally had to spell it out for him in baby terms, just like Commander Kriv'tik and that survey deal. Then he started to realize just how valuable he really was, as opposed to all those highly trained professionals he was throwing away. You almost need to feel for the guy at this point. He was given knowledge Darumon was going out of his way to cover up, so witnesses become expendable. The project to build the weapon is a one-time affair. You only need just so much to blow up a universe. After that, he moves on, and Ytani is out of a job, and probably out of life, as well. Worse still is there's no one to cry over it. His parents are gone, and he's probably absent from view by anyone else. Otherwise, I would imagine someone, like a grandparent or other relatives, would be screaming for a lost child."

"Right," Petrith accedes. "Darumon wouldn't want anyone to know HE has him. That wouldn't go over well with whatever Child Services agency they might have over there."

"And then, he's sent to a secret military base that doesn't officially exist. So, who cares if HE should suddenly not exist? There aren't any records to identify him. But the military side of it…oh yes, they might get reassigned, because it takes time to train skilled labor, and THAT carries value. But an uneducated runt with no life…?"

"Got it…and with no one to claim him to bring him home."

"Poor guy," Marelle relents. "It's no wonder he turned out so bad."

"I said to him," Kaliya adds. "Murder is still murder, and the law is still the law, no matter who you are or what someone like Darumon might say. If you have someone like Ayene, who has a university law degree, that says they DO have law and justice over there, despite Darumon pretending to own everything. So, you still need to expect your tail to get chewed by it."

"But a guy like him," Sulíma offers. "He wouldn't even know what that means, since at seven decades, you might not even have enough education to realize what it's like to have an education."

"Right…skilled labor, that's what it's all about. And he was throwing it away with the base staff, which means Central would do something, at the very least, assuming he didn't lie to them about it. I might even think Darumon would have a word or two for it. He needs that military to do his other work, but he could pick any kid off the street to do the Prodigy skill. And more, if it weren't for him falsifying his reports, and if Central should ever figure something is wrong for all these lost crewmembers, that they want to call an investigation, it won't matter what Darumon thinks he owns. If he tries to interfere by putting people on active simply to stop the questions, I don't think he could do it fast enough, not with so many already becoming restless for those chips. They might rise up and point their guns at him next, simply for the favor of it."

"Good for you, Kali!" Sulíma smiles.

"He apparently held such a belief that no one ever defies the Marshal, the same as they never defied the Council, even if they ever

DID try to show personal opinions. But the Marshal shouldn't hold any legal claim of authority in our world. He's an alien, after all."

"Yes, that too…technically, at least…if you don't count what he did to us over there."

"Jiggers," Relissa moans. "No wonder he was playing this like a game. It's all just one big bugaboo of a game for him, and he never really grew up at all."

"I'll bet this also relates to how he treats girls," Marelle suggests. "He grows up, probably without any proper supervision, except what the base staff might offer, which at this point might not be much. He matures and starts getting those urges, like guys do, and starts to realize that girls are useful for something."

"This is also where that Alpha Male syndrome comes in," Kaliya adds. "Which he didn't know anything about, it seems, as no one ever explained to him what happens when you're one of us, a male, and play with weightlifting."

"Oops!" Sulíma yips. "That could be a problem."

"Aye!" Relissa nods. "And if those girls can help him satisfy those urges, he'll want more of them, and with no control over it."

"That's right!" Marelle suggests. "He's probably got nothing else to do in there, so he ends up dwelling on it…that, and his toy city."

"And there you have his mania," Haran concludes. "Developing to the point where it goes wild, and he thinks the Marshal will give him the world with a ribbon tied around it."

"I'm trying to imagine something here," Túfula muses. "Just think if he ever did have the idea to try something, even if just out of boredom and looking for something to do. He wanted girls, so could he pop into their bedrooms? Can he molest them like this?"

"Probably not to his satisfaction," Kaliya reflects. "If he's not corporeal, he wouldn't get the physical sensations, but he sure could scare them, maybe even abuse them."

"And that would surely encourage some part of his mania," Haran returns. "Terror attacks, at the very least."

"It would. And quite realistically, I can't see how he should NOT have been able to get at least some little idea in his head. If he understood how to flash to another location, ANY location, even line-of-sight through a window…how hard can it be to figure that one out? He could then walk up to their barracks and enter inside any of those rooms."

"Then it's just a case of attacking them in some way," Marelle admits.

"This simply makes matters worse," Túfula relents. "Kaliya, you can carry objects from place to place, but can you carry people, like if to abduct someone?"

"I don't know. I've never tried carrying a person… Well, actually, our team did manage to carry him along the road to toss him inside the transport, so I guess that's a result. But wait a minute…" she pauses in thought as she tries to recall the events. "We had multiple people on him. This reminds me of that book. I couldn't pass it off from one person to another in projected mode, but we had multiple people grabbing and moving him."

"How does this play out, do you think?" Petrith wonders.

Kaliya tries to replay the scene in her mind.

"Will power… Yes, it must be related to conscious will, a struggle against us. He was resisting, so he was applying his conscious will, even though it wasn't intended this way, but it worked out that we could move him as a group because his will was focused on his efforts to resist us independently."

"That's an interesting perspective."

"This might also reflect on him trying to free himself, and us trying to hold him down. We had to exert ourselves to overcome his will to break free. It was literally a contest of will here, and this might go independent for each of our efforts."

"I think I'm losing you," Marelle winces.

"Losing?" Relissa teases. "Did you ever have it to begin with?"

"Look at it this way," Kaliya considers. "That book we were playing with once. It was an inanimate object, and I could pick it up, but it phases with me and my manifestation. Therefore, another projection cannot interact unless I set it down and let it re-phase with the natural environment, thereby allowing the next one to pick it up."

"This is your workaround for passing things around each other, right?" Marelle asks.

"Right, and so far, this is the only way for us to do it. But Ytani was a conscious being with his own perception of existence…his own manifestation, if you will, and corporeal as opposed to a projection. Therefore, multiple of us can interact with him successfully because he's not phasing with any of us. Each of us is in contest with him for our will versus his."

"This sounds like something to take up with Aelwyn."

"Yes, this would make a good study. And then, can a projection actually carry a person like this. If Ytani tried abducting someone, and if we say the subject is conscious and opposing the effort, the real question is, can he pick her up and fold back to his house, or does he have to drag her physically out the door? And next would be if she's unconscious, for instance if she was sleeping. Hmm…"

"Sleeping might be a bad thing," Petrith grimaces. "It would probably work more like the inanimate object, in this case. Next thing you know, she wakes up tied to his bondage rack."

"That would be bad," Marelle moans. "The perfect kidnapping, because you can do it behind closed, and also locked doors."

"All right," Kaliya shrugs. "So, we'll add this to the list of possible criminal actions. That regulatory body of ours is going to have its hands full trying to set up rules for all this, to say nothing of enforcement. Still, I doubt Ytani would realize this if he was so limited in his skills. And yet, Túfu is right. In four centuries, he should've done something, even if by accident. Maybe if to play with toy action figures, shrinking down like you're one of them, or to flash back home and visit with someone…anything!"

"Wow, that's a dull-horn and a half," Sulíma moans. "How did he even manage to figure out his basic job?"

"Darumon must've given him some very precise instructions," Petrith considers. "And likely told him there's nothing else he CAN do with it. I'd like to see Darumon's face if he ever DID actually learn something, if only to pop into his office to say hello."

They again share a tender laugh, but the suggestion caused Kaliya to delve into deep thought.

"To pop in and say hello..." she muses distantly.

"Uh oh...I think I just opened something here."

"Jiggers, Petrith," Relissa groans. "I think you just gave her some wacky new idea."

"I didn't mean to."

"But think about it," Kaliya smiles impishly. "He only told him how to do one thing with it, so like with everything else, he was hiding most of it. But four hundred years, Petrith...how many times did Darumon actually check on him? Ayene said he got almost no visitors, and this included Darumon himself."

"That guy is not much of a father figure anyway," Marelle winces.

"No, he's not...and without any OTHER kind of proper supervision...who's to say he didn't actually invent a few new tricks?"

"Um, are you asking us or telling us," Petrith wonders.

"The base staff had no idea what Ytani was doing in there where the Prodigy skill goes. He was mostly isolated in that house. He was a megalomaniac with dreams of owning everything around him. AND..." she asserts with a finger. "We have evidence to prove it! Those spy videos, and I also know the Commander made recordings of his recent conversations."

"Um, all right, but what do you have in mind to do with it?"

"Give me a moment," she offers. "He imagined himself becoming king of the world over there, with a slave population of dwarves and with Suuden'kai taskmasters in active mode, and he gloated over the idea of having girls who would bow down to him. I've played god figures before, but he believed he WAS a god. Why should he even bow down to Darumon at this point?"

"Oops!"

"And the message...that one unit of Arcanicium... Darumon might wonder who it was, but what if we GIVE him a target to point a finger at? He used distractions often enough on everyone else, so here we use one on him. The base staff, and even Ytani, knew it was highly explosive. And since we had an uprising downstairs turning on him anyway, his dreams of playing god with a toy planet just got turned upside-down, so he's a little upset now," she smirks.

"And that's a bigger oops."

"And now he's gone missing…WITH the Arcanicium."

"And that's a massive oops. But where?"

"Where…hmm… One thing that comes to mind is he might not want to go home directly, or else Darumon might be upset for losing his weapon. And he might not want to stay on Morndindor, because it's a given that's where they KNOW him to be. So, in all that free time living alone, he…learned…a few things, like how to travel to distant stars, or some such. With a little work, I can project and fold myself to distant objects, if I can maintain a constant effort to keep moving. All I need is line-of-sight to focus on, and a star is simply a very distant object to focus on with line-of-sight, so there you go."

"Interesting, and this would be a fascinating way to explore the stars around you."

"And along the way, he met someone. Now he's got friends. He'll need someone to help in removing that weapon, anyway. Otherwise, how do you explain the missing stockpile?"

"Right, you got that much."

"And with the clear failure of losing his toy city, therefore his excuse for more girls and toy soldiers, he'll need a replacement. And where do you think he'll find an unlimited supply to kiss his hooves?" she grins brightly.

"Oh dear…"

"And so, we turn Darumon the wrong way while we set down in HIS backyard. And sweet little Ytani is going to create a scene for us."

Another weekend had come and Thaelyn was in a meeting in his office at the guildhall. The meeting involved several city planners and construction foremen, along with representatives from the merchants'

guild about his plans for redesigning and rebuilding the former Daanen'kai city on Ruuki uy'Daan.

"My Lord," mentions one of the city planners. "We will need to clear space for a permanent gateway node there, and likely we will be building a hub terminal in this case, since I would expect the city to serve as a future capital for that world."

"So far, it is the ONLY city in that world, but this is reasonable. And considering the devastation and decay of the existing structures, at this moment it might be just as easy to demolish most of it and rebuild from scratch, much like we did in Rolsklinde. But I would wish to make a few alterations to our building codes on this occasion. Eventually, we may need to modify these codes universally."

"And what might that be, my Lord?"

"It would be to raise the ceiling height somewhat, to better accommodate our taller friends. Recently, I have noticed they seem to be somewhat cramped with our traditional building sizes. If we raise the limits, it will more appropriately resemble their own structural dimensions and allow them greater comfort. And at some moment, I think we should also consider allocating space for a memorial park, to reflect upon their losses during the attack."

"That would be most gracious."

"I feel it would be unconscionable not to give proper mention to the lives lost in that city. And even though the Elder Council has relinquished its authority over the territory, I would still feel it worthy to make the appropriate accommodations for a Daanen'kai population making their homes there one day. We are already working to relocate our recent Suuden'kai inductees there, so we will begin with that. Who knows, we might be building a colony base for them along the way."

"Very good, my Lord. And by the way, do we have a name for this new addition to our most glorious kingdom?"

"We do. Ultimately, I would wish to give a better name to the world as a whole, but I will save this for later. As for the city, I have given this careful consideration, and I feel it needs to take on the aspect of the Daanen-Aryku and their desperate hope to escape from their oppressors. It must take into account their suffering, and their desires to find peace. So, we will call it Daazh uy'Sodrad, which in their language translates as Spring of Freedom."

"A most excellent choice, my Lord! I will make the appropriate recording in our registry."

The delegation offers a parting bow and departs back to their respective offices to begin their work.

Thaelyn now exits his office and strolls outside as he begins on his way to Rolsklinde. Kaliya and her team were convening in the courtyard, discussing their daily plans for exercise and training, when he came into view. They were waiting for him with an important announcement.

"My Lord," she calls. "Can we have a moment, please?"

Thaelyn diverts himself from his course to meet with the group.

"Yes, Kaliya," he replies jovially. "What do you have in mind today? You look like you might be conspiring on something again."

"Again? Would I do that to you? Um, wait, don't answer that," she giggles. "Actually, my team is the one with the message. We were just waiting for you to come out so we could catch you before you got busy with anything else."

Kaliya defers to her teammates, directing the squad leaders to step forward to represent the rest. She calls on Navina to make the presentation.

"Your Lordship," she announces. "We've all been in deep discussion on this and have come to a decision. Considering our recent training, our practice and mission accomplishments, the new studies we're engaged in, and many other factors, not the least of which is our recent revelation of who and what we are and what we must represent as we move forward, we find ourselves in a situation where we wish to take this to the next step. And we're not the only ones. We've held meetings with those who are involved in the conjoined training, sharing our experiences and perspectives, and they also feel the same, especially considering where we are going and what it means for our people."

"I see, and what would this next step entail?"

"With your permission, we would wish to submit ourselves fully into your military service. We want the Stormhooves to hold special meaning again. It was once a noble service of knighthood under a king, and although we can't be sure exactly how that history played out, we feel it should still be a noble knighthood and still under a king. Therefore, we want to be your creation and serve under your leadership, bringing back our ancestral honor and taking back our homes."

Thaelyn smiled warmly at the suggestion as he passed his gaze across the full assembly.

"I would be most honored for your service. I know we have shared many words together, and Kaliya has been involved in several of our more important discussions about your history, as well as Adalon's prophecies, and what these Stormhooves might represent in the modern day, if we consider this as a form of revival."

"Yes, about that. We feel this would be the most important of all, to take something that holds such a romance for us and turn it into something truly functional to serve our people and a higher purpose. If we are an example of a Celestial-grade society, we need role models to follow, and there is no better role model than one who is also a Celestial."

"Indeed, this does make good sense. You are still a young society, so to have something akin to a tutor would be very valuable for you."

"Absolutely. It's our way of taking control of our lives and demonstrating to Darumon, if he was the one to create all this in the first place, that we are now using his creation for our own purpose, not his."

"This is very reasonable. To think of you who are pursuing the roles of paladins and other such noble adherents, at least in part as to serve as role models for so many others to follow, due to these Gifts of yours and other noteworthy principles, this incarnation of the Stormhooves will be one for the history books, and likely even more romantic than the first. But before we take this step, I feel I should ask about your Commander and his feelings on the matter, as well as your Council."

"The Commander fully understands and gives his blessing to it. I wouldn't be at all surprised to see him join us one day. As for the Council, while we all wish to honor them for their work, at the same time this is war, and due to circumstances outside our control, they must take a back seat to it. Therefore, the choice becomes obvious, and the future of our people demands we make this choice."

"Indeed, I suppose I must agree," he sighs. "And for these same reasons. But now, if you hold such a desire to join our military, have you been briefed on the entrance requirements?"

"Absolutely! And we have already covered that, Your Lordship."

The group leaders, along with the rest of the group, all reached into their pockets and pulled out badges adorned with ornate ribbons and pinned them to their lapels. Thaelyn examines the full group. The shiny badges each bore a colored design on the front…violet.

"By the Powers, all of you?" he gasps. "But then, I should not be so surprised, as we had this with Kaliya's friends. But to see so many of them…all at once."

"And not only us, Your Lordship, but many more in training as part of our conjoined efforts. They have all taken up practicing these new methods based on our examples. We are becoming something of a new standard."

"How many are we speaking of here?"

"The full assembly, just under five thousand by now…"

"Five thousand…" he wheezes. "And all violet?"

"Yes, Your Lordship, we all took the test. Poor Master Sagrid will probably be taking an early retirement, but we all got violet."

"This is enough to make up a full brigade! This new Order we are creating will be more than just an elite group of operatives, it will be a full Special Forces unit, and an exceptionally unusual one, at that!"

"I'm actually envisioning something more than that," Kaliya notes.

"Oh, and what is that now?"

"This is just the beginning. I'm basically pioneering this revival, and I don't expect it to end here. We're taking this home, and I'm expecting it to continue to grow into a full military body. It may be composed entirely of our own people, if only due to the nature of these Gifts we are sporting, and as a way to govern and regulate how they are applied. Therefore, this will be the new military body for our society. We who would call ourselves…Suuden-Aryku."

"Suuden-Aryku is it?" he muses affectionately. "No longer Daanen-Aryku?"

"If our purpose is to retake our home and bring it back to order, we must become one with our people again, no longer in exile. And as I mentioned before, the reason for us to make this example must be to offer this standard of excellence, and to lead our people into a new future where we must evolve to hold these virtues close to us. We cannot simply pretend to be normal people, not with half of Darumon in our blood."

Thaelyn felt a warm sensation of parental pride flow into him.

"Kaliya, when I first met you, you were a hot-tempered young lady with too many reckless ambitions and biased opinions. You have grown tremendously in this time, and I think I cannot take full credit for it. A fair portion had to come from somewhere else."

"Some of the credit clearly comes from all your work here to set the examples we are now drawing from. This is where a Celestial society finds its roots, even though this society is even younger than ours. And I suppose a part of it should also be given to Lord Oghma and what He teaches."

"Indeed, this should be included," he nods.

"And I think all our past conversations of where we came from, and how we were made, has opened our eyes to a lot of things, and made us realize if we are to fight back against what Darumon represents, we need to break free from his illustration and rewrite it for ourselves."

"And indeed, I think that represents the finest example of all," he now turns to the group in general. "Very well, then I shall have you pass the word around, and I will give the appropriate instructions on my side. We will attend to the formalities when time permits, but for now I think it would do us best to put you into an accelerated form of education to meet up with Kaliya's level. This includes mage studies, as she is already Seventh Circle, going on Eighth, and the rest of you are…what by now?"

"Most of us are in the Fifth," Navina reflects. "And we would be very eager to accelerate to meet her level. And you can be sure we will work hard for it, the same as she did."

"Does this include blowing up the lower mage training field?" he raises his brow.

"Well, we can try to avoid that, but if this is her standard…" she smirks.

"Oh, Powers help us. Very well. Then, I will give the word to our educators to see about adapting a schedule similar to what we used on her, at least for this occasion to hurry you along. Though I should still caution, for future training, it is best to take the standard flow. We will only use this for our crisis of this war."

"Thank you, and would it be appropriate to start calling you… my Lord?" she grins.

"Indeed, it would," he smiles. "Your society has not followed a monarch for apparently a very long time. Naturally, there are a few cultural differences, but I think we can attend to those as we move forward."

Kaliya instructs her team to draw to attention and give their salutes as Thaelyn makes his goodbye and continues out of the courtyard to Rolsklinde.

As he enters the WIC building, he takes up his seat at the strategy table, along with Kailen and the General. Kailen glances at him with a curious smirk.

"Commander," Thaelyn notes. "It would seem I am not the only one in this room with the occasional mischievous glint in his eye. How long did you know about this?"

"A while, now. The word has been spreading for a long time, and I finally told Kaliya, if you are going to do it, you need to jump in with both hooves."

"Indeed, and she apparently made quite a splash along the way. We have nearly five thousand violets in need of heavy training to meet our war needs. We will be accelerating some of this to push them along, as this represents where we stand on Morndindor and whatever lies in wait for us later."

"My Lord," the General considers. "If this is to be a new unit of particularly elite standing, we should give it the appropriate ornamentation. An emblem of some sort representing their ancestral mention."

"That would be a fine idea, but do we know what the original Stormhooves wore in this regard? Would there still be a record of it?"

"I cannot be sure, but if the Commander could do a bit of research on it, maybe someone might still hold some of the old teachings of their history."

"I think I might know who to talk to about this," Kailen considers. "Elder Vankkar always held special interest in that. I think I also remember some kind of mention coming out of Commander Kriv'tik during the interrogation. He mentioned something about a historical story relating to a king uniting the world, so I wonder if he could point us at something."

"Yes, I recall that now," Thaelyn reflects. "So, it would seem we might have another fan of the old history."

"Next on my mind is the base, and our future direction to reach Azgarén. What's next for us there? Do we try to maintain it and put on a show for the rest until we can do something about it?"

"Yes. We must now consider any Suuden'kai arrivals, or even Darumon himself, coming by to investigate anything at all. According to our observations, and the details given to us by Commander Kriv'tik, the only real concern, unless something unusual occurs, are their supply deliveries and our periodic reports going out, of which he will assist."

"And Ytani? Kaliya told me a little while ago she had an idea for him, but she still needed to develop it into something functional."

"What sort of idea is that?"

"First of all, that he essentially flubbed up and lost the city, which is a given. This might cause him to become concerned over Darumon's reaction. But more importantly is his lust for girls and a pet world under him."

"Indeed, this is a curious direction."

"We also have Adalon's message relating to the weapon, which Kaliya thinks she could possibly play into, but here is where she says she'd like to develop her idea a little more before presenting it. She was hinting at Ytani turning renegade."

"Oh dear, I think Darumon is in trouble, if this is going where I think it is," he chuckles. "Very well, we shall give her some time for this. The last report coming out of there was about the mine in the city running low…not depleted, but simply low."

"As opposed to the stories we were giving Ytani during this time?"

"Correct. So, I must wonder how low we can go before their Central Command gets anxious for a resumption of their operations. How much patience does Darumon have to see his weapon finished?"

"I don't think I could answer that, but perhaps if we confer with Commander Kriv'tik, maybe he can offer something."

"Good, but in the end, we want them to leave entirely. However, unlike my play here on Therinë, we cannot let them know we are present. Therefore, to say the Estelar are coming to Morndindor might not be such a good choice. If the dwarves hold an uprising due to their fellows from the outside contradicting their Thane's stories, this could serve as a good excuse for Darumon to pull out. But then we must consider how this pull-out will likely involve dismantling that base and recalling the crew."

"Yeah, about that," Kailen grins expectantly. "How do you recall a crew that has been replaced by projections?"

"This is a good question, but one that does not have an easy answer for now. If Commander Kriv'tik was planning an escape of some sort, as part of his mutiny, and we cannot simply send him home, we must deny their simple return."

The morning review continued with reports of the scouting runs still searching for more survivors on Morndindor, and a report from the base about a new supply shipment received and acknowledged by the fake staff members. Apparently, their deception was working. The visiting Suuden'kai troops delivering the supplies didn't notice anything unusual. Then, a knocking came at the door as a scout entered with Eiki making a visit from Glimmerheim.

"Ah, do we have a special occasion for this pleasure?" Thaelyn asks as he notices the arrival.

"Yer Kingship," she replies reverently. "I be so very grateful for yer help in these times, an' yer scouts have been a-tellin' me of the fine work ye be a-makin' for us. But now I come before ye with a wee mite of a question, an' a bit of…um…fixin' t' answer a clear worry back home. I had a word with yer scouts t' pass through yer Captain, an' we all agree this needs t' be attended, if only t' keep things in hand."

"I believe I understand. With the new stories being told down there, and so few complete answers to be given due to our situation of security, it was difficult to know how far we could reach before breaking the silence in the eyes of our enemies. What do you have?"

"The Chancellor an' I agreed that the people need t' have at least enough t' fill them up, but at the same time nay so much as t' make things hard on ye if that Darumon should come back makin' trouble. So, we made a decision t' tell what we could, an' make them know there be a right grand bit of trouble waitin' if the wrong words be spoken out in the open. I think we got the message across fair enough, an' the people yay be with ye on this much."

"This is good to hear. We must move very carefully to be sure they only speak about those things otherwise possible to know from the people outside."

"Right ye be, an' we made this sure an' true in their minds. But now we have a new bit t' ask of ye, if ye don'na mind, an' I be a wee bit short of an answer t' it me'self. Mayhap ye, with all yer fine wisdom, can find the right way for it."

"Very well, Eiki, what sort of problem do we have here?"

"We don'na want t' simply sit on our duffs waitin' for the next blastin'. We nay be warriors, but our honor be a-hurtin' bad from all the foolin' they gave, an' we want t' be a-makin' somethin' t' d' our part in the war, even though we know we nay can be a-makin' a great showin' for it. Yer men said mayhap ye would want t' open up some trade for our wares, an' there be many a fine fare we be a-wishin' for since closin' the doors so long ago. Mayhap we could also trade such as Adamant an' Mithril, if we can find any more of it, t' help yer army. The trouble here be we know we can'na make an open trade if this Darumon be a-comin' through, but mayhap there can be another way?"

"Indeed, this would provide a good opportunity for us to join together and give you the possibility to rebuild somewhat. Then let us consider what we have to work with here. You have a well-developed city down there with many potential crafts for trade. We already know you could use to improve your food, and perhaps also cloth and leather, and I am sure there are other things you could find of value that might not normally be found underground. The difficult part would be how to interact with a predictable and persistent trade route while still not making a large display. It would need to be hidden somewhere."

"If it need t' be hidden, then I think it nay be a good idea t' put it outside on the barrens where the Suuden-Aryku or this Darumon can pop their noses out t' see it."

"Yes, but inside your city would also be a poor choice if he should try sneaking in under an illusion of a local citizen."

"D' ye think he would make such a surprise visit if he be a-thinkin' his servant the Thane be a-runnin' things so well for him?"

"Hmm, this is an interesting point, and I would actually tend to believe he might not make a surprise visit as he should clearly hold the opinion that he owns that operation. Therefore, it would make greater sense to simply arrange a common visit, and then we would know ahead of time his arrival. If this is the case, we could make quick plans to hide our evidence, but the manner must be simplified in some way for efficiency."

"Like mayhap t' simply close a door that he might not look in t' see our work. Hmm…oh! Wait now, this brings a clever thought t' me mind. The men who were a-diggin' out the upper town cleared away a lane from the store t' get through, an' the foreman actually had the idea t' make up a false door t' cover in case anyone from above be a-comin' in the other way. It looks just like the rubble they cleared out. An' so if ye were t' close it, ye would only see what looks t' be a filled lane."

"Good, this was very clever. And I recall some parts of that area were still useable. Therefore, if we could establish some shops in there, possibly along with a portal to help move our wares in and out, we could establish some fine relations while at the same time keeping a low profile. Then if Darumon should make any sort of visit, we could send a quick word to close that door and he would never know the difference."

"Aye! That be a fine one!" she yips eagerly. "Then d' ye think this mayhap be somethin' ye an' yer folk can d' for us?"

"Indeed!" he nods. "I will send word to make a close inspection to see what we have to work with, and possibly some laborers to begin some form of construction effort, then to our merchants to start arranging deliveries to the new marketplaces. We might need to arrange this as a sort of embassy district, since we are a foreign society. But I think, if your people do not mind us taking up a bit of space, we can more than compensate for the imports we will bring to you."

"Aye. I can speak t' the Chancellor about this, but I nay be a-thinkin' it t' be a problem for us. We nay be usin' it, anyway."

"Excellent. This reminds me, our people brought out a fair amount of adamantium from that mine south of your city. This technically belongs to you, so we will deliver this back into your hands for you to decide how you would wish to use it."

"Yer Kingship, that be a fine gift, an' I yay be sure the people will take t' makin' something grand for ye."

She gives a modest bow and returns to the scout still standing in the doorway. They leave the building, but before going home, she turns to make a quick detour to visit her husband first.

Chapter 4

A QUIET MOMENT

The end of the school year had finally come. Kaliya had finished one of the toughest periods so far in her academy course, having gone through two years of compressed mage studies in order to push her high enough to mark a rune on Ruuki uy'Daan so she could bring the troops across. This next year would revert to a more routine schedule, but still difficult as she would be entering the Eighth Circle, which by its own merit would be hard.

Relissa and Haran were preparing to enter their next year of study, both going into the Sixth Circle by now, along with all their other studies for their individual professions.

Sulíma, Túfula, and Petrith were soon to be finishing up their language classes, but at the start of the new school year they wanted to enter into formal study. So, they made arrangements to fill in the remaining language classes during weekends, since they were proficient enough by this time to enroll.

Marelle, on the other hand, had other plans for this year. She wanted to become a mother before it was too late.

"Roddy," she mumbles as she runs through her objectives list. "We have the formal dress and gown ready, and the flower wagon will be present with a wonderful display. I really need to thank Aerlie for her help on that. Then we have the banquet hall arranged... Oh, and the portraits! We need to get ourselves over to that nice little gazebo in Solinaia to have our paintings done. Can you think of anything else?"

"Marelle, this is my first time as much as it is yours, and it sounds like you've got everything nicely lined up for it. All I can say is my belly is twisting up in knots just thinking about it."

"I know, mine too. I'm especially nervous that we're trying to pinch this into such a tight schedule between my classes. I've got a year for this, and in that time, we need to get married, now that we have a free moment to get away for it, and then immediately try to have a baby, and in those last few months try to raise it just enough that I can break away to return to the academy."

"We'll need a nanny to cover for you while you're away."

"Yeah, but Aerlie promises she'll help with that, since we're in such a tight spot."

"It's good to have friends like that. And so, we're scheduled to do this just after this year's graduation."

"Yeah, and that's only a week away now. The closer we get, the jumpier I am."

"I know the feeling, but we'll get through it. We'll just take it one step at a time."

"And don't forget, when we're done with that, I need to visit Aerlie almost on a daily basis for her to check me for this fertility thing. When she gives the word, well, you know."

"Right, that's when we jump into bed together for that happy little moment," he grins.

"But we need that blessing first. Aerlie mentioned stopping by the temple in B.T. for a blessing by Lathander. Lots of people apparently do this to ensure strong healthy babies, and I really want this to work."

"All right, Marelle, we'll go in together. Why not get both of us blessed, for a double-hit on the healthy part."

She giggles and leans into him for a tender hug.

As the week passes, Marelle and Roderick make a visit to Solinaia and a gazebo setting specially arranged with flowers and ornamental vines. They wore their ceremonial dress and held their position for a painting to be made of the wedding couple. Relissa had been chosen for the bride's maid, and Haran as the best man, and another painting was made with them included. By week's end, classes were out, and they made their official appearance in the Temple of the Planes in Bya'an Tamoranth for the special occasion.

"We are here, gathered together in this place," Aerlie announces to the assembly, "to give witness to this, the most joyous of occasions in our lives, where a man and a woman come together in blessed matrimony, in the eyes of our Gods, to love and to share their joys and their tears, for the better as well as the worst that the fates may bestow upon us, for all time."

The temple was packed with visitors and students from the academy. Thaelyn stood in the front row, along with his officers. Kaliya, Sulíma, Túfula, and Petrith were lined up, along with Kailen and Ankhia. Tristeen stood in front on the other side of the aisle, along with Lady Amariyn and Lady Sehnisavain, and others who played such a prominent role in the lives of the loving couple.

Relissa stood on one side facing Marelle wearing a flowing gown and a flower circlet around her head, which was entirely atypical for the dark elf's usual decorum, while Haran stood on the other side facing Roderick in an equally impressive formal coat, pants, dickey, and cummerbund.

"On this day," Aerlie continues. "It is my most honored pleasure to bring these two into wedlock and grant unto them this union that they may forever share their lives as one."

She turns to Roderick to begin the holy rites for his vows.

"Here stands Sir Roderick Sabastian Kholgard, of noble honor and valor, who comes before us to offer himself to this woman in his moment of promise that he shall bestow upon her his love, devotion, and commitment for the duration of his lifetime, to attend and support her in her moments of need, and to grant her his dedication of home and family. Is this, in truth, your deepest vow?"

"It is," he announces boldly.

Aerlie next turns to Marelle, who was only barely holding together during this time.

"And here stands Marelle Elena Carronel, of virtue and compassion, who comes before us to offer herself to this man in her moment of promise that she shall bestow upon him her love, devotion, and commitment for the duration of her lifetime, to attend and support him in his moments of need, and to grant him her dedication of home and family. Is this, in truth, your deepest vow?"

"It is," she offers up strongly.

"Then let it be said that on this day, I bring these two together into this union as Husband and Wife. May the Gods we adore give them their blessings of a long and endearing life."

The assembly in the room gives up a loud applause and cheers for the newlyweds. Flower petals rain down on them as they make their way along the aisle to meet with friends and patrons, receiving handshakes and hugs all the way out of the temple to a carriage waiting outside to carry them around the city. The temple bells ring to sound off the special moment, and people in the streets usher up well-wishes and waves to the couple as they make their marital drive.

In the days following, life goes somewhat back to normal, with Marelle making a visit to the temple for her check-up with Aerlie. The two of them were in consultation in the Healer's Ward, with Marelle preparing to lay on one of the beds for her examination.

"How have you been feeling these last couple of days, Marelle?" Aerlie asks.

"Relieved that the first part is over... Getting ready for that wedding was tough."

"Yes, it usually is for many people. You should've seen me at my wedding with Thaelyn. It was such an extravagant affair, him being a noble. And me, I felt so small in all that."

"Why?"

"Well, I was not born to a noble family, so it felt like I was being lifted out of a hole and placed on a pedestal, and the glamor of that pedestal was overwhelming for the notability Thaelyn carries."

"Wow, that must've been hard."

"I had a group of friends supporting me as my bridesmaids, but it was still a struggle to hold myself upright...well, until Amaree, one of my friends who was standing there with me, started passing hidden sign language messages to the priest," she giggles.

"Huh? Now wait a minute. Are you saying I'm not the only one making trouble around here?"

"Yes, we've had a few in the past, as well. Thaelyn has a long list of accomplishments during his lifetime, including a number of titles. I didn't have that much to offer to make it seem worthy in comparison. So, dear Amaree started passing these messages to involve all the cute little quirks of my life, just to break the tension. It worked, too, I actually felt better for it."

"What kinds of quirks, or should I even ask," she grins.

"For one thing, there was the moment where I brought the Elixir of Visions to the guild, which was prophesied by Adalon and involved some very strange circumstances over where it must've come from and why it was here at all."

"Yeah, I've heard of that."

"Then was an unfortunate occasion where Thaelyn brought a group of us out on a field mission patrolling for orcs, and I accidentally hit him in the back with a lightning spell."

"Ouch, yeah, I remember your story about that."

"And then was my time in the circus, where it all began."

"Right, I recall Kaliya telling us that one once."

"So, if you put it all together, even though it's not quite as noble as to be a knight of this or that, or accomplishing great deeds, this became my legacy," she sighs. "But it's alright. It makes life all the more interesting for us."

"And that's the important part, I guess."

"Yes, it is. But then Tyr showed up. That was downright shocking, and not only to me!"

"Wait a minute. You actually had Tyr show up at your wedding? Gracious, does that sort of thing happen often?"

"No, it does not, but mine was an exceptionally unique case. Do you remember my story of how Ecco made her deal with Tyr for her contract and ultimately to become me?"

"Yeah, that story is a little hard to forget."

"It was even harder to learn about. At the moment Thaelyn and I shared our vows, and we were turning to face the assembly, the entire temple was bathed in divine light. It was magnificent! Then the face of Tyr manifested into the room over the altar looking down on all of us. I nearly fell over when I saw it."

"That's a little scary, I should think."

"This is when he announced my contract was complete. The trouble was that none of us had any idea what he was talking about, especially me."

"Wow, so how did you react to that?"

"Shock would be a good place to start," she giggles. "Fortunately, where my voice failed, Thaelyn offered up his to inquire as to the meaning, and Tyr explained it to us."

"How did that go?"

"Here is where he told me that my contract was complete and now I must choose my blessings of his Favor. Of course, this made about as much sense as the rest, until we further learned that I had apparently made this contract in a prior incarnation. He didn't actually tell me who it was, however."

"Then how did you know about Ecco in that case?"

"During my attendance in the academy, people started whispering in the halls. Apparently, my arrival, and some of my actions, as well as that fated appearance by Adalon where this elixir is concerned, started giving people ideas, and they began recalling those lines in her prophecy. At the time of Tyr's appearance, and this sudden mystery of my contract, Adalon made another showing and called on my friends, which included Vonafel, by the way, to chant the full passage. I had no idea over the meaning of it, but Thaelyn literally fell to the steps as he made the connection."

"Dear gods, was he alright?"

"I don't think anyone has ever seen him as emotional at any moment before or since as he was on that day...well, except for the death of Tyr. That would certainly count. No one knew who Ecco was, not in our world. This was old history, known only to a handful of people from Sigil, including Thaelyn. So, the mystery of the reference was extremely cryptic to the people here since Thaelyn never shared that experience."

"And I guess this made that passage of the prophecy almost meaningless to most, right?

"Yes, it did. Vonafel has mentioned in the past how some of these passages seem to demand private knowledge from someone to interpret the meaning. And you know how Thaelyn feels about chasing prophecies. So, he didn't ever put a great deal of thought into it until that moment."

"Incredible. And what happened after?"

"I had to make some very carefully considered decisions as to what sort of Gifts I wanted bestowed upon me by Tyr. It was also technically at this moment when I joined the ranks of the Eladrin. The blessings completed me as a Celestial being."

"That sounds like a dream come true for some. A little bit frightening, however."

"In the end, I can't see how I would wish it any other way. Our spirits know each other; we can feel it on a very deep level. It is not so easily described to a mortal being. Those of us with origins of this sort have a different level of sensation."

"That's fine by me, I'm just happy the two of you found each other."

"Now, I'll have you lie down here and expose your lower abdomen for me."

Marelle lies down and draws her shirt up partway, then pushes away the waistline of her pants to give Aerlie access to examine her reproductive center. Aerlie leans over to study the region, engaging her special Healer's Sight, which causes her eyes to glow softly and allows her to peer inside the body.

"When was your last monthly cycle, Marelle?" she asks.

"It was the week before the wedding, so that makes about two weeks by now."

"Really! Then you should be very close. I would say in the next few days, perhaps up to a week. I will monitor you during this time and let you know when I see it. But for now, you look very healthy. The organs are firm, the tissue appears normal, I think you should not have any problems bearing a healthy child."

"That's great to hear. So, I'll just keep coming back till I'm due for it, I guess."

"Yes, I would say to come back in two days for another examination, and we will play it by ear from there."

"Sounds good to me!"

Marelle pulls herself back together and waves as she departs the temple. And since she has some free time on her hands, she decides to go up to the guildhall for a little mage practice.

✦✦◆✦✦

"Your Lordship! I'm going to start pulling my horns out now!"

Chief Technician Lapäli was storming into the WIC strategy room with Professor Cogswoggle following up closely behind displaying a contented grin on his face.

"More so than usual?" he smiles tenderly. "Very well, is there a problem?"

"You bet there is! This little cupcake down here," she angles her finger downward at the gnome.

"Has he been staring up your lab coat again?" he smirks.

"No, he…well, actually yes, that too. But this is another thing."

They arrive at the table, and she directs the attention to a strange device she held in her hand. She set it down for Thaelyn to examine.

"Just when I thought I was beginning to understand how these things work, he comes along and breaks another law of physics."

"Oh, come now, Chief. The Professor is not one to go around breaking laws. There must surely be a logical reason for it. What is this I am looking at?"

He picks up the device and studies it. It was crude, blocky, and had two small mesh screens on the front at opposite ends of the facing. The unit was simple in design and Thaelyn saw it opened into two pieces of folded metal forming a casing, so he pulled it open to examine the inside while the Professor explained.

"Well, my Lord, it all started with that knowledge quest you gave a few years back. Do you remember that? Of course, you do," he smiles.

"Ah, yes, when we were still engaged with the war here and beginning to make use of the Daanen'kai trans-com devices to enhance our communications in the field. I had you start work on a project to create a variation of that, though in a simpler form by compare, which we could use to enhance both civilian and military capacity. Is this the result? I was wondering about that. You usually do not take quite as long on your projects, though with all your other efforts, I suppose it is reasonable under the circumstances."

"Actually, my Lord, I finished that about a year and a half ago. I have a functioning prototype out and ready for market, and I think you would be happy with the results. I was holding back on my release, however, when I had an idea for this little darling."

"Very well, and how does this compare to the intended project goal?"

"This would more likely be useful for our military objectives, I think, considering we're hoping to invade Azgarén. I don't know if we would release it openly, at least not yet if we are keeping so many tender secrets, but it could prove useful in other areas as we move along. It uses a slightly different principle, and I wanted to get it right before bringing it to you."

"Slightly different?" Tanjhira wheezes.

"And of course, I also wanted to show it to the lovely Tanjhira, as well, just to hear her girlish rant."

"Yes…" Thaelyn muses cautiously as he passes his gaze between them. "I recall you mentioning she is not prone to do that often. Did you elicit anything special?"

"Oh! She delighted me to no end on this occasion!" he laughs energetically.

Thaelyn looks up at the distressed technician, grinning and shaking his head modestly.

"So, what is the principle here, Professor?"

"First, I got the original project design running a while ago with something our people will surely take great pleasure from. My thoughts on that are it should prove quite useful as a local form of communication amongst our people. But this one, oh ho! This is special! I recall you mentioning time and again how you want to move around as a kind of enigma in front of those Suuden-Aryku. When we captured some of their own communications equipment, I had a chance to study it for comparison to the Daanen-Aryku variation, and I discovered a little flaw."

"A flaw?"

"Yes. It also uses the same principle, at least on some of the circuitry, as our new project, and we believe this would be for local channels. You know, like from an outpost to a home base."

"Yes, this might make sense."

"But, if you turn it just the right way, and set the frequencies just so, you can hear your enemy talking! If you don't want them to know anything about you, I think I would call this a flaw."

"This is true, but I would also think the Daanen-Aryku, as well as the Suuden-Aryku, have their methods of encoding information so it is not so easily interpreted."

"I'm sure this is true, and I know I've had this discussion with Tanjhira here, but in my mind, you can still listen in, and if you're smart enough, you can figure how to decipher it. This is where I consider the flaw to be. It's not a one hundred percent guarantee."

"And am I to interpret this device here is your answer to it?"

"It may look a little crude, and surely with room to add improvements, but basically yes. And when I showed it to Tanjhira here, once she stopped her girlish rant long enough to speak again," he giggles, "she associated it with another design they are apparently familiar with."

"Uh huh, and no doubt the reason she wants to pull her horns out now. Very well, but is this why she is accusing you of breaking laws?"

"Breaking laws?" he feigns innocence. "Why, my Lord, you know me! I didn't break anything that couldn't be broken if you know how to break it without actually breaking something."

"And that is precisely why I have you in my employ. So, what did you do?"

"This uses a specially enchanted crystal as the main feature, custom grown, then separating small fragments using a process I'll describe as ensorcelled phantasmal segmentation into what we'll call whisper shards."

"Ensorcelled phantasmal segmentation?" he winces. "That sounds like you are creating ghost images of the original body."

"Indeed! It's a process I started researching many years ago as part of an old idea I was working on. We need to use this technique in order to maintain the linkage association, because to cut away actual pieces using traditional methods wouldn't offer the desired effect. Add to that a few other components that we most often use for our arcanic devices, and further combined with the final result of that other project, and you have my latest and greatest masterpiece."

"This sounds rather interesting, and so this might borrow from your original project, but with a twist of some kind. I see. But now, Chief, why do you suggest this to break your laws of physics?"

"Try talking into it, Your Lordship. You'll understand."

"Very well then," he reassembles the unit and holds it up to his ear. "This is Thaelyn speaking. Is there anyone there?"

"Oh! Hello, my Lord," ushers up a clear voice on the unit. "Such a fine thing to hear your voice, how are you this crisp wintery day?"

"I am quite well…but just a moment, I believe it is actually autumn here."

"Oh no, where I am, we have a brisk winter breeze blowing in off the water, carrying up the salty air here by the dockside."

"Water? Dockside!" he utters sharply. "Good man, to my knowledge we do not have any cities on a seacoast around here as yet."

"Ah, but I beg to differ. This here is such a grand city, with such a fine long history to it. And, oh look! The fishermen are pulling up the nets from the water. They brought in a fine haul this afternoon."

"Afternoon?" his voice was escalating. "It is still morning here! And even if you WERE on the coastline, which is west of here, you would be at an even earlier time than ours. Where are you?"

"Oh, didn't I tell you? My deepest apologies, my Lord, I'm standing dockside here in the grand city of Lordan Bay."

"What?!" he shouts as he stares into the unit. "General, did you hear that?"

"Yes, my Lord, and this might explain the poor Chief Technician now. Should I prepare your list, simply to have it on hand?" he smiles impishly.

Thaelyn glares incredulously at the General for the suggestion, but he was not convinced just yet.

"Good man," Thaelyn speaks into the unit again. "Perhaps my hearing is failing me. Did you say you were standing on the docks in Lordan Bay?"

"Aye, and it's such a fine day here. We have children running around in the streets enjoying the afternoon air, and shopkeepers hawking the local catch of the day."

"Excuse me, Your Lordship," Kailen inquires tenderly. "But I'm probably not as familiar with the geography as I should be in this case. Where is this city of Lordan Bay?"

"It is to the far northwest corner of Sein'amar!"

"Huh?" he shouts. "But that's on Tae'Eladar! We're on Therinë!"

"And now do you see why I'm accusing him of breaking laws?" the Chief cries. "We're not only on a different planet, but also a completely different universe, and speaking in real-time to someone on your world."

Thaelyn gaped at the unit in his hand as his breath caught in his throat. His mind could barely conceive of such a thing coming out of the hands of anyone on this side of the planes.

"This goes a little beyond anything I might expect of our society," Thaelyn mutters. "At least not at this moment in our history!"

"The only thing I can even remotely suggest out of this is quantum entanglement. But your society is WAY behind that level of tech. And it doesn't involve crystals!" she asserts strongly.

"Yes, I might have to agree. Um, General, with all due respect to the Professor here, I think I need verification on this. Find a page and send him to Lordan Bay immediately."

The General calls a page from outside the room and sends him on his way. He runs off to the city gateway hub and crosses to Tae'Eladar, then through the hub network to Lordan Bay, where he takes a local transit to the docks district.

Thaelyn waits for the page to arrive while the Chief gripes about breaking laws concerning the speed of light barrier, relativity theories, quantum mechanics, and the space-time continuum, to say nothing of violating dimensional boundaries. After a few minutes of waiting, a voice comes through on the unit.

"My Lord," the voice issues with an obvious panting. "I've just arrived here on the docks of Lordan Bay, and here we have one of the Professor's colleagues with a box similar to the one you're holding. Do you hear me?"

"Indeed, I do, but I can barely believe it. I will be most eager to hear how he made this possible. Thank you, page, you may return to your former post. I will also put in a few extra chips for your long run."

Thaelyn pulls the unit away from his ear and studies it one more time.

"Slightly different..." he mumbles softly to himself. "All right, Professor, can you give me an example of how we can communicate across such bounds as these with your fellow in Lordan Bay?"

"Well, it's a funny thing, my Lord..."

"Oh! A funny thing. General..." he raises his brow.

"Ready here," he smiles.

"All my life," the Professor continues. "I actually wanted to create something like this, but with all my other projects and such, and then most recently working on these new technologies with the lovely Tanjhira here, I put it on the back burner for a while. It was actually very similar to that project you ordered, as it was becoming very clear we needed a way to communicate more efficiently than sending notes through rune portals."

"Yes, this does make sense. And as we are now entering an Age of Electricity, it is certainly time for it."

"Right, the application of electricity in our culture can open up a lot of new possibilities. It also works with frequency waves, and this gives the idea of sending signals of some kind. But the downside is you need to string a lot of wires everywhere, and this can get us all tangled up before you know it. Then you hit me with that knowledge quest for the air transmission, and this also reminded me of my old project."

"But this unit here cannot be based on the same principle."

"No, hardly that. Although I'm sure the other one will find a lot of good uses, this one is another thing entirely. But I got stuck in a rut after a while trying to figure out how to link everything together. I had the idea of everything broadcasting at once, but this would simply clutter things up so much, it would come out as gibberish. Then I got a peek at those trans-coms and the hub relay they use. That's what gave me the final piece to make it work. Channels, as well as addressing."

"All right, so we can say this helped you over a minor hump in the road. You know, this could just as easily be described as sending postal mail to a house on a street by its numbering."

"Oh, absolutely, my Lord. If only I didn't get stuck in that rut, we might have had it earlier," he giggles. "But anyway, after I got a working example for that new project, I pulled out my old work again and gave it a new twist. This here is basically a prototype. But I'm sure, with a little work, we could add to it to make it even better."

He picks up the device and opens it for demonstration.

"The crystal is the key, and the beauty of it is we can segment out as many pieces as we desire without harming the mother body. Now, you mentioned coding techniques. I'm sure we could add something into it if we wanted, as a way to isolate and address certain links to certain people, so we're not all talking at the same time and getting all jumbled up. But the loveliest part is the crystal enchantment and how the crystal itself operates. We'll call it metaphysical synchronicity. I'm borrowing knowledge we have about the practices and philosophies used by beings in the Outer Planes, when they use such terms as to 'Know' a thing, which is effectively the intellectual perception of existence. My original design was to draw from this idea, where you have the mother crystal and one or more child crystals that can all link up and share the harmonics passing through the mother."

"Wait…" he lays a hand on his brow. "This is to say you created a kind of network, where the only material body, assuming we can even call it material at this point, is the mother, and these children are more accurately described as phantasmal emulations in a kind of collective synchronization? Powers help us…"

"That's what I say!" the Chief groans.

"This would transcend the limitations of a physical universe," he whispers. "And certainly not the sort of thing I would expect to see in a common mortal society, especially ours in the modern day. This would be better described as a form of technology you might find in a Celestial society, at least."

"Well, my Lord," the Professor admits. "We do have someone special teaching us a great many things, and I suppose we have other technologies that your common mortal society might not otherwise have, as well as a lot of privileged wisdom."

"Indeed, we do," he concedes ironically. "And so, it comes back to me, in this case."

"But anyway, the phantasmal nature of the crystal, and the method we use to segment the shards, keep them all working with a single resonance, so each shard can commune with the mother, and through that to its other siblings, all while inside an arcanic conduit. If you apply a vibrational stimulus to it, such as to talk into the unit here, the core of the mother will also hear it. Here is how we can associate with the Daanen-Aryku hub for their trans-com network. From there, as you said, the mother will pass it down to the other shards, causing them to similarly resonate, and you have communication."

"Would this represent a one-to-many form of communication?" Kailen asks.

"I believe we could do this," the Professor responds. "If one were to address it to multiple endpoints, it could serve as a type of broadcast source, much like this other one using the air transmission."

"Which we might refer to as radio. This, as opposed to quantum communication which uses a matched pairing for one-to-one. But this combines BOTH aspects into one unit. Cu'Nar help us."

"I'm getting the part of the hub and a networked communication line," the Chief accedes. "But that crystal blows my horns off. And I hold a high-level university degree in engineering."

Thaelyn leans on the table with his head in his hand as he contemplates this discovery, trying to rationalize where this stands in comparison to his original project goal, or any other form of technology he might have expected.

"Professor," he sighs. "This takes us to a level... I cannot even calculate the measure of it. But this is certainly far above anything we might otherwise have under normal conditions for our current state of technology in our world. I would agree with the Chief here. As I said, this is more befitting of a Celestial race, as they would involve concepts and physical laws you would not necessarily find in a Prime domain."

"Sounds a little like a cheat, if you ask me," she smiles softly.

"This is clearly an anomaly, Chief," he nods amiably. "But as the Professor said, my involvement here changes things for the direction of our society. I was teaching lessons about the Outer Planes and the various philosophies we have out there, and then the associations we share with some of the societies, including the Estelar. So, when you take all this together, I must admit this can invoke us to jump over a few of the natural evolutionary steps you might normally expect."

"Yes," she relents. "I suppose this might impose a few deviations here and there."

"We should also remind ourselves of the Elixir of Visions. This allows our full society to study and learn great volumes of wisdom. And this has had an effect on us for a great many new developments, of which I have found myself on several occasions trying to contain, if only to keep our development from racing out of control."

"That could be a problem too, a society of super geniuses with the potential to outpace themselves technologically."

"And yet, Adalon did once mention something as a consolation in our case, and that being our isolation from any other local societies, where we could actually make these advances, some of them out of sequence to the natural path, and not be a hazard to anyone around us…well, at least within our local fold."

"Uh huh… Well, Your Lordship, you're not in your local fold anymore," she chuckles.

"Indeed, but fortunately, your society is sturdy enough to manage it," he grins.

"Oh thanks! Is that with or without the horns?"

"And so, here we find ourselves with another example, and I must give credit where credit is due. Congratulations, Professor, you discovered it fairly," he offers his hand to shake with the Professor.

The Professor hops in a quirky little dance as the Chief pulls up a chair and nearly falls into it, then leans on the table.

"In all the nether-space," she moans. "You passed us up! And you barely understand electricity!" she covers her eyes. "Worse, we've barely known each other for a few years, and you were writing notes to each other before this! How long did it take us to develop quantum communications?"

Thaelyn leans over to lay a hand on her arm to comfort her.

"Patience, dear lady. We will all share the benefits from this, and I think we are far from finished in our relations. Your people will quite likely develop a few of your own revelations one day."

"Maybe. But now what do we do?"

"Indeed! Now that we have it, we should put it to good use. Under the circumstances, as the Professor just mentioned whether or not to publish this, I think, as would be the tradition of any new technology discovered by fair means, this should be published."

"Great cu'Nar! There goes your so-called Seas of Creation," she chuckles.

"Perhaps, but we should still exercise the proper discipline where our cultural philosophies are concerned. This, plus the other, can be introduced to our people, as I suspect we will need this, in one form or another, as our people are, in fact, now spreading out to multiple worlds, and having an efficient form of communication between them becomes important."

"That would make sense."

"And I would share this with you, as thanks for your participation in so many things, that you are deserving of a few treats here and there," he smiles.

"Thank you, Your Lordship. I just need to find my horns again."

"Perhaps you could check with Kaliya. She may have a few spares available."

They all shared a round of laughter as Thaelyn continued.

"Now, I will have you and the Professor develop it further. Install these into our new ships, and any other items we are building that need communication. Perhaps you can borrow from your trans-com encoding methods, at least for now, to get us started quickly with a functioning example. We will surely need those channels and private conversations as we move forward. Such an invention as this would place us at least on par with the Suuden-Aryku, and likely above many things. We will be able to carry our conversations right under their noses and they will not even know of it."

✦✦✦✦✦

The upper town district of Glimmerheim was becoming a busy center of trade after having been refurbished in the weeks following Eiki's return with news of new relations with Thaelyn and his people. Several new marketplaces were opening up with crafting materials, unique foodstuffs, tools, herbal mixtures, and alchemical healing aids. The lanes through the main part of the city were flowing with heavy traffic as people would make their way through the secret entrance in the storeroom next to the former home of the Thane.

Deep into the upper town, secluded within an alcove at the end of one lane, they set up a small portal gate leading to Rolsklinde, again with a dedicated node on the other side conveniently placed in the plaza district off in a corner. This was only a temporary solution until more permanent arrangements could be established at a later date when the situation of war settled. Visitors could now travel to-and-fro, including Chief Bronzeheart and his fellow workers who had been living in Rolsklinde since the end of the war on Therinë.

Although the issue of security was still present, the citizens of Glimmerheim became more familiar with the details of the story they were allowed to reveal openly, and what to keep secret if anyone came looking. It was developing as a social custom by this time.

The Chancellor had been informed that if the people operating the Suuden'kai base should become aware of any visitations by Darumon, a messenger would arrive to relay word so he could take the appropriate steps to ensure their security and put on a good show. In the meantime, he found himself busy with the chores of interfacing the local economy with the one used by Thaelyn's kingdom, and the stream of new income was bolstering the city's wealth tremendously.

The crews operating the Suuden'kai base were taking turns on short-term shifts as Kaliya's teammates, as well as other Daanen-Aryku trainees, worked a careful schedule between their academy courses to maintain a presence in projected form as the Commander and his officers. Another crew of engineers, sent from the Naarg uy'Sodrad, would similarly manage the critical operations, such as monitoring the reactor and the conveyor.

Meanwhile, the real Commander Kriv'tik and his officers were making themselves at home in the city on Ruuki uy'Daan. They were taking up occupancy in the homes previously restored by Captain Lapäli and the Daanen'kai refugees living there as they waited for Kaliya to bring her troops across to rescue them. Several more homes were being repaired by this time, and a small marketplace with basic goods was being built. But most of this work was temporary until the city could be officially restored.

Commander Kriv'tik and his officers had taken over the operation of the old Sentinels' HQ building to coordinate the workforce and local security, and some of the Suuden-Aryku work crews were being retrained to serve in the local factories to help support the reconstruction efforts. Work had also begun to renovate the old medical lab building for emergency support.

On this day, Ayene was visiting Rolsklinde for a briefing with Thaelyn and his officers.

"Your Lordship," she submits. "I'm sure many of us could assist in training new pilots, if you think you need extra help. I was speaking to Marelle about this, and she invited me to observe her technique…although I'm a little unsure what to expect out of it after our experience of travelling to Ooduan with Ytani."

"Yes, I heard of that," he grins. "Our dear little Marelle has been experimenting in pushing her limits, and while I am not specifically against this, as one should know what they can and cannot do with the tools at their disposal, I do hope she can restrain her ambitions when the actual duty calls on her."

"I think she knows this, and that one example was indeed a tense one. Still, I would like to see what else she has to offer, and maybe share a little of my own experience."

"Very well, we can have you make a visit and see where it takes us. But now, as for your society on Azgarén, you say most of you hold some level of piloting skills?"

"Yes, if you look at Ytani and his shuttle, this is representative of the average citizen. All our traffic is hover-enabled, and our cities often have two layers of flow, one at ground level and another at altitude above the streets. But we also have regulations and procedures to maintain a smooth flow of vehicles. I once served as a security patrol officer, essentially to enforce the traffic laws and provide for the occasional emergency support in case of accidents."

"This is interesting to me," Kailen mentions. "For all the experiences we had with your military in the past, we expected your full society to be like this. But this would actually suggest your society is not unlike any other for how you typically live your lives."

"Yes Sir. Except for the Suppressor chip dulling our senses, and the seed entity climbing our backs, we're still normal people, mostly. The Marshal's influence on us seems to have taken its toll, but life still goes on."

"So it does. Then maybe we might find a few opportunities over there to give us a small advantage. I recall His Lordship once mentioning how even in a society so carefully managed, there are still a few here and there who ask questions. We should keep our eyes open for this."

"That sounds good to me, but then what. How do we use it?"

"This is something in need of careful consideration," Thaelyn suggests. "Darumon has become well-known for his propaganda and misinformation. So, we should turn this back on him. Kaliya's recent suggestion to use the image of Ytani as a renegade is an interesting one, and might do well for us in one or another instance. But ultimately, if the people are so deeply influenced by his stories, we will need to break this somehow. We want him to lose control of his pet population."

"A pet population," she sighs. "How right you are, and how depressing it sounds for us."

"We will work to correct this, Lieutenant, but we are in a delicate position. For now, we must focus ourselves on what manner of defenses he might throw at us once we do arrive. What sort of air force do you have on the ground?"

"We do not have a formal air force, but we do have our local security patrols. We don't apparently consider there is anything in our local vicinity to bother us...even though we have these alleged insurgents invading our galaxy on all sides."

"That seems a little imperious, if you ask me."

"I suppose it does. We never had anyone or anything approaching us directly, and according to the Marshal, our military is keeping it at bay very effectively."

"This reminds me of how he played the Governor here in Rolsklinde," Kailen reflects. "Nothing ever coming at their walls, but the enemy was out there...somewhere."

"Indeed," Thaelyn infers. "And this security force, where might we expect to find it most heavily concentrated?"

"If you were to take our conveyor through to Azgarén," Ayene continues. "You'll find yourself arriving in our Central Command

Headquarters. Not a very polite destination if you have in mind to infiltrate our space under hostile conditions. This is a large military installation located outside our capital city, and it's where most of this originates. There are smaller facilities in other locations, but this will be your biggest challenge."

"Likely so, and what about scanning and detection systems?"

"We have a network of detection grids that are used for tracking air transportation, which is fairly common and necessary to monitor flight paths."

"Do you have anything for extraplanetary detection?"

"Yes, there are scanning arrays to monitor our ships in space, as we have a number of space docks, starbases, and manufacturing platforms throughout our local star system. But you shouldn't have any trouble with that unless you have some way of approaching from that direction…or do you?" she asks tenderly. "How do you actually expect to arrive there?"

"This is a question we are still debating, but one way of answering this is to turn Darumon's game against him with a false play on one side while we sneak in from the other. He would not expect anything like us to arrive on his doorstep, so we are going to make a curious show for him."

"Uh oh…and does this involve Marelle in any way?" she smiles cautiously.

"I would imagine she might play a small role," he grins. "But this is jumping ahead of things, as we still need to develop some of our technology, including that Dynamistic Harvester. Still, what sort of space-based defenses do you have out there?"

"Once you reach above the planet, you get into our space navy. We typically have patrols circling our local area, although nothing ever really happens out there, and we have our main fleet, which is divided into task forces involving frigates, cruisers, and of course our pride and joy, the glorious Han'amaku class battleships."

"You sound as if you admire those," he smiles.

"Well, I've seen a few images and some design specs, and they are very impressive."

"But do we have any numbers associated with all this?"

"The scuttlebutt I hear is the fleet is huge. But this is to go along with all that supporting industry polluting our environment, therefore our need for these seeds to survive, and all those imaginary insurgents we have to fend off. So, at this point, I don't know how to answer you accurately."

"Indeed!" he chuckles. "Could it be that Darumon is making yet more statements to mislead you? Hmm, but you must still have something to support all that carnage your Commander described."

"Yes, I suppose, at least during his career we did. But as you have said in the past, this was during ten millennia of the Marshal's occupation. A lot can change in that time."

"Yes, it can. And yet this statement also limits us. If we are to suggest an invasion of some kind, it cannot so easily be explained as a local issue, not when so much within your local galaxy has been destroyed already."

"But Ytani wasn't found locally," Kailen notes.

"No, he was not."

"Could we say he found new friends of some sort?" Ayene offers. "If he's becoming a renegade, he wouldn't represent much of a threat by himself, with or without that superweapon. He still needs a way to deliver it, and that tiny shuttle of his doesn't do interstellar travel."

"Actually," Kailen reflects. "Kaliya already suggested this as a means to justify him turning renegade and having any capacity at all to remove that weapon. Therefore, we're going to say he had a lot of free time in that house of his to experiment with his Gift, and along the way, he found someone new out there."

"Oops!"

"Right! And if they are a space-capable society of unknown origin, this opens a lot of possibilities, especially if they come from a completely different universe, and with the flows involved."

As Thaelyn listened to the exchange, he began to form a mischievous grin at the implications.

"An unknown enemy with an unknown form of technology," he muses. "This would likely draw his attention. Furthermore, if there are no valid suspects within your local galaxy, this would clearly impose a fearful mystery, and one that is entirely appropriate, if you recall my initial conversation with Commander Kriv'tik. Why would any enemy body with jump-capable vessels bother attempting to establish a hidden base for a surprise hit that is so easily put down by your military? Therefore, in Ytani's case, he will arrive out of nowhere and go straight for the throat."

"Ouch!" Kailen winces. "But if Ytani is going to launch any attacks into Azgarén local space, he still needs that index mark for his jump-capable ships to lock onto."

"And we do not have one as yet. This will be a handicap, unless we can somehow sneak in one of our ships sight-unseen and take it outside to make our own."

"I seriously doubt you would be successful in that," Ayene cautions. "Not with all the detection systems in place. Someone will see you, if not arriving through the conveyor, then at any of the intermediate stages of leaving the planet and travelling into space."

"Then we need an alternative, as this would indeed make for a fine plan, if only we had a means of...um..." he halts as a new thought comes to mind and his grin broadened.

"Uh oh..." Kailen moans. "He's got that look again."

"Is that a bad thing?" Ayene inquires gently.

"That all depends on whose side you're on."

"Lieutenant," Thaelyn resumes. "You mentioned these detection arrays. Explain this a little more. You have a ship arriving in your local space. How would this appear on your scanners?"

"Um, well," she considers. "Most likely, we're speaking of a ship returning from a long-range patrol or some other star system, and jumping home to some predetermined arrival point. This would automatically send an alert to our main military starbase, which we call the Saakerav Space Dock."

"Saakerav?" Thaelyn perks up.

"Saakerav!" Kailen retorts strongly.

Ayene drew back at the sudden responses.

"Um, did I say something bad?"

"Lieutenant," Kailen responds. "You're using the name Saakerav for this base? Do you know the history of that name?"

"Yes, actually," she recalls. "King Saakerav and his rule to bring our world together as a united body…it's a favorite romance for us in our history lessons. And I recall from my training it was part of the Marshal's build-up of our new military, to establish a large space dock for the construction and management of our main fleet. And using this we would step out as part of his Grand Plan to spread our civilization across the stars. At least until these insurgents came along and stifled us," she smirks indifferently.

"This sounds like a carefully engineered motivational incentive."

"Yes, he presumably pulled the name out of our history to reflect on a powerful leader directing our people on some great crusade."

"Oh, naturally!" he emits ironically. "Another of his blasted crusades. Only in this case, against his illusionary insurgents to test your new military against while he secretly prepared to attack his real enemies. I wonder what his ultimate goal would be for you. With respect, Lieutenant, you're not very good at fighting, not with that seed on your back, and without these chips in your heads. And if he doesn't give you enough information to know WHY you're fighting, he probably doesn't have much of a future for you once his immediate goals are accomplished."

"I don't know, and personally, I don't want to know. I was telling my Commander once how I was getting so very close to resigning from my position due to the conditions we had in that base. And the more I hear about the Marshal, the less I want to be a part of HIS military at all."

"You are welcome to join with ours, Lieutenant," Thaelyn soothes. "We can always use good soldiers like you."

"Thank you, I might end up doing that one of these days. But my service, if you can call it that, was mostly to manage the base supply deliveries and a few other procedural elements. I was never an actual soldier."

"You said earlier that you were involved in local security. What sort of role did you serve there?"

"I was in administration for a while, and sometimes on city patrols. I hold a law degree at CPU, which is our local university, and a very prestigious institution. I once had in mind to go into law as a profession, like a legal consultant, but as I got up to the point of making a decision, I didn't really care for a simple desk job. I wanted to get my hands involved with something more, um…I'm not sure how to describe it," she sighs.

"Something…meaty, perhaps?" Thaelyn smiles tenderly. "Maybe to say tangible, demonstrable, quantifiable…profound?"

"Wow! Yeah, sure, any or all of those," she giggles. "Then I saw that flier for this special project and thought this might be a good alternative. Unfortunately, my new desk job was worse than the old one."

"Perhaps we can find you something more substantial if you would like to donate more of your time to work alongside of us."

"Are you offering me a job?" she smiles. "Well, I would need to talk it over with the Commander. I wouldn't want to just run out on him."

"Of course."

"But anyway, back to Azgarén, what is it you want to know about jumping into our local space?"

"Yes, my thoughts were related to how it might appear on your scopes, but then to ask about cloaked ships."

"Cloaked? Well, the jump signature is a little hard to miss, cloaked or not. And our scanners are actually quite advanced, so if we are speaking of a simple refraction of light, it wouldn't stand up. We're not speaking of a simple ping method used to detect objects in space. The scanners are capable of detecting energy signatures, spatial warping, such as from mass density and gravity wells, then elemental composition…if it represents a solid body, we'll know what it is and where it's going."

"Very well. And what if it is surrounded by an energy sphere, such as a spatial distortion field?"

"Wow, are you saying you can actually make one of those? Well, the scanners CAN detect the field, which would represent a spatial inversion drive, and they can also penetrate to detect the object inside. So, do you have any other clever ideas?" she smiles inquisitively.

"Perhaps…" he returns a grin. "What if the craft also projects a type of shield layer that represents a solid barrier, and as such is otherwise impenetrable by your scanning energies. We are speaking of something that might absorb your scanning emissions and thus possibly not even show up as a body at all."

Ayene gaped at him for the impossible suggestion.

"A stealth cloak? I am not aware of any such technology, not as a counter to ours. What are you talking about?"

"One of those unknown technologies your society might be so afraid of. We have a magical shield we were using on occasion against your troops here during the war. It proved to be very effective against your weapons. With some fine-tuning, we could probably alter it somewhat to absorb not only hostile forms of energy, but other emissions, like those used in your scanning equipment. This would likely leave it to appear more as a hole in space, rather than a body."

"That might make things very difficult for them back home, and not simply for scanning, but I should think also target locks and anything else we need to pinpoint the object in space. But you still need a way to deliver this into our local environment, and for this you need that starting index."

"This is true, and for that, we need a ship to create that first link."

◆

The day wore on, and Ayene was sent over to the Bahlaie Center to visit Marelle, who was attending another of her practice sessions on the new simulators.

"So, you think you can give me a few lessons in flying, Ayene?" Marelle asks cheerily.

"Well, you did invite me to examine your style, and His Lordship also thinks it might prove worthwhile to compare notes."

"Is that before or after you lose your horns?"

"Yes, I recall our last excursion together," she smiles timidly. "You should probably know I used to pilot some of our security shuttles around Capitol Prime as part of my early career duty. If I were to meet with you on our streets, I might find it necessary to pull you over and write a few citations for your...style," she grins. "But I believe we're only using a simulator this time, right?"

"Yeah, we recently upgraded them with new software and custom flight controls. I actually helped design them."

"You helped design the flight controls? Do you hold any kind of engineering degree?"

"No, and if you really must know, my early discussions also involved Relissa and Haran, my brother."

"I probably need to meet with that Relissa one of these days. She sounds like a very unusual individual. And your brother? What sort of skills does he have?"

"He's in training as a mage, so he specializes in magical studies."

"Magic, which has nothing to do with engineering..."

"Not the way you do things. Although there are a variety of crafts which can offer a few ideas for our technology and how it might use the flows. Then we got together with the Chief Tech and Professor Cogswoggle to hammer out the details."

"Hmm, well, I suppose the only way is to take a look and see the result."

Marelle leads Ayene into the training room where they met with her instructor. She then directs the young officer to the new simulator, where she has Ayene sit down and study the layout of the flight controls. The first thing she notices is none of the controls match her previous experience.

"But... How do you control your flight? Where is the flight stick? And the throttle? And what about a flux field monitor? And what are these odd domelike things mounted on the arms. And this here... Is that some sort of holographic matrix? This isn't an aircraft! This looks more like a virtual interface for an architectural design board."

"And this is exactly the reason none of you would ever be able to figure it out," Marelle smiles. "For us to use our magic, we need special controls, and those can't be a part of your standard configuration. These domes are channeling orbs for the weapons, and they can work independent of each other. And since I need those to work my magic, the rest of it needs to function separately, and with minimum mental focus."

"Minimum mental focus…because you need so much for this magic of yours?"

"Well, on those occasions when I need to use it, yeah. Normally, a mage isn't flying an aircraft, or operating any other kind of heavy machinery while casting spells. So, we needed to reinvent a few things to make this work."

"This should be interesting to see. Can you demonstrate?"

"Sure, hop out and stand behind me here. There's enough space for an observer. The video screens offer a type of surround view, so you can get a good feel of flying in here."

"But standing up might be a bit disorienting."

"Maybe, so just hold on. And remember, it's only a simulation."

"And I will wait outside," the instructor suggests. "Her flying technique turns my stomach."

"Instructor, can you set me up with one of my new scenarios? How about that urban assault plan; that's my favorite."

"Whatever you wish, Marelle. But I think His Lordship was hoping to get a little more service out of the Lieutenant while she still held enough sanity to be of value."

"Oh, instructor, you're such a kidder. Don't pay any attention to him, Ayene. He knows I can handle myself."

"Marelle, I flew with you once," she chuckles. "So, I think I will listen to him more than you for this point."

The instructor activates the simulation scenario as Marelle takes her seat. Ayene takes a position and kneels just behind the chair inside the partially enclosed environment of the simulation chamber. The video screens come alive with computer-generated scenery of rolling hills and grassy plains. On the far horizon was a metropolitan city skyline. The starting point was a lone landing pad.

"This looks like a good starting point," Ayene mentions. "That skyline looks a little like Capitol Prime…not quite though…"

"What's different about it, anything special?"

"Well, Sargeras's sanctuary building would be one example. I could probably think of a few industrial centers as well."

"All right, fair enough. I think this view was based on some historical detail someone pulled up once. But now, hold on. You're in for a ride."

Marelle dons a set of specially designed virtual gloves and runs a power-up sequence on the front panel. She then inserts her hands through oversized circular cuffs mounted on the armrests, which served as a safety catch in case her arms go flying around the cabin. She then sets her palms on the channeling orbs, and extends her index fingers onto the holographic controls. Ayene studies the procedure enthusiastically.

"Are you trying to tell me you developed a virtual interface?" she asks. "A kind of fly-by-wire control system? Whose idea was that? Yours? But I thought you people said you were Early Industrial!"

"Well, yeah, but we also have the Chief Tech who added a few thoughts. This particular arrangement was mostly her solution to our problem."

"Ah, of course."

Marelle smiles over her shoulder, and then applies her left finger to a cross-shaped touch control, sliding upward gently. The simulation shows lift-off from the ground.

"All right," Ayene mumbles. "You moved the flux field control. Not bad, it's under your hand now."

"Yes, but it's not a flux field. We dropped that antiquated piece of junk a while ago."

"Antiquated?" she gasps. "Excuse me, who is the space-faring society here?"

"Technically, you are. But ours has to beat yours if we should hope to make any kind of impression."

"Impression. Yeah, I've heard a few things about your impressions. And what sort of impression are you aiming for here?"

"Well, as Thaelyn calls it, overkill. But we call it a transport sphere."

"A what?" she mutters distantly.

"Here, let me show you," Marelle answers with a broad grin.

Marelle hits the throttle…hard. The video screens lurch forward with the surrounding scenery showing through simulated cockpit windows quaking through a shock wave almost immediately, accompanied by a sonic crash. Ayene shuddered and ducked behind the chair.

"What was that?!" she shrieks. "Is this thing supersonic?"

Marelle flew close to the ground in the direction of her target, gently managing the holographic matrix with her right finger, intently focused on her course.

The city approached rapidly when she tilted up and to the right in what appeared to be a circular banking maneuver over some low foothills. Ayene watched hesitantly as Marelle throttled back to subsonic, but rather than swooping around in a gentle arc to the city, she made a sharp reverse corkscrew maneuver, twisting back around as she came out and lined up with a main boulevard. The disorienting inversion caused Ayene to yelp and fall over. She reached up to grip the chair again to pull herself back upright.

"What just happened?" she wheezes.

She glanced around frantically at the scenery outside as it raced past.

"We have speed limits here; did you know that?"

The city was a large metropolis with many skyscrapers. It bordered a row of hills on one side with roadways and bridges connecting main avenues and side streets, as well as a tunnel representing a high-volume thoroughfare passing underground from one side to the other along an intercity highway.

Marelle eased back the throttle to a comfortable rate as she passed between the city structures. She aligned herself along one main avenue. Ayene kept low behind the chair as she stared alarmingly at the tall buildings rushing past on both sides. Then Marelle ducks between a pair of them along another avenue, followed by dodging around the next side, and zigzagging between two more buildings. Ayene struggles to follow the sights.

"You were supposed to yield to that other vehicle," she mumbles. "And that last intersection had a crosswalk. I think I saw a pedestrian."

Marelle then circles a spiral around a nearby structure before realigning along the same avenue she came in on.

"That's a clear safety violation!" Ayene charges.

Marelle turns along another avenue to find a series of skyscrapers with skywalks crossing between them. She spirals around one building, gaining altitude to meet with the curious architecture.

"Oh no," Ayene whispers. "You're not going to play with those, are you?"

Marelle straightens out and aims directly for the first of the two skywalks.

"This is a restricted no-fly zone!" Ayene shrieks.

Marelle rides a wave over one and under the next, while Ayene simulates a need to jump and duck to avoid hitting anything, even though it was only a video. When Marelle passes the second of these bridges, she pulls up sharply into a loop, causing Ayene to fall over backwards with a screech as the world turned upside-down on her. The simulator came full circle under the second bridge and leveled out again.

Ayene's breathing was becoming shallow, and she felt faint.

"I swear, if I had my citation book, I could make a career out of you."

She peered through the front window again as Marelle set her sights on something new, and began a low altitude weaving pattern along the avenue dodging surface features and under bridges. Ayene found herself shouting a volley of legal infractions.

"You were supposed to stop at that last intersection! And that was an illegal lane change! And again, you're going too fast! And you just cut off that hover-bus! And watch out for that bridge!"

Ayene instinctively ducks as Marelle speeds under a bridge crossing the road, then to line up with her next target. She found the entrance of the freeway tunnel coursing its way underground back to the other side of the city.

"Oh please! Not that!" Ayene cries.

Marelle makes a sharp twisting loop and dives inside. Now she moves her left finger to the cross-shaped control, centering herself and preparing for a series of quick jerks.

Inside the tunnel was simulated traffic, two layers of it following lighted guideways, and moving in both directions. She took up a central position within the lanes of traffic. Ayene was beginning to panic. Marelle used her new strafing control to make quick lateral movements either up-down or left-right to avoid any oncoming vehicles and other objects. This was a secondary control to her normal flight directional pad.

Ayene ducked her head and tilted to the sides as hover-coaches and low-flying shuttles zipped by on all sides, above and below.

"You're in the wrong lane! Watch out for that truck! Stop weaving in and out of traffic! Take the upper or lower lane, but not both! Look out for that pylon!"

The corridor of the tunnel passed by swiftly as Marelle made one maneuver after another to avoid the local traffic. Ayene found herself trying to scream, but her voice was paralyzed. They eventually reached the end of the tunnel and Marelle pulled up sharply into a vertical climb, hitting the throttle again full.

"How are you able to move like this?" Ayene gasps breathlessly.

The simulation went supersonic again, and Marelle hit a magnification scale control on the throttle to increase speed for escape velocity as she directed the ship into space.

"Now wait just a moment!" Ayene objects. "What sort of drive system are we using to go up like this? This breaks the dynamics of flight!"

"Oh, you might be surprised at what this baby has," Marelle replies serenely. "Now, this next part is still a little experimental, but we put it in so we can get a feel for how the system is supposed to work, at least in theory."

"What do you mean? What else can you possibly do to this simulator?"

They had penetrated low orbit by this time. Marelle brings her hands out of their restraining cuffs and up to the front console, where she begins programming a navigation panel. Ayene studies her motions, but the language of the control panel was alien to her. The HUD on the front video screen altered to a new configuration showing some status indicators and a tactical display with a course projection on it.

"That looks like a navigation coordinate schematic," Ayene states.

"Very good…"

"Well, among other things, I also served as a helmsman in a few sector patrols, so I know this configuration."

"Sounds good to me."

"But what are you actually doing?" she asks.

"This is an alternate mode of operation for space travel over longer distances. It overrides my manual controls. I hit an auto-scale switch for my speed, and I can set my destination here on the console."

As Marelle set her waypoint, she returned to her flight controls and hit a small enabling switch next to her throttle. Ayene studied her motions as she prepared to engage the new drive system.

"But wait a minute! There is no way on this side of nether-space you can tell me…" she begins, but before she can finish, Marelle hits the actuator.

The view outside shows a characteristic rippling effect as a distortion bubble forms around them and the entire scene goes into a blur. Stars turned to streaks, and wisps of ethereal vapors whisked by as the bubble draws the nearby compressed space around the ship, sucking them through a pipeline like a pea through a straw. Ayene could only shake her head at the audacity of the suggestion for a small craft like this.

"What sort of drive system are we using here? I didn't recognize that term you used before."

"You people would call it a spatial inversion drive."

"In THIS thing?" she yelps. "Just how big is this combat fighter of yours? You need some serious space to squeeze one of those into a ship."

"Remember, we're using our own tech, not yours. So, whatever YOU need for it, we can probably do it in much tighter spaces. I was talking to the instructor about this once and we settled on the idea that this is bigger than your average fighter craft, which might associate to your security shuttles. This might better fit what he calls a corvette class vessel."

"A corvette class?" she muses. "Interesting, I know the design concepts, although we don't actually use those. But it's still much too small for what you're suggesting…at least by our tech."

"We're able to use this on our gryphons, so if we can do it there, it's just a matter of adapting it to this."

"I need to take a look at those gryphons of yours. But can they fly in space?"

"Well, no, that one is only designed for air travel. But it's a junior version of this, at least in concept."

"In concept, and this from a society that doesn't even have real aircraft."

"And my understanding of it tells me they had it for a few centuries on Tae'Eladar, which places it well before electricity."

"I find all of this very hard to believe."

"You're not the only one."

After several moments, the computer signals the arrival at their waypoint, which represented a jump point to exit the local space and end the simulation. Once again, Marelle played over the controls to engage a new feature, setting a destination index from a menu, and moving a hand over a channeling orb on the left side of the console. Ayene observed the status indicators, and a new display that looked like a power meter charging up, both graphically and with digits cycling underneath it.

"I'm afraid to ask, but what is that?"

"We call it an arcanic jump drive."

"A jump drive?!" she shrieks. "In a combat craft?"

"Hey, if we can use portal rune stones to carry people, why not here as well?"

"In all the nether-space," she moans. "Azgarén is doomed. We're going to be conquered by Early Industrial people using one-man fighter craft with spatial inverters and jump drives."

"And speaking like squirrels," Marelle grins.

"Oh, yes! I love that one."

In another moment, the power bar reached its maximum and Marelle slapped her hand on the domelike orb. The scene outside appeared to turn inside-out, and the simulation took on an approximation of a voyage through a dimensional conduit, and thereby ending the simulation.

"You surely must be joking, Marelle," Ayene relents. "The power and size requirements for this sort of technology can only be applied into capital ships, not small craft like this."

"Using traditional physics," Marelle admits. "But using the flows and the technology we're able to build from it, we're not limited to only traditional physics doing the work for us. The flows can be channeled by the will of the mind, and that changes the equation significantly."

"So, in the real application, you are operating the craft partly by your mind?"

"Some aspects of it," she nods. "Others are specially designed subsystems taking charge of that role for me, so my mind can focus on other things."

"Such as?"

"Weapons would be a good example. For instance, these orbs require my focus in order to use them, and you need to hold a certain level of mage training before you can even qualify for it."

"How much?"

"I'm aiming for the Seventh Circle for this, which is fairly high in the academy studies."

"Would someone like me be able to take any of these lessons?"

"They have both civilian as well as military study courses. The military has some entrance requirements to qualify for, but if you can do that, I don't see why not."

"All right, maybe I can ask about this someday. But now, how do you plan on using this? It was my understanding you don't actually want to cause that much damage, and instead try to help my people."

"Right, the weapons have two modes of operation. One is based on your plasma blaster tech, which we're borrowing from the weapons you people were using on the Daanen-Aryku."

"Oops, so you're turning this around on us?"

"It's important to have something serious in case we actually need it for some reason. But the other one is a type of EMP weapon, to disable rather than destroy."

"Ah! And therefore, not cause so much physical damage, thus killing a lot of people. Yes, I understand. That's actually very clever. And if we include that cloaking tech His Lordship mentioned earlier... In all the nether-space, I don't think we would stand much of a chance against you. Our ground forces would be wide open to you, and I think even our navy would find it difficult to follow you under those conditions."

"But just remember, Ayene, it's Sargeras and Darumon we want. The rest of you just need to get out of our way."

✦✦✦✦✦

A new week was beginning, and classes were coming together in the guildhall. Relissa, Haran, and their friends were anxiously looking forward to their new school year, but silently missed their companionship with Marelle as she was taking the year off. This would put her a year behind, but she had good reason for it.

Marelle was making another visit to the temple for an examination. This was the third time since her marriage. Her first two went at two-day intervals, but on this occasion, Aerlie suggested reducing it to a daily event as she expected to see the appropriate signs occurring very soon.

"I'm getting more nervous about this the closer we get," Marelle concedes. "I don't want to miss it because then we miss a whole month, and I'm already cutting it so close."

"Relax, Marelle," Aerlie comforts her. "I know this is your first time, and you want to get it right. I'll be with you through the whole process. Just lay back and let me take a look at you. We should be just about there by now."

Marelle lies on the bed and pulls her shirt and pants away to reveal her abdomen. Aerlie takes a close look, once again engaging her special Healer's Sight and peering under the skin to examine the organs. She checks one side, and then the other of Marelle's reproductive tract, and discovers what she has been waiting for. She offers up a gentle smile.

"Marelle, it's time! I see it occurring just now."

"Really? Oh, thank the gods!" she rambles worriedly. "So, now what? I mean, I know what I'm supposed to do, but…um…well, this isn't something you just run home and jump into bed for, like on a scheduled appointment. What I mean is, well, a girl needs to get into the right mood for it, doesn't she?"

"Will you calm yourself, Child!" Aerlie giggles. "I am sure you will do just fine. It is only just beginning, so now would be a good time to start preparing for it. Go find Roderick, tell him the news, and maybe later you can return for your blessing to charge yourself for the occasion. Then I might suggest a little relaxation, such as a nice meal in a pleasant setting, some gentle music… This often helps put a lot of people in the right mood."

"Oh, yeah, that sounds great. Right, so I'll go let him know, and then come back this afternoon. How much time do we have for this? Oh, there I go setting dates again!"

"You have plenty of time for it, although we generally suggest it is better to begin sooner rather than later to give yourself the time to make a successful conception. I would suggest you might even wish to make a couple of attempts in the coming days, for assurance. But you'll have a much better chance this way than if to take it at random."

"Right, of course… Then I'll see you a little bit later."

Marelle brings her clothes back in order and hops off the bed, giving her final thanks to Aerlie and leaving the temple to find her husband.

Aerlie returns to the main hall of the temple with the other priests to review the service currently underway, and to check on the new class of young clerics starting up their training.

"My Lady," mentions one of the high priests. "I couldn't help but notice that young lady leaving in such a rush. She seemed quite nervous."

"Yes, this is her first time to have a child. We are all wishing her our best, and she will be returning for a blessing by Lathander later with her husband."

"Ah, the delight of bringing forth a new life. We will offer up a special prayer for her."

"I'm sure she would be very happy for it. In fact, I think maybe I'll put in a good word for her ahead of time so that Lathander knows how special she is to us. Maybe he can offer her a little something extra for this most joyous of occasions."

"That would be a wonderful gift, my Lady."

Aerlie steps across the dais to the row of deific icons that includes the symbol for Lathander, also known as the Morninglord, whose domain includes such blessings as life, birth, youth, renewal, and others. She kneels down and summons the mind of the deity, offering a brief communing to describe her friends and their most heartfelt desires.

Marelle rushes through town to the city gateway hub, then across to Rolsklinde. She hurries over to the city Watchman Security Office on the other end of the plaza where the old barracks was found. This was the new building established for local city law enforcement and legal processing. Her husband was assigned here as the new head of civil authority. She charges into his office with the news.

"Roddy, dearest, I'm ready," she announces hurriedly.

"What? You mean... Are you saying it's time for us to, um, you know...?"

"Yeah. It's not like we have to do it right this minute, but it's happening for me."

"All right, that's good to hear. Now it's just a question of getting away for a quiet little moment for us to enjoy that special time together."

"Right, but let's not forget the blessing. Lady Aerlie suggests going back soon to get charged up for it, as she tends to put it."

"Charged up?" he chuckles. "That's a cute way to describe it. When do you want to do this?"

"I would say let's go back today, maybe if you can finish your work for a little while and we can make a visit this afternoon. She also says we might want to make a couple of tries in the next few days to be sure we get it."

"That's probably a good idea. This doesn't come around very often, as I understand it, so we want to get it right while we have the chance."

"That's how I feel, too. And maybe, since I don't have much else to do right now, I can help you with your work for a little bit until the time comes. That might help get my mind off things for the moment, I'm so nervous."

"Sounds good, then come over here and sit down, and we'll see what sort of trouble we can make for the city together."

The day wears on as the classes in the guildhall come to a close. Relissa and Haran take up their usual seating out in the courtyard to discuss their new schedules. Petrith, Sulíma, and Túfula were just starting up new classes as well, and joined the others in the courtyard for a visitation.

Tristeen had been visiting Bya'an Tamoranth to meet with several other High Council members in the parliament building. Among other things on the agenda was an issue concerning Rolsklinde and future expansion to decide on a prospective new mining interest, as well as a plan for a new township development over on the western coast.

Kaliya had gathered up her team members, along with a number of other Daanen'kai trainees recently admitted into the Order. They were gathered in the lower athletic field for a group session where she could impart a few of the lessons and exercises she had been practicing while in her own training.

Thaelyn and his officers were in their usual meeting at the WIC building going over the recent scouting reports of Morndindor and their continued efforts to gather up any survivors still out in the wilderness and bring them together for better support. The trade routes into Glimmerheim were prospering, and relations were improving nicely.

"All right, Marelle," Roderick submits. "I guess that's as much as we can do for now. I don't want to miss our chance to meet in the temple for that blessing, so maybe we can put the rest on hold here until tomorrow."

"Yeah, things here look like they're holding together well enough. It's a lot different from how it was when we were working here before. The people have a completely new perspective on life in the city now."

"And I think we both know who to thank for that."

Marelle smiles pleasantly as she and Roderick get out of their chairs and walk out the door of his office. They make a casual pace through the building to the front doors, trying to keep themselves calm for the upcoming moment of intimacy that would follow after they receive their blessings, and then seek the comfort and relaxation of a good meal and a little inspirited music. They cross the plaza to the city hub and through to Bya'an Tamoranth, then take the local transit to the Palace District, where the guildhall and most of the government buildings were located, along with the grand Temple of the Planes. They cross the avenue from the gateway terminal to the temple and enter inside.

"Ah, Marelle, Roderick," Aerlie calls as she sees them enter. "We are so glad to see you. Have you managed to calm yourself since I saw you this morning?"

"Yeah, a little bit," Marelle relents. "But it's starting up again."

"Oh, there is really nothing to it. People do this all the time, and we never have this sort of tension. This is just a simple blessing to empower you for health and strength to bring forth a wonderful new life. Will you both be attending, or just one of you?"

"We'd both like it, just to be extra sure."

"Excellent. I even made a little mention to him earlier just to let him know this is your first, and you want this to be special."

"Thanks. So, what do we do here?"

"It's very simple. Follow me and I'll bring you up to the icon for Lathander. Then you just kneel down, set your hands on his icon, and allow him to lay his blessing on you. I'll even help by calling his attention to it, since I think he'll be expecting you."

"That sounds great. How does it usually feel?"

"Different people tend to offer their own interpretations for this. Some feel a warm fuzzy feeling, others a tingling. Some say the room feels brighter, or they have a lighter bounce in their step."

"Interesting. Well, I guess we're ready, right Roddy?" she looks up at him.

He smiles back nervously and nods.

Aerlie leads them to the row of icons and motions them to kneel in front of the one belonging to Lathander. The icon, like so many others, was a golden plaque on a short pedestal set in front of a statue depicting the god. The symbol on the plaque portrayed a sunrise over a green field, with sunrays in pink, red, and yellow hues.

The high priest had several other clerics in a study session during this time on the other side of the large dais. He noticed the new arrivals and called his gathering of clergy to lower their voices to give the couple their peace. Several people were in attendance in the pews seeking their comfort and offering their piety. They watched inquisitively as the couple approached the altar.

Marelle and Roderick each placed their right hand on the icon and waited for Aerlie to perform her ritual. Aerlie also places her hand on the icon to summon the mind of Lathander, and then pulls back as he turns his focus to the aspiring couple. The statue displays a subtle glow as the classic sign of the deity manifesting himself within the body to offer his service.

And then the glow begins to surge.

Aerlie's eyes roll around the room as the entire scene begins to radiate brightly. The sudden increase in illumination draws the attention of everyone in the room. The high priest and his class all turn to find the source, eventually focusing on the statue. The attendees in the pews abruptly raised their heads to see what was happening, and quickly homed in on the couple kneeling in a daze as they gazed uncertainly into the eyes of the marble icon.

Soon, the brilliant glow surrounding the statue took on a distinctive form. Aerlie staggers back as she sees an image emerging into the local space.

"Great gods above," she whispers. "And here as well."

The divine apparition calls the attention of the high priest and his group. They observed a distinctive shape coming out of the statue. It was Lathander himself, manifesting physically into the temple.

Aerlie drops to her knees. The group of young clerics all crumpled to the floor in a penitent grovel. The commotion of their sudden collapse briefly draws the priest's attention, only to return nervously to the image as he also falls to the floor. The people in the pews jump out of their seats and huddle down low, ducking their heads in a respectful bow.

"Roddy," Marelle whines tenuously. "Do you see that?"

"Yeah," he whispers anxiously. "What do we do now?"

"How am I supposed to know! This wasn't on the lesson chart. Just hold still!"

Lathander leaned forward out of his iconic likeness, gazing down upon the couple who seemed paralyzed at his feet. He reaches out with both hands, lowering them placidly to the heads of his two seekers.

"Let Thou This Day Bring Forth This Gift," he intones potently, his voice resonating throughout the room.

He lays his hands on Marelle's and Roderick's heads and holds them there for an enduring moment, where a softly pulsing wave of light washes through their bodies. The expressions of the loving couple contort. Their eyes turn crossed, and their lips pucker. The glow permeates their bodies, and they seem frozen in this position. Aerlie and the other priests watch in apprehension as it becomes clear the duo is receiving something more than your average blessing.

After a long moment, Lathander pulls up and retracts back into his icon, allowing the statue's glow to subside. All returns to normal soon after.

"Gracious, I've never seen that before," Aerlie mutters to herself.

The high priest and his students rise back to their feet, and the people in the pews slowly return to their seats, cautiously scanning for any other anomalies.

Aerlie also rises, but holds her place while she studies the couple kneeling on the floor trying to recover from their own shock. The room goes silent waiting for their reaction.

Marelle and Roderick sat motionless, barely able to move their muscles or to find their voices. Their faces slowly relaxed into a blank stare. Aerlie leans to one side as she discreetly attempts to peer around and look at them. A long moment passes as they gradually return to their own senses.

"Wow..." Marelle utters gently. "That was weird."

"Yeah," Roderick responds curtly. "You got that much right. How do you feel?"

"I'm not quite sure yet. Give me a moment to feel my body again."

"Me too..."

They wait a few short moments until Marelle is able to respond further.

"Roddy, I'm feeling a little bit of a tingle. Do you feel anything?"

"Yeah, the same actually... Strange..." he offers a quick chuckle.

Another moment passes. They were still sitting motionless and staring into the distance.

"Um, Roddy?" she mumbles a little more determinedly. "I'm feeling, um, kind of...frisky, you know?"

"Uh huh, me too, a little..."

Aerlie and the other priests look on as the two slowly returned to life.

"Oh dear," Marelle declares anxiously. "I'm actually feeling a lot more of it now."

"Yeah, same here, it's getting stronger. Um, do you think we should run home real quick?"

Marelle suddenly started to twitch. The sensations similarly spread to Roderick, and the two of them were now compulsively fidgeting. The movements escalated.

"Roddy!" Marelle sounds off impatiently. "I don't know if I can make it that far!"

"Well, what then?" he denotes firmly. "We can't do it here; this is a temple!"

"No! Um…" she springs to her feet with her knees rubbing together and hands clutching at her sides.

Roderick also sprang upward, bobbing up and down while his eyes darted around the room as if desperately looking for a place to run.

"An inn!" Marelle shouts urgently. "Someplace close! Um, wait! I know…across the street. Do you have any money?"

"Yeah, lots! Let's go!"

The two of them now make a mad dash away from the dais and out of the building.

Aerlie and the other priests, along with the people in the pews all watch the couple sprinting through the doors.

"Good gracious!" Aerlie emits amusedly. "So much for that nervous fret!"

"My Lady!" the high priest mentions. "Have you ever seen anything like that before?"

"No, but I certainly wish Thaelyn and I could feel such energy. Now I'm a little jealous."

She smiles affectionately as she redirects the priests back into session, now that the immediate excitement was over.

Outside, Marelle and Roderick burst onto the sidewalk and hurtle themselves across the avenue, dodging passersby and carriages on their way to an inn on the other side of the street a couple of doors down. They crash into the lobby and stagger up to the counter where a young woman stood as the clerk.

"We need a room…with a bed!" Roderick shouts.

"Ah, welcome to the…" the girl begins merrily.

"No talk! Room! Bed!" he yelps hastily.

The girl sways back from the fervent surge. She turns and

fumbles with the doors of a cabinet on the wall behind her, pulling out a key, and then turning back to her customers.

"That'll be fifteen…"

"Here's my coin purse! Take it!" Roderick issues as he slams the item on the counter and snatches the key from her hand.

He turns impatiently looking for the hall with the inn rooms.

"What room?" he demands quickly.

"Six, upstairs," the girl points at a stairway on the side. "Midway down the…"

Before she could finish her statement, the ambitious couple chase up the stairs and down a hallway leading across. The stomping of their feet halts above the lobby as they locate the door, then fiddling with the lock, and finally stumbling into the room. The noises are further compounded by the thrashing of hopping and jumping as they tear off their clothes, and lastly a firm thump as they dive onto the bed.

"Gods above, what was that about," the girl wonders quietly.

"Dear, what just happened out here?" calls an elder woman as she emerges from a rear room.

"Mom, I don't know. A couple ran in here, and they looked very eager for something."

"A couple? My goodness, it sounded like a stampede just ran through."

On the walkways outside lining the street, life continued in its usual manner for the city. People were passing by while wagons and carriages were led down the avenue by teams of horses. It was a prominent roadway in the city, with many fine shops and taverns, and of course the temple and various government buildings all attending to their daily business, when above the lobby of the inn, a distinctive sound began reverberating through the walls and out the window.

The clerk and her mother stared at the ceiling as a rhythmic thudding sound was knocking on the wall and flooring in the room overhead, accompanied by intimate moans and cries of pleasure.

"It's a bit early in the day for that, don't you think?" suggests the mother.

The girl can only shrug.

Outside, a woman and her young child are walking by when the sounds arose from a window overlooking the street. She orients her head to examine the window, but realizing the nature of the sounds, she quickly covers the ears of her young child and hurries him along the walkway.

A wagon passes by, and the driver also hears the sounds. Curious as to the commotion, he pulls to a stop and turns to find the source. Another carriage behind him is forced to stop, then also turns to locate the noise. Other people on the walkways are similarly brought to a standstill as the curious attraction draws an audience.

In the lobby of the inn, the thumping was growing in intensity. A man rushes out of the back room to investigate.

"What in the names of the gods is going on here?"

"Dad," the girl issues. "We've got a couple, you know…doing it. That's all."

"A simple couple?" he balks. "That sounds like a small army complete with their horses."

The rhythmic sounds were turning into a rambunctious hammering, and the moans were becoming howls.

"Oh Roddy! YES!! More! Come on! Ooh, I love it!" the voice screams.

In the temple across the street, Aerlie was attending to her most recent clergy students when her Avariel hearing took notice of a conspicuous disturbance occurring outside. She abruptly halts her service and turns to the door.

"What is going on out there?" she inquires mutedly.

She steps off the dais and proceeds along the aisle to the doors. Her unusual announcement brought the attention of the others in the room, causing many of them to follow.

The people outside on the street were gathering in front of the inn. The wails coming out of the upstairs window echoed off the neighboring buildings. Both male and female were involved now, moaning with such intensity as to be heard nearly a block away.

The hammering above the inn's lobby was pounding harshly on

the ceiling. Additional laborers from the rear of the building came forward to investigate. The howling of delight rumbled through the structure.

Aerlie emerged through the temple doors and turned to locate the origin of the sound. The other priests joined her on the front steps.

"Oh dear…" she mumbles.

Additional people were gathering on the street, coming out of surrounding buildings and taverns. The two guards at the front gate of the guildhall directed their attention to the avenue below.

"What in all the nine hells is going on down there?" announces one of them. "Watch Captain, we have some sort of commotion out here."

The Watch Captain was inside the courtyard when the shout came in. He turns to respond.

"What do you mean?"

"It sounds like a bloody riot down there! And I see people gathering up in masses."

The Watch Captain hurries out the gate to examine the disturbance. Relissa, Haran, and their Daanen'kai friends all listen to the shouts and get up to see what's happening. They run outside the gates to take a look.

"In all the bleedin' hells," Relissa emits. "What is that now?"

She leads her group down the hill, followed closely by still others from the courtyard.

The Watch Captain observes the scene, trying to decide the best course of action. He turns back into the yard and shouts to one of the pages.

"We need support out here! Call out the guard, and someone go fetch His Lordship over in Rolsklinde."

Word was spreading further out along the avenue. Pedestrians were shouting into nearby buildings calling the people out to gawk at the strange event. A man runs into the parliament building to pass the word.

"Everyone, there's some sort of ruckus happening two blocks down the road! We have a large mass gathering up outside!"

Tristeen and the other members of the High Council were shaken out of their debate at the announcement, along with the full delegation of parliament members on the floor. The collected body exits from the building and orients to follow the flow of people along the avenue.

The howls from the inn were bellowing into the street. Inside, the duo crashed and banged on the floor and the walls as the bed seemed to be jumping around the room. The sound of shattering pottery and cracking furniture was heard amongst the fierce pounding of their nuptial consummation. Dust wafted down from the beams in the ceiling of the lobby below.

"Mom, grab that vase over there! Dad, watch that painting!"

The young clerk franticly tried gathering up whatever she could find that was loose. She turned to secure the key cabinet on the wall, only to have it bounce out of her hands and fall to the floor. And a maid and custodian chased falling ornaments and decorations as they leapt off their hooks.

Aerlie studied the scene from outside. The streets were packed by now. Carriages were halted and pedestrians were gathered along both sides of the road, stretching blocks away.

"This is going to go bad as soon as he arrives," she reflects as she watches the guards from the guildhall charging outward.

"OH!!" Marelle screams. "Harder! More! You can do it! I need more!!"

The sounds were now reverberating over the rooftops of houses, to be heard even as far as the combat training yard on the side of the guildhall. The noise caught the attention of the people in the outdoor field.

"What is that I hear?" shouts one of the students in an after-class practice session.

"Sergeant!" cries another. "We've got some sort of disturbance out here!"

"Aye," he responds. "I'm hearing calls from the front. They're saying there's some sort of racket out on the street."

"On the street? And we can hear it up here? Great gods above!"

Kaliya and her team heard the noises, as well as the shouts from the yard above, and she paused her practice session.

"What's going on up there?" she shouts to the people in the yard.

"There's a rumpus occurring out there," calls one of the students as he points in the direction of the road.

Kaliya turns to follow his direction and waves for her group to chase after it. She leads them along a walkway circling around the front of the guild and onto the avenue leading down the hill away from the front gate.

"My Lord!" shouts a page through his panting as he arrives in the WIC building. "You need to come quick! There's something bloody wonky occurring on Providence, just outside the guild!"

"What is it?" he asks imperatively as he turns to follow the young man.

The General and the other officers follow behind Thaelyn as they all leave the building and cross the plaza to the hub terminal.

"My Lady!" Relissa calls from across the crowd. "What's that going on over there? It sounds like they're tearing the place apart!"

"Gracious," Haran moans. "Look at that!"

"What exactly is that noise?" Sulíma hesitates.

"Suli," Petrith contends. "If you don't know that sound, you haven't yet learned what all that tail-spinning of yours actually results in."

She glares at him and jabs her elbow into his ribs.

"Dear cu'Nar," Túfula yips. "Can someone actually be so loud?"

The building was visibly jarring by now. The outside wall was flexing, the window shutters were flapping side-to-side, and a soft glow seemed to be emanating through the curtains.

Kaliya and her group arrived and joined next to Petrith and the others. Tristeen was working her way across when she noticed Aerlie on the temple steps, and then Haran and the others nearby. She struggles to get through.

"Haran!" she shouts. "What's happening?"

Haran turns to find the voice and raises his hand to draw her attention.

"Tristeen! What are you doing out here?"

"What am I doing out here?!" she shrieks. "The whole of parliament is out here! And you know how they are. Anything that can shout louder than those people demands attention."

"Roddy, my love!" Marelle screeches.

"Oh, Marelle, it's wonderful!" he howls.

"Criminy!" Relissa moans. "Haran, did you hear that?"

"Oh dear gods!" he pleads as he looks around the massive crowd. "Please don't tell me."

"Haran?" Tristeen whines. "Did I hear that correctly?"

Thaelyn barrels through the city hub portal, along with the other officers. They dash off to the local transit, but Thaelyn halts as he senses Aerlie's emotions emanating out. He hurries outside looking for a crack between the buildings to find his mark, but the local arrangement obscured his line-of-sight. So, he runs into the street and halts a nearby wagon from passing, opening up a clear spot.

He takes a position on the road and pulls up a fist, charging himself with energy, and then slamming it into the ground, causing the earth beneath him to ripple and flex, then drawing downward like a trampoline. The surface recoils and catapults him in a somersault onto a nearby rooftop, where he has a better sighting on his target. He then circles his fingers like a bull's-eye to the avenue leading up to the guildhall gates and swings his free hand in an arc toward his goal. His body is transformed into a brightly glowing wisp, a ball of light that shoots across the rooftops to his intended destination. As he zips across, Aerlie caught a glimpse of him as he passed overhead, and the apparition made impact on the ground, where it transformed back into his natural body.

Aerlie could only cover her eyes briefly and shake her head for what was surely to follow after.

The sounds attracted him to the avenue below the slope. He turns to see a huge crowd of people massing on the street, stretching for blocks in all directions. He rushes down to see where the noise was coming from, pressing his way through the people as they tried to part in front of him.

"Aerlie!" he shouts. "What in the names of the Powers is occurring here?"

"They only came in for a little blessing!" she begs. "How could I possibly know this would happen?"

"What are you talking about? A blessing?! This is abnormal, my dear! How could a simple blessing do this?"

"But... He..."

Thaelyn manages to fight his way across to the temple where he found Relissa, Haran, Kaliya, and others standing amongst a crowd numbering in the thousands by now.

"I need more!" the screams insist. "Give me more! Harder!!"

"No!" yells the clerk in the lobby. "Not harder, the ceiling can't take any more!"

"Bring some chairs around!" the innkeeper orders. "Get up on them. We need to hold these beams up. Put your shoulders into it!"

The ceiling supports were cracking as the pounding from the room above was weakening the structure. The crashing of furniture upstairs was replaced by the tumbling sounds of loose pieces.

"Aerlie, who is in that room?" Thaelyn demands.

"Um, well, my dear...uh..." she falters.

"Aerlie," he intones gravely. "What are you hiding?"

"It's, um... Well, it's Marelle...and Roderick."

Thaelyn gawps incredulously at her, and then brings his hands to cover his face as he stoops over.

"Oh no..." he whimpers. "Not her again. Why does it always have to be Marelle?"

"Marelle! I feel it!" the voice yowls from the window.

"Yes! Oh Yes! Give it to me!" she screams. "Give it hard!"

The two of them each let out tumultuous wails, blasting out the window and resounding across the entire district. The duration of the moaning extended to their full breath, and slowly faded into silence. And in the street followed an uproarious applaud and cheering.

"Gods' pity," Haran mumbles solemnly. "My sister is famous. And not for anything I can tell my children about."

"Is this how they do these sorts of things?" Túfula wonders.

"If it is," Petrith notes. "We need to be sure to take this girl…" he thumbs assertively at Sulíma, "…far away from here for her turn."

"Aerlie," Thaelyn mutters. "You and I need to talk."

"But I didn't do anything," she pleads. "It was supposed to be just a normal blessing. You know the sort."

"Yes, I know the sort, but this was not one of those. Did something…extra…occur during this occasion to invoke this demonstration?"

"Well, maybe…"

"Oh, indeed!" he incites enthusiastically. "And what, pray tell, is this maybe about?"

"Well, he sort of manifested into the temple briefly."

"How much of a sort of is that?"

"He came out of the statue and laid both hands on them. And it took a while. And then it took another while for them to simply recover from it. And then, um…well, they sort of couldn't hold themselves still."

"Dear Powers," he rolls his eyes. "What are we in for now, I wonder?"

In the lobby of the inn, all had gone quiet. The clerk and her parents slowly removed themselves from the furniture and gazed uncertainly at the ceiling over their heads. Portions were bowed and some of the beams were splintered. They silently wondered if anything was still alive up there, asking themselves if someone should go up and check. Then they heard soft footsteps. The sounds thudded around gently for several moments and finally traced into the hall and towards the stairs.

Marelle and Roderick ambled downstairs into the lobby. Their clothes were only loosely adorned, with the shirts unbuttoned and the pants barely held together. They were barefoot and carrying their shoes, their hair was disheveled, and they wore an unnaturally contented grin on their face as they meandered lazily up to the front desk.

The clerk eyed them hesitantly as Roderick set the key down on the desk. His eyes were unfocussed and staring off in the distance while the expression on his face was unchanging. Marelle shared the same visage.

The girl searched the debris at her feet for his coin purse, handing it back over to him.

"Here's your purse," she declares timidly. "I only took out what was needed to pay for the building repairs."

"Did I have enough?" he ushers dreamily.

"Yes, actually, and there's still a few coppers left over."

"Wonderful…" he coos.

The two of them turned and moved towards the door. The girl's parents stepped out of the way, pulling the chairs to one side, and kicking away some of the rubble, allowing them space to pass through. As they emerge outside, the crowd ushers up another rousing applause.

"Look, Roddy," Marelle observes placidly. "We're celebrities."

"Whoopee…" he sings.

She sees Thaelyn standing across the way near the temple, along with her friends, and staggers over to meet them.

"Hiya!" she announces giddily. "What are you doing here?"

Thaelyn studies them apprehensively.

"Someone came and told me there were two people trying to destroy six centuries of my work. And how are you this fine day?"

Marelle and Roderick each began giggling uncontrollably as their gaze drifted off absentmindedly.

"Yes, I can see it in your eyes," Thaelyn admits. "In some ways, you look nearly as bad as those dwarves we found once."

He casts off at Aerlie, and then the others around him before continuing.

"I wonder if we should describe this as a successful venture," he muses paradoxically.

"You must be joking!" Kaliya moans.

"Oh, one cannot be too certain when one tears up half the city for it," he affirms cheerily. "Then again, perhaps this might be an obvious example," he chuckles. "But now, I think these two should go home. Relissa, Haran, could you possibly assist? See to it they arrive safely and, dare I use these words, put them to bed."

"Buggers, my Lord," Relissa groans. "Don't you think they had enough of that by now?"

"Yes, but I think their energy is spent, and now they need rest."

Relissa and Haran each wrap their arms around the couple to lead them away through the gateway network back to Rolsklinde. Thaelyn gives instructions to the assembled public to give way and return to their previous activities while he and Aerlie go inside the temple for a little chat.

Chapter 5

SEEDS OF INSPIRATION

"Knock, knock," ushers a shy voice from the door of the WIC strategy room. "I hope I'm not disturbing anything, but I thought maybe I should poke my head in for a quick hello."

Marelle was making her first appearance in public since her momentous ordeal at the inn.

"Ah, come in," Thaelyn welcomes. "We have not seen you for two days. A few of us were beginning to worry. Are you well?"

"Yeah, Roddy and I apparently just woke up. Two days? Wow, that was some hit we took."

"Do you recall anything from it? If not, we saved the town crier report for you to read. It became quite a newsworthy event. I think the papers are reporting it all across the kingdom by now."

"Oh wonderful…" she blushes. "Well, from what I can remember, I guess it was worth it. Did anyone get hurt?"

"No, but the inn is currently undergoing some rather extensive repair work."

"Oops! I'm sorry, my Lord. I'll tell Roddy and we'll try to offer up some money to help pay for the damage."

"Never mind that," he waves it off. "I spoke with Aerlie on the matter, and it seems Lathander took a special incentive to offer his thanks for your service. As you may recall, since that day you and Kaliya made that mission to dispose of Darumon's weapon, the Estelar have offered their special thanks. It is extremely rare that the Estelar would ever find cause to give thanks to a Child Race, so we are guessing this to be Lathander's contribution."

"Wow, that's some contribution!" she smiles bashfully.

"Indeed! Therefore, Aerlie and I pulled some money out of the emergency disaster fund to help pay for the repairs."

"The emergency disaster fund, right... So, that's my new notoriety, causing a city disaster," she chuckles softly.

"Marelle, do not concern yourself," he smiles. "The occasion met adequately with the epic standards to qualify," he winks.

"Oh gee, thanks, I think."

"But anyway, from this moment, I would suggest you find some minor occupation, nothing too stressful, until your moment arrives. Perhaps you could spend some additional time on your flight training, at least until it becomes too inconvenient for you, and Aerlie will assist from there. She also desires you to make routine visits on a monthly basis for a check-up."

"All right, that sounds fair enough. I'm feeling hungry right now, so Roddy and I were heading over to one of the taverns for something to eat. And I think we should probably keep a low profile for the time being."

She waves goodbye and turns to leave, joining Roderick in the lobby, and then proceeding outside.

"Now, General," Thaelyn continues with his meeting. "It would seem our relations with Glimmerheim are progressing nicely, and Belrum was able to further cement a relationship with those small villages we found near the western coastline. The people there are doing just slightly better than the rest, if only for their fishing efforts."

"I would agree," he offers. "But considering the rest of the world, I hesitate to wonder how long that might last."

"Those are my thoughts as well; therefore, we must also consider our long-term objectives and what aid we can provide to restore that world. I wonder if we can assist them in further developing that region. Our scouts have found other such villages along the coastline, many of them very small. If we could combine them, and link them with a portal to Glimmerheim, we could establish a better sense of communal support."

"That would be a fine suggestion. The exchange of goods, and especially food, could bolster them on both sides."

"I am also looking at this space directly in front of Glimmerheim, this so-called outer city region. Although it is devastated, and the land is barren, I would wish to make this our foothold to begin redeveloping their ecology. We will need a set of accurate maps of the full continent so we can plan the placement of trees and their accompanying shrines. Each of them will need a significant level of support in the early years until they grow strong enough to manage their own."

"And each tree with its own reach will need to be spaced at reasonable intervals, perhaps with a small amount of overlap in some cases, for a complete coverage of the land in order to see a reversal of the damage occurring."

"Correct, and this will require a lot of seeds as well as a lot of shrines."

"And a lot of people attending to them, with a lot of resources supporting them," the General sighs.

"If we recondition this area outside Glimmerheim," Thaelyn asserts. "We can provide some important local support venues. This will reduce the need to import everything."

"But we still need people, specifically mages and druids, to invoke a few alterations of the local elements, such as occasional weather patterns, to bring rain to the area in order to prevent the dry wastes from taking over again."

"Yes, this will be an ongoing battle lasting for decades, to be sure. At least until the trees can govern this themselves."

"But the scale of it," the General muses. "We are effectively engineering the ecology on a global scale. This is something we have never done before. In fact, our only example of this would be the Sarrukh and the efforts they made to restore Tae'Eladar in those early days."

"This is true, and now it would seem to be our turn to make this effort on another world. This will test us to some rather extreme measures to see it through successfully. But if we pace ourselves and put our best people to work for us, we might just be able to succeed."

"Then, where do you suggest we begin?"

"Our starting point must be to conduct a careful examination of the local flora and fauna and how it interacts within the ecology. We should take samples and see if we can culture them for reseeding. Then, as we spread outward, we must try to reestablish the local environment along the way."

"That will require a tremendous effort."

"Yes, it will. Fortunately, we have a world filled with many volunteers to add into it."

❖

The months pass by while the school year progresses at the guildhall. Petrith, Sulíma, and Túfula were deeply involved in a series of make-up courses to bring them in line with the requisites of their full academy training, including the first two circles of mage training which would be combined during this first year. Kaliya was in her Eighth Circle while Relissa and Haran each entered the Sixth.

Marelle took up part-time occupation with Roderick at the Watchman Security Office in Rolsklinde serving a familiar role behind a desk, a role which harkened back to her days in the Allegiance Guard during the time of the war where her biggest concern was the occasional barroom brawl.

She longed to return to the academy and continue her training, but the cautions of pregnancy restricted her to a simpler duty. Next year, she thought to herself, she'll go back and resume her education. She expected to go two more years until she reached the Seventh Circle, as this was the estimated level she would need to fully operate the controls on her new combat craft. It was a lot of training just to fly into battle, but she would represent a formidable opponent by that time.

Her scheduled appointment date was approaching, and she made a trip to Bya'an Tamoranth to visit the Healer's Ward for her monthly check-up. It was her second month at this time.

"Marelle!" Aerlie chirps as the mother-to-be enters the room. "How are you feeling today?"

"Much better… That first month with the morning sickness was a bother, but it seems to be getting under control now."

"Yes, it usually is for new mothers. Here, lay on the bed and I'll take a look to see how you're progressing. You look like you might have found your second wind. Your eyes, your face, you seem a little brighter on this occasion."

"Actually, you may be right. I'm feeling a little more bounce in my step lately. Maybe it's just my imagination, but I feel a surge of energy making me want to get out and run the streets again, like I did in my early days serving the Guard. It's probably just old memories since I've been helping Roddy over in Rolsklinde."

"Well, by the look in your face, you seem to have found that youthful zeal again. Sometimes, becoming a new mother can bring up that perspective in a woman when she's looking forward to bringing forth a new life."

"Yeah, and even Roddy is showing a new side of himself," she giggles. "He's chasing around the yard drilling the new guard members like a young Watch Captain fresh with his stripes."

"Really! And how old is he now?"

"Forty-eight, going on forty-nine this year."

"That sounds wonderful! I am so pleased to hear of his enthusiasm."

"Yeah, I was saying to him just recently how he looks so much better, too. His face looks younger, and I noticed some of his gray hair is changing back."

"Excuse me?" Aerlie pauses. "His gray hair?"

"Yeah, you remember he was getting a little bit of gray here and there, right? Well, I've been noticing lately it's growing out at the roots a darker color again, more like his natural color."

Aerlie stops her examination and stares blankly at Marelle. The two of them gaze at each other and Marelle begins to feel an odd shiver tingle across her skin.

"My Lady, why are you looking at me like that?"

"Gray hair doesn't revert back to its natural color. In humans, this is a sign of aging, and typically only develops more as time passes."

"Um, alright..." Marelle responds uncertainly. "So why am I seeing it in this case?"

"What did you say about his face?" Aerlie asks intently as she leans in to study Marelle's features.

"Well, he looks a little different from before..."

"In what way?"

"Um, actually, now that you mention it, it seems some of the lines in his face, like near the eyes and forehead, are smoothing out."

Aerlie takes a close look at Marelle's face, concentrating around the eyes and forehead, then the cheeks and mouth, massaging the skin with her fingers to test the firmness. She also peers into her eyes, and then along the length of her body.

"Marelle, I would ask you to stand up briefly and remove your shirt for me."

"Is there something wrong?"

"I need to check several aspects of your body for comparison with an average woman of your years."

Marelle stands up and removes her shirt. Aerlie further directs her to remove her undergarment as she makes a careful examination of her breasts.

"Can you also lower your pants for me briefly?" she asks.

"You're making me worry, is there something wrong?"

Marelle complies with the latest request for the ongoing inspection. Aerlie continues her study, making a pass around her waistline, hips, and thighs.

"Marelle, you will be thirty-seven soon, correct?"

"Yes, in a couple of months."

"This is amazing. You look much younger than that. I would also like to have Roderick come in for an examination. I want to see him for myself."

"Yeah, sure... Younger? What do you mean?"

"Marelle, as a woman ages, certain features tend to show the effects of time on them. Humans show this more prominently due to their shorter lifespans as compared to the other races. You look like you have the body of someone only in their late twenties, not their late thirties. I'd like to see Roderick before making any judgments on this matter, but I'm wondering if Lathander's blessing did more than just create a public disturbance."

✦✦✦✦✦

Ayene was sitting at her desk in the old Sentinels' HQ building on Ruuki uy'Daan, the former base for Captain Lapäli and his scouting teams while they were still stationed in the city. The building had been repurposed as a local city management office during the reconstruction efforts to rebuild the city after centuries of decay. She had her own desk and assisted Commander Kriv'tik with the service of coordinating the work shifts in the local factories, which were also being refurbished and staffed with members of their former base crew and processor facility workers.

On this day, Ayene was feeling sluggish, sitting at her desk for long moments studying the reports and periodically drifting off in unfocussed thought. As she leaned forward on her desk, she would make frequent glances at the biotech entity wrapping around her midsection. From time to time, she would make sighs and whimpers, just barely audible, but enough to get noticed after a while.

"Lieutenant," Commander Kriv'tik calls out from his desk across the room. "Are you alright? You've been staring at the same papers for hours now."

Ayene perks up abruptly at the mention, realizing her depression was becoming noticeable.

"I'm sorry, Sir, I've been distracted by a number of thoughts recently. You're right, I need to better focus myself."

"Just a moment, Lieutenant," he suggests as he stands up from his desk and walks over to join her. "This has been going on for several weeks now, and I think it's getting worse. Maybe we should talk about it."

Ayene looks up at him from across the desk. She was embarrassed that her display had been noticed, but quietly pleased that she might have an opportunity to talk about it. She and her Commander had become friends over the years, being stationed at the mining base, so she felt reasonably comfortable in talking to him.

"Sir," she sighs. "It's nothing new, just old thoughts and disturbed feelings that keep coming back...maybe a little more so now than before."

"Ayene," he comforts as he sits on the edge of her desk. "I'm probably no different from the rest when considering our new situation. As His Lordship once said, we were on the edge of mutiny in that base. Now here we are essentially defecting over to the other side."

"Yeah..." she chuckles. "Who would've imagined that...us joining the enemy, but the enemy is actually our friend."

"Yes, it's an interesting twist. So, what is it that's bothering you today? You seem distracted."

"Well, maybe I am, and it's probably not just for one simple reason, but multiple reasons. You and I, and Lieutenant Az'krun, and the others in our base, became very familiar with each other, but in the eyes of Central Command, we're still just soldiers assigned to a job. Now here I am, doing a job...which I'm happy to do...but it seems a little empty when I think of the things I've seen on the other side."

"The other side..." he muses. "You mean those people and their operations to take down Sargeras? Would you instead like to join as part of their team?"

"Well, he did actually offer me a job once," she shrugs. "But I don't know if I could offer anything worthy. They're all using such strange methods. I once signed up with our military hoping to serve an important purpose. Then we discovered the only purpose we're serving is to destroy worlds and ruin the lives of innocent people, all for some creature that shouldn't even be alive right now, so he can destroy something else, and then release more of the same so they can take over whatever is left and ruin the rest of it."

"That's a bad situation for anyone to be in."

"And then I see these people, who don't even have the full set of technology to do a job, but they're boldly charging forward to do it anyway, just because it's there to do. And they're doing it successfully!" she balks. "It's enough to twist my horns around!"

"You're not the only one," he smiles. "You know, since our arrival here, our people have been struggling to cope with our new situation on multiple levels, not the least of which is emotional for all that we've learned. None of us can go home until we can find a way to remove those creatures from our world, and we can't even go back to warn the others without some concern for the repercussions Darumon might lay on our own society."

"All his so-called death toys, as the Med-tech described them. I wouldn't want to see what he might have in mind for our own people if they start misbehaving. But where does that leave us? I want to play a role in it somehow, to carry this home and serve our people. But I don't hold any of the skills these people are using to fight this battle."

"What about taking up a few classes? His Lordship once invited us to take some courses in their language. Have you considered this yet?"

"So far, we've been too busy trying to build up a basic infrastructure in this…refugee colony," she smirks ironically. "Refugees…living in a destroyed city that once belonged to people we were describing as traitors…now smashed, burned, and decayed due to abandonment all because that Marshal and his OTHER pet minions hunted and slaughtered them for his personal pleasures. Traitors? I think the Council is a bigger traitor, for this point."

"Most likely. As I recall it, when the Marshal and Sargeras first arrived, the Council bowed down to them very quickly with this offer of great wisdom. They saw a mountain of wealth raining down on them, and nothing else mattered after that."

"What about the next group? They go up for reelection every decade. Didn't we ever get anyone new in there to replace them with better senses?"

"From what I've seen, the turnover rate is actually very low. Once you hold the top position, it's hard to overturn you unless you make some critical mistake that gets you thrown out. And the people have a habitual tendency to simply mark the box to reelect whoever was in there from the last term."

"A habitual tendency..." she ponders uneasily. "Sir, I'm actually getting very tired of belonging to a race with so many habitual tendencies. We have the habitual tendency to follow the leader, even if they tell us to jump off a cliff. We have a habitual tendency to take our medicine without asking why, and a habitual tendency to listen to excuses without analyzing the causes. What kind of species would do that, other than one bred to be a servant?"

"Ayene, I don't know, and I don't like it any more than you do."

"And finally, there's this..." she glances down at herself and the seed entity. "We were told once we were going to spread out across the stars. Then we were told to stay at home, but we still need this because we so inconveniently poisoned our native habitat that we're living in our own hostile world. You know, Lajivi, we could just as easily populate other worlds without this thing. What am I expected to do, run around in a poisonous environment tail-naked while I build a treehouse for myself? If we're going to populate a world like that, my first thought would be to involve an enclosed, pressurized habitat, not open-air grass huts. We DO know how to build enclosed habitats, you know? They're called space stations, and space is probably THE most hostile environment you can build for!"

"You're absolutely right, and this is one of the reasons I objected to it so much in the beginning. If it wasn't for our Council and the Marshal's new military forcing it on us, I doubt we would have it now."

"And the people all following directions as if the Council was a god entity you don't argue with."

"Yes, I think they've always done this. More of that following the leader off a cliff mentality."

"And further," Ayene asserts. "How do you justify this hyperreactive reflex it has to injury? If we're so technologically advanced to design this in the first place, how do you justify designing something that kills you if you simply scratch it, then to mandate this for every person on the planet, emergency procedure or not. I would think colonizing other worlds would involve a lot of rough work, and therefore a lot of potential injuries, minor or otherwise. It seems so counterintuitive."

"I can't say…other than the people who were inventing it weren't very intuitive to begin with."

"More likely the Marshal was directing the whole thing, even in those early days. The intuitive ones were the ones who rejected it."

"You're probably right," he chuckles. "And of course, he wanted us to have it, and not likely to remove it once it was applied, if it serves to provide for his master."

"Oh yes! We're a life support machine for him, so why should we want to remove it, unless we simply can't stand looking at it. But if we TRY to remove it, it kills us," she shakes her head. "And then to hear Med-tech Tad'vaal has a solution to it. Those same people we once called traitors did what we who invented it could not," she sighs painfully.

The Commander watched her as she made this final statement.

"Right," he affirms. "And this is where you're lost in thought. You want it. I don't blame you. I wouldn't mind it either. But if her only solution involves experimenting with an unspent core, we need to collect that from Azgarén. And right now, I doubt His Lordship would authorize any visits that could disrupt his other plans."

"But Sir, what if we were to simply write up a requisition, like you did with those probes? All I had to do was run back home, visit the ARC, fill the order, and return back. It was so quick and easy, and virtually no one asked any questions about it."

"Virtually no one?" he considers. "What about Central? They

would surely want to know the reason for you arriving at the base. They still have their protocols and log entries to record."

"Well, yes, but once I reported this custom order and the excuse you gave for our environmental conditions getting to us, they didn't bother me after that."

"All right, so this one might work for us. But how do you justify the need to order a seed core? If any of them should require you to report in, and you give any excuse at all, they might want to review your orders before passing it."

"And if the orders involve a seed core…right, it might look a little strange. What about a fake requisition for something else as a cover?"

"While that might provide a way, my first thoughts are to lay low and not draw as much attention to our activities on Morndindor. We don't want them thinking we're doing anything strange over there that suddenly we're making so many odd requisitions for things that wouldn't normally be a part of our usual operations."

"All right," she sighs heavily. "But you know, we still have the issue of how he intends to move on Azgarén. He needs to make an advance on it somehow, and so far, this still infers using the conveyor, which again needs to get past Central's security checkpoint. He also mentioned creating a distraction for the Marshal using a ship programmed with a jump index. But how do you get a local index unless you find a way into it using the conveyor, which automatically defeats the purpose, as you're arriving right in front of them. The only other way would be to jump in…"

Ayene halted her words as a thought suddenly entered her mind. She furrowed her brow as she tried to develop the idea.

"But that wouldn't solve the problem on the ground," she mumbles. "And if you can't use the conveyor… How did they do this before?"

"According to His Lordship," he reflects. "His people were able to establish their own once they arrived on these other worlds."

"Yes, but how did they actually arrive on those worlds without ships of any kind? I recall you telling me of the orcs using mini conveyors to Theriné, and also to Morndindor."

"Right, but it all started with that one young lady of theirs, that

Lieutenant Nazég, using this skill like what Ytani had, and then carrying some of their technology here to Ruuki uy'Daan for the first jump."

"This skill… Hey, wait a minute. What about this. If they used this skill, like she did here, then she could arrive somewhere outside Central, and no one would know about it. This could work for their arrival, as well as bypassing Central for that seed core, couldn't it?"

"I don't know how to answer that. This skill is very strange to me. Maybe it would be better to ask her instead."

"All right, but then, if she could do this, she could carry more of that conveyor tech with her, and bam! You have access."

"All right, that works for the ground teams. But what about this distraction you were talking about?"

"They need a way to deliver their ships into our local space, so they need a jump index. But according to Marelle…you recall my visit to their research center where she was in training, right?"

"Yes," he grins. "And I recall you moaning over all her traffic violations along the way."

"Well, aside from that," she smiles. "Her ship is expected to involve a jump drive, so all she really needs is a way to set the index. And for this, she needs to be present for the operation. But the question, which becomes our next paradox, is how to bring her to that place to mark the initial index…unless she hitches a ride on another ship already capable of it."

"Another ship? Do they have any others they can use? Or maybe those Daanen-Aryku, but I thought they were stuck with their nav systems wiped."

"Sir, I'm not talking about any of THEIR ships, but one of ours. He's talking about using a ship as a distraction, and Ytani is stealing stuff," she grins timidly. "How would you like to join me in a little of our own covert planning?"

✦✦✦✦✦

Relissa, Haran, and their Daanen'kai friends, Sulíma, Túfula, and

Petrith, were gathered in the courtyard of the guildhall, as usual, for another afternoon discussion of their classwork and general gossip.

"It's amazing," Túfula reminisces. "It's only been a few months, and yet I've learned at least as much as I might expect in a year back home. That language course went so fast, I feel as if it was a dream."

"I still remember that little prank Marelle played on us those first days," Sulíma recalls teasingly. "You people all know how to speak our language, and yet you pulled that little trick just to watch us struggle."

"Aye, that was a fun one, alright," Relissa retorts. "But you seem to be doing fine enough with it now. Where do you think you'll go from here?"

"They're pushing us through a lot of requisite courses. My favorite so far is the mage study program. I'll finally get a chance to see how it all works. I almost can't wait to see where it takes me once I progress far enough to start picking up my new professional curriculum."

"Yes, but Suli," Túfula asserts. "My point is that we're learning so much, and in such a short time frame, it puts everything in question on how we were made to learn things back in our old school."

"But there's one main difference here, Túfu," Petrith offers. "We're using this odd elixir here, which seriously alters the rate at which we can memorize things. We didn't have this before."

"Granted that... But the fact that we actually CAN learn so much faster, with or without the elixir, should suggest something in and of itself. That's what I'm questioning."

"How do you mean?"

"Our old schools extend on the order of decades for us to finish each of them. We have the junior school, the senior school, and then the university."

"Yes, but remember, we're also spending time growing up, as well. And it takes a couple of centuries for that, so everything is calibrated to meet the needs."

Relissa shakes her head morosely at the conversation.

"I'm trying to imagine you peeps taking two centuries to learn what it might take me only a few decades, at most. And that includes all my bad behavior and frustration I had in my early days."

"But you're not Daanen'kai, Relissa," Túfula notes. "My point is why does it take us so long? Is it simply to pace the lessons with our growth cycle, or is there another reason? Why couldn't we compress it all down to within one century, or maybe less than that? Why does it take us so long to grow up?"

"Wow, is someone a little grumpy today?" Sulíma giggles. "Maybe you slept on your tail the wrong way last night."

Túfula gives a playful shove on Sulíma's shoulder as she forms her reply.

"It's not like I was hoping to grow up any faster. I didn't really have so many desires to be an adult before my days, especially considering the living conditions we were under on Ruuki uy'Daan. Being an adult just didn't hold as much promise when you're surrounded by orcs on all sides."

"Being a child didn't hold much for us either," Petrith concedes. "So, are you actually so grumpy that it might take you centuries to learn something back home whereas you could learn it here in a matter of years?"

"I don't know, but it seems like a lot of time spent on something that shouldn't actually take that long."

"Let us not forget," Haran adds. "You have exceptionally long lifespans, and this might carry its own complications, extending each part of your life cycle to the extremes."

"He's right," Petrith admits. "It's not just about the schooling, it's the life cycles."

"It's not easy being Daanen'kai, I guess," Túfula relents.

"Personally," Haran suggests, trying to comfort the girl. "Even though it might seem like such a tragically long period for you to grow up, I should think you would get to look forward to an exceptionally long life to observe the development of wisdom and the world around you. Certainly, this offers its own rewards."

"Thank you, Haran," she smiles. "That's very kind of you. And you're right, a lot can happen during a full lifetime."

Ayene was just arriving at the front gates of the guildhall as the conversation was wrapping up. She stumbled into the courtyard moderately out of breath, as she didn't speak the local language and therefore didn't know how to use the local city gateway system. So, she ended up running the distance from the hub terminal.

She scans the courtyard hoping to find a familiar face, or at least someone with whom she can ask directions, and sees Relissa's group, along with the Daanen'kai members. As she came into view of the group on the bench, the others turned to see the statuesque, if also a misshapen figure, due to her seed entity infestation. Sulíma and Túfula both displayed a subtle revulsion for the Suuden'kai officer, but they kept their feelings silent. The rest examined her closely.

Ayene took quick notice of the Daanen'kai members, including Petrith, which at this point was the only face she recognized, so she steps forward.

"My apologies for interrupting you," she states through her wheezing. "Petrith, can you help me a moment?"

"Yes, Ayene," he responds politely. "What is it?"

"Ayene?" Relissa mutters. "Are you that new girl Kaliya's been raving about?"

Ayene jerked around to find the young elf in her cadet uniform. She had not expected anyone other than the Daanen-Aryku to enter the conversation, due to the language differences.

"Raving? Well..." she blushes slightly. "I don't think I'm one to rave about, but yes, I'm her. So, you speak our language?"

"Aye," she admits merrily. "A good many of us are taking it these days. It's becoming something of a fashion craze, especially since we're moving so close to Azgarén now."

"Interesting. But I suppose this is to be expected, if you're hoping to make any kind of future interactions. It's nice to know, actually. I may try to take a few lessons of my own one day. But anyway, I was hoping to find Kaliya here somewhere. You say she's been raving about me? I wonder, should I ask why?" she smiles timidly.

"Sure! She was telling us about how you've been helping out with things lately. And then Marelle told me a wee bit about you too. She said she gave you a good run with her story when you were getting ready with the modrons."

"Yes! And she gave me an even better run with her demonstration of what she calls flying."

Relissa, Haran, and Petrith each ushered up a tender laugh, while Sulíma and Túfula barely smiled. Ayene took quick notice of the two girls and their hidden scowls.

"All right, I guess not everyone around here feels the same for me, so if I can just get some simple directions, I won't bother you any longer."

Túfula relented and gently jabbed an elbow into Sulíma, then she spoke up.

"I'm sorry, Ayene. It's not you. It's probably us, at this point. They told us we have some new people helping, but it's a little hard to get over the history we have together."

"I'm not any happier for it than you. When I learned of it, I basically wanted to resign from my service. If it weren't for my Commander, who's actually a good man, I don't know where I'd be right now."

"All we ever saw were cold-hearted killing machines hunting us for nearly ten millennia. We lost so many people, and many generations of them. We didn't even know of Darumon until fairly recently when he was discovered running the show as the Governor of Rolsklinde. Only Master Velen actually remembered the name by this time."

"Master Velen?"

"Yeah, that's how we address him these days. It became something of a habit for us after a while, as he was like a mentor and a leader for our people."

"Interesting. So, the rest of you didn't even know who Darumon was?"

"We knew of Sargeras, but that's the only name that stuck for some reason."

"He's likely regarded as the primary figure," Haran notes. "So, that name may tend to stand out."

"You know," Relissa adds. "I think I heard it said Darumon might have been keeping his name out of it, even downplaying it as part of his game to defray attention."

"Maybe so."

"Ayene," Petrith announces. "Let me introduce you to some of our friends. Over there is Haran, Marelle's brother, and then we have Relissa. On this side we have Túfu and Suli."

Ayene promptly perks up at the mention of the dark elf's name.

"Oh, are you the famous Relissa who talks to animals?"

"Aye, but I wouldn't say I'm so famous for it. Do you know me from somewhere?"

"Marelle told me about your little joyride in that heavy transport."

"Oh, buggers! She gave you that one, ay? All right, I suppose that marks me well enough."

"And you keep them in your clothes?" she winces.

"Aye, would you like to see them?"

Relissa pulls open her oversized jacket to reveal the large pocket inside. She waves Ayene to come closer for a better look.

"Do they bite?" she mutters cautiously. "Remember, I'm fragile with this seed entity on my back."

"Nah, don't worry about that. Here, let me introduce you…"

She coaxes the two furry creatures out of hiding and onto her shoulders.

"This is Scratch and Snickers."

Ayene gazes at the two adorable little faces with their twitchy little noses and bushy tails.

"Aw, they're so cute! I don't recall ever seeing anything like this back home. Of course, in the city, you don't see much of anything crawling around, and even in the wilderness, most things are kept in sanctuaries and artificial shelters these days."

"I've heard of what you people did to our ancient home," Sulíma moans bitterly.

"Suli," Túfula interjects. "Remember what Kali was telling us recently."

"Yes, Túfu, and I'm trying. But at least you still have a father to look up to. Except for Ankhia, I'm basically an orphan because of them."

"Not because of them, Suli, because of Darumon…and in our case, the orcs. I doubt the Suuden-Aryku were even involved, and I seriously doubt Ayene was a part of it anyway. So, lighten up."

"They had to be involved in the sabotage. You don't get Flame Elves popping inside your engineering section by accident, you know. And what about those rifles?"

"All right, fine, but just keep in mind the chips and everything else these people are suffering from, and again because of Darumon. By the stories Kali was giving us, they have their own problems, and they don't even know what those problems actually are, which makes it even worse."

Ayene listened to the exchange and lowered her head. She sighed heavily.

"You refer to us as 'The Suuden-Aryku'…" she mumbles. "That puts a few things into perspective. You regard us nearly the same as an alien species, and not a friendly one at that…not that I can blame you."

"Ayene," Túfula offers. "Just ignore us. I have old habits, and she gets grumpy if she's not the center of attention for all her tail-swinging."

"Tail-swinging?" she muses. "And how old are you?"

"Four," Sulíma submits tenderly. "Túfu's right. Forgive me. My mood was spoiled when you showed up because it reminded me of all the stories handed down to us. When all you see is that horrid military of yours, you begin to wonder if there's any normal people left alive over there."

"Normal people…" Ayene considers. "While I'm sure there must be a few, my Commander and I were just recently speaking of how they all took up such shameful habits of following their leaders off cliffs. So, if this is what you call normal, I do not blame you for your opinions."

"Yeah. It's hard to forget the history you hear passed down from your parents, grandparents, great grandparents, and who knows how many more we went through since we left Azgarén. Now, my sister and I are all that's left of our family. It's not supposed to be like this."

"In all the nether-space, so many of them…" she moans. "Suli, if it means anything, I'm already very angry over what that beast did just to those of us on Azgarén, and your story simply compounds that. I'm trying to help your cause, and ours as well, so if you can aim your venom some other direction, maybe we can work together."

"You're right. Kali said some good things about you, but it's still a little new to us. She's on the front lines, she sees everything. We're just students receiving a few words here and there. Other than for that Ytani guy of yours, you were all still…well, Suuden-Aryku."

"The enemy. Right. I have a feeling it's going to take time for any of us to settle down from this, so maybe I should just get on with the reason for my being here. Where is Kaliya right now? I need to talk to her about something."

"Um, the class schedule is finished for the day. Petrith, do you think she's out on the training field again?"

"Yeah," he affirms. "I saw her gathering up a group of students for another practice session. She's been working those people hard lately."

"She's certainly got enough of them to train," Sulíma suggests.

"And so many more on the way," Túfula adds.

"She actually trains people?" Ayene wonders.

"She's not only training them," Petrith responds. "She's setting the example for a full military unit to follow."

"But that's impossible! She looks so young. How old is she?"

"We're all the same, right around four centuries. We were classmates on Ruuki uy'Daan before the attack."

"Four! And at ONLY four, she's a military drill instructor? In all the nether-space, you people move fast around here!"

This statement causes a sudden round of laughter among the Daanen'kai members of the group, soon to be followed by Relissa and Haran. Ayene glared at the assembly, wondering what just happened.

"Um, what's so funny here? Did I miss something?"

"We were just having a little discussion a short while ago," Túfula reflects. "Our studies here go so fast as compared to what's normal for us, and I was complaining about why it has to take so long for our normal schools to get anywhere."

"Uh huh… So, you don't like taking centuries to go through your traditional schools, and moving up the ladder almost instantaneously is suddenly more appealing. Wow, there goes our education program back home. I hope none of you are planning on becoming teachers."

The group ushers up another round of laughter, this time with Ayene joining in.

"Why do you want to speak with Kali?" Petrith wonders.

"My Commander and I were trying to devise a possible solution to a problem presented by His Lordship about invading Azgarén and applying his distraction for the Marshal. But the questions being raised also created paradoxes. We think we have an answer, but I need to confer with Kaliya and see what she has to say about it. Some of it has to do with her special skill."

"How so?" Haran asks.

"It's our understanding she used this to leap from Therinë to Ruuki uy'Daan, right?"

"Yes, she did. She was born there, so she knew how to find it."

"Um…uh oh, that might be a problem then. I was hoping she could help with Azgarén, but if she's never been there before…"

"Yeah, she can recall her image to places she's familiar with, but I don't think she can take a shot in the dark at an unknown location."

"Dammit, and it was such a good idea, too. Well, let me speak to her anyway. We still have that distraction idea to play with. Maybe we can find a workaround somewhere along the way."

"I say we call her over and ask her," Relissa suggests. "She's a smart one, and she knows these bits better than most. This gives me an idea to try out some of my new training. Petrith, you said she's in the lower training fields, ay?"

"That's where I saw her leading out after class," he recalls. "Why? What does this mischievous little prankster have in mind this time?"

"Oh, this should be a fun one…"

Relissa calls on her two little companions who were perched neatly on her shoulders. Ayene watches the scene intently.

"Is this where you start talking to animals?" she wonders.

"Aye, I'm in training as a ranger."

"Just what is a ranger, in this case?"

"It's a scouting profession where we learn to use animal companions for support. Some of us have a special gift, a lot of it with my people since we share a close bond with nature. We learn to train them and use a special kind of language to give instructions where we teach them to do tricks. They can be our eyes and ears, and if we use bigger ones, they can also serve as protection in the wild."

"Do you keep the bigger ones in your clothes as well?" she grins tenderly.

"Nah, but keeping them close by sure is nice on those cold nights, or if you need help hunting for food."

"Right. I was never one for wilderness survival. But then, I guess none of us are back home," she glances at herself again for the seed entity. "We tend to keep away from anything with sharp or pointed edges."

"That must be tough," Sulíma winces. "Just how do you manage if you can't afford to take even the slightest scratch?"

"Well, perhaps I'm exaggerating a little. Scratches aren't usually as bad, but slices or full lacerations, that's bad."

Relissa coaxes the small creatures off her shoulders and into her lap. She then begins uttering a series of clicks, chirps, and whistles, intermixed with several well-chosen words from the old Sylvan tongue used by the dryads, giving a set of instructions to the small creatures.

"Petrith," Sulíma mutters nervously. "Did I say I wanted to study in this academy, or was I just delirious?"

"You wanted to study here; I heard you pronounce it very clearly."

"And we have people who talk to animals here…"

"Not just that, but look at them!"

Relissa finished her chittering and the two squirrels dashed off across the courtyard, climbing the wall and over to a walkway on the other side, then chasing along towards the lower training field.

Kaliya was engaged in another training exercise with a large group of Daanen-Aryku practicing combat moves out on the field. The trainees had paired up and she was running them through a sequence of martial arts drills, when suddenly she lets out a well-pronounced yelp as she feels herself being assaulted by two tiny creatures crawling up her legs.

"What in the...!" she shrieks.

The assembly turns to see the two furry messengers climbing Kaliya like an awkward tree, and then settling on her shoulders.

"I swear, this place has no end of surprises," she announces with a jolt.

The troops in the field all let out a boisterous laugh at their instructor's unfortunate predicament.

"Yeah, you just go ahead and laugh," she retorts playfully. "We'll see who has the final say here."

Kaliya examines the two squirrels, with one on each shoulder, and exchanging stares with the small visitors as they sit stoically awaiting her reaction.

"So, you must be Relissa's little friends. Is she playing a joke on me, or do you want something?"

The two passengers began chirping excitedly and angling off towards the walkway they came in on.

"Do you want me to go somewhere?"

Kaliya lifts one arm to point in the direction of the walkway, and one squirrel travels along the length of it to emphasize its desire to follow, still chirping and turning in that general direction.

"Got it, I'll follow you," she assures the anxious courier as she turns back to the assembly. "Navina," she calls to her assistant. "Come take over for me. I think I'm being summoned somewhere."

Kaliya moves off the field while her next-in-line takes over the session. She attempts to follow the motions of the two chaperones as they guide her along the path back to the wall they had originally jumped over.

"I can't climb that," she explains, though she honestly has no idea why she's talking to squirrels. "But I'll bet you're leading me into the courtyard, which makes sense if Relissa is calling me."

Kaliya makes a brisk strut around the front towards the main gate. The guards at the gate observe the tall female parading by with her two escorts and couldn't help but to let out a muted chuckle.

"Are you going to laugh at me, as well?" she teases as she passes through the gate.

She spies the group sitting on their usual bench inside the courtyard, so she gently reaches up to pluck the two riders from their perch and set them down, allowing them to return home as she made her approach.

"All right, so who sent these rats after me?"

"They're not rats, those are squirrels!" Relissa giggles.

"Girl, from this altitude, they all look the same."

They all let out a round of laughter, leaving Ayene to ponder the mysteries of what just occurred in front of her. She closes her eyes and shakes her head.

"And this is your friend, Relissa," she relents. "Yes, I think I understand now. And here I was almost...I say ALMOST...ready to admit to this thing you call magic and this strange skill of yours, until I met these people. Now I think every one of you is as insane as our Council, and it spreads like an infection around here."

"And this is only your first day at the academy. Just wait until you try taking classes."

"I was actually wondering about those language courses of yours, but if my classmates are these people here..."

"We already finished ours," Sulíma affirms. "So, don't worry. It's only if you want to take any mage studies or anything else. That's when we'll be sharing classes."

"I'll keep that in mind."

"So, let me guess," Kaliya considers. "I was dragged by the horns by a pair of nut gatherers to talk to you about something?"

"I hope I'm not bothering you by coming here, but my Commander and I had an idea, and I needed to consult with you on it."

"An idea... All right, I'm open to ideas. Let's sit down and talk."

They take up seating with the others and make themselves comfortable.

"We actually had two ideas," Ayene relates. "But I think one of them is shot down already after talking to these people."

"Which one was that?"

"It involved a way to infiltrate Azgarén without anyone seeing you. We were also talking about this distraction you were thinking of using on the Marshal."

"All right, let's see what we have. Where do you want to begin?"

"Let's go with the distraction first. Marelle and her people are developing this weird technology of yours that'll use spatial inversion drives and a jump drive, right? And you need a way to bring that into Azgarén space, but of course you need an index for it. Using the conveyor is out for several obvious reasons, but what if you could load up those combat ships inside a carrier and use that to jump into Azgarén space?"

"A carrier would be fine, but you still need the index for the carrier to make a jump."

"Yes, and then you said you were developing some sort of an idea for Ytani turning renegade and stealing stuff. What if he steals a star cruiser? Do you think you can take control of one of those? How good is this magic of yours?"

Kaliya pauses to envision the scenario, and further reflects on her training sessions with her team. The suggestion was a very enticing one, and not simply for the covert tactic. She began to form a broad grin.

"I think that's your answer, Ayene," Petrith accedes. "When she gets one of those, we're in a lot of trouble."

"Aye," Relissa adds. "And more than likely, she'll get another mark on that famous list for it. And you too, Ayene, for even thinking of it."

"A mark on a list?" she wonders.

"Aye, Thaelyn has this special list he keeps for those peeps who come up with crazy ideas and other gibberish that gets them noticed.

It's all well and good, but you need to be really wacky to get the mention."

"Uh huh…I'll take your word for it…whatever that actually means. Kaliya, what do you think?"

"First, we should ask, what kind of ship, and why is it there to begin with. Then, I think it would depend largely on the size of the thing and how many crewmembers are onboard. And I'm sure there are certain key areas we would need to control to ensure our success."

"Right. As for what kind, we were speaking of surveys for more minerals. You know; because our existing veins are running out," she smiles softly. "Therefore, we would need to call in a science vessel to conduct a surface scan."

"Oh, those unfortunate people…" Petrith moans.

"As for taking control, my suggestion would be the bridge and engineering to start."

"All right, this is good," Kaliya nods. "And if we use stealth, maybe also a distraction, like we did before at your base…hmm. But I would need to bring this to His Lordship before we decide on anything."

"Good, this is reasonable. And then you have a ship capable of jumping your other ships into the local space. The only thing we need to consider here is the size of the shuttle hanger. After that, I suppose you can make your own index, right?"

"I should think so, and then jump in and out as needed. And if we suggest Ytani somehow pirated this thing, and if it's later seen in Azgarén space…ooh, I like it."

"I have training as a helmsman if you need it. And the Commander can help as well."

"All right, this is a good idea to play with. So, we have our potential distraction. I'll add this to my list. But now, what was that other idea?"

"Well, it was originally an idea on invading Azgarén sight unseen and without using a conveyor. But according to him," she points at Haran, "you probably couldn't do it, which is really unfortunate, as I thought it would be a great idea."

"Well, tell me anyway. Thaelyn teaches us that even bad ideas can lead to better ones with a little bit of talk. How did you see this occurring?"

"Jiggers, Kaliya," Relissa moans. "You're starting to sound like him now."

"Well, he's a good teacher, so why not."

"It involved using this skill of yours," Ayene reflects. "Like you did with Ruuki uy'Daan. But Haran said you need to know of the place before you can go there with this…um, what do you call it?"

"A projection… Yes, I would need to hold a memory image of the place I wish to travel to, and I've never been to Azgarén."

"What about someone else in your team? Can they do this?"

"The only two people remaining who are still native to Azgarén are my parents. But neither of them knows how to use this, and my father needs to keep out of our military affairs in case Darumon comes back to spy on us."

"Oh wonderful. So, like with Suli here, and all her horn-pulling about the people you lost along the way, this grinds you down to just two people who even remember Azgarén, and neither of them are part of your military. Well, alright, back to the beginning."

As Kaliya listens, she suddenly gets an idea. She quickly reflects back on her meeting with Thaelyn and Adalon's most recent prophecy. She now finds herself studying Ayene very carefully.

"A Child with a gift…" she murmurs privately.

"Huh?" Ayene wonders curiously.

"In a place of pits and people stout, a foreign Child is found; her gift revealed, a journey made, the corruption in rebound."

"You just lost me."

"Jiggers," Relissa moans softly. "You think it's her? From the prophecy?"

"Well, Ayene is a female…"

"I can certainly vouch for that much," Petrith grins.

"Hey you!" Sulíma elbows him in the ribs. "You've got three already!"

"Well, you stopped wagging your tail, so my mind is drifting now."

"Oh! So that's how it goes now!" she smirks heartily.

Ayene watches the play with curious interest.

"Um, do you do this with all the young men?"

"Every chance I get!"

"But he's supposed to be HER boyfriend, isn't he?" she directs at Kaliya.

"He's the boyfriend for all of us," Túfula affirms. "We're all sharing him."

"Sharing? In all the nether-space, how do you do that?"

"It comes down to another issue we have due to..." she coughs gently, "...the trouble we have back home. Too many females and not enough males, so we need to double up in order to survive now."

Ayene winced at the suggestion, as it made very quick sense for the discussions they just shared. She closed her eyes and shook her head at the implications.

"The things people can be reduced to simply for the tragedy of war."

"Ayene," Sulíma asserts. "It's a bad thing for a lot of people, but we're struggling to make the best of it. And besides, Petrith is a fine catch...if only he'd live up to some of the promises he keeps making," she smiles flirtatiously.

"Promises?"

"Yeah!" she urges. "This handsome stud keeps telling us he'll take care of our needs, but so far I'm still waiting for my turn."

Ayene gawked at the audacious statement.

"And is this why you need to keep wagging your tail?"

"Don't forget the soap, Suli," Kaliya giggles. "This is the key to holding his attention."

"Oh no," Petrith moans. "Not that again."

They all shared a quick laugh at Petrith's dilemma.

"Actually, Ayene," Sulíma responds. "I wag my tail as a matter of habit. I've always been like that. In fact, I also give lessons. But the four of us share a special relationship where we tease a lot."

"Teasing, all right," she nods. "I think I'm getting the picture. Hmm, and you give lessons?"

"Sure, you want a few?"

"Um, well, I don't have a boyfriend right now, so maybe later."

"But now, Ayene," Kaliya resumes. "You might hold the key to our invasion of Azgarén. Adalon is a prophetess, and she's been leading us with a long list of prophecies telling us what to expect next...within reason. She's very cryptic, so she doesn't just give us the answers. Most of the time, she makes us work for it."

"This sounds like what I've heard of these Estelar."

"Yeah, she probably took private lessons from Maker Kuroku. But one of these came to us just when we captured your base crew, which means something happened on that occasion to clue us in to the next step, and that must be to find someone who could take us to Azgarén. And I'm betting it's you."

Ayene drew back at the mention. Suddenly, the small spark she had earlier which desired to serve an important purpose began to flare up a little.

"Me? I would be honored, but how can I possibly do this? It's my understanding this has to do with the Tav'ageen Anomaly, and according to our history, this relates to children, right?"

"They were just the lucky ones who accidentally found it."

"Lucky is a subjective term here, Kali," Petrith cautions.

"Well, yes, if not for Darumon and what he did. But what I mean is they found it as a precursor. We believe this is only now starting to show itself in our species, along with perhaps a number of other advanced qualities. This is both good and bad, as it could be used for all sorts of reasons, and not all of them favorable."

"Really?" Ayene wonders. "What else are you thinking here?"

"Crime and corruption would be an example. Imagine a projected body stealing stuff from a shop and vanishing without a trace."

"Oops! Right, I got it."

"And so, I'm pioneering this skill and training my full team in methods to use it for a greater purpose. We're going to need to set an example…a governing example to demonstrate this to the rest of our people."

"The rest of…what people…" she glances at Sulíma and Túfula briefly. "Because if these two regard us as hostile aliens…um…"

Kaliya followed Ayene's direction and saw the other two girls ducking their heads.

"Were you two behaving badly out here?" she chastises. "What did I tell you about our new movement?"

"Yes, Kali," Sulíma emits tenderly. "I'm sorry, it's mostly me."

"Not entirely," Túfula relents. "I'm the one who described them as 'The Suuden-Aryku.' It's an old habit now."

Kaliya huffs silently, but excuses it as a casual error. She pats the distressed girl on the shoulder.

"All right, but from this moment forward, just remember what I'm creating, and it's bigger than any of us."

"What you're creating?" Ayene muses. "Kaliya, you're only four, and they have you working as some kind of drill instructor? Just how did you qualify for that?"

"It's not a choice, Ayene. At this point, it's demanded of me, as I'm the first into it, therefore I need to carry this on my horns. I was the first to discover this skill and begin developing it. My experiences and accomplishments along the way have also gained recognition for my talents and the lessons I've learned from Thaelyn and his people. From this, I began to share it with others."

"Wow, that would actually be quite an honor."

"They even created a special commendation in my honor, which was rather unexpected."

"A commendation? For what?"

"Diplomatic interactions, where I used my Gift to represent a figure that could deliver vital information while also resolving a very delicate situation of misinterpretation and wrongful actions, and this to a society where their culture might not take it by more conventional means."

Ayene gazed at the young officer in disbelief.

"Do you know how long it takes for anyone to learn these sorts of skills back home? To say nothing about delivering it to a foreign culture."

"Not precisely, but they teach things fast around here."

"And this military unit of yours, what is it you're actually building?"

"We're reinventing the Stormhooves, Ayene."

"The Stormhooves!" she shouts incredulously. "You? In all the nether-space, why would you do that?"

"First, some of us think Darumon was impersonating Saakerav to unite our people under one rule. The reason being to keep us from spending everything we own fighting each other. He wanted us for his minions, so it doesn't serve HIM if we're all running off in different directions starting wars with each other."

Ayene gaped and retracted abruptly, and she could feel the blood rushing out of her face.

"The second reason," Kaliya continues, "is largely because many of us, at least those of us who recall the history, regard it as a romance."

"Yes! And mine as well! And right now, you're destroying it, thank you very much."

"You and Túfu," she thumbs at the girl. "But Ayene, we're reinventing it BECAUSE of him. If it's so much of a romance for us, it's because of the image it creates…bringing the people together in unity and prosperity. But OUR Stormhooves will rub it in the face of that creature who wanted this so he could use it against us later."

Now Ayene stared stone-faced at Kaliya for the audacity of the proposal.

"And you think you can actually do this?" she emits softly. "At only four centuries and with barely enough rank to lead a small squad?"

"Yes, Ayene," she affirms confidently. "I must. And I have Thaelyn's support. Our Stormhooves will serve under HIS rule, using HIS teachings and HIS philosophies, and we will involve everything Darumon would otherwise hide from us. Ours will use the Prodigy Gift, our magic, and our new psionic skills."

"Psionic skills? What do you mean?"

"I'm trained in telepathy, and the rest of our team is also involved in this now. We believe we might also have other Gifts not yet discovered. We are half…whatever Darumon might call himself, but he's nearly a godlike creature…and as such, we might have some remarkable talent available to us. Furthermore, we are devoting ourselves to a member of the Estelar named Lord Oghma. We're all paladins, holy warriors with a religious devotion to the true gods out there, and this demands some exceptionally high standards of excellence. Due to our hybridization, and these skills we seem to possess, it has been decided we could stand on par with a young Celestial society, if only for our LACK of knowing what that actually is as a society that MUST hold itself to those higher standards. And by the way, Celestial societies become students under the Estelar as a requisite demand. So our ideas of taking up a religion become moot. Therefore, if anyone could be described as qualified to set any sort of standard, it would be us."

Ayene felt a cold shiver running down her back by now. She was almost ready to run away, feeling meek and uncertain in front of this absurd, but also strangely commanding display.

"And for what ultimate purpose?" she asks timidly.

"Those people back home need an education. Call it payback, if you like, for tossing my father out. We could say the cu'Nar called us out on a pilgrimage to seek knowledge, and we found it, right here…" she waves around her. "Now we need to bring it back, because once you people start turning off those torture device chips of yours, you'll have a planet full of Ytani's and a Council that STILL refuses to acknowledge my father's teachings, which is the ONLY way to define it. Now, who do you think will set your new educational standards, if not us here. And I'm leading it, simply because it is demanded of me to do so…age notwithstanding."

"All right, I'll stop arguing, especially if you're going to throw Ytani's name into it. But Kaliya, just how many are you actually training in this unit of yours that you could hope to pose any sort of standard in front of a full population."

"So far, our ranks are composed of just our own people, but we number close to five thousand by now."

"Five thousand!" she screeches. "And how does a simple Lieutenant command that many?"

"Well, technically, I don't, and they're still mostly in training. But I'm in line for a promotion one day to Captain, and the way it's looking, I might have more than that heading my way."

"More…" she hesitates. "But still, five thousand is not an army."

"Not yet, but I envision one day it will be. Everything has a beginning, Ayene, even this. And this takes us back to Azgarén, with the rest of OUR people joining in," she raises her brow at the mention.

At this point, Ayene felt a sudden gush of emotion rushing through her. This statement turned the others fully around. Kaliya was referring to the Suuden-Aryku as part of her people, and this would naturally involve Ayene for her role. She could almost feel her eyes becoming wet.

"And are you saying you would have me work as part of this somehow?"

"Why not? The more we speak of this, the more I'm thinking you must be the one Adalon had in mind. She has a tendency to point out certain people in her prophecies, and those people must then carry some kind of Fate with them to serve an important role. She mentioned someone would be found on Morndindor, and that someone would help the rest of us find our way to Azgarén. Tell me, Ayene, where did you live before this?"

"I was born in C.P., and my parents still live there."

"Then you should know the area quite well, right?"

"I grew up in the city, so yes, I know it very well. I worked as a local security officer, I made occasional patrols around the streets, and I served a few administrative jobs, but um… I don't have any idea how to use this skill you talk about, and our people aren't religious, so this god of yours…uh…"

"They'll need to learn. We need this as a way to distance ourselves from Darumon and everything he represents. We also think Maker Kuroku instructed the cu'Nar to give us this blessing they shared once as a way to burn away his essence within our bodies."

"A what? You just lost me again."

"Our eyes, Ayene, the glow is because of the cu'Nar, which are a race of beings known as Positive Primes, and made up of energy. They shared a little with us when they first brought us away from Azgarén. It was said to offer some kind of protection and a cleansing effect. Thaelyn thinks it might be the Maker's way of saying she wants all mention of Darumon and Sargeras burned out of existence."

Ayene gasped at this latest announcement.

"Burned out of existence…" she wheezes. "She must hold a deep revulsion of him. How did it feel when you got it?"

"I was born with it. My parents, and all those who came away from Azgarén, were the ones to get it. The rest of us simply inherited the effect as it was passed down."

"Oh, but you're saying we'll all be expected to take it at some moment, and that means me. But just how do you expect to fight something like Darumon and Sargeras, if they're supposed to be godlike figures, with or without our military on their side? You have only five thousand troops, most of them still in training. Even if you use this magic stuff of yours, can you actually stand up to something like this?"

"Ayene, our magic is probably stronger than most of your technology. As for standing up to them, I don't know the full answer to that right now, but we're not just simple people trained to fight. We're members of the Order of Tyr, which is dedicated to other members of the Estelar, like Tyr, Torm, Helm, and more, and our bodies are augmented with Adalon's blood, which makes us, in a very real sense of the word, super soldiers. Even the gods should fear us."

"Are you serious?!" she winces. "Or simply lost your mind!"

"Ayene, let me reiterate. Augmented. Stronger, more durable, more capable…you can't kill us in a simple…conventional…way. Or at least, it would take a much stronger effort to do so. I've heard of these people going up against extremely powerful foes…beasts and monsters that could destroy whole cities…and being tossed around like rag dolls, but then standing up again and running back into it. You know…augmented."

"Wow, that, by itself, sounds mythical, if also a bit insane simply to do it," she chuckles softly. "Not even our own science can provide something on that scale…not that I think we would use it even if we had it…and then with the seed entity like it is…"

"Yeah," Sulíma notes. "That seed thing would probably defeat the whole purpose."

"And not only that," Kaliya continues. "Unlike our people, who are probably too pacifistic to do any real work, the Order is a military body known to push the boundaries simply to get the job done. And it isn't just a military body, it's a special case. It's founded on some very precise principles, and built on a foundation that is guided by the wisdom of the Estelar, backed by a Draconic and a Celestial, and won't back down no matter what you might throw at us. Don't underestimate these people just because they don't have as much tech as we do. That's what I did when I first saw them, and I lost my horns on several occasions when I was proven wrong. Regardless of their tech level, they're highly intelligent, extremely clever and resourceful, and follow a philosophy defined by no less than gods. You simply can't compare that to anything normal, and certainly not by our standards back home."

"In all the nether-space, just what did he open up when he found you?"

"Maker Kuroku's little surprise," she smirks playfully. "So, are you in, or do I need to drag you by the horns into one of our classrooms to see it for yourself?"

"Um, Kaliya?" Relissa raises her hand. "Just a wee thought here, but I'm thinking you might want to hold back on the full registration for a bit."

"Why is that?"

"Well, I'm looking at this thing on her back, and if Darumon had any play in it, it might flub up the Spirit Test for her. Maybe you should wait till she ditches it first."

Kaliya studies Ayene's seed implant for a moment.

"Actually, you may have a point. We can't be sure what sort of result it'll give, and we want her score to be pure."

"Kaliya, Relissa…" Ayene flusters. "Once again, you people are losing me."

"It's alright, Ayene," Relissa comforts. "You need time to learn, and that's fine. You should probably start by dropping everything you thought you knew about life and starting over. The Spirit Test is a test to measure your spiritual energies. This probably wouldn't make sense to you unless you understood your spirit has a certain polarity and purity of nature. The test measures this and gives you a score, and your score can qualify you to join up."

"All right, so help me to understand, why is this important?"

"Thaelyn is a Celestial, meaning he's pure Positive, and he's a wee bit particular on who he allows to take up sides with him. We all need to be Positive to earn his teachings."

"Oh, well, all right, that makes a little more sense…but only a little. And this seed entity might skew the results?"

"It's just a thought, but you only get one try, so we want it to be a good one."

"All right, I'll keep this in mind. But then, how do we go about this?"

"My first suggestion," Kaliya considers, "would need to involve your idea of using a projection to reach Azgarén. Adalon said in one of her prophecies how we might have someone like you discovering the Gift, and taking what she called a dreamy path to shores where others peek. She uses some very strange terms in these things. But what this says is someone with personal knowledge leading the way using projections."

"Uh huh, if you say so. I guess this goes along with what Relissa said about me having to learn something. I just hope I don't need to speak squirrel for it," she grins.

"Ay!" Relissa yips. "Are you teasing me now for all this? I'm already getting enough from these peeps here," she points at the Daanen'kai friends.

"Let's see if we can develop this a little and go from there," Kaliya asserts. "This is an important step for us, and we need to solve this before anything else happens relating to that base or our future plans for the war. We can work on the rest afterwards, although I think you'll probably need to go to school and brush up on a few things if you want to take any formal classes."

"She's new here," Petrith notes. "Will you put her through that process using the incense? That's how most of us got started."

"Incense?" Ayene wonders.

"Yeah," Kaliya reflects. "When we first started testing people, they were very leery of the idea, so we had to use a special blend of incense which offers a mild hallucinogenic effect. This helped to loosen their inhibitions and free their minds enough to take that first step. This is actually how I first discovered it, and that was by accident."

"Do you still use this even after that first step?"

"No, not for long. Once you get the feel for it, you stop using the incense and learn to project yourself anytime you desire."

"And the part about getting naked?" Petrith winces at Ayene's body.

Ayene grimaces as she considers Petrith's mention.

"Naked? I have to get naked? Oh please, don't tell me that. It's bad enough that I can't bear to look at myself in the mirror. I don't want to go flaunting this in front of other people."

"I think we can forego this," Kaliya submits. "The early tests involved this mostly due to the idea that it helped reduce any possible distractions, including clothing on the body. But I think we've moved far enough beyond that by now that we could skip a few steps. Most of the new trainees are jumping right into it, now that it's so well demonstrated."

"Thank goodness. Then, if you're willing to take me as your student, I'll do as you ask and hope I can succeed at this."

"Now wait a minute!" Petrith protests. "You mean I stripped down to my over-prominent masculinity and paraded in front of a room full of darling young ladies when I didn't actually need to?"

"Oh Petrith!" Sulíma chides. "We all know you didn't strip down because you needed to. You did it because you wanted to!"

Sulíma and Túfula both started giggling at the poor young man's misfortune, soon followed by Kaliya and her other friends. Ayene watched and couldn't help but to feel a similar urge welling up inside, which spontaneously erupted in a moment of bold laughter. She tried covering her mouth to hold it back, but it was already bursting out. This caused her to marvel at the sensation returning to her after nearly a lifetime without.

"Look at me!" she declares warmly. "I'm laughing! For the first time since I was a little girl, I can feel it again. Oh, thank you for this. It made my entire day seem brighter."

"That's great!" Kaliya praises. "Personally, I think you tend to be a little too straitlaced. You need to loosen up more."

"I suppose I would have to agree. When you grow up in a society so restricted in their emotions, it's hard to enjoy even the simplest pleasures in life. Even trying to find friends or love interests is stifled, and it becomes more of a mechanical process simply to maintain any semblance of a functioning society."

"Wow, that's bad. And you get this chip at only four decades?"

"Yes, and that's when I lost all sense of what it feels like to laugh or cry...at least not without that horrible feedback effect. I shared a very dry relationship with my parents, and so I once pretended to have an imaginary friend to talk to. That was until I got my chip, and then it ended."

Kaliya pulls out a timepiece from her pocket to check how much time is left for the afternoon. She then reflects on her previous engagement with her team out on the field, but with Navina filling in, she could maybe take a little bit of time away.

"Ayene," Kaliya asserts. "Maybe we can make a quick lesson today to get you started. I'll show you around and explain a few things, and we can make some plans for tutoring you. It'll probably take several lessons, if you're anywhere as tough as our first examples, but if we can get you over the first hurdle, the rest comes easier."

"All right, I'm in. And maybe I could also try some additional practice in my home on Ruuki uy'Daan during my free time, if you can brief me on the basic principles."

"The most important is not to be afraid of that first step. You can't really do anything wrong, other than simply not move beyond your body. It's a bit like going to sleep and waking up again, but you maintain conscious control over it while your body is still sleeping."

"I hope I can pick this up quickly. I know you're taking time away from other important duties, and I appreciate this very much."

"If we can get this to work, we can present it to Thaelyn, but he'll probably want you to take a formal training course with Aelwyn."

"Is that your instructor?"

"Yeah, she's another Celestial, so this gives you an idea of what you need to understand the Gift."

"Wow, yes, I think I get it now. I'm only barely able to comprehend everything you're throwing at me, but I'll try."

Kaliya and Ayene both get up and stroll away from the others towards the administration office where the testing chamber was located. Kaliya then leads them inside to introduce Ayene to the local staff.

✦✦✦✦✦✦✦

"Thaelyn, my love, do you have a moment?"

Aerlie was peeking into the strategy room of the WIC building late in the afternoon. She was arriving from Tae'Eladar after a busy day with her new students in the city temple.

"Ah, this is a bit of a surprise!" he calls to her. "What brings you out of your refuge of divine providence?"

"If I mention it, you might have another episode."

"Then I should probably ask, affectionately of course, for you to return whence you came," he chuckles. "Does this involve Marelle in any way?"

"My dear!" she teases. "How could you possibly suggest such a thing, especially after that sensational performance she gave for the public? In fact, I hear talk about how the entertainers at the local circus are considering this as a new side show."

"Oh dear Powers, please not that. And will you be participating in the exotic attractions again?"

"Well, it's been a few years..." she muses casually.

"Of course. Very well, what has she done this time?"

"Actually, to be honest, this is not her doing at all. So, you can rest at ease that there will be no new disasters this week."

"Ah, but the week is barely half over, so that does not give us much time to rejoice. What is this about then?"

"Well, as you know, I've been asking her to come in on a monthly basis for a checkup, just to be sure all is well with her pregnancy."

"Indeed. And how is she doing with it? I hope she is alright. It would be terrible if she should suffer any complications, especially considering...ahem...that incident."

"Oh, don't worry about that. I had her in this morning, and she looks as healthy as a woman ten years her junior."

"Fabulous. I am so pleased to hear that."

"And so is Roderick, by the way."

"You had him in your office as well?"

"Yes, I decided a little review would be in order...you know, because of that...ahem...incident. And he's also looking quite strong and virile, just like a man ten years his junior," she smiles brightly.

Thaelyn was beginning to sense something amiss. He rolls his eyes around at the General before returning them to his wife.

"Aerlie, why are you using these terms?" he asks suspiciously.

"What terms?" she wonders innocently. "Ten years their junior? Oh, nothing special. Just a bit of curiosity over something that came up, due to that...ahem...incident."

"Aerlie..." he announces sternly. "I doubt you would be standing here giving me a health report if there was nothing special about it. What happened?"

"They both appear to be rejuvenated by a fair decade, it seems. Roderick's gray hair is fading back to his natural color, and his lines are smoothing, while Marelle is showing more…um…perk to her feminine physique.”

“Rejuvenated? This due to Lathander’s blessing, no doubt.”

“Remarkable!” the General commends. “Such a wondrous gift, they are both truly deserving of it.”

“Wait,” Kailen submits. “Are you suggesting they’ve both been restored by this much to their ages?”

“Lathander presides over birth, as well as youth,” Thaelyn states. “It is therefore within his power to perform this feat. But it is unlikely you would ever see him offer this to someone without a very special mention prompting it. Like with most things, life must go on by its usual rules, and not be modified by any unconventional means, such as a god tampering with the natural aging process. However, Marelle was involved in disposing of Darumon’s weapon, and no doubt this is his way of saying thanks.”

“That must be a great honor then. I’m very happy for them. But this also means we’ll have an additional ten years of Marelle’s antics,” he chuckles.

“Indeed,” he shrugs. “But at this moment, I would consider that a privilege. Aerlie, how are the two of them taking this?”

“They’re both a little surprised, but otherwise very pleased for the gift. This also offers them that extra time to spend with their children as they grow up, which is always nice.”

“Excellent. And thank you for sharing this with us. Perhaps, the next time I should see them, I will offer my own congratulations.”

Chapter 6

RISING POTENTIAL

Ayene was returning to her office on Ruuki uy'Daan where she worked alongside Commander Kriv'tik at the old Sentinels' HQ building. Her spirits had been lifted by her newfound friendships and her hopes to learn the projection skill. It had been a couple of days since discussing the projection training, and Kaliya had been counseling her on some of the principles and her personal experiences.

So far, they held one session to test her abilities, but Ayene's tense expectancy made it difficult for her to relax successfully. The two of them suspected this might take some time, so they planned another session using the incense as an aid, hoping to carry her through the initial steps in a more deliberate manner.

Ayene was keeping this new ambition a secret, at least until she could feel confident about her success. She felt inspired to be a part of something as important as this new incarnation of the Stormhooves. It represented an opportunity for her to build something meaningful. Her dissatisfaction over her former military service, for all the good it actually did, and being used as a tool for Darumon, caused her to rethink her career choice. And if this new skill could be developed, it would automatically provide her with a very valuable role, even though she knew it would take her away from her existing post and virtually demand her to participate with Thaelyn's military.

As she entered her office and approached her desk, she was greeted by her Commander.

"Lieutenant," he announces. "You seem more attentive today."

"Yes Sir! I'm feeling inspired after some recent interactions with Kaliya."

"That would be Lieutenant Nazég, correct?"

"Yes Sir. She's actually a very gifted young lady. I like her. She even invited me to join a little circle of friends she has. And you know, for the first time since I was a little girl, I'm able to laugh again."

"That sounds wonderful."

"She's been encouraging me to participate in some group sessions with them lately. We're describing it as a form of therapy…you know, to help me reconnect with my emotions after a lifetime without."

"I think this is a very productive effort. We could probably all use a little of that."

"Yes, I would imagine our whole culture back home has been severely damaged by these chips, and whatever else the Marshal did to us along the way. These people seem to have maintained most of our pre-Sargeras culture, despite all the troubles they had to endure. She also mentioned something when I went to speak with her that day about our ideas. She hopes one day we might all come together again, and she can help rehabilitate us."

"You mean those of us here?"

"I'm talking about everyone, here and on Azgarén. We're not the only ones who suffer from this emotional handicap due to the chips."

"Ah yes, of course," he nods. "Speaking of that meeting, what about our suggestion relating to this invasion of Azgarén and the distraction?"

"Oh, right! The idea of the ship is a good one, so she'll add this to her own thoughts. We're still working on how to play the other one for the invasion. But this is a little more complex and requires some research."

"Very good, and I would like to stay informed of your progress."

"Naturally, Sir."

The day progressed into the afternoon, and Ayene asked to be excused from her work shift to begin her rest period. She made her way to the gateway node, and eventually to Tae'Eladar, where she then used the local transit network, now that she understood how it worked, to travel up to the guildhall again. There she found Kaliya and her friends in the courtyard for another meeting.

After their initial greetings, and some light gossip to soothe Ayene's nerves, Kaliya once again led the young woman on her way for a tutoring session. But unlike the previous occasion, which was simply to a local conference room, as Kaliya had been using, she made arrangements to use the ritual testing room to apply the incense, hoping this time to find better results.

"And you said this incense is a mild hallucinogenic?" Ayene asks gently.

"Yes, but don't worry, it's nonaddictive. I learned it's used sometimes in the city of Sigil by the Guild of Sensations to help them free their minds as part of their study practice."

"Uh huh…if you say so," she grins tenderly. "Is this where you'll also require me to get undressed?"

"No, I think we can skip that part, especially if you're so self-conscious about it."

"I am. I hated my appearance ever since I got this thing. I still remember it. The day before my appointment, I stayed in my room and stared at myself in front of the mirror. I wanted to remember what I looked like, and I was almost crying…well, as much as I could for the chip in my head. It would be the last day I'd ever see this beautiful body again."

"Easy does it, Ayene. We'll see to it. We just need to take it in steps."

"Right, if the Med-tech says she can do this, I'll do whatever I can to help. I want that body back."

"Good, keep that thought in mind, it gives you focus, but try not to let it influence you. We need you to relax for now. First, we will do the incense, and then we'll go into the ritual chamber and see if we can get a result."

"What is this ritual chamber? How does it help as compared to any other room?"

"This is part of a testing process we call the Spirit Test. Recall what Relissa said about your seed entity and signing up for service here. For those who don't pass the test the first time, there's a possibility, depending on the score, that you can take this ritual to correct whatever anomaly it was that interfered with your testing. We're speaking of maybe a psychological condition, perhaps relating to repressed feelings or blocked memories. The incense loosens the mind, and the room is enchanted to allow these memories to manifest themselves in front of you."

"Manifesting in front of me? Like images of some kind?"

"Generally so... We need to speak in terms of metaphysics here. They describe it like being in a quasi-dreamlike condition, and these images are interactive, forming out of your thoughts into physical space."

"That almost doesn't make sense to me. But then, metaphysics doesn't make sense either," she smirks.

"Yeah, such as it was for the rest of the world back then. But this allows you to resolve these feelings in a manner that seems real, and this provides a sense of accomplishment, such that now you could possibly pass the test on a subsequent try. But you only get one chance at this. If it works, great. If not, they have to draw the line that it might be irreconcilable."

"Wow, so do it right the first time or don't do it at all. Got it. But I'm not taking the test on this occasion, right?"

"Not this time, we're just trying to follow a process to help you loosen up a little. And the ritual room provides for a curious advantage to make things easy."

"All right. But can you now explain a little more about this test, like how it measures something as insubstantial as a spirit?"

"Think of it as your bioelectrochemical cellular activity, and your complex neurology applies a focusing effect to congeal the collected body of energy into something with a directed intent. Your mind is not just an organic computer processing a lot of relational signals. It's the center of your consciousness, and these energies develop over the course of your lifetime into a potent force that holds the capacity to transcend beyond your corporeal form."

"That sounds strange. I'm not a scientist, but this doesn't relate to anything I ever learned in my old university days."

"I doubt it would, as it's not generally a part of your classic sciences. Try it this way. You are standing in a room, all alone, facing a wall, and someone sneaks up on you from behind, very quietly. Once they arrive in close enough proximity, suddenly you can feel something within your conscious awareness of a person right behind you. Have you ever had this before?"

"Actually, I can't think of it personally, but yes, I believe I know what you mean."

"That's your spiritual energies interacting with the other body, once it gets close enough. Your consciousness is essentially your spirit essence within your body, and it emits a kind of aura effect. This aura carries a certain radius, and if you have another body within that radius, you can feel each other's presence in space."

"Wow. All right, that much I think I can wrap my horns around, as it now carries a bit of empirical substance."

"This was part of my father's science, and likely why it was so often discredited by the Council. He was a visionary, and this was still fairly new to our people in those days. Then, unfortunately, Sargeras and Darumon came along and spoiled things."

"Right, I suppose they did, at that. So, how do I do this?"

"Sit down here on the mat," she points at the floor in front of a series of racks with candles. "I'll light these candles and the incense, and then I'll leave you alone for about an hour. Relax, breathe deeply, and allow it to take effect."

"Um, when you say breathe deeply, should I remind you of this thing on my back. It's supposed to filter out harmful stuff in the air. This is one of the functions it's supposed to serve, especially if you recall the pollution back home."

"Yeah, you're right…" Kaliya muses. "Dammit. Well, we'll give it a try. Maybe some of it will get through. Breathe extra deep for this point," she chuckles.

"Uh huh…sure," Ayene smiles cautiously.

Ayene sits down on a mat in the center of the meditation circle while Kaliya moves around to ignite the candles and incense sticks. She weaves her fingers in loops around each candle, then snaps to ignite the flames. Ayene watches in awe at the candle flames popping into view with not so much as a spark of ignition from any recognizable source.

"In all the nether-space," she whispers. "And this is what you call magic. You just wave your hand, and it literally goes poof."

"Basically. It's all governed by the mind. But we have some very precise rules to follow in order to control it. Just like with everything else, it's a powerful force and demands respect."

"I hope one day I can learn something about this."

"They have classes here, so that shouldn't be a problem. It's much easier for me these days to light a simple candle than it was in the very beginning when I first started. Just like you, and everyone else, this was a mystery beyond anything our science could explain."

"Then what manner of science does explain it? Surely, there must be some form of empirical study to give definition to it."

"The term empirical is subjective here. In a manner of speaking, there is a form of science, but the empirical part is based on conceptual perception, and it all relates to the dynamistic flows. But you need to study this here where you have access to it."

"That's one thing I never would have expected. I was always under the impression that the laws of physics, at least as we understood them, were universal and there simply wasn't anything else."

"This is reasonable, for those of us who are born in a barren fold like our home universe. Unfortunately, our misfortune of being born in that barren fold, which is absent of the flows, limits us to only those laws of physics. The flows represent another side of it. So, while you may be right, at least in part, how can you say we know everything, if we never travelled to the rest of that universe…or any other universe…to see and study it? We might suggest gods to know everything, but we are not gods."

"Now there's a philosophy to wrap your horns around," Ayene smiles. "All right, I won't argue any more. Just feed it to me slowly, and give me time to absorb it."

Kaliya smiles and exits the room, allowing Ayene time to attempt her meditation, which was a practice she was not especially good at. About an hour later, Kaliya returns to call Ayene out of the room and lead her to the ritual chamber. Master Sagrid had agreed to supervise the procedure as the two women selected a door and stepped inside.

"Kaliya," Ayene mutters. "I'm barely holding myself upright."

"Then you do feel the effects of the incense? The seed entity didn't filter it out completely?"

"It would seem that way. How did you feel when you were in here?"

"Dizzy, barely able to stand up without leaning on something. I felt woozy, like I was ready to fall asleep, which I apparently did once I got inside."

"Is that when you had your visions, or something?"

"That's when I projected, but I didn't actually realize it. I thought it was a simple dream."

"Interesting. All right, but where are you? I can't see anything in here."

"I'm standing right next to you," she replies. "Let's take a few steps forward."

"Aren't there any lights in this place?"

"No, this room is completely empty of everything. It's just you and your imagination."

"I see, so now what?"

"Well, the first thing I would suggest is to call up some light."

"Um, but wait, didn't you just say…"

Before Ayene could finish her statement, Kaliya was focusing her mind to conjure up a light source. She reflected back on her time in testing with Aelwyn, where she discovered her ability to create objects inside this room using only her thoughts and directed will to alter the reality of space. This led to some additional practice sessions to see if she could develop this even further. On this occasion, she imagined a single gentle light beam angling directly down on them from some undisclosed location overhead.

Ayene took immediate notice of the localized illumination centered on the two of them. She strained to look up to find the source, but there was nothing apparent to be found.

"I don't understand what I'm looking at...and not seeing. You said the room is empty, and yet here's a light...without a source."

"This room behaves like a pocket dimension resembling the Outer Planes, which is where the Estelar tend to live. The properties are very strange, to say the least. But the mind holds a potent influence here, where we can alter the reality of space. And I learned from my own training, my mind can do this, at least on a small scale."

"You must be joking! So, you simply think of something, and it becomes real for you?"

"This is the thesis behind my father's faction. But not even my father ever went this far. We generally describe it as the riddle of metaphysics. Try to imagine this if you can. The riddle goes like this: Perception enables recognition, existence demands definition, and from this, substance becomes our reality."

"Yeah, easy for you to say. That doesn't make any sense at all to me."

"And if you think that's bad, try this one. In a metaphysical reality, nothing unknown exists. It only exists after it is known."

"Uh huh. No wonder the Council threw him out. So, what does it actually mean?"

"It means the MIND, not physics, defines our existence. I must first Know a thing by defining it within my thoughts. I perceive it in my thoughts, and my perceptions recognize its existence by applying a definition to it. Then my mind applies this onto the substance of reality. My mother once coined a phrase: In this space I have will, and my will can alter this space. This is a derivative of the same idea, and I think she came to this conclusion as she discovered my Prodigy Gift when I was a girl and was trying to study it. She had no idea how close she was to a revelation. So, if you think the Council back on Azgarén has any idea what they're talking about, they're not even close. Watch this…"

Once again, Kaliya directs her focus to create a chair, the same sort she once made for herself during her original training sessions. It was a replica of the type of lounge chairs used in the Naarg uy'Sodrad rec area.

Ayene watches Kaliya as she places her thoughts into a space just in front of them. The bewildered girl then turns to see a strangely blurred form appearing out of nowhere, slowly becoming solid and materializing into the local space. She shakes her head disbelievingly at the bizarre apparition.

"If I had not seen it," she wheezes. "I would never have believed it possible."

She steps forward to test the object. It was solid. The plush cushions were smooth and welcoming. She turned back to see Kaliya grinning over her accomplishment.

"Just what is the full definition of this thing you call a Prodigy Gift?" she asks. "It seems to transcend well beyond anything like what Ytani was said to do."

"I'm sure Darumon only gave him enough to accomplish his task. Ytani didn't even seem to have enough gumption to try experimenting on his own. So, for all his bravado about being so unique, he was actually very limited in his capacity. This Gift, on the other hand, is described as a godlike ability, and we're still learning about it. If you recall from our earlier discussion, we're also capable of a few psionic talents, and I remember once, when we were moving on your base, you were wandering around saying you felt as if something was creeping up on you. That could be a sign of another latent ability."

"Meaning what? I hold some hidden talent, maybe?"

"Maybe, and all the more reason to suggest you might hold special interest in Adalon's prophecy."

"Incredible…" she glances at the chair again. "Can you do this elsewhere?"

"I haven't tried yet, and so far, this is a low priority for me. But one day I might give it some more study. According to Aelwyn, she says it can be done, but it's not nearly as easy out there as it would be in here. The malleability of Prime space is different from the Outer Planes. But anyway, sit down and let's try some practice."

+ + ◆ ◆ ◆ + +

"Your Lordship," Kailen begins. "I just got a short memo from Ankhia. Do you recall Tana Lar'akan? She's the one Kaliya says would like to try out as a druid."

"Ah yes, has she made any new decisions on this?"

"From what I understand, she's already enrolled in a few courses to fill in her studies. Suli tells me she's sharing some classes at the academy, and she's taking up some private tutoring with Ankhia and a few others at the Naarg uy'Sodrad, since we don't have any formal study courses ready yet. But she's very interested in following a career in biology studies, as well as the druid courses. Ankhia tells me she would like to combine the two into a conjoined practice."

"That sounds rather ambitious. For this point, I would direct her to meet with Priestess Rumoren to begin her lessons."

"My understanding is they already shared a few conversations, but until she can enter her formal studies, Tana is asking if she could take up a kind of apprenticeship. She's been hearing of our conservation efforts on Morndindor, and we think this would be a good exercise for her."

"Indeed, it would. Very well, we shall have her work with the Priestess during her free time, but let us not interfere with her classroom hours. Those are still very important."

"Absolutely."

"And this would be an excellent time to conduct some of this work; now that we have control of that base. Since we are able to monitor what occurs up there, we can move about in the fields and plains without much concern. I am aware that Priestess Rumoren has been sending out biological survey expeditions to map the different forms of flora and fauna, at least those that still remain. But we must move quickly in order to catalog and collect enough specimens that we might have a viable assortment in which to reseed the land."

"That's a monumental task, no matter what level of technology you have to work with."

"And no doubt, as we proceed, we will need to devote many resources into it."

"My Lord," the General offers. "We should probably think about establishing some manner of research center to store and process these specimens."

"I agree, and this will surely become necessary in the near future. We have more than enough space available to us, and since our current access point is opposite of Ruuki uy'Daan, perhaps we could begin planning a conservation facility somewhere nearby. What if we were to allocate some space in the vicinity of that city? We have a large amount of open land out there to work with, and this will likely be a rather robust research and cultivation center."

"Yes, this sounds like a wonderful idea. I'll pass it along to the Priestess and some of our native zoological foundations. Commander, perhaps some of your people would like to contribute some ideas into this, if you have any previous experience."

"I'll send word back to Ankhia," Kailen responds. "I know we have a few specialists in the biology profession, and we probably have a lot of old historical records in our archives we could research for ideas."

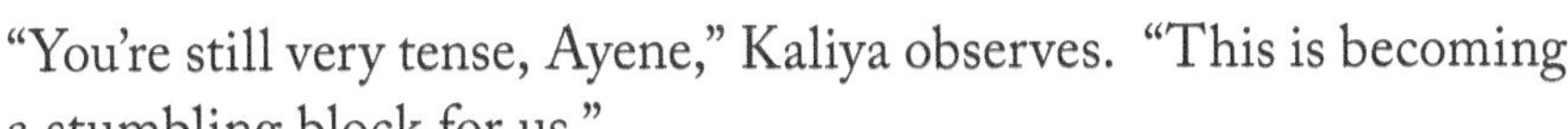

"You're still very tense, Ayene," Kaliya observes. "This is becoming a stumbling block for us."

"I'm sorry, it's getting a little frustrating for me. This effort was supposed to yield more assured results, and it's still not working."

"Don't let it get to you. Our people had the same problem in the beginning, and some of them took a long time to admit they could do it. So, don't let the frustration discourage you. We'll work it out. We know it's in there, so let's see where we can make improvements to our technique. Tell me how you feel at the moment. I'll compare this to my own experience, and maybe we can find some common ground."

"All right, I'm trying to believe this to be true, and I'm sure it must be true as I know Ytani did it, you also did it, and all those people working at our base are doing it, so there is a lot of evidence to support it."

"Good, so the belief is there. It must be something else, then."

"Maybe it's centered in how I'm theorizing the separation of mind and body. I'm attempting to evaluate how the spirit is anchored to the body, as you were explaining at one time, then to detach from that anchor, allowing the spirit to separate away. Unfortunately, every time I make that attempt, I find the anchoring mechanism is still engaged."

Kaliya studies the girl sitting in the lounge chair and listens to her statement, but then she begins to notice something.

"Ayene, do you always think in such terms as 'to theorize' and 'to evaluate'? You speak in such technical terms."

"I'm sorry, it's a habit, probably due to my military training."

"Maybe also to your long time without emotions, and this may have limited some aspects of your development."

"Yes, I'm sure that probably played a role. It's hard to grow up in a society like that."

"No doubt, and this might be another aspect, a society that so often demands their empirical evidence, and all of it being so mathematical. How old are you now?"

"Thirteen-point-two."

"And again, another term that seems unnaturally technical."

"Oops…sorry, that's another old habit. But a lot of people back home use terms like these. How would you say it?"

"Using decimal terms is something you might use in a science class. We tend to use the older methods, as it feels softer and more organic. Do you people still remember those?"

"Ah…" she croons. "Those were the days before the chips. Thirteen and two."

"That's right! Or else to say you're just shy of thirteen and a quarter. It carries a warmer feel to it."

"Yes, I see your point. This is what we call the Classic Era terminology on Azgarén. It sort of faded away sometime after Sargeras arrived and we were all convinced to move into a new era due to the Marshal and his directives to spread out. It coincided with his counseling to evade from this infestation, as he called it, which then resulted in these seeds and everything else he pushed on us."

"So, in the process of him trying to 'help' you overcome this horrible disease thing, he ruined your lives not only with these seeds, but also by spoiling some of the warm and fuzzy social comforts we loved so much. How nice of him."

"Yes, well, I was born into this, so I'm not sure how else to behave."

"Then that's probably where we might be having our troubles. You grew up without any real experience using emotions. And worse, in such a technical culture. When did you get your chip, four decades?"

"Yeah, and that's barely enough time to enjoy anything, especially if you don't have anyone else with emotions to share it with."

"What about friends at school?"

"I had a few in those early years, but things changed for me once I got my chip. It seemed like those friendships simply flattened out."

"That sounds bad. When I was in school, I had a lot of friends. We played sports, travelled up to the beach, went shopping, joined together for birthdays and decennials… Did you do anything like this?"

"I recall a few times at a beach we have west of the city. I didn't do much shopping with anyone other than my parents to buy school clothes, or other personal or household items. Sports… Well, yes, I played a few school activities. And decennials were popular too. My first centennial was really nice, but that one is considered special."

"Yes, it is," Kaliya smiles affectionately. "But sports? What kind?"

"Field ball was one. Do you know that one? You have a ball, and you kick it around the field trying to move it to the other side to make a goal."

"Yes, I know of it. We had that back home, although I didn't actually play that one as much. I was more into gymnastics and track."

"Really! A gymnast? That takes talent."

"It does, and a lot of practice. I was good, too. I won a few awards for my performance on the floor."

"Wow, do you still remember any of it?"

"Oh, this was a long time ago. Then the attack came, and like everything else in my life, it was spoiled."

"Oh, I'm sorry. But yes, I suppose I can relate, at least in my own way. I remember in those early years, I would spend a lot of time in my room playing with my dolls, and at one time I also had an imaginary friend to talk to. I called her Tuka."

"Tuka? Why that? Did you know someone with that name?"

"No, it was from a popular brand of doll we had at the time. It came with a built-in AI to simulate lifelike behavior. She could talk and respond to conversation, and was generally intended to serve as a surrogate for the emotions until we got our chips."

"Cu'Nar's Grace, Ayene!" Kaliya moans. "So, it's basically a crutch to lean on until they neuter you?"

"Yeah," she sighs. "But I suppose, after a while, I began to imagine her as a real person. I would sit next to her, even though she looked like she was sleeping, and I would pretend to have conversations with her about things. I don't think she was actually talking back at the time, but I would imagine us sharing all our little secrets together. It's silly, I know. Just the rantings of a little girl lost in her dream world."

"Ayene, it sounds like you had a few problems growing up, but I suppose it couldn't be helped. Maybe if I share my own story with you, it could help you feel better. When I was little, and we're talking maybe half a century, I apparently had these odd dreams."

"Dreams?"

"Yeah, I don't recall much by now, but my mother discovered it one day, and as a researcher, she wanted to study it."

"Why study dreams? Are they so important?"

"Well, I suppose that depends on who you talk to. Some people believe they carry visions or perceptions we can interpret somehow to understand something in our environment that isn't directly apparent. In my case, it was the Prodigy Gift making its initial appearance. But I was very young, so she decided not to tell me for fear it could cause some unknown psychological aberration."

"Really. Was she afraid of something bad happening to you?"

"No one could be sure, as this Gift was as unknown to us as those first cases on Azgarén. They had those death syndromes, which were entirely unexplained, and I guess they were trying to avoid a repeat. But then the attack came, and everything in my little world came crashing down on me. I had a good life before this. I was a star athlete in our school, an award-winning gymnast, I had lots of friends and a lot of good times. I was a very happy girl."

"And the attack destroyed all that."

"Not just destroyed physically, with our city burnt and our people killed, but all my dreams and my beautiful life was gone. I suffered a terrible emotional trauma from the event, and this seemed to close my mind to a lot of things. The shock clouded my judgment, and I didn't show this Gift anymore."

"Then how did you find it again?"

"Thaelyn…he turned it around for me. There were several stimulating factors involved. When he first arrived on Therinë, I was on a scouting patrol with Relissa and Haran. We were observing a large influx of orcs coming through some kind of portal. We thought it was yet another invasion, but then some of his scouts followed through. At first, we were unsure who they were, and while we were discussing it, which effectively stalled our response to run away, we found our answer when Thaelyn and a moderate guard showed up right in front of us."

"Oops! Did he announce himself at that time?"

"He didn't speak our language, being foreign to our world. We have our language, and many of us shared a native form with the other races, but we didn't understand him at all. Relissa tried a little of her Elvish, but she was very bad with it, so Thaelyn apparently had an idea to solve the problem, and this is where I got my first hit."

"A hit?"

"Well, that's what I call it. I had this terrible emotional wall built up in my mind. It blocked a lot of repressed feelings. To solve our language issues, he decided I would make a good example to employ a kind of telepathic mind meld on me to share languages, allowing him to speak ours and me to speak his."

"Are we speaking of literally unloading an encyclopedia of knowledge into your head? Ouch! But that sounds like a potent skill."

"Potent isn't the word for it. I was so dazed afterwards; I could barely recall my name. But it hit me in such a way that it opened up a crack in that wall."

"Ah, I think I see where this is going. And this crack allowed you to begin to reconcile yourself?"

"It was a start, but it wasn't easy. In those first days, I was spending time in his camp, speaking to his priests, listening to their philosophies and beliefs, and it echoed the words my brother and others had been trying to teach me for so long, until finally some of it started to sink in, and that crack began to split open."

"What happened after?"

"Aerlie, our Queen here on Tae'Eladar, is also a priestess. She introduced me to one of their gods named Ilmater, also known as the Crying God. He presides over such things as sorrow and misery, relieving it from others and taking it into himself."

"This is one of those Estelar?"

"Yes, we can commune with them from time to time and receive guidance. I knelt down at his altar and touched his symbol, and soon felt a nurturing presence enter into me, lifting my worries right out of my body."

"That's very interesting. They hold such power over people?"

"They are VERY potent beings where such as telepathy and other mental abilities are concerned. They are a society of beings who are easily eons old by now. No one really knows precisely how old they are, or where they came from, other than they originate from the far reaches of Creation."

"This sounds a little like how Sargeras was described once. One who belonged to an ancient race, and far-flung across nether-space."

"Could be, as they're also described as godlike and from some forgotten moment in time."

"Please tell me again about these Primordials, and how do they compare. Do you know?"

"Our discoveries since Thaelyn arrived have expanded our understanding somewhat, but the original stories are that they were once discovered by the Estelar to be in possession of worlds here in this fold. Tae'Eladar is said to be a survivor from that time, so we think maybe it was involved. And on these worlds, they planted one or another pet species of life to be used in their games. The games were a form of gladiatorial sport where whole armies were placed into contest very literally to the last man standing…or at least until one side was obliterated. Whoever lost the battle, lost all favor with their 'god', and the remainder of their species was wiped from existence, to be replaced by something new."

"In all the nether-space," Ayene winces. "So, these creations of theirs don't even hold enough value for a second chance? What does that say for us, Kaliya?"

"Just look at my father and our people, Ayene. That should give you an idea."

"Thank you, but no. I wouldn't want to see that happen to the rest of us. What about these Estelar?"

"They revere life. They believe it must be nourished and allowed to grow, to evolve, and perhaps one day, all things willing, become godlike in its own way. The Primordials would never allow something like this. Some of our more recent discoveries tell us they were a precursor society to the Estelar, a society of overseers who loved their position of power. They regarded themselves as the absolute masters, and nothing else should come close."

"And, I suppose, this fits nicely with how the Marshal behaves with us. The seed entities, the chips, all these stories of insurgents… But it's all just a game to him."

"In your case, he probably needs you to assist in his revenge attack.

What comes after that, I don't know. Anyway, as I was making repentance for all my bad manners, speaking to priests, going to the temple, and consulting with Thaelyn, I felt I wanted to join with him. My previous military experience was a mess, and this offered me a chance to start over."

"You know, Kaliya, this part sounds a little like where I am right now, as I look back on mine and how the Marshal treated us."

"Well, second chances are possible, Ayene, and Thaelyn's Order is a good way to go. And this is where I got what I suppose could be described as my second big hit."

"Another one? What happened?"

"I had to take my Spirit Test, but I expected I might fail since I still felt something missing inside of me. I got a substandard score, but was given the chance for this ritual I mentioned. In this room, I found my answer, and most shockingly of all, I accidentally found my Gift again."

"Accidentally. So, it sounds like this crack finally opened up completely."

"Yeah, blasted wide open, but I had no idea what it meant at the time. I was expecting just a dreamlike experience. They explained the incense and the room, like I did with you, and I had a little experience by this time with their magic, having had a chance to actually try a small bit. So, this was just enough to allow me to move beyond that early idea of everything being myth and mysticism."

"Mysticism," she smiles gently. "Like lighting a row of candles just by waving your hand over them?"

"Oh, Ayene…I had a few occasions like that, and didn't expect any of it. You think you're ready to lose your horns? I had mine splintered, shattered, and more, when I discovered they hold such technology to create what is effectively a perpetual motion device. And our science says that's supposed to be impossible."

"Like what he was saying about that fusion reactor on Ruuki uy'Daan. A perpetual feed of fuel by converting this energy into it indefinitely."

"That's one example. With a few careful twists in how they

combine their technology with magic, they can do all sorts of curious things. Try a hydroelectric plant using a fixed reservoir, and a portal to recycle the spent water back up to the top, rather than simply allowing it to drain away."

"Oh dear…a closed loop interaction. Kaliya, that sort of thing could revolutionize our technology back home!"

"I know. Tanjhira is hoping to apply this on Therinë once we develop our little settlement better. But now, getting back to the story, I was so dizzy on entering this room, I didn't really know what I was doing, but my mind must've been conjuring things simply because I wanted them. I created a chair, just like this one, and then decided to sit down. I guess I fell asleep, but a few moments later I projected."

"Did you understand what you did at this time?"

"No. Keeping in mind, I did this as a little girl, but didn't actually know about it as my mother kept it a secret."

"Oh, right. So, how did you interpret it?"

"A dream, mostly. I expected a dream experience, so I decided this was it."

"And what did you do next?"

"Thaelyn and the others tried counseling me on what to expect, which can be different for each person. I allowed myself to follow my senses, which started to pull me somewhere. I found myself being drawn, as if through a long tunnel. Again, I had no idea what it was, but in hindsight I now realize I was folding my projection across space back to Ruuki uy'Daan."

"Explain how this works again. This is what Ytani used to enter that city, right?"

"Yes, you imagine a sensation of movement, where you envision a location, whether line-of-sight or recalled from memories. And depending on who you talk to, you might try to push yourself, or else feel a pulling sensation, but motion to carry yourself across space directly to that spot. It's like using a jump drive on a ship, but here a personal journey."

"Fascinating. Just imagine if we could one day use a power like this for our technology. Do you think it might be possible?"

"I think this is what Marelle is pioneering right now…technically speaking."

"I'm actually jealous now! She comes from a society that doesn't even have powered flight, and she can jump a ship across space using her mind?"

The two of them share a brief laugh as Kaliya continues.

"So, I was standing there on the streets of our city on Ruuki uy'Daan, but it was so desolate and decayed. There were occasional orcish patrols, and the buildings, what was left of them, were overgrown with vegetation, and falling apart. I still thought it was a dream, but a nightmarish one. I started to run, following some instinctive urge to course my way up to our old house. But here is where it gets really strange."

"Uh oh…"

"Inside, I met with my mother, who was one of the victims of that weapon Darumon invented."

"With the altered seeds?" she winces.

"Yeah. Part of my original trauma was that we were running together to escape from the orcs during the attack and she got hit. I was standing right over her at the time watching this seed take root."

"Ugh!" she grimaces. "Oh, you poor thing. And you were what, half a century? They put us to sleep for the procedure, but I've seen a few videos of the growth cycle, and it's awful to think of someone going through this while conscious, to say nothing of a young child watching it."

"Especially if we didn't even know what it was. We thought it was some horrible magic the orcs used on us. Then to discover it was actually some old tech YOU people invented and then weaponized…"

"Please, Kaliya, I'm in no better condition than the rest, other than I went through an official medical procedure for it. But that doesn't make me feel any better for what it did to me."

"Yeah, I know. Sorry. I don't blame you for it. But anyway, in this odd dream, I walked up to her and told her I loved her, which I think was the one thing I missed most of all since the day of the attack."

"You effectively lost your mother."

"When she was hit, I could only just scream and run away. I couldn't even turn back to help her."

"I doubt there was anything you could do. But then, when did you actually learn of this Gift?"

"Oh, this was good," she giggles. "It was from her. We were talking, and for some odd reason, the conversation seemed to be travelling in directions I couldn't understand, not so much like a dream, but rather like an interview."

"An interview? How do you mean?"

"I felt like I went there to see her again, or at least to see an image of her in my dream. Then she started talking about life on Ruuki uy'Daan and asking me about life where we landed…or rather crashed. Asking about my father, my brother, our new friends, and I felt compelled to respond with a report of what's happening out there."

"That's interesting," she grins. "Like a debriefing."

"But it was hitting us from both sides. She had been suffering from isolation syndrome during this time, and didn't realize I was actually in the room with her. She felt SHE was having a dream and hallucinating my visit as part of her own delirium."

"Oh wonderful. So, who figured it out first?"

"She did, and much to my own surprise. She had this revelation that I was actually projected and standing in the room with her. I still had no idea what she was talking about, and due to the effects of the biotech seed, she wasn't able to communicate very effectively. Also, I had apparently projected myself using my old childhood image."

"Huh? Why would you do this?"

"No idea, other than to say to relive some old memory. I was a child at the time when we had the attack, so I was recalling that image here."

"Did you use this image when you first projected?"

"Actually no, this came out after I arrived. So, in my mind, I was returning to that moment, complete with my half-century body, and even my clothing. It was probably due to all my old nightmares of the occasion, now manifesting in this projected form."

"Incredible. You created this new image, and overlaid it on top of your projection, forcing it to conform to this new shape."

"That's right. Now you're getting it. You need to believe in it to make it real. Your perceptions create this image, and your force of will consolidates it into physical space."

"It still sounds like something out of an old vid-com sci-fi program."

"I suppose it does, but the amazing thing is it's real at the same time."

"Then how should we continue this session? I think that incense has worn off by now."

"Let's give ourselves a break. Maybe we need to approach this a little differently in your case. You grew up in a very restricted environment, deprived of emotions and apparently with some twisted social values that make you behave almost like machines. Let's see if we can revive the true you in there, and help you find that little girl who once played with imaginary friends."

"Even though it was just a silly little dream?" she smirks.

"Especially for that reason," Kaliya affirms. "Adalon said this Child would apparently discover its Gift. So, if I'm right, and it's you, maybe you'll find it even without my help. Either way, let's bring you forward with some renewed social values."

Chapter 7

UNBOUND

"So, this girl saw it up close?"

"It was right in front of her. Kali apparently needed a body…you know, so she could take the form of a local orc. At this point, we had no idea that she even existed. Petrith and I had hoped she escaped on the Naarg uy'Sodrad, but it was kind of an empty feeling, not knowing for sure."

Sulíma and her friends, along with Relissa, Haran, and on this occasion, Ayene, were gathered in the guildhall courtyard for their usual meeting. Ayene had been making routine visits these past few weeks as part of her therapy to reestablish herself with her natural social habits after so much of her life being governed by the Suppressor chip.

Today, Sulíma was telling a story of their time on Ruuki uy'Daan. It was a story that was becoming epic amongst many of the students.

"She lured one of the orcs out of the camp," she explains. "And into the bushes using the image of a small creature called a pixie, then dove into a nearby bush for cover while she folded her image to another bush behind the orc and reshaped herself as this big nasty predator thing called a tiger."

"I've never actually seen an orc," Ayene admits. "But I've heard of them. How big a predator are we talking about?"

"Orcs stand only about chest height to us, to give you an idea. But this tiger, according to Tana, was apparently bigger than she was, and these are fierce, muscular, predatory animals. They stand on four legs, with strong claws and sharp teeth. Kali took this form and leapt on top of the orc's back, sending it to the ground, then grabbed his head in her jaws and twisted to snap his neck. It was dead instantly."

"She can kill in this form?" Ayene winces. "That's dangerous. And all this, just barely an arm's length away from this girl? In all the nether-space, even with my Suppressor chip, I think I would still be frightened by that."

"Probably not nearly as frightened as to see what came next," Petrith suggests. "Kali dragged it off into the bushes to study it. When she was done, she took its form, stood up, and casually walked back to the camp. Now THAT would be scary!"

Ayene shudders as she shakes her head in wonder, trying to imagine the shock of seeing it with her own eyes. The group had been enjoying the storytelling, and Ayene felt a surge of enthusiasm flowing through her as she shared these experiences with her new friends. Then Túfula recalls another moment and offers it up for consideration.

"Should we tell her the one where Kali was playing god, and poor little Suli nearly jumped out of her skin from it?"

"No, Túfu," Sulíma protests. "She doesn't really want to hear that one. In fact, I don't think ANYONE..." she sneers mockingly, "...wants to hear that one again!"

"Oh," Petrith offers. "Then we absolutely MUST share it again."

"Curious," Ayene wonders. "Did someone pull a little trick on the Mistress of Pranks on Ruuki uy'Daan?"

They all laughed at the young woman's cleverly formulated tease.

"This is a good one," Petrith continues. "Kali was apparently making a visit to the city to pick up some old holo-disk records from the medical lab. This was to aid in the research they were conducting on the biotech seed. Suli also happened to be in town looking for more salvage as part of our rebuilding efforts."

"Was this before or after you were discovered by the others?"

"This was still before that, but after the tiger incident. Kali had only recently made that first mission, shut down the conveyor in their camp, and also retrieved the weapon they used. But now, we had a new problem. The orcs were bored and were starting to make incursions back into the city looking for fun."

"What kind of fun would they hope to find in a destroyed city?"

"The mutants... They made a habit, so it seems, of making periodic visits to hunt and abuse our people who were affected by that seed."

"How horrible! But I suppose they thought they held a superior position if they were worshiping Sargeras."

"That's true, but we didn't actually know this at the time, only later after Suli witnessed this one occasion. On this day, one such patrol was coming in, and both Kali and Suli saw it, but not each other, apparently, as they were each hidden from view. Suli could only watch the scene; she didn't have much else to do at that moment. But Kali..." he grins impishly.

"This should be good, what did she do?"

"Poor little Suli," Túfula giggles. "It's tragic, but it's also funny."

"Yeah, you laugh at my misery," Sulíma gripes. "But I was really frightened."

"I know, Suli, but we can look back on it now and feel differently. You see, Ayene, Kali wanted to go out and rescue that mutant, but she couldn't just go out and fight the orcs, or else it might inspire more to come later looking for more excitement. So, she came up with an ingenious spur-of-the-moment idea to solve the problem, while at the same time preventing the possibility of more coming in to investigate."

"She won a medal for this, too," Petrith recounts. "Remember that?"

"Yes, she did, and not just the one, but that other one for her dealings with that shaman."

"A medal…" Ayene considers. "An award for her deeds… We might sometimes earn commendations for our service, but a medal is something more from our ancient history books."

"Anyway," Túfula continues. "Kali created this huge stone giant, a kind of god figure, and stomped her way down the road towards the orcs and the mutant. She shouted at them to run away, and then told the mutant not to be afraid and to go home. This scared the wits out of the orcs, so they didn't dare come back into town. But Suli also saw it, as it walked right past her, and it scared the wits out of her as well. She ran nonstop all the way back to our hideout, which was clear across the city, out past the fields, and inside that old mine. By the time she arrived, she could barely breathe, and only spoke a few words before collapsing."

"Oh no!" Ayene gasps. "Were you alright?"

"I woke up later, early the next morning," Sulíma recalls. "I was still very shaken. The Captain asked me about what happened, but I was just barely able to answer. Later, as I was sitting in the large room we used for our social gatherings, I heard whispers talking about some new speculation that it might be some sort of creature, new to our world, which could change shape. This got me to thinking about that tiger again, and the orc from the camp."

"But you still didn't know it was Kaliya."

"Not yet. That came later. We first started to notice the mutants becoming very active, whereas before they mostly kept in hiding. Now they were making patrols around the city. Our people studied this, eventually following a few, discreetly of course, until we found Tyanna directing the whole thing."

"She must be a strong woman to lead such an effort while under the effects of that seed."

"Yes, she is, but it was all really Kali's idea, and her mother was put to work on our side to make it happen. After talking to her, we realized what was going on with the mutants and the orcs, and this strange new creature fighting some kind of battle, so we felt we should join forces. It wasn't long after this when Kali made her appearance."

"What did you do then?"

"I fainted…again," she shrugs and sighs.

"You're kidding me!" Ayene laughs. "Your long-lost friend shows up and you faint?"

"It wasn't the sort of meeting any sane person might ever expect. Túfu and I were in the camp after lunch, getting ready for work, when we saw a strange bird inspecting some of the equipment in our warehouse, then making a determined search of the camp. It was much too suspicious simply to be a bird looking for food. It was spying on us!"

"But this wasn't a bird, I suppose, just another projected image?"

"Yeah, Kali was sent to find the reactors used to power the conveyors, to ensure they were disabled, so His Lordship could relax the situation of war on his side. We had them in our possession at this time, powering our equipment, and they were hidden on one side of the camp. The bird was flying around trying to find them, and Túfu and I started to panic. She went to find the Captain while I tried…um…talking to it, thinking it might be that alien thing come to investigate us."

"You were talking to a bird?" she raises her brow.

"Yeah," she giggles. "Of course, me talking to a bird might stand out that I was losing my mind, but fortunately the bird didn't hold it against me, as we all have our tender moments," she smiles innocently.

"Uh huh. Tender moments," she shakes her head.

"I asked what it was doing, and it said it was looking for the reactors. It was on a mission, and being very stubborn about it, and needed to solve that much before it could relax into any kind of casual conversation," she grins timidly.

"Oh, naturally. Are you sure it wasn't Relissa and any of her pets?"

"Probably not…" she smiles. "I don't think any of them can travel to other planets yet."

"Thank goodness for that."

"So, I decided to help out, pointed to where it could find the reactors, and once it was happy, we came together for a little chat."

"I'm trying to imagine a group of people having a chat with a bird."

"Yeah, it was definitely a strange one. And as a side note, you need a lot of acting skills to do this right. Kali tried very hard to ease the tensions until she could feel the situation was secure enough to open up about the bigger details. That's when she finally reshaped her image on the ground in front of us. Of course, my surprise at seeing something as crazy as that, then to see my longtime friend, whom I thought might be dead, come out of it…well…" she shrugs. "This is the last I recall until I woke up again with her kneeling next to me."

"Wow, that's a terrific story, Suli. I wish I had something even remotely worthwhile to compare with it."

"Ayene, do you have any stories to tell?" Túfula asks.

"Unfortunately, my life is very dull compared to that. You don't get much adventure when you live in a world filled with emotionally stunted people."

"Well, don't worry about it. We had three and a half centuries of hiding in that mine, which was very dull. Just tell us what you can."

"All right, I'll try. The most interesting part of my life was probably when I was a little girl, but after getting my chip, things smoothed out considerably. I grew up in C.P., went to study at Capitol Prime University, or CPU, and held a dual major in law and politics."

"A dual major? Wow! What were you aiming for as your career?"

"Originally, I had hoped to enter a career as a legal councilmember, maybe to find a position as a local city official and work my way up the ladder. But this is a tough market, and I was also developing an interest in something more hands-on. So, I chose to fill in as a law enforcer working for C.P. Security, at least as a way to pay for myself until something better came along."

"That sounds so much like trying to live a normal life," Petrith muses. "And here we are seeing your smilitary behaving as anything but normal."

"Our people do live as much of a normal life as we can, despite the Marshal and the chips. We still have homes, families, jobs, and all the things a society needs to survive."

"But how did you get involved with the military?" Túfula continues.

"C.P. Security is a division of Central Command to manage civilian law enforcement. So, I needed to take courses in our military academy to prepare myself for the position. They have a special course for this service. I think this is a leftover from the old Sentinels' service. When I graduated, I was initially employed in several administrative positions, and occasionally some city patrols, which became very repetitive after a while."

"In a society controlled by these chips," Petrith wonders. "Do you actually have that much trouble with crime?"

"Technically, no. The chips effectively obliterate the underlying psychological causes of crime, such as greed and lust, which tend to be the traditional elements that invoke it. We also have some strong social values which dedicate our efforts to the research and development of science, technology, and a general desire to pursue greater wisdom."

Ayene pauses as she reflects on her statement, and then breaks out in a dry giggle.

"Yeah, listen to that," she relents. "The pursuit of knowledge… us, a society that allowed an alien creature to come in and tell us to infest our bodies with these horrid parasites. And then we all jump off a cliff at his request because he tells us it's good for us."

"Easy does it, girl," Relissa soothes. "We all have our part because of him."

"Right, I'm sorry, Relissa. But it does bite you in the tail. We threw out Elder Nazég because he couldn't give us our necessary empirical data for his faction. But that alien being and his promises? Oh yes, we'll bow down and kiss his tail for that one."

They all broke out in a tender laugh at the suggestion.

"But anyway," she continues. "My duties often involved ensuring the proper flow of city affairs, like monitoring the traffic on the main throughways, responding to accidents, and similar matters."

"Well, I suppose even in a society of robots," Sulíma grins sheepishly. "You still need to maintain some order."

"You're right. Sometimes we do have incidents, not always due to the people losing control, but sometimes due to equipment failure or natural causes."

"Of course," Petrith agrees. "That could probably happen to anyone."

"But does this mean you are civil duty, or military?" Túfula wonders. "You say it's part of your military, but this makes it sound like you're a police state."

"I, um…" she flusters. "At this point, all things considered, I'm not really sure how to answer that. We typically describe it as a subsidiary service that answers to the military as a supervisory body, largely due to our condition of pseudo-war with the Marshal's so-called insurgents. C.P. Security, like many city security agencies, is managed as an autonomous authority, with an independent administrative structure. But if the military needs them, they submit to the demand and hand over control on a case-by-case basis."

"That sounds like an excuse to me."

"It sounds a bit authoritarian, to me," Haran muses. "Like some of the things we had in Rolsklinde. We serve our own needs, but THEY can come in whenever they like and take over."

"Yes, it does," Petrith affirms. "A convenient way to explain why Darumon wants complete control of everything, while making it sound like the people still have some aspect of their freedom."

"You're probably right," Ayene admits. "What about you people? How do you do it?"

"Ours is a Sentinels service, just like it used to be in the old days on Azgarén, according to our history lectures. A law enforcement and security service working for the Council. We didn't have a true military."

"So, you kept most of our traditions after you left, while we jumped off that cliff at the Marshal's request."

"I suppose so. And here on Tae'Eladar, they have their military called the Order of Tyr, which is a strange one as compared to us."

"How so?"

"Well, first, it's a true military, which in itself is strange because we're not a naturally militaristic society. Unlike us with our Council, they follow a King, and apparently this world was engineered by this Maker Kuroku we keep hearing about, so whatever she has in mind, we're something special. Haran, you've been in some of their political studies, so what do you have to say about it?"

"Yes, I have, actually," he offers. "The Order might sound like a police state, if you look at it a certain way, but it doesn't behave like one in the traditional sense. They act more like a regulatory body to set the standards for the rest to follow, behaving as much as a parental figure as it does a true military. For instance, civil law enforcement is governed by what we call the Watchman Service."

"A Watchman Service, how quaint," Ayene muses.

"Yes," he grins. "It's a division of the military dedicated to civilian law. They train a subset of military protocols, in part for the standardization of the practice, as well as to employ the Spirit Test to ensure the integrity of their membership. After that, although they might follow certain military codes of honor, the Order mostly serves as an administrative body, holding them accountable for their practice."

"Administrative..." Ayene nods. "This sounds a little like ours, at least on the surface."

"With the exception that they don't just come in and take over on a whim. If something dire occurs, like a disaster, they might go into action, but more often as an accessory to the civilian service. It would take something really big to demand them to actually take control and correct it. And to my knowledge, other than for war, or that one occasion they call the Spellplague, which was a worldwide disaster event, I don't think we've seen anything like that."

"Ouch! I'm not so sure if I want to ask about that. You also said something about holding them accountable. So, if anyone within this body should become reckless or greedy with their perceived position of authority, the Order reins them in?"

"Precisely! The same for education and health care, both of which serve civilian roles, but if left to privatize, they could just as easily move off in separate directions, and with little or no discernable cohesion of their standards. The Order keeps them all in check, so that no matter where you travel, you can be sure the service you receive is uniformly consistent, and adheres to the same high standards."

"That's a fascinating system of service. Our system of health care is a structured network of medical wards and laboratories governed by our Council. Our education system is also governed by the Council, but law enforcement is a military affair."

"But isn't your Council ultimately controlled by Darumon?" Túfula inquires.

"I suppose it is. We're made to believe the Council is OUR planetary government, and simply cooperating with Darumon during this unfortunate period where we have these insurgents threatening us. Therefore, Darumon was granted authority over our military body, while the Council is in some kind of deliberation no one knows anything about."

"Um, wait. Deliberation over what, and why doesn't anyone know anything about it?"

"No one has seen them for a long time. They locked themselves away inside the inner chamber and haven't come out since. Rumor has it they went into a long deliberation over what we presume to be Darumon giving them some of his secret knowledge. Meanwhile, nothing else seems to be getting done while they're sequestered away."

"That sounds suspicious," Petrith muses. "Especially when you consider Darumon and his schemes."

"This might then reflect on the rest of it, like our health care. We already know he controls what they do or do not research, and if it doesn't serve his needs, he simply denies the privilege. I suppose I should also mention we have a state-controlled media service. I learned this once from Commander Kriv'tik when we were having a private conversation in our base one day concerning a recent news report we saw."

"What was it about?" Petrith asks.

"We get these occasional reports about outposts and trade routes we're supposed to have as we try to explore the local stellar cluster for potential colony sites. He said once not to believe everything we see because he knew there were no such efforts being reported within the military circles. It was mostly a form of propaganda to keep the public calm relating to the insurgents, and also the Tav'ageen Anomaly we were trying to escape from. The Marshal was apparently trying to maintain an image of trying to solve our local issues, even though they weren't really getting solved."

"Sounds like he's got his fingers in every pocket…" Sulíma moans.

"More like inside every head," Petrith conjectures. "Especially if it involves schools, media, anything to keep them under his influence for whatever he wants them to know."

"This sounds so much like what he was doing back home," Haran reflects. "He was posing as our Governor and doing exactly the same thing, using the Dean of our old academy in this same manner."

"Aye," Relissa ponders. "It must be a regular show he puts on. Same as on Morndindor and Ytani. He must've learned from the best."

"But Ayene," Sulíma resumes. "How do you actually see this thing you call the Tav'ageen Anomaly? According to what I heard, Master Velen described it as a Prodigy Gift, and then later it was called a disease of some kind."

"I don't know the history of it as precisely as that," she considers. "We mostly learn of it as an infestation of some awful alien parasite of unknown origin that found its way into our world and nested itself."

"Nested?" she grimaces.

"For lack of a better word, yes. The early discoveries found this strange apparition moving around independent of the native body, and this didn't correlate with any known medical or physical anomaly. Then the Marshal came along and suggested this idea of the infestation. He said it could be trying to take over the bodies of our children, and therefore this apparent image they found. And if that wasn't frightening enough, he said we could be in danger of losing control of our society. He encouraged us to prepare to vacate our home world, using any available planet we could find that would allow even a haphazard colonization effort, and using the seeds as an enabling factor to survive until we could stabilize later."

"And so, this is where the seeds came from."

"Then we started having troubles with these insurgents, which suddenly kept us at home. We needed this big military, and therefore this big industry to supply it, and since we were going to vacate anyway, we shouldn't bother with so many eco-friendly techs. Therefore, we polluted our world so bad."

"How convenient, and this enforces the need for these seeds, even at home."

"We were also experiencing more of these strange deaths, same as those early children, but now at random throughout the public. This raised even more fear and paranoia that this infestation was growing. More people were encouraged to take the seeds, until we hit a threshold where we could no longer plan the evacuation for the war outside."

"And here is where he locks you up," Haran relents. "You have these seeds he wanted you to have, and according to Kaliya, she thinks they act as a feed to support Sargeras in that barren fold."

"And that part hits me the hardest," she shudders. "It's bad enough they forced me to deform my body with this thing, but to use me as food for that creature," she grimaces and turns away. "It wasn't until after all this when they came out with the chips, saying THIS will stifle the infestation from targeting anyone else, so we should be safe…for now…to stay at home until the rest of it is resolved."

"And how long ago was this?" Sulíma inquires ironically.

Ayene glared at the girl, knowing the meaning of the request. She couldn't help but to sigh and shake her head.

"Long enough that you might think someone within that society of scientists and scholars would try to seek higher knowledge and realize something was wrong with this picture. But like my Commander said to me during our meeting in that detention center, we were probably born and bred to be docile animals that jump off cliffs on demand."

"I'm sorry, Ayene. I don't mean to say something bad, but I think I have to agree. Maybe we're also guilty in our own way. That attack on Ruuki uy'Daan should've had everyone running to the ship. But it seems most of them stopped when the alarms cut out, and the school simply followed orders that it was nothing to be worried about. We're just as much dumb animals that jump off cliffs."

"Suli," Relissa ushers. "I don't think you're such dumb animals, but you might be a wee bit quick to follow orders without proper thinking. It's one thing to follow your supers, but it's another to jump off a cliff without looking first. If he made you so easy to push around, you need to learn how to push back."

"Thank you, Relissa, those are very kind words. I think after all is said and done; we need to realize this most of all."

"And this is where your new Stormhooves comes in," Ayene considers. "You're finally learning how to push back."

"It's a hard lesson, but yes. And using one of his games to rub it in."

"It actually runs a bit deeper than that," Petrith suggests. "We're not a naturally predatory species. But in our position, where we've come so far that it becomes imperative to learn a few things, we need to overcome that docile side with some self-preservation habits. We also hold some very peculiar qualities, and this might force us to consider if we have a higher calling to apply ourselves to. And living as prey animals that jump off cliffs doesn't do it."

"After that day," Ayene recalls. "When Kaliya was talking about this, I've come to realize this is probably the best suggestion ever. It holds recognition, a sense of historical tradition, and considering everything we've been talking about, it would carry the authority to correct all these errors. The only thing I'm not so sure about is how our people will take this religious aspect. Remember, we're not a religious society, so they might describe this as some kind of cultist mysticism, and try to discredit it."

"They can try if they want," Túfula admits. "But the way things are developing, this final battle will likely change some of that. I would expect the people of Azgarén will NEED to learn who the Estelar are, and simply accept the fact that there are indeed gods out there. Religion or no religion, this is tangible, especially if you consider Sargeras is right in their backyard, and he's one example."

"Likely so, Túfu. And if you consider what I hear of Sargeras himself, it's said he stands extremely tall."

"Jiggers, Ayene," Relissa winces. "Just how tall is that when it comes out of you?"

"I only know of a few rumors passed down from the original arrival. Sargeras was weak, and we all believed this was due to him and the Marshal barely escaping from these insurgents. The Marshal told us he needed special medical aid, but our science wasn't properly equipped for it. One of his early requests was to build a temporary shelter until a more permanent structure could be built. It was described as a sanctuary building, and we had to clear four city blocks for it in the downtown section of the city."

"Buggers!" she shouts. "Just how much space does this blighter need for himself?"

"And worse," Haran frowns. "How do you justify removing so many other buildings, which were probably important commercial buildings, just for someone to take up residence?"

"Yeah," Ayene chuckles ironically. "That one is the worst of the horn-pullers. The building is one of the tallest in the city, and needed a wide margin space around it as a buffer zone for his privacy demands. The Marshal custom-designed it, and he claimed he would attend to Sargeras's needs while he helped the rest of us organize everything else. But I recall some rumors about how Sargeras was already as tall as a house, and the early medical attention the Marshal gave seemed to cause him to grow even more. But this all sounds like nonsense to me. How does someone grow out of medical aid?"

"If he's not a corporeal creature," Haran cautions. "Lots of things become possible. The Estelar can grow in strength due to the worship they receive from their followers. And strength, in this case, could also relate to their manifested size. And if the Marshal's alleged help was to infuse him with souls from your so-called infestation killing your citizens, along with these seed entities and whatever contribution they offer, that tallest building in your city could suggest his full healthy proportions."

"And buggers to you too, Haran!" Relissa gripes. "So, what are we saying, he could be as tall as a mountain by now?"

"Does anyone ever enter inside that building of his?"

"No," Ayene asserts. "Other than maintenance workers, which only attend to the utility areas, he's alone in there, with the only exception being the Marshal making visits."

"Then I might assume, after this long a period, he is probably regenerating to his full strength. The only question here is how much of this energy he needs for it. Maybe also how much he can gain for his life support if those seeds only provide enough to barely maintain him while inside that barren fold. I heard once he might be mostly sleeping, and his strength, if we judge by his control over the Flame Elves, which wasn't apparently very strong, could be only a minimum level."

"Captain, this is becoming very bothersome for me."

"I couldn't help but to notice that, Priestess. You're sitting there at your desk shuffling mountains of reports and boxes full of journal books. I wish I could offer some way of helping you, but this is much more your line of work than mine."

Priestess Rumoren and Captain Hagmaert were sitting inside the officer's hut in the outpost on Morndindor, both busy at their respective assignments, and both feeling the pressure of increased workloads due to the extended efforts they each had in front of them.

The Captain had been importing additional scouts to scour the land at further reaches looking for survivors in the vanishing landscape. He continued working with members of the dwarven society he had already rescued, including Belrum and his fellows, but between the extensive cartographic missions to cover the full continent, and then to see about any other continents across the sea, as well as to check every nook and crevice for potential refugees, his desk was overflowing with papers.

The Priestess, however, was in even worse shape.

"Yes, Captain, and I'm very eager to see it through, but the methods I started out with are showing a severe lack of efficiency for the volume of detail I'm slogging through. I have an army of druids, as well as rangers out there studying every plant and animal they can find; some on horseback, others on gryphons, and many with wagons carrying crates and bags to collect specimens. But this little outpost simply doesn't have enough space for all of it. Where do we expect to put everything when the first deliveries start coming in?"

The Captain makes a cursory glance around the hut and through the door outside, but can only shake his head.

"I'm aware from one report we received a while ago," he states, "about the development of a new conservation center they're planning to build on Ruuki uy'Daan. But I think they're only just starting to break ground on it so far. My only suggestion is to do the best you can with what we have to work with until we can find more space for it."

"Then we need to expand our operations here. We're trying to conduct these surveys across the whole world, and all in short order. This is more than anything we have ever attempted before. For instance, do we still need this shield wall? We could set up a number of shelters out there where we can store some of these specimens, maybe install some power units, enclose a few areas for the wildlife, and create some small greenhouses to get us started."

"That sounds like a wonderful idea. You should write this up for His Lordship and begin requisitioning the supplies. I'm sure we can find a number of commercial franchises back home to supply you with goods, as well as the labor to get started."

"Excellent. Maybe I could take this straight to him and present my case personally for a few additional ideas."

The two of them continued their work through the day until evening came. They enjoy their meal and some casual conversation, until the Priestess feels the time is right to be on her way. She excuses herself politely, and makes her way through the gateway node.

It was midmorning on Therinë, and Thaelyn had been in conversation with his officers, as well as receiving a visit from the researchers at the Bahlaie Center with a status update on their latest projects.

"And so, Your Lordship," reports Chief Technician Lapäli. "We were able to decode the data from that concept prism Adalon gave us. Creating the containment field shouldn't be a serious issue, I think. The details for constructing the bubble stabilization grid and maintaining the subverted spatial pocket can be conducted using mostly existing technology we're already familiar with. Although I need to point out it will require some specialized industry to construct the components. All we have after that is to figure out how to populate the space with arcanids, and then keeping them happy enough to produce for us."

"What about storage? The size of this bubble will be trivial in relation to our full multiverse, and the volume of arcanic energies the average mage needs may vary between applications. Therefore, we must conserve our charge between uses."

"The Professor and I have discussed this. Your mages can eat this stuff up quick once they go into action. So, a storage cell might not be entirely practical unless it can somehow compress the charge into a smaller space, allowing us to store more of it. We also need to concern ourselves with the recharge rate."

"Yes, and with the relatively small colony we might have to work with, that could move rather slowly, forcing us to pace ourselves carefully. Professor, have you solved the riddle of how to maintain the arcanids yet?"

"I'm working on testing several theories," he responds. "The concept prism provided some useful information to get started, but I also need to test a few applications to make sure they're functional. But it's hard for me to obtain any viable results while inside an arcanic cloud, since the arcanids are feeding off the natural space, rather than anything I might otherwise provide to them. So, I think I need to conduct some preliminary testing outside the cloud, and for this I'm reminded of that moon called Madzurki. Do you think we could make use of that?"

"We could, but I should remind you to take care around that

atomic device we stationed over there. We have it stored in a remote area of the processor, out of easy view of anyone looking around, but I do not want any accidents, such as tampering with it or the detonator device. I should also point out we cannot be sure if the Suuden-Aryku would ever make any surprise inspections."

"I think we can solve that with a little careful planning, my Lord. According to Tanjhira, we should have easy communications from there to the base. And if we build a few of my new communicator devices, we can stay in close contact with those of you here in case we need it. We've also been finishing up some of our construction efforts to build a small fleet of transport shuttles. Nothing fancy, mind you; it's mostly just to move people and cargo around. The Daanen-Aryku like to use these since they're so familiar with them, and not all of them are in training for mage courses, as you know, to use rune stones."

"Of course, and we could use one of those for a quick escape. But now, speaking of that device of yours, have you managed to bring any new innovations to it?"

"Actually, yes, we have. It's still in the development stage, but the lovely Tanjhira here had some of her people conjure up some interesting design concepts for us, and you won't believe how simple it is to implement!" he giggles.

"Indeed! Tell me."

"Your Lordship," the Chief Tech explains. "Using his whisper shard might be as simple as plug-and-play for us. The reason being it could very easily replace the standard antenna we use in our existing designs, with only a few slight modifications to the circuitry to channel the signal through. We could probably have a working prototype out before the end of the year."

"Fantastic. I see this is moving forward nicely. And with this, we should be able to find similar solutions to replace your trans-coms and other communications equipment. This provides us with a superior advantage for our future operations. But now, what about our combat vessel designs?"

"So far, we've made several design changes to our old model.

One major revision was to provide the ship with a lateral strafing control, as Marelle suggested once. But incorporating this feature also completely alters the way we think of flying, based on our previous technological designs. The flux field is out completely now, as is the magneto-graviton drive. In fact, we're working to incorporate this feature into all our ships, including the shuttles."

"Very interesting, and how do you apply this now?"

"We applied a hybrid form of our spatial inversion field with your magical transport sphere to create a bubble of inverted space that can slide through physical space using spatial compression techniques. In theory, the only limitation is the power output of the reactor feeding into the field, and thus driving it through space. The more power, the faster you can cycle the compression event horizon, and therefore the faster you can pass through space."

"This should be a most enjoyable sight to see."

"Of course, there are a few variables to consider, like the physical size of the vessel, and therefore the volume of the pocket space, which relates to the surface area of the bubble, and this then relates to the dimensions of the compression field event horizon. So, simply having a bigger reactor doesn't always mean a faster ship, as a bigger ship would require more power to drive the broader event horizon."

"Indeed, this is a fascinating aspect of it. A small vessel might be good for interplanetary travel, while a larger one would serve better for interstellar travel. But there may be an upper limit of how fast you can go unless you can design more efficient technology."

"Right. But there's a curious aspect here that's always fascinated me. In theory, this field subverts you into a kind of sub-spatial pocket. The object within the bubble doesn't represent a physical object in physical space since the pocket isn't part of that same space. Even the bubble itself isn't part of physical space, instead representing a, um, maybe if I describe it as a blister-like pocket underneath the skin of space…if that makes any sense."

"This is a curious depiction, but I believe I catch your meaning."

"Right, so if space…that is to say physical space, real space, what we're standing in right now, is warping around the bubble, then anything and everything in that space bends around it as well. Theoretically, a ship using this method of transport would be able to pass through anything in our physical space without interacting."

"Chief," Kailen interjects as he listens intently to the discussion. "What do you mean to pass through anything? Are you saying it could pass through other objects?"

"This is a technical theory that goes along with the principle, but no one, to my knowledge, ever tried to prove it. The bubble slides through space using spatial compression. Space in front of the bubble is compressed, then pulled around the shell and decompressed behind it. But the bubble doesn't represent a creation within physical space. Instead, it represents a zero-dimensional object embedded underneath physical space. And the body inside doesn't feel inertia, as it's not actually moving. Space itself is the only thing moving, philosophically speaking, if only due to being compressed and uncompressed, sucking this blister along like a pea through a straw, and with the rest of us being outside the straw."

"Incredible."

"She is actually correct in this, Commander," Thaelyn asserts. "If you are moving along within a bubble of distorted space, which is detached from our physical space, whatever is within our space will simply bend around you along with the space itself."

"Why didn't anyone ever try proving this before? A person could pass through a building, a mountain…a planet…"

"Indeed," Thaelyn concedes. "And so, I suppose the idea of Marelle crashing into a mountain is no longer an issue."

"But Chief, how does this affect engaging in combat?"

"She might not represent a material object," she advises. "But energy is another thing. The membrane, in this case, is permeable. Light can still pass through, and so would other forms of energy, both in and out. But some things may need to be calibrated in a phased condition, like our weapons, which use plasma energy. Then, once through the shell, it behaves as expected."

"This brings us nicely to the next concern," Thaelyn submits.

"Azgarén is said to have a network of detection grids. The vessel may be visible to the eye, but we must obscure it from their scans."

"Right, and we are working on a variant of the shield modulator to block those scans. The tricky part is to have it block their energies, but not our own, so the modulation needs to be very specific. Fortunately, these flows are very flexible, so I'm confident we can find an answer. The shield should then be able to absorb not only hostile energies, but also detection emissions as well."

"And the jump drive?"

"Using your runes as a basis, we were able to create a few prototypes for testing. The difficulty here is to ensure we are creating a rift large enough to draw the full vessel through. For this, we need to make sure to have an adequate volume of energy to create a distortion field around the ship, which then opens a rift event. We need to share the same power source for this as what's used by the main drive system, so it's a case of either-or. You'll need to come to a full stop to jump."

"Very well then, if we can put a safe distance between us and anyone else, I suppose this is acceptable. Hopefully, the charging process will not take an excessive amount of time or cause too much misery. We shall see with our new prototypes, and maybe future refinements can offer us more flexibility later."

"My Lord," a page enters the room. "Priestess Rumoren has arrived and awaits your audience."

"Send her in."

The Priestess had been waiting patiently for the meeting to allow an opening for her. When the page waved her in, she entered with a bow.

"My Lord, I hope I am not disturbing you too greatly."

"Not at all. How is the study progressing on Morndindor?"

"It is progressing nicely enough, but it is becoming very cumbersome for my small station. I had a conversation with Captain Hagmaert about this, and we came to a few ideas, but I wanted to present this to you for your approval, as well as any refinements you might wish to add into it."

"Indeed, one more aspirant hoping to pick my brain. Why not," he chuckles. "What do we have on this occasion?"

"I'm aware of the project for the new conservation center on Ruuki uy'Daan, but this will take time, and I am already collecting a lot of details, reports, and soon-to-be specimens as my people return back to me. I need facilities now! Therefore, I would wish to requisition materials and labor to construct a number of shelters and greenhouses, at least on a temporary scale, outside our outpost on Morndindor. Also, I would like to ask about that shield wall. Is it still necessary? I think by now the situation should be secure enough to take it down."

"Yes, I would agree. General, will you kindly send the orders. Let us begin expanding our presence to involve this new capacity until the conservation center is ready. We can then relocate as needed and continue our work there."

"Of course, my Lord," he nods.

"But you know, Priestess," Thaelyn continues. "As much as I am eager to see this through, I am beginning to feel concern about the budget we will need to allocate here, as this will drain a sizable amount of our war and disaster relief funds away. We should see about finding some other form of funding to aid in this, as this effort will extend over a long period."

"Yes, I'm sure you're right," she affirms. "I wonder if there's any way we could… Oh wait, what if I could submit some inquiries for grants from some of the other biological study centers, maybe also some botanical gardens and cultural centers. We could also involve exchanges of scientists and scholars who could offer some of their time as part of a large research and study program. What name do we use here when studying life from other worlds?"

"That is such a fascinating question, Priestess," he grins broadly. "And so very appropriate for the occasion, but I must admit it is completely unexpected for where we stand in our local level of technological prestige. This would be the study of exobiology, and it would typically be the domain of societies more like the Daanen-Aryku here, for all of their capacity to travel to other worlds. It is a curious and deeply intriguing form of science, as life tends to pervade across many worlds, and to have such an opportunity to study it would be any proper biologist's dream. If you could drum up enough support for this, I think you will have contributors knocking down your door after a while."

"Good gracious, my Lord! Then I guess that solves the problem of funding," she chuckles.

"Truly amazing," the Chief Tech muses. "I'm watching evolution in the making here."

"I've seen a few occasions like this so far," Kailen adds. "The frightening part is how fast they're moving with it."

"They'll be up to our level before we even have a functioning city again."

"And no doubt," Thaelyn offers. "We will likely need to cut a few corners in this case when designing that conservatorium. We should involve your hydroponics technology, probably also to incorporate a power source that is not dependent on the city grid, at least not until we can design a better infrastructure, plus water filtration and recycling, and a way to isolate the collected specimens so we do not have any cross-contamination with the native flora and fauna."

"You'll need enclosed habitats then," Kailen suggests. "And probably with localized environmental controls. This will probably involve more of our technology than yours."

"It cannot be helped at present; we have a pressing need and time is against us."

"Understood, I'll pass the word on my side to provide the technologies, and the Priestess can work on her funding and labor support. This will also give Tana a good exercise in her studies."

Thaelyn leaned back in his chair as he pondered this new evolutionary development.

"Powers behold," he sighs. "Where are we going in this war? We started out so simple, and now we are crossing worlds and developing technologies to cross entire folds of Creation. In addition, we hope to remake some of those worlds we find along the way."

"I don't envy you for this point. This is a big jump for your people."

"It causes me to recall the Sarrukh and what they did on Tae'Eladar. And although Morndindor is not quite as severe an example, it is nonetheless a challenge we were not ready for. In fact, I would not have expected any such efforts as these for at least a few or several centuries when we came upon our own Space Age, ready to reach out beyond our world."

"But where would you go?" the Chief Tech wonders. "If you're inside that Shell, there's no place to travel to."

"This is true, other than to examine the other planets we share that space with. For this point, we might find a little help from the Estelar to seek a valid destination to start us on our journey. And yet, if only for Darumon and his orcs, we now have not one, but two new folds open to us. And let us not forget the Sarrukhan Gate, which could offer yet another destination."

"The Sarrukhan Gate?"

"Yes, several centuries ago when we were trying to understand the origin of life on Tae'Eladar, we discovered a time capsule, as we tend to call it, left behind by the Sarrukh. Within that body we found a message of their passing and the work they apparently made; plus a highly advanced technological portal device we call the Sarrukhan Gate. In fact, we had to borrow from this some of the technology we use now for our own design."

"How interesting..." she smirks. "So, we're not the only ones you're cutting a few corners with?"

"Yes, I must admit, we had another pressing moment with the Spellplague forcing my hand."

"I remember that from my grandpappy," the Professor muses affectionately. "Oh, the stories he shared with me!"

"Indeed, that was a special moment...a turning point for us in many ways. The Gate leads to the world they once used as a resource for all the life they imported into our own. Although, I suspect they must have used some of their science to create a few unique species to fill in, like the gryphons. When we found that time capsule, I gave instructions to open the portal to see where it led, and then sent a long series of expeditions into it to discover what was on the other side."

"What did you find?" the Chief Tech asks.

"A world not unlike our own in many ways, and fully populated with humans, as well as variations of many of the existing plants and animals we know so well. But the people were not, at that time, as sophisticated as we were, so I gave instructions to close the Gate for a later moment, hoping one day we could return to see how they are developing."

"Well, soon you'll be able to do just that once we get these new ships up and running. You could send one of these through a portal and launch into their local space to mark an index, and use that to make later returns to check on them."

"This would be an interesting turn of events. But I would wish to do so discreetly, so as not to disrupt their local culture with alien visitations. Also, they do not apparently have access to the dynamistic flows in that space, much like your people. Hmm, this makes me wonder where they are in relation to your home. Could it be the same barren fold?"

"That would be a curious twist, but cu'Nar's Grace, I hope it's not the same galaxy, not after what Darumon did over there!"

"Indeed, but this world did not bear any marks of a disaster, so perhaps we are fortunate."

It was another month into Marelle's pregnancy term. Aerlie had instructed her to enroll at a local civic center where they offered courses for citizens young and old on health and fitness, as well as domestic arts and crafts. Marelle was put on a schedule to perform a type of yoga exercise for young mothers on a regular basis, as well as a recommended nutritional diet for the remainder of her term. Aerlie's advanced medical knowledge, which she learned as part of her Celestial studies, had improved the health and welfare of the people considerably over the years, and now it was Marelle's turn to take advantage of it.

Elsewhere, Ayene was still making regular visits with her friends at the guildhall as part of her emotional therapy, which she had adapted to very quickly, thanks to the thoughtful support of each member of the group sharing their own styles of humor and drama. She had Haran with his sophisticated wit, Relissa and her quirky temper, Sulíma and her overly coquettish manners, and Túfula with her tendencies towards dry humor. The young Suuden'kai lieutenant sampled them all and chose among them her own style. But even though she enjoyed her time with friends, she found herself occasionally reflecting on her home and early life.

"You know, Suli," she ponders. "I sometimes find myself thinking about what you said that one time when I first came in here."

"What was that?" she replies. "Was it that part of me behaving badly, as Kali calls it?"

"Well, yes, but I think you have justifiable right. You mentioned losing your family."

"Oh, that. Yes, but please don't take any more offence at it. It hurts, but it's a hurt I had to get over a long time ago."

"Maybe so, but it reminds me a little of mine."

"Why? Did you lose someone?"

"Not the same as you did. I have my mother and father in the city, and some grandparents who live elsewhere...and then great grandparents, and well, you know...it goes from there with all the rest."

"Sounds like a good full family. So, what's the problem?"

"Well, the chips would be a good place to start."

"Oh, right. So, as a family, how do you get along without emotions?"

"The relationship is a cool one, you can be sure of that. You can't feel any true love due to the chips. I did when I was little, but it cut out as soon as I got mine. I don't see people talk about it or try to display anything..." she sighs. "But then, I don't get out much, I guess."

"You said you don't have a boyfriend, right?"

"Yeah. I was hoping one day it would happen, but then I got wrapped up in my career. After working in C.P. Security a while, I decided I wanted to get more involved with a hands-on career, where you actually go out there and get physical with it, rather than my original idea of a straight legal practice, which is much more of a desk job. I got a taste of military security along the way, as part of my training, acting as a helmsman for some of our sector patrols, and it felt more…vigorous, as if my actions held more of a quantitative purpose. I guess I was itching to get out there and do something useful…as His Lordship said once, more tangible."

"Nothing wrong with that," she smiles. "You should've seen me on Ruuki uy'Daan. We couldn't go out because of the orcs, but I was iron-horn determined to get this one machine working in our mining camp. It was a materials processor we used sometimes to recycle some of the old scrap, at least until it started breaking down."

"Oops, and I'll bet you had a hard time trying to fix it without a proper industry to provide the parts for you."

"That's right."

"Well, I had my chance at what I thought to be a possible opportunity at doing something useful when this special project came up at Central. They were looking for recruits to take on a secret mission, which happened to be that mining base. It was classified, so applying for it, and even just to inquire about it, placed you under a high security restriction. Fortunately, I held a good security rating due to my work at C.P. Security, and my local Captain recommended me for it. It didn't seem very extravagant, but at the same time it involved working away from home and travelling to new places. And with the Marshal's name attached, it felt like the time had come for us to push forward."

"Oh great, but pushing forward, in this case, really isn't the sort of thing you want to be a part of."

"Not with what I know of it now. But at the time, we all believed the stories about this Great Cause we were supposed to be following. This base was only a small piece of it, but it was described as an integral part of our service to Sargeras, so I applied. But as I reflect on it now, I'm asking myself if it was so much because I wanted to serve, or was I simply trying to escape from something back home."

"Like what? You didn't like where you lived?"

"Um, well, I was living in an apartment before this. Not that it was a bad place to live, but I'm not so sure I would want to go back there now. Not after spending time here with all of you. I like it here…the people, the atmosphere…the clean air," she looks up at the clear sky.

"Aw, that's very sweet, Ayene. I'm sure we're all happy to have you, if you can forgive us that initial rough spot we had together."

"Don't worry about it, I think we've gone well past that by now."

"So," Túfula wonders. "What is it you're trying to escape from, if not your apartment, or the polluted air?"

Ayene sighs heavily as she tries to reconcile her feelings, which at this point held a number of deep implications.

"I always wanted to show myself to be worth something to someone. Maybe it's a hidden insecurity from my childhood. I had a hard time growing up at home."

"How come? You didn't get along well with your parents?"

"Túfu, getting along is a subjective term here. I would like to think my mother has feelings for me, though many times I've questioned this, and my father also tends to behave rather distantly at times."

"How do you mean distantly? Like as if he doesn't care for you?"

"They both seem to behave like this. It's been this way for a long time, and I don't know why. I tried on many occasions to justify it with the Suppressor chip affecting their attitudes. But when I spoke of this with a few others I knew during my life, they gave me some very different stories of their own experiences. This just left me feeling lonely and sometimes dejected, even with the chip installed."

"That sounds bad, especially when you consider the chip. Do you ever visit them?"

"I've made a lot of routine visits since my graduation and joining the Service, but the reception always seemed flat. We share some basic conversation, and then I leave. It was less like a homecoming and more like a status update. Like saying: Hi Mom, Hi Dad, I'm still alive, so I'll be going now."

"That doesn't sound very nice at all. Was it always like this, even as a little girl? Surely, they must've felt something for you when you were young, didn't they?"

"Once again, we have to remember these chips. As for when I was a little girl..." she pauses. "I'm not really sure, that was a long time ago. A lot of things are fuzzy now. I recall doing things, going places, so maybe it was better. Once I got that chip, however..."

"Those chips seem to be a big stumbling point here," Petrith observes. "They're interfering with your personal feelings, family relations, love interests...how do you even function like this?"

"Different people cope with it each in their own way. Maybe mine just took a bad turn somewhere. I once had this imaginary friend named Tuka. I think this was probably my outlet. This was before my chip, but afterwards she was gone, so I guess the chip negated my need for her anymore."

"An imaginary friend?" Sulíma inquires. "What was she like?"

"It was based on an old AI doll I used to have. Then I guess my imagination took over to exaggerate on things. I would see her in my bed, just lying there, she didn't do much else," she shrugs. "I remember sitting with her and imagining we were telling stories together. I'm sure I was just dreaming...you know, some kind of daytime fantasy in the privacy of my room."

"Sounds just like a girl," Petrith smirks.

"Oh!" Sulíma snaps. "And you boys don't have any fantasies?"

"Suli," Túfula cautions. "His needs soap before it becomes interesting."

"Oh, right! I forgot..." she giggles.

"I swear," Petrith shakes his head. "No, mine involved huge alien robots tearing up the city."

They all shared a laugh at the thought.

"I was talking to Kaliya about this," Ayene continues. "She was suggesting this doll might be something like a crutch until we get our chips. That's a little depressing."

"A doll," Sulíma muses. "But this is as a young child. Is this to say, once you get your chips, you don't play with dolls anymore?"

"Not necessarily. As children, we have all sorts of toys. Even as we get older, we still like to enjoy some kind of entertainment, even though the emotion of joy is absent. This might involve toys as well as vid-com entertainment, like cartoons."

"So, life still goes on, generally speaking," Túfula considers.

"Yeah. Tuka was my favorite doll from about three to four decades, which is where I got my chip. The brand name was Little Sister Tuka. She was a popular model with a built-in AI to simulate natural behavior for conversation and other things."

"Sounds cute, actually. Just like any normal society making up toys for their kids."

"Yeah," Sulíma relents. "With the exception of this society stealing away half their mind once they're no longer allowed to feel anything from it."

"Maybe..." Ayene concedes. "The part about the Suppressor chip affecting emotion is said to be coincidental, although I have to wonder about that. To my knowledge, we haven't seen any more incidents of the Tav'ageen Anomaly, or at least there's no word of it on the newswires, so it does seem to counter that. If the two centers are so close together, it may be unavoidable."

"I don't know. It seems a little too convenient for my taste."

"To your knowledge and not on the newswires," Túfula muses. "Didn't you once say those newswires are controlled by Darumon? Would he WANT anyone to know, even if it was discovered again?"

"That's a very good question!" Ayene affirms. "So, this could be an indication why we don't hear anything. It makes me want to walk into that news office and start interrogating them for their publication practices."

"If he has people inside there censoring the news, maybe you should go in and haul them into a prison cell. That would be a much better application of law enforcement and security than anything else you were doing."

"That's not a bad idea. But anyway, after I got that chip, it spoiled my time with my imaginary friend, and since she was an extension of the Tuka doll, that came to a close as well. Convenient or otherwise, it does seem to carry its effect. I think this is about where I started having my issues with my parents, also."

"One of these days, Ayene," Túfula suggests. "You'll need to go back there and correct this. Now that we know about these chips and everything else Darumon did, you need to heal these old wounds."

"I suppose you're right. This might change a few things. And if any of that is a contributing factor, it could make a big difference. But it's a little difficult for me to do this right now being stuck here on this world."

"This actually brings up a good point," Petrith considers. "With things as they are now, you might not be visiting home for quite some time. How do you think they might react to you suddenly disappearing from their scanners? That ought to invoke some kind of reaction, I should think."

"My visits were restricted when I took that assignment. I was mostly limited to vid-mail. But I suppose you're right. Now that I'm over here, there will be no more of that. And since my earlier visits often felt so empty, I began to restrict myself to long occasions, excusing myself as being too deeply involved in sensitive work to get time away from it."

"Now you're just trying to avoid things completely," Túfula admits.

"I don't know, Túfu. Maybe I was looking for excuses from being reminded of all the old memories. My Mom and I have already had too many arguments about this in the past, and I really don't need any more. But I'll tell you what. Once I get my horns turned around with all this, I'll give it another try. Maybe this new knowledge will make a difference. But I don't expect it anytime soon, and things might get worse before they get better. We still have that base, and in order for the Marshal to lose interest in it, he has to lose all of us along the way."

"Uh oh…what do you mean?"

"Well, think about it. We committed treason by turning ourselves over to the enemy. Now, Central might not know who the real enemy is, but they're still of the opinion the Marshal is our friend, therefore…"

"Right, I get it. Now you're working for us, and essentially against him."

"And the Marshal's going to lose that base," Petrith adds, "along with the planet, as part of Kali's Master Plan. So, this naturally means the base crew, as I doubt any of them would be returning home after this."

"But how would this affect your family?" Túfula wonders. "And the families of all the others? Can't you send some kind of note to break it to them gently?"

"Our vid-mail goes through Central," Ayene admits. "And it's sometimes monitored for security reasons. So, I doubt I could send anything to warn them about it. I'll just have to repair the damage later…somehow."

"Dammit," Sulíma scorns. "This just complicates matters! In the process of getting that monster off our tails, we're ruining lives."

"Suli, there's not much we can do about it right now. Right or wrong, good or bad, like it or not, we're stuck with it until we can finish our work."

"All right, Ayene. This just grinds on me now for all the compromises we have to make."

"I know, but we're not the only ones. You want to talk about ruining lives, what about all those worlds we blasted. What about all those dwarves we pulled out with that drug? My problems are small compared to that."

"Aye, now there's one for you," Relissa pipes up. "We were wondering where you found those wacky mushrooms you were feeding the dwarves. I remember the reports we got from that mine up north of Rolsklinde. Where did you get those things, anyway?"

"Yes, good, let's change the subject," Ayene affirms. "We found those as part of our surveys after first discovering that new universe the Marshal brought us into. According to the reports I read once, we sent out a series of expeditions to investigate the local star clusters for anything interesting. I'm assuming this was part of his study to find his minerals. Along the way, we apparently found a number of worlds with primitive forms of life, like that fungus."

"What was the world called?" Túfula asks. "Did you give it an actual name, or just a discovery code?"

"It was a rocky moon around a gas giant in a star system we named Lyeenka. The star, in this case, was a red dwarf, which is cooler and longer-lived than most others. The planet was barely within the habitation zone on the outer edge, but as a gas giant, it's not going to be a good candidate for holding life."

"Right, but if I'm not mistaken, a rocky moon, especially if it has water on it, and if in a position to allow the right temperatures, could possibly work."

"Very good, you remembered your lessons. It also helps if it has a strong magnetic field, or in this case, can borrow one from its parent. This would protect the local atmosphere from being blown away by the solar wind. It was just warm enough for liquid water, and it apparently had a substandard atmosphere on it, which was high in methane due to a lot of organic matter."

"Jiggers," Relissa whimpers. "I wonder if I'll ever live long enough to understand any part of that."

"It's alright, Relissa. This usually comes from studying astronomy for a long time, but if you didn't spend as much time doing it, well…"

"Aye, I get it. Maybe we'll have time for it one day. I'm still young, and now that we have a few things turning the right way for us, I might see a wee bit. But you know, this sounds like what they found with that farm in the mine."

"Yes, the farming chamber is designed to simulate this environment artificially. I'm not entirely sure who did the research for it, but we got the results shortly after we set up our base and began the mining exploits both to our south and on Therinë. We would then borrow the drug from the local mine near us to deliver into that feast Ytani hosted on occasion."

"Ayene," Sulíma muses. "How do you feel about giving drugs to people? I mean, you did this for what, four centuries?"

"Suli, please don't ask me that. I think we all felt guilty for what we did, but it was being justified that they were hostile to our efforts at procuring the metal, and apparently sympathetic to these insurgents."

"And since Darumon wanted his metal," Petrith offers. "Everything else becomes moot, especially if he can rob you of your emotions, and worse, put you on active with that other chip, if you still hold any objections to it."

✦ ✦✦◆✦✦ ✦

"Chief Tech, I think we finally made a breakthrough on the jump drive addressing feature."

"It's about time. Trying to scan those runes of theirs to figure out how the data is stored was no easy gambit. What do you have?"

Chief Technician Lapäli and her team were still hard at work in the BRC facility. Slowly, piece by piece, small parts of it were coming together.

"As for those runes," the technician notes. "It's not digital data. At least, not in any form we might ordinarily use for our own nav systems, like in the Naarg uy'Sodrad."

"Are we speaking of analog, then? As I recall, the way they described it, it's like recording a mental perceptive image."

"Yes. Essentially, I think this is correct, but likely in a format we can't easily identify with our equipment. But we think we found an alternative, and it involves those mini conveyors."

"Ah! Are we borrowing something from Darumon, on this occasion?"

"Why not? We took those things for analysis, so we'll just borrow his algorithms. The Professor assisted in the study, and we think we can simulate this as an object definition interpolated by a heuristic AI."

"Very interesting, but how do we do this?"

"Our first objective will be to design the AI. Those conveyors used a fixed target, but ours has to be dynamic. Therefore, it needs to be able to interpret the local environs through scans and what the Professor calls a Knowing algorithm. He'll work on that using some of his native technology, which is derived from something that looks like an iconic circuit board he showed me once. They apparently used something like this for Kaliya's rune marking apparatus."

"Yes, I recall her showing this to me. It uses some kind of conceptual icons to simulate certain parameters in a sequential language chain, and this creates some manner of nether-wild interaction that caused me to simply pull my horns out," she chuckles.

"Well, you're not alone, Chief!" he smiles. "Then, once we have this, the data can be stored into a nav system and recalled as necessary for return visits to that same location."

"What about dynamic addressing, as to jump to a calculated location like we did in the ship?"

"One thing at a time, Chief," the technician grins. "If we can get this part working, that's an important move forward. The algorithm can probably be expanded with more functionality later. But one thing I like about this idea is you only need to log a jump point one time, using any ship you happen to be flying. The data can then be shared with an entire fleet, if necessary, all to return to that same point."

"Good, but it would be nicer if that fleet didn't all jump into the same point at the same time, instead allowing a little room for each ship."

"Well, yes," he laughs. "But like I said, one thing at a time. The Professor already mentioned this, and associated it with their ability to link multiple gryphons into a flight group for their transport spheres. If we can do something like that, it might help."

"I like it, at least in theory. Try to get a prototype working. I want to see this in action. But let's hope we don't lose anyone inside nether-space along the way."

Ayene was returning to the office from her afternoon visit at the guildhall. She was checking in briefly before making a routine inspection of the factory workers downtown, to ensure all was proceeding smoothly. She made this tour on a regular basis, as it was part of her work assignment for civil management.

"Sir, I'm just on my way out. Did we have any calls while I was on my break?"

"No, all is quiet today," he responds. "You seem to be enjoying your rest periods lately. Is it allowing you any new insights with your therapy?"

"On occasion, I see different sides of it. Sometimes we laugh, sometimes we cry. It's not all about the good side, there is also the bad, and we need to understand all of it. Today, I reflected a little on my family."

"Did you come to any conclusions?"

"Nothing special, it was mostly just calling up old memories. We spoke about my childhood. I explained a few things about life back home. But I doubt I'll ever understand what happened there. Now, it's just circling around in my thoughts again."

"Well, try not to let it bother you. They're on Azgarén, just like all the rest, and subjects of the Suppressor chips and everything else the Marshal did to us. There's not much we can do about it right now."

"Yes, I know. I just wish I could answer one question… Did they love me?"

She turns and heads out the door to make her rounds. She borrows a utility hover-shuttle parked outside and drives toward the industrial district, visiting several workshops along the way where she found both Suuden'kai and Daanen'kai workers employed, along with a new crew of people being trained from Tae'Eladar. She stops briefly at the medical ward, which had been refurbished and made operational again for clinical service to the local residents.

She continued along the road on a tour of the local shops. It was a segment of industry put to work to aid in the restoration of the city, providing tools and materials for repair and new construction.

When she was finished, she returned to the office to report in before closing up for the day and returning home.

Ayene had taken up residence in one of the neighborhoods on the west side of town, where Sulíma and her friends, along with Captain Lapäli, once began their restoration of the old homes during their recapture of the city. Now it was home to the displaced Suuden-Aryku from the mining base on Morndindor.

She enters her home and finds her way into the kitchen, where she prepares a simple meal and sits down for a light dinner. She was feeling depressed, still thinking of her conversation with Sulíma and the others about her old family life. The house seemed especially quiet on this occasion. She felt alone in this big space. During her time in the mining base, she at least had the fellowship of the base crew in communal living, even though she had her private officer's quarters to retire for rest.

The city was still mostly under renovation, and there was talk of building taverns, marketplaces, entertainment venues, and other such attractions to offer diversion from her personal worries, but much of this work would take time. She didn't feel a desire to travel to Tae'Eladar again, or even to Therinë. Instead, she felt worn from the day's activities and wanted to retire to bed early. And so, she finished her meal and cleaned up.

After attending to her chores, she went to the bedroom, where she disrobed and took a quick shower in an adjacent bathroom, and then donned a nightgown. She stood in front of the mirror, examining herself. It was a habit she had developed recently, trying to imagine herself without the seed entity. Her body was deformed from the parasitic lifeform permeating her tissues, mostly around the midsection, as it interacted with her internal organs, but also into the neck as a few tendrils reached into the base of the cranium.

"One of these days, you little creep," she muses silently. "And not just on my behalf, but for so many others…"

She returned to the bedroom, but now she felt restless. She was weary, but also uptight about the day's conversation and the memories it invoked.

"Mother, why did you always seem so distant?" she mumbles softly. "Every time I made a visit, you appeared as if distracted by something unnatural. Is there something wrong with me that you just don't like?"

The absence of the Suppressor chip allowed her feelings to carry the old memories with renewed vitality. She walked across to a vanity table in a corner of the room and sat in a chair facing another mirror. There she stared at herself, not so much at the seed entity this time, but simply her reflection in general. The room was silent, but she could hear the echoes of her life ringing out in her ears. Monotone voices, distant words, discussions, debates, until one series began to emerge above the rest. It was a memory of a conversation she overheard once by her mother and father.

She was young at the time, a first-year student at the university, but living at home. She was in her room reading a book. The door was slightly ajar, allowing her to hear noises from other parts of the house. In the family room, her parents were in discussion about having a second child.

"I do not want another," her mother declares. "I am concerned of seeing that condition appear again."

"But Lenya, the med-techs say the situation is easily controlled, and this condition is supposed to be extremely rare. In fact, they tell me there have been no new incidents reported ever since the development of the corrective procedure."

"No new incidents reported...then what was it I saw in there? Do they simply not report it for the sake of keeping it quiet? This... thing...whatever you might call it that forces us to take these steps, is still as virulent as ever. You did not see it, and I cannot get it out of my head. I do not feel comfortable to bring another child into the world if this thing is so near to us."

"Very well, Lenya. But you must still try to resolve this anxiety of yours for Ayene's sake. She needs our support to finish her development."

"All right, Yulin, I will try. I just hope that thing is truly removed from us."

Ayene had not heard these words echo in her mind for a long time. Originally, they were meaningless to her, as her mind was focused on her studies, not her home life. But the words seemed to carry a new meaning now. Something happened.

"Mother, what did you see?" she wonders tenderly. "What thing? Was I sick or something? But I feel fine now, so why do you behave like this?"

She continued sitting in the chair, allowing her mind to drift, and hoping to find some clue within her childhood memories of the occasion, but nothing came forward. It seemed like an isolated incident with no further repercussions. Finally, she pulled herself out of her thoughts to realize it was getting late and she needed to find some sleep. She stepped across to the bed and laid herself down hoping to relax, but her mind simply drifted back to her childhood again.

"Anxiety?" she considers. "Even with the chip? Whatever it was, either it was serious, or you must be very tender on the subject."

She was rolling from one side of the bed to the other, trying to find comfort and force herself to relax so she could sleep, but the memories kept nagging at her as new thoughts began to surface.

There was an occasion when she recalled waking up for breakfast one morning. Her mother fixed a simple meal and served it only at arm's length from across the table. Ayene shook her head, trying to dislodge the thought and again search for sleep.

Another recollection came to mind of her returning from school. She was sitting in the living room watching the vid-com while her mother seemed to eye her from the side. Ayene felt as if she was being studied.

"No, it was just my imagination. She was busy with…something. I'm sure."

She recalled feeling the hair on her neck rising. Even though, at this time, she had her chip installed, she could still feel eyes burning into her from behind a corner.

"Ayene, clear your mind!" she commands. "Let's try some of that meditation again. You need sleep!"

Hours passed, and she simply rolled across the bed, turning one way trying to find relaxation, only to turn the other way and try again. The night crept forward. From time to time she peered over her pillow at the clock on her nightstand. It was midnight… It was after midnight… It was early morning, and still she had not dozed off.

"This is ridiculous!" she mutters angrily. "Ayene, you need sleep, or else you won't be able to function well tomorrow. Let's try that meditation again, just like Kaliya was describing. You need to clear your mind, release your body, and drift away. That's how we go to sleep. And stop talking to yourself. You're starting to behave as you did when you were little again."

She fluffs the pillow and throws herself back onto it, bringing up the covers neatly. She lies on her back staring at the ceiling, taking deep breaths, trying to focus on something other than her thoughts, directing herself to another point in space, and then closes her eyes once more. She struggles to release her anxiety, but stress and curiosity itch her to check the time again. She rolls onto her side to peer over the pillow. It's getting close to the time when she would need to start the day, only another couple of hours.

"You've managed to waste the whole night," she decrees. "Oh well, I guess it won't kill you. And you're still talking to yourself."

With only the wee hours remaining, she settles herself to simply wait it out. She tries now to fill her head with other thoughts, first the stories that Sulíma and her friends told, then Kaliya's tale of her youth and her own discovery. She recalled when Kaliya created that chair in the ritual testing chamber. It felt soft, but even though Ayene was under the effects of the incense at the time, she couldn't find her center to transcend out of her body for some reason. She wanted to, but something held her back.

"Inhibitions, probably," she mumbles. "And being too… mechanical, I suppose."

She closes her eyes again and reflects upon Kaliya's soothing voice.

"The way we teach it," the echoes murmur in her thoughts, "is you relax your mind and your body, then piece-by-piece, try to send each part of your body away from you, leaving only your mind..."

She repositions herself, rolling onto her back again and taking another deep sigh. She first directs her thoughts to her legs, starting from the bottom up. She imagines her hoofed feet dropping into nether-space, then her elongated ankles, her calves and finally her thighs. The hardest part for her was to restrict her analytical mind from rationalizing those body parts to still be present and accounted for in reality. She considers her hands and arms next, up to the shoulders. She felt light-headed after a while, but rather than fight it, she simply allowed the sensation to waft over her, enjoying the relaxed euphoria of finally resting after such a hard night. Her worries were starting to drift away, and she did not care to retake them.

Her torso was next on the list, peeling away from her hips, through her abdomen, and lastly to her chest. All that remained now was her head. This would be the hardest part, but she did not demand herself to debate the issue. She delayed her next move, revisiting the apparent numbness of her body, and then imagining her head falling out from under her. And at last, she drifted to sleep.

She laid there for a while longer, wondering what to do next. She felt very relaxed by now. The weariness seemed absent. It was pleasant, but her conscious mind still seemed active, and now she was curious about the time again. She rolled back onto her side to see the clock. It was almost time to get up now. She sighed solemnly.

"All right, that's it. No point in trying anything else."

She pulls herself to a seated position on the edge of the bed. Her eyes were focused on the doorway leading into the bathroom. She stood up with her mind now in duty mode. It was a common habit for her; it was time to go to work. The night was over, and another day was dawning, so her first order of business would be a quick shower.

As she made her way to the bathroom, she pulled her nightgown off over her head and wadded it up. Then, just as she passed through the door, she tossed it at a hamper sitting along the bedroom wall. The nightgown flew out of her hand and mysteriously vanished.

But she didn't see it, as her attention was on her reflection in the mirror again.

She stared at herself for a moment. Her image was the same familiar shape she had seen so many times before. Nothing had changed. She turned on the water in the shower and stepped inside. But the water didn't seem normal to her this time. It didn't feel hot, like it should. She tried adjusting the valves, but it didn't help.

"Great, something's wrong with the plumbing today. I'll need to check on that."

She continues running the water, then takes the soap bottle and squeezes a little into her hand, and finally lathers up and rinses off again. But even though her military mind is running at full throttle; a tiny sense feels as though there is something not quite right this time.

When she finishes, she turns off the water, steps out of the shower and grabs a nearby towel from a rack. She ritualistically dries herself off, even though she didn't feel especially wet, and wraps the towel around her head as she moves back in front of the mirror for a quick inspection.

Her obsession with her disfigurement draws her attention to follow her image as she now turns to leave, this time to study the seed entity at the point where it was first implanted on her back. She gazes at it over her shoulder while creeping forward through the door.

"That's where it all started," she muses privately. "I was asleep for it, but when I woke up, there it was."

She drifts out of the bathroom while still studying the mirror, reaching out a hand to find her way, then curling around the corner into the bedroom to approach her vanity table and a dresser.

The vanity table had its own mirror, and naturally this became the newest attraction to draw her attention. She begins pulling out a set of clothes for the day's work, first with the undergarments, then her pants and a shirt, and finally a vest. As she applies each item, that small spark in the back of her mind is now suggesting how something is not quite normal to the sensation of getting dressed today. But she simply shrugs it off. After all, these are the same clothes she's been wearing for years. What could possibly be wrong?

"You're probably going to have problems all day if you keep up like this. Let's just get through it. Maybe tonight you can get some real sleep."

When she is finished getting dressed, she pulls the towel off her head and lays it over the back of the chair, then grabs a brush from the table and neatly grooms herself. Afterwards, she studied her presentation. At this point, it was more about her professional appearance, not her deformity from the seed.

When she was ready, she stepped back for a final review, first from the front, and then turned to the side. Everything looked neat and orderly. And so, feeling satisfied that she was ready for the day, she casually exits the room, bypassing the bed located in the opposite corner behind her, and therefore completely oblivious of something still lying beneath the covers.

She proceeds out to the kitchen, but she doesn't feel at all hungry. She opens the refrigerator to examine her inventory, but nothing comes to mind that appeals to her. She realizes she must try to eat something, and so she takes out a bottle of juice and opens a cupboard to fetch a glass. She pours a little into the glass, and then brings it to her lips. But as she takes a sip, she halts suddenly, spitting it back into the cup.

"Agh! That's not right. It's tasteless! It must've spoiled or something."

She examines the cup, and then the bottle, and sets them both on the counter, then reaches for a piece of fruit in a nearby bowl. She pulls out a knife from a drawer and cuts off a slice. The fruit appeared juicy and ripe, but as she brought it up to take a bite, the sensation was awkwardly unexpected, causing her to spit it back into her hand.

"What is wrong here?" she gripes. "Am I going crazy, or is this thing on my back making trouble for me. Maybe it's getting back at me for my comment last night. Wouldn't that be unfortunate," she huffs.

Now frustrated, she sets the fruit down on the counter next to the cup, and puts her hands on her hips to study the situation, finally to shake her head.

"Well, I'm not hungry anyway. I'll just go, and maybe get something to eat later."

She turns and leaves the kitchen, passing through the house and out the front door, then strolls down the road to her office.

On her arrival, she reports to the Commander and sits down at her desk. She examines her data terminal with a list of inquiries posted to her inbox. She opens one up to see a report from one of the workshops sending a requisitions order. This would be her routine for the morning, processing these orders and coordinating the work crews.

The day progressed, and Ayene was deeply involved in her work. She did not feel at all hungry during the day, so she skipped lunch. Officers and staff members came and went, and she took each one in turn, writing reports and filing them on the computer. It was a job she was very familiar with, especially after her time at the mining base. But this one held a more symbolic meaning to it, as the city was slowly brought back to life, even though it was more like building a ghost town for the low population count.

Along the way, she would occasionally reflect on what Kaliya said about her new military unit. She considered the prospect of holding a role in it. Adalon apparently predicted someone like her, but it seemed surreal to have someone directing your actions from something as mystical as a prophecy. During the lulls in her work, she allowed herself to envision returning home as part of this new military body, the Stormhooves. The name alone held its own romance and prestige, but according to Kaliya, this incarnation would be unique.

Her work shift ended in the early afternoon. She usually took this time to visit Tae'Eladar, but today she wasn't sure if she felt right for it. She still felt uneasy, suspecting it was due to her bad night and a sense of something misplaced. So, she decided to go home and rest, maybe to try again to eat something, or to find some other distraction to get her mind back in order.

As she arrives back home, she enters the living room again,

and then the kitchen, where she sees the glass of juice and the fruit still sitting on the counter. She considered trying to eat again, but strangely she still didn't feel at all hungry.

"What is wrong with me today?" she moans. "I hope I'm not getting sick."

She sighs and returns back to the living room.

The house was very sparsely furnished. A home decorator, she was not. Her military career didn't afford her much of a home life, neither did she develop much desire as a young Suuden'kai with no emotional content to find pleasure in collecting memorabilia. This, of course, was aside from the fact that she was currently a refugee in a foreign habitat. She decided to sit down in a leisure chair, one of the few items she had available to decorate the room, and here she ponders for a moment.

"I should probably try going to bed early today. I didn't sleep at all last night, which could be why I'm having so much trouble now."

She looks around the room for something to do. She did not have a vid-com unit in the house, not that it mattered as there were no entertainment programs to watch in this city. She then looked outside through a window, and eventually stood up and walked over to it. She peers out into the yard, which was overgrown with weeds and tangled vines.

"I wonder if I could find some tools and see if I can do something about that. Maybe I could take up gardening. That would be a nice hobby."

She reflected on the neatly manicured gardens, shrubs, and trees found all around Bya'an Tamoranth on Tae'Eladar. The scene was so lovely and peaceful, and it often smelled so refreshing. She opened the window to let some air in, sniffing it to see if she could experience the same here in any way. Nothing... There was no scent to tingle her nose. She was disappointed, hoping to at least feel some pleasure from the fresh air. The air in this world was clean, very clean as compared to Azgarén. On other occasions, she had noticed how nice it was to breathe deeply the crisp breezes, often tinged by the salt from the nearby seashore. It was exhilarating. Why couldn't she have at least this much today? Nothing was working for her. She was now becoming even more concerned about her health.

She closed the window and turned back into the room. Her mind rumbled with conflicting thoughts and feelings, made worse by the strange experiences of the day and the lack of sleep the previous night. And still, she did not feel hungry, or tired for that matter. But regardless of this, she decided to go lay down.

She strolled along the hall and into the bedroom. As she passed through the door, her mind automatically turned towards the vanity mirror again, passing the bed along the way and approaching the table. But just as she was making her advance on her reflection, something caught her attention out of the corner of her eye. It was on the bed. She reflexively jerked her head around for a better look, and she instantly froze.

On the bed, lying serenely under the covers, and apparently asleep, was a body. It looked remarkably like her reflection. Her mind went blank, her mouth fell open, and the scene suddenly felt surreal, as if she had entered a bizarre delusion.

She held her position for another moment before cautiously moving forward for a better look. She tenuously approached the side of the bed, keeping her eyes locked on the impossible shape resting under the covers, until she finally halted while standing over the figure. She could conjure up only one thought.

"Tuka..." she mumbles quietly.

She stood there for a long moment, trying desperately to justify what she thought she perceived laying silently before her. It had to be a dream.

"Tuka?" she whispers disbelievingly. "What are you doing here? I haven't seen you for so long."

She continues to study the form of the young woman in the bed. She hadn't seen this image since childhood. But this image was different.

"Tuka, how did you get here?" she asks in childlike tones. "And look at you... You're all grown up now. But they got to you too, didn't they."

The body in the bed was silent and still.

"How are Mother and Father? Are they still angry with me? Did they send you here to take me home again?"

Ayene began feeling a gush of emotion welling up inside her. She did not even know how to interpret it, but she knew it was the sense of loss she always felt, or wish she felt after having the chip installed.

"It's been so long since we talked. I missed you. You were the only one who would listen to me. Mother just turned away after a while. But why are you here if she didn't send you? Maybe Father sent you? He always seemed a little more concerned."

The body did not alter its condition, nor did it respond to her dialog.

"Yeah, I know, but still, I can't go home now. I don't think I'll be able to go home for a long time."

She continues staring at the body, as if hearing an imaginary voice ushering out of it.

"Why? Because of a lot of bad things that are happening there! And if I go home now, they'll try taking me back again, and people will get angry, and they'll ask all sorts of questions, and a lot of other things."

The room remains still for the activity on the bed. Ayene continues hovering next to it.

"It's all because of HIM, you know? He told us a lot of lies…"

She halts as if to listen to a rebuttal.

"What kind? Everything!" she shouts. "Those insurgents, the chips, the seeds, all his promises…in all the nether-space, Tuka!" she waves her hands. "If I could tell you all the things I've learned after we left the mining base…"

She abruptly halts again, this time catching herself as if barely realizing what she was saying. She frowns and rolls her eyes around the room trying to judge her surroundings.

"The mining base…" she mumbles softly. "But wait a minute… Tuka, how did you actually get here? Why were you gone so long, and where did you go?"

She quickly turns around to locate the vanity mirror again. She jumps in front of it to examine herself, then turns back towards the bed, taking an awkward step forward.

"What is going on here?" she muses quietly in thought. "What am I looking at?" she hesitates as she stares at the bed. "I know you!" she points affirmatively at the body. "But where did you come from? Not from Azgarén!"

Her mind was now turning over hard on itself. Her logical analysis was starting to churn. She was no longer a child, and this imaginary playmate should not be real. She needed to investigate her day's affairs. If this was a dream, what was she doing all day? Or was she doing anything at all? She stormed out of the room and out of the house.

She walked briskly at first, then started to trot. Her mind was burning for an answer. She wanted to revisit the office. Her trot turned into a run as she set her sights on an intersection a couple of blocks ahead where she needed to turn down the main avenue to the management building. Anxiety was kicking in as she urged her body to move faster, driving herself to reach that endpoint with such determination as if she could simply fly to it. Finally, this rising anticipation climaxed, and the world turned to a blur.

Ayene's form suddenly streaked across the roadway in a wispy vapor, landing neatly on the corner of the intersection, precisely where she wanted to make her turn. She yelped and stumbled out, there to pause rigidly as she examined her new surroundings, then cautiously to glance over her shoulder to see where she had just come from.

"All right, that wasn't normal," she whispers gingerly. "And it probably goes without saying, there is something wrong here. And I think that tells it all. Either you're going crazy, or this is a dream."

She timidly turns to continue her course, walking slowly until she gains her confidence again, eventually arriving in front of the building. She pulls open the door and enters inside.

Several staff members were still at their desks in the lobby as Ayene ambled through to a hallway where she finds the large management office she shares with the Commander. He quickly takes notice of her as she enters the room.

"Lieutenant, I thought you were finished for the day."

She pauses inside the door, gazing carefully around the room.

"Sorry Sir, I'm having…some difficulty…or something."

"What's wrong?"

"I was doing reports today, wasn't I?"

"Excuse me?"

"What I mean to say is," she stutters. "Yes, I was doing reports and, um, I need to check on something."

"Is there a problem?"

"I'm not sure yet, let me check my terminal to see where I left off."

She proceeds to her desk and sits down, activating her terminal and selecting several icons on the touch screen to pull up her day's work.

After reviewing several pages of requisition forms, work orders, and status reports, she is convinced the day's work, as far as she could understand it, was done according to her previous recollections. She gets up from the desk and walks slowly into the room. The Commander studies her motions.

"Ayene, are you alright? You seem disturbed about something."

"Lajivi, I'm not sure what it is. I didn't get any sleep last night, and this day has been proceeding very strangely for me."

"In what way?"

"I'm sure it's just because I'm tired, although I don't actually feel tired," she titters. "Nor do I feel hungry…all day so far. I tried eating something this morning, but it didn't taste right. It didn't have any taste at all, in fact."

"What was it you were trying to eat?"

"Just a glass of juice and a piece of fruit, nothing unusual. At least, I don't think it was unusual. In fact, it's still sitting there on my kitchen counter," she chuckles nervously.

"Ayene…" he begins.

"But it's alright. I'm not really hungry anyway. Maybe Tuka will eat it later when she wakes up."

"What? Who is Tuka?"

"Tuka? Oh, she's a friend."

"I see. Maybe you should go lie down and try to rest. If you didn't get any sleep last night…"

"Yeah, I tried, but she's taking up the whole bed. I suppose I could try pushing her out of the way, but she looks so peaceful, and it's been so long since I last saw her. I don't want her to go away again."

"Huh? What are you talking about? Who is this Tuka?"

"Oh!" she begins giggling mindlessly. "Yeah, that's right. Never mind, Commander, I'm tired, it must be. I thought I came to work this morning, but I must be asleep instead," she continues laughing. "After all, Tuka's not real. She's just an imaginary playmate I used to have as a child!"

She turns and stumbles out of the room, meandering through the building while cackling insanely at the absurdity of her actions, believing herself to be losing her mind. She exits back out onto the sidewalk again, then turns towards the corner. When she reaches the intersection, she glances up the road in the direction of her house. She pauses, and the laughter stops.

She studies the line of buildings and homes, then glances briskly at the management building before returning to the road again towards her house. She breaks into a sprint, this time trying not to have another accident like she did before, keeping herself to a methodical gait until she reached her front door. She halted momentarily, hesitating to reach for the doorknob before carefully opening the door and entering.

"Tuka? It's me again," she calls gently into the house. "I'm home. Don't be afraid, I'm just a little tired and would like to lie down. Do you mind?"

Ayene cautiously enters the house and moves along the hallway to her bedroom. She half-expected to find it empty, but also hoped she would still see her friend lying there. She peeked into the bedroom. The bed was still occupied.

"Tuka…" she mumbles distantly.

She enters fully into the room and carefully walks over to the bed, standing alongside it as she did before. The dream didn't seem so dreamlike this time. She studied the body carefully.

"You're wearing my nightgown…"

She quickly glanced over her shoulder to find the hamper she used to discard her gown. She steps up to it and starts digging around inside to find the used garment she tossed into it earlier in the day. It was absent.

"Did you steal my nightgown?" she demands. "But if it's not here, and you're just imaginary, and you're still in my bed…"

She glances down at her body and the clothes she put on this morning.

"All right, let's see. I got up this morning, took a shower, and got dressed. Right! But where did the nightgown go? And these things," she examines her current clothes. "These came out of the dresser drawer."

She began taking off her clothes and dropping them on the floor. She watched as they piled up next to her until she was fully naked, then she studied the body on the bed again for comparison.

"But if these clothes simply pile up, and yet my nightgown is missing…or at least from where it should be…but now it's on you… and you're there…while I'm here…" her voice drifts away. "Standing… here… In the room… And you…sleeping… Oh no…"

She twisted abruptly back to examine the hamper.

"It didn't… It wasn't…" she mumbles uncertainly and turning back to the bed. "And you…and me… In all the nether-space! In all the NETHER-SPACE!!" she screams.

She jumped in front of her vanity mirror for another quick examination, then back to the bed for confirmation.

"I lost you at…what was it? Around four decades…because of that CHIP!" she shrieks.

And here, the final piece began to settle into her mind.

"You're not my imagination! You're me!"

As the realization became apparent, a massive surge of anguish came flooding forward. She screamed fiercely, such that her voice bellowed through the house, causing the windows to rattle. She raised her fists and fell to her knees, then pounded her fists into the floor with such perceived intensity, it caused the walls to shudder.

"Darumon!" her voice reverberates. "I'll rip your infernal heart out for this! I swear it!"

She now doubles over and covers her face, then begins sobbing. She wept for many long moments as she reflected on her childhood friend and playmate.

"I had it…" she moans. "It was in my hands. And HE took it away. Oh Mother, if only…"

She suddenly halted her outpouring as a new thought flashed into her mind.

"Mother…" she wheezes. "Sick? Me? Of course! Something happened. Blast it!" she scorns harshly. "She must've seen it. No wonder she pulled so far away from me. She must've thought I was contaminated or something with that STUPID alien infestation nonsense. Oh, Mother…he sent you into a panic the same as all the rest, didn't he!"

She slowly collected herself, stood up, and dimly browsed the scene, ultimately to find her vanity mirror again. She stepped in front of it one more time.

Her reflected image was that of her nude body, seed entity and all. She stood there motionless for several moments, wondering how she managed to create this. Then a new thought came to mind, and a faint surge of inspiration began to form.

"I'm projected. It was accidental, but here I am. Adalon was right. Kaliya was right. She said you normally come out in whatever is natural, and this is it for me. Right, I get it. And Tuka was me when I was a child back home."

She turned sideways to examine herself, especially the seed entity.

"You nasty little bug, your days are numbered now. I can almost taste it. What do you think, Tuka?"

She glances at the bed and smiles naughtily, but her body simply lays there.

"Oh, I know what you're thinking…it's the same as me. Don't worry, your time will come too. We'll both get a little bit. But now, what to do with it? I got this far…hmm. Tuka, what do you think… this probably happened this morning, right? I couldn't sleep all night, but then… Oh, wait, that last bit of meditation, I'll bet that did it. Wow, I actually learned how to do it. Now, if only I can remember what I did so I can do it again," she giggles ironically.

She reflects on Kaliya's teachings during their attempts at the guildhall, and finally recalling Kaliya's special caption line.

"In this space I have will, and my will can alter this space. Dammit, Kaliya, what did he make of us? We're as much half-god as Thaelyn and his people. This could be dangerous in the wrong hands. No wonder Ytani went wild with it."

She studied herself for another moment, and an idea began to form.

"I can be anything I want to be. I just have to create the image in my mind and impose it onto this shape."

She considers an example for testing.

"Any shape my mind can imagine. I imagine it, believe in it, and make it real. I am that thing, whatever I create. My will is strong, and I want to create…"

She places an image into her mind, recalling from her old memories and drawing her attention to her projected body, as if to sculpt it by her simple thoughts and desires. Slowly, her figure undulates, becoming fuzzy and indistinct. She concentrates on the outlines, bringing substance back into it. The figure reconstitutes into a new shape, and now she was looking at a new interpretation of her body…without the seed entity.

"That's more like it," she muses privately.

She turned to the side to check from behind, studying her shape and refining her vision to add better definition to it.

"Of course, the last time I saw this was a millennium ago, but I don't think I would have changed too much since then. Still, it's not a bad effort."

Her reflected image was beautiful. Her body was slim and smooth, her arms and legs were slender and well-toned, her contours were nicely feminine, and her skin was clear of the unsightly red blotching.

"This is how you might look if it were not for that horrible little parasite," she remarks to no one in particular. "Ayene, you did it."

She turns and steps back over to the bed, then leans onto the edge to gaze at her real body.

"Just you wait, girl, we'll take care of this. I'll see to it, one way or another. We'll get our seed specimens, the Med-tech will do her research, she'll find the antidote, and we'll peel this horrid piece of biotech trash off our backs and throw it right in the Marshal's face!"

She continues peering down at her body as if once again in an imaginary conversation with herself, but this time enjoying the novelty of it.

"What was that, Tuka? You think I shouldn't throw it directly in his face? Well, maybe you're right. After all, he is a near-god, so that could be dangerous. But figuratively speaking, we're going to throw a lot of things in his face soon," she grins brightly and laughs. "Meanwhile, I need to turn this in. Don't go anywhere, I might need you later."

Now Ayene feels the rush of achievement. She dashes out of the room and down the hall, bursting out the door and onto the street.

Thoughts began flowing through her mind, like her little accident where she flashed to the street corner.

"Line-of-sight... Folding your image..." she muses.

She focused on that same point on the street corner and placed a desire to arrive there. She recalled that first experience, intensely pushing herself mentally to that location while she was running, but this time she halted her motion and interpreted this thought independently. She raised her hand to zero the location with her fingers.

She pressed her mind to deliver her figure to the intended destination, and the world around her turned to a blur as she drew herself to that point. Images of the surrounding buildings zipped by as the focal point on the street corner zoomed into place. She was now standing on the corner making a quick scan of her new surroundings.

"I could get used to this," she admits contentedly.

She now dauntlessly turns and walks up to the door of the management building, once again pulling it open and boldly stepping inside the lobby. As before, several staff members were at their desks. They all jerked up to gawk at her as she confidently strode through the lobby and down the corridor. She arrived at the door to the office where she would find Commander Kriv'tik and promptly enters, then formally marching up to his desk.

"Commander, I have a report," she announces firmly.

The Commander looks up from his data terminal at the fully nude form of his second officer standing affirmatively in the middle of his office. He is stupefied and speechless.

Ayene waits for him to respond to her announcement, though curious as to why it's taking so long, or for that matter, why his eyes were bulging out of their sockets, and his mouth was hanging open. The Commander gets out of his chair for a closer inspection.

"Ayene?" he gasps. "In all the nether-space, what happened to you? Aside from the fact that you're out of uniform, where is the seed entity?"

At this time, Ayene suddenly realizes she was still in her imagined nude form from the bedroom. She quickly glances over her body and attempts to cover herself bashfully.

"Oops… Um, sorry Commander, I guess I need to pay a little closer attention to these details."

"Closer attention?!" he declares incredulously. "It takes a determined effort to remove all your clothes and parade around like that. But that's only a minor detail as compared to the seed entity. Where is it?"

"Commander, I finally understood what happened earlier…and I'm angry!" she roars.

"At ease, Lieutenant… I think you should probably report to the medical ward. From your earlier conduct and what I see here, I think we need to perform a full examination."

"Lajivi, wait! Listen to me, this isn't my real body. My body is lying in bed right now. This is a projection! I'm a Prodigy Child!"

The Commander is taken aback, not only by the suggestion, but also her strong assertiveness. He had never seen her display such passion in her behavior before. He searches for his words, but is cut off prematurely.

"And what's more," she continues sternly. "I want to kill that bastard Marshal for what he did to me!"

"Ayene, slow down, what are you talking about? Are you saying that what I'm looking at right now is a projected image, like what Ytani was doing, and what Lieutenant Nazég described?"

"Exactly, and apparently, it's not the first time. I finally understand who Tuka is…was. She wasn't an imaginary childhood friend, she was me."

"Wait, you lost me. Explain this Tuka."

She takes a quick sigh before responding, although realizing along the way that it didn't have any effect in this form.

"When I was little, and this was before I received my Suppressor chip, I had an imaginary friend. In time, I thought I was dreaming, but I would see her in my bed asleep, and would sit next to her and carry imaginary conversations with her. She was like a personal companion to share my inner thoughts with. I would tell her about my feelings and sometimes invent stories with her, since my parents were both completely without feelings of any kind."

"Due to their chips."

"Yes. I suppose you might say this was a defense mechanism as a young child in that sort of environment. I called her Tuka, as an extension of a doll I used to have called the Little Sister Tuka AI doll. Do you recall those?"

"Ah! Yes, I remember those were a popular brand once upon a time."

"Anyway, then I got my chip, and she was gone. I never saw her again."

"Then, this is to say that chip effectively disabled this skill they spoke of. Well, as unfortunate as it is, I guess we can actually call that an empirical result."

"Yes, I suppose we can. And as for that result, I want to take the one who invented it and rip him limb-from-limb."

"All right, but for now, just try to contain yourself. We're not fully ready for that yet. Now, can you explain your earlier behavior, and why you're naked and without the seed entity."

She once again peeks down at her body. She was embarrassed at the situation, but she didn't care anymore, so she shrugged and relaxed her posture.

"It's not my real body anyway, so what do I have to worry about. I should be happy about it. After all, it's a dream come true to see this again, even if it is a projection."

"Maybe so, but in my office?" he smiles cautiously.

"I'm sorry, but I guess I was so excited to accomplish this, and I don't technically feel anything in this form, not like my natural body, so it's a little hard to tell the difference. It feels a little like wearing a costume."

"All right, but do you think you should at least return home and get dressed before parading around any more like this? We have a lot of young men in this building that might stare."

"I say, let them stare! At least it's for a good reason, and I could use the attention. Besides, it's good for morale," she grins coyly and shrugs.

"Really!" he chuckles. "You know, it sounds like you're starting to take lessons from that young girl you spoke of once…Suli, right? But anyway, as for what's going on?"

"Right. Last night, I went home and had a lot of thoughts going through my mind after my meeting earlier in the day with my friends. I guess it brought back a lot of those old memories of my family and the frustration and loneliness I felt. I had something to eat and went to bed, but I couldn't sleep. I just kept rolling from one side to the other, dwelling on those old memories."

"I think you need to reconcile yourself of those memories, especially if they conflict with your other actions so much."

"I will, and I think I also came to an important conclusion during this time as I found myself like this. If my parents happened to take notice of it at any moment, well…"

"Ouch, yes, I think I get the picture. It would be like those early moments of the panic. That might explain a few things."

"Right, but anyway, this morning I tried practicing what Kaliya has been teaching me about meditation."

"She is teaching you meditation? For what purpose? Is this part of your emotional therapy?"

"Oh, um…well, yes and no. If you will recall, I went to her about these ideas we had on the invasion and a jump index."

"Yes, I recall that."

"Well, this is an extension of our research for the invasion aspect. She's never been to Azgarén, so she can't project there directly, having no personal memory of the place to recall an image from. But I'm a native, and it would also seem Adalon had another prophecy predicting someone from our base as one of these Prodigy Children. How do you like that?"

"Incredible! And so, this somehow relates to you?"

"Kaliya guessed, by my past participation in their work, that I might hold some relevance, so she took me in with some private tutoring to see if I could do it. But I was too rigid in the beginning, and this is where she suggested I join her circle of friends to loosen up a bit, as she calls it, in order to find my inner self. Well, I guess it finally worked, because here I am."

"That is truly fascinating, and it simply makes me wish I understood more of what this was. But now, what are you going to do with it?"

"Among other things, this prophecy talks about this new Prodigy Child sharing her memories with others, and this probably means Kaliya's teammates. She tells me they're all learning telepathy, so I'll be the source and they all tap into it."

"Is that safe?"

"Oh, I'm sure they'll go easy. After all, I want to be a part of their team, and this is where I might need to ask you about giving me at least a partial leave so I can start taking more time with it."

"I see. Well, I know you always aspired for something more, and if this Adalon is calling for you, who am I to refuse."

"One thing I was hoping for one of these days is to find those seed specimens for the Med-tech over there so she can start her research on the solution. I hope this to be one of my missions."

"Would this have something to do with your being naked right now?" he raises an eyebrow.

"It might," she smiles and looks away innocently. "I wanted to try this out to see how I looked."

"Uh huh…"

"It must've happened this morning," Ayene reflects. "I tried this meditation technique again, and I guess I finally went to sleep. But it didn't feel like sleep, as I thought I was still awake. So, I finally gave up, got out of bed, and I think I must've had my mind so intently set on my work that I didn't notice my body still laying there as I left the room."

"This morning? So, all day long when you were at your desk…"

"Yes Sir, and this might also explain some of the other anomalies I've been experiencing today, including the food. Maybe I can't eat or taste things this way, which I suppose makes sense if I'm not actually inside a body with taste buds."

"Very well, that explains that part. How about your previous visit? I thought you might be going crazy with that maniacal laughter of yours."

"I probably was," she nods. "I didn't understand what was happening to me. But when I got home again, Tuka was still in my bed and wearing my nightgown, which I was sure I took off and threw into the hamper before going to the shower. Then I had this revelation that I'm standing in the room with this body in my bed, just like those early children were said to be doing. That's when I realized what happened."

"You were seeing it from the other side. That must've been at least a little scary."

"I think scary isn't the right word for it. The whole scene started out really eerie, but as it began to settle, the shock of realization hit hard. Then I started asking myself if I could do anything with it while I was standing there. So, I tried a little practice to see if I could alter my image. And this is the result."

"Right, and then you simply had to go around town to show it off, I suppose," he eyes her suspiciously.

"Well, it wasn't my original intention, but like I said, I don't feel the traditional tactile sensation like this. Also, I think Kaliya was right on a few things, like I tend to be too mechanical. Nevertheless, I apologize for being out of uniform, but since I'm here, um, maybe I could ask you for your judgment of my success?" she offers timidly.

"Ayene, I'm actually a married man, although I haven't seen my wife for a long time due to being stationed at that base. And you're a fraction of my age," he smiles tenderly. "Not to mention, that's a very curious question to ask of your superior officer."

"Lajivi, just cut to the chase. You're a man who ought to know something about women. In all the nether-space, by this time I would certainly hope so!" she chuckles. "So, just give me your best objective opinion on how I look. You know…body shape, skin tone, general appearance to make it look convincing… Remember, this works a bit like a costume for me. And I need an outside perspective to judge if I'm doing this right."

"A costume…uh huh. All right, then give me a moment to drool," he grins.

He makes a careful examination of her from all sides, trying desperately to be modest while also thorough. He visually inspects her contours and skin tone, attempts to estimate her bone structure and muscle tone, and her alignment of limbs and tail.

"You seem to have made a good effort on this occasion. Your proportions are in line, nice form, good color and complexion, skin texture… You know your body well…and so do I now," he chuckles.

"Good! And I'm not even embarrassed by it…quite amazingly. Maybe that's what happens when you have a chance to ditch that horrid bug. I'll just let it pass that it was a necessary work effort to try out a new skill, and from a more scientific perspective to analyze the result."

"Excellent, but before you go out again, do you think you might want to get dressed before approaching anyone else with this?"

"Absolutely, I think that would be a wonderful idea. Just give me a moment to change my image."

Ayene now redirected her mind to her projected body and began to apply her uniform overlay. She recalled the clothing she had been wearing earlier in the day, which was a very familiar image in her mind, and just like she altered her body in her room, now she was attempting to overlay her new image with the clothing included.

The Commander observed as her image began to change right in front of him, at first applying a soft blur in the general pattern of her uniform, and slowly materializing in sharper detail as it came into focus. The final result was Ayene now properly adorned in her usual outfit.

"Amazing..." the Commander muses softly. "And so, this is how it's applied. For instance, with Ytani and whatever he did for his impersonation in that city."

"Yes, and I doubt we would have ever figured this out ourselves if we took that initiative for our, um, mutiny."

"You're absolutely right, Ayene. So, we would've been limited to either attempting a negotiation, or simply evading altogether."

Ayene peers over her shoulders to examine her work on both sides.

"Commander, your opinion?" she asks.

The Commander once again makes a pass around her to study this new image.

"It appears complete. Very good! Such a skill as this could serve a considerable potential."

"More than that, I can be anyone or anything. The only limitation is my imagination."

"And that's probably the scariest part. Be careful, Ayene, and don't become another Ytani."

"Absolutely, Sir! I'm going to take my lessons from Kaliya. I believe she can teach me how to use it right. But now, would you excuse me? I wish to report to Kaliya and see where this takes me."

"Very well, dismissed..."

She leaves the office contemplating what she'll say when she meets with Kaliya. As she exits the building, she begins walking along the sidewalk in the direction of the local gateway hub, which was her habit by now whenever she visited Tae'Eladar, until she suddenly stopped in her tracks.

"Wait a minute, why am I walking?" she giggles. "Let's see, guildhall courtyard, right there near the bench where Suli and the others sit... Recall the memory and pull yourself to it."

She closes her eyes and brings up the memory of the location, making it appear sharply in her mind, along with that same mental draw to her destination.

✦✦✦✦

"Still no sign of her," Sulíma relents.

She and the others were in their usual spot in the courtyard waiting for Ayene to arrive for their daily gathering. But Ayene's extended delay was starting to cause concern.

"Do you think she'll be coming at all today?" she wonders.

"Maybe she got busy with something," Petrith suggests. "After all, she's a working girl."

"Maybe, and we don't really have any way to check on her with a trans-com from here. I hope everything is alright."

"I'm sure it is," Túfula affirms. "She's just got a lot on her mind over there. So, what were we talking about again?"

"I'll be moving to a new line of training soon," Relissa announces.

"Oh? What kind?"

"Coming up soon, I'll be looking to train...BUGGERS!" she jumps, as an image pops into view in the courtyard just in front of them.

The entire group flinches at the sudden appearance of a tall young lady, seemingly Daanen'kai in her general shape and poise, but without the glowing eyes, and with a uniquely recognizable face.

Ayene appeared in the yard, though a little startled by her travel experience, and twisting side to side to study her surroundings.

"In all the nether-space, that took a little more effort than I was expecting. And wow, those sights along the way…"

"Jiggers!" Relissa snaps. "Ayene, is that you?"

Ayene's posture was that of one trying to catch herself after jumping onto the ground out of her folded space. She turns around to see an array of surprised expressions gawping at her. She returns with a shy smile.

"Hi everyone, have you seen Kaliya around? I need to find her."

"Ayene!" Sulíma yips. "What happened to you? And where did you just come from?"

"Suli, I finally have a good story for you, but right now I need to find Kaliya. I'm projected!"

"Criminy," Relissa mutters amazedly. "You did it, girl? But you don't look the same as you normally do."

"Yeah, well… When I first realized what I did, I decided to try a body without the seed entity, just to see how it looks. My Commander seemed to like it. It certainly left him speechless long enough when I strutted into his office naked."

"Would you care to explain that story, Ayene?" Petrith inquires charmingly.

"Hey! You!" Sulíma elbow jabs him in the ribs. "Remember the tail?!" she points and begins wagging it vigorously.

"Do Daanen'kai boys actually lose their focus so quickly?" Haran muses wittily.

"It's alright, Suli," Ayene soothes. "I wasn't carrying my soap on this occasion."

The group lets out another laugh at poor Petrith's history, as the young man covers his eyes.

"I think she's back out on the fields again," Relissa considers. "Here, follow me and I'll show you. Come on, everybody, let's go."

The group all rise to their feet, and Relissa leads them through the guildhall with Ayene in tow, coursing their way through the corridors to the training hall, then out the other side and down the stairs to the athletic field.

"Kaliya," she shouts. "We need you a minute. We've got something wonky to show you."

Kaliya was once again on the field with her team when she heard the call. She turned to see Relissa and the gang, along with Ayene, or at least what generally looked like Ayene, on the bleachers behind her. She calls a pause in the exercise and trudges up to meet them. When she arrives, she takes a long gaze at Ayene.

"What happened to you?" she asks.

"I'm projected!" Ayene declares delightedly. "And do you want to know something else? I'm a Prodigy Child!"

"What?"

"I think you and Adalon were right. But I didn't realize it until just a short while ago. And I'm just about ready to tear someone's horns out for it," she scowls.

"Um, who's horns, in this case?" she asks mildly.

"That beast who makes us take his horrid chips to cover it up!"

"He has horns?" Haran wonders openly.

"Yeah, thick black ones coming out the sides and angling forward. Do you remember when I told you about that imaginary friend I had as a child? Tuka, named after that doll I had once. Well, I finally realized who she was. She was me, lying in bed after I apparently projected into my room. But I thought it was a dream in those days."

"That sounds a little like me and my strange dreams as a girl," Kaliya reflects.

"I'm also guessing this is the reason for my parents and their behavior. They must've seen it once, and boom! There I go into the first medical clinic with an open surgical room to get my chip. No doubt, our family med-tech put a rush order on it."

"Cu'Nar's pity," Sulíma moans. "And this is how you people treat the Prodigy Gift?"

"We don't even know what it is, Suli, so how are we supposed to know anything? No one talks about it, and they all see it as a horrible disease or alien parasite. Once, in the very early days, and probably no thanks to Darumon, we had this big global panic. We called it the Tav'ageen Scare. There were bodies showing up at random everywhere, and this sent the people into a frenzy looking for a way to escape. It was described as an alien parasite thing that found its way into our local environment and had settled itself, but none of our science could locate or identify it. This is where Darumon comes along and says, 'Here, take this, and everything will be just fine…' And here you have the incentive that drove everyone to take the seeds, and later the chips. After that, no one wants to talk about it. And this is also why people like my parents lock themselves in a closet whenever they see it."

"That's bad," Petrith shakes his head. "And in a way, this also reflects on Master Velen's faction and what he tried to offer, but no one would listen."

"I'm really very sorry for that because his faction is probably the ONLY one that could've given us the answers we needed. But anyway, last night I had trouble sleeping, so I finally tried some of that meditation Kaliya was teaching me to see if I could get any rest at all. I must've dozed off early this morning, but rather than sleeping, I guess I projected instead. Then, stupid mechanical me, I got tired of lying in bed, so I got up, started my daily routine, and um…well, sort of missed the fact that my body was still in bed."

"Jiggers, girl," Relissa winces. "You need to pay closer attention to where you leave stuff like this."

The group enjoys another moment of laughter at the predicament.

"I spent the whole day at work," Ayene continues. "Then went home to relax a bit, but instead, I found Tuka taking up my bed. Well, I think I went a little crazy at about this time, thinking I was that little girl again with my playmate, until my mind started asking what I was looking at and how it got there. I made another visit to the office to see if I had actually been working today, and then back home again to confirm if Tuka was really in my bed. When I saw her again, I realized this couldn't be a dream. Then I recalled those early children, and here I was doing the same."

"Wow, that must've been a surprise," Kaliya notes.

"Yes! I screamed at the top of my projected lungs and blasted my rage at that creature who dares call himself our benefactor back home.

Then, once I calmed down a bit, I pulled my horns back around and decided to try playing with it a little. I wanted to see what I could do with it, and my first thought was to see myself without that horrible little parasite again."

"Aye!" Relissa smirks. "And is this where you ran up to your Commander stark bloody naked?"

"Um, yes..." she coughs subtly. "I was apparently so lost in my success; I forgot I was still naked in my projection. So, I ran through the streets all the way to the HQ building, stormed through the lobby in front of a small army of lonely young men, and then into his office, where I stood at full attention to present myself," she grins bashfully.

"Cu'Nar Grace, Ayene!" Kaliya giggles. "Not even Suli is THAT bad!"

"And to think," Petrith muses thoughtfully. "I was sitting over here this whole time, when I could've been on Ruuki uy'Daan watching the entertainment show of the month!"

Both Sulíma and Túfula gawk at the young man for his remark, then turn to glare at each other.

"You know, Suli," Túfula notes. "We need to put a lot more effort into our tail swinging around him. His mind is drifting far too much lately."

"Yeah," she nods. "We might also want to change our fashion style to reinforce the idea. Something light...and very revealing," she turns to glare at Petrith.

"If it helps any," Ayene adds. "It's not like I was trying to show off. But I don't have the traditional tactile sensation in this form, and neither do I seem to be able to taste or smell anything like this."

"This much you have right," Kaliya affirms. "Without a physical body, you don't have any of those physical senses. So, you need to pay closer attention to detail by other means. With your mind properly conditioned, you can simulate some of the tactile sensation, but it takes practice."

"All right, I'll keep that in mind. Anyway, here I am. Kaliya, you and Adalon must've been right, as crazy as it might seem to someone like me. I guess I simply have to admit I'm your link to Azgarén, and whatever else you have in mind for me."

"So, does this mean you want to join up?"

"Well, like Relissa said, I might need to hold back from that test for now, but if you can put a word in to get me started, I'll do what I can."

"All right, good. My guess is he'll want you to practice a lot more before going on any serious missions. Still, we need to get that link established before we can decide on that base, or anything else. So, are you ready to do this now?"

"No better time than the present to get this started, especially if he'll want me to practice more."

"Naturally. But don't forget your body. You still need to eat on occasion."

"At least it's getting some much-needed sleep. I wonder if a person can work during the day, and then sleep and project during the night. They could run a full cycle without stop!"

"Oi, girl," Relissa moans. "Don't you have anything better to do than work all day? Kaliya, we need to hook this kid up with a boyfriend."

"Yeah," Kaliya relents. "Unfortunately, Likha is still using the last one we made."

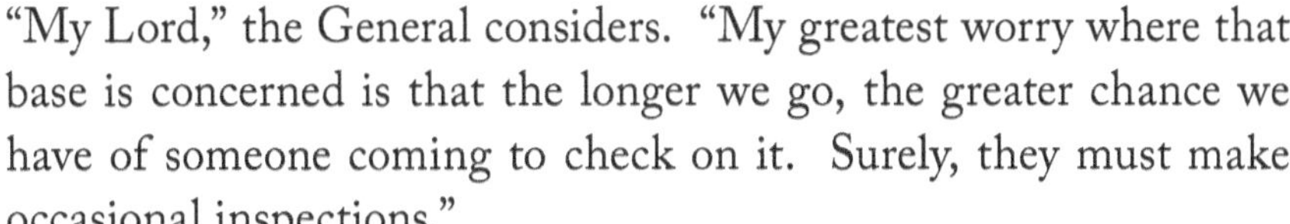

"My Lord," the General considers. "My greatest worry where that base is concerned is that the longer we go, the greater chance we have of someone coming to check on it. Surely, they must make occasional inspections."

"I must agree with you, General, and if one of those should occur with any significant amount of detail, they might notice certain discrepancies we may not be accounting for."

"In addition, although Commander Kriv'tik is assisting us with these false reports of his mining operations, I am wondering how long this will hold up for us. We are really just assuming they need full capacity in those storage warehouses. What if they need something less?"

"Indeed, something less, or if they simply become so frustrated with the diminishing returns on their operations that they decide to proceed forward as is. This could be a problem, at least insofar as them discovering the weapon is missing altogether."

"And all the more reason I hope Kaliya can bring us this plan she promised before we see anything on the other side."

"This is true," Thaelyn reflects. "But at the same time, I suspect either Adalon or Maker Kuroku is aware of this and has a contingency plan of some kind. I just wish I knew what it was."

"Yes, I must agree. Our objectives include discouraging Darumon from making any further efforts in that world, but at the same time we need our link to Azgarén by means their Central Command would not so easily detect."

"And this would involve that other Prodigy Child, whoever she is. And then to find a means of applying our distraction, and what form this might take, but my feelings are it should involve a true invasion of their local space."

"That's what I'm looking forward to the most," Kailen muses. "To see what sort of alien invasion force we bring, and how they respond to it."

"It will likely be a good show, and ultimately it cannot be so limited in appearances that their media service, which I hear is regulated and censored by their Council, fails to reveal it, at least in part, to the public, therefore preventing them from realizing their little paradise is not so paradisal."

"Are we trying to start a new panic?"

"Not so much a panic as to simply cause them to realize the reality of war is not an entertainment sport that occurs only on someone else's doorstep. After ten millennia, these insurgents ought to realize how to find their mark."

"Agreed...and this will bring into question Darumon and all his successes in his campaign to eliminate them."

"A bit overdue, if you ask me," the General muses distantly.

The conversation is interrupted by a knocking at the door, with Kaliya and Ayene stepping into the room.

"My Lord, may I trouble you for a moment?" Kaliya announces. "We have something important to offer."

"Kaliya, come in," Thaelyn waves at them. "We are simply in careful debate on how to approach Azgarén without giving them cause for celebration. What do you have for us today?"

Kaliya and Ayene proudly stepped forward to the table to make their presentation. At this time, Ayene had changed her image to her standard appearance so as not to draw immediate attention to her condition.

"My Lord," Kaliya announces proudly. "I would like to present to you Lieutenant Ayene Ti'van, the solution to our problems."

"Oh, how nice, and a pleasant greeting to you, Lieutenant... But one moment here, I thought we were already introduced at one time," he raises an eyebrow.

"Oh, my apologies," Kaliya smirks. "Then perhaps I should approach it this way. In a place of pits and people stout, a foreign Child is found..."

Thaelyn and the other officers reeled back, and each raised their brows in wonder.

"Indeed!" he intones boldly. "And how did we come about this marvel of marvels?"

"Well, perhaps if I let Ayene explain. She has a rather interesting story to tell. Ayene?"

"Uh huh," she smiles. "Put me in the spotlight, as if my Commander didn't already lose his voice once along the way. Your Lordship, some time ago, my Commander and I were discussing ways to help you with your dilemma of approaching Azgarén with your invasion force, which as we understand it would resemble a ground force, and also this distraction of yours, which sounds more like something arriving from outside our local star system, right?"

"Yes, and in fact we are still in debate on these issues. Do you have something interesting to offer?"

"I believe so. Between the two of us, we had an idea come to mind, and I consulted with Kaliya here for her opinions. As for this distraction, I think we can solve this with a little play based on the existing facts we have to work with, and how to twist them into a new game for the Marshal."

"Oh dear…here we go."

"First, the most difficult is to have an index of any kind into our local space, and for this you need something to either mark one or that comes preprogrammed with one. This is easy…one of our ships. But the question is how to procure one. For this, Kaliya and I came up with a cute little plan, and it involves that mischievous young man, Ytani."

"Of course, and how is Ytani involved with one of your ships?"

"He's going to steal it."

Thaelyn glares at her a moment before glancing at the other officers in amusement.

"Very well, I suppose I need to ask this. How is he going to steal a ship? First of all, perhaps I should ask, what sort of ship are we speaking of here?"

"I'm thinking of a cruiser class vessel. But of course, we need an excuse for one to be present in the first place. Well, Kaliya and I have been discussing a few things relating to this, and the way that mining base is experiencing so many shortages lately, it would seem very reasonable for us to conduct a survey for new deposits. In fact, my Commander and I were discussing this once with Ytani as an excuse to occupy him."

"Yes! And I do recall this mention in our spy videos. So, you would call in some manner of survey vessel for a study, I suppose."

"Right, and Ytani will want to oversee it personally, being the remarkably responsible fellow that he is."

"Oh! General, did you hear that? A remarkably responsible fellow…"

"Incredible, my Lord!" he muses humorously. "And he seemed so young. Gracious, they do grow up quickly."

They share a quick laugh before Thaelyn continues.

"And how does this remarkably responsible fellow go from conducting a survey to stealing a ship?"

"First," Ayene responds. "He needs to bring along his newly recruited team of dwarven specialists, which naturally would be needed to take core samples and perform other forms of testing for the viability of the mineral veins."

"Ah, but of course! But, um, how do we explain the minor detail of your people being alien to that world?"

"Well, the dwarves had to be pulled out under the influence of that drug, in order to bypass the questions."

"Uh huh…"

"And along the way, they were also equipped with some strange alien weapons I once found in our supply stores."

"Um…" he coughs gently. "And when did you actually find these alien weapons?"

"When I was conducting a recent inventory and found a number of unrecognizable crates stuck in a corner. The markings were clearly very strange. At first, I thought it might be Ytani ordering more of his entertainment equipment, but I guess I was wrong," she grins innocently.

Thaelyn gawks at her, and then lays his head in his hands and moans.

"General, would you be so kind as to fetch my list, please. And do take care to spell the name correctly."

"Indeed, my Lord, this is surely a noteworthy one."

"Well, Ayene," Kaliya muses. "Welcome aboard. You've just been entered into a very exclusive club."

"Yeah," she smiles gently. "And given what you said about it earlier, at least I'm in good company."

"Very well," Thaelyn resumes. "So, we are saying Ytani must be in possession of something alien, but where did he find it?"

"Most likely from his long time living alone and getting bored," Ayene shrugs. "So we figure he probably…finally…figured out how to experiment with his Gift."

"Ah! This would make for a good ruse to play. Let me see if I can guess from this point. We can possibly say he tried projecting his image to some far distant point in the sky to see if there was anything noteworthy to discover. Or perhaps we could simply say he found some other latent ability that allowed him to detect something in the near proximity. And therefore, he now has... What do we say here, new friends?"

"Very good! And these friends just happen to be very technologically advanced, with advanced space travel, therefore they are helping him to steal a ship, as well as that weapon, leaving one piece behind as the message for the Marshal on who took it."

"Oh dear... And considering his true nature, how are we applying ourselves?"

"Well, I know my Commander recorded some of those recent conversations, so if we simply deliver these back to Central as part of our tidying up and filing our reports, we have something on file to demonstrate his wild ambitions, including his mania of becoming a god-king. And with that weapon in his hands..."

"Powers pay witness, that would put a sweat on even Darumon's brow, I should think."

"Now, we can play into this later, maybe by a message or something demanding tribute. He loved tribute, especially in the form of female pleasure victims. And if he wants to play god, the Marshal will probably get very angry."

"And no doubt, he would have a very strong interest in pursuing him, if such a thing were even possible. But what about this ship?"

"The ship would offer us our entrance into Azgarén local space. Depending on the ship class, I think it should be able to carry a flight of your combat ships in the shuttle bay. And if those things are able to mark their own index, there you go. Then we pull out before the Azgarén security forces can do anything about it."

"Maybe also to make a little noise before doing so..." Kailen notes. "We don't want to simply jump in and jump out again. We want them to know who it was jumping in."

"Yes, I believe this would do well for us," Thaelyn affirms. "We could jump in, allow our people to conduct some minor mischief, and then depart. This will lay down the foundation of Ytani and his friends making our true incursion of their local space, and therefore a true threat for Darumon and his shiny military. But simply to have that ship in our possession will give us an important travel route. Therefore, we can make this move when we are ready. Good. Then Kaliya, you will need to prepare your team to capture a ship for us. This will likely prove a very good test of your skills."

"Yeah," she muses. "This will be a good one. But before we go this far, I want to be sure we build up a good excuse for it. We need to check our reports and make sure we have an adequate need, so their Central Command doesn't argue too much."

"This is reasonable, see to it. Coordinate with Commander Kriv'tik as necessary, and file the reports to build up a good image for us. Now, as for the land invasion..."

"Right," Ayene continues. "Your Lordship, Kaliya and I were talking about this new military unit of hers, the Stormhooves. I think it goes without saying this represents a kind of romantic image for many of us back home. We learn of this in our history, at least for the nostalgia aspect of it, and even though it dates back to a bygone era, there is still a lot of glamour involved. Then she started going into all the new facets of it, which had me pulling my horns out after a while."

"No doubt! Our incarnation will involve many elements your romance might not have imagined even in your wildest fantasies."

"Yeah, this Prodigy Gift, your magic studies, new forms of combat training, and whatever else you give your soldiers that makes you seem almost supernatural on the battlefield."

"Well," he chuckles. "I do not know if I would use such a word as that, but in comparison to many other examples, ours would surely pose a formidable force."

"Right, and I find myself in a situation where I think I would like to be a part of it, if only due to Adalon and her suggestion that someone would come forward to fill this role she mentioned."

"Indeed! But are you familiar with our application process? It can be a rather selective one."

"I learned about this when talking to Relissa and the others at the guildhall. She mentioned I should probably wait on that Spirit Test of yours, if only due to my seed entity that could skew the results."

"Most interesting, and she may actually have a point. We would not want to confuse the results with this additional and generally unknown entity."

"Of course, so for now, if I could simply enter some of the preliminary courses as a form of preparation, this shouldn't be too much to ask until we can correct this other issue."

"I suppose this is reasonable. But then I must ask, why do you and this other mischief-maker think you are the answer to Adalon's prophecy?"

"As I understand it, the prophecy mentioned something about a foreign Child coming out of that base and presenting herself as a potential component to your cause. First and foremost, I always wanted to serve a valuable purpose, maybe as a personal desire to feel myself an important member of something. Secondly, Kaliya thinks, for all my past participation, that I must be the one to apply here. I can't be sure where she came up with such affirmative determination in this regard, unless she holds some unusual skill to seek out talent. But then we got to talking about this military unit she's putting together, and this other suggestion I had about this land invasion, and how it could possibly apply. Well, one thing led to another, as they usually do, and we started testing a few theories."

As Thaelyn studied her and listened to her explanation, he started to feel a new sense of dread come over him. He set his elbow on the table and leaned his head into his hand as she rambled on.

"General," he mutters gently. "I am getting a delicate sense that we may have another mark on that list coming up."

"Yes, my Lord," he replies. "I think I see it as well."

"And finally," Ayene continues. "I feel that I should comment on the Med-tech's statement relating to these seeds. This is surely a good incentive to want to join up for something, if to be able to find a solution for that along the way. I mean, in all the nether-space, do you honestly think I want to go through life looking like this?" she glances at herself. "No way, I want to look like this instead…"

She steps away from the table and centers her focus on her body, reimagining it as her unaltered form, just as she had it before, although this time complete with clothing. And as the image changes, the officers at the table draw back in astonishment.

"Cu'Nar's eyes," Kailen gasps.

"Dear Powers," Thaelyn wheezes. "I must truly pay closer attention to those who pass through this room."

Ayene now represented her desired unaltered form, or at least a close facsimile, and stepped up to the table again.

"And using this, along with her telepathic skills, we have access to anywhere I can deliver you on Azgarén, although I would imagine C.P. would be your first goal. I can also use this to provide the Med-tech with her specimens, or anything else you ask of me."

"Lieutenant, how and when did you come about this?"

"Your Lordship, I'm apparently a Prodigy Child, although I didn't know about it until today. Originally, I asked Kaliya if she could project to Azgarén, but without the personal memories, this was impossible. Then we started talking about me doing it. After all, if this is universal in our species, it stands to reason I might be able to learn how to use it, right?"

"It would!"

"So, she took me on for a little private tutoring."

"Oh, she did, did she?" he eyes her suspiciously. "General?"

"Yes, my Lord," he relents. "I am already scribbling it in."

"Oops!" Kaliya mumbles. "Oh well, I guess it's for a good cause."

"Initially," Ayene resumes. "I wasn't able to do it, probably due to too much time under that chip, and then the rigid nature of my old military training. So, she admitted me into her circle of friends for a little therapeutic socializing."

"This is an interesting mention," Thaelyn notes. "We should probably keep this in mind for later. Those chips might impose a handicap for this point."

"Probably so, at the very least. Along the way, I started to recall some of my life stories and old memories, one of which was when I was a little girl and had an imaginary friend I called Tuka. This was until my fourth decade, when I got my chip, and then she was gone. So, this probably represents an empirical result for the chips."

"This is reasonable. And therefore, the removal of the chip would allow the renewed discovery of the talent."

"I originally thought Tuka was a dream playmate, but in fact, she was me lying in bed after I had accidentally projected."

"Indeed! How interesting it is to hear of it from the other side now. You might want to share this story with Aerlie for the psychological study."

"All right, sure," she nods. "Last night, I had difficulty getting to sleep, so I tried a little of Kaliya's meditation therapy to relax. It was early morning by this time when I think I finally dozed off. But then I got tired of waiting for the clock to tick down, and rather than pay attention to my body still lying in the bed, I simply got up, and with my mind on my work, I took a shower, got dressed, and started the day."

"Cu'Nar's pity," Kailen winces. "You simply walked out of the room without noticing you forgot your body? I think I would not wish to be your body for this point."

"Well, I didn't get any sleep, but I still had to start my day, so I consider I got both at the same time here."

"Oh no…" he shakes his head.

"Anyway, I went the full day until my work shift ended and I went back home. This is where I found my body still in the bed."

"This should be an interesting point," Thaelyn muses. "How did you react to that?"

"I felt like I had suddenly entered a dream. A surreal delusion that just didn't seem plausible. I stood there thinking my long-lost imaginary friend had returned, so I started talking to her."

"Did she talk back?" he raises his brow curiously.

"Well, in my imagination, yes, and we started talking about things back home, like my family, maybe me going home again, and some other stuff."

"Uh huh… Commander, does your wife perform any neurological scans to check for anomalies? I think we have a patient here," he smiles gently.

"I'll need to check," he responds amusedly. "But this one may require special handling."

"Oh, come on you two," Ayene jests. "Eventually, I figured it out. I had to make another run to the office to see if I did in fact spend my day there, then back home to find Tuka still in bed. This is where I began to turn my horns back around and realize I was posing as those original children did one time. Then I got angry for that chip, the Marshal, his lies, and what they did to my life and my family."

"I can be sure of this much," Thaelyn affirms solemnly.

"Once I settled down a bit, I decided to experiment a little."

"Ah! And here we have a curious suggestion. You are barely a few moments into realizing what you are doing, and already you want to experiment. Where was Ytani for this point?"

"Good question!" she tosses her hands up and shrugs. "I wish I had an answer to it. All I can say is I had a better teacher," she glances at Kaliya, and smiles. "So, here I am, standing in front of the mirror. My first thoughts go back to how I looked before I got this awful seed. Now I want to try altering my shape to what I recalled of myself in those early days. This has always been my deepest grudge. They forced me to deform my body all because of some rule laid down by an insane Council. So, I tried to recreate that image one more time, just to remind myself of how I looked, and how I wanted to be once again."

"I can fully understand, Lieutenant. And I am sure you are not the only one."

"And after I had my new body, I was apparently so happy that I succeeded in this, I ran naked through the streets all the way to the HQ building and up to my Commander to get his opinion of it," she smiles and shrugs innocently.

Thaelyn gaped at the young officer, and then turned to Kailen, who was staring blankly at her. He turned further to the General, as he was gazing in astonishment.

"General," Thaelyn notes tenderly. "Perhaps you should highlight that mark."

"Absolutely, my Lord," he gasps. "Good gracious, this young lady is indeed a courageous one."

"Um…" Kailen wonders. "Just out of curiosity, what sort of response did he have?"

"Well, once he found his voice again," she responds pertly. "I asked him to give a thorough review for an objective opinion of how I looked…you know, to be sure I did it right."

"Oh, naturally…very professional, I'm sure."

"Anyway, here I am for your assessment, in the hopes I can join your service."

"Indeed," Thaelyn accedes. "But let us limit the public streaking to just the holiday occasions," he grins. "Very well, first, I would wish to fulfill two primary objectives. If you are the one to fill Adalon's role, we need you properly trained. And although we have that issue of your seed, I would wish you to apply for at least a few courses to see you through until we can attend the rest. My first suggestion is the language class. Perhaps you could call in a few of your fellows for efficiency's sake to fill a classroom."

"Of course," she nods. "This makes perfect sense."

"Now, are you actually suggesting becoming a part of our military? And do you realize to do so is also to become a citizen of my kingdom?"

"Kaliya is almost dragging me by the horns to join up. And I was very nearly ready to resign my post in our military even before coming here. Ytani and all he did, the Commander and his stories… this is enough for me to lose interest in Central Command. Not that I would turn against my people, but that service, and under the Marshal, isn't something I want to represent. And yours is far more appealing for the potential it offers. I would hope to apply myself as perhaps the first of my people to sign up for this promising new direction, and if that means also to become a citizen of your kingdom…well, Kaliya seems to like it, as do Suli, Túfu, and Petrith. It's been a thousand millennia since any of us followed a King, and our Council, last I heard, isn't doing its job very well."

"So it would seem. Very well then, let us first attend to these smaller matters and work our way along. As for your projection training, it would seem you have at least a small amount of practice by now, but I will have you fill in with a formal preparatory course. Kaliya, can you see to this?"

"Yes, my Lord," she affirms. "I'll help out as I can, and let Aelwyn know, as well."

"In addition, have you spoken to your Commander on this matter?"

"We spoke briefly on it," Ayene admits. "And he understands that if I have a special calling of some kind, I should follow it."

"Then it would seem we have inherited another very special young lady into our service. Welcome aboard, Lieutenant."

Ayene smiles brightly as she and Kaliya both salute and return out the door.

Chapter 8

PARTURITION

"My Lady, I'm here for my monthly exam," Marelle announces as she enters the Healer's Ward.

"Ah, good to see you again," Aerlie responds. "How have you been since the last time?"

"I'm holding together, but my old clothes don't fit very well anymore. I can't wear my usual uniform pants because they're becoming a bit too snug around the waist. So, now I have to wear this dress instead."

"Are you following my exercise program, like I asked?"

"Yeah, and I feel good from it, but this little fella inside here is putting it on lately."

"Let's see…you're at six months, going on seven. We'll take another peek and see what's going on in there. Have you and Roderick given any more thought to my question about discovering whether it's a boy or a girl?"

"We talked about it a few times. It's so strange for someone to ask that. The way I remember it from back home, you get what you get, and then you buy your clothes and stuff later. Here, we have a chance to make our plans before the baby is even born."

"That's the beauty of being a healer in our society. My Sight

"

can see inside there and tell you what to expect…assuming you wish it. Some people actually prefer to wait and let it be a surprise, but many seem to like this idea of knowing ahead of time so they can take the time to prepare."

"For now, let's just see if everything is still cooking like it should be. I'll try to get Roddy to sit down with me and make a decision. Maybe later, after this visit…"

"All right then, lie on the bed here and let's take a look."

Marelle was making yet another monthly visit. She was showing a prominent bulge by now, and it was starting to slow her down. But she was determined to keep up her work for as long as she could. She lies down on the bed and draws up her dress to reveal her midsection.

Aerlie makes her usual pass to examine Marelle's body and peers inside with her Healer's vision. This is a process she has performed countless times before and on just as many women who passed through the Ward over the years.

"Well, it certainly looks like things are coming along nicely," she declares. "Since we are going into the late term now, I think there is one detail I should mention to you, regardless of whether or not you would like to know the gender."

"Oh, what's that?"

"You are carrying twins."

Marelle gawps at Aerlie's statement.

"Twins?" she gasps. "Oh…wow… That'll make a lot more work for us. Do you think I'll still be able to go back to the academy in time for the next school year?"

"It will be hard, I'm sure. One will take a lot of time; two will take something more, not necessarily twice. I might suggest you keep a short class schedule in the first few months to give you extra time. Maybe you can focus on the most important classes during that time to bring you to where we need you for your work, and leave the other topics for a later study period."

"Yeah, sure, and I think I'll definitely need to get Roddy to decide with me on what to do about this. Two of them? Oh my…"

"Having twins is a most delightful occasion, Marelle," Aerlie twitters. "It's not very common in humans. Is this something you have ever had in your family before?"

"Not in my family, not that I'm aware of, at least."

"Maybe in Roderick's family? Sometimes it runs in family lines."

"I don't know, but I'll ask."

Marelle's thoughts begin drifting to all the bits and pieces she will need to assemble for this occasion, but now doubled in quantity.

"Two babies..." she begins to feel giddy. "It's a little like making up for lost time."

"You're right! This gives you a very good start for a wonderful family."

+ +◆+ +

"How much longer for your language class, Ayene?" Relissa asks.

"They're estimating maybe a week and a half more, the way things are going."

"Are you still having those problems with the elixir?" Sulíma wonders.

"It still occurs, but only mildly. It was bad that first day, but we got used to it after a few days of experience."

"Jiggers," Relissa recalls. "I remember that first day. You caused such a stir; they brought in the full crew from the temple to check on you."

"Yes, I'm still a little embarrassed that we caused so much of a disturbance..."

"But it wasn't actually your fault, Ayene," Túfula reminds her. "It's that...thing. It just reacted badly to it. What's it good for, after all?"

"The seed entity is advertised to give us higher resistance to toxic environments and substandard conditions, which is supposed to be valuable when we travel to other worlds. Initially, we were made to think we were going to colonize those places, at least until things turned sour on us for all those insurgents the Marshal claimed were harassing us, and we got stuck at home with our native environment so polluted that we needed them even there. I'm guessing it reacted to the strange substance in that elixir we were made to drink before class. But once the entity decided it's not actually toxic, it allowed it through…somewhat."

"Yeah, but it cuts the efficiency of the elixir down by almost a third."

"At least it's working, and we are learning our lessons. This is why we're doubling up the four-hour bottles instead of using a single six-hour dose. It's not perfect, but it's good enough, I suppose."

"Well, you seem to be doing well enough with the language by now," Relissa admits.

"Yes, it's nice to be able to speak in your native form now."

"Have you had time to speak with any of the other instructors?" Petrith asks.

"I had a few conversations so far, nothing extensive as I'm still in my language training, but this next week and beyond should get busy as I start signing up for a few things."

"What about your regular work?" Túfula inquires.

"Until I go into a full classroom schedule, I'm still working part-time to fill in a few of my duties. But he's assigning someone to replace me while I'm here now, so this should relieve me to focus on my new direction."

"What kind of studies do you think you'll take up," Sulíma wonders. "Once the language course is done."

"His Lordship is suggesting a number of preliminary courses to fill in my prerequisites. Just like Relissa said, I should refrain from that test until later, so this might restrict me for now, but there seems to be a lot I need in the interim. One thing I would like to try for is the magical studies, as I'm fascinated by this every time I watch the mages practice out on the field."

"Aye," Relissa snickers. "Just make sure you're not standing in front of them when they start throwing out fireballs, like a certain girl we all know did on her first day."

"What do you mean?"

"Oh, Kaliya got a little carried away that one time, thinking of her old home and what the orcs did to it. Next thing you know, they're rebuilding the testing field."

"Sounds like another interesting story to be told. I have never heard so many of these in my lifetime as I have in this brief moment with all of you."

✦

"Likha, we're going to need some additional help around here while I'm on maternity leave. I'll try to do what I can, if I get the time for it, but the first two years will be hard on me until the baby develops enough that it can manage on its own."

"Yes, Ankhia, I was thinking of asking Lady Aerlie if she could offer some of her people to supplement our staff, since they've been so helpful in the past with those mutation victims from Ruuki uy'Daan. They really moved up quick on the ladder to meet the needs of our people."

"I wonder if any of our own staff members would like to take up the study of their practice. We're technically following a religion now, so why not have a few take formal studies and see if we can combine the two."

"That would be a sight. So, does this mean I need to go back to medical school, Tae'Eladaran style?" she giggles.

"That might not be a bad idea. And I can barely even imagine how it might appear."

The two of them were discussing Ankhia's upcoming pregnancy, which began more than a year ago, and was soon to come due. Ankhia had been preparing for her leave, once she gave birth, and would not be able to fulfill her professional demands during this time, as her child would require a lot of attention for an extended period due to the slowness of their babies to mature past that initial stage of newborn dependency.

Likha was her next-in-line, having served long enough and learning the trade sufficiently to take up the reigns as a resident staff member. Her promotion was an exciting moment where she would take more responsibility and a greater role in the future medical needs of their people.

"Speaking of Lady Aerlie," Ankhia recalls. "She asked to be present and offered assistance when the time comes. As it turns out, it looks like I'll be the first one giving birth in a new baby boom around here. Just imagine."

"Another month, that's all. How do you feel?"

Ankhia looks down at her enlarged belly, gently caressing it with her hands.

"This is my first, Likha. I'm nervous, but also excited, because this time we might finally have a chance for ourselves. If only we can finish this war before any new disasters strike."

"I hope you're right, Ankhia. Maybe my time will come one day, and I can join you in motherhood."

"You haven't chosen anyone yet? Remember what we were talking about. You're old enough, have you thought about it?"

"I'm not quite ready yet. Maybe for the next wave. Let's get you and the others stable, and then I'll think about it. There's no sense in all of us getting sent home at once."

"Good point, but don't wait too long. I want to be able to trade mothering techniques with you one day."

✦✦✦✦✦

It was a weekend with Kaliya and Petrith running a practice session at the mining base. Petrith was still in training to develop his skills with the Suuden-Aryku equipment, in this case using the Commander's data terminal. The Commander had given his access codes to log into his terminal so that Petrith could examine the data network linking to Azgarén. This would allow Petrith to browse the network and gain some familiarity with it.

Kaliya stood behind him to oversee the process, in case he should discover anything of special interest, as well as to monitor the effort in case there was any unusual feedback from Central Command.

"Make your accesses casual," she suggests. "Don't try anything that might otherwise require a security clearance. Let's just see what's out there so far."

"Right, so a simple data feed, maybe from a media source. That shouldn't raise too many questions."

"Sounds like a good start. We'll see what the local headlines read and go from there."

He calls up a browser application which defaults to a home page at Central Command. The page reported several articles of recent news, including security events, meetings of ranking officials on the local politics, some military operations around the regional star systems, and finally an old review from Marshal Darumon about his most recent engagement.

"Wait a moment," Kaliya issues. "Here's what Commander Kriv'tik said once about that staging post operation being cancelled."

"You mean on Therinë? Yeah, it says here it was due to a flaw in their approach. His so-called insurgents were investigating the condition of that planet after being out of contact with the locals for an extended period of time, and he had to pull back in order to prevent them from discovering his covert ops deployment."

"Yeah, how unfortunate," she smirks. "And also, how unfortunate that those so-called insurgents are now pursuing him across his other holdings without HIM knowing about it. But this also tells us that he makes up just as many stories with them as he did everywhere else."

"If we're hoping to drop a few of our own in there, it needs to be done very carefully."

"You're right, but we apparently have those regulators in the way. So, we need to bypass them somehow while at the same time invent a few stories to contradict his."

"And all the while not making so much noise that he gets any funny ideas for a new death toy to correct things."

"That's one of our biggest problems, so we might need to find where he orders these things and see if we can cut it off."

"All right, good," he affirms. "And then we just need to tap into their network. We don't want them to be able to track us, so it can't be from here. Maybe if we could rig up a wiretap and plug it in to a router junction, then tap into it remotely and address our feed through one or more false nodes. That would make things hard for them to track."

"Leave it to a hacker to figure that one out."

They continued studying the news feed, reading through a few stories, and searching for other information that might be easily available. Petrith punched in several search terms and keywords, trying his luck to see if they could find anything on specific subjects. He typed in a search based on the Daanen-Aryku, using different keywords in hopes of returning a valid result, but no information came up using this name.

"Is it that they don't call us Daanen-Aryku back home?" Petrith muses. "Or do they use another name?"

"I have no idea," she reflects. "I don't recall anyone ever stopping by and asking us how we identify ourselves. At least not with anything less than plasma rifles."

"That's probably indication enough. What about this. Let's try a more straightforward approach."

He now inputs Velen's full name to see what comes up. The result showed a list of articles dating back in history, with the most recent being several years prior.

"Here we go," he states. "Do you want to see what they have to say about us?"

"On a personal level, not really," she offers. "But we probably should take a peek, just to see what we have to work with. We already know they call us traitors who escaped with unknown help. And according to Commander Kriv'tik, we're supposed to be dead by now, found on some previously unknown world in some far distant corner of our home galaxy, and then blasted to nether-space by their remarkably efficient military after ten millennia of effort."

"Yeah, I like that last part the most. Well, here it goes."

He calls up the article, which appeared to be a vid-com news report.

"Good evening, this is Ileani Ur'paran for C.P. News reporting.
At long last, Marshal Darumon and his forces were able to track down

the final remnants of Velen the Traitor and his criminal organization. They were discovered in an unchartered sector on the far side of the galaxy, coordinating with a previously unknown race believed to be associated with the insurgent forces that have been causing so much havoc among our remote outposts and survey expeditions. This finally brings to a conclusion this long pursuit, along with the associated fear and suspicion relating to the former Council official and his connections that have led many to believe his involvement with the insurgent forces is the direct cause for their persistence to locate Sargeras and prevent him from returning to his former position of authority…"

"How interesting!" Kaliya barks. "So, not only are we traitors, but we're also directing these insurgents now. Wow, my father has really gone up in the world, from a lowly unappreciated Council member to a celebrity terrorist."

"Yeah, we should probably go tell him…but wait. No, dammit, he was killed on the far side of their local galaxy. I guess we can't tell him after all," he chuckles.

"My mother will be so disappointed to hear about that one, unless she was with him at the time."

"It doesn't mention her specifically, but I guess she would be included with those remnants."

"That part is probably the ONLY thing here that holds any truth to it…remnants."

"And what's with the language being used here?" he muses. "For a bunch of people with inhibitor chips, that sounds like a lot of buttering up, if you ask me."

"I'm sure it has to do with their media embellishing things, like the Commander said, to keep up the image. I don't know who this Ileani Ur'paran is, like if she's a normal person made to do a job that's just reading a script, or if she actually has any real ambition, but stifled like everything else."

"Her introduction sounded like she's a regular on the airwaves."

"Maybe. Hmm, alright, so if we say she's a regular image, and the people listen to her, probably thinking they're getting real news out of her, could we use this somehow?"

"Not standing where we are right now. This would have to work its magic along with that wiretap and our own propaganda campaign. Maybe if we could make contact sometime and see just how ambitious she actually is, we could turn this around for us."

"All right, keep this in mind for later. But it has to be discreet."

A Suuden'kai staff member arrives in Commander Kriv'tik's office with a report just received from the local construction crews in the city. He was standing in for Lieutenant Ti'van during her time away at the academy.

"Commander, I've just received word from the supervisor working on the new city hub terminal building. They're putting the final touches on it and will soon link it to the network connecting to Rolsklinde on Therinë and Bya'an Tamoranth on Tae'Eladar, giving us easy access to both for travel and trade. But the bizarre aspect is they say they will be using wheeled vehicles for transport, as a service feature. This, as opposed to us who might use star cruisers for interplanetary travel…assuming we actually had any."

"Yes, I heard of that once. It should make for an interesting experience, but like with so many other things we're seeing around here, I don't expect it to last long as they evolve up the ladder to their own versions."

"Incredible, and to think of how long it took any of us to move up that same ladder."

"That's apparently the difference in our cultures, where ours moves very slowly, it seems. Anyway, when it goes online, we can deactivate the mini unit outside and stow it for later. The new hub facility should make our efforts much more productive, but now we need to begin producing more industrial products to trade with the other races, and for this we need to expand those small workshops. We also need raw materials."

"As for the raw materials, that mining facility out west seems engineered to provide a variety of minerals out of the local terrain using a nano-molecular processor. It's not a bad piece of hardware, although the results are falling short of our demands. We will need to survey for more productive mineral deposits, and probably apply some of our own technology to it for better efficiency. We also have a similar issue with these small workshops and the associated machinery."

"I understand, but we also have to remember this isn't our world to fill up with our own brand of heavy industry. Lieutenant Ti'van already mentioned this once when she had a consultation with His Lordship. Apparently, they have a variety of alternative technologies they can apply to solve this without the associated pollution. So, I will submit a few ideas to his people and see if we can work out a coordinated effort to meet our needs. What about the reactor and that new extension for the fuel input?"

"The extension is currently in the framework stage and being poured with concrete. I would imagine perhaps a few more months for this stage to be completed before the installation of the infrastructure and the equipment. But I swear to you, Commander, if this thing works as advertised, I'm not simply going to pull my horns out, I'll also throw away my university degree in Engineering and take up praying to one of their gods. There is simply no other way to explain how you can make energy out of a system that runs perpetually with no recognizable fuel input. This hydrogen generator of theirs simply makes the stuff out of thin air, as far as I can tell, and this will provide free and unlimited energy for as long as it's running… which amounts to an indefinite period of time."

"I guess that's why they call it…magic!" he emits theatrically and grins. "But if it's really running off this energy layer they call the dynamistic flows, this would be your source, and a renewable one at that, by the sound of it. This reminds me of some of those early survey missions by the fleet into this new universe we found. They were detecting some kind of unusual energy layer, which they naturally described as abnormal energy."

"Yeah, I heard of that. And here we are using it with a form of technology that's about as abnormal as the energy itself."

"But just imagine if we could adapt any part of this to our own technology back home. It could change the way we live."

"Oh, I'm sure of it, but before we go that far, I think it would be prudent to take a few of their classes on the topic. Aside from this, we are also looking at a shortfall of a labor force, if we make any significant expansion. We currently have some imports from Tae'Eladar helping with the existing workshops, and this is another thing causing my horns to sag. These people are said to be Early Industrial, but here we have them training and working in automated facilities and using computerized data terminals. It's starting to put a few of our own people to shame for the expediency of their efforts."

"Ayene once told me their education system over there uses an unusual substance which she called an elixir that enhances their function considerably. As a result, these people are simply geniuses, no matter what tech level they have," he sighs and shakes his head. "Ensign, we're going to be in trouble unless we can learn to pick up our tails and push hard to keep up. Just try not to have any accidents along the way."

"Yes Sir!"

◆◆◆

"Commander," Thaelyn announces. "Have you received any word yet from the crew sent to examine that facility on Madzurki?"

"I did," Kailen responds. "We have a couple of possibilities here, depending on how much space the Professor needs to perform his studies. The mess hall represents a large room with enough space to set up a number of tables and desks, and since we're not supporting an active work crew, that space would not be required for a dining area. We also have the crew quarters, none of which are being used. They were all cleaned out of the personal items a while back as the former crew relocated to Ruuki uy'Daan. So, with a bit of work, we could possibly reclaim some of that, maybe also to remodel some portion of it to open up a larger space by taking out a few walls."

"This is promising, and it might also afford us a little privacy in case anyone comes looking. We could simply close off that section, as I would doubt any inspection crews would poke their noses into someone's personal quarters, especially if that someone is a civilian."

"That's my thought as well, and this could all be done fairly quickly and easily to get him up and running as soon as possible for his side of the Harvester research."

"Good, then let us begin with the dining area, and if he needs more, we can consider the rest. We should keep a number of additional people on hand to serve as support in case he needs it, including a pilot to assist with transport. And if anyone comes along for their inspection, we will try to hide everything in a closet while we put on a show with a few projections, if need be."

"That should be fun."

"My Lord," the General considers. "Having an inspection team is one thing, but I feel we should touch upon the idea of Darumon himself making a visit of any kind, especially if he should wish to inspect their progress for his weapon. How should we proceed on this?"

"While this is certainly possible, Lieutenant Ti'van once mentioned that he would most likely call ahead, although this does not necessarily ensure us a great amount of time if he intends to make his visit immediately after his call. But my hope is it will afford us just enough time to tidy up. After that, we may find ourselves pressed into some manner of play to give our excuses for Ytani and his actions. However, this also creates a rather significant complication whereas obtaining a ship is concerned. If he should discover his operation in such a state, we might lose that opportunity. All I can hope for at this point is that Adalon's prophecies about finding our way will continue to hold up. At the very least, we will have a chance at our ground invasion. And perhaps another possibility might arise elsewhere if we lose this one."

"Then I might suggest we formulate one or more contingency plans for this occasion, just in case. We are already describing Ytani as a rebel, but without that ship, he is a rather impotent one, especially if he has nothing to transport the weapon for his own use. Therefore, we will likely need an alternate excuse for that."

"Very well, but keeping in mind, these friends may come with their own ships."

"Granted."

"Alternatively, we could possibly excuse it as a natural disaster, such as something occurring on that moon, like a collision with another object. Such things can occur if you have asteroids or comets in the area, though a moon is a very small target to hit. This could buy us some time, but not much. We could also suggest an error in handling, but one that went unnoticed until recently."

"He won't be happy for either of those," Kailen admits. "But then, I suppose you can't expect perfection in such places as these."

"Indeed, but then we might also need to explain the work crews at the processor, and possibly the condition of the city and the low mining output, which I understand is still being reported as substandard by our people, correct?"

"Right, Kaliya tells me her people are playing with the numbers a little, suggesting a struggle to find new deposits, but they turn up too thin and running out more often."

"As if to say they have finally run out of the mineral within that mountain of theirs," Thaelyn muses thoughtfully. "This would represent a stall tactic, at the very least. I do hope this can hold up for us while we investigate our other objectives. But it would surely give us adequate reason for that ship. We could then play the role of Ytani and Commander Kriv'tik suggesting this new survey. I think Darumon would not want his production line to quit entirely, so he might submit to a continuation of his operations if we can play out a convincing scenario for him."

"And Ytani himself?"

"Assuming Darumon takes our bait, we can follow this with Kaliya's idea for his rebellion. Even if not for the ship, and if we say he is losing control, he might still try to escape with his newfound friends. And his mania, which must be a part of our play either way, can be applied to either of these."

"Yes, it most certainly could."

"But we should also direct ourselves to how this might play out if all things come together as we would desire them. We need a viable alibi. First, he was using his Gift to deliver the metal in trade for his female pleasures. We have Kriv'tik's recordings of those recent statements, and this clearly illustrates his abusive attitude and god syndrome. We have Belrum's stories of the outside world, which contradicts Ytani's own storytelling, and this is causing an uprising within that population. Therefore, his loss of containment, which is escalating out of control by this time, and this will incur our own form of a dwarven army on the move to take that base," he grins.

"And there goes the operation, as well as a clean-up."

"Indeed! If Ytani loses this, he loses his pleasures, and therefore he becomes irate that he can no longer play god. As such…well, who knows what he might do in retribution."

"Including sabotage and the theft of Darumon's weapon?" Kailen smiles mischievously.

"I think this is well within reason. After all, he was so remarkably responsible to go up to that ship in order to find these new deposits," he chuckles.

"Cu'Nar help us, you are as bad as Kaliya with this stuff."

"Perhaps, but I suppose I must admit she does carry some good points and fine ideas. I will say it again, Commander, she simply had to find her niche. Anyway, this means we must put on a show, and we naturally want Darumon to see this, to lodge it in his mind that he is losing his operations entirely on that world, and therefore to pull out. This must then follow with the apparent demise of the base along with the staff."

"This reminds me a little of our exploits during the war here," Padriyl notes. "For instance, the orcs and that phantom transport you had flying all over the place making trouble," he grins.

"Indeed," Thaelyn smiles. "And let us not forget a certain young man who played a collaborative role in a little joyride using that transport."

"I tried advising against it."

"Did you now! How unfortunate you were so unsuccessful."

"Yes, well, Marelle was very convincing."

"So, the loss of the mining base," Kailen continues. "Which sounds like another play on the com-link, is essentially cleaning house, leaving Ytani to take what he can and run with it. This leaves us with Lieutenant Ti'van's story of his alien friends, the specialist crew of armed dwarves, the theft of the ship and the weapon, and his rabid ego and delusions of godhood making threats against Darumon, and perhaps all of Azgarén. I'd like to see how that one turns out."

"This may be a curious one," Thaelyn nods. "But as with all things, we must temper ourselves, at least somewhat, so as not to cause the local military to panic. We want to bring them to our side if it is at all possible. So, rather than an outright threat using the weapon, the Lieutenant suggested making demands for tribute. This would serve to portray his desires to play god, and giving demands that should be light enough to afford our distraction until we can make our own move."

"Good, but let's hope we don't have any unexpected surprises along the way. This represents a lot of variables to play with."

"It does indeed. Therefore, I think it goes without saying, we should press forward with all due haste for our own objectives before any of this actually occurs. This might also demand us to conduct a few tests to find our operating parameters in that space using such as our scrolls."

Kaliya was once again on the field with a team of recruits practicing their combat technique, this time using a selection of practice weapons to simulate the ones they would use in actual battle.

The females were given sword-staffs, similar to the one Kaliya was granted during her mission to Ruuki uy'Daan, but this was a simpler design for training. She had been working with them to share her personal experience in how to spin, twirl, swipe, and slash with the weapon, as well as the gymnastic dancing moves also associated with the combat style. It was a style well-suited to the females due to their inherent grace and dexterity.

The males were each given a dire mace, which was an oversized metal ball on an elongated shaft, designed for two-handed use, and preferably by someone of sufficient strength to wield it. These troops were practicing with the weapons in the open spaces throughout the field, positioned well enough apart so as not to conflict with each other.

The art involved swinging, spinning, and hammering the weapon on either the enemies or the ground, which in the case of the actual enchanted version, would invoke a localized earthquake effect. Also included with the technique was to toss it into the air, much like a two-handed hammer throw sport to hurl the item over distance to land on a target marker. Again, the enchanted version would apply an effect on impact, in this case a fiery explosion.

A page approaches on the bleachers above, after passing through the training hall. He calls into the field.

"Lieutenant Nazég, your presence is requested in Rolsklinde."

Kaliya turns to him and nods, then calls up one of her squad leaders to fill in her place. She follows the page through the guildhall and out the front gate, joined by Master Sagrid as they make their way to their meeting. On arrival, they are greeted by Thaelyn, his officers, and Marelle who was standing by.

"Yes, my Lord, you sent for us?" she announces as she approaches the table.

"Kaliya, we have an assignment for you and Master Sagrid. This is to conduct a small experiment for us to determine the viability of a theory."

He directs them to sit down, and further brings their attention to a spell scroll laying on the table.

"During the course of this day," he instructs. "We have sent multiple deliveries of these scrolls to Madzurki, each at one-hour intervals, for a total of five deliveries. This example will make six. The idea is to test if the arcanic energies of these scrolls will bleed away from them in an area absent of an arcanic cloud, therefore giving us some empirical data for their duration before they go inert. We will send this one with Master Sagrid as he makes his journey with Marelle, but Kaliya, you will go into projected form and meet them there."

"Are we looking at any specific time limit here?"

"The scrolls would normally last for months, even years, depending on the spell Circle being inscribed and the quality of the materials used. Higher Circle scrolls tend to be inscribed using much finer materials with a longer lifespan than the lower ones. But until now, we really have no data on their performance in a universe without an arcanic cloud, which might affect the rate of decay."

Kaliya nods as she picks up one of the scrolls to examine it. She reads the name of the spell.

"A Scroll of Marking... So, this is to mark a rune. But if he's going there physically to cast this, what is my purpose in projected form?"

"We also sent your effigy apparatus there, recently modified with an arcanic capacitor. The Professor finished a design concept recently, in part using some of our existing technology, and in part borrowing a few ideas to improve the efficiency from those plans for the Harvester device. As a result, he installed a prototype on your unit, so this should give you the ability to use it in a barren fold."

"Ooh! So now I get to try it out," she grins.

"Correct. We really only need one example from you on this occasion. If it works at all, multiple efforts should follow along predictably."

"Of course, and the scrolls? What's the purpose of those if I'm using my semi-automatic rune marking device?" she smirks.

"Semi-automatic?" he raises his brow.

"Yeah. That machine could put a mage out of business. All you need to do is read the glyphs and the machine does most of the work."

"Indeed, I suppose it does at that," he chuckles. "In fact, between this and those mini conveyors we found on Ruuki uy'Daan, the Professor is suggesting we could completely renovate our existing portal technology with something new and perhaps more flexible. This might come out as a derivative of the new jump drive technology."

"Really! Wow, that should give poor Tanjhira another case of Horn Loss Syndrome."

She leads the group in a moment of laughter as Thaelyn continues.

"Yes, and I truly feel for her at this point. If I had any of my own, I might feel the same. But anyway, as for the scrolls, this is for any alternative methods we might find ourselves in need of pursuing. For instance, if we have physical bodies present and need to make the traditional use of portal runes. In the immediate term, if we find ourselves using this as our initial infiltration team, we need to discover if we have enough duration of time to allow them to find a safe haven in which to cast the scroll and mark a rune for a later return."

"As an alternative…in case something goes bad with our primary plan, I suppose."

"Correct. A few contingency plans are always desirable."

"Naturally."

"And since we must investigate both of these scenarios, we might as well do it together. We have everything waiting at the facility on Madzurki, along with some assistants to help process and catalog the runes you create. We need to be precise to keep yours and his separate for analysis, to see which of them, or perhaps both, provide viable options."

"Sounds like you've been working a few tricks behind MY back this time," she grins.

"Indeed, we need to keep our people on their toes," he smiles. "Or perhaps hooves, in your case. And when you are finished with this, I will have you report to Aelwyn for a review of your telepathic study. If we are to borrow memories from another individual, we need to be sure you are well enough practiced in the art. This becomes another aspect of our testing."

The month passes by with Kaliya appearing periodically for her enhanced tutoring session. By this time, Ayene was also in training with Aelwyn to hone her projection skill. She had also signed up for a number of introductory classes at the academy to begin her new studies, and along the way she held meetings and consultation with several instructors to teach her the protocol and etiquette of the Order.

Ayene marveled at the prim and well-structured etiquette used in Thaelyn's military, as compared to her own which seemed very methodical and dry. The Order was much more like a family, being a Fellowship of Knights, and as she listened to the lecturing by her new mentors, she began to understand how the local society held such high esteem and dedication to their cause, no matter what challenges they faced. And with each new experience, her determination grew to take this battle home and liberate her people.

As the month came to a close, a new event was occurring. Not a war causing the destruction of life, but instead a new beginning. In the Naarg uy'Sodrad could be heard the classic fussing of a pregnant mother struggling with the pangs of childbirth.

"Grace of the cu'Nar!" Ankhia screeches. "This is worse than anything my mother ever warned me about!"

"Ankhia, I told you we should use the anesthetic," Likha implores.

Ankhia groans as the contractions were increasing in magnitude. Likha and her team were standing over her as Aerlie and several others from Tae'Eladar aided with the delivery. Kailen stood off to the side, feeling helpless as his spouse suffered through her spasms. Sulíma stood next to him to afford comfort, while at the same time wondering if she should discontinue all future engagements of her flirtatious manners.

"I wanted this to be natural, but…ARGH… What in all the nether-space is he packing in there?!"

"Ankhia," Aerlie suggests. "Childbirth, for most of us, is a very difficult process. I've seen this so many times."

"Do you use…UGH…anything like drugs to take away the pain?"

"Not drugs, we use something different. And I think maybe

you should try it. This is your first, and that's usually very hard on a new mother."

"What is it...AHH...oh, forget it, just hit me!"

Aerlie reaches a hand behind Ankhia's neck and offers a gentle pinch, rubbing both sides lightly and applying a divine touch to soothe the pain. Ankhia feels the effect immediately and relaxes onto the bed. Her tensions and boisterous grumbling eased into a placid smirk.

"Wow, that's potent," she remarks peacefully. "What did you do?"

"It's a little trick we learn in our training as healers. It's a pinch on the nerves in the rear of the neck. Not enough to cause paralysis, although we can do that as well, as a temporary remedy in case someone is severely injured, and we need to fully immobilize them. In this case, it's a minor application to halt the sensation of pain, but again the effect is temporary, so we should see about hurrying you through this."

"Yeah, if you can convince the little monster to crawl out of there, I'm all for it," she grins.

Aerlie moves alongside Ankhia's body to her midsection and makes a quick examination. She takes a small bottle filled with a medicated oil and pours some into her palm, then applies it to Ankhia's belly. The oil makes Ankhia's skin tingle slightly. Aerlie then begins caressing the young mother's belly in rhythmic arcs along both sides.

"When I give the word," she issues. "I want you to push very hard and keep it up until we're done."

"You mean you can just bring him out on demand? I really need to learn how you do this."

Aerlie smiles as she continues her circular motions, building up tension within the abdominal walls, while at the same time bringing a momentary pause in the contractions.

"This is part of my Celestial training," she admits. "And now I teach this at the temple."

Likha and the other interns study her motions carefully. Kailen and Sulíma watched curiously as Ankhia lies there serenely awaiting her cue.

Aerlie's rhythm continued for several enduring moments, first to one side, then to the other, and with an occasional set of swipes across the middle. It was a rhythmic pattern that repeated several times, along with a subtle murmuring, until finally she felt the time was right.

"Ready… Now, Ankhia, push hard."

Ankhia bore down hard on herself as Aerlie slid her hands alongside the woman's oversized belly. The group watching the spectacle observed as the bulge made an assertive motion through the birth canal following Aerlie's hands as she moved to catch the baby on its way out, then easing it gently onto the bed just below.

"Great cu'Nar above," Likha gasps. "Yeah, I think I do need to go back to medical school…Tae'Eladaran style!"

"Likha," Sulíma mumbles faintly. "Nothing personal, but when my time comes, I want her to do it."

"Maybe by that time, I'll learn a few things on how it's done."

"Fair enough."

Ankhia relaxes from her struggle and looks down in astonishment at the new life she just brought forth.

"That defies everything we thought we knew about physiology," she chuckles weakly.

Likha assists in tying off the cord, and further to receive the afterbirth, while Aerlie and her attendants clean off the baby and wrap it in swaddling.

"You have a very handsome young son, Ankhia," she announces. "Congratulations on being the first of your people to bring new life to this world."

Ankhia takes her newborn child in her arms and gazes down at it, beaming brightly at the fresh young face. Kailen and Sulíma come closer to join the affair and offer their support. Aerlie and her people finish cleaning up and move to one side to allow the new family their moment.

✦

Another month passed, and Kaliya was tutoring Ayene on some of the finer points of projecting. Ayene had been given the same beginner set of study materials that Kaliya received when she was in training, including stuffed replicas of a hawk, a squirrel, a tiger, an insect, and a tree. The list of objectives in the training course had grown by now to involve greater precision of a person's observational skills to pick out small details quickly in order to replicate the image as a projection. Kaliya also helped her expand her imaginative qualities to conjure up freeform images, as well as her acting performance to impersonate those creatures.

At this moment, the two of them were projected and standing in the conference room of the guildhall that Kaliya so often used when called to service.

"Ayene, I need your assistance for a moment."

"What kind?"

"At some moment, I will need to impersonate my own Suuden'kai disguise. I think I should be alright to use my natural form, but with the seed entity on it. Would you mind allowing me to examine your body up close so I can get it right?"

"You mean without my clothes? It's not a pretty sight."

"Don't worry about that now, I just need to get the basic image."

"Um, do you need me to take everything off?" she grins modestly.

"We'll try to keep the sensationalism to a minimum this time," Kaliya smirks. "I think just the outer garments will be enough."

Ayene complies and reimagines her form down to her undergarments, allowing Kaliya to see most of her body with the seed entity attached. Kaliya walks around the Lieutenant's form studying it from all sides until she is satisfied.

"All right, now let me try."

She steps away and reshapes herself, also in her underwear, to match the seed entity on Ayene's body.

"What do you think?" she asks.

Ayene walks around her briefly to study the new form.

"It looks good, but don't forget the eyes. And you also need the interface unit."

"Ah yes," Kaliya readjusts herself. "What about rank insignias, in case I go as a military officer?"

"What rank, a Lieutenant maybe?"

"Yeah, good enough for now, I guess. It's not as noticeable."

"Gee, thanks," she smirks. "All right, you can borrow from mine."

"Oh…" she huffs playfully. "What I mean is, it won't draw as much attention to me walking around out there."

"Yes, I understand."

Ayene recomposes her image with her military uniform, and Kaliya mimics the arrangement. Ayene then makes yet another inspection to confirm the accuracy of the display.

"Now," Kaliya continues. "I want to show you a few tricks I learned along the way as I was scouting on Ruuki uy'Daan. Let's go to the city just in front of your civil management building."

They recall their memories of the former Daanen-Aryku city and vanish from the local space to reappear on the street just outside the building where Ayene worked part-time with her Commander. Here they pause briefly to study the local surroundings.

"Looks like you've been busy over here," Kaliya observes.

"Yes, I hear they finished work on the city hub, the research center and library, and a few more industrial workshops. The trouble is we're running short of staff to fill all the positions, so my Commander is negotiating to hire and train some more people from Tae'Eladar, and maybe a few more of your people."

"Maybe we can find more on Azgarén one day, also."

"We're hoping that, as well."

"All right, we're going to change into birds and fly off over those mountains to the south, and I'm going to show you how to zip along through the air without the need to have a solid line-of-sight target to focus on."

The final month was progressing forward, and Marelle was getting ready for her delivery. She had been collecting baby gifts from showers given to her by friends and family, and had a room set aside in her home neatly decorated and waiting. During this time, she and Roderick had discussed once more if they wanted to know the genders of their twins, but both decided to allow nature to take its course. The gift of Lathander would be a blessing no matter what they received from it.

In the WIC building, Thaelyn and his officers were in a meeting with both Kaliya and Ayene, and under Aelwyn's supervision. The day had come for another important experiment.

"I wish to call the attention of the room," Thaelyn announces. "This is a continuation of our experiments to test our capacity when interacting in unknown environments, such as that of Azgarén which is believed to be located in a barren fold. Previously, we tested ourselves to use our spell scrolls, as well as Kaliya's special, um, semi-automatic spellcasting machine," he winks at her, "in that same type of environment, in this case using Madzurki, to see how well they performed for us. Our results were favorable, at least insofar as our immediate operational concerns are involved."

"Your Lordship," Ayene wonders. "What sort of test was this?"

"We conducted a series of tests to mark portal runes, some of which involved scrolls that had been imported to that processor facility at intervals over a five-hour duration, and then Kaliya with her effigy device, as we tend to describe it, which allows her to perform this while projected. The purpose was to see how long a scroll might hold its charge during this time to give us a safe operating margin."

"So, this is to ensure you can actually mark your runes in that space to create a portal."

"Yes, it is. We needed some data just in case we find ourselves in need to use physical bodies, as opposed to her projection. But we also needed to test her device, as well. As such, we now know her device works, if to give it a fresh charge to work with, and we can trust the scrolls to provide a good five hours in which to find a safe hiding place. I cannot see how it might take longer than that to escape from a large city, but this is a good start."

"Do you think these scrolls could go longer than that if they needed to?"

"I am fairly sure they could, and I suppose we will conduct more tests later to find our limits. Overall, this gives us a very important advantage, and now we need to see how best we can use it, therefore today's experiment."

"I see," she grins and glares at Kaliya.

"My Lord," Kaliya wonders as she notices Ayene's smirk. "What have you been up to this time?"

"Oh, nothing too extraordinary," he grins. "At least, not in comparison to certain people recently in my employ. After all, we know of this one certain young lady who, for all her four centuries of ambition, needs a bit of exercise now and then."

"Uh huh."

"Therefore, this next test must carry us another step to confirm our proposed methods can indeed bring us forward. To this end, this delightful young lady," he smiles at Ayene, "has offered herself to help us in a small demonstration. Kaliya, you will recall your recent advanced tutoring with Aelwyn. Now is the time to use it. I will have the two of you sit here facing each other."

The two women take up chairs and position themselves close together face-to-face.

"This is how we will proceed," he continues to the group. "Ayene has recently been to a place, with the aid of an escort to help her find her way, and studied the local surroundings. If need be, she could project herself and travel there by recalling the memory. And we did have her test this to confirm the scenario. However, this is a location I do not believe Kaliya has yet visited in her own travels."

He pauses briefly to study the two women in their seats.

"The objective here is to see if Kaliya can learn this location by using her recent advancement in telepathy to peer into the mind of the other and study that same memory, thereby absorbing it as her own."

"I don't think even our father went this far," Kailen moans.

"This does in fact travel into a higher realm of sensory absorption. As a Celestial, I can perform this by merging my mind with another as a form of clairvoyance, to see with another person's eyes, hear with their ears, and so on. And since your Petrith once demonstrated this skill..." he coughs quietly, "...while peeking into the women's shower..." he smiles, "...we will use a variation of this skill for our needs."

"Oh dear...that poor guy."

"Once we have what we need, Kaliya will then go into the other room and project herself, then attempt to travel to that location. As proof of her deed, I have a man standing at that location holding a trinket which Kaliya will return to us here."

Kaliya and Ayene turn to each other after Thaelyn finished his briefing. Ayene relaxes herself as Kaliya leans over and places a hand on the woman's temple. Aelwyn supervises the process and conducts a passive telepathic scan to ensure it is proceeding appropriately.

Kaliya projects her mind at Ayene, penetrating her thoughts calmly as the woman recollects a vivid image of the location she had previously visited. She envisions a bleak landscape, flat and barren. Ayene's experience during her visit revealed a warm dry breeze. As Kaliya purveys the memory, she notices an impossibly high column of rock jutting out of the land. Although she had never seen this before with her own eyes, she knew what it must be from her lessons.

"The Spire..." she mutters quietly with a distant grin.

She peers deeply into the image to absorb it fully while Ayene continues to recall her experience, including the local space, the environmental conditions, and the general perception of where she had to travel to arrive there. When Kaliya had seen all that was available to see, she pulled out.

"Ready, my Lord," she declares calmly while still trying to hold onto the image.

"Now go and project yourself."

She stands up from the chair and moves away to the door, continuing through the hall to a small conference room where she can find peace. Thaelyn and the others wait. After several moments, Kaliya reappears in the room near the table.

"I am ready."

"Go."

She attempts to recall the image she so carefully burned into her mind, once again grasping for the sensation shared by Ayene from her own experience...and her projection fades from the room.

She found herself flying through a misty veil in multiple hues, an unimaginably massive cloud of vapors and swirling energies. Ahead of her was a dot that represented her goal. She focused her thoughts on that dot, imposing the memory of what it represented. Then the veil shifted, as if she passed through a membrane separating that from a clear sea of light and energy. It seemed like infinity in all directions, but still with that dot directly ahead. She needed to maintain her concentration on it to continue her course, yet the sights were so enticing.

The dot began to grow in size, and she knew she was nearing her target. She struggled to push forward, demanding herself to reach the endpoint of her course as it came closer. Finally, she could see details, including colors and a shape forming in the window of her destination. She made another push to touch it with her mind, and the dot began to envelop her, transforming the scene as a new environment formed.

She was standing at the base of the Spire, the massive mountain of rock reaching high above the center of the Outer Planar realm known on Tae'Eladar as Cynosure.

"Well now," ushers a prominent voice from behind her. "What do we have here? A young velvet horn who thinks herself so grand that she can stand with the gods now?"

Kaliya turns to find the familiar face of her training sergeant. She instinctively pulls herself to attention.

"Ease it off, Lieutenant. This isn't a formal review. How do you like visiting this place, ay? Not quite the same as your old home, I'll bet."

"Not nearly, but I'm very pleased to have this opportunity. I believe you have something I need to return to His Lordship?"

"Indeed, I do. Try not to lose it along the way. And while you're at it, tell him I'll be sending him the bill for a new set of boots after walking all this way."

"Not to worry, Sergeant, I'm sure he'll compensate you nicely for this. I assume you have a ride back home?"

"I sure bloody hope so, if I can ever get that old coot over there sleeping away his days by that rock to open a portal for us."

"Well, if you should have any trouble, I'm happy to lend a hand. For now, I need to report back."

The Sergeant holds out his hand to reveal a small silver medallion, much like an oversized coin, with the image of the Order heraldry symbol imprinted on it. She picks it up and makes an honorary salute before departing away.

Back in the WIC building, Thaelyn and his officers waited patiently. Ayene still sat in her chair, wondering if Kaliya was able to find her way. She was fascinated at how proficient her friend had become with such skills that seemed mythical to the people of Azgarén. And yet, she was not only able to use it, but to gain such knowledge from it that she could find her way to foreign shores by borrowing from another person's thoughts. As the group continued to ponder the possibilities of this experiment, Kaliya made her reappearance in the room, neatly positioned near the table and wearing a proud smile.

"My Lord," she begins. "I wish to thank you for the chance to see such marvelous sights. I would like to sit down with you sometime and tell you how it appeared."

"I would look forward to it. But now, did you actually reach your target in this case, or did you simply go sightseeing?"

She steps forward and offers him the silver medallion in her hand.

"By the way," she grins. "He says he's looking forward to a new set of boots after the long walk. I just thought I'd pass that along."

"Oh, is that so? Well then, we should not disappoint him. I will have you return to your body and report back here. We must now make plans on how we might use this."

Kaliya gives a salute and vanishes from the room, only to return a few moments later to find the group reassembled around the table. She finds a chair and sits down.

"Good, now listen carefully," Thaelyn directs. "We need information more than anything else at this time. Naturally, this means conducting a considerable amount of scouting to survey the local terrain and to locate a suitable campsite for our initial operations. Ayene and her fellows have provided us with some good information relating to the landforms and a world map, as taken from their data terminals at the base. This gives us a starting point, but now we need details, and these details will likely revolve around strategic targets and their military operations."

"As far as I know," Ayene comments. "The Marshal spends most of his time in his office, which is located onsite at Central Command."

"Good, for as long as he stays there, we can hope there will be no new worlds obliterated. But no doubt he still wants to pursue some of his other goals, and at this moment, I think one of those is likely to involve the prison portal where he can investigate the means of releasing the other Primordials."

"But, my Lord," Kaliya recalls. "We still have the Lady up there watching things for us, right?"

"Yes, and she will inform us if anything should occur. Until then, we might suggest he is laying low until one or another of his current projects comes to fruition."

"Or until he discovers one or another of those is currently a big gas cloud."

"Indeed!" he chuckles. "And for this, we must be ready with our own plans. The first of these is to dispose of that base, and this is where your idea of Ytani comes into play. What is the situation of our reports about the mining yields?"

"We're still playing with the numbers, and Central sent a reply once to confirm the condition of our operation, which is to ask if the mine in the city could be failing completely. Our response was that we believe it might be, but we're waiting for a confirmation before taking further action."

"A stall tactic... Good. We will continue this and hope the Professor finds his results soon so we can close that part of it down. Meanwhile, I want your team to be ready in case we have an urgent need to push forward with that ship. Ayene, what sort of ship do you think they would offer if we should call for a survey expedition?"

"For a mineral survey," she responds. "The most likely would be a science vessel, like a deep space planetary exploration ship, and probably with deep penetrating scanners to study the mineral content of the subsurface. These are usually a midrange cruiser category with a crew complement of several hundred members. It's still part of our space navy, but categorized as a research vessel, which is not as highly militarized. I think you shouldn't have too much trouble taking it, if you're careful and don't trip any alarms."

"Very good, then an infiltration shuttle loaded with Kaliya's team under a cloak will probably work nicely for us if we can take the most critical areas before descending to the rest of it. Now, as for the base itself... If we say Ytani is stealing a ship, how do you suspect Central will respond initially?"

"I think they would first try contacting it by comms, and if that fails, they might try sending a scout vessel to investigate the local region for any signs of a tragedy. If that turns up negative, the next likely action will involve an investigation of the last known contact and operating parameters, and what events might have led up to the disappearance."

"That seems fair enough," Kailen admits. "After all, if a ship goes missing, this would be a standard procedure to follow. But if we then start giving out the story of Ytani, this might turn ugly, at least as far as how Central will interpret things."

"Yes, I'm sure of it. First, we would need to build up the image. This might involve us filing those recordings of his last communications with our office. We can then finally reveal his true manners and demands to cover up for his actions where our female staff members were concerned, and this lets out that he's been behaving very badly. Along the way, we can also mention his god syndrome, and his threats to us concerning the chips and his private army."

"How do you think Central would respond to that, especially the chips?"

"One thing I would like to hint at," Kaliya offers. "Is Darumon's custom military and their determined lack of information sharing. If those people have no more idea of the mining operation than just a destination to send supplies on occasion, they need their eyes opened to ask questions a bit more often."

"This is true," Thaelyn affirms.

"As far as the chips go," Ayene continues. "My Commander and I both feel there are those within Central that would likely feel the same as we do, including the HC. I doubt any of us fully appreciate having those things installed. They're described as augmentations to improve our performance in battle. But those of us, like the Commander, who may have ever had them turned on, would quickly realize how unpleasant they can be. So, I think most of Central will sympathize with us, at least privately."

"Privately, but this suggests not in front of Darumon," Kailen wonders.

"Yes, it does, as he ultimately drives us to our Great Cause in the name of Sargeras. Therefore, we need to maintain a certain level of professionalism in front of him."

"If this is how he behaves with you," the General muses. "This is clearly an indication that he desires you to perform as his trained pets that do not question his motives."

"It does," she sighs solemnly.

"All right," Kailen resumes. "So, the message is delivered to Central. How do you see it following through?"

"I would expect it to follow our usual chain of command. We have a Watch Captain who oversees the operations inside the control center. He would chain to High Commander Geilv, as he would need to make a review of the details before any big decisions can be made on what to do about it. The loss of a ship is a rather significant affair."

"I should think so!"

"And since we're also speaking of the mining base, this will ultimately demand the attention of the Marshal. What happens after that, however, is another thing."

"And this is where my team goes into their act," Kaliya affirms. "I've been working on scripts for several members of the team, including Ayene to play herself. I would like her to be present just in case we need any of her inside information along the way."

"This is a clever strategy," Thaelyn nods. "She would be most familiar with their protocols, and this could serve us in case we find ourselves in a pinch."

"The biggest unknown here is whether our projections will be good enough to fool someone like Darumon. If he plays it like you, with apologies, and doesn't extend his higher senses to detect the veracity of our images, as opposed to physical bodies, we might be able to sneak in under the wire."

"And this would be a good test of your abilities, but it is also a gamble. However, I understand your meaning, and if he has been working with them for so long…indeed much longer than I have on Tae'Eladar…he might very well have relaxed his posture to the point where he takes everything at face value."

"That's the hope. Then, from here we want to drive him to make a few discoveries, like the absence of Ooduan by way of the conveyor status console in Madzurki, and the city below after we start our little playhouse riot."

"Then," Ayene adds. "We hope he will take the action we are expecting him to take, meaning to simply pull out, as there is nothing left for us there."

"After that, we need to dispose of the base. If he gives us a simple evac order, and with the condition of the city as it is, he might not order a full dismantling of the base, as there might not be enough time for it. Instead, I'm thinking he might use that reactor technique again, like he was trying to do with Rolsklinde."

"This would certainly follow with his practice," Thaelyn accedes. "And it would do a fine job in his absence to remove his evidence."

"Unfortunately, the dwarves will find it first…" Kaliya smirks. "And much to their chagrin, as well as the base crew, they simply get physical with it, which isn't something you normally want to do with a fusion reactor."

"Indeed, it is not!" he chuckles. "I must feel for those who are unfortunate enough to be caught in the blast effect. But even with this being played out on their com-links, we still need to remove the physical evidence in case anyone comes to investigate the remains at a later moment."

"Our people could do that easily enough," Kailen offers. "That base, from the way it's described to me, is modular and designed to be packed and unpacked, at least within reason."

"Very good, and this alleviates our concern of the future outcome for that world. From here, we move forward to our next objective."

"Azgarén…" Ayene muses. "I wonder what we'll find once we get there. I know what we'll find inside Central Command, but I wonder if we can find any help along the way."

"Sympathizers would surely be welcome, but we would be operating very close under the eyes of our opponents, so any form of interaction must be handled with the utmost discretion."

"My Lord," Kaliya notes. "Petrith and I were browsing some media files on the Commander's terminal to see if we could find anything useful. We found a news article on my father, where Darumon created this fanciful story of how he apparently found and dispatched him…finally…in some remote unchartered star system on the far side of our home galaxy…if you can believe such rubbish."

"I recall that report," Ayene affirms. "He was discovered taking sides with some previously unknown race as part of this insurgency, and also said to have been coordinating some portion of the attacks we were suffering. You know, at the time, I felt a subtle sense of relief that this part of our troubles was at an end. Now, I just want to laugh at it."

"Is that before or after pulling your horns out?" Kaliya smiles.

"Both!"

"Well, all laughing aside, I'm actually wondering about the woman who was reporting that bit, and what kind of person she is on the inside. For instance, is she someone who might find it exciting to report on some real news, or is she just a mechanical voice to read canned statements set down in front of her?"

"Um, who was it that gave that report? Was it Ileani Ur'paran? She's a regular at C.P. News, one of their main anchors."

"Is she popular? Do the people pay that much attention to what she has to say?"

"I believe so, actually. She's something of a celebrity image in journalism. Although, when you consider those regulators, well..."

"Yes, but my point is, what would she do if someone should come up to her and make an offer for real news, and further to evict those regulators so she could actually report it?"

"They work for the Council, remember. How do you explain to them that their regulators are being kicked out of the building?"

"Do you have any real laws in that place? How do you explain the application of censorship in your society? Is it regarded as legal or illegal."

"Actually, illegal. According to my law degree, Article Nine, Section Fourteen of the Charter of Laws, otherwise known as the Truth in Reporting Act of 3752 CTD..."

"CTD?" Thaelyn raises his brow. "Is this a calendar date?"

"Yes, actually, and measured in centuries. CTD, Centennial Time Delineation...very scientific, like everything else in our culture. We can further involve decimal values to include decades or individual years."

"Powers help us. And when was this calendar based if we are already involving dates in, what is it..." he waves a finger in the air briefly trying to calculate the numbering, "...hundreds of millennia?" he winces.

"Good gracious!" the General wheezes.

"Yeah," Ayene smiles. "It dates back to King Saakerav and the transition to our new social organization with a Council of Elders and the beginning of what we call the Enlightened Era. Our current calendar date is up to 9862.44."

"Ugh…" he moans and covers his face. "While the numbers themselves may not be so bad, to hear them spoken in this context is rather disturbing."

"Sorry…" she giggles. "Anyway, according to this Article, which is old by now, dating back even before our industrial era, but where we were developing our first media services using old-style wired telegraph relays, it says the news media is required to report true and accurate statements, to the best of their ability. We're supposed to be a society of intellectuals with freedom of information, if you recall, not a police state. So, intentionally giving out false or inaccurate information over the media stream would be regarded as a felony, assuming anyone in our authority positions was actually following this rule. But it would seem the Council isn't, and neither is the military."

"To the best of their ability?" Kaliya muses. "I can see a flaw in that statement, if their 'ability' is being curtailed."

"Very cleverly stated, Kaliya," Thaelyn nods. "And this ultimately reaches back to Darumon with his regulators curtailing their ability. Especially if we apply some form of justification to it, like these war protocols demanding some form of discretion."

"I swear!" Ayene huffs. "Such a nasty little trick to play on us. So, technically, we can say they're not actually breaking any laws under these conditions, if the news is being fabricated, and all they have to report, to the best of their ability, is what's given to them, and likely to prevent any new panics for the real news."

"Let's try another approach," Kaliya offers. "Does your law degree offer anything we can use as a technicality to override this?"

"Well, I suppose we do. They always teach us it's the spirit of the words we're supposed to honor. So, by the spirit of the words, they are supposed to report THE truth, to the best of their ability to report anything at all."

"The spirit of the words," Kailen chuckles. "We still teach it using that principle."

"Do you still use the original Charter with your people?"

"Yes, the famous Charter of Laws is still with us, and our teachers still carry those same principles to educate our students. It's a time-honored tradition, I guess."

"All right," Kaliya leans forward. "If it's the spirit we must honor, then we need to teach these people what this spirit actually is. What if someone were to blow the whistle on those regulators? Doesn't anyone actually tell the world there are regulators inside your media services?"

"No, apparently not," Ayene concedes. "Which simply points to a conspiracy to keep it secret."

"Fine, but we need to break that conspiracy. Do you at least have a functioning court system over there?"

"I would like to say yes," Ayene responds. "But all things considered, with where we stand on so many questionable topics, it's a little hard to say."

"All right, add this to the list. Investigate a valid court system, and magistrates who can be brought to our side."

"Certainly! And I can think of a few people I knew of during my university studies."

"Good. So, here is what we need to do. We need to start playing this back on him."

"By playing it back on him, are you saying to call someone like C.P. Security on those regulators?"

"We need them out of the way before we can impose any of our own propaganda. But we also need people on the inside, and in such positions that we can flex a little of our own authority muscle."

"Sounds reasonable."

Thaelyn watched the two women as they plotted their schemes. He turns to Kailen and the General.

"Gentlemen," he mutters softly. "We will need to monitor these two carefully. I think we are observing a multitude of new marks in the making."

"Cu'Nar help us," Kailen moans. "And I thought ONE of them was bad."

"Indeed," the General grins. "And this might also prove to be rather entertaining along the way."

Kaliya continues, "We'll need to gently point a few fingers at the suspected offenders and where they come from. But someone will have to be in-the-know deep enough to follow our game. We'll also need evidence to hold up our claims, and those regulators are an obvious starting point. Then we need someone inside the news media to join up so we can feed them our own news stories."

"And if you have in mind to use Miss Ur'paran for this," Ayene surmises. "You'll have a reputable image speaking for you. The question then becomes, what sort of message are you planning to release?"

"We should begin with something innocent, but realistic, to start picking apart Darumon's machine. And it has to be done in small pieces, as if to say something the regulators might not otherwise think is in need of censoring."

"I would agree. And this can begin to open their minds to some of these long-standing discrepancies the people were too dull-horned to realize during these past ten millennia," she chuckles.

"Yeah, to stir things up enough to untwist a few horns. Those people need to remember what it means to think with their own heads. For instance, ten millennia and no one ever remembered you have eco-friendly tech for all that dirty industry? What do you have for laws relating to environmentalism and pollution?"

"Um, let me see..." Ayene reflects. "Article Twenty-Three, which is known as the Environmental Preservation Act of 6210. This basically demands any industry that pollutes in any way that is harmful to the environment to clean up their act with decontamination technologies, or else be shut down, along with being fined or have other penalties placed on them."

"Perfect. It's nice to have a legal expert on our side," Kaliya smiles. "Too bad your Council didn't see this coming a long time ago. This should actually be their job, shouldn't it?"

"It should, assuming they were actually doing it."

"This is quite reasonable," Thaelyn affirms. "This ought to follow a natural progression of action and reaction. It is very unfortunate that no one ever did this previously, or else that it never resulted in any affirmative action. Even more so that no one ever questioned it, or demanded a result based on these laws."

"I believe it's all being kept under a war declaration. Therefore, no one holds the authority to do anything about it. Not for as long as those awful insurgents are out there."

"Oh, but of course, how silly of me to forget that," he shrugs.

"This does bring up a good point, however," Ayene considers. "I have my law degree, but I'm not the only one. What about all the OTHER law degree holders out there and anything they might have to say about it. If we could get a movement going..." she ponders thoughtfully. "You know, if Darumon needs so many falsehoods and misinformation to control the show, he wouldn't fare as well if the full world population should discover his lies."

"Unless you factor in another of his death toys," Kailen mentions.

"Well, yes, but one of our primary objectives will need to be to find who makes his death toys and take them out. We also need to take control of his military machine somehow. If he loses that, he loses his control mechanism. He would be reduced down to just his personal means."

"But this can still be dangerous, if we consider what he did when he first arrived here on Therinë, and what we think he did where that Tav'ageen Anomaly of yours is concerned."

"We will need to expose that, as well," Kaliya admits. "But I'm sure this is getting ahead of ourselves. So far, we need to dismantle his machine, as much as we can without exposing ourselves, and probably also expose the Council for their part in things. In fact, I'd like to know where they are and what they think about their own laws if they're so obviously breaking them. If they were to become aware of who and what he really is, I think the game would change a little."

"Maybe so," Ayene relents. "But good luck trying to tell them. According to our illustrious news feed, they mostly hand out nothing more than simple press reports saying nothing new is happening today, please try again tomorrow."

"Really! And who is it that actually says this?"

"Their press agents, they're the only ones I ever see quoted by the news, not the Council members themselves."

"Incredible. So, what is your Council doing if not proposing any new government mandates, initiatives, new laws and policies, press releases over new discoveries, and whatever else it is they're supposed to be doing?"

"That's a really good question. I actually recall from people I've spoken to in my lifetime that no new developments have been reported for as long as anyone can remember…"

Suddenly, Thaelyn perks up. His relaxed posture now abruptly lurches forward on hearing those last words spoken by Ayene. His unexpected reaction drew the quick attention of the meeting. The General jerked around to stare at him nervously.

"My Lord? Do we have something important?"

"Powers behold," Thaelyn whispers. "But it would surely follow with his pattern."

"Your Lordship," Kailen mutters timidly. "What is it?"

Ayene studies the group, suspecting something bad just happened. But being as yet unaware how to interpret Thaelyn's manners, she was at a loss to understand it.

"Um, did I say something wrong?"

"You said…" Thaelyn responds. "According to these people… for as long as they can remember, nothing new has occurred. Is this how you describe it?"

"Gods above!" the General wheezes. "But of course, that would make sense."

"Yes, it would," Kailen admits softly.

"And this would afford us a reason for their apparent absence," Kaliya adds. "They might not even exist at all by now."

"Um," Ayene flusters. "What are you people talking about?"

"Rolsklinde…" Thaelyn declares boldly. "When Darumon was impersonating the local Governor, he interfered with their education system, as well as whatever news and information on world affairs they might generate, leaving the people ignorant of virtually everything occurring around them. All they could recite to themselves were those same words…for as long as they could remember, nothing new is occurring. Could he be doing the same with you? He controls your news media as well as your military, which translates as your source for all the interesting facts your seekers of free information might otherwise expect to receive. He then fabricates his own stories as fetishes for your public rather than any actual news."

"Incredible!" she wheezes. "And with regulators to oversee it from the inside…"

"Then we have your Council, which does not seem to be conducting any of the affairs you would normally expect them to be conducting…and for as long as any of you can remember. And in your case, this would be a respectable length of time. So, the question becomes, where are they if they are not otherwise where they are supposed to be? In Rolsklinde, Darumon eliminated the former government of the city and replaced it with his own."

"In all the nether-space!" she shouts. "He would do that to us? And on top of everything else?! No wonder they always seem to be missing from the public view. They're always said to be hiding in some private chamber doing…whatever it is they're supposed to be doing, and it's always top secret and highly sensitive."

"And for how long? This is the question I think we should answer. When was the last time anyone actually saw one of them physically?"

"And if they actually are missing in action," Kaliya muses. "How closely is Darumon paying attention to his minion regulators, and anyone else he expects to be doing their job while he's off destroying worlds."

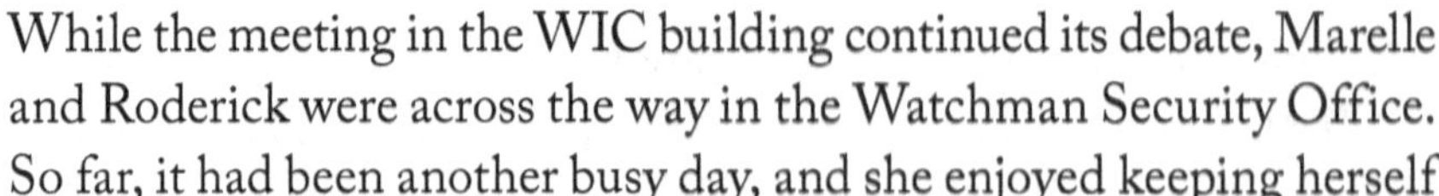

While the meeting in the WIC building continued its debate, Marelle and Roderick were across the way in the Watchman Security Office. So far, it had been another busy day, and she enjoyed keeping herself occupied next to her husband. Her work had become increasingly difficult as she had grown so much due to her pregnancy, but she found herself to be too unsettled and filled with boredom to just sit around the house waiting, so she continued her work as best she could under the circumstances.

During this last month, she found it very uncomfortable to sit in one place for long periods. She had replaced her usual chair with a more extravagant leisure chair and added an extra pillow to it for better comfort. Still, it was hard for her to conduct her work, as the desk was now just on the edge of her reach.

And then it happened…

She felt a twinge erupt in her lower belly, soon followed by a soaking of her garments. She looked down at herself.

"Um, Roddy…" she calls across the room. "I have a little situation here."

"Oh, what sort?" he responds casually, not realizing the severity of the condition as yet.

"I'm wet, I think my water broke."

He quickly jerks up at the mention and turns towards her, his nerves instantly spiking.

"Oh great! Do you think you can make it to the Healer's Ward?"

"I'm not sure, but I'll have to try. The thing is I was hoping Lady Aerlie would do it, but she's all the way over in B.T."

"That's a good bit of walking from here."

He jumps to his feet and helps her out of the chair. She leans on him as they leave the room, making their way out of the office and into the yard.

"Lieutenant!" he shouts at the yard officer. "We need a wagon over here, now! And someone fetch a blanket or something for us."

The yard officer dashes off into the plaza to find a convenient wagon while another one runs up to take Marelle on the other side. Together they struggle to support her as the yard officer locates a suitable transport. Yet another man brings out a blanket from a supply room to wrap around her.

"And someone fetch His Lordship!" Marelle shouts. "He asked to be made aware of this when it happens."

<hr>

"Ayene," Thaelyn begins. "Tell us about the arrangement of your government buildings. For instance, is it anything like what we have on Tae'Eladar, with the parliament building, another for our High Council, and then office buildings and so on?"

"Yes, generally so," she responds. "My mother once took me there when I was little, but since then I rarely ever visited it for any reason. It's a very neat and well decorated plaza with large buildings all around representing offices and meeting halls for our public officials, like legal councilors and top-ranking political officers. At the center is the Council's Grand Hall. It's generally a round building lined with offices for the individual Council members and their division agencies, as well as secretaries and other public offices. In the middle is the Grand Hall itself, the inner chamber, which is a large room with the Council bench positioned within a semicircle of seating for a viewing audience of legal advisors and research division executives. This is for those occasions of people submitting ideas for new directions in our science and discovery."

"Sounds rather nice... Then here is what we will do. Once we settle a few of our more immediate objectives, I will give you an assignment to investigate their chambers. We must be discreet, but I want to know if that Council of yours is actually inside and doing any manner of work. Further would be to discover the last time anyone ever saw any results of this work. If Darumon is so closely controlling your government, we need to see who he is controlling, assuming there is anyone at all."

"Or if it's just more of his lies and minion servants telling people not to ask questions. I swear, I'm almost ready to go up to my old Captain at C.P. Security and tell him to arrest everyone involved with this fiasco."

"Perhaps, but let us follow a predictable path here."

As the meeting considers this recent dilemma, the conversation is interrupted by a voice shouting into the room.

"My Lord!" shouts a watchman officer. "Lieutenant Carronel is in labor!"

The room turns to the attention of the officer just arriving from outside. Thaelyn stiffens his posture at the announcement.

"Great Powers… Very well, send word that I will be out in a moment."

Thaelyn turns back to the meeting at the table.

"We shall adjourn this for now. General, send a page to B.T. to inform Aerlie. And find a mage!"

He jumps out of his chair and dashes out of the room, followed by the other members close behind.

Marelle was sitting on a wagon by this time, waiting in the middle of the plaza. She was wrapped in her blanket to keep her warm and to cover her soiled garments. People had collected around her to offer support, and several priests were arriving at her side from the local temple to give comfort. Thaelyn emerged from the WIC building in a hurried jog, followed by the other officers and a mage.

"Mage," he charges as he pulls out a rune from a special slot in his belt. "Take this and open it as secondary."

The mage takes the rune and begins casting the enchantment on it.

"My Lord," Kaliya inquires hastily. "Is there anything I can do?"

"At this moment, I think we may be in good hands, if only to take her to B.T. for Aerlie to attend. If you desire, you may follow. I am aware there are many who are curious to see what we have arriving here."

"All right."

Thaelyn steps up to the wagon as the mage engaged the portal energies in the rune. Ayene observes the scene in wonder at the flurry of attention.

"Kaliya," she asks softly. "Is it commonplace for people to behave so frantically over a woman in labor here?"

"Somewhat. It's often considered a very exciting occasion for them. But Marelle is special because she had a…um…very peculiar moment of conception."

"What do you mean by that?"

"I'll tell you later. Just follow close behind."

"Marelle," Thaelyn calls to her. "Come close, I will carry you."

"I'm wet, my Lord. My water broke a few moments ago. I have this blanket around me, but…"

"So I see. Very well then, so be it. Never mind it for now, just come to me."

Marelle slides across the bench on the wagon into Thaelyn's arms. He grips her gently, but firmly.

"Sir Roderick," he directs. "You will follow after me, and the rest after that. This rune takes us directly to the guildhall. From there we shall have but a brief walk to the temple."

He next turns to the mage.

"Hit me with it."

The mage reaches over and touches Thaelyn's shoulder with the rune. He and Marelle both vanish in a flash, arriving on a platform in the guildhall courtyard.

"Watch Captain!" he shouts as he steps off the platform. "Send word to Aelwyn to meet us at the Healer's Ward."

Relissa, Haran, Sulíma, and the others were again gathered on the bench enjoying a pleasant afternoon chat as the arrival came through.

"Jiggers!" Relissa shouts. "Haran, it's happening!"

"What's going on?" Sulíma wonders urgently as she jerks around at the commotion.

"I think Marelle is having her baby."

"Kailen, I want to be there," ushers the voice on the trans-com. "Just give me a moment to find some help."

"Ankhia, are you sure?" he intones cautiously as he waits for the others to pass through the portal. "I remember you wanted to see this, but you're still recovering from your own…"

"Kailen, I wouldn't miss this for anything, the way you described it to me that day. I'll call Likha and have her assist me."

"Very well, should I wait for you here?"

"You go ahead, I'll meet you there."

The link on the trans-com ends and Kailen takes his turn passing through the rune portal, leading up the rear of a procession following Thaelyn and Marelle out of the guildhall and down the avenue to the Healer's Ward at the temple.

Marelle looked over her shoulder at the long line of people forming up behind them and sighed.

"Wonderful. So, am I going to be on the morning review again?"

"Take ease, Marelle," Thaelyn offers soothingly. "I think this time the city is safe. Or at least that is my hope."

"Oh, thank you, my Lord," she chuckles weakly. "You're so comforting in your words. But I will admit one thing. Where else would you find yourself being carried along for something like this by your own king," she giggles.

"Indeed, I would imagine you might not see this quite as much, if you look at some of our early history."

They arrive at the temple entrance to the Ward, where Aerlie and a group of priests were waiting for them.

"This way," she announces. "We have a room ready for you."

She leads them further into the Ward to a private room where Thaelyn lays Marelle on the bed. Marelle repositions herself for better comfort while Aerlie and the priests help with her garments. Thaelyn then directs the other prominent guests to move back, affording the expectant mother some breathing room.

Relissa, Haran, and their Daanen'kai friends, formed a group on the side of the room. Kailen joins with the General, along with Kaliya and Ayene, in an adjacent corner. Roderick stood next to Marelle holding her hand. Soon to arrive was Aelwyn, who took up next to Thaelyn, and several minutes later, Ankhia and Likha arrived from the Naarg uy'Sodrad. Ankhia was carrying her newborn in a sling pouch provided by Aerlie to keep the child cozy as it nestled in front of her.

By this time, Marelle's dress had been removed and a blanket laid over her, folded up to allow Aerlie access for the delivery. Aerlie made several passes around Marelle's body to check her condition.

"How do you feel, Marelle?" she asks.

"The contractions are slow so far, but other than that, I'm alright."

"Good. We will allow the contractions to build a little before we begin. The body knows when it's time."

Marelle relaxes on her pillow, looking up at Roderick with a gentle smile.

The assembly waits patiently for the contractions to increase their frequency. Whispers of casual conversation circle around the room to keep things calm and pass the time. Kaliya, Relissa, and their friends tell Ayene the story of Marelle's sexual exploits, bringing her in line to the significance of the affair. Roderick was tense, but remained under control, confident that his beloved was in the best of care.

Aerlie continued to make periodic exams as Marelle's contractions increased, until finally the moment was approaching.

"All right, Marelle," Aerlie advises. "I'll help bring them out, and I want you to follow my instructions on when to push. Until then, you should try to refrain from the urge. Simply breathe calmly and allow the sensation to pass."

Marelle nods as Aerlie performs another examination of her midsection. She peers inside to observe the orientation of the two unborn babies, making sure they were properly aligned.

Ayene watched the affair with fascination, turning to Kaliya on several occasions asking about the procedure.

"How is it possible she can see inside there without any sort of medical scanner? What about bio-monitors and pharmaceutical delivery tubes? And where is the incubator tray and atmospheric filtration apparatus?"

"Jiggers," Relissa moans. "Do you peeps actually need so much hullabaloo just to have a baby?"

"Well, some of it isn't so much hulla…um, whatever that word is, but necessary for our pollution content. Other parts are necessary to monitor the mother as well as the baby for their condition."

"Our environment here is much different," Aerlie offers. "First, we do not have that same pollution content, so the filters are simply not necessary. As for the rest, we have our own means of monitoring things, and I suppose one day, as the technology improves, we may apply some of that, but perhaps not to such invasive need as what you are suggesting."

"Do you at least use drugs to help with the pain?"

"Not drugs, specifically, but we do have a technique we can apply. You can ask Ankhia about it, as she had this just recently. Speaking of which, Marelle, how do you feel about this?"

"I feel a lot of pressure, but so far I'm handling it."

"All right, if it changes, you tell me, and I'll give you a little pinch to ease it off."

Aerlie once again applied a handful of her medicated oil and started rubbing it onto Marelle's stomach. She then began a set of rhythmic passes around Marelle's abdomen. It was a very similar pattern of caressing movement as she did before with Ankhia, but this time since there were two babies involved, it was mostly oriented to one side, selecting the first child to be made ready. She repeated this process to massage the body, once again building tension within the muscles, occasionally making a pass along the other side to offer balance, but specifically preparing the body to bring forth the first child. Her motions allowed the babies within to position themselves so that one would be ready while the other held in reserve.

"Are you ready, Marelle?" she begins. "And…now, push!"

Marelle gives a strong push while Aerlie slides her hands downward along the surface, directing the first child to make a smooth passage out of the body. The other priests stood waiting to receive it, tying off the cord and cleaning it up, then removing it to a small, cushioned table to the side and wrapping it in swaddling.

"Criminy," Relissa mumbles softly. "My Mum never said anything about it going this easy."

"I don't ever recall a conversation like this," Haran relents. "It was much more of a womanly thing."

"All I can say is," Kaliya considers. "My mother had it hard trying to deliver me."

"I have nothing to say about it," Ayene adds solemnly. "My mother never had this discussion with me."

"Is it because it never came up, or you just don't talk about it?"

"Um, I'm not sure how to answer that. Maybe it just never came up. I was young, before the time when it might become an issue, and then I just got busy with things," she shrugs casually.

Aerlie makes ready for the next one. She continues her pattern of massaging to bring the other baby into alignment for the birth canal, and once again continues her caressing movements to build tension within the muscles.

"And here we go for Number Two, are you ready? Now, push."

Again, Marelle gives a sturdy effort while Aerlie brings the next baby out, and the priests take their role once more to prepare the child.

"Wonderful, Marelle. Now you can rest. We'll clean up."

The new mother relaxes into the cushions, breathing a sigh of relief and gripping Roderick's hand as he stands over her brushing the hair out of her face and laying a gentle kiss on her cheek.

Aerlie turns to examine the two newborn babies, now neatly wrapped in swaddling.

"Marelle, it seems you are the proud mother of two baby girls, identical twin sisters from the looks of it."

She brings the two little girls over to Marelle and sets them carefully into their mother's arms. Marelle and Roderick both looked down at their little faces just peeking out from the hoods of their wrappings. They were fair-skinned, with thin light copper colored hair, which seemed to shimmer in the light. They had not yet opened their eyes, appearing serene and relaxed.

Thaelyn moved in carefully to peer over the bed. Relissa and the others stepped in quietly to take a look. Aelwyn moved around to the other side for her review. The room was filled with smiling faces and warm feelings.

And then the babies made their first gentle peek at the outside world.

Marelle and Roderick gazed at them as they slowly opened their eyes, blinking lazily, then to look up into the face of their young mother. The two little girls seemed to respond together, as if on cue by mutual agreement. Their eyes were glazed over at first, but as they cleared, the two new parents got their first chance to exchange glances with their lovely new daughters and their beautiful…golden…eyes.

Marelle felt a sudden anxiety come over her.

"Roddy, is it just me, or… Do you see that?"

"Yeah, what is that? Is that normal?"

Aerlie moved up quickly when she sensed the heightened tension building in Marelle. She studied the newborn faces.

"Thaelyn, look at this!"

Thaelyn comes in closer for a better view, as did Aelwyn on the opposite side of the bed. Relissa and the others strained to catch a glimpse of what was happening while trying not to crowd the scene.

"Well now," Thaelyn whispers. "I think we have our answer."

"Would someone like to tell me what this is?" Marelle urges nervously. "I mean…" she glances up at Thaelyn and his eyes. "Oh dear…"

As the group gazed at the new babies, they could see their eyes clearly now. The color was unmistakable. It was the same golden color as Thaelyn and Aelwyn.

"How lovely," Aerlie decrees. "And the hair color is rather unique, too."

Aelwyn's empathic senses begin detecting a new sensation arising from the bed. She extends her hand to hover over the nearest child's head.

"Thaelyn, see here," she bids. "Place your hands over these children."

He follows her instruction, first with the baby on his side, then to the other. Aerlie also brings her hands near their heads. Marelle and Roderick waited nervously to hear their reactions.

"Well?" she demands lightly.

"I am sensing a Celestial aura between them," Aelwyn issues. "Positive, and transitional to Ordered…"

"Transitional? You mean, like from Bitopia? Part neutral, part ordered?"

"Indeed!"

As Thaelyn examines the two babies, he senses a passive telepathic bond.

"Aerlie, do you feel that?"

"They're linked!" she declares. "Barely out of the womb, and they're already linked."

"I must wonder for how long. Perhaps they spent some amount of time like this already, maybe even to peek into the rest of us along the way."

Marelle felt a welling-up of uncertainty inside her.

"I gave birth to Celestial babies?" she whimpers. "I don't know how to raise Celestial children!"

"Rest easy, Marelle," Thaelyn assures. "We will help you. But this is a most extraordinary occasion! Do you know what you have here? These children carry Lathander's aura, meaning they are as much his children as they are yours. They are telepathically bonded, in a way similar to Aerlie and I, and perhaps even more so...being identical twins. I must wonder what other powers he has bestowed upon them."

"But how do you raise children like this?"

"In much the same way as you would most others, but their capacity will be much more pronounced than the average example. Aerlie and I, and perhaps also Aelwyn, if she can pull herself away from her classes long enough," he smiles, "will likely need to spend a fair amount of time tutoring them in their Celestial training. They might also need to spend some time up in either Celestia or Bitopia for special study sessions."

"For this much," Aelwyn suggests. "I think we should call Aristan down here to help. Maybe even Nemelle."

"Who are they?" Marelle wonders. "I mean, I've heard the name Nemelle before, I think..."

"Yes, I believe we spoke of this once before up in Sigil. Aristan is my personal love, and would be my beau if I could ever pull him away from his service in Bitopia. And Nemelle is a close friend of mine from the guild up in Sigil, in her case derived from a Morier."

"Wow! So, more Celestials like you?"

"Yes, the remainder of our little circle, along with Thaelyn and Aerlie. In Aristan's case, he is Aasimar, and Nemelle, much like with Aerlie, is an Eladrin. Aristan's father is Oghma, and he possesses considerable talent in inspirational enthusiasm and intellectual growth. He also has a tendency to be very flamboyant in how he presents himself," she grins brightly. "And Nemelle gravitates more to the chaotic side, being part Morier, and her father is Corellon Larethian, the leader of the Seldarine."

"Oh dear, this should be fun," she chuckles.

"But Marelle," Thaelyn soothes. "For now, you should rest at ease knowing you have two exceptionally special children, and all of us to support you. It would seem our meager numbers have grown a bit."

"Aye!" Relissa yips. "Now, all you need are a few boys to toss into it."

Marelle and Roderick attempt to force down their anxiety. They exchange stares and reflect on the events that brought them up to this moment.

"Well," she considers meekly. "I guess this explains that wild ride we had. It must take a lot to make children that are half-god."

"Yeah," he concedes. "But let's hope it doesn't happen again. I don't think I dare show my face again inside that inn over there."

Thaelyn steps back, along with Aerlie and Aelwyn, to allow the others in the room to pay their respects. Each of them gazed in wonder at the incredible sight. The children were completely at ease, as if already aware of their surroundings and welcoming the attention.

Chapter 9

PREPARATIONS

Thaelyn and his officers, along with Ayene and Kaliya, were meeting in the WIC building again. It was a new day after Marelle's delivery, and they were still deliberating how to make their approach to Azgarén.

"Your Lordship," Ayene begins. "Among other things, since you're already assigning duties to me, is that I would like to make a visit to the ARC one of these days to pick up a seed specimen for the Med-tech to study."

"This would be to initiate her research on a solution to it, correct? Yes, this will need to be one of our objectives. But as I recall from the Med-tech's last statement on the matter, she would not be able to invest as much time into it until she could stabilize her scheduling with her new child. I would desire to give her this moment so we could find ourselves with the finest talent available to provide our answers."

"All right, this is reasonable. I can wait for it. But I find myself trying to imagine how I might approach it. I could have my Commander write up a requisition for the seeds, saying we're conducting a special test, but we need a really good excuse for it, as this isn't something I would expect any casual military division would get involved with."

"I would have to agree, and so you will need a few contingency plans in effect to answer the questions as to the reasoning."

"Well, one thing is for certain, sitting here with you and listening to your strategic planning has already broadened my perspectives in this area. So, what do we do next? We need to make that first landing, don't we?"

"We do, and for this, we must conduct another test. At the same time, once we make this step, perhaps we could begin installing a few operatives for some preliminary intelligence gathering."

"I've been working with Petrith," Kaliya notes. "He's progressed far enough in his studies to project himself consistently, and Aelwyn has been working on his telepathy. He's nearly up to my level by now."

"You seem to be working him hard. What about his other studies?"

"He's coming along nicely in his classroom studies, but I also need him on the field, so I'm hoping to have him spend a little time with some extracurricular activities."

"Oh dear, and what sort of extracurricular activities are we speaking of here?"

"The kind you hired him for," she grins. "Ayene and I have been spending some time in private tutoring sessions, with Ayene teaching him how to impersonate a local military officer…junior grade in his case. I need him to infiltrate Central Command and access their local data terminals for a little peek at their system software, security codes, and network configurations. If we're going to hack into anything, he needs to know how to hack into it, and there's no better way than to learn from the source."

"That's simply dangerous!" Kailen winces. "Elder Vankkar was afraid of pure telepathy being a security risk, but if he were to see this, his horns would shoot through the roof!"

"Maybe so, but there's only just so much you can teach Petrith about hacking without having the stuff he needs to hack into available to play with. So, I'm preparing him for a little field study. He'll keep a low profile and try to gain access to any data files that could be useful for later; in case we need to break into anything that might hold critical information we can use against Darumon."

"And I can further assist in this operation," Ayene adds. "I can lead him into certain areas where he could pose as my assistant to take notes and perform tasks for me. I doubt anyone will ask questions, especially if we use disguises with rank insignias high enough to bypass their curiosity."

"Very good," Thaelyn nods. "And along the way, maybe he can learn ways to tap into their networks for our propaganda campaigns. Then our next step should include the three of you making our initial infiltration so that each of you can begin a few of these operations. Time is the only limiting factor here, so we should make use of it as best we can before Darumon gets any new ideas for another of his crusades."

"All right, then we should begin once we have Petrith up to speed on his covert ops."

<hr>

Over the following weeks, Kaliya and Petrith spent their after-class time with Ayene as they all worked together to make preparations for their initial incursion of Azgarén. So far, this would represent a limited scale invasion to establish a foothold arrival zone. Finally, when they considered themselves ready, they scheduled some time on a weekend to meet in the WIC building in Rolsklinde.

"We are here to make our first effort at Azgarén," Thaelyn announces to the room. "On this day, we will keep our movements small in order to maintain a low profile until we can learn more of what is around us. This is an important step for us, as it represents a leap into the unknown, and a voyage to places none of us would ever have expected to travel to...except for Ayene of course," he smiles. "It also stands as a testament to our ingenuity and resourcefulness to accomplish deeds otherwise deemed impossible for such as us. May the Powers guide us in our future directions and what new mysteries we unveil along the way. Kaliya, Ayene, Petrith, take your seats. We will proceed one at a time, so as not to overwhelm Ayene with too much extraordinary attention," he grins.

The three young agents all take up seating in a tight circle facing each other. Kaliya positions herself for the first turn at the telepathic bond to share Ayene's memories.

"Ayene," Thaelyn directs. "I will have you conjure forth an image of your home city. My impression of Capitol Prime is that of a major metropolitan affair, is this accurate?"

"Yes, it is," she affirms. "It's one of our largest cities on Azgarén."

"What is the population, approximately?"

"I believe it was last tallied at around five million."

"Indeed, no small matter, that. Then you must consider your choice carefully. It must be somewhere inconspicuous in case there are people moving about. We cannot allow you to be seen suddenly popping into view of a crowd. Perhaps if to choose an alley, or behind a building, maybe a utility area…someplace largely unused or infrequently travelled."

Ayene ponders the situation, recalling several prospective options and subtly shaking her head as she discards a few, then finally deciding on one that seems promising.

"Your Lordship, if we're to go into the city proper, which is where most of my clearer memories take me, it would need to be a place I visited enough times to hold a firm memory of. At this moment, I'm thinking of the underground vehicle storage lot belonging to C.P. Security, where I used to work. You don't have much foot traffic in the area, unless someone is either coming or going to their vehicle, and if we arrive in a disguise, like a small insect, no one should even notice. Then, once we can survey the area, we can reshape ourselves to our normal disguises."

"This is quite reasonable. Proceed ahead and recall a secluded location in your mind and hold it there. Kaliya, it is your game now."

Kaliya turns to focus herself on Ayene, carefully merging her thoughts to observe the imagery flashing through the young woman's mind. She sees a shadowed enclosed space, illuminated by artificial lighting, and supported by synthetic stone columns. The space included a driveway leading through the center and around a corner in the distance. The air was cool in Ayene's experience memories. The sensation hinted at being underground beneath a large building within a bustling city. When Kaliya felt she had gained sufficient enough detail, she pulled out.

"Ready, my Lord," she states distantly as she mulls over the image.

"Good, now Petrith, it is your turn."

As with Kaliya, now Petrith takes a turn to peer into Ayene's thoughts. Once again, she holds the memories of the parking lot for him to study. He draws in the same image and local sensations of the area, and when he feels himself ready, he retracts away.

"Ready here," he states calmly.

"Excellent," Thaelyn instructs. "Now we will have each of you project and depart. Travel together, peruse the area, and find a location preferably outside the city, study it and report back here. We shall await your return. And try not to become too distracted by conversing with the locals. There will be time enough for that later," he grins.

The three of them leave the room to find their chairs in the adjacent conference room. After submersing themselves into their meditative sleep, they emerged as projections. Kaliya led them briefly back to the strategy room to confirm their departure, and the group folded out of the local space.

They could not technically see each other during transit, as each was in their own perception tunnel, leaving them each travelling to the location in the memory independently. The scene enroute was a dazzling array of stars and spiral galaxies zipping by so fast that the images left trails behind them. Then a translucent wall appeared as they approached the dimensional membrane, passing through to an impossibly vast expanse outside the local universe.

Indescribable shapes and other-dimensional images flew by while each of the travelers strained their focus on a tiny dot directly ahead of them. Their practice in training hardened their discipline of mind to ignore the outside anomalies and keep to their intended goal. The fight to reach their destination would not be won until they stood on solid ground again. Then another wall came into view. It was the dimensional universe where Azgarén would be found.

They penetrated the membrane and again found themselves hurtling past more stars, with the image ahead now beginning to grow more distinct. The dot became a circle, slowly refining with imagery, the shapes appearing much the same as the memory of the underground lot. With a final effort, they merged into the vision and the world came into focus.

They had arrived as a set of insects sitting on a concrete floor. There were several hover shuttles and other vehicles nearby, neatly parked in marked stalls. The garage setting was lit by rows of lighting on the ceiling, which was supported by columns interspaced along the length of the area. There were no people in immediate view, so Kaliya signaled the others to reshape into Suuden'kai form.

"All right, good," Kaliya observes. "Is this how you recall it, Ayene?"

"Yes, this is the place. We're underneath the C.P. Security building. I can show you the way out from here to the street. I don't think anyone will pay any attention to us outside. We'll just be an average group of people walking along."

"Good, lead the way."

Ayene leads them along the driveway and around the corner at the end, then along another driveway leading up a slight incline, following the route through a small maze of lanes until an opening appears ahead.

"Well, I have to admit," Kaliya relents. "I don't think we had anything this complex on Ruuki uy'Daan, but then we weren't a metropolis with millions of people.

"Neither of us was old enough to drive either," Petrith smirks.

They emerge outside to find a busy street, and Ayene directs them onto a sidewalk.

Kaliya and Petrith both gazed in wonder at the magnificent city skyline. It was brilliantly lit from all directions. The roadway was streaming with a constant flow of hover vehicles. The margins of the lanes were a long line of glowing traffic guide markers, and the sidewalks were lined with lampposts. The buildings reached skyward higher than anything they had ever seen before, with lights shining through windows and along sidings. It was apparently nighttime, and the city glowed brightly.

"Fascinating," Kaliya mumbles amazedly. "I was just a little girl the last time I saw anything like a city, or at least of the sort we might be familiar with."

"What we had back home didn't even come close to this," Petrith notes. "The tallest building we had there would only be a fraction the size of these."

Kaliya looked up into the sky to see several flying vehicles soaring by between the buildings.

"Are those the patrols you mentioned once?"

"Yes," Ayene responds. "Some of them, but there are also lanes of traffic that fly at altitude. Not everything is on the ground."

"Incredible!"

They strolled along the sidewalk to the nearby intersection, passing several native residents along the way. Kaliya glanced at them casually, trying not to appear overly interested in their appearance. She noticed they all looked very much the same as Ayene and the other members of her base crew, with the seed entities, and in this case also with the cranial interface units. When she reached the corner, she peered around the length of the avenue.

The roadway extended out of sight, all brightly lit and filled with vehicles travelling in both directions. She could see a long line of tall buildings of different architectural designs, some of which were connected midway up with skywalks.

"We need to find a way out of here to a higher vantage point where we can see the broader region."

"We should try to reach a rooftop," Ayene considers. "We could change to birds and fly up to one, though it will be a steep climb from here," she chuckles.

"Yeah, but not outside. We need to find cover again."

They turn and head back to the garage, ducking inside and

cautiously looking for a secluded corner. They take one last peek to be sure no one is looking, and then change to birds.

"I'm going to make a wild guess and suggest you probably don't have birds like this in your world, right?" Kaliya squawks in her bird voice.

"No, this one would not be native to us," Ayene returns back the same.

"All right, we need to be discreet when we move, regardless of how inattentive these people are outside. Follow me."

Kaliya leads them back up to the garage entrance, carefully peeking around the corner to make sure the coast is clear of anyone moving in their general direction. When the last of the pedestrian traffic passes by, she takes off in a quick flurry, followed by Ayene and Petrith. They angled upward sharply to gain altitude and to avoid any observers below.

They fly together between the buildings, circling upwards to locate one with a reasonably accessible rooftop, then settling on the edge to take a perspective. Many of the buildings around them were much taller, obscuring their view, so Kaliya leads them to another building, even taller than the previous one.

"Do you have any idea where we are in all this?" she asks.

Ayene makes a quick scan of the area to gain her bearings.

"We arrived near the center of the city. You can see over there that large structure," she points with a wing. "That's where Sargeras resides."

The building was massive, both in girth as well as height, made of a dark stone-like material. It stood out prominently against the other city features. It was essentially square with beveled edges and slightly tapered as it ascended upwards. One side made a gradual swooping inward curve about midway up, then flattening out and continuing to the top floor.

"Wow! That place is big. And it's the last place I want to visit right now. Which direction is the quickest way out of town?"

"Um," she hesitates as she looks around at the other sights. "This way…"

Now Ayene takes off with the others in tow. They fly up higher, gaining a better view of where they were. They had risen above many of the other buildings by now, affording them a truly bird's-eye view of the area. Kaliya looked around at the sights, still in awe at the expanse, and density of the city.

They travelled many minutes between buildings and over rooftops, until the city began to blend with residential complexes. At first, it was large apartment buildings, but later came the outskirts with suburban neighborhoods and individual family homes.

"This is going to be impossible," Kaliya mumbles silently. "How do you find your way around something like this, to say nothing of locating and coordinating any kind of military activity?"

Ayene was leading them generally eastward out of the city. She glanced off to the right and saw the telltale glow of another sight well familiar to her.

"Kaliya," she calls out. "Look there; do you see that glow in the distance?"

Kaliya follows her motion.

"Yeah, what is it?"

"That would be Central Command. It's a large military spaceport, so if you have any ideas of spying on them, that's where you want to be. I can show you later when we start the real work."

Petrith studied the sight in the distance.

"And that's where you want me to start hacking their computers? Wonderful."

"Step by step, Petrith," Kaliya states. "But now, where are we going to set down? This damnable city just keeps on going," she chuckles.

"There are some hills over there. We can use that. It should give us a good starting point that's easy to identify, and it also affords a view of the city."

They continue towards a row of small hills just outside the city limits. The housing below was petering out and changing to sparse woodlands. The trees appeared bare and sickly. They descended to the ground.

Kaliya took a quick look around the local area. It was devoid of any civilization, the last of it ending a few miles away. She changed back to her normal form, along with the others.

"Are these trees dead, or is it a seasonal thing?"

"Some of them appear dead," Ayene admits. "But for most, I think it's also probably seasonal. We do still have trees, many of them struggling with this pollution. They're surviving, but there are also patches where they are thinning out."

"What about other natural areas? Forests, fields…wildlife?"

"I am aware that many species are endangered. There are many conservation efforts in effect to preserve them, and in most of these cases you will only find them in protected shelters, like habitat zoos."

"Ayene…" she sighs.

"I know, Kaliya, you don't need to tell me. I've seen Tae'Eladar with its beautiful skies and fresh air. It's a wonderful place. I even passed by that dryad grove once, although I was too afraid to enter it. I honestly wouldn't mind living there. The air was fragrant from all the flowers and bushes…not like this place. If you had a real nose, you would know what I mean."

"Is the air here actually so dangerous to breathe that you need the seed entities as a form of filter? What about other people, like any of ours, if they should come here?"

"That's a good question. I doubt you would die from it…well, not immediately. It might cause illness after a while, so if you're going to spend long periods here, I might suggest you wear a mask of some kind."

"Wonderful. All right, I'll keep that in mind. Let's make a good study of this place and report back. I'm sure by now Thaelyn is wondering what happened to us."

✦ ✦ ✦ ✦ ✦

"My Lord," the General mutters. "How do we approach a city of five million? We are speaking of twenty or more times that of even our own large cities, especially if you consider the recovery we are still making after the Spellplague."

"Yes, that moment took a lot of good people away from us. The numbers may not sound very inviting, but I think it should not be as much a concern if we focus on just those key points of interest that are most relevant to our needs. The bulk of it would likely fall into secondary categories or none at all, leaving it mostly as an obstacle to carefully step around."

"And this is just the one city," Kailen offers. "We can't be sure how many more we might need to cover and whatever strategic points of interest they have."

"This is true. We are looking at a large civilian population, and depending on how many games Darumon is playing, our scouting activities might need to involve a bit of research to see if we can narrow things down somewhat. There is probably no need to investigate everything door-to-door, just to locate those elements that hold the greatest value and step our way through them. No doubt, this will take some careful consideration, and we cannot know at this time how we will proceed without that surveillance. So, for now, let us simply establish our foothold."

Thaelyn directs the group's attention to a bag sitting at the end of the table.

"We have Kaliya's effigy here," he states. "Once she and the others find a suitable location, we will mark a rune on it. One way or another, this will serve as our starting point. We will proceed forward from there."

"This gives us a way in," Kailen muses. "But what about the return, like if we send in any real people, we will need those scrolls to come back, right?"

"Yes, this is correct, at least until our people can finish the research on the Harvester. But I am holding out hope that this will find its way soon enough. Until then, we will use what we are most familiar with, and we know this will work based on our testing on Madzurki."

"Good."

The discussion in the strategy room debated over these and several other issues since Kaliya's team departed. But it was soon interrupted as the group returned into the room.

"My Lord," Kaliya announces on her arrival. "This is going to take some work. I've never seen anything that big before, not even in my school days on Ruuki uy'Daan with my vid-com history lessons."

"Then we can assume you found your way? Good."

"Yes, we found our way, and Ayene led us to a set of hills off to the east of the city where we found a peaceful setting in a half-dead wooded grove where we'll make our first incursion."

"A half-dead grove," he raises his brow. "That does not sound very inviting, but with the pollution as it is…" he sighs. "Very well… can you describe what you see over there?"

"The city is big…huge…lots of skyscrapers, lots of traffic on the roads. It's nighttime over there, so everything in the city is brightly lit. We travelled a long distance to find the edge of the city, passing over outlying areas and suburbs until we finally found that set of hills. To the south, Ayene showed us a glow on the horizon that was supposed to be Central Command."

"Excellent, this gives us a few bearings to get started. Now, before anything else occurs, I will have you establish our foothold. I had your effigy brought in. Take it and mark a rune at that location, and then return back. Ayene, go with her and wait. We will send a small trinket through to test the rune. Watch for it and return it back to us."

Kaliya and Ayene both nod in acceptance. Kaliya picked up her bag and they were off again.

They arrived back on the hillside. Kaliya finds a fairly level spot and unloads her bag, where she begins to assemble a tripod stand to mount her casting device. Ayene watches as Kaliya attaches the induction unit, with an arcanic capacitor plugged in underneath, and finally the conjuring program board plugged into a docking port. Lastly, she inserts a rune stone in the cradle socket.

"Such a fascinating piece of equipment," Ayene muses. "It looks like it would defy anything we might call science."

"I'm sure it would. This thing that looks like a large breadboard is configurable with these resonating iconic glyph plates, which are designed to harmonize with my voice calling out their names. They form a conceptual algorithm which invokes the arcanic energies to perform whatever sequence is laid out. It's a little like a computer program for casting spells. There's a microphone here to capture my voice since I'm not actually physical. Otherwise, I would simply do this myself, maybe in physical contact with it. But this machine could effectively make me obsolete."

"Oops!"

"Except for the projected aspect of things. But I suspect, once we refine the technology, even that part could go bye-bye. A future device might be as easy as pushing a button."

Kaliya positioned herself in front of the unit and placed her attention on the program board. She hit the switch on the side, causing the unit to come to life. Ayene peered down at the odd contraption, observing from above a series of small wheels and gears turning a framework of rings with mithril disks and counterrotating sets of channeling crystals. She studied the icons as they softly pulsed with electrical energy, lighting up with their independent hues. She simply shook her head at the absurd mechanical interaction of components.

"If the Council could only see this, I think they would lose a decade's worth of horns."

Kaliya smiled as she began calling out the glyphic icons in sequence, causing each one to brighten with an intense radiance as it went active. Ayene studied the action, stepping back cautiously and keeping silent so as not to interfere with the process. As Kaliya completed the sequence, a soft hissing engaged, and the crystals flashed with a surge of energy channeling through the apparatus. This followed with a flat swirling vortex erupting out of the device. The vortex expanded outwards as a broad disk, then retracted back as it condensed into the rune in the middle, causing it to glow as an indication of a successful marking operation.

"In all the nether-space," Ayene whispers. "I've never seen anything like that before."

"And that's what we call…magic," Kaliya declares jovially as she flutters her fingers.

Ayene lets out a giggle while Kaliya packs up her bag.

"One of these days," she muses. "Maybe I can learn that."

"All right, you wait here," Kaliya directs. "I don't think this should take too long, but if we have any problems, I'll come find you. Otherwise, I think success will be obvious if something flashes into view here."

"Understood."

Kaliya returns back to the WIC strategy room and presents the rune on the table.

"Here you are, my Lord. This leads to a quiet little mesa on the hillside. Ayene is standing by."

Thaelyn directs a mage to take the rune and cast the enchantment on it. Then using the same small silver trinket Kaliya retrieved from the Sergeant in Cynosure, he drops it onto the rune and watches it flash out of sight. A few moments later, Ayene returns holding the trinket in her hand and sets it on the table.

"It would appear to be successful, Your Lordship," she states confidently.

"Most excellent," he ushers contentedly. "This is an important step for us. We now have access to Azgarén, with or without a conveyor or any other device. The next step would be to create a return process, and for that we shall allow the Professor some time to carry forward with his experiments. Meanwhile, let us sit a moment and contemplate how to proceed from here. Since you are still projected, perhaps we could take advantage of this and make a few casual surveys…"

On Tae'Eladar, in the city of Bya'an Tamoranth, in the Royal Historical Archives, Vonafel Windsong was at her desk busy reading through several papers her team of historians had been reviewing recently as part of some old research.

She made it a habit to keep a personal copy of Adalon's book on a stand on her desk and open to the final pages where the last few prophecies were apparently hidden behind a form of magical encryption. With the prophecies holding so much relevance in recent times, she kept one eye on her work and the other on the book, waiting for any of the hidden passages to suddenly reveal themselves.

As she was studying her paper, and taking a few odd notes along the way, suddenly she thought she saw a glimmer of something occurring out of the corner of her eye. She paused from her work and turned to find the strange anomaly, only to realize she was being pulled towards the book again. She stared at it, asking herself if she was simply going crazy with her obsession, or if something had actually occurred. Then she saw it.

Her eyes grew wide, and she gasped unexpectedly. She instantly dropped her paper and reached for the book, then let out a squeal of excitement.

"Ooh! Another one! We have another one!"

The ranting calls in her assistants from another room.

"What is it?" asks one of them. "Another line? Ooh! Let me see!"

The group hovers over the book as they read the newly revealed quatrain.

"I wonder what they just did over there," the first researcher muses.

"From the looks of this," the second researcher considers. "I would say we just made an important step forward."

Vonafel studies the wording and reads it aloud.

"Upon the birthing shores they fall, the Exiled Ones return; for she who carries forth the flag, the Hooves of Storm will yearn."

"Grandmother!" the first woman exclaims. "That's another reference to those Hooves of Storm. We need to get this to His Lordship! I don't know what they just did, but this looks important."

"Yeah, and that poor girl is setting herself up as a new messiah."

It is nearly the end of the year, and soon graduation time will be arriving at the academy. Kaliya and Ayene were making a visit to the WIC building to report on some of their latest scouting activities.

"We have a few possibilities for Central Command using our cameras," Kaliya relates. "They have ventilation ducts we could use, same as at the mining base. There's one inside the control center with a good view of what they're doing in there. So, if we're careful, and disguise it with some camouflaging colors to blend it in better, we should have a good source of intel from their operations."

"Very good," Thaelyn admits. "But under the circumstances, I would also like to watch the Commander himself, as he is an important figure in their operations, and I suspect he might not spend as much time in the control center."

"Right, we found him in his office, and again, there is a ventilation duct in a convenient position to watch him. We could put another camera in there. After that, it's just a matter of checking the chips and power cells on a routine basis."

"Excellent. We will begin with this and see where it takes us. What else do we have so far?"

"I've been showing Petrith around the place," Ayene submits. "When we first arrived, I decided to check in at the lobby, as I figured we are going to be seen on a few occasions wandering around. So, I registered us as specialized military analysts, myself being a Captain," she grins mischievously, "and Petrith a Lieutenant. And we are working as part of a classified project relating to some newly proposed security upgrades based on these insurgents and their persistent attempts to invade our space. In other words, I'm playing the Marshal's game against him with his suggestion of Morndindor being corrupted by some covert plan, and therefore that cleansing procedure he used on them. This, combined with his excuse for withdrawing from Therinë due to that discovery, and we need to work on protecting ourselves from any more of this."

"How interesting, as well as clever. And this fits nicely with their existing game, so I cannot see how they might argue. What sort of progress have you made thus far?"

"We're accessing their data terminals and investigating the existing encryption protocols they use with the excuse of evaluating their functionality so we can make our new improvements."

"You know, Lieutenant," Kailen offers. "You frighten me. Petrith was bad enough when he was a boy on Ruuki uy'Daan playing his pranks with our Security Council mainframe. But YOU…you're simply dangerous!" he chuckles.

"Maybe so, Commander," she smiles. "But I would much rather be dangerous to Darumon than to any of our own people. I will admit one thing, however. This skill is one to be afraid of. Now I understand how Ytani went so wild with it, and all he ever did was to play an angry dwarf. I can only imagine the possibilities if this should fall into the hands of another like him, but this time one who actually knows how to use it."

"How true, but let's hope we can contain that somehow before it gets out of hand."

"Anyway, Petrith now has access to their terminals, and with justifiable reason, as well as a security pass, so he should be set for a while. I'll simply make visits as part of my own operations and progress checks."

"This aspect of our operations seems to be moving forward nicely," Thaelyn concedes. "We have barely even started, and already we have some important avenues to investigate. Perhaps we could also have you see about any other operations they are pursuing, such as their investigation of the prison portal."

"All right," Ayene nods. "I'll see if we can tap into that sometime. But I should caution not to push our limits too quickly."

"Absolutely. Now, I am aware Aelwyn is currently working on developing the rest of Kaliya's team with their enhanced telepathy. We will place them into operation once they are ready. This will expand our capacity considerably to scout any important or strategic targets relating to Darumon's operations. We know he has used one or another research facility, such as this ARC, to invent his death toys, so we need to investigate those to see how we might gain access to them and disable that aspect of his control."

"We also mentioned sending me to investigate the Council and see what they're actually doing; if anything. And we still have those regulators in the media stream. But relating to that, I had an idea, if I may."

"Of course…"

"My former boss at C.P. Security," she begins. "He and I go back a long way from my service in that office. If our purpose is to remove those regulators, who are a clear and obvious violation of the laws…or at least those laws we're made to believe in…I could bring him in, maybe with just enough information to clue him in on these wrongdoings, and tell him I'm part of a covert operation working to uncover some kind of conspiracy. He knows I was sent on that secret project for the Marshal, although he didn't actually know what it was, like everyone else. But if I play into that a little, I think I can work up a story for him."

"Interesting. Very well, but how do you think he would respond to the greater level of intrigue out there, for instance if to involve the Marshal and any of his plays?"

"I know he doesn't like the Marshal. He's an old-timer dating back to those early days. If I involve the Council and their illegal regulators, and if the Council really is missing, this should be enough to spark a few fires. But we still need to keep things under wraps because the Marshal, with his chip-controlled military, is very dangerous. So, my covert ops project needs the freedom to move around without a lot of public sensationalism."

"Cu'Nar's Pity," Kailen winces. "Did I say you were dangerous? I think maybe I understated it."

"Hey, I'm learning from your little sister," she glances humorously at Kaliya.

"Yeah, and I already know what sort of mischief she can get into."

"These are some very clever ideas, Ayene," Thaelyn considers. "But I would suggest before we make this move, we verify a few of our facts so we know exactly who to point our fingers at. If your former employer…eh, what position does he have, by the way?"

"His name is Captain Bein'talan," she responds. "He's the Chief of C.P. Security in the downtown precinct. And I'm sure he knows people in other offices we could possibly bring in if we need it."

"Good, so if this Captain is a law enforcer, we can say he holds some valuable potential to remove certain elements, possibly to incarcerate them until we can make further movements on other fronts. In addition, if he can do it quietly, this alleviates us of a few variables on our side. Next would be our own news media campaign and whatever propaganda we might offer, but for this we will need an agent on the inside."

"And this is where Miss Ur'paran comes in. Got it. But we need to move on her carefully, as she's still a variable we need to settle."

"Indeed, so we should spend a bit of time to study the situation and look for our opening. We still have our own needs on this side for the research and development of our new military, and this limits us as to when we can actually apply ourselves."

"One thing I can report on relating to this," Kailen submits. "I am aware our people are close to finishing a prototype drone unit using the new jump drive. We'll be experimenting with that soon to see how it works, but so far it simply draws from the local arcanic sphere, so it's only useful in our own environment."

"It is a beginning, and we must always start there. Perhaps, if we can refine that arcanic capacitor a bit more, it can carry a greater charge to allow more efficient usage."

"I'm waiting to see what this does to the existing portal tech around here," Kaliya smiles.

"Yeah, and that can sure twist a person's horns," Ayene muses. "Instantaneous travel from anywhere to anywhere… Would we even need ships at that point?"

"While I am sure there will still be a need for ships," Thaelyn affirms. "And I might even suggest they will serve a valuable role for many applications, but where travel is concerned within any single planetary sphere, at the very least, a gateway network like what we have on Tae'Eladar, could revolutionize the travel industry. But before we go out and celebrate, we should still temper ourselves with the reminder that the Harvester technology we are working with now is only temporary. We still need to mount that hurdle manually if we should wish to truly earn it."

✦✦✦✦✦

In the city of Bya'an Tamoranth, in the Hall of the Order, a commencement ceremony was taking place as the current year's graduating class was assembling to receive their citations. Trumpet heralds played an opening anthem as people gathered in the ceremonial Great Hall at the center of the guildhall fortress. Thaelyn stood by silently on the dais to make a formal showing, but on these occasions, he did not actually play a role, instead leaving it to the Master of Ceremonies.

Slowly, the congregation was processed as the MC called each graduate forward to receive their official induction as a full Brother or Sister of the Order. As they received their document, Thaelyn gave a nod before they were dismissed back to their former positions.

Kaliya waited patiently for her name to be called. Like all the others, she wore her ceremonial uniform, along with her rank insignia and valor medals, and stood at full attention among the rows of cadets. She was twitching with emotion, both nervous and excited at the occasion.

Relissa, Marelle, Haran, and their Daanen'kai friends, along with Kailen and Ankhia all stood on the balconies with the other guests overseeing the ceremony. The crowds also included Tyanna and Velen, Kaliya's parents, and the Daanen-Aryku Elder Council who were offered a special invitation to observe the spectacle. Padriyl positioned himself with his video camera to record the occasion, and Ayene also attended, but due to the fact the Elder Council was present, she had to conceal herself using a projection and a Daanen'kai disguise.

"Lieutenant Kaliya Nazég," the MC calls out.

She steps forward from her row and turns to proceed out to the runway carpet, then turns and marches towards the stairs in front of the dais.

"A Lieutenant?" Elder Vankkar whispers. "How did she make that? Last I heard she was a Corporal."

"Aye," Relissa responds softly. "They made a special case out of her when we moved to Ruuki uy'Daan. They pushed her by a wee bit, and borrowed from her old experience in the Sentinels to boost her along."

"Experience? With respect, her experience there wasn't much to speak of."

"Aye, maybe so, but they ran her through a lot of drills and special training to meet the need. She even set a few new examples for herself, and now, here she is."

"Amazing. She must've grown tremendously in this time."

Kaliya arrived at the base of the steps, where she offered her traditional salute and knelt down, while the MC prepared his customary speech.

"On this day," he announces. "You who have come before us do hereby honor us with your devotion. Now, the time has come for you to choose, with final determination, your course to become a member of our brotherhood, the Order of Tyr, fully and completely, and for the duration of your lifetime. And good gracious, what a lifetime THAT will be!" he chuckles. "How do you plea?"

"As the first of my people," she replies boldly. "And with many more to follow, I regard this as a personal privilege to lead the way for a new generation and a new future. And I will hold this honor as a symbol to light the way for those who seek true enlightenment and prestige of spirit...my youth notwithstanding, and neither my ridiculously long lifespan," she smirks. "I plead yay."

"Then in the eyes of our gods," he smiles. "Rise, Sister of the Order, Kaliya Nazég."

The audience ushers up a rising applause as the MC hands over a scroll with her academy completion record on it. An attendant then steps forward and pins the guild heraldry symbol just below the neckline in the center of the overlapping fold of her vest. The fixture would be placed more permanently at a later time. She then steps back and gives another salute. Thaelyn nods at her with a proud smile, as she is sent back to her former position.

At the end of the ceremony, the observers who were standing on the balconies came down to meet with their friends and loved ones and offer their congratulations. Relissa and her group, along with Velen and the others, all worked their way through the crowd to find Kaliya.

"Girl, you passed me up!" Relissa teases. "You'd better not go off and finish this war without me, or I'll be sending critters up your tail for the rest of my days."

"Don't worry about that, Relissa, I think we still have some time. We're still waiting for Marelle to get back into her studies, as I think she has an important role to play one day."

"Aye, so I guess I won't moan too much over it, since I'm a year ahead of her by now," she winks at Marelle standing next to her.

"My little girl," Tyanna beams emotionally. "You've come so far, and you're still so young."

The two of them embrace for a tender hug, followed by another hug from Velen, and then Kailen and Ankhia.

"My precious daughter," Velen croons. "How I've longed to see a day like this. But for all the troubles we encountered, I thought it would never come."

"Father," she utters gently. "I think we had a few higher powers watching over us and guiding our paths."

"Oh?" he chuckles mildly. "Are you now taking on a new religion with this association we're being directed into with these Estelar?"

"Why not," she smirks. "It sure beats following someone like Sargeras."

The group shares a tender laugh.

"Kaliya," Elder Vankkar begins teasingly. "I still remember when you were young and running your tail off out there making trouble for everyone. I hope we won't be seeing any more of this now that you've apparently earned yourself a new command role."

"Who, me?" she gasps mockingly. "Elder Vankkar, do you honestly think I would make the same mistake twice?" she grins cutely.

"Twice, maybe not, but an entirely new one…hmm…"

"Well, just hold on to your horns. I'm not finished yet."

"Right, that's what I'm afraid of, especially that part I'm not supposed to know about because of…you know who."

"Yeah, that's the hardest part of it. But one of these days, I hope this will change."

"All right, I'll try to be patient."

"So, what's next on the list for you?" Marelle asks.

"My first goal," Kaliya considers, "is to make an appointment with the runemancer's parlor again, this time for my official enchantment glyphs."

"What does that involve?" Kailen inquires.

"Once you finish your studies and accept your oath as a full member of the Order, you go in for a special set of these glyphs. They're a little like tattoos, but magically enchanted. This becomes a permanent feature for the rest of your life. There are different kinds, depending on your primary studies, and they typically augment you with such things as increased strength, dexterity or agility, mental acuity for mages, as well as durability, making us a lot harder to kill."

"Aye!" Relissa yips. "This brings us back to the time with that demon. He was tossing those paladins around like dolls, but they just stood up and came back at him."

"And this also brings us back to that first day," Haran reflects. "Do you remember when we were talking to him, and he explained to us this military he was building?"

"Yeah," Kaliya affirms. "He's making an army of super-soldiers. But the enemies we might face are not always simple people. Like Relissa said, they can also involve demons, or maybe fierce beasts, like dragons and undead creatures. There was a moment of history

I was reading about once where they were up against whole armies of those things. And if you count such as Sargeras, we may also have to involve the gods themselves."

"Grace of the cu'Nar," Ankhia winces. "Is that the sort of thing they usually go up against around here?"

"And here I thought we had it bad with the Suuden-Aryku," Kailen relents.

"Maybe so," Kaliya admits. "But this isn't necessarily the norm. Most things around here are generally under control. But Tae'Eladar isn't the end of it. One day, we might reach out and find new places, and who knows what we'll find out there, to say nothing of what we might need to do about it. We may find ourselves coming to the rescue of some entirely new society one day."

"Well, you just promise me you'll be careful out there, Kali," Tyanna begs. "You're my only daughter, and I don't want to lose you."

"Mother, I think that'll be a little hard to do now. Between my training, these glyphs, and then the custom armor they made for me, it'll take a lot to get rid of me. Nevertheless, we still need to keep our tails straight and our horns curled."

✦✦✦✦✦

Several days have passed and the new school year was beginning. Marelle was taking up new classes, but only a half-day schedule to give her time for her new family. Her primary focus was the Sixth Circle of mage study since that was the most important topic at the moment to bring her up to par for her pilot training in the new ship designs.

Relissa and Haran were continuing into the Seventh Circle of mage study. The budding ranger had her sights set to finish this year, while the young mage had his eyes on the full range of study, all the way up to the Ninth Circle, and he couldn't be happier.

"Relissa," he remarks as they sat on the courtyard bench. "In all those years I attended the academy in Rolsklinde, I never would've expected to travel so far, or so quickly, and with such proficiency in these studies as I am here. It's exhilarating."

"Aye, and here I was calling you a bunch of wacky names for it. Now I'm doing it too, and this is the last thing I ever expected to be learning. I just keep thinking of my younger days, sitting in that stuffy old lecture room. It almost put me to sleep sometimes."

"Nothing stuffy about these classes though. They inspire you to learn, and then to want more."

"I'm with you on that! But you're pushing three more years of it, counting this one. I'll be done after this set."

"You can always take more," he winks.

"Aye, sure," she chuckles. "But I've got the itches to get to work, too. I want a little piece of this bit before it falls away."

"Just remember to keep your head. War isn't something to get excited about."

"Aye, I get it. But I don't want Kaliya running a dizzy dash out there all by herself. Someone needs to watch her tail."

"I thought we had Petrith for that."

Relissa giggles boldly at the thought.

"You're right, but I'm talking about keeping it attached, not the other part."

"Still, I can't see much for you to do out there if it's mostly scouting Azgarén as a projection."

"Maybe so. But I need to get busy with something, and maybe along the way I'll see a wee bit come around."

✦ ✦ ✦

"Control, make ready to test the arcanic index marking actuator."

"Powering on… The drone is ready. The flux field is active."

Chief Technician Lapäli and her team, along with the Professor, who was taking a break from his research to supervise this demonstration, were running a test of the new arcanic jump drive subsystem. The device had been installed in a remote-operated drone unit, which was being controlled by an operator at a console in the Bahlaie testing range.

The drone was a pilotless aircraft fitted with the traditional Daanen-Aryku flight technology, and proprietary actuators to provide the function of marking and recalling to a rune jump location. The vehicle was positioned out on the range and being brought online for a trial run. Tensions in the control booth were moderate, even though many aspects of the technology had been tested in a laboratory environment.

"I just hope it doesn't collapse into a singularity," the Chief remarks candidly.

"Oh, Tanjhira," the Professor reassures. "I don't think we'll have anything like that. The flows don't usually behave that way. Instead, it's more likely to erupt in a fantastic fiery blue explosion, igniting the surrounding energy cloud, and sending out violent world-shattering shockwaves that tear open the fabric of space, rippling across the planes and rending the entire multiverse down to wisps of ethereal vapor," he finishes with his typical theatrical exuberance.

The Chief slowly turns around with horrified appeal as she stares down at her diminutive cohort standing gleefully at knee level by her side.

"Or..." he continues merrily. "It could do nothing at all."

"Thank you, Professor," she croaks. "It's always so delightful working with you."

She turns back to the operator at the console and tries to clear her throat again.

"All right, bring it up."

The operator moves a control slider which powers up the drone's flux field, lifting it off the ground to a comfortable height. Cameras were following the unit, and the Chief watched the affair on a monitor inside the control booth. The drone was stable and hovering in place.

"Power up the capacitors," she orders.

The operator programmed a charging sequence to gather the local arcanic energy into a series of specially designed capacitors inside the drone. He watched a status indicator count up the load charge.

"Those capacitors are the biggest part of this, so far," the Chief comments.

"Yes, but I had an idea on how we might make them more compact," the Professor considers. "It's one of the things I've been thinking about while working on my other project for the arcanids."

"What do you have in mind?"

"Well, part of it is derived from Darumon and his weapon, and the aspect that you can actually compress this energy by so much. But gods forbid we compress it by so much that we create another like that!"

"Yes! I would have to agree."

"And yet, if we could make even a partial effort, I think we could squeeze a sizable amount into a smaller space, maybe resembling a heavy plasma, and further to support it in a neutral-buoyancy suspension vessel, a little like what he used at his processor."

"Interesting, and you think you can do this without causing it to blow up, shatter, rend, and otherwise rip the universe in half?" she smiles gently.

The Professor giggles at the Chief's lighthearted remark.

"We actually have part of our answer in some existing technology from our Dynamistic Spires," he suggests. "If we borrow from the design of the accelerators, and increase their efficiency while at the same time reducing their overall size..."

"Ah, I think I see where you're going. Make them into something like a superconducting conduit. So, the vessel you're referring to would behave like a strong magnetic bottle."

"There you go! And this might be useful to increase our current charge, and even bring the size down to fit on a battle suit."

"Just one more thing to add to my to-do list," she sighs.

"But think, Tanjhira, how many innovations would you have the chance to make back home if left to your own devices?"

"I have to admit, not nearly as many as I'm making here in this short time."

"Chief," the operator calls. "We have a full charge. The diagnostics check is good, and the actuator is ready."

"Then let's hit it."

The operator hits a switch on his console and the drone unit emits a soft hissing. The hull of the device quickly begins to glow, followed by a flash emitting a wide circle of energy waves spiraling inwards to the core of the vessel. The glow fades as the wave is reabsorbed into the core of the unit.

"I need a status report," the Chief issues.

"The perception array appears to have captured the environmental parameters. Our data integrity validation check is good, and it looks like we have a successful marker."

"Good. Now, take it to the other end and let's test it."

The operator flies the unit remotely to another point on the range marked with a flag. The cameras continue to follow the drone, and the Chief and Professor study the monitors in the control booth.

"Ready, Chief," the operator announces.

"Now we see if it pays off. Worst case scenario, despite the darling Professor's theatrics, is we might blow up the drone, or else lose it in nether-space. Charge up the recall actuator, and give me a count."

"Charging... Ten percent...twenty...thirty...forty..." the operator ticks off the numbers.

The Chief and the Professor study the monitor intently as the drone begins to glow, forming a soft spherical aura around it.

"...Seventy...eighty...indicators show a spatial bubble forming... ninety...mark...the rift is open; the drone is passing through."

They alternate between the monitor and looking through the window to see the drone encompassed in a bright bubble of light, and then flashing away in a radiant burst out of sight. A mere instant later, another bright flash erupts at the location of the previous operation where they marked the jump index, with the drone reappearing in view.

A rousing cheer cries out in the control booth as they celebrate the successful test of their new jump drive. Team members pat each other on the back and offer congratulations, while the operator brings the drone back into the hanger for further review and analysis.

Kaliya was attending a scheduled meeting at the WIC building. Another month had passed, and she had just sent away the most recent progress report from the mining base.

"What do you have to tell us on your recent report?" Thaelyn asks.

"They're getting anxious, as you can probably expect," she declares. "We've been giving reports of discovering new veins, but then those veins give up before they pan out into anything useful. So far, we're still going strong on the southern mine, and we dropped a hint that we might need to conduct a new survey. But to do so would require special planning, as we…meaning the original base crew… do not hold the proper methods to mine it ourselves, and therefore we need another work crew. But for this, we need to make special arrangements with the local population to supply one."

"Does Central know what these methods entail?" Kailen wonders.

"Commander Kriv'tik says Central is aware we are using what he calls persuasive methods to encourage their participation, but the mention of using drugs is apparently not a part of that," she smirks.

"Oh, how convenient… So, once again, Darumon doesn't give anyone enough information to know what anyone else is actually doing out there."

"Yeah, it's a lovely juggling act he must be playing. Anyway, I figure we could work this into our larger plan with Ytani, once the Professor is ready."

"This is beginning to cut close to the line," Thaelyn cautions. "I hope we are able to contain it."

"This is true, but according to Commander Kriv'tik, they've had other occasions of shortfalls in production. Surely, Central can accept that this one mine has to run out eventually. So, while the promise of trying to correct the situation might placate them for now, I have a hunch the Professor will find his answers soon."

"Oh? And what joyous new gift are you using on this occasion to predict this miracle?" he raises his brow.

"Well, nothing really extraordinary. I was over at the BRC to check on things recently, and Chief Tech Lapäli says they have a prototype containment unit ready. It's small, but enough to demonstrate a theory of operation. From there, we just need the Professor to give the results of his testing on Madzurki. He says he'll be conferring with the Chief Tech in a few days to go over his notes. It sounded promising."

"Very well, this is good, and it will allow us to finally move forward. I should applaud Adalon for giving us these plans and making them simple enough to actually find a solution quickly."

"Yeah, this is for sure. I think I would also wish to thank whoever it was that originally supplied them to us. That was a generous offer, even if it is only temporary."

"Yes, I would agree. The Maker must have a few very special contacts she can call in."

"After that, we can hit Central with Ytani's little rebellion."

"Indeed, and this causes me to wonder about your statement concerning this new mining crew. I recall you once mentioning him taking a recently recruited crew to the ship with him, correct?"

"Yes, but unfortunately, the people down below are becoming too frustrated by now to continue cooperating, even with these persuasive methods we're using, so they're turning rebellious. Especially after the southern mine recently cut out with the local crew expiring, and we had to call for a replacement team. But this new demand for the survey simply pushed things over the top, and now Ytani is taking that other team and running away with it."

Thaelyn glared at her for the audacious plotline. He then glanced at the other officers at the table, finally settling on the General, who returned an amused stare.

"Should I bring out your list again, my Lord?" he asks tenderly.

"Keep it on hand. I would like to see if this idea actually plays out as she describes it, and THEN we will mark her down for it."

"Absolutely, my Lord!" he grins.

"Oh dear cu'Nar…" Kaliya rolls her eyes. "How many more?"

"You know," the General muses. "All things considered; I am actually thinking of starting up a real list in her case. Considering her lifespan, and all she has done in this short time, to keep a proper record of it, maybe like a biography, might not be such a bad idea."

"Indeed," Thaelyn admits. "If you feel this way, then by all means. She is certainly noteworthy enough with all her innovations that we should record her progress. And I suspect this movement of hers will create even more. But now, Kaliya, if we are making such preparations as these, have you had an opportunity to visit the runemancer's parlor yet?"

"I did," she affirms. "And I picked up all my official glyphs."

"Good, and what about the rest of your team? If we are to plan our assault on that ship, we need them fully functional with at least the see-invisible glyph."

"You have one of those, too?" Kailen muses.

"We do, and this is an important one, as it allows our people to see each other even if they use the cloak."

"I swear, if to say you people are dangerous, that just doesn't give you enough credit!"

"Traditionally, these are most often used on our scouts and certain other specialized operatives. Although, in modern times, we are seeing more people applying them simply because they are so functionally valuable."

"I would have to agree," Kaliya infers. "So, I'll pass the word along. Although they're all still a few steps behind me on some of their lessons, but we should be good to go for this mission."

"Excellent," Thaelyn nods. "And we will also need to coordinate with the dwarves. You should make a visit with Eiki soon to let her know."

"And I hear we have those new trans-com units in production now," Kailen adds. "At least on a limited basis so far. We've been installing some of them into our com-systems to augment our existing capacity. In fact, the Chief Tech is so happy with it, she's recommending we replace our existing networks with the new ones."

"This is encouraging news. But I might also suggest we do not completely abandon the older technology, as we might still find a use for it when tapping into our enemy's networks."

"Yes, of course. But as for this new one, she and the Professor are suggesting we give it a new name. So far, they're calling it a shard-com; since it's based on these whisper shards."

"Very interesting…and quite appropriate. But this now causes me to wonder. As we consider this new movement, we must also recognize that we will be going into dangerous territory with many new complexities to manage. If we are upgrading to a higher form of communications technology, we will need to augment this with other data collection and management techniques. Commander, we have used your camera devices in the past, and I know our people have developed similar technologies…which is to say using our native methods, although perhaps not as advanced as yours from the digital data storage aspect…yet…" he chuckles.

"Cu'Nar's grace, but I know what you mean. At the rate you're going, I don't expect it to be too long before that."

"Nevertheless, this simply complicates things for us to manage what I will assume to be a growing influx of information. We will be assaulting a world filled with many elements to study, and using many operatives collecting photos and recordings that will likely overflow our existing capacity. Therefore, Commander, we may be forced to consider a few other important upgrades."

"Computers, I'll bet."

"Yes, but as with everything else, we must try to maintain some amount of control for the current level of technological savvy our people have versus what we must apply to achieve our goals. So, we will use this locally to improve our needs in this war, and then allow our people to follow their natural course as time and opportunity permit."

"All right, then I'll get together with the Chief and let her know, and have our people at the Naarg uy'Sodrad start putting a few things together for us."

✦ ✦ ◆ ✦ ✦

"Lieutenant, how are the little ones coming along today?"

"They're keeping me busy, you can be sure of that," Marelle responds cheerily.

"Good. I'm sorry we have to pull you away from your mothering detail, but we still need to train you in several key areas."

Marelle was visiting the BRC for another flying lesson. She was taking time away during a weekend to continue her training with her instructor in preparation for adapting her to a new role she would likely play in future operations. The two of them were meeting inside the flight training center and reviewing several of the new developments recently added to the prototype model of her new fighter design.

"I hear we finally have a jump drive, is that right?" she asks.

"Not only that, but we managed to modify that transport sphere used on the gryphons and combined it with our spatial inverter to create a hybrid design. It's still mostly a prototype in the laboratory, however. We haven't actually put it on a functioning ship yet. In order for it to work properly, we need a more efficient arcanic collector and storage vessel, but the Chief has some people working on a new design the Professor recommended that could boost our energy production enough to make it viable."

"That's good to hear. And the jump drive?"

"We ran a demonstration of the technology, and it worked. But again, the storage bottles we're using are a little too inefficient to make it fully practical. Once the new design is ready, that should make all the difference."

"What about my new flight controls? Do we have anything on that?"

"The software is mostly ready, and again we tested it in the lab on a minor scale. The next step would be to install it on an actual ship. This is one of the things we'll need you to help test. I just hope you don't go crazy with it."

"Sir, I'm not going crazy with anything. I'm just doing what needs to be done."

"Yes, Marelle, I understand. It's just that our manners of flying are a lot different from yours. But then, we never went into combat with it, either."

"So, what is it we're doing today? Going in more circles?"

"In a manner of speaking… Come outside to the trainer and I'll fill you in on your flight plan."

They proceed outside in the direction of the training craft Marelle has used on many occasions before. As they make their way up to the ship, her instructor gives her a review of her course plan.

"On this occasion, you'll be making a single low orbit pass, and then back to base. The nav system has your trajectory all laid out for you."

"Um, wait a minute, low orbit?" she pauses. "I'm going into space this time?"

"That's right, Marelle," he smiles. "On this occasion, we need you to learn what it's like to travel beyond the planetary sphere. Not counting that little trek to Madzurki and Ooduan, you'll be the first of your kind to make this step. Congratulations."

Marelle stared at her instructor in a moment of wonder, and briefly reflected on the words Adalon once shared at the guildhall.

"I'll be travelling to places I never thought I'd see. Gods above, Adalon wasn't kidding, was she."

She quickly pulled herself together as she considered her new assignment, and comparing it to her mission with Kaliya. This would likely be an easy assignment in relation to the rest. All she had to do this time was to go up, once around, and come back down again. She had already practiced something like this on her simulator. She smiled modestly at the honor of taking this important step forward.

"Yes Sir, are we all set for it?"

"The ship is ready when you are. Try not to get lost out there."

"Me? Alone? You're not coming this time?"

"This time I'm keeping both hooves on the ground," he chuckles. "I'll be in the control booth monitoring your flight. We'll be in touch the whole time, so don't worry. We're using those new shard-com units now, and we recently installed one inside the training craft."

"Ooh, I've been waiting to try one of those. All right, I'll be on my way."

She makes a salute and walks around to the hatch leading into her ship. She closes the door, makes herself comfortable, and runs her power-up sequence. She examines the nav display for her projected course. It was essentially a moderate climb at maximum power, which would allow her to leave the atmosphere and enter a low orbit. From there, she would make one pass around the planet and descend back to base.

"Control, this is Lieutenant Carronel, ready on deck," she announces into the com-system.

"Lieutenant," a voice returns back. "You are cleared for departure."

"Acknowledged."

Marelle powers up the flux field. The vessel still used the original flight controls common to the Daanen'kai model. As the ship lifts gently off the ground, she hits the switch for the landing gear and applies motion on the throttle. The ship begins moving forward. She increases the throttle, accelerating away from the base and pulling up on the stick to give more lift. She maintained a steady incline, gradually throttling forward to maximum thrust. The air outside was gusting past, breaking the sonic barrier, and still accelerating, while the ground receded away at frightening speed.

She studied her nav display, following along the flight plan. She was in the tube and on course. She could see clouds in the distance falling beneath her, and the land below losing its detail. The sky above became thin, as wisps of vapor rushed past the windows, eventually to fade altogether. Then she looked out the window to see the world beneath her. It was amazing.

From her vantage, she saw a sight she had never considered she might see in her lifetime, except for the fact of her recent training. It was the broad curvature of Tae'Eladar, seen from high above and still rising. She could clearly make out the atmospheric layers as they condensed on the horizon, in contrast with the emptiness above. The landforms below afforded her a view of nearly the full continent, and ahead was darkness, if only for the illumination of the sun, and the dim glow of the Ethereal Maelstrom beyond the distant Shell of the Tae'Eladaran planar domain.

"Beautiful," she mutters unconsciously.

"How do you like travelling in space, Lieutenant?"

"Sir, this is beyond a dream. Running this on the simulator just doesn't compare to doing it in real life."

"I understand your meaning. I can't say I had this pleasure personally, as the last time I made a flight like this would've been on Ruuki uy'Daan, but not into low orbit, only a high-altitude scouting run. Still, the sensation of flying high above carries a certain feeling of spiritual freedom."

Marelle studied her nav monitor, watching the numbers as they continued to rise until she made her intended altitude, then leveled out to make a single orbital pass. The world below seemed to revolve under her. She looked out the window to see the continent of Sein'amar, followed by the neighboring continent of Shulan Tau, and then an ocean. In time she saw another landmass, and then another ocean. The flight took almost an hour and a half to make her way around, finally to come up on the other side of Sein'amar again. And along the way, she had the occasion to examine the local moon, Selûne, as she passed by.

"All right, Lieutenant," issues the instructor on the com-link. "It's time to make your descent. Remember to watch your angle of approach as you make reentry."

"Yes Sir, engaging reentry now."

Marelle adjusts a downward angle on her flight stick while pulling back on the throttle slightly. The world turns into her path as she begins making her way back toward the atmospheric layers. Slowly, she glides into the upper atmosphere, checking her speed and vector alignment. The nav display guided her course with statistical details and correctional guidelines. She felt the buffeting of the upper layers as she passed through, with wisps of vapor gusting by at high velocity.

She kept a careful watch on her flight path, flying mostly by her instruments at this moment, throttling back on occasion to control her rate of descent, until the ship settled into a stable flight characteristic after that first phase of reentry. Now she was able to fly more naturally, as she was accustomed to from her previous experience. She made a series of turns, following the nav point indicator for her landing zone, and descending lower to the ground. The world came back into focus, with details of hills and forests, roads, and then buildings, as the base came into view.

She finally lined up with her glide path back to her landing pad, making a relaxed approach, lowering the landing gear, and setting down neatly.

"Very nicely done, Lieutenant," the instructor offers on the com-link. "We'll practice this a few more times in the coming weeks before moving on to the next step."

"Thank you, Sir. It was truly a pleasure making this exercise," she replies as she powers down the ship.

✦

"All right, Haran, let's try this again."

"Is this really necessary? I mean, isn't this why we have training dummies?"

"Aye, but the dummies don't offer any challenge. Now, we'll have you run to the mage upper field. When you get there, do something wacky. I'll send this guy away and have him spy on you, and then report back here."

Relissa and Haran were in the athletic field after class working on her latest project, training a pet hawk. It was part of her ranger study, which consisted of testing her skills on different types of animals. Haran was assisting on this occasion as a live test subject.

He nodded in agreement to his assignment, and took off in a dash up the stairs and through the combat trainting hall, then through the corridors of the guildhall to the lower mage field, and finally taking the teleport pad to the upper field. On his arrival, he pondered briefly what he might do to make a sufficient scene for her hawk to report back on. He looked around at the other mage students, who were all busy at their practice sessions, and an idea came to mind. He began conjuring up minor water sprays and shooting them off at the students.

"Erm, Haran," the Mage Master calls out, taking note of the display. "What is it exactly you think you are doing?"

"Sorry, Master, but I'm helping a friend train her pet hawk. Would you like to help?" he asks by shooting a small spurt in the Master's direction.

"What the…" the Master yelps. "And how does this help train a hawk?"

"It's conducting a spy run, and needs something interesting to report back on."

"Oh really! And who is it we're supposed to be helping on this occasion?"

"Relissa, so you can probably guess where this is going."

"Ah! Yes! And it figures. Very well, if this is how you desire it."

The Mage Master fires a shot back at Haran, and the students engage in a water fight game. Spurts of water begin flying in all directions as the students exchange potshots in the playful sport, drenching themselves and the general scene of the field.

In the sky overhead, a graceful figure makes a series of circles, gazing down at the chaos on the ground. Students were zigzagging across the field shooting squirts of water at each other, some shouting to coordinate their attacks, while others screeched as they got hit. The bird made several passes, and when it had seen enough, it returned to Relissa's arm and reported back in a sequence of squawks and chitters.

Relissa then made her way up to the field, cautiously peeking around the wall from the teleport pad.

"'Ere now!" she shouts. "Haran, I said do something wacky, not start a war!"

On her announcement, the group turned at her and started firing off shots in her direction. She was hit multiple times before she could even duck out of the way. The barrage sent the hawk quickly fluttering off, and so Relissa decided to jump out and conjure up her own volley, firing off in any direction she could set her eyes on.

◆ ◆ ◆◆◆ ◆ ◆

The Professor was making his scheduled visit to Chief Tech Lapäli at the BRC facility. His arrival was highly anticipated as it was hoped he might have the final pieces to add into the Dynamistic Harvester design. He was accompanied by his assistant, and called Tanjhira and a few of her colleagues to attend the meeting in one of the conference rooms.

"I would like to call this meeting to order, please," he issues. "First, I would like to offer my personal thanks to Adalon for her most gracious gift to aid us in this time of need. I would also wish to offer my thanks to all those here who have participated in these projects, even though we are in a time of war, and most of this will be placed back on the shelf once we're done…at least for now."

"Thank you, Professor," Tanjhira smiles. "I have to admit, it's been an extraordinary experience working with you, even if I do catch you peeking up my lab coat at least once each day," she giggles.

"Yes, well," he grins. "I have my reputation to uphold, and you've been such a good sport about it. But now, as to our purpose here… To understand the intimate nature of the dynamistic flows is to understand the arcanids that create it, along with how and why. We have heard in the past how this is a flow of energy that pervades our space and regenerates over time, replenishing what might be lost or used by others. When the event we call the Spellplague occurred a few centuries ago, it ripped through our multiverse like a storm, tearing up worlds and tossing many of the Outer Planar bodies around as if they were toys scattered on the floor. Even the Estelar were affected by it, where some were lost to us, and others had to flee the local space to find shelter."

"Professor, I've heard this referenced before, and I think Padriyl also mentioned something once when he was in conversation with His Lordship. But can you remind me again what happened?"

"It was said to be a wicked play by one of the Estelar we call Shar, who conspired with another one named Cyric. There was one we used to call Mystra, Goddess of Magic. Shar apparently never really liked her much, but Mystra was the one who used to manage this layer we call the Weave."

"The ambient layer of this energy you use now, right?"

"Yes, although ours is managed locally by now. The natural flows tend to ebb and flow like a tide, leaving ripples with highs and lows, sometimes resulting in dense areas we might call wild zones, and thin or empty areas we might call dead zones. A mage who might try to conduct his spellcasting in these areas would experience unexpected results or maybe no results at all. The Weave was an effort by Mystra as a favor to her Children, meaning such as mages and scholars, to provide a consistent layer to work with."

"How nice of her. So, what happened to it?"

"Shar and Cyric happened to it by conspiring to murder Mystra and steal her creation."

"Murder? These gods would actually stoop to something like this?"

"Apparently so. It seems that no matter how high you go; you might still find those one or two individuals who behave as ruffians. Shar once created a variation of this, and now she wanted both. But unfortunately, Mystra had stretched hers so very tightly by this time, that when she died, her control of it snapped back and rent everything apart."

"Wonderful, and because of this, we have this Spellplague of yours. Cu'Nar help us. Whatever happened to Shar?"

"It's my understanding the other Estelar laid down some heavy punishment, though I'm not really sure what they use on these occasions. Cyric was also punished, once they pulled him out of hiding, but after that, it was mostly a waiting game for the natural flows to heal themselves."

"All right, but that sounds bad no matter how you define it."

"This is also where His Lordship took the initiative and helped us to develop the Spires, so we could make our own Weave locally, and not be dependent on anyone else."

"Yes, and this is where we've been borrowing a little of that technology for our new inventions."

"That's right! Now, to ask about the flows and how they are formed, then how to contain and use them for something like this is to ask a few other questions along the way. We already know from past discussions with His Lordship, among others, that the Estelar use this as a kind of support layer. I've heard it associated to how we might need air to breathe."

"Right, I've heard this as well from a few things we've been suggesting about Sargeras being on Azgarén, and how he might be able to survive over there."

"And so, this leads us to the suggestion of those seed entities, which isn't at all pleasant. We know we have it here on Tae'Eladar, and also in such places with Therinë, Ruuki uy'Daan, and Morndindor. Lieutenant Ti'van once mentioned to me that she was aware Therinë was in the same universe as Morndindor, due to her team picking up the adamantium ingots from there, and her observations along the way. So, we're going to assume Ruuki uy'Daan is found there as well."

"Probably within the same galactic body, I would imagine."

"Maybe so. We took measurements of the harmonics of the arcanic energies in those places and found they are all very similar. They also seem to match what we have here on Tae'Eladar, that is to say the original energies, not our modified version from the Spires."

"Does this mean it could all be combined within one big cloud?"

"It's possible, unless we are suggesting this is simply how it comes out. The way these arcanids behave, by the depictions we have of them, is that they form a kind of symbiotic relationship with other forms of life. Think of plants and animals and the air we breathe. What we exhale, they take in. What they release, we breathe in."

"All right, and so these arcanids work the same way, but I also recall them being found in another dimensional layer, so what is it they actually take in?"

"This is one of our questions. I'm also asking why they are not found around Azgarén. When we use the term 'a barren fold', my impression is we place it into a context of an abnormal condition. We have it in our universe with Tae'Eladar, in another universe with Therinë and the others, but not your universe with Azgarén. Why? What's different about it that we call it barren?"

"Yeah, that's a good one."

"We also have the Estelar who are said to cover most of Creation by now, and this further implies this stuff is everywhere."

"And this simply exacerbates the statement."

"This also raises a most curious question of why Sargeras and Darumon would choose to hide there in the first place, especially if it is barren and he should not be able to survive there at all. But then a thought came out when I was speaking to His Lordship once. We were speaking of Adalon's prophecies, then of your long trek out this way, the message you were carrying, and the anguish you suffered along the way. He mentioned a meeting he had with Commander Nazég and Archivist Windsong, and it was stated that we might not have been able to take any earlier action if that universe of yours is off-limits to the Estelar for some reason."

"I recall the Commander briefing me on this once, but this simply makes me wonder why a society of gods would mark anything as off-limits."

"I wondered about this as well. The statement seems to demand one to ask this question. His Lordship said he once learned, probably as part of his Celestial teachings, that there may be Folds of Creation out there they hold in reserve for some reason, maybe to keep them pristine from their personal influence, or perhaps for study reasons."

"Study reasons?" she muses. "I can probably see the part of staying out if you don't want to influence something, but to study… Wait a minute, like a science project, perhaps? Ah, yes! To physically avoid it in order to prevent the contamination of the contents," she nods. "That's an interesting concept. So, is this to say our native universe might be a study project for some reason? A barren fold, one without the flows, and possibly to see how life develops in its absence?"

"It certainly offers a possibility. And if they're all told to stay out, a Primordial might find it very convenient to use this as his hideout."

"It sure would! And much to our misfortune, it seems that's exactly what he did."

"But now we have this mystery of how he's actually surviving in there. It's been said he was probably in a dormant state before he found you. But then, I believe it was young Kaliya who said that Darumon might have created these seed things as a feed to support Sargeras in the absence of these energies. And this led me to a few curious ideas."

"All right, I'm listening," she smiles.

"When we offer our worship to our local gods, it's a special practice we make to place our focus of mind and devotion as a service to contribute some of our mental energy to supplement their natural strength. The gods aren't beings like us. I recall from our history where we had a few precious occasions when one or another of the Estelar actually came down and spoke to us personally."

"Wow…that must've been a sight. How do they appear usually?"

"Most often, they take a form which appeals to our senses as one of us. But there was one occasion that was carefully documented when one we had never encountered before came to us to offer her favor if we would perform a service for her. This is where we have the story of Lady Aerlie first coming to us. This individual is known as Aerdrie Faenya, the goddess that presides over winged creatures, like the Avariel."

"They have their own? Amazing."

"And she was said to be truly astonishing to behold. She apparently arrived in her native form, which looked like an amorphous body in the middle, hovering above the ground and with many long fin- or wing-like appendages fluttering about…all gossamer thin and glowing. I think there were some drawings made once. You could probably look it up in the library back home."

"Yes, I would like that very much."

"Anyway, we give our energy to them with our thoughts and emotions, and they often return the favor with their blessings and other gifts. If we associate this to those seeds and Sargeras, we might be talking about something similar, if only on a more primitive scale, and therefore I'm thinking he needs quantity in trade for the lower quality."

"And therefore, involving the full population of Azgarén…all right, I'm with you so far."

"Now, this by itself doesn't answer the question for the flows and the arcanids, unless you consider a much more generalized scenario. In our world, we as a collective body of life create the environment around us. Animals interact with plants, which then interact back with animals."

"I am truly fascinated by your society, Professor. Regardless of the fact that you are still Early Industrial, you hold some very advanced wisdom in many areas."

"Thank you," he smiles. "If we say we work a type of symbiotic relationship with them, and we work another one with the arcanids, then we might be saying life, as a general quantity, is working this relationship. The Estelar use the flows as their support layer, but are we saying they interact with arcanids like we interact with plants? I think not. Even the gods had to start somewhere, and we understand them to be beings of a supremely high level of development, well above us. So, my proposition was to ask which came first, the arcanids, and therefore the flows, or the gods who might find it useful."

"This is good, and how did you conclude this one?"

"Simple. Evolution. Those of us here are not gods, and yet we can use the flows for our personal needs. Now, imagine if you develop this by millions and even billions of years. Just as life may have once crawled out of the ocean to breathe air, so too did the Estelar grow to depend on the dynamistic flows, rather than the original air their ancient ancestors might have once used."

"Great cu'Nar!" she gasps. "That certainly puts things into perspective. So then, these arcanids are likely a precursor form of life, much like the earliest forms of life you might find in those oceans that created the air in the first place."

"And the Estelar simply evolved to learn how to use it, like we are now, but in their case continuing to such a refined state that they completely evolved out of their original corporeal forms into what we see today, and are therefore now dependent on the flows as their support layer."

"Incredible," she sighs as she lays a hand on her brow. "And your worship simply adds into that, I suppose, which is the reason you share this relationship. You give a little to them, and they give a little back, like a form of barter."

"Precisely! But now, as for the arcanids themselves, if the Estelar behave this way as incorporeal creatures in their modern day, and they live outside our Prime domain, and if these arcanids also live outside our Prime domain, I'm tempted to suggest that creatures of any sort that fall into this category live out there as opposed to those of us who are called Primes living here. This brings me back to our local universe, maybe also that of Therinë, and then Azgarén."

"Uh huh, and here we come full circle, where our evolution might one day carry us outside such a universe as this."

"And therefore, if these clouds all have the same harmonics, could this simply be a standard feature of the flows in their natural form given arcanids of any sort interacting with corporeal life of any sort as part of this symbiosis. The data we have might suggest this. But the hole in this theory is Azgarén and your barren fold. Where are all the arcanids if they're not performing this same function over there? I say, maybe there aren't any."

"Um, alright, so why don't we have any around Azgarén...or anywhere else over there?"

"This could relate to the same reason the Estelar put up a Keep Out sign around it. It's a study project. Something must've happened and they're studying it. But this raises a big whop-a-doodle of a question."

"Yes, I think it would, especially on the scale of gods."

"What might cause a god, of all things, to want to study something? Gods are so often described as All-Seeing, All-Knowing, but these are infinite terms, and not very practical for a finite creature to lay claim to. How do you squeeze infinity into a finite body, or even a finite mind? And the Estelar are definitely finite, even if they are still called gods."

"Now there's a concept I never really thought of before."

"Therefore, my proposal is they found something new to study in that barren fold. And if the fold is currently barren, that means the arcanids haven't moved in yet. It must be a comparatively young universe in relation to the others."

Tanjhira wheezed and pulled back into her chair. She gaped at the Professor for the remarkable conclusion, at least as much that it came out of an Early Industrial scientific perspective, but also that in her mind it made perfect sense.

"And therefore, it hasn't YET developed the flows. And...wait, this would further suggest the Estelar are studying it, maybe to learn how life...maybe even THEIR form of life, once got started way back in the beginning. Grace of the cu'Nar, talk about learning the mind of God."

"It's a surprising one. This might also cause one to ask when the arcanids first arrived, and from where. Everything needs a beginning. Maybe this is why the Estelar want to study this. Even the arcanids need a beginning. Maybe that beginning came from elsewhere, perhaps even a Prime space. But then, how did they get up there?"

"How..." she ponders. "Could they have migrated somehow? But then, if they're so primitive, they might not hold the capacity. But..." she raises a finger. "If they're such a primitive form of life, could we be speaking of something on a microcellular level? And if so, all you need is someone with a jump-capable ship entering that space and maybe leaving a bit of trash behind. And bam! Contamination, which might then evolve into this. But then...ah! I think I get it. This would precede the existence of the flows. Therefore, if a god society needs the flows, none could've existed at this time. So, what we're saying is, the Estelar are trying to understand how it all got started. Can someone invent a jump drive in a space without the flows offering their shortcuts, and then, following with the rest of it, ultimately leading up to the presence of the flows, and thus enabling a god society like theirs."

"Abso-double-lutely!" he cheers.

"And then what... These gods draw strength from the worship of people, and this amounts to a form of trade using, um, mental energies, I guess. But these arcanids are probably a more primitive form of life, so the simple presence of living organisms like us, maybe with our general activities and the energies we give off naturally, feed into them much like plants and animals complement each other simply by coexisting together."

"Very nicely done, Tanjhira," he beams. "But now we need to figure out how to coax these little fellows inside our containment chamber. If worshiping the gods invokes a reaction with them, I wonder if praying to these arcanids would do anything," he giggles.

"Um, I kind of have my doubts if they're not otherwise a sentient form to realize we're asking them to do something for us."

"Yes, I think you're right, therefore we'll need a lure, a bit like going fishing. But I think a group of priests might still be needed if we place a special worship icon to focus on inside the chamber. This will be our bait."

✦

"Fishing?" Thaelyn raises his brow.

"Well," the Professor smirks. "This was a cute term I coined, as it seemed so appropriate to the need. And it certainly seemed to work, because we caught a bucket-full of arcanids along the way."

"I see..." he intones warily.

The Professor and Chief Tech Lapäli were reporting their findings at the WIC building of their recent success with the Harvester technology. In attendance were Thaelyn and his usual officers, along with Kaliya and Ayene.

"At least this takes some of the focus off me for a change," Kaliya chuckles.

"Indeed, and I must say, Professor, your story has left me very impressed with your work. I would wish to offer my congratulations to everyone on your team, including the Chief for all of her work in this, and so many other recent efforts."

"Why, thank you, Your Lordship," Tanjhira offers.

"This new discovery brings us an important step forward in our war efforts. But Professor, I think I might have to go even further in this case. Between you and the Chief here, you pulled together a very fine piece of research using mostly preexisting knowledge and testimony from people who have brought about their own revelations and statements outside the scope of this research project. For this alone, I feel compelled to grant you the official discovery of this principle, as it would easily fall into the same category as if I were to give it out as a knowledge quest."

"Woohoo!" he squeals. "This might even nominate me for another science award!"

"I would surely hope so! This is a most noteworthy discovery. While the Harvester itself must still be kept as a classified project, this one component brings our people a little closer to understanding the ways of the flows and the means to further control them."

"Good for you, Professor," Kaliya smiles. "And you too, Tanjhira."

"But now that we have this," Thaelyn adds. "I think it is important for us to temper ourselves with the reasoning that the official invention of our own Harvester technology must be conducted by another who is otherwise independent of this research, to allow the full challenge of combining these principles into an appropriate growth exercise to bring our people forward."

"That's fine by me, my Lord," the Professor accedes. "I'm sure there may be a small mention in there of our work once the official discovery is made. But as is the tradition of our society where such things have been made in the past, we need to give credit to those who make this without the added help of any higher minds."

"And here we go again with that restrictive ruleset," Ayene mutters.

"Yes, Lieutenant, but it's necessary. We can't say we actually invented anything, other than this bit about the arcanids. Everything else is simply following someone else's design work. We follow the wisdom of the Estelar here, and we respect this philosophy that we learn what we learn only when we're ready to learn it."

"Right, so once my horns untangle from that statement, I hope to be able to understand something from it," she chuckles.

"Our next step," Thaelyn continues, "is to develop this as a full-scale application. We need to ramp it up to a working model capable of serving our needs."

"Right," Tanjhira affirms. "The numbers we were registering coming out of the gathering nodes in our scale model are still preliminary due to the recent acquisition of our arcanids. The focus we were using was small, but the projected energies it emitted once we had our people, um, praying to it...and it's funny to say such a thing," she grins, "began to demonstrate our capacity and the amount of energy we might get out of it. Our next objective has to be to calculate what size we need as our full-scale model, and how we're going to use it. But I'll caution you ahead of time; this thing isn't cheap on materials."

"I might expect as much. What are we speaking of here?"

"Adamantium...lots of it. The full casing of the containment module is solid adamantium...well, adamantium plates welded together to form a housing. One solution is to make it modular, where we can attach segments or panels to regulate the interior volume. We can then scale the whole thing up or down, depending on our needs. But this also multiplies the volume of materials needed. We also need some heavy-duty power to supply the containment field. This one small unit is using up just about every last spark of energy we have available from our existing power supply out there, so I'm going to suggest nothing less than a fusion reactor for a larger application."

"Very well, I will have you begin building one of those onsite. You could borrow the design you were using on Ruuki uy'Daan, but in this case, modify it using our own fuel inputs rather than yours."

"Yeah, I'm still trying to put the curl back in my horns after your suggestion on that. How to power a fusion reactor with a perpetually renewable fuel resource. Dear cu'Nar above, your arcanic technologies could revolutionize just about everything we ever invented."

Chapter 10

AN ALIBI

"Eiki, are you busy?"

Kaliya was making an unexpected visit to the woman's home in Glimmerheim. Eiki jumped at the sudden presentation of the young officer's oversized form popping in and crouching low to fit in the confined space. She was in projected mode so she could bypass travelling through the city and appear directly inside the woman's cozy little home.

"Oi, Kaliya! Me dear, I still can'na get used t' ye poppin' in like that. An' look at ye. How can ye feel comfortable standin' there like that, hung over so low in this wee space?"

"Don't worry about that. I'm just here to pass a few instructions along."

"Good t' hear… I've been a-wonderin' what be the word up top. Ye've been a mite quiet since the day ye took that nasty Thane down."

"I know. We've been very busy with a number of important projects to prepare ourselves. We recently made our move to Azgarén, and set down a foothold. Now we're conducting scouting operations to see what we have to work with."

"Oh!" she croons. "I remember when ye said that would be a hard one t' make. D' we know anythin' from it yet?"

"So far, it's still early. But what we know for sure is it'll be a lot of work," she chuckles mildly.

"Aye t' that, I'll bet!" she giggles.

"But for now, we're making plans to free this world from Darumon's interest, and for this I need to call on your help again. You and the Chancellor have a job ahead of you."

Eiki had been busy sewing a dress at her worktable. She put down her materials as she listened to the report.

"The first thing we have in mind," Kaliya continues, "is to make it seem Ytani, who was impersonating your Thane, as you recall, lost control of the city. Between his abusive behavior, his constant demands, his growing belligerence, and so on, you people finally had enough of it, and now you're rebelling."

"Rebellin' ye say?"

"Yeah. Our story up there is going to paint the picture that the mining down here is thinning out too much, and they need to make a survey for more minerals. But for this, he needs more of you to come out and do the deed. But if you recall, he doesn't ask politely."

"Oi! I know that old tale by now!" she frowns.

"Right. Now, just recently, we're saying that southern mine quit on us with the work crew expiring from this drug, so he called up a new one from down here…nothing especially new where that goes, other than you people getting tired of losing your men to it. Then we have this survey, where he is going to call for yet another work crew, but here is where you go wild. It's too soon, and you're too upset over losing all the previous men to let another crew go out."

"Blessed Mother, this sounds like we'll have a lot of ragin' goin' about!"

"This is where you start asking these questions, ultimately to dig yourselves out to see what's really happening out there, and then Belrum's story."

"Aye, an' I can see where this be a-goin' now."

"Good. Now, we'll put a little time in here between his demand for the survey crew and when he actually expects it to be ready. This gives you time to do the work, therefore the questions and the rioting in the streets when you start complaining over his lies and storytelling.”

“Aye, but then what? This be where methinks ye wanted that Darumon t’ come ‘round t’ look at things, so he gets up an’ walks out on it, ay?”

“It is. We’re going to make our play up top to ask for help for this survey. We need them to send a ship to help us conduct the work.”

“A ship?” she ponders, trying to associate with her own teachings for what that was.

“Um, right…” Kaliya chuckles. “You people don’t go out much, and I guess you don’t often travel on water, even when you do. A ship is a kind of transport that carries lots of people. In a world like yours, and many others, this might normally travel the seas, but my people also have a kind that can travel the space between worlds. We’re going to make a play for one of those, and Ytani is going to steal it.”

“Truly now!” she smirks. “An’ why would he go an’ d’ a fool thing like that?”

“Well, initially, as I was explaining this to Thaelyn, because he’s such a responsible young man, he’s going to take that new crew of miners with him to help begin the excavation of this new mine, once they find it. However, he has ulterior motives to escape from all his obvious failures down here. So, he’ll use them, plus some unknown weapons from an unknown friendly source he apparently found somewhere, to steal the ship and run away.”

“Really now!” she laughs boldly. “Dear, d’ ye often go ‘round makin’ up such wild tales? What does yer King think of it?”

“He’s already written me down a few times for it,” she sighs. “But it’s all in good spirit.”

“Aye t’ that! He be a truly grand ruler, if I d’ say so!”

“Anyway, this is where we need to call in the loss of the ship, which we hope will call Darumon’s attention, thus causing him to make a visit to investigate. And here we need him to see your people rioting in the streets for Ytani’s errors and poor management. From here, we will play our final piece that this world is apparently lost to us, and hopefully he'll want to pull out."

"Ye say hopefully…"

"Yeah, this part is the only one we can't fully predict due to how he so often behaves. But if we play it right, he might see no reason to stay, as there is nothing else to do here."

"Right, then," Eiki considers. "So, I'll be a-needin' t' get with the Chancellor t' make up our work for the people outside."

"I'll come tell you when we're ready, and you need to follow a plan to work the people through these discussions, all the way up to a riot ready to go to war with whoever is responsible for all this."

"A riot, ye say? Aye, the people would sure be a-fumin' at all the Thane's wild tellin'. An' if ye take in Belrum an' his tales, that just makes things worse for all the pummelin' an' so many people lost outside. If that Darumon should dare think himself right enough t' d' this t' us, we'll have a few good words for it shoutin' out in the streets. But when will ye know the final word for all this?"

"Now that we have what we need to move forward, we're going to make this call very soon. First, we need to file a report with the expiration of that southern mining crew, just to have it on record that it happened. This will probably occur with the next monthly report we send out. Then we'll wait a little bit for Ytani to order up the replacement, since those people don't know the exact timing of it, and not long after that, we'll do the rest. When we're ready, I'll give you the word, and when it's all done, I'll come back and report to you on the results."

"Aye, then," she nods. "Kaliya, ye be a good sort, ye an' yer King. I want t' thank ye again for all yer kind help with me sewin' supplies. I hear tell in the streets of how the folk be so grandly welcome for the coin an' trades. For such a long while, we be a-wantin' for many a fine trade from above, but with the doors closed, things were a-runnin' thin down here."

"Yes, I can certainly understand that," Kaliya sighs.

"The Chancellor, bless his heart, he be a-tryin' his best t' keep the city workin' hard, but without a Thane t' rule, some folk be a-wonderin' who t' call the next one."

"Do you have anything like a noble lineage around here that would normally take up this position?"

"I think, once upon a time we did, but nay anymore. The Thane was s'posed t' belong t' a long family. The Chancellor did a wee bit of searchin' through some old tomes an' scrolls relatin' t' our history. The Thane as we know him was an only son, an' he took over at the time his father died…which brings me t' wonder how THAT happened."

"Oh great!" Kaliya throws her hands up. "And so typical! So, we might say Darumon eliminated any potential competition to get in his way. Therefore, Ytani could play his role for four centuries unhindered by any relatives vying for the successor role."

"Aye, an' with nay any t' follow, this simply broke our leadership 'round here."

"This makes perfect sense. And all the more reason you have this problem of who comes next now that HE is out of the way."

"Aye, an' there be nay anyone among us with the right breedin' for it."

"You know, Eiki, there are other forms of rule that don't follow a royal bloodline. You can create a body of voters who elect a ruler. It's called a democracy."

"Mayhap so, but I don'na think any of our folk would know what this be, nay off the top. An' this would call for a wee bit of schoolin' afore we can catch the full meanin' of it."

"Actually, you're right. Political studies, at the very least, just to learn the practice of it."

"An' ye should also know, we dwarves hold high regard for those who show up the strength t' lead us. I think, simply t' hire up any soul off the street would nay bring the sort of kinship we favor for the one holdin' the seat."

"Again, you may be right. Your society is kind of finicky," she grins.

"Aye t' that!" she giggles. "An' when we look at all the help ye've been a-givin' us, t' the folk above an' t' us down here... Lass, I'll tell ye true. The tales of the world above be hard for us. Nay a one of us knows how t' fix all the blastin' an' the dyin' land. But Tol an' the others, they've been a-whisperin' a few tales in our ears of the world ye come from, how grand it be there, an' how ye know of a way t' help us with ours. Be this the way of it?"

"Yes, though it won't be easy. But Thaelyn and his people have some very good ideas on how to restore your world, and he has plans to do exactly this, once Darumon is out of the way. It's not quick; it'll take time, many decades, maybe centuries, to say the least. He's already got people out there collecting specimens of plants and animals as a way to try to preserve them so that later we can bring them back and reseed this world."

"Reseed?" she asks curiously.

"That's what we call it when life on a world comes so close to extinction that we need to start almost from scratch. We're trying to save what's still out there so we can make this effort. It's not just about your people, but also whatever else is out there."

Eiki pauses from the discussion to take a deep sigh, trying to reconcile the scale of the destruction she's been hearing about from her husband, as well as trying to imagine an entire world being brought back to life. It was too big for her mind to comprehend, but one thing did stand out about it. She held the conversation as she stood up and strolled into another room where her family kept a personal library of old history books. She returned back with a thick book in her hands and sat down again, now opening the book to look inside.

"Lass, in our days, we had many a tale told of great Thanes come an' gone. They be heroes t' our people, makin' such great deeds, an' leavin' behind legends t' tell our children. This here be a book with some of the old tales me family kept. It has been a long while since I looked at it. Me mother would tell me tales from it when I was a wee babe."

"I know a few things about dwarven culture. The dwarves of Tae'Eladar kept a lot of old history, and they tried to keep their culture alive even through all these years."

"'Tis good t' hear how our kinfolk kept true t' our traditions. An' now t' see them followin' such as yer King, it speaks t' me that they know a thing or two. An' then Tol, with all his tellin'…"

She pauses to glance at the book, and sighs in recollection of her memories.

"Our world yay be a wreck now. None of us here would know how t' fix it. I've heard a few people talkin' about it. Belrum's tales of the blastin', the dyin' land with nothin' growin', an' how he an' his kin had t' leave an' find better land t' live on. We nay be a people anymore, Kaliya. We be but the last of us, an' now without a ruler t' lead us. An' even if we did have a ruler, he could'na hope t' fix all this…nay in his lifetime, an' nay any of his children. Ye an' yer kin know how t' d' this reseedin' bit, but d' ye think we would know about it? Belrum an' his folk could barely eke out a few bits t' eat in that old cave of his. An' they lived out there all this time. All they could d' be t' watch the land die."

"I know, Eiki, and it hurts me just as much for how many you lost in all this."

"Aye, but here ye are helpin' us with things we nay can d' ourselves. An' did we ask ye for it, mayhap? Nay! Ye just came in an' did it because it was the right thing t' d', an' ye don'na turn the other way because it yay be too hard, or ye don'na want t' spend yer time with it. This be the way of a true leader, the legends that built our world in the old days. I'll bet there nay be a man or woman in the land who would argue this. An' those of us here in the city, we already know the tales."

"Eiki," Kaliya hesitates. "What are you actually saying in all this?"

"What I be a-sayin' yay be that we need a strong ruler in this land t' bring it back from the dead. D' ye think we can find it here? I think nay. We can barely build up our own city from the dead, an' this be WITH all yer fine trades. The folk outside yay be but wee hovels barely scratchin' their backsides tryin' t' figure out how t' live with twigs an' scraps. D' ye think they can bring the world back from the dead?"

"Well, um…"

"Aye! Ye know me meanin'. But yer King, lass, he nay be one t' let people fall behind. He be half a god, by the sound of it from Tol."

"You're actually a lot closer than you might think," she chuckles weakly.

"Be it true then?" she grins. "An' more, ye have a world over there, part of it filled with our kin who travelled far from here on their pilgrimage. What were they a-lookin' for, d' ye think? Be it t' find their god? Mayhap... But how d' ye think they got there in the first place? We don'na play with this magic like ye an' yer kin. I'll bet me uncle's whiskers they had help for it, what d' ye think?"

Kaliya was suddenly stifled at the suggestion. Eiki was right, and Kaliya knew it. Dwarves were not traditionally known to play with arcane spell craft. So, unless they miraculously created a portal, and even more miraculously aimed it successfully at a valid target on a completely different world in a completely different universe, then there had to be something else involved.

"Cu'Nar's Pity, Eiki..." she wheezes. "I know the elves made theirs somehow, but I don't think I have the details on how the dwarves did it."

"Mayhap the All-Father saw somethin' bad in store for us, so he paved the way for some of us t' travel ahead. An' this paved the way for the rest of us t' follow."

"Eiki!" she gasps. "Are you actually saying you...here...would, um..."

"Aye, lass. Yer King an' his folk be already makin' more work here than a hundred Thanes. An' this reseedin' bit...I can'na begin t' think of what that would bring, but I think it would mark him a hero among heroes, the greatest of them all. Ye can'na top that. An' so, if any man be worthy t' take the throne here, it would be him, an' I can'na see how any among us would argue with it."

"But it's not like he came here to attract new people. I mean, um..."

"I know what ye mean, lass. He came here t' chase that nasty old Titan. But did he simply run past us after seeing the land out there?"

"No, he didn't."

"An' did he stop t' ask, that he yay or nay spend his time tryin' t' help anyone?"

"Well, technically, no, that's not his way. He did the same with us on Therinë. You should've seen him when I used that word Titan on him," she grimaces. "Next thing I know, he's not only liberating our world and everyone on it, but he united all of us on a campaign to travel to places we didn't have the capacity to travel to, just to finish it."

"Really now!" she chortles. "An' look at ye, lass. Look at where ye be now. Be that the mark of a true leader? An' why be it we nay can say the same for all he be a-makin' right here for us. We have nothin' after that Thane rolled us on our bellies for so long. I say, if Tol thinks so grandly of him, an' ye an' yers think the same, an' so many others behind ye, then it be clear as day he be the true an' stout soul t' lead us back t' the way it once was for us. An' more, we can join back with our kin who made the pilgrimage. They found our hope, an' this hope found the rest of us."

"Eiki, I don't know what to say right now. I'll tell him, and I think he'll also be without words in the beginning, but if this is how you feel, I know we would all love to see you join us. But let's not get too far ahead of ourselves. We still need to contend with Darumon."

✦✦✦✦✦✦✦

"Kaliya..." Thaelyn sighs in deep contemplation. "I do not know how to respond to this. Another world...possibly?"

"It would certainly appear that way," she replies softly. "For all that they suffered with their Thane, they need strong leadership to make a comeback. She said they don't have the knowledge or the resources to do it themselves, so the impression is they would need to find something else regardless. And for all the work you have planned, as well as what's already made, none of it with any question for the need, or consideration of the expenditures you would make along the way...you are simply doing it. Among their people, and I'm sure you would know this about dwarves, they would regard you at the top of the list of their greatest heroes. Therefore, it simply follows.”

“Yes, dwarves are like this, although I had no idea any of this would lead to such a thing. Powers behold. Then it would seem we might inherit even more Children.”

“She also hinted at the old pilgrimage of our dwarves on Tae’Eladar…how did they find their way there, and for what reason. Although it might be impossible to demonstrate this, they couldn’t have done it themselves, so they must’ve had help. And if they’re calling it a pilgrimage, could it be their god foresaw something and was planning ahead for it?”

“This is a fine suggestion, and one I might actually wish to submit to him to see if he has anything to say about it. The primary dwarven god, out of their pantheon which they call the Morndinsamman, is named Moradin. Although I have never spoken to him personally, I certainly do know of him, and by now I would expect he might know a few things of us on Tae’Eladar. Maybe he has been watching during this time.”

“I would imagine so, by now,” she smiles.

“Very well then, we should see to a few of these steps once we rid ourselves of Darumon. This restoration project will be an extraordinary one, so we should be on with it at our earliest opportunity. I will give instruction for Shescellaie to produce a new life-seed, and we will introduce this into the valley just in front of their city. I think we will break ground there and restore that part to full operation, then to use it to aid the rest.”

“All right, good. In the meantime, we have a couple more weeks to go before my next report. This one will mention the mine to the south cutting out and a new work crew being selected. Then, not long after that, we play our game.”

The weeks passed by, and it was time for another monthly report to

Central Command. Kaliya was visiting the mining base for a final review.

"Spook Kriv'tik," she calls to the teammate impersonating the base commander. "Do we have our report ready?"

"Yes, Lieutenant, would you like to review it before we send it off?"

"Yes, I would, let's take a brief look."

The two of them step inside the Commander's office to examine his data terminal where they had been preparing the false reports on the mining operation. She scans the document on the screen, and quickly checks the numbers.

"All right, so we have the southern mine that cut off two weeks ago, and we say in here we're currently acquiring a new team. I'd like to know what Central thinks about all these mining teams mysteriously vanishing if they don't otherwise know we're using deadly drugs on them."

"I can't imagine, Lieutenant. For that matter, I'm having a hard time trying to imagine half the things those people are doing over there without eventually asking questions about it."

"It kind of makes you feel sorry to be part of the same species after a while. Ten millennia... How long does it take for any scientist or scholar to ask even a single question about anything Darumon is doing out there?"

"Apparently more than that, and he seems to be doing a good job of covering for himself."

"Yeah, that story the real Commander Kriv'tik gave sure might seem convincing...if you have no idea how to fight a real battle. Insurgents that never win a fight, but successfully keep the people locked down on their home world so they can't escape from this horrible infestation everyone wants to get away from. Wow, if I were a horror film producer, I could make a fortune off that one."

"One thing I think we should keep in mind after all this is to be sure to record our history for the people to learn from. We sure wouldn't want them doing this again. We need to learn from this mistake not to be so foolish as to simply give ourselves away to someone without at least asking a few questions and seeing the evidence to back it up. Apparently, Darumon simply came in with some very elaborate stories, and because he represented himself as a reliable source, he just naturally had to be believed."

"A superior being from a superior society," Kaliya muses. "One that presumably has superior technology our people wouldn't understand anyway, so don't bother asking about it. But..." she emphasizes with a finger, "...if we give everything we own to him, he might share some of it, and then woohoo!" she waves her hands theatrically. "We all become gods."

"Personally, I'm waiting to see what their Council looks like after that suggestion you and Lieutenant Ti'van had together. That could answer a few things right off the top."

"And it simply takes us back to how Darumon was running Rolsklinde, using people like the Dean of the old academy to distribute his lies. If he's doing the same thing here, we have trouble."

They study the data terminal a few moments longer, reviewing the details and pondering the sequence of events that might soon follow.

"All right," she relents. "Send it off. The city down below is running out, and we have a firm suggestion of a survey in here, so it's just a matter of putting together the pieces for our next report."

"How long for that, do you think?"

"I'm not going to wait very long for this. We'll give it a week, maybe a little more for Ytani to rally up his new survey team. And this is what finally breaks them downstairs."

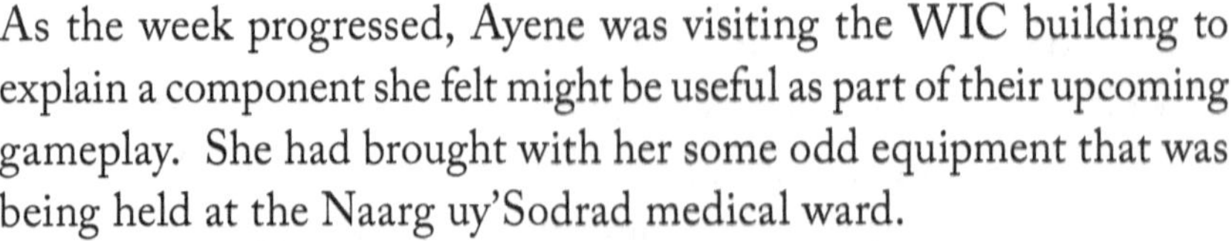

As the week progressed, Ayene was visiting the WIC building to explain a component she felt might be useful as part of their upcoming gameplay. She had brought with her some odd equipment that was being held at the Naarg uy'Sodrad medical ward.

"Commander," she begins. "Here are those diagnostic probes we ordered once from the ARC. Kaliya tells me she took them when she captured the base, and now I wish to present these for our future operations."

"Ah, good," Kailen responds. "I recall this from one of our spy videos. But now, can you explain how they work, and what exactly they're supposed to do?"

"Yes, although without my interface unit, I can't offer a proper demonstration. However…" she reveals a small box she was carrying. "Likha, over at the Naarg uy'Sodrad, gave me this to help me explain. This is one of the interfaces taken from our staff during the time you had us in the operating room."

Ayene opens the box to reveal an interface unit nestled on a foam pad. She pulls it out and holds it up for everyone at the table to study it.

"If you look here…" she points at the interface, "…this port is where you would attach the probe in order to reprogram the unit or conduct a diagnostics function. I would recommend using this as opposed to your previous methods of those scrambler devices. This would be much more effective, as it will disable the unit completely."

She picks up one of the probes and holds it near the interface.

"You have this short cable and attachment fixture," she directs at the unit. "This attaches and locks into place with a small twist. From there, you have a control panel on the unit with several small buttons to perform a series of functions. You use these to follow a menu system on the display panel. For our purpose, we are using a custom function to deprogram the interface completely, which will result in the chips being disabled."

"And this would basically release them from their control, right?" Kailen asks.

"Yes. As you engage the unit, you will see a progression bar display on the panel, and hear a soft beep when it's done. We have three probes here, all the same, so we can distribute them among our team members to offer a little bit of coverage."

"What about any kind of alert signals…for instance, if the units lose connection with your network. We once suspected they're all linked to a data network of some kind that might send out an alarm if something bad happened. Is this correct?"

"It is true that they do connect to a security network for status updates and operating conditions, but unless the individual is found dead, it doesn't necessarily send any kind of alarm if that person is simply disabled or unconscious. Therefore, if you use that sleep spell on them, or if you hit them with that stun technique Kaliya once explained to me, it shouldn't do anything, unless the electrical zapping effect shorts something out. But I still don't think that would do anything other than maybe cause an interruption in the signaling."

"All right, so we can skip the area jammers on this occasion, and once the interfaces are disabled, I doubt we would need the personal units either. Then it's just a matter of removing them from the area."

"Right. I feel a little guilty for conspiring against my own people, but this is for a necessary cause. I just hope they'll forgive us later after we explain the situation," she smiles tenderly.

"We'll let Commander Kriv'tik handle that for us. His rank and past history should come in handy here."

"As for our approach," Thaelyn submits. "We will use that transport shuttle from your base to make our arrival. Kaliya's team will lead the way, but you and yours will need to hide under a cloak due to your missing interfaces that might cause you to stand out. The first objective is the bridge, where she will take down the crew members, and your team will replace them. From there, it is simply a matter of systematically progressing through the rest of it until we have containment."

"And once everything is secure, we jump out of the area. But now, where are we going with it?"

"I suppose that depends largely on the richness of your destination choices. Personally, if we have Ruuki uy'Daan or Therinë on the list, I would choose one of those. I doubt Darumon would think of returning to either of those for any reason, and certainly not to look for a missing ship."

"All right, good. And afterwards, we return to the base and prepare for our next act. This will be a good test of my acting skills."

"Lieutenant," announces the spook commander at the base. "Central is sending a follow-up on that survey idea. They're asking if we have an official requisition ready, or if we're still pending with our local preparations."

Kaliya was once again in attendance with her projected operatives at the mining base. It has been several days since the last report went out.

"Do we have the Commander's requisition form ready?"

"Yes, it's on the data terminal in his office. I've checked it once already, but if you'd like to take another look..."

"I reviewed it when the Commander was putting it together, and it looks good. I would like it scheduled to arrive in the next few days. This gives Ytani enough time to make his new demands, and subsequently the people down below becoming fed up listening to him and start digging their way out to see the world for themselves. Then we have the resulting riots for all of his lies," she chuckles mischievously.

"You know, Kaliya," he grins. "You must have a mean streak in you."

"Well, nobody's perfect, I suppose," she shrugs innocently. "All right, let's send this off as our response, and put a date on it for this coming weekend."

"Understood."

The officer fills in the last few blanks and submits the form. Now, it's just a matter of time before the show begins.

Over the course of the next few days, Kaliya and Ayene, along with Marelle and Petrith, Lieutenant Az'krun, and Commander Kriv'tik, were in a last-minute briefing in the WIC building.

"As I mentioned before," Ayene recounts. "It's likely to be a science vessel with deep penetrating scanners, what we often refer to as precision subsurface scanners used for mineral surveys on moons and asteroids. These ships are most often a midrange cruiser category with three or four hundred crewmembers, depending on the vessel."

"Your most critical operations centers," the Commander adds, "would be the bridge and engineering, but there might also be an auxiliary control station in case the bridge is compromised for some reason. From there, you should be able to use the ship's internal sensors to locate and defeat any other crewmembers who might still be moving around."

"Keep in mind," Kailen offers. "Unlike with the base on Morndindor, these people are going to be awake, and likely much more aware of what's happening, although admittedly they probably won't be expecting a military assault. Still, you need to treat this no differently than with your initial training."

"Yes Sir," Kaliya grins impishly. "In other words, they'll never know what hit them."

"That's what I'm actually afraid of," he chuckles. "Then, once they're down, you will use rune transport to remove them from the area. As before, we'll send them to the outpost with Captain Hagmaert for further processing."

"Do we use the sleep chant on this one, or simple stun attacks? Personally, I don't think we'll have as much a luxury for the chant, and we're not trying as hard to conceal who we are as we were before. We're simply kicking tails and counting numbers here."

"Other than for keeping to the shadows before you actually kick those tails," Thaelyn muses wittily. "Yes, I think we will allow Captain Hagmaert and his people to handle things for us, if need be. Simply take them down quickly and remove them quickly. Our primary objective is to capture that ship. It is not as important if they see our faces, so long as they do not have time to react to it. Then later, once we have them in our custody, we will allow the Commander and his people to inform them of the situation at their leisure."

"Got it. I'll pass the word along."

"One more thing that comes to mind," Ayene wonders. "If we are saying Ytani is transporting as many as three hundred newly recruited miners, you're not going to fit all those in that little transport. We'll need to use the larger cargo transport for that, although it would still be a tight fit…it always was before. So, we should remove it from the area first before anyone comes to investigate. It might make things a little more convincing, or at least save a question or two."

"Good point," Thaelyn accedes. "Marelle, once you return to the base in the smaller transport, we will have you take away the other one for us. Perhaps you can move it to the Captain's outpost for storage."

"All right," she affirms.

"We will use our new shard-coms to communicate between us. I want status updates on our progress, as well as a listening post inside the control booth at the base so we can overhear the conversation. Now, if there is nothing else, I will have you be on with your work. Good luck."

Kaliya and her assembly pulled to attention and offered a salute. The group then departed from the room and made their way to Morndindor, where they met with Captain Hagmaert for a quick briefing before taking a rune transport up to the base. On arrival at the base, Kaliya met with her assault team, as well as her projected base crew. And when the real Commander Kriv'tik arrived in the room, he stared at his doppelganger projection.

"There is something especially creepy about seeing yourself like this," he mutters privately.

"With apologies, Commander," the projected member bows politely. "But someone has to do it."

"Right, just as long as you stay out of my wife's bedroom," he smirks.

"All right people," Kaliya announces. "This is it. Spook Kriv'tik, do we have a response from Central yet on the ship?"

"Yes, Lieutenant, we just received a message a short while ago that one is available and standing by. I told them I needed to reconfirm our readiness before we could proceed. They are currently waiting for us."

"Good. Well then, comms, call them up and tell them we are in a go condition."

"Yes Ma'am," issues the officer at the com-station.

Kaliya pulled out a spare shard-com and set it in the corner of the forward console to serve as their listening post. In the WIC building, Thaelyn, Kailen, and the others could now hear the general chatter on a conference channel.

The comms officer opens a channel at his station.

"This is Morndindor Base to Central Command, are you receiving?"

"Morndindor Base," ushers the voice on the link. "This is Central Command. Affirmative. Do you have a response for the survey expedition at this time?"

"Affirmative, we are in a go condition to commence. Our team is assembled and ready."

Kaliya quickly waves a hand in front of the officer's face and makes a quick hand signal at him. He nods as he continues in the speaker.

"By the way, Central, what vessel are you assigning to this mission?"

"We have assigned the Ghan'aju research vessel. This should satisfy the need to fulfil your request."

"Very good, Central. When the vessel arrives, have them contact us and we will prepare our team for departure."

"Understood, Morndindor Base. We will signal their crew to begin underway immediately. Central Command out."

The link ends and Kaliya glances around at her team.

"Commander Kriv'tik," she begins. "Do you know this vessel?"

"Not personally," he considers. "But then, I've been out of circulation during my stay here, so if this is a recent addition, I might have missed it."

"Maybe I can help," Ayene offers.

She sits down at one of the front consoles and logs in using her security access to gain the necessary clearance. She then pulls up a browser to the Central Command military page and conducts a search in the military naval registry for the name. A moment later, she has a detail page exhibiting the Ghan'aju research ship. She croons over the resulting design specs.

"Ooh, this is a nice one. A deep-space exploratory cruiser with a category six spatial inverter, a deep penetrative scanning array, exobiology lab and hazardous specimen containment, radiology lab…"

"Um, Ayene," Kaliya addresses supportively. "While I'm sure you're fascinated by the technical specs, can you tell us about the crew compliment?"

"Oh yes, that…" she chuckles. "It says here the standard crew is four hundred thirty."

"Yikes! Well, it looks like we've got our work cut out for us on this one."

"Do you have enough space to detain that many?"

"I don't know, but we'll have to put something together, and quick."

Kaliya picks up the shard-com unit she set down on the console earlier.

"My Lord, are you listening?"

"Yes, I am," issues the voice.

"Ayene says the ship they're sending has upwards of four hundred crewmembers onboard. We're going to need help to hold them still, at least until we can talk to them."

"Agreed. We will have Captain Hagmaert and his priests use sleep chants on them. This will keep them for now, and we will remove them to Ruuki uy'Daan under heavy guard until we can work on the rest."

"All right, sounds good. We'll keep you posted as we move forward."

She sets the unit back down and again reviews the plan with the group.

"Now, once they call in, we will inform them that our away party is launching and will arrive shortly. Lieutenants Ti'van and Az'krun will pilot the transport with everyone else hiding in the rear. Once we arrive, Marelle, Petrith, the Commander, and the two Lieutenants will go under cloaks. Marelle will need to stay in the transport, but the rest will follow us up to the bridge once the way is clear. Remember your spacing so you don't bump into each other. We rehearsed this a little back home, so keep to the numbers."

"This will be fun," Ayene muses. "Trying to find your way when you can't see your body or those around you that you're trying to avoid."

"This is why we use the count. We practice this during our field training to time our movements."

"You must have some very interesting methods."

"We need projected members to impersonate Ti'van, Az'krun, and Kriv'tik. We'll have the three members inside the booth here accompany us on the transport."

"Um, Lieutenant," remarks one of the projected members. "We never actually practiced riding in a transport before while projected."

"Yeah, I know. We'll just mark this down as another learning experience. It all comes down to your perspective relative to your surroundings. We don't usually have an issue with this on the ground, even though technically the planet is in motion. But I think inside a transport, you need to narrow your focus to the local environment and place yourselves relative to follow along. Maybe if to take a small form, it might help in the beginning."

"If you say so."

"I think it's doable, and probably easier than it sounds. Then, once we arrive, you'll make your appearance through the door while the rest of us hide."

✦✦✦✦✦✦

"Marshal, I have an update."

The cool monotone voice of High Commander Geilv issues over the com-link. He was sitting in his office at Central Command and reporting to Darumon over his vid-com terminal.

"Yes, Commander, what is it?" he responds in a stern gravelly voice.

"I have just received confirmation from Morndindor Base requesting the delivery of the research vessel. The Ghan'aju is currently departing."

"What was the last report from the base?"

"Their last report indicated the apparent discontinuation of the mineral supply within the primary mining venture. The secondary venture to the south of their location seems stable except for the expiration of the previous work crew. A new crew is being acquired."

"So, it finally happened. The mines inside that city ran out. I knew it would come eventually; after all, nothing lasts forever. I'm actually surprised it held out as long as it did. And now we are embarking on a new survey. This should be interesting. But who is it they hope to use on this occasion? Your technology does not provide you with the means to extract the metal in its purest form, and we need this for our little project."

"Understood. Morndindor Base reported a recent investigation to identify the mineral's characteristics sufficiently enough for the survey ship to locate them, and the report also suggests Ytani will be acquiring a specialized work team to serve this new operation."

"Good! That young man is developing well for us. I might just keep him around for some other application, should anything come up that would require his...ehm...special talents. Yes..." he chuckles wickedly. "I will be very interested to see the results of this, Commander. Perhaps, in time, you might learn how to use this metal yourselves, and we won't need to suffer the inefficiencies of an inferior labor force again."

The link ends and the High Commander sits back in his chair as he returns to his other duties, completely unaware that he is being watched by a tiny surveillance camera tucked away neatly behind a ventilation grill at the far side of the room above the door.

At the same time, in the control center of the base, the Watch Captain gave his orders to prepare the ship for launch. He and his full staff were also under surveillance by a camera, again hidden inside a ventilation duct with a clear view of their operations.

Orbiting high above the planet in the Saakerav military space dock, a smartly designed research and exploration vessel of substantial size and accouterments had just finished the recall of its crew complement, and it was now powering up for departure.

"Control, this is the Ghan'aju, ready for departure," the Captain announces in his own characteristically flat Suuden'kai voice.

"Ghan'aju, you are cleared for departure. Releasing docking clamps…now…"

The noble ship slips out of its moorings and begins drifting backwards as a catapult launching release gently sends it away. The helmsman applies a lateral thrust to turn the ship outward from the space dock, then forward to gradually steer away from the station.

Even though it was part of the Azgarén space navy, the ship was not a combat vessel. Rather, it was used for exploration, stellar cartography, and planetary studies. As such, it was only minimally armed, with light security, and staffed mostly with researchers and technicians. The military body consisted of the bridge and engineering crews, security staff, medical technicians, and auxiliary support staff that would serve to supplement the primary crew during alternate work shifts.

The design of the vessel resembled an elongated oblong main body mated to an angular wedge-shaped engineering section protruding to the rear and underneath. On either side of the engineering block were the large nether-space inversion nacelles. And nestled behind the main body was a concave niche for the shuttle landing bay, complete with landing lights leading in through an atmosphere curtain to shelter the bay interior.

The ship made its way out from the dock into open space, setting course to reach a minimum safe distance between it and any other objects before engaging its nether-space drive.

"Captain, we are approaching our jump point," announces the helmsman.

"Our destination is Morndindor," he declares smoothly. "Set the jump coordinates. All hands, prepare for nether-space jump."

A brief klaxon sounds throughout the ship as a warning for all hands to secure their stations before the jump. The navigator sets his coordinates in the jump drive indexer, selecting from a navigation chart of previously recorded exit points.

"Ready, Captain."

The Captain makes a cursory pass around the bridge to judge the readiness of the crew before giving his order.

"Proceed."

"Engaging jump sequence," the helmsman responds. "Powering up the nether-space inversion field... Ten percent... Twenty... Thirty..."

He rattled off the numbers as the power relays charged up. A modest hum could be felt reverberating through the ship as the reactor power revved up to capacity.

"Sixty... Seventy..."

The view through the large forward monitor of the outside space began to ripple as an inversion field formed a bubble around the ship.

"Eighty percent...the inversion field is stable. Ninety percent... Mark. Phase-shifting is active, we are entering the conduit."

The ship is surrounded by a visibly luminescent bubble of energy. It flashes in a dazzling surge, then vanishes from sight, leaving a rippling echo effect as the rift closes behind them.

They passed through a long tunnel-like conduit. The helm was set to a computerized autopilot to navigate the convoluted channel as it makes the occasional twisting and bending through hyperspace. The images outside were surreal, but to the Suuden-Aryku, with their past experience and professional manners, to say nothing of their inhibited emotions, it held no specific value. It was procedure, nothing more.

Their passage through the slipstream was smooth and well-practiced. Ahead of them, they could see where the tunnel connected with the domain of the destination universe, the exit point where they would reemerge back into normal space. As it approached, the scene outside blended with a natural star-scape, and the ship penetrated into the region of local space outside Morndindor.

"Helm," issues the Captain. "Bring us to within low-orbital scanning range. Comms, signal the base of our arrival."

The communications officer engaged his console to transmit the message, and in the mining base on the ground, Kaliya and her team waited tensely.

"Morndindor base," ushers a voice on the local com-system. "This is the ASN Ghan'aju. We have arrived in orbit and await your response."

Kaliya's team was ready, along with their supplemental partners. Her team was dressed in their typical covert black leathers, with hoods and masks, along with padded boots to keep the sounds of their hoof steps silent. They each carried belts with a variety of potions, a combat knife, some tools, and an emergency escape rune, since by this time they were each in the Sixth Circle of study, which was enough to learn how to open a portal.

Kaliya directs the real Commander Kriv'tik to answer the com-link, while the projection steps back.

"Commander Kriv'tik, speaking," he announces coolly. "We have a team ready to depart. I will accompany and direct our efforts once we arrive."

"Commander," the ship's Captain interjects. "We will need to configure our scanning arrays in order to serve our objective. Do you have the specifications?"

"We will bring the configuration details with us. My officers will oversee the operation."

"Acknowledged. We shall await your arrival. Ghan'aju, closing."

"That's our cue, folks," Kaliya calls to the room. "Let's go! Ti'van and Az'krun in the pilots' seats, everyone else keep low. We'll close the blinds on the windows for cover."

The assembly files out the door and loads up in the troop transport, taking up seating wherever available, as they had more bodies than actual seats. The three projected members altered their forms into smaller shapes to assist in adjusting their perceptions to accommodate the local environment.

Kaliya makes a quick call on her shard-com as they settle into the transport.

"This is Thaelyn," answers the voice.

"My Lord, we are mobile. They've arrived and we're on our way."

"Good. Stay alert and follow your training, Lieutenant."

"Acknowledged."

Ayene sat herself comfortably in the pilot's seat and powered up the craft, while Lieutenant Az'krun assisted with the diagnostics and status monitors. They lifted off and swung around over the base, heading in a southerly direction out of the mountains and angling up sharply. She boosted the throttle speed incrementally to maximum power, rising over the landscape rapidly, then to break through the sound barrier and accelerate to supersonic velocity. The world fell effortlessly beneath them.

"This is so much like my last flight run on Tae'Eladar," Marelle recalls.

"You're really lucky, Marelle," Kaliya coos. "Your society isn't even ready for this, and already you're going places none of you has ever gone before."

"Just like Adalon promised."

They continued higher until they began to see the upper layers of the atmosphere.

"All right, here's the plan," Kaliya orders. "When we land, we go dark. The three spooks go out as the Commander and the two Lieutenants. They'll pave the way for the rest of us. Our first goal is the bridge. Take that, and we control the most critical operations of the ship, including the helm and comms. This becomes our foothold. We bring in the real Commander and his officers to start their work. Next is engineering, followed by a systematic run-through for a bit of housecleaning. But everybody has to move together and under cloaks."

"Lieutenant," issues the Commander. "Most often, according to our design standards, the bridge and engineering segments are primarily accessible through the magneto-lift service. The size of a typical lift car is not adequate to hold all these people."

"Then we do it in turns. Depending on how the situation looks, if we have a simple button to press, or if it's motion sensitive, we may need to use spooks or possibly real bodies, if the area is clear."

"The lifts should have call panels that allow you to call a car to your service. These would be pressure-sensitive buttons your projected forms can use. Critical areas also use detectors for greater efficiency."

"Good to know. So, we'll work our way to the bridge, and then to engineering. I'm expecting someone to meet us as we land, and escort us to the bridge for you to meet with the Captain. From there, hopefully we won't have any trouble finding the engineering section on our own."

"That should actually be very simple. The lift service will take you to any station on the ship. It represents a network of shafts running through the vessel. There are stations located at different areas, some of them designated as home stations where the cars will park for critical traffic, such as the bridge and engineering. You'll have a panel of buttons to direct you, and we also use a voice interface for efficiency."

"I've never actually been on a ship like this before. What happens if one of these cars gets stuck?"

"There is a bypass in that case. Normally, when you enter a car, it will take you to your desired stop, while in the process sending other cars in your path forward to the next home station. There is also a security lockdown to isolate key areas of the ship, again such as the bridge and engineering."

"How nice! So, we go in, take over, lock it down, and that gives you a little privacy to do your work."

"I can perform this task once your people are on their way to the next station."

"Good, so we've got three spooks to play with. We'll run them through individually, if need be, to fill up the cars. But I want everyone on the bridge for our first move. Keep in mind, you need to remain quiet during this time until we have the situation under control. And stay out of the line of traffic through the corridors. Meanwhile, Marelle, you will stay on the transport for now until we're ready. There's no sense in dragging you all over the place."

"Understood," she nods.

Ayene guided the transport into low orbit, lining up with the rear of the ship. Outside the front window, they could see the body of the ship coming into view. It seemed to be hovering gracefully in the distance, innocently awaiting the arrival of a technical team to begin a casual survey operation.

"Ooh! That's a nice one!" Marelle coos. "So, when do I get one of my own?"

"Easy does it, Marelle," Kaliya begs. "Let's first take care of your pilot's badge, then we can work on your captain's bars."

As Ayene made her final alignment, she called them up on the com-link.

"This is Lieutenant Ti'van of Morndindor Base to the Ghan'aju, requesting permission to land."

"Lieutenant Ti'van," returns the voice on the link. "Permission granted. You are clear to land."

She continued forward towards the ship, calmly approaching the landing zone and flight bay on the rearward segment.

Kaliya watched as the ship loomed ahead. She was fascinated by the sight of a true star cruiser, the sort of thing she had only seen in old vid-com programs as a child. Now, here she was, a military officer on her way to capture one and steal it away, along with its crew. But the operation had to be carried out with the utmost precision and care.

Ayene descended towards the arrival zone, guided by a navigation HUD directing her on a computer-generated glide path into the flight bay. The transport made its approach, crossing over the marked landing zone and gently passing through the atmosphere curtain into the bay. She hit the switch for the landing gear and settled on a nearby pad.

"This is it!" Kaliya urges. "Squad leaders; cast cloaks on our guests, and everyone else go dark. Spooks; make ready at the door."

Kaliya and the squad leaders begin casting cloak enchantments on Petrith and the Suuden-Aryku members, while the projected members lined up at the door. As the group goes under their invisibility shroud, the projected Commander and his officers open the door and step outside. They were greeted by a lieutenant standing outside in the flight bay.

"Commander Kriv'tik?" the Lieutenant solicits. "I have instructions to escort you to the bridge to meet with Captain Va'tyn."

"Proceed, Lieutenant."

The Lieutenant leads the spook Commander and his officers through a door in the rear of the flight bay. They follow along a corridor a short distance to a door accessing a magneto-lift. The Lieutenant presses the call button. A moment later, a car arrives, and the door opens. He steps inside and waits for the Commander to enter.

The lift car was small, only large enough for perhaps ten people at a time, if neatly packed. The Commander and his officers made a quick, but discreet, examination of the size, realizing it will take multiple runs to transport all the people up to the bridge.

"Commander," the projected Ti'van begins. "With your permission, Lieutenant Az'krun and I should visit the lab briefly to discuss our details for analyzing the specimens we will be collecting with the ship's researchers."

"Agreed," he nods. "I will proceed to the bridge with the Lieutenant and await your results. No doubt, I will need to brief the Captain on our procedure before we begin."

The Commander now follows his escort into the lift, taking a cautious stand near the front of the car, as he expected some of Kaliya's team to have taken up positions along the back wall by this time. In his projected form, he couldn't see them, but the team each had the special enchantment glyph applied by this time, so they could see each other under the cloaks. The rest of the team waited in the hall for the car to depart.

The projected form of Lieutenant Ti'van glanced casually around the corridor to make sure it was clear. The immediate area was absent of any crewmembers. She waited a brief moment, directing the form of Lieutenant Az'krun to walk along the corridor to an intersection to observe if anyone was coming along in that direction. All seemed clear.

She pressed the call button, and a new car appeared a few moments later. She motioned silently for the next group to enter as she stepped around to examine the control panel inside the car.

The panel was a matrix of buttons indicating different decks and specific sections of the ship. This was an alternate method of control in addition to the voice command the car would normally respond to. She searched the panel for a hold button to keep the door open long enough for a team to enter. She counted to ten in a low whisper, just audible enough for the teammates to hear as a timing mechanism to coordinate their movements. Then she released the hold and pressed the button indicating service to the bridge.

The Commander arrived on the bridge with his escort. When the door opened, he made a conspicuous effort to delay his exit by engaging in a brief conversation with the other officer.

"Lieutenant," he issues, pausing by the door to allow the hidden members to exit. "Once my officers return, we will need to spend some time to recalibrate the ship's scanners to identify the minerals we are looking for. It is my understanding this vessel is equipped with a deep penetrating precision array, is this correct?"

"Yes Sir," he nods as he compulsively presses the lift's hold button. "This ship holds the latest design specs for research and study of planetary bodies. You will not be disappointed."

"Very good. Being stationed in that base for so long, I find myself a bit out of touch with our newest fleet arrivals."

"I suppose so. But we are quite proud of this one, so I am sure you will find everything you need here."

"Excellent. I will be looking forward to our results together."

The Commander turns casually to orient out the door, by this time hoping the cloaked members had fully departed outside. He steps out onto the bridge with the Lieutenant in tow to meet with the ship's captain.

The bridge was a large room lined with operations consoles along the rear and side walls. The helm and navigation stations were positioned ahead of the Captain's chair, and the front wall was a large video display depicting the forward view outside the ship.

"Commander Kriv'tik," announces the Captain. "I am Captain Va'tyn. We are ready to proceed with our survey mission. What do you require?"

"My officers are making a review of your research facility and will arrive shortly. They carry the details of the calibration specifications, but we will also need to examine specimens to ensure we have a viable resource deposit."

"Understood. I hear the Marshal is interested in learning about this new technique of yours. He believes it could lead us to learn how to harvest this material directly, rather than employing the service of other races."

"I am sure this would offer a viable result once we become more familiar with the practice after a bit of field exercise. The method has been tested in a laboratory environment and we believe it holds some valuable potential in our future operations."

Lieutenant Ti'van arrived several moments later with her delivery of hidden agents. Like the Commander projection, she pauses and counts quietly inside the lift as a delay tactic while seemingly studying a data-pad she was carrying. At the end of her count, she proceeded outside the lift to meet with the Commander.

"Commander," she begins. "The research labs appear to be ready. If all is well up here, I should bring our sample specimens up from the shuttle for our comparison studies."

"Affirmative, proceed."

The Lieutenant makes a quick nod, then returns to take the next lift car back to the flight bay.

The form of Lieutenant Az'krun arrived a few moments later, again delivering more hidden agents. He paused in the same fashion as Lieutenant Ti'van, and then exited the lift car into the room, joining by the Commander's side.

"Lieutenant," the Commander asks. "Are the details delivered?"

"Affirmative, the primary components should be in place by now. We are ready for our operation."

"Excellent. We shall begin with the return of Lieutenant Ti'van."

The Ti'van projection returned back to the corridor where they first arrived from the flight bay. She expected there to be a few people still standing nearby under a cloak, in this case Petrith and the Suuden-Aryku members, who would go up last. She glances around the area to ensure there are no crewmembers passing by, then further to peer around the corner of the nearest intersection leading deeper into the ship from the flight bay, before returning to the lift door.

"Lieutenant, are you present?" she mutters softly.

The scene is disturbed by the appearance of Kaliya shedding her cloak momentarily to respond.

"Who is left?" the projected Ti'van asks.

"The replacement crew, that's all. We'll follow you back up."

"All right, Spook Kriv'tik is probably stalling for time while we assemble."

"Good…" Kaliya nods as she turns to a seemingly vacant space next to her. "Now, we go by the numbers. Commander, you're two, Ti'van is four, Az'krun is six, and Petrith is eight. We'll count to ten, and you go in single file on the even numbers. Line up on the back wall, left-to-right, and allow space so you don't bump into each other. You can't see each other, so use your best judgement. I'll follow up the rear."

She casts another cloak on herself as she finishes, and the Ti'van projection calls up the next car. When the door opened, she stepped inside and began another soft count.

Kaliya observed from under her cloak as each of the Suuden'kai members made their moves according to the numbers, followed by Petrith and lastly herself. They took up comfortable positions along the rear wall of the car. The Lieutenant then pressed the button for the bridge, and they were on their way.

"The research we were conducting at the base," the Commander projection explains as a means to occupy time, "was based on the speculation we would eventually experience a shortfall with the existing mines. These mines have been in operation for an extended period. It was inevitable that they would become exhausted."

"This is quite reasonable," the Captain accedes. "And therefore, you prepared this as a contingency in anticipation of this event. But is this solely to identify the minerals, or does it also afford us to devise our own extraction method?"

"So far, we are still limited to foreign labor, but our studies have provided us with a curious result."

"Really! What result is that?"

"First, there seems to be an ambient energy source in this space. It is unlike anything we have ever experienced back home."

"Ah, yes, we are familiar with this phenomenon, although our science is still trying to understand the nature of it, as it does not fall into any previously defined category. So far, Central is simply calling it abnormal energy."

"Yes, for lack of a better term, I suppose it is, at least by our standards."

The projected Commander appeared to mull the term. Privately, he almost felt like laughing at it, if only due to the obvious ignorance of how 'abnormal' the arcanic energies truly were.

"Do you feel an alternate definition would be in order?" the Captain asks.

"I suppose the notion is subjective. Abnormal as compared to what? We might first wish to ask this question, as it could be very normal...for THIS universe...and perhaps it is abnormal for us NOT to have it in ours. Did anyone at Central ever consider this aspect before?"

"Actually, I have never heard of this concept expressed before, but it certainly is a viable one."

"But anyway, we found that this mineral seems to carry a trace signature of these same energy readings."

"It does? Is this to say it might be a source for it?"

"A source, no. But it does seem affected by it somehow. It seems to carry a type of charge, for lack of a better term, and this may affect some of its properties."

"How interesting. I wonder if this might hold any industrial value to us."

"In time, we think it could," he nods casually. "One thing we noticed in our tests is it seems to excel beyond the typical qualities of something like steel for its tensile strength. But it is also apparently a rare mineral, so the potential would likely be limited in scale, or at least very expensive."

The projected Lieutenant Ti'van was just arriving on the lift as the conversation was progressing. As before, she paused inside the lift car counting quietly to allow time for the hidden occupants to exit before making her own appearance on the bridge. She stepped out and crossed to the Commander's side, where she stood and waited patiently while the two senior officers continued their conversation.

"I see," the Captain muses. "Well, perhaps we might find our answers at a later moment. May I ask what the Marshal is using it for during this time? Stronger than steel, but also very rare. This might suggest something specialized. It is my understanding this operation has been underway for an extended period, correct?"

"Yes..." the Commander responds. "But unfortunately, this entire operation has been classified, as the output of his process seems to involve some proprietary technology. We are under orders to deliver it to a processor where a specialized work crew refines it further, and then stores the result in a depot. From there, he apparently has a purpose for it, but again, he is keeping this classified."

"As with so many other things..." he asserts concernedly. "Commander, with respect, I would not wish to violate any restrictions, but I will admit I have a few colleagues back home who are aware of this operation from their past interactions. First is the obvious question of a mining base conducting any kind of operation that might be classified. This, in itself, is unusual, as a mining operation does not seem like the sort of thing one would normally classify."

"I suppose, if you consider what might be normal operating procedures."

"Normal, yes. Even if we found something new, and from the industrial perspective, it might hold value, and further if to say it might be a rare substance, this in itself does not sound like the sort of thing to classify. Not unless you want to tell me it carries something volatile or dangerous, and the reasoning falls under a safety protocol."

"This would indeed be reasonable," he nods.

"Then to see it used to produce something that is also classified, and next to hear you tell me his plans for it are once again classified. These could lead one to easily question the integrity of the entire project. Further, if I may, is for you to suggest this mineral seems to reflect this abnormal energy our science does not otherwise know how to interpret. If the Marshal is using proprietary technology to process this material, how does HE know what it is if he is not otherwise telling US anything about it, especially if it might hold a valuable industrial potential, or anything else for that matter? And this could potentially also infer that safety reasoning, or whatever other cause is behind it. I am reflecting on this long overdue promise of his to grant us some of his privileged wisdom, and this would surely be one aspect of it, would it not?"

"I suppose it would. Furthermore, is that one should also consider where we are located in that statement, and whether this could be normal or abnormal relating to that."

"Absolutely!"

"Well, these are all very good questions, Captain. But unfortunately, at this moment in time, I am unable to oblige you. Our instructions are similarly restricted by these limitations, so we can only assume the Marshal must maintain some very carefully considered principles where his objectives are concerned. And since my officers are now assembled, we should be on with our work. Perhaps at a later time we might find these answers together."

"Very well, Commander, and I thank you for allowing me this moment to voice my perspectives. Now, where do we begin our operations?"

Kaliya had been listening to this last portion of the dialog, when suddenly an idea came to her. She held up her hands to draw the attention of her cloaked teammates and gave a series of hand signals to direct their action, once the 'go' signal was given.

The projected Kriv'tik would be personally unaware of this change in tactic, as he could not see her giving out these orders, so he simply continued according to his script. He proceeded to direct the two Lieutenants away from the crewmembers to allow space for the hidden teammates to operate. He also steps away, as if studying the forward monitor, which was displaying an image of the planet below.

"Captain," he begins. "Our operations will begin with a brief review of our objectives. The first of these is this…"

The Commander now holds up his hand and closes his fist. This represented the go signal to the hidden teammates. Suddenly, the room erupts with a flurry of activity as cloaked figures in black bodysuits pop into view surrounding each of the bridge staff. The unexpectedly abrupt arrival of the foreign bodies took the entire bridge crew by surprise. But before anyone could react in any way, Kaliya's teammates were slapping stun strikes on each staff member's forehead…all except for the Captain, where two teammates rushed up to his sides and grabbed him.

"What in the…!" he yelps. "What is the meaning of this? Who are you people?"

The sudden rush of activity in the room left him dazed. He glanced around the room to see the full company of his staff now lying motionless on the floor. Kaliya emerged from her cloak and approached calmly in front of him.

"Easy now, Captain," she soothes. "They're not dead, simply incapacitated. We need your ship, that's all."

"Who are you?" he shouts. "And why would you attack us?"

"Technically speaking, you and your crew are being taken as prisoners of war."

"Prisoners of war? What war?"

"The one Darumon started with us on the other side. He's not who he says he is. Initially, I was simply here to take all of you in this condition," she waves at the rest of the crew. "However, I overheard some of your conversation a moment ago, and it gave me an idea, if you would like to hear it," she smirks softly beneath her mask.

"Oh dear…" the Kriv'tik spook moans. "Are we applying another love and kisses method?"

"Hey! It worked the last time," she shrugs.

"An idea?" the Captain gripes. "You assault us in a hostile takeover, and you have an idea of something?"

"You were asking questions. These questions concern the integrity of this, or any other of Darumon's operations. This hints at suspicions concerning his veracity."

"Um…"

"So listen up carefully."

She begins pacing across the floor as she continues.

"You're right. That mining operation is a cause for concern. We regard it as illegal. Darumon is producing a weapon of tremendous destructive potential, and it also reflects on this thing you call abnormal energy. Where we come from, this energy isn't so abnormal. In fact, just the opposite… It's abnormal for Azgarén NOT to have it, and this handicaps those of us who are native to that world, as we have no idea what it is or how to use it, but HE does. And so inconveniently, he's not teaching anyone, even WITH his promises of great wisdom."

"He, meaning the Marshal?"

"He, meaning that creature who is undeserving of a title of any kind, so we simply call him Darumon. If that weapon were to be set off in our native universe, without this energy we call the dynamistic flows, it would blow up on a huge scale. But it if were to go off in THIS universe, or any of a multitude of others out there, where this energy is quite commonplace, it would start a chain reaction rippling through the entire cloud. And Captain, the cloud could very easily span the entire universe. This is a doomsday weapon on a godlike scale."

"You must be joking! Why would he want something like this?"

"The reason why also involves why he is telling people like you to do his work, but doesn't explain what that work is or why he wants YOU to do it. He's a terrorist, a criminal on the run, along with his master, Sargeras. And the people they are running from are the ones who OWN all those other universes."

The Captain glared at her, and then glanced at the Commander projection, as well as the other teammates.

"And just who are you and what relation do you have in all this? You look like one of us, but you speak like someone NOT from Azgarén, by your indirect referencing."

"Very good, Captain, it's good to find someone who still remembers how to use their head independent of what Darumon demands out of you. I'm not native to Azgarén. I was born on a world found in this universe. As a result, I had the good fortune to learn a few things about him, because we met those same people he's hiding from. Now, we're working for them. We're part of a covert operation to put a stop to him and to bring him and his master to justice."

"Then why are you here on my ship? What does this have to do with your justice?"

"One at a time, Captain, and I'll explain. First and foremost, he likes people to do as he commands and not talk back, or to ask questions. This is why you all have chips in your brains. If you start asking those questions you just put forward to my agent here..." she thumbs at the Commander projection, "...likely he would do to you the same as so many others, and boom, active mode. Get the picture? THIS is the reason for those chips."

The Captain instantly understood the reference, and he reflexively tried lifting a hand up to his interface unit.

"So, we need to take away his toys first," Kaliya continues. "Meaning to say a chip-controlled military that kills on command with the push of a button. This will bring him down a bit closer to our level before we can take further action."

"He actually does this?"

"We have statements from those who were a part of his grand crusade against his mythical insurgents where this is exactly what he did, and likely to completely innocent worlds, many of which are suggested never to have seen it coming."

"But just a moment here!" he asserts urgently. "Why would he use us on innocent worlds?"

"Two words…target practice, to test his shiny new military he worked so hard to build, and to make sure you didn't turn tail on first sighting of who his REAL enemies are. Captain, we are speaking of beings on the scale of gods. You can't oppose that, not unless you have some truly nether-wild tech, and people in active mode of these chips who make suicide runs without even thinking of what they're doing."

"In all the nether-space…so that is the reason for it. All right, I understand this much. And the ship? And what was this story of a survey expedition?"

"A ruse, part of a complex play we're working on. He blasted that world down there, which used to be fully populated by even more innocent people, simply to remove any interference with his highly classified mining operation. I would imagine those people would probably object to you stealing their most precious minerals."

"Stealing!" he shouts. "Argh…" he groans as he clutches at his interface.

"Ah yes, and then we have those."

Kaliya turns to her teammates.

"I need someone to bring one of those probes over here and disable this thing."

One of the team leaders diverts and pulls out a probe, making ready to attach it to the Captain's interface. The Captain flinches as he sees the device being brought into play.

"What is that? What are you doing?"

"Disabling that little tyrant stuck to your head. This is from the ARC back home, custom-made to turn those things off. Take it, you'll love me for it," she smirks.

The teammate plugs in the probe and activates the reprogramming function. The Captain feels a slight twinge as his interface unit goes dead.

"Now, to continue," Kaliya glances around the room. "We need that beast to get out of here. This world doesn't belong to him. He destroyed a full civilization just to take their minerals so he could make his doomsday weapon no one is supposed to know about. We want him out. But we can't just go up to him and ask him nicely. He doesn't do anything nicely. He kills you for disobeying him. Therefore, we need to make a very careful play to make it look like he lost his operation. The purpose here is to cause him to simply walk away, hopefully without any further destruction of the remaining population."

"He must be extremely determined to cause all this just for minerals."

"I would say, 'determined' isn't the right word for it. Determined might be better to teach US how to do it and leave the middleman out. But his kind treats little things like us as toys, so this can give you an idea of who he is. If he once gave you a promise of some sort of wisdom, or whatever, it was all a lie. Just look at your body, Captain. THAT is his gift to you, and nothing more."

The Captain briefly glanced down at his body, but he didn't need any special direction to understand her meaning.

"And what kind of play requires a ship and a false notion of a survey?"

"The survey is based on the idea his mining is running out. This means his resource is drying up. He had an agent down there oppressing the locals and using them as slave labor. We changed that, but Central doesn't know yet. None of this can be shared with Central because Darumon is hovering right over your shoulders."

"All right, I see your point, and this is where your covert aspect comes in."

"We consider lives are at stake here. Not just people like those below, but ours as well. If he went to such extremes as to force all these chips and seeds at you, this is indication enough that he has ulterior motives. And in those ten millennia you were waiting for his blessed wisdom, all you got were excuses and a heavily polluted world."

"You got that much right!" he huffs.

"Furthermore is the prospect, although maybe not as critical if we can contain it, but if he is known for destroying whole worlds, well, we have Azgarén and everyone down there who is otherwise not asking those questions you're all supposed to be asking by now. He keeps you right under his thumb, and he likes it that way."

"So, everything you're doing out there is outside our local authority?"

"Essentially, yes, because your local authority is more accurately HIS authority. As for this ship, that agent of his is going to realize soon he fouled up this top-secret mining operation when the locals finally held an uprising, and he's going to steal your ship to run away. This will give Darumon a false target to distract him while we sneak in from behind."

"You can't just run up to him and grab him?"

"Not precisely. It's not that easy. He and Sargeras are in hiding, and probably watching for those people who would normally run up to them. We're afraid they could run and hide somewhere else, and we don't want that."

"And so, you take this covert approach. But then, if he is not who he says he is, then who is he?"

"He and Sargeras are leftovers from an ancient war where Sargeras and his kind were found conducting criminal acts, in some ways like what we see down below, and the REAL authorities punished them. But apparently, Sargeras and Darumon escaped from their justice and went into hiding. This is where Azgarén comes in. He found our world, gave all sorts of cute little stories about his misfortune, and unfortunately for you and yours, you simply didn't know any better. Now look at where we find ourselves. Your full population was apparently sent into a panic with this thing you call the Tav'ageen Anomaly, and likely due to HIM forcing it on you so you would take his seeds and chips, none of which is as advertised for their primary function."

"None of it? But wait, how would YOU know this if you are not from Azgarén?"

"We've had some time to study these things outside of his view.

He probably wouldn't be very happy with us learning his little secrets. He sure doesn't let any of YOU learn what they are."

"Um, well, alright, I suppose I cannot argue that point. But I am still wondering who you are that you are not from Azgarén, as I was not aware of any colonists taking up space out here, and then how you made contact with these others along the way."

"Colonists, yeah. As if we EVER had colonies. All right, this is fair. But I'll caution you, Captain, as this information is probably going to shock you. At least NOW, your chip is disabled, so you won't take any hits from it."

"Yes, and I would actually thank you for that. I never did like that horrible little torture device."

"Yes, torture device is right. That's probably the best way to call it."

Kaliya pauses to glance around the bridge again. By this time, several of the other crewmembers were beginning to recover from their stuns. She knew that she needed to bring this to a close quickly if she was to succeed in her objectives.

"Captain, we are the result of that monster chasing us all around your local galaxy, finally into this universe, where we set down on a world, hoping to find peace from his pursuit, only to be hit one last time and pushed into a trap he had waiting for us on yet another toy world. Perhaps you've heard of us. My father is apparently a world-famous traitor to the people, or so it is said."

He frowned deeply at the suggestion, but he didn't dare make any assumptions at this time, because he couldn't accept the assertion based on what he thought he knew from the news media back home claiming Velen was dead by now.

"A traitor?" he wonders cautiously. "And now you are at war with us?"

"My people were NEVER at war with you. We were trying to run away from HIM after YOU joined with that beast that wants to destroy all of Creation. Unfortunately, Darumon and your Council vilified us so badly that it justified you chasing us all across that same Creation trying to murder us simply because we didn't want to become his toys, like the rest of you."

"Um, alright, I can already see where this is going."

"Right, so let me introduce myself…"

Kaliya takes this moment to remove her mask and hood, pulling them down to reveal her features. The Captain glared at her for the strangely glowing eyes.

"What happened to your eyes?" he asks tentatively.

"A little gift from those people who evacuated us away from Sargeras. My name is Lieutenant Kaliya Nazég, daughter of your former councilman, Elder Velen Nazég. Ten millennia ago, when all this got started, my father received a warning from a neutral body telling us to come away with them. The ultimate purpose was to meet the real authority figures out there, but we had no idea what this was at the time. All we had to go on was to say Sargeras is bad, don't listen to him, and run away."

"I see. So, someone came to remove you, and this is where that ship came into play, I suppose."

"Yeah. But Darumon apparently took exception to this and gave chase. He knew where we were at all times, we think, because we would jump, trying to escape from you, only to have you arrive on our doorstep and take several shots at us, just enough to panic us into running again to another world, where the process repeats."

"Taking shots only to panic you? But, what about his stories of those insurgents?"

"There are no insurgents. You destroyed a full galaxy of innocent worlds, many of which were probably lesser developed and had no idea you even existed, just to play target practice with your shiny new military. And unfortunately, we led the way as he was chasing us… or perhaps I should say driving us in front of you."

"Oh really!" he scorns. "And this is how he uses our favor of offering aid?"

"Yeah, makes you want to pull your horns out, doesn't it? His kind uses beings like us for entertainment. This is why those others, whom we refer to as the Estelar, brought their justice on them. Life is not an entertainment sport you just blow up whenever you feel an itch under the tail."

"Unbelievable!"

"My father is still alive, by the way, as I heard recently Darumon tried making a claim that he killed him finally. But we are in a completely different universe, Captain, and his stories said we're still supposed to be in your local galaxy."

"Yes! This much I can attest to."

"When we finally met with these others, some of whom represent these Estelar, we learned who Sargeras really is, and they took up the task of pursuing HIM now, to finish what was started so long ago during that war. He's not even supposed to be alive right now, Captain. Neither of them. And until recently, when Darumon attacked yet another world, which was where these people live, none of them knew he WAS alive."

"Oh great. So, this must mean he was making a sneak attack on them, maybe with intentions of using this super weapon of his… ugh…" he lays a hand on his brow. "And now, you're helping them. But what position do you have with the rest of our people?"

"Other than to be ashamed of being part of the same species after all you did back home? You let your horns be dragged so low that you can't even remember to ask why the skies are so cloudy," she shrugs and shakes her head. "We have our work cut out for us, Captain, all of us. But those two creeps need to be taken out first. We'll work on the rest later…all of us, together."

"Then, you are not hostile with us, even after all we did, and you are simply doing a job, I suppose. All right, I think I can agree with you on this, at least in principle. Your statements were very informative, if also very sensational, and very passionate. Clearly, you must not have the Suppressor chip installed, and especially if you are going around disabling them."

"Yeah, we were gone when those became a fashion, along with the seeds."

"You know, some of this is what I was trying to convey to the Commander here. There are those of us back home who are wondering about these old stories and several long-time inconsistencies. Not all of us are simply sitting around with our horns sagging, but we are limited in what we can do about it, as we need evidence to support any kind of review."

"Yeah, the society of scientists and scholars, where we need that ever-popular empirical evidence to show off. I won't argue with this, but Darumon doesn't let you have it. Just like we were saying earlier, he only gives you what you need to do your immediate job… nothing more. And if you question it…"

"Got it…active mode, be silent and do as you are told."

"Even worse, he classifies everything and denies anyone simply to talk to each other. So, Captain, I'll make a deal with you. I'm a military officer on a mission. My team is specially trained in methods our science back home doesn't have a horn-twisting clue over, and it's largely based on these abnormal energies Darumon doesn't teach you about. You saw us as we came out of our invisibility cloaks, and that's just a small part of it."

"Yes, and I find myself curious as to how this works."

"Well, I can offer to answer all your questions, many of which you probably won't like to hear about, but we regard our entire population to be in danger because of him. We need this ship…well, any ship will do, but this one is conveniently available, and to use it as a form of distraction while we sneak in behind. We'll take good care of it. We just need it to disappear from their scanners as part of our play. We'll give it back to you once we're done."

"That is very kind of you," he attempts a soft chuckle.

"So, let's do this the polite way and cooperate together for a common cause. HE is the enemy here, and WE need to fight back. Now, I could go with my original plan, which was a hostile takeover of this ship. But if I could gain your support, it would be a lot nicer for all of us."

"I might agree to this, but just for the sake of argument, if this is your full team, do you actually think you could take over a vessel of this size with only these few people?"

"Quite assuredly, yes. With respect, did you see us coming just now? This abnormal energy, which we refer to as the dynamistic flows, is miraculous stuff to those who know how to use it. And the people I'm working for taught me and my team some rather advanced lessons. So, taking a ship like this, with people like you inside, is barely enough for me to break a sweat. I once ran a training scenario against a fortified outpost with a full company of soldiers on active alert, and using this same team. I finished the scenario in record time and without anyone knowing what hit them. All I need is to use our cloak to sneak up on someone, hit them with a stun, and then use a technique that resembles a conveyor function to remove the bodies. How do you defend against that?"

"You do not," he concedes. "And neither would you leave any evidence behind of your movements for anyone else to discover what you are doing."

"Absolutely! Then we use this ship as a decoy for his Pride and Joy agent down there who will turn renegade. The original base crew was also being used for Darumon's games. That man, named Ytani, used threats and coercion, some of it involving those chips, to take advantage of people."

"Ytani? Just Ytani? I believe I've heard that name, but it seems incomplete."

"I don't know his family name, not that it likely matters. His family is apparently dead due to an accident, and he, starting at only seven decades, was recruited by Darumon for this otherwise highly classified, and technically nonexistent operation, if only due to a special skill he was taught to coerce the local population to do Darumon's work. I would imagine HE would be made to disappear once the operation was complete. This is how Darumon operates. We're just tools he uses to perform his work. Anything that doesn't serve his needs is wiped from existence. Just look at that planet down there. Your military hit it so hard, it's experiencing an environmental meltdown."

"In all the nether-space," he wheezes. "And is that why it appears so barren?"

"The ecology is dying, so we're trying to save whatever is left of it. And I hear Azgarén isn't much better for all the pollution."

"Yes, you are right. This is one of those inconsistencies some of us have asked about. We have industrial technologies that would not be so harmful, but he never gave instruction to convert that other industry to use this."

"This is an excuse he uses to keep you in those seeds. They hold a service to him."

"A service?!" he shouts. "What service?"

"We don't have the precise evidence to prove this yet, but based on the stories the Commander gave after we captured their base a while back," she smirks. "We think the seeds are custom designed to provide a supplement, maybe similar to the flows, but as a feed into Sargeras. Beings of his kind use this as a type of support layer, much like we need air to breathe. So, this serves a bit like a life support mechanism."

The Captain grimaced at the notion, and Kaliya could hear several others groaning as they also felt the revulsion, along with feedback hits from their chips.

"Team leaders," she asserts. "Let's at least start disabling these chips while we're here."

The Captain watches as the team leaders pull out more probes and systematically move from one to another body plugging in and deprogramming the interfaces.

"You are doing this for everyone?" he asks.

"The military chip is an obvious slave device," Kaliya declares. "But the other one also causes trouble, and not simply for that feedback effect. So, we're doing all of it."

"What about the aspect of the Suppressor being a curative solution to the Tav'ageen Anomaly?"

"The Anomaly is a lie, much like that story of the alien infestation. The only aliens infesting Azgarén are Darumon and Sargeras. My father's science faction, which none of you ever gave credit to, was perhaps the ONLY faction to give you a proper answer to it. But Darumon wouldn't want that. Why? Well, here... Let me show you what the Anomaly REALLY does. Spooks, present forward natural."

The projections of the Commander and the two Lieutenants now line up and reimagine their images as their original Daanen-Aryku shapes. The Captain jerked back at the surreal transition.

"Captain," Kaliya continues. "The Tav'ageen Anomaly is a latent ability in our species that is only now coming forward in some examples. But a creature like Darumon, being who he is, doesn't like little things like us having such an elaborate quality, thus the chips to disable it."

He gazed at the three Daanen'kai teammates in their military cadet uniforms. But the unnatural transformation wasn't the only thing that stunned him. Their clean figures without the seeds or the interfaces, and the strange glowing eyes struck him with awe, even though he had been studying Kaliya for hers during this time.

"More of those eyes…"

"This is how we appear in the modern day after we received that gift from these others. We sometimes call it a blessing from that neutral entity we encountered on the ship. The glow reflects an infusion of positive organic energy, and it's described as a way to cleanse us of any impurities that might be left behind by Darumon and what he did to our species."

"Wait, what do you mean by that?"

"He partially engineered us, which is why he has such an interest in us serving his needs. We know of this by notes left behind from one of these Estelar who was watching him during this time. We're the answer to pursue him now."

The Captain was becoming visibly disturbed by these new revelations. Kaliya watched his reactions, feeling a mote of sympathy for his condition. She surveyed the rest of the bridge crew to see their reactions as the team members continued to disable the chips.

"Captain, as much as I've enjoyed this conversation, I'm still on a mission, and I would imagine my command is probably wondering what happened to me during this time. I should've reported in some time ago on taking the bridge, at the very least. So, we need an answer here. My job is to take this ship, with or without your cooperation. Our mission to liberate this planet is paramount, then to chase Darumon back to Azgarén. I would truly love to have your help…for our people, for our world, and for all that monster ever did to us. Will you help us, or do I have to get physical again? Please say yes, and we can all benefit together."

The Captain glanced around the room as he saw his bridge staff in a seated position on the floor where they once laid. The team members were in a standby condition, waiting for an answer. Silently, he knew he probably couldn't fight these people, not with this strange ability of theirs. But at the same time, he also understood who the real enemy was by now, and these people were working on putting things right.

"Am I expected to hand over command of my ship to you? What sort of command authority do you have to take possession of it?"

"I'm only a Lieutenant, to be honest," she shrugs. "But if it's real command authority you want…"

Kaliya now steps back and conjures up a Truesight spell to reveal Petrith and the Suuden'kai members still under their cloaks. The real Commander and his Lieutenants popped into view standing along one wall on the far side near the lift.

"This is the real Fleet Commander Kriv'tik," Kaliya directs. "We have him on our side after he and his base staff submitted themselves to aid us in our cause."

The Commander and the others stepped forward. The Captain studied him carefully, hoping it was not just another illusion.

"This is a rather interesting method you use, Lieutenant," the Commander smiles. "Is this more of that love and kisses technique I heard about?"

"Well, it certainly beats body-slamming them on the floor," she grins.

"I can see that. Now, Captain, like she said, we could do this cooperatively, or she could finish what she started…or maybe I could simply pull rank, which you know I could do if I wanted to. The

Marshal wants his metal, and he doesn't bother giving explanations or excuses for anything that gets in his way."

"Yes Sir," he relents. "I think I am beginning to understand that now. But if you are not actually serving him anymore, what exactly do you hope to use our ship for, and what will you do with us in the meantime?"

"Like she said, the ship is needed as part of their diversion tactic. But we also need it to provide a jump index to Azgarén local space. This is to deliver their ships into our space, as they don't have an index of their own."

"They do not? But if they came from there…"

"Captain," Kaliya interjects. "While we did come from there once, Darumon installed saboteurs on our ship this last time which caused us to crash on this one last planet we're on now, and this also wiped our nav systems. So, we need fresh ones. Also, that agent of his, who will be stealing a ship, is going to claim discovery of new friends, and using this ship as a carrier for their own."

"Really! That is a new one."

"We need the people back home to see actual invaders of an actual unknown and unknowable technological capacity invading our home space. This is to break your idea that you might own everything, especially as HE is supposed to be so superior."

"Yes, this is one other issue I always had…our success record against his insurgents and how persistent they were to keep trying."

"And we can't use the conveyor in our base," the Commander adds, "as it opens up directly under the Marshal's nose, and this is a covert operation. As for your crew, we need to offload them completely. We're currently managing a world called Ruuki uy'Daan. It's the former home of her people before the Marshal launched the last of his surprise hits on them for his pleasures."

"Surprise hits…" he huffs. "Pleasures. And all for our…shiny military…to have something to shoot at? Is that all Elder Nazég was, a scapegoat for his entertainment value?"

"And we lost a lot of people along the way," Kaliya mourns. "A LOT of people."

Now the Captain was getting angry. And with his chip disabled, he simply allowed himself to let go. His breathing increased and his face contorted in disgust.

"So, he comes to us with his stories, tells us to go out and shoot anything he does…doesn…" he frowns as he finally begins to realize something new occurring.

"It's the chip, Captain," the Commander advises. "It does things to our language center, among other things."

"Oh, how unfortunate," he intones ironically. "Let us try that again…doesn't. Yes, I remember this now, way back when I was a boy. So, to shoot anything he doesn't like. And then, he makes up this story about Former Elder Nazég, blasts entire worlds to dust, and THEN he conducts this illegal mining operation to build a doomsday weapon to destroy the rest of the universe?"

"Well," Kaliya offers. "It's not necessarily, um, OUR universe he hopes to destroy. It's all the others out there, where the Estelar live, which is even worse."

"Oh! My apologies, but this sounds more like a revenge attack now."

"Exactly, Captain, now you're catching on. So, will you help us?" she smiles innocently.

He glares at Kaliya, and then the Commander, and eventually turns to survey the rest of his bridge crew, all of whom were propped up and listening in to the conversation.

"What do you need from me?"

"First, shut down your comms. As far as the outside world is concerned, you no longer exist. This includes comms, your ship ID broadcast, and whatever else you use to tell someone you're still alive out here."

"In other words, we're running silent. Comms," he orders. "Do it. Shut us down to silent running. Next?"

"We need to remove your crew to Ruuki uy'Daan. Our original plan was to knock each of you down with our stuns and use what we call rune transport, which is that conveyor method I spoke of, and this will deliver you to a collection site below. From there, you would be forwarded to Ruuki uy'Daan."

"A conveyor transport method sounds interesting, but on an individual level?"

"Yes Sir, we use it all the time. This thing we call magic blows our old tech completely to nether-space. Then, we'll relocate the ship out of sight, and begin a little play on the ground saying…oops, we lost you. And, uh oh, we need the Marshal to come in and see all the trouble his pet agent has caused down there that has otherwise lost his mining operation."

"Uh huh…clever. So, you're essentially shutting him down. All right, then where do we begin?"

"Well, if you're actually helping us, we could make this really easy. Call your people up here, and I'll have my people disable your chips. Then we'll send you down for further processing on the ground. I'll call ahead that we have the situation under control, and to have your people moved to Ruuki uy'Daan where we'll arrange support to find temporary shelter and occupation until the situation sees our final objective complete."

"Your final objective being…the Marshal?"

"Him and Sargeras, they both need to be removed. But I'll caution you. Many of our plans are still in the development stage, so it won't be anytime real soon for us to move forward. We need to understand all his little tricks and how to disable them, but without any unpleasant repercussions."

"All right, I understand. Then, Commander Kriv'tik, I suppose I must submit myself and my crew to your authority."

"You're a good man, Captain," he assures. "We'll take care of you, don't worry about that. Now, you need to place all active subsystems on automatic. Once we relocate the ship, we'll place it in station-keeping and monitor it as needed, but your crew will need to stay grounded until further notice."

"Understood. Comms, give me the ship-wide intercom so we can inform the crew."

The comms officer initiates the intercom system so the Captain can give his announcement to the crew. Kaliya had her team reassemble themselves, with the team leaders moving to one side of the room in preparation to reprogram the interfaces, and another set of teammates on the other side to manage the transport runes.

Meanwhile, as the Captain and the Commander worked on organizing the crew, Kaliya pulled out her shard-com to report in.

"This is Phantom Prime to base," she announces.

"This is Thaelyn. We were beginning to wonder what was happening up there. You have been silent for an extended period."

"Yes, well, we had a little unexpected situation to resolve, but everything is under control now."

"Ah, very good, so what do we have so far?"

"We have control of the ship, my Lord. The Captain surrendered to us."

Thaelyn's voice caught in his throat, and he gaped at the odd communicator device he had lying on the table. He glared at both Kailen and the General before returning to the unit.

"Eh, just one moment..." he flusters. "Where did the part about the military assault vanish to that we are now jumping ahead to someone surrendering to us?"

"Um, well," she emits timidly. "This was that little unexpected bit I mentioned."

"A little one?!" he shouts. "Young lady, how does one arrive on what is essentially an enemy vessel as a hostile assault team...a covert hostile assault team...and simply have them surrender to you?"

"Well, as the Commander just now mentioned, I used my love and kisses approach again."

"Oh! But of course!" he throws his hands up. "I forgot about that extraordinary new maneuver. General, my list, if you please..."

Thaelyn leans over in his chair and covers his eyes.

"Oh no," Kaliya moans. "Not another one," she chuckles weakly. "All right, let me explain, and you'll see my meaning."

"I am going to have a headache the size of the Great Wheel before this is finished. Very well, Kaliya, what sort of fanciful story do you have for us this time?"

"It makes perfect sense," she begs. "And it was also very convenient for us. We arrived on the ship, just as planned. We began our movements to the bridge, again as planned. And while my team was assembling, I had my spook impersonating the Commander stall for time by engaging in some idle banter."

"Very good, this is reasonable."

"Once I arrived with the final pieces, as we had to move up there in stages for the size of the lift car, I overheard some of the conversation. It seems the Captain was disgruntled by a few things back home."

"Oh, really! What sort of things?"

"Well, the conversation I caught was asking about the mining operation being so classified that it might cause someone to question its integrity for the ultimate purpose. This is essentially to question Darumon for his motives using such an innocent thing as a mining base to make something so heavily classified."

"Indeed! This is fascinating."

"This got me to thinking. Maybe I should try my love and kisses approach and see if I could sweet-talk the situation into my favor. So, I ordered my team to take down everyone except the Captain, and simply restrain him while I had my conversation. After some careful talk, I got him to understand Darumon is a criminal doing a lot of bad things and hiding it from the people back home. Afterwards, I brought out the real Commander, and the Captain surrendered himself and his crew, and right now he's helping us process everyone for the chips, and we'll use portals to send them down. I will then ask Captain Hagmaert to assist in directing them to Ruuki uy'Daan, where we will help them settle until things move forward."

"Incredible!" Thaelyn muses avidly. "And with barely any effort. Kaliya, you are going to rewrite the book on military conduct if you keep this up. Very well, Captain Hagmaert, are you listening to this?"

"Aye, my Lord," he responds on his side. "Great gods above, Lieutenant, you're going to give the rest of us a bad name," he chuckles boldly. "I'll have my people standing by down here. But we're probably going to need some additional support to help these people settle down. Last I heard, we're expecting a lot of people to arrive at one time."

"Yes, Captain," Thaelyn affirms. "So, do your best. We will send some additional troops your way, as well as some interpreters. And Kaliya, I will have you keep us posted as you progress until the crew is away and you are ready for the next step."

"Understood, and thanks for not yelling…too loud," she giggles.

They end the link, and Thaelyn leans back in his chair.

"And with barely even a fight…" he muses. "This is surprising, but at the same time, I suppose it could also be promising, if we can find more like this."

"Indeed, my Lord," the General offers. "And I'm tempted to suggest this could qualify her for another merit badge."

"Yes, but how do you define such a thing. Ingenuity, creativity, taking advantage of an opportunity, using reason in order to avoid a fight… Powers behold, General, this might even need something new…again."

"Much like her first one. Good gracious, she's creating her own military service, complete with its own honors."

"My little sister," Kailen reminisces. "She doesn't even seem old enough, and yet she's doing more than I ever did. I'm a little jealous now."

"Perhaps you should take time to learn this Prodigy skill, Commander," Thaelyn suggests.

"Maybe one day I will, though I'm not actually sure what I would use it for. By the time I learn it, she'll have this war won already," he chuckles.

"I cannot speak for that, but even without the war, there may be other possibilities."

"Still, I think I would prefer to keep my hooves firmly on the ground and see things through from this side. She's clearly got talent with this Gift, and her team is becoming very well coordinated by now."

Back on the ship, they were still processing the crew members. Marelle had been listening in on the shard-com conference channel when she decided to come out of hiding and survey the scene. She stepped out of the transport and found her way to the lift, then called a car and studied the control interface.

"Let me see…" she mumbles. "I want to go to the bridge, which button is that… Oh, wait…a voice interface."

She clears her throat and begins speaking the Suuden-Aryku language.

"Take me to the bridge."

An automated voice response issues over a local speaker.

"Destination: Bridge. Stand by…"

"I like it already," she muses softly.

"Lieutenant Ti'van," the Commander issues. "Take the helm. Az'krun, you take Tactical, and Mister Girhani to the Engineering station."

"Captain," Kaliya muses. "How many more, do you think?"

"We are almost there, Lieutenant," he notes as he observes the continued processing of the crew. "I will be honest with you on one thing, I am very happy to be relieved of that damnable chip."

"Which one, the military chip or the other one? We often call it the emotion inhibitor chip for its most apparent function."

"Yes, I will have to agree on that. Both, actually, but the military chip most of all. I never had it placed on active, but I know a few people who did."

"Just ask the Commander here. He told us he had it multiple times whenever he was told to go out and smash something."

"Tragic… Maybe he and I can find some time to sit and talk. I'd like to hear more of this story. I don't like people saying I let my horns sag."

"I'm sure of it. I'm very happy we were able to come to an understanding, and it offers hope for us to find more on Azgarén, rather than having to fight every step of the way."

"But unfortunately, I suppose this will mark me as a renegade, or a mutineer."

"Let's describe it as liberators. But, welcome to the club. The Commander and his people are the same. Although, technically, you'll just disappear. Ytani is causing a lot of people to vanish along the way. So, your reputation shouldn't be affected, just your existence."

"Oh, thank you," he chuckles. "But I suppose it does follow logically. This reminds me of my wife and family, however. Is there any way I could pass a message to them that I am alright? If Central thinks our ship is lost, they might send some kind of death notice to them, and I would hate to think of what that might do."

"Granted. I'll pass the word and see if we can offer something. But they would need to know to keep it extremely quiet. Yours won't be the only one, and we can't allow any of this to filter back up to Darumon."

"I understand. That sort of defeats the purpose of a covert plan."

Marelle was arriving on the bridge. As she stepped out of the lift, she marveled at the elaborate arrangement of consoles and video monitors. She found Kaliya in conversation, so she strolled up to meet her.

"Hiya!" she announces cheerily. "Remember me? You left me all alone down there in that little transport while you were up here having your party."

The Captain glared at the diminutive young lady with her clearly alien features.

"Um, Lieutenant, who, and could I also ask, what is this?"

"This is a good friend of mine and a fellow military officer, Lieutenant Marelle Carronel. Excuse her manners, it runs in the family."

"I see. Is she a part of this covert team of yours?"

"She's part of our military body, yes. She was going to help return our transport to the ground while the others take the ship away."

"Ah," he nods and turns to Marelle. "So, are you a pilot of some kind?"

"Yes Sir," she affirms. "I'm mostly in training as a combat pilot. But I just had to come up here and take a peek at the place. From the outside, this is a beautiful ship."

"Thank you. Well, this is the bridge. Would you care to take a look around?"

"I'd love it."

"Um, Marelle," Kaliya wonders. "How did you find your way up here so quickly?"

"I took the lift and tried the voice interface, rather than trying to search for a button. Fortunately for me, it doesn't speak squirrel, so I didn't need Relissa for it."

"Oh dear..." Kaliya ushers nervously. "Ayene, could you take over for me, so we don't lose our new friends to her bedtime story?"

Marelle smiles brightly and strolls over to meet with Ayene for a brief review of her station.

They continued calling in the remainder of the crew, where one side of Kaliya's team would disable the chips, and the other side sent them away with the runes.

On the planet below, in Captain Hagmaert's outpost, his people were assembling the refugees and passing them through the gateway unit to Ruuki uy'Daan, where Thaelyn had additional troops directing the flow towards the city to find temporary housing.

On the bridge, the First Officer was monitoring the flow of crewmembers.

"Captain," he announces. "I think this is the last of them."

"There are no more on the ship's scanners?"

"Affirmative, all decks are clear."

"Good. Commander, it would seem our people have fully departed, and it's just us now."

"All right, Captain, you and the remainder of your bridge crew should go now. We'll handle it from here. Lieutenant Ti'van, what sort of destinations do we have over there?"

"I'm showing both Ruuki uy'Daan and Therinë, just as His Lordship suggested. Which one do we want?"

"Let me call this in and check," Kaliya notes.

She pulls out her shard-com again to make another call.

"Phantom Prime to base..."

"This is Thaelyn. What do we have?"

"The ship is clear, and we are waiting for your opinion of our destinations. Both choices are available, so which do you prefer?"

"My personal choice is Ruuki uy'Daan. Darumon abandoned the orcs, and at this moment, I find it unlikely he would hold any desire to return there. It would also make things more convenient to monitor the vessel, along with the native crewmembers."

"All right. We're sending Marelle back now to attend to her duties. I will send my team home to project themselves, and Ayene and I will return to Rolsklinde, so we can join the others. We will then converge on the base to follow up with the next stage of our plans."

"Very good... Proceed."

They end the link and Kaliya sends Marelle on her way. The Captain and his remaining officers are sent down with the runes, and Kaliya's team takes their own leave with their recall runes. But Kaliya stayed behind to oversee the final operations.

She studied the main viewscreen, which Ayene switched to a rearward angle to observe Marelle's departure. The small craft was seen leaving the flight bay and orienting towards the planet. The operation seemed so professional, as if it was an old habit.

"It almost seems unreal," Kaliya mumbles.

"What is that, Lieutenant?" the Commander asks.

"Marelle and her people... I'm thinking of us, where we come from and where we are now, and then people like Marelle, how big a step they made to help us."

"Yes, the way it's been described to me, they not only took this enormous leap, but they did it without hesitation, and with very little difficulty. It puts us to shame, in a way."

They continued monitoring the scene as Marelle departed from the area, leaving the ship free to make its own move.

"Now for the fun part," Kaliya mutters. "Commander Kriv'tik, it's time to secure this ship. Our destination is Ruuki uy'Daan if you please."

"Lieutenant Ti'van," he instructs. "Set our course and begin the jump sequence. We'll do this right where we are to leave a signal trace for them to find."

"Acknowledged, Commander."

Ayene punches in the destination index and engages the drive system.

"Powering…" she announces. "Ten percent…twenty…thirty…"

Ayene rattles off the numbers as she monitors the status readouts on the helm.

Kaliya recalled that last day on the Naarg uy'Sodrad, how she heard very similar callouts as the mighty colony vessel lifted off Ruuki uy'Daan and made ready for its final jump. She could still hear the whimpers of the survivors as they huddled together, shuddering from the attack, and wondering where they would end up next time.

"Fifty percent…sixty…" the count continues.

Kaliya felt a sensation of anxiety building in her. It didn't make sense that she should feel so tense. This was a fine ship, fully functional, and this time no one was chasing them or trying to sabotage their flight mechanics. Her people were on the offensive now.

"Seventy…eighty…the inversion layer seems stable. Ninety… Phase-shifting engaged; the rift is forming."

On the main viewing screen, the starry sky and planetary scene blurred into a bright flash, followed by a long tunnel stretching out ahead of them. Kaliya stared at it, comparing it to how travel through a gateway appeared. So familiar, and yet so different in how it was applied.

Ayene allowed the computer autopilot to carry the ship through the slipstream, guiding the large craft with precision turns through the twists and contortions of the conduit. The travel time did not seem as great as the apparent duration from the conveyor at the base to Madzurki. Kaliya took notice of this. She could already see where the conduit pierced back into the dimensional body.

"This is a short one as compared to the others."

"Yes," Ayene confirms. "This would associate as being within the same galactic body, so the travel time would not measure as much."

The end of the tunnel came into sight through the monitor, and Ayene was ready on the helm controls. As the ship made its exit, she took control to scan the local stellar region.

"Setting course to intercept Ruuki uy'Daan Prime…"

"Ruuki uy'Daan Prime? Is that how you would describe it?"

"Well, unless you want to say the planet itself is called Ruuki uy'Daan, which I suppose you might in your case. But traditionally, we refer to the star system as the body with the name, and then number the planets, where the Prime world is the main colonized body."

"Really! All right, I guess you learn something new every day."

Ayene pilots the vessel across the stellar plane until a planet comes into view on the monitor. Soon, the screen shows the full face of Ruuki uy'Daan.

Kaliya gazed at the monitor. Ruuki uy'Daan… She had never seen it from this perspective before. She was born there, but all she knew were the maps and charts created by the scouting surveys, not an outside image of her home seen from space. Now, her anxiety was replaced with melancholy. It was once her home, but no longer. She had to forcefully remind herself that her home on Tae'Eladar was a worthy alternative, with caring people, lots of friends, and opportunities to make a prestigious life. And yet, this world, though it may not be her home now, at the same time was not lost to her. It was part of the kingdom, and still available.

"Lieutenant Ti'van," the Commander states. "Bring us into low orbit, and set up for automatic station-keeping."

"Understood."

"Commander," Kaliya begins. "Will you and Lieutenant Az'krun be able to find your way back to the city on one of the resident transports?"

"I'm sure we can figure it out. We can scan the planet to create a tactical map, and use that to program the nav system with the coordinate points."

"Good. Then I need to steal Ayene away from you so we can attend to our other work."

"Acknowledged, and good luck, Lieutenant. The Marshal is not one to be taken lightly."

"I won't be taking him lightly, simply taking him for a ride," she grins.

Kaliya pulls out her return rune and enchants it. She then directs Ayene to go first and Kaliya follows up after.

❖

"My Lord, just checking in…"

"Kaliya," Thaelyn muses. "We are sitting here discussing how to commend you for a job that was surprisingly tactful, as well as remarkably efficient. Although we might have found ourselves with a unique opportunity on this occasion, it strikes us that if such things can exist in places like this, we must be vigilant for any others."

"Absolutely, I would agree, especially after listening to that conversation. I only got the tail end of it, but it was enough to make me wonder about a few things."

"And perhaps," Ayene adds. "As we make a little progress on Azgarén, we could carefully investigate a few possibilities. Like you said, having sympathizers could be a very good thing."

"It would," he accedes. "So, if you should happen to notice anything out of the ordinary, keep it in mind. But I think we should keep to the essentials, at least within reason, rather than shouting it in the streets."

"Of course."

"Meanwhile," Kaliya notes. "We're on our way back to the base. But first, we need to get spooky," she giggles.

"Young lady," he intones wittily. "If I did not know better, I might think you were enjoying yourself. Actually, wait. I DO know better," he chuckles.

"Well, the term does hold a certain appeal."

The two young officers move to the next room where they often performed their projections, and settle themselves in. A short while later, they emerge and take on their respective Suuden-Aryku disguises, then check in again with Thaelyn before moving on.

On their arrival at the mining base, Kaliya checks with her team, which had reassembled after their return home, then projected and travelled separately to wait for her. But her first objective was to check in with the currently active crew.

"Spook Kriv'tik, do we have any word from Central yet?"

"Not as yet, Lieutenant. They do not seem to be aware of the absence of the ship."

"Maybe they don't monitor these things as closely as we thought. But then, why should they if it's just a simple survey expedition, and nothing bad is supposed to happen to it. Well, we're about to put a crimp on that. This simply allows us to play our game on our own schedule. But for now, I'm relieving the replacement crew. Go back and find something interesting for yourselves."

"Yes Ma'am. And good luck to you, especially as you'll be dealing with Darumon himself, or at least that's the expectation. I don't envy you that."

The active crew folds themselves out of the local space, leaving Kaliya and her primary team taking up their stations.

"Now," she announces. "We've studied our lines and we each have our scripts for our little act. Let's see if we can recall some of our junior school theater class. Our first objective is a little reconnaissance. I need two spies inside Central. Take up positions in that ventilation duct, one to observe and one as a go-between, since we don't have a direct line of communication. Observe briefly and report on what they're doing right now."

Two team members take the assignment and flash out of sight, reappearing as small insect-like creatures behind the ventilation grill in the main control center of Central Command on Azgarén. From here, they were able to peer through the grill into the room. Sitting nearby was a spy camera they set down earlier and were maintaining on a regular basis.

The scene inside the control center seemed routine. The operators at the various stations were directing military traffic on the ground, as well as monitoring the patrols in the local region of space around the Azgarén star system. There were no emergencies calling the special attention of the High Commander, so at this moment he was absent from the room.

After a few moments of study, one of the visitors in the duct gestured a signal to the other to report back, and the creature vanished in a puff.

"Lieutenant," the teammate announces on his return to the base. "Central appears SOP at this time."

"Very nice, so they must not have any knowledge of what happened to the ship yet. Well folks, that's about to change. Put on your best acting performance, it's showtime!"

Kaliya makes a cursory pass around the room at the various members standing ready, including several Daanen'kai engineers still stationed to monitor the reactor and conveyor.

"I need all nonessential personnel out of here. Report to Captain Hagmaert's outpost."

The Daanen'kai members file out of the room, along with a resident mage to open a portal, and depart from the area.

Kaliya takes another look outside at the base compound, noticing the troop transport had been returned to its location, and the large cargo vessel was absent. It would be used as part of her little play. She could almost feel a sensation of nervousness, or whatever might be possible while in projected mode.

"Spook Kriv'tik," she issues. "It's time to unbutton our drawers, as they say on Tae'Eladar. Make a call to Central. Tell them we have a little problem."

The projected member portraying the Commander steps over to the com-station, while another operator sitting at the console activates the link.

"This is Commander Kriv'tik to Central Command," he states in the classic flat tone.

"Central Command responding. What do you require, Commander?"

"I have a report. It is uncertain and needs confirmation. We have lost contact with the Ghan'aju."

"Stand by, Commander."

Kaliya points affirmatively at the agent recently returned from his spy post, sending him away again. He disappears in a puff, arriving back at his former position.

In the control center at Central Command, the spies in their hideout observed the scene.

"Ghan'aju…report," repeats the officer on the com-link.

They had been attempting to raise the ship on the communications channel since putting the Commander on hold, but there was no response.

"Captain," reports an officer sitting at another station. "There is no telemetry link from the Ghan'aju."

"Run a system check. Submit a ping semaphore to locate the vessel."

The operator configured his console to broadcast a special multithreaded signal across their hyperspace com-link network. This was an operation sometimes used to locate a lost vessel, in the event their primary channels were inactive. He waited for the response while the comms officer made another attempt at hailing the ship. The operator continued to wait until a timeout condition returned a default result.

"Captain, the ping is negative."

"Switch to Morndindor Base again."

The communications officer redirects the link to the base.

"Commander Kriv'tik," the officer announces. "This is Captain Ta'yeen. We are unable to locate the Ghan'aju. What was the last reported condition of the operation?"

"A detail was dispatched shortly after its arrival. We are aware they were received, but that was their last communication to this station. We attempted to contact them for a status report, but there was no response."

"Who was present in this detail?"

"Ytani and a selected work crew."

"Ytani? Does he hold the qualifications for this procedure? My interpretation of his position did not carry this level of expertise."

"Correct. His duty here was the interaction with the local

population to procure the metal, not the technical aspect of our operations, or a science expedition for that matter. In fact, I am unsure what level of professional training he might have at all…if any."

"If any? But Commander, why would you allow him to go on this mission rather than your own technical team?"

"The technical team, in this case…" he pauses deliberately for the effect. "Well, yes, I suppose this is where we are at this time."

"What do you mean, Commander? Who was on this technical team?"

"A group of natives who were supposed to hold the expertise to locate and sample the metal. Captain, in the absence of Ytani from his usual station, I am forced to deliver our operating conditions directly to you. Ytani had previously denied us this liberty, instead to fabricate our reports and to falsify data relating to certain operational difficulties and procedural anomalies that have been occurring here."

"Excuse me?" the Captain winces softly. "Commander, this sounds serious. First, it was my understanding that Ytani is not a registered military officer. Why would you, as a Fleet Commander, submit to his authority when he technically has no proper military authority at all?"

"Why? By order of the Marshal, of course. He was assigned to his position and given certain privileges over my position, despite the fact that he is a civilian, and probably should not be in a military base to begin with."

"What?! Commander, this violates protocol. Why would he do this?"

"Captain, this is likely due to the same reason he classified this entire mission, along with the substances we were working with and the reason he wanted them. As for Ytani, my belief is due to his ability to interact with the native population on their natural level. I do not understand the method used here, as the Marshal apparently trained him in something proprietary, and once again without explanation on my side to understand the nature of it. But this seems to carry a special innate value, and that value elevates his authority to a position that is superior to mine, if only due to the fact that he was able to provide the metal in ways our own methods might not."

"Commander..." the Captain pauses in thought. "I do not think I care much for this level of violation, regardless of what value he might hold in relation to any other, and especially if he was using it to falsify his reports. But we will leave this be for now. Continue with your report. I think this will require a review at some moment."

"A review? As if you ever bothered to question this in the past, even after I submitted several complaints due to these same difficulties we had here. The Marshal, for all his security protocols, seems to deny our people to question anything he does."

"All right, Commander, point taken. And I will admit, yours would not be the first time I have heard this particular complaint."

"Understood, but it becomes frustrating, especially for all the events we had here, that no one back home ever paid enough attention to finally ask those questions. Are you aware of a few fatalities we had during this time?"

"Yes, actually, I do recall a few occasions."

"Good, but did you do autopsies on any of them?"

"This would fall to our resident med-tech, although I do not recall any special reports from him. Is there something you would wish to report on this?"

"Allow me to continue, and we will come to it. But I would advise caution, Captain. According to Ytani, he believed the Marshal desired his mining output at all costs. And the rest of my report might confirm this for the experiences we had to endure here."

"Understood, Commander, I will take this under advisement. Please continue."

"Over the course of our operations, and with increasing severity, especially during this past century, Ytani has been exhibiting aberrant behavior with my base staff, especially our female members. In more recent times, I took the liberty to record a few of my communications with him to keep as evidence of his manners, which by this time have developed into a highly agitated form of psychosis for his attitude towards me, his demands on my crew, and his overall treatment of my staff."

"What do you mean, can you give an example?"

"I can give you many examples, and I will submit to you some of these recordings to keep on file as my evidence. Ytani is a young man and apparently given special privilege to avoid the Council mandates for any alterations, including the An'gamu seed and the Suppressor chip. In fact, one of my officers recently discovered the Marshal explicitly ordered his Suppressor chip removed as a favor to entice him into his current service."

"Removed?" he blurts. "Why?"

"Unknown. No reason was given, so I am forced to consider this as a form of incentive, bypassing the Council mandates and affording him freedom from the inherent control effect it applies. And he certainly seemed to enjoy this aspect. He had full emotional content and an unaltered form, which further seemed to invoke a sense of narcissism and a severe loathing for our altered physiques."

"I see. And with no seed, which means the Marshal must have pulled him out before his implantation," he muses privately. "Did he make any offensive comments or gestures during this time?"

"Many, and often… He was known to my staff to use obscene language, vulgar references, and lewd suggestions to our female staff members."

"Very well, Commander, this is one mark I will put down against him. Civilian or not, this manner of conduct is unacceptable."

"Agreed. Although, according to him, he felt as if it was moot for our opinions, as the Marshal would likely override it."

"Oh, he would wish to override our military protocols?"

"I suppose this depends on whether we include those same security restraints and information quarantines. Furthermore, that he seems to expect us to perform regardless of explaining to us what he has us performing."

"Uh huh. Got it. What else do you have?"

"Back to Ytani, he further demanded female attention as a form of payment for his services to provide the metal."

"Excuse me, Commander? Are we saying he is treating your operation as a bordello?"

"Affirmative. And his sexual demands were frequent, occurring each time we delivered a shipment to the processor. Furthermore, his conduct with our female staff members was abusive, often resulting in injury, and we also suffered three fatalities…those same three you were supposed to be conducting autopsies on to confirm the reported causes."

"What?! Aargh…" he shouts, and then takes an abrupt feedback hit. "Dammit…" he wheezes softly. "Commander! Why, in all the nether-space, did you not report this to us earlier?"

"Here is where we come back to that notion of overriding things. He threatened to use his favoritism aspect with the Marshal to place us all on active so we would no longer complain. This might give you an idea of how determined the Marshal is to keep his secrets."

"Incredible…" he groans.

"Ytani also developed a form of mania from his interaction with the local population, believing he could rally them up as a private army to attack our position. This placed me into a situation where I held no true authority at all, especially if you consider the aspect of the Marshal's demands to serve at all costs. And those costs, it would seem, may include using the military chip as a governing factor."

"Dammit, Commander. Is there anything else you wish to report?"

"I might further report his most recent behavioral anomaly as having gone fully insane with his mania, believing he would rule this world as a god-king with his own private slave population and military authority…on active, by the way…serving his every need, including his female attention whenever he desired it. I also have one recording where he suggested bringing in random civilian females, and then leaving their corpses in the desert out here."

"Unbelievable! Aargh…" he groans from another hit. "I swear," he moans silently. "Whoever invented these chips… Commander, I would very much like to review these recordings. This is simply criminal, and on multiple levels. All right, what is your current operating status? You said something about him taking some kind of crew up there? What crew?"

"Our current operating status is in a standby condition. The mining operations in the city below have been depleted and are therefore nonoperational. The mining operation to our south is also currently nonoperational. The work crew he took with him was apparently the one he most recently acquired for the southern mine."

"And why would he do this?"

"It was my understanding he was attempting to acquire a new work team to supply us for this expedition to begin the initial excavation. But his behavior with the local population, by the reports he filed with me during this same period of time, also demonstrated a high level of abusive behavior. I do not know the precise condition of the city, but my suspicion is he was unable to acquire that second work crew, and therefore took the first one instead."

"Commander, this is very disturbing, and for a number of potential reasons. Is there any way for you to investigate the situation with that local population to confirm their condition?"

"Not without revealing ourselves to them. Ytani has been using deceptive methods to fool them into believing there is a condition of war outside their city, and he was calling for this metal and the work teams as a supply route to a counterforce effort. It therefore follows that if they should ever discover us up here, and worse, that WE are the ones stealing their metals, our position will be severely compromised."

"Wait! Did you say stealing?"

"Yes, this is the best definition I can offer. If they do not otherwise know we are here, are not otherwise cooperating with our efforts, and therefore are not otherwise GIVING us these materials, there is only one other word for it."

"I swear! Aargh..." he yelps with another hit. "Commander, do you believe your position to be in jeopardy at this time?"

"Unknown. It is my understanding he has made an excuse that the path we use to retrieve the metal is controlled by friendly forces. But if the local population should ever become curious and make their own investigation, this could easily change. I might also suggest one other complication to which I am recently considering."

"And what is that?"

"Our impression of this metal, given the mining outputs, suggests it to be a rare substance. And as a rare substance, it might hold value, such as with precious materials representing wealth."

"Yes, and I think I can already see your point. We are taking up what could be regarded as material wealth…to them, at least, and doing so by subversive means. Ugh… Commander, you are right. This is tantamount to theft, and likely on a grand scale by now."

"It does seem that way. But this also causes me to ask why the Marshal would request it this way, as opposed to using some other method. Negotiation comes to mind, or perhaps the metals could be found elsewhere, and we could set up our own operations, where he simply explains to US how to do it, since he seems to know what it is and how to use it as part of his own knowledge."

"Oh! Really! Yes, that would be a very good suggestion."

The Captain pants as he hovers over the com-station inside the control room. He glances into the faces of several of the other officers before continuing.

"Commander, I do not like the sound of this. And if Ytani is currently MIA, those locals might become restless, especially after your depiction of his behavior. Is there anything else of pertinence you wish to report? I am going to need to give this over to Commander Geilv for a review before we can proceed."

"This is all I have at the present time. But I am growing concerned for the Ghan'aju. He was the only member of our base staff to join that team. He demanded the rest stay here. And his work team was under the influence of that drug we use to coerce the local population into our service," he flashes a mischievous grin to the other teammates.

"What?! Aargh!" he screams from another feedback hit.

Another voice comes on the line now.

"Captain? Are you alright? Someone call a Med-tech in here!"

"Negative, Ensign," the Captain responds feebly. "I just need to survive this one conversation, and then I will have a few words of my own to share with him. Commander, what was that you said just now?"

"Captain," the Spook Kriv'tik responds. "Perhaps I should refrain from including this part."

"Negative, hit me with it. You said something about a drug, and coercing someone?"

"My apologies, but I thought this was included as part of our mission directive as filed during the initial engagement. I am fairly sure it was known we are using persuasive methods to get the metal, since the natives were not regarded as friendly. The Marshal established our operation using a strange fungal growth that produces a strong mind-altering drug effect. The local population was not otherwise cooperative to our needs, and so this was to be used to extract our mining teams and put them to work."

"I do not believe what I am hearing today! Just what is it he is pulling out of the ground out there that would demand such outrageous methods to procure?"

"To my knowledge, the mineral is undefined."

"When you say undefined, Commander, is that to say you simply do not know what it is?"

"Affirmative, not even a name. Other than to say it is a metal that carries some unusual properties as compared to other substances we are more familiar with. I once heard a name mentioned that the locals use, but it is generally meaningless by our terms. And our science has no definition for it, therefore our need for the local population to extract it for us."

"And what is he making with it? Do we know, or is he keeping that a secret as well?"

"My answer would need to be yes, it is also undefined, other than to say it is a substance that is declared to be explosive and highly volatile."

"Highly volatile... Explosive... Undefined... Did he at least give a reason for producing it?"

"Negative. At least not directly. This operation is supposed to relate to his crusade, but this here…I cannot say. To my knowledge, the processor is being managed by a civilian work crew, but according to the reports I have received during our inspection tours, they only understand enough to operate the equipment."

"So, no one knows what it is or why he is making it, and he is using drugs to coerce the locals into our service because they are uncooperative to give us their support for any other reason."

"I might suggest the term 'uncooperative' is subjective, as I do not recall any mention to negotiate for the metal, or otherwise use diplomatic or political means to acquire it. In fact, the only explanation I received when we first arrived was that the full population of the planet had been corrupted by these insurgent forces, but without any true evidence or demonstration of fact. Their society is not space-capable to make contact with anything, and it is irrational that a society as advanced as what the Marshal represents would trouble themselves with something that better resembles a preindustrial condition."

"Preindustrial?"

"Yes, Ytani made numerous crude remarks regarding their lack of having even as much as electricity."

"I do not believe this!"

"Therefore, this claim, which seems irrational to hold any relation to the Marshal's society, as this one would not even qualify as appropriate. And then we have the need for this drug to 'coerce' their compliance, at least in this one city we are managing."

"I see."

"Furthermore, I must also say, this drug seems to be fatal after a while, demanding us to replace the work teams on occasion."

"Oh! Is THIS the reason?" he shouts.

"Yes. And this corruption, and therefore the uncooperative behavior, as it was stated, is also the reason the Marshal ordered a planetary cleansing, to reduce the threat potential from the remainder of the population opposing our efforts."

The line was silent for an extended moment, with the only sound being that of a distant groan escalating in the background to a scream, and then a notable thud as something fell to the floor.

"Um, Captain?" the resident Ensign ushers. "Should I call for the Med-tech now?"

"Maybe you should call for one anyway," issues another voice. "I think he cannot respond to you like that."

"Yes, I think you are right. Commander, stand by a moment. The Captain seems to have passed out from a severe feedback hit."

The link goes on hold as the command base crew deals with their local issue.

Kaliya gazes at her team, especially the Kriv'tik projection.

"I really feel for that guy right now," she mourns. "But these people need to know a few things about what's happening outside their little information block."

While they wait, one of the projected spies returns.

"Lieutenant?" he calls.

"Yes, what do we have?"

"Well, you managed to send that Captain of theirs into shock. Just like they said, he had a bad feedback hit which sent him to the ground."

"I hope it's nothing critical, but with those chips installed, there's no other way. They need to know what's happening out there, and it isn't good."

"Understood. But now, I wonder how the HC will take it. We're fairly certain he's in active, so if he has any reaction at all, it won't be pretty. Not to mention, I should probably warn you, from our spy operations, he looks like an elder."

"Oops, that doesn't sound good for the age grouping. All right, we'll see if we can soften it a bit, if we can. Get back over there and check on it for us."

He nods and departs in a puff, as Kaliya and the others continued to wait for someone to come back on the line. After a few more moments, the Captain returned.

"Commander..." he ushers dimly. "Captain, um, Ta'yeen here

again. Would this be all you have to report at this time, or do you have any more surprises for me?"

"I am sorry, Captain, but I suppose after four centuries working at this post, I thought you would know about some of this by now. But then, I am reminded again of how this is such a highly classified operation, that our objectives, as well as our methods, might not be as openly defined, particularly if you consider those…security restrictions, and that…information quarantine, the Marshal seems to like so much. I have heard it described as…private detail."

"Yes, Commander, I believe I have heard this as well on occasion. But in truth, I think I would not be able to excuse any part of this, classified, restricted, quarantined, private, or otherwise, as well as to claim it must be done at all costs."

"I submitted several complaints about Ytani during our time here relating to his past behavior and other issues we had with him, but none of them resulted in any kind of corrective response. Not by Central, not by the Marshal, not even by his parents coming to visit on occasion to offer any manner of childrearing support."

"What? Childrearing! In all the nether-space, Commander, just how old is he?"

"Oh…" he muses innocently. "Was this also concealed from view? Very well, when our operation first began, he was seven decades. We never once saw him receive any family visitation, and the Marshal only briefly visited on a very few occasions. Our base staff found itself acting as surrogates, at least until he started demanding his female companions. From there, it began to escalate as I mentioned before."

"Commander…" he sighs. "All right, the Med-tech just gave me a mild sedative, so I would like to keep it under control from here. This represents a series of violations I cannot even begin to reconcile, and at this point in time, I cannot even be sure of who to talk to about it. I wonder, do we know who his parents are supposed to be?"

"Personally, no, I never heard a name mentioned, and since I once learned that his parents were described to have died in some freak accident, I would not know who else to talk to."

"Eh, a freak accident?"

"Yes, Ytani himself actually mentioned this once while in a private conversation with one of our people. Then the Marshal came along to recruit him into our…highly classified and virtually unknown…operation here, along with his fabulous…incentive…of removing his chip."

"Commander, I am tempted to ask why you placed emphasis on that statement."

"Well, we are in another universe at this time, did you know this?"

"Actually, yes, I did, although I am also aware THAT is classified, as well. All right, I think I am getting another picture here, and it is not pretty. Do we know of any OTHER family that came along asking questions?"

"Not that I am aware of, and without anyone complaining about a lost child, this leaves very few possibilities. Therefore, Captain, I would wish to offer some advice based on my own perspectives, and the experiences I have gained during my lifetime which have directed me to one or another suspicion."

"Very well, Commander, what do you suggest?"

"First, those complaints I submitted were rejected. I cannot be sure what level of authority rejected them, but if it was not Central Command following any of our native policies, like you mentioned we are supposed to have, then it must be the Marshal keeping to his demands to serve at all costs. Ytani's favorite threat was the authority chips. This might represent the aspect of serving at all costs."

"It might, by the sound of it."

"The security restrictions and information quarantines might also be a part of it to prevent anyone from asking those questions, or analyzing those actions we are made to perform. In this way, no one knows anything outside of personal knowledge, and this is quickly covered up with more restrictions."

"Uh huh, thank you. So much for our proud military and its policies, which can apparently be reprogrammed with the push of a button."

"Therefore, Captain, if the Marshal wants his metal so badly as to serve at all costs, including to wipe this planet of its native population down to the last surviving city, and then to use drugs to essentially enslave those mining teams, and this as opposed to simply teaching us the process to do it ourselves, we must ask what he would have to say about us asking questions about it. How do you feel on this?"

The link went silent again. Kaliya and the others waited. This was a test to see who among them would begin to realize the gravity of the situation, and therefore to keep it under control for their own good. Kaliya's team was planting the initial seeds of malcontent here. After a long moment of silence, the Captain came back online.

"As opposed to simply teaching us..." he moans. "As if to say, granting some of his superior wisdom he kept promising for so long," he sighs. "Commander, you are one of our most esteemed officers. Do you have a premise behind this suggestion?"

"I do, and regrettably it was also...classified. It relates to every occasion when I was sent out on his missions to destroy things."

"Every mission...to destroy things...and, um...at all costs again?"

"Yes. I was placed under those same security restrictions and information quarantines on each occasion. And personally, I am tired of complying with it by now. Especially if we are never allowed to share this with other parts of our military. Last I heard, we are supposed to be...voluntarily...offering ourselves to assist him. But those chips and security restrictions make us virtual slaves, and nearly as much as that drug for these miners."

"I understand. Can you give me an example, if you are so opposed to following HIS security restrictions by now?"

"Certainly. My military service has provided me with a number of experiences while serving the Marshal. For instance, my full task force was placed under active mode during those moments. We would be assigned to strike at an insurgent outpost, but using a blanket effect to cover the full planet, rather than a point target. And it seemed as if they never saw it coming. The reason we were given said this corruption effect represented some manner of contagion that could be infectious and spread to other worlds."

"How lovely."

"It does, however, cause one to wonder what we actually hit, and why halfway across the galaxy that it might pose such a problem to us on Azgarén."

"Oh yes. Unless those infected people have personal jump drives, I might find it interesting to know how they could even find us. Did they appear as more preindustrial?"

"Actually, some of the scans did indicate energy production and pollution levels, but of a lesser grade to our own. Others, not even this much."

"Lesser grade and worse, but never high enough to fight back, I suppose. And without even a space industry, how could they pose a threat to us, especially from halfway across the galaxy."

"Indeed. And unfortunately, much like what I see with this planet and the resulting wipe, my crew did not have the occasion to ask questions, or to analyze the criteria. And these occasions were also highly classified such that no one was allowed to know of it."

"Naturally."

"Therefore, the Marshal seems to have some very demanding needs if he wants us to serve him to such extremes, and those needs do not involve our opinions, and neither our independent analysis in our…voluntary…service to assist him. I suspect he will not be pleased by our current situation here, but how many of us want to be placed on active if we ask too many questions or make too many complaints about it?"

"Understood, Commander. And this represents a very disturbing scenario. I have heard it said that only he knows his opponents, and therefore the reason he holds the position to guide us on this campaign. So, unless we are missing a critical detail to explain anything, do you have a suggestion on how to proceed on this? We will need to report something, I believe."

"Affirmative. The chain of command would lead to the High Commander. What condition is he currently in?"

"Active, as is often the case when the Marshal has special need of him. Although, what need this is if he is simply sitting in his office, I cannot be sure."

"Does the Marshal interact with anyone else in our military? This is to say to issue orders, directives, and other instructions."

"It mostly goes through the HC, as far as I know."

"Then I think that is your 'need,' Captain. To ensure the job gets done."

"Right. So then, do we include him in this?"

"I feel it is necessary. He needs to be made aware of this situation, for his own information. But perhaps if we were to reveal it in smaller portions, we can avoid the more severe reactions to it."

"All right, but who will tell him, you or me?"

"I suppose you may need to inform him of the initial details, and then give it over to me for the fine-tuning."

"Acknowledged. Stand by."

In Central Command, the Captain places the link on hold again while he considers his options.

"Ensign, call his office. Tell him we have a problem with Morndindor Base and to meet us here."

The operator makes the call, and they wait.

In the ventilation duct, one of the small spies departs again to report in.

"Lieutenant," he announces on his arrival in the base. "I have a report from Central."

"Let's hear it," Kaliya instructs.

"The Captain has issued a summons for High Commander Geilv. He looks very disturbed, even with his sedative and the chip, and many of the other officers in the room are not too far behind. We have the full attention of everyone in there by now."

"This is actually good. Spread it around a little and maybe start some gossip. But so long as they understand the repercussions of what that gossip might bring if it reaches the wrong ears."

"Yes Ma'am! So, are we hoping to have all of Central go mutiny now?"

"Well, it would certainly put a crimp on the Marshal's control mechanism. The only problem after that would be how he might react if he should ever figure it out. This brings me back to that Tav'ageen Anomaly of theirs and his panic procedures."

"You just can't win with a creature like that."

"Not at all. All right, back to work," she thumb-points at him to depart again.

The spy vanishes, and now they wait for Commander Geilv.

"What do you think we can expect of him, Lieutenant?" asks Spook Kriv'tik.

"If he was on active during the full time we had our troubles on Therinë, that's already three and a half centuries, maybe four, if you count when they first found it, and who knows how much before that, especially if he was the cause of our troubles on any of the other worlds we crossed, or during any of Commander Kriv'tik's campaigns. You have to wonder what this does to a person, and if there's anything left of him afterwards. What if one day it's ever turned off?"

"No idea…"

✦✦✦✦✦✦

"What is occurring here?" the stoic Commander Geilv demands in his cold monotone voice.

"Commander," the Captain begins. "We have a serious situation occurring at the Morndindor Base."

"Explain."

"The situation is complex, and it reeks with potential conspiracy, corruption, cover-ups, and it also brings into question the whole purpose of the operation to begin with. It is further complicated by the apparent demands of the Marshal to conduct these procedures, and we also have a mention of the possible implications regarding those who might not follow orders as he would desire."

Commander Geilv stood there glaring at the Captain for the laundry list of charges suddenly being brought into conversation. He glances around at the other officers who were in attendance in the room, all of whom were focused on him by now.

"Understood, Captain. Where do we begin?"

"First, Commander, I would ask to speak freely, and outside of protocol during this occasion. The situation is simply too absurd to follow a normal procedure here."

The Commander gazed at him a moment before responding.

"Granted, Captain."

"Thank you. I would now wish to preface this with a statement. Commander, we all respect your authority, and we honor you for your service. But at the same time, we also know you are currently on the active mode of your authority chip, and we know what this does to a person. Furthermore, during the time I was in conversation with Commander Kriv'tik, I experienced several feedbacks from my Suppressor chip, the last of which sent me to the ground, and we had to call in a Med-tech to give me a mild sedative to bring me back up again."

"This sounds unfortunate. How do you feel now?"

"I am standing on my own two hooves, but just barely. But this brings me back to you. Commander, I do not know how much you are aware of concerning the operations at Morndindor, but as the HC, I would imagine you should know of their operating parameters. Is this correct?"

"I am aware of their reported activities and their purpose to conduct their operations."

"Yes, but does this include the classified nature of the material they are harvesting, what it is they are producing, and why?"

Again, Commander Geilv stared at the Captain, followed by a brief circuitous glance around the room.

"Did Commander Kriv'tik suggest something?"

"He explained a large amount of detail which I was previously unaware of, much of it is apparently a part of his classified directive, to which he is going off-protocol to reveal, despite the Marshal and his security restrictions, and none of it appearing legal, to say nothing of conscionable."

"Conscionable…" he furrows his brow slightly. "And off-protocol? Explain, Captain. What happened over there?"

"First, you should know the Ghan'aju has vanished from the scopes. They do not respond to comms, and the ping locator is not returning a result."

"Did Kriv'tik give a reason for this?"

"Only that Ytani, that special operative the Marshal installed, took a group of drugged natives with him on this survey mission, and the Commander lost contact with the ship shortly thereafter."

"Wait! Explain why Ytani would go on this mission, and also this statement of drugged natives."

"Then you do not know of it? All right, according to Kriv'tik, the planetary population was deemed to have been influenced by these insurgents. Were you aware of this much?"

"I recall a statement regarding this, and a military mission to enforce compliance in order for us to conduct our future operations."

"Compliance. Is this what he calls it? Interesting. Did that mission involve the complete wipe of what appears to be a preindustrial society down to one surviving city, and the operation uses a type of narcotic to drug these mining teams into our compliance? They do not apparently know we exist; we are using lies to fabricate a false image in front of us, and with these drugs, we are effectively turning them into slave labor, and with US stealing what could be precious resources."

Commander Geilv glared sternly into the Captain's eyes as he tried to reflect on this procedure through his chip-controlled mind. By itself, it seemed obscenely excessive, resulting in a large-scale loss of life, which might not otherwise seem warranted if an alternative could have been found. Then a tick erupted in his face from a minor feedback hit.

"Containment procedures…" he ponders distantly. "They were described as supporting our opponents."

"But Commander, one might ask why to use such extreme procedures on an entire planetary population. Kriv'tik suggested this one could not possibly offer any true threat potential, especially if they are preindustrial. They should not even qualify as associates to the Marshal's society if they were not space-capable to reach them.

We might even want to ask if the Marshal's society would bother with anything that low to begin with…unless you want to say HE uses them as slave labor, and these insurgents simply removed them from his authority. But this also brings up a curious twist of the horns for the implications."

"It does. It also brings another twist of the horns for the wipe."

"And none of it with any real evidence to prove anything. Surely, there ought to be other planets out there that might offer us a solution rather than to invade this one and destroy the native population. As Kriv'tik suggested, the Marshal, who seems to know all about this material, could teach us how to do it, and therefore send us elsewhere without harming anything else along the way. Why did he not do THAT?"

"He did mention something to this effect in my earlier conversation with him…but only in this conversation, not as a process to pursue as an alternative."

"Not as an alternative. Again, interesting, Commander. You know, I once recall how he promised us some form of wisdom. I would think mining some alien mineral would qualify for that, if it is so important to him."

"Granted."

"And this is only one aspect of Kriv'tik's report."

"One aspect? What are the others?"

"I would say the theft of these minerals is one. Then the drugs… It ought to be regarded as a criminal act to intentionally drug someone in order to get them to perform any sort of service for us. This represents forced servitude. And worse, this is the reason for those teams expiring so often. It appears to be fatal. So, not only are we drugging them, but we are also poisoning them."

The Commander held his poise as he stared into the distance. The other officers in the room watched as another tick crinkled the Commander's cheek.

"Commander," the Captain notes. "I see you must be feeling a reaction of some kind."

"Affirmative, but continue. I would agree with this statement, and even worse for the deaths. What else did he say?"

"Were you aware that Ytani was a child when the Marshal first employed his services?"

"Affirmative. The Marshal described him as holding a gifted talent he could use on this occasion."

"He was apparently only seven decades at the time. This should represent illegal child labor, especially if he was stationed over there and NOT going to school as he should have been."

"Not going to school?" he muses quietly. "What about his parents and their influence?"

"What parents?" the Captain raises his brow. "According to a statement Kriv'tik says came out of Ytani himself, they died in something that might, at least on the surface, resemble a freak accident that so conveniently allowed an underage kid to be recruited into this highly classified and unknown operation where he disappears off the scope from anyone who cares. That sounds suspicious right there."

"But do we have any evidence to support this statement?"

"Evidence? I doubt it. After all, the Marshal classifies every little thing he does and prevents anyone, including our top officers, from knowing about it. Our people do not even know we found a new universe out there, if you recall."

"Yes, you are correct."

"Further is that the Marshal intentionally ordered his Suppressor chip removed, perhaps as a form of service benefit."

"And removing his chip... But a service benefit?"

"Yes, and one that clearly went to his head, as well as the absence of the seed implantation. And Kriv'tik says he never saw Ytani receive visitations from anyone other than the Marshal on a few rare occasions."

"So, we have no proper education, and no family visits, which would result in a very unattended condition, as well as excusal from the Council mandates, and this is going to his head? In what way?"

"Here is where we move to the difficult parts. Ytani apparently matured in that place without proper supervision or childrearing, other than what the base staff could provide as surrogates. But this was apparently inadequate to give him any proper form of culturing, as he began to develop a series of severe psychological abnormalities. One of these involves his sexual desires, to which he began demanding members of the female staff members to service him."

Now the Commander furrows his brow even deeper, and another tick clenched his cheek.

"How do we describe this, Captain?" he urges. "He is using our female staff as sex partners?"

"More like sex toys at this point. Over time, his manners at interacting with the base crew became vulgar and belligerent to the point of using obscene language, derisive statements, and frequently debasing them for their altered forms, that is in relation to his otherwise perfect unaltered body. And he became excessively abusive of his female playmates to the point of injury..." he pauses as he considers his next statement. "...And, um..."

"What else, Captain."

"Commander, what comes after gave me a number of hard feedback hits. Maybe I should call a med-tech up here to offer some support."

"Is it that bad?"

"Yes, so I think I must insist. Ensign, call him up here again."

While the Ensign makes his call, the Captain puts his conversation on hold. At this moment, one of the spies inside the ventilation duct takes an opportunity to report back.

✦ ✦ ✦ ✦ ✦ ✦ ✦

"So..." Kaliya reflects on the report. "He's trying to break it to him easy? Good, let's go gently on him. The poor guy has been through a lot, I'll bet."

In the control center, a med-tech has just applied a gentle sedative to the Commander's neck.

"How do you feel, Commander," the Captain asks.

"Better. Now, continue with your report."

"All right, but keep in mind to remain calm. This is not at all pleasant. Kriv'tik tells us he had three fatalities because of Ytani abusing his sex partners."

Even though the Commander was now under the effect of the drug, his brow furrowed even more, and he stared deeply into the Captain's eyes. Then, another tick erupted, clenching his cheek even harder. The Med-tech standing next to him took notice of this, as well as the obvious statement that caused it.

"Captain," he mentions. "Three fatalities? I am aware of one we received about a year ago. She passed through our lab for an autopsy."

"What did she look like?"

"Badly injured, with multiple lacerations, bruises, and several burn marks. I also recall she appeared as though she might have been restrained somehow. I saw marks on her wrists and ankles, where we thought she was struggling against some sort of prisoner restraint. Then I recall vaginal injuries, evidence of rape, and finally we found a slice on the seed entity that appeared as if made by a sharp bladed item. This was accompanied by the resulting necrotizing of her internal tissues, which we believe was the final cause of death."

The Commander was now groaning as his face contorted.

"Captain," he demands tensely. "What did the report say from Morndindor? Did they give an explanation?"

"Oh yes, Commander," he retorts. "And Med-tech, you too..."

"Me?" the Med-tech protests. "Why me?"

"Commander, Ytani has been forcing Kriv'tik to falsify his reports to us for his activities over there under the threat of subjugating the full crew to the active mode of their chips, or possibly to bring up a private army of his native servants to attack their position. Kriv'tik has been pressured to comply with these demands because he believes the Marshal wants his product at all costs, much like he wants us to behave as his personal attendants, not asking any unfortunate questions or arguing the facts, as our opinions on the matter are rendered moot. Hereto we have the statement...at all costs...if you catch my meaning...Sir," he glances at Geilv's interface unit for emphasis.

The Commander began groaning harder, and his hand was shaking as he reached up to his interface.

"Falsifying his reports?" the Med-tech reflects. "Well, I can confirm this from that last example, as it stood out in our review as a preposterous explanation for what we saw. It was reported as an animal attack."

"An animal attack?" the Captain balks. "Ridiculous! With evidence of rape and burn marks? Why does no one report anything so blatantly obvious to the proper authorities around here! In all the nether-space…"

"To be honest, I was tempted to inquire on this, but unfortunately, I had assumed you people up here knew what you were doing. I guess this was in error," he shrugs. "So, the principle must instead be no one knows what anyone else is doing around here for all the secrets being kept behind our backs."

"Precisely!" he groans. "You know, you could have said something, and this could have prompted an investigation, if it was really so obvious. Kriv'tik was probably hoping someone over here would have the horns to do exactly this, since his position was apparently being leveraged. You should know as well as the rest that no one speaks to anyone around here about anything."

"All right, Captain, I admit, you are right. So, who do we blame this on, the Marshal?"

"Exactly. He hides everything behind his overly excessive security protocols that deny anyone to ask questions or investigate things."

At this point, the Commander was struggling to hold himself still. His groaning continued as he clutched at his interface.

"Captain!" he growls. "What is the current situation over there? Finish your report."

"Yes, Commander… Kriv'tik tells us Ytani demanded to take this work crew, which as I said was under this drug effect, with him to the Ghan'aju. Ytani's developing psychosis, as he calls it, had elevated to the point of a mania where Ytani believes himself to be some sort of god-king who would take control of the world, with his slaves on one side and us in active mode on the other side, all serving under him. Kriv'tik further suggests his abusive behavior might extend to the local population he was managing, and a second work crew he was supposed to be gathering for this mission may have failed as a result. Therefore, the work team he collected for this mission was taken from the second mining activity they were working, leaving them in a full standby condition with no mining occurring at all."

"Captain, Commander..." the Med-tech infers. "As a medical professional, I recommend we approach this carefully. If Ytani is falling into some manner of psychosis due to his belief he can control a slave population and us serving him on active, he could turn on us with that private army of his."

"Worse than that, Med-tech," the Captain offers. "The Marshal might want this metal at all costs, and this could extend to the point of..." he halts abruptly as he gazes at the Commander. "...To the point of putting us all on active if we complain about it."

"That should be a violation of our rights! Military or otherwise, we do still have those, do we?"

"I suppose this is subjective with his demand to HAVE the chip in the first place, if this is how he uses it. It follows what Kriv'tik mentioned of some of his earlier career experiences. He is going off-protocol here and admitting, despite the Marshal's information quarantine to the contrary, that his task force was placed on active on multiple occasions simply to blast worlds, and due to some nether-wild reason that ought not to hold any relevance to our own planetary security halfway across the galaxy from them."

"Nether-wild? How so?"

"First, all or most of them were beneath us, technologically speaking, and likely not space-capable to fight back, or even to know we existed as we blasted them from orbit. How do you like that for starters?"

"I do not. Thank you."

"Next was something about a localized infection that could bite us in the tail later...if we let it get this far. Therefore, boom, dead planet. You know, I recall some of those reports claimed an OUTPOST was found, not an infected world. Therefore, a blanket effect rather than a surgical strike. So, this might give you an idea of how things work. The Marshal must be very demanding of results if this is how he wants us to behave."

"How he wants US to behave? As I recall the story, we offered our aid voluntarily, and this is how he returns it?"

"Med-tech, how he returns it, by whatever definition you or I, or even HE might use, is more like this. He does not apparently ask politely. He ordered a complete wipe of a planetary population to prevent interference of our efforts to effectively steal their minerals, which, by the way, might represent a considerable amount of material wealth to them."

"Incredible!"

"And Ytani, the one doing it, used lies and falsehoods as part of his story to make them simply hand it over to us. They do not apparently even know we exist over there."

"I swear!"

"So, clearly, the Marshal does not care about other people's opinions. Instead, he uses such as drugs, or in our case, chips to enforce compliance. And then, he tells us to do things we might otherwise object to if we had enough of a mind to actually think about it."

"But..." the Med-tech issues nervously. "Could there be a legitimate reason, rather than just accusing him of something?"

"If there is," he responds. "He never explains it to us. He just does it. And then, all his security restrictions and information quarantines, as Kriv'tik describes it, keep us ignorant of what he is using us for."

"Containment procedures..." Commander Geilv grumbles.

"Commander," the Captain interjects. "Before you blow a fuse, listen to me. Kriv'tik is waiting on the line to talk to you. I believe he has a course of action to suggest in this case. The Ghan'aju is missing with Ytani and what might be an army of his slaves under his control. I cannot be sure what this means for the crew of that ship, but if they are not expecting an attack of any sort, he could potentially overwhelm them and take control."

"Captain!" the Med-tech snaps. "Would he have the technical training to pilot it?"

"Who knows what he has if he received private tutoring by the Marshal and was otherwise completely unsupervised in that house of his while he was growing up."

"Huh? Growing up?"

"Med-tech, we were apparently denied knowing certain critical factors where that operation is concerned. You spoke of secrets behind our backs? Try this one. Ytani apparently started at seven decades, with no formal education, and his family seems to be missing from the picture. He was excused from all Council mandates for the chip and seed, and seems to hold favoritism with the Marshal. They are mining an unknown mineral, to be refined into an unknown and highly explosive substance, and for unknown reasons. And if we now reflect back on the Marshal and his demands, if you do not like something, bam, active mode. How do you like that for our most beloved benefactor?"

"I do not! This is starting to smell like a conspiracy here."

"Captain," the Commander submits. "Get Kriv'tik on the line."

They return to the com-station, and the Captain orders the comms officer to open the link again.

"Morndindor Base, are you still there?"

"Affirmative," Spook Kriv'tik responds.

"Commander Geilv is here with us. I explained the situation to him, although his horns are nearly smoking from it. And now he wishes to speak to you."

"Understood."

The Commander steps up to the console.

"Lajivi, what is happening over there?"

Kaliya perks up and glares in astonishment at the com-station on her side. She quickly glances up at the Kriv'tik projection, and then spins around to find Ayene.

"A first-name basis?" she whispers urgently. "He uses that?"

"I...uh...never heard this before."

"What's his name, quick?!"

"Um…Geilv…Teranu…"

Kaliya points assertively at the projected member to pass it along.

"Teranu," Spook Kriv'tik begins. "We have a situation developing here that is not favorable. Did the Captain explain to you our current condition?"

"Affirmative," he responds. "Ytani is AWOL with a small army of drug-induced slaves on the Ghan'aju. Then, we have the mining operation at a standstill, the remainder of the local population may be unsettled for his errant behavior, and he is reported to have been abusing his position in your base with your female staff members to the point of committing murder, and then ordering excuses. Further, he seems to be experiencing a manic disorder and delusional behavior, using threats of the chips and a private army to enforce a perceived position of authority. Is this correct?"

"In summary, yes, it is. This situation is further compounded by the fact that our mission was classified, and the Captain was unaware of many of these procedures we were made to follow at the demand of the Marshal to obtain his mining output."

"Yes, we spoke of this. Information quarantines, and the use of those chips as a form of enforcement to achieve his goals."

"Good. Combine this with the unknown aspect of what we are mining and why we are mining it, and further that I filed several complaints in the past which were rejected by someone of authority within Central Command, but I suspect it was not you, correct?"

"I was unaware of any of this prior to this moment."

"I understand. But here we have our most important concern. Do you recall the missions I was sent on in the past when I was in command of my old naval task force?"

"Yes, and I recall we shared several discussions on those. You felt the targets you were assigned were incorrect for your observations as compared to your mission declaration."

"Yes, good, you remember."

"And now you are going off-protocol? I sometimes wondered about that…when you would finally break from it."

"Indeed, I suppose it was inevitable…"

The projected teammate glances at Kaliya with a look of apprehension in his face. He was being made to go off-script and improvise for this part now.

"Well," he continues. "This world resembles another of those examples. They are not technologically adept enough to oppose us in combat, and yet my information tells me the entire planet was wiped as part of a cleansing procedure to prevent interference of the Marshal's mining exploits. When I combine all this, I see a pattern emerging that the Marshal has a very strong demand for this output, to the point that all else becomes expendable, including us, if you factor in Ytani and his fetishes, and whoever it was with sufficient authority to reject my previous complaints."

"This is beginning to remind me of a conversation I had once on a recent mission he pulled out of."

Kaliya cocked her head at the statement, and then turned to her teammates to see their reactions.

"And so," Spook Kriv'tik offers. "I have a recommendation on how to proceed. The Marshal will need to be informed of this operation shutting down, and Ytani being at fault on multiple counts. However, we must remain blameless. I do not wish to be placed back on active again simply for arguing these aberrant details. We should investigate the Ghan'aju first. Perhaps the disappearance is something minor, maybe even innocent...an accident, perhaps."

"Agreed, this is a reasonable exercise. Captain, call up a scout frigate and send it out there to investigate. But tell them to be on alert for anything unusual."

"Acknowledged," he nods.

As they wait, the spy returns again to relay the most recent observations. Kaliya and Ayene meet with him away from the com-station for a little privacy.

"What do we have?" Kaliya asks softly.

"This is getting a little hairy. Geilv was facing away from us in the duct, so I folded across the room and made like a spot on the far wall to get a better view of his face. By the time the Captain explained everything, Geilv was turning purple. Then we had a few words from their Med-tech on that last victim, where they did an autopsy on her, and it showed all her injuries. He later mentioned it was described as an animal attack in the report."

"I remember that," Ayene nods. "Ytani forced the Commander to do this."

"Right, and this caused a strong rebuttal from the Captain, calling it ridiculous, and why doesn't anyone report something so obvious."

"Really!" Kaliya smirks. "Well, wouldn't THAT be truly amazing to see…what with Darumon preventing so much of it."

"Yeah…" he chuckles. "There was an exchange on this. First, the Med-tech suggested he thought about it, but assumed the people up there knew what they were doing, but apparently this is incorrect. Then, the Captain asked why he didn't do it anyway, as it should've stood out, regardless of anyone knowing what they're doing, so to push an investigation. After all, it should be common knowledge that no one talks to anyone, so why assume anything to begin with."

"Ouch!" Ayene yips. "Yeah, I would say that ought to do something."

"It should bite a few tails, to say the least," Kaliya nods.

"Anyway…" the spy continues. "We have a few revelations finally opening up. Meanwhile, Geilv's horns were nearly shooting off sideways by this time. So, even with his chips AND a sedative, that man is a strong one."

"All right," Kaliya notes. "Maybe this is a good thing. Now, let's get back to it and see what comes next."

The spy nods and flashes out of sight, and Kaliya and Ayene return to their posts.

Commander Geilv and the control center staff waited while a scouting frigate was dispatched to Morndindor to conduct a search for either the survey ship, or its remains, whether in orbit or elsewhere in the local space. Soon after, a report came in.

"Central Command, this is the Niv'zatan reporting."

"Niv'zatan," the Ensign responds. "What is your report?"

"There is no indication of the Ghan'aju in orbit of the planet, nor any indication of debris, either in orbit or on the planet's surface.

And our scanners are not detecting any noteworthy energy readings in the local star system from other bodies."

"Check for signs of a recent jump. See if there is any residual energy from the power-up sequence."

"Affirmative."

The staff waits several more moments for the ship to make its new survey and report back.

"Central Command, we have a faint reading in low orbit of what we believe to be residual energy from a nether-space jump sequence."

"Acknowledged, Niv'zatan. Commander?"

"Then this would mean the ship was pirated," he asserts. "But I still find it unlikely that Ytani would hold the capacity to do this himself. Not the way I heard him referenced by the Marshal on those occasions he would speak of him. And if those natives are not technologically advanced enough to meet our level, who was flying it?"

They switched back to the mining base.

"Morndindor Base," the Ensign announces. "We have received word back from our scouting frigate. There is no sign of the Ghan'aju in the local space, but they are detecting a faint energy signature suggesting it might have jumped away recently."

"Then Ytani must be in control of it," Spook Kriv'tik offers. "I can see no other reasonable explanation."

"Commander," the Captain interjects. "Even if Ytani is in control, a ship of that size requires a substantial crew to operate, and these locals are not described to be sufficient enough for this purpose."

"I cannot offer an alternative, unless it involves the coercion of the existing crew."

"Coercion? Oh, but of course. Then we will need to call on the Marshal for this point. Stand by."

The link goes on hold again.

"Here we go, people," Kaliya smiles. "It's time for our finest work. Let's hope he gives us at least a few moments advanced warning before he makes a showing, so I can tell our friends down below. We need to be sure of our timing."

Several minutes pass as the Marshal is summoned to the control center. As he enters the room, all eyes are on him, some of them apprehensively. The Captain and Commander Geilv take up the front.

"Commander," the Marshal growls as he arrives. "What is this about a missing ship?"

"The Ghan'aju appears absent from its duties at Morndindor," he replies formally. "It does not respond to hails, telemetry requests, or a ping. There is no sign of debris in the general vicinity, or on the ground. Commander Kriv'tik reports his situation is stable, but on standby until further notice."

"Standby? Why standby?"

"Marshal," the Captain steps forward. "Commander Kriv'tik filed a report just now describing a situation of worrying concern where Ytani was involved. The report tells of abnormal behavior, obnoxious and abusive conduct with the base staff, demands for sexual favors from the females, and even developing as a form of psychosis, as the Commander describes it, inflicting harm on them in the process."

The Marshal grimaces at the depiction as the Captain continues.

"He further demanded the Commander make excuses for these injury reports, and even a few fatalities, all suggesting external causes for these so-called accidental deaths."

"Accidental!" he shouts. "How do you describe murder as accidental?"

"According to the Commander, Ytani has been developing a form of mania relating to his service in managing the native population, expressing himself as a King who would control the world, and he further used threats of activating the base staff's chips if they complained over his methods. He used this, as well as a threat of a private army of these natives to force Commander Kriv'tik to falsify his reports to us over his true activities."

"Intolerable!" he shrieks. "And just when I thought he was proving himself to be useful."

"He recently extracted the new work crew he ordered for that one external mine they were managing and brought them to the Ghan'aju as part of this alleged survey operation. This was in place of another crew he was supposed to be acquiring, but apparently failed, as the Commander believes, due to his abusive behavior in the city he was managing."

"So, let me see if I understand this correctly. That little pest took a bunch of dwarven miners with him to the ship, and then what... hijacked it?"

"This is the impression we have so far. And it leaves the mining operation in a stagnant condition with no work crews operating anything. It also leaves our installation in a potentially vulnerable position if the locals are unsettled due to his treatment, and now his absence."

"Yes, it would at that. And it could also leave us in an incomplete standing where the final output was concerned. What were the last numbers we had?"

"I, uh... Ensign, get the base back online for us."

The Ensign reactivates the com-link.

"Morndindor Base, this is Central Command. We have the Marshal present and have briefed him on the situation relating to Ytani and the Ghan'aju. He is requesting your current output volume and stock supply."

"Our last report shows the processor is currently running at very low capacity due to the low output of the remaining mining operations. But with the loss of the mine to the south, we anticipate it will go offline very soon. The last reported stockpile was measured at eighty-six-point-seven percent."

"That's not what I was hoping for," the Marshal muses. "But all things considered, it's not bad, either. Commander, do you have any further information on Ytani's management of the city? I wonder if it might be possible to salvage anything out of it."

"Unfortunately, our position does not afford us to investigate personally. Ytani was using a false premise to persuade the native inhabitants to provide their service to us. This false premise would not permit us to make a personal investigation."

"Yes, of course, then I might need to check into it personally.

I have a…eh…special technique I can play to enter inside without them taking notice."

Kaliya watched and listened, but she was starting to worry if this would actually involve arriving locally or if to use some other method. So, she decided to offer a suggestion to reinforce the notion of following her preferences. She turns and begins whispering at the projected Kriv'tik.

"Suggest an inspection if we're compromised here."

He nods and turns back to the com-link.

"Marshal, given these circumstances, it is our belief we may be in a compromised position. If Ytani was behaving errantly in the city, we may need to pull out. Therefore, perhaps it might be necessary for you to make a quick inspection of the base, maybe also the processor, to ensure we leave no loose ends behind for them to discover."

"Hmm, yes, this might not be a bad idea. We certainly wouldn't want any of those little troublemakers picking up any ideas from us. Even if the city is in an unsettled state, it might still be possible for us to return one day and make another attempt. Very well, maintain your condition until I arrive. Captain, ready a ship for me."

They end the link, and the Marshal leaves the room, allowing the other officers to breathe a minor sigh of relief after the nervous upset they just went through. The Commander and the Captain gazed at each other for the implications of this disturbing turn of events.

"All right, people…" Kaliya emits excitedly. "Here we go! I'm heading below to get them started."

Kaliya now prepares herself to visit the city below. She quickly draws her focus and vanishes from the room, reshaping to her natural form as she arrived inside Eiki's home.

"Eiki, it's time!" she urges. "Get your people together in the square!"

"Oi!" the middle-aged woman yelps at the sudden announcement. "Blessed Mother, Kaliya, ye keep spookin' me with that. What d' ye mean? Be it time for Darumon?"

"Yes. Sorry, but he's coming now. Get out there and call up the people. Get the Chancellor and start up your show."

"Great blazes of the abyss, right ye be! I'll be sure t' tend t' it quick as I can."

"And don't forget to close that door to our people."

"Aye t' that!"

Kaliya flashes out of the room and Eiki jumps to her feet, throwing down her sewing materials and dashing out of the house.

"Here ye, citizens!" she shouts as she runs through the street. "Come t' the square, it be time for a town meetin'!"

She runs through the city shouting out to the people. Word spreads quickly through the shops and taverns, and a large congregation forms up following her to the town square in front of the Thane's Hall. She hurries up to the Chancellery, shouting out as she flings open the door.

"Chancellor, it be time! Get yer frizzled old whiskers out there, we need t' put on our show!"

The Chancellor shot up at the abrupt notice. He lurched to his feet and followed her into the plaza.

Kaliya arrived back in the base towards the rear of the complex, and strolled through the door into the control booth, just to be sure there was nothing unpleasant waiting for her should she try popping directly into the room. The team was still waiting, and all eyes were on the conveyor at the far end of the base.

"If I had nerves," Ayene notes. "They'd be jumping right now."

"Stay calm," Kaliya soothes. "We can do this. Just stick to your lines as best you can. We need to paint a new picture here now."

A few moments later, a ship arrives through the conveyor and settles down on one of the pads.

"Play the game well, people," Kaliya mumbles softly.

The Marshal appeared as a tall and neatly adorned officer of high esteem. His uniform consisted of black synthetic plates sectioned by red seams. His full body was covered, except for his head, which appeared rough and leathery, with numerous small barbs and ridges, and two thick horns protruding from the temples, curving forward slightly to tapered points. His complexion was a dark red with softly glowing yellow eyes.

He approached determinedly, with his posture revealing his obvious displeasure at the local situation. Kaliya felt queasy, but she had to carry this through, and do so with no outward emotional display. This would be her most difficult exercise yet, and not only her, but her whole team.

He approached the control booth door and entered the room.

"Now, let's see here," he muses. "I think our first objective should be to investigate the city. I want to know what we're working with, and if it can be salvaged or not."

"Of course, Marshal," Spook Kriv'tik offers. "The last report I had from Ytani was his usual demeaning accusations and derisive statements about them. I must therefore assume he does not treat them well down there."

"Really! Then we need to see how they feel about it. Give me a few moments and I'll be back with my impressions."

He heads out the door and pauses on the roadway as he apparently tries to decide how to approach this. He glances over his shoulder at the booth and the people inside who were watching him, then turns back around and seems to shake his head gently. He then raises his hands and places his thumbs and first fingers against his temples in a moment of deep concentration. Kaliya and the others studied him closely.

"What is he doing?" she wonders distantly.

Kaliya and her team watched silently as the Marshal drew in his concentration and a rippling effect began circling around his body. The anomaly represented a two-dimensional plane of warped space which enveloped him and folded his image away from the local scene.

"All right, that confirms it," Kaliya states confidently. "He can fold his body through nether-space directly."

"That requires some serious mental power right there," Spook Kriv'tik mentions.

"It also confirms our suspicions for Therinë and the elven trees, the sabotage on Ruuki uy'Daan, and everything else we think he did to us."

The Marshal reappeared in the city under the mountain, altering his form as he emerged in an alleyway, taking the shape of a dwarven commoner. He could hear shouting from around the corner in the town square, so he cautiously stepped into view to listen.

"Aye, good citizens!" the Chancellor announces to a seemingly enraged mob. "That be the tale of the folk outside! When our people finally punched a hole through the mountain that came down over our doors, we found folk who yay still be alive out there. An' the tales they gave say there nay be a war an' nay any point-ears ragin' across the land, as the Thane was a-tellin' us for so long. Instead, they tell the tale of some mighty blastin' comin' down on their heads, pummlin' the land an' destroyin' every city an' town that ever did serve the fare up there."

"An' there nay be a war with point-ears?" argues one male citizen.

"Nay, lad, the folk outside say the point-ears quit floppin' through their portals only a hand or two of years after they first popped their eyes out. Then came this blastin' t' finish off the land, an' us folk here bein' told t' dig deep t' hide from a war that nay be a-ragin' at all, while our kin outside be a-burnin' in a hellfire nay a man ever knew what was about. An' then there be the mine the folk found that day."

"Aye, what be that about again?" shouts another man.

"The tale was the folk outside found a mine t' the south of us, filled with what they think t' be our men servin' up Adamant bricks, the same as we be a-makin' here. But if there nay be a war t' serve up t', where d' ye think the bricks be a-goin', ay?"

"Where d' ye think they be a-goin', Chancellor? There be a lot of holes in the Thane's tales here."

"Our kin tell how they saw this wild-lookin' crew of folk, ugly as a wart-ridden boar an' twice as tall as any dwarf. They were seen one time comin' t' the mine t' pick up the bricks. If this be the true foe, it nay be any point-ears by the old tellin'!"

"An' what d' we say of the bricks we make here? An' the men we send up? The Thane was a-tellin' these wild tales of a war for four hundred years!"

"Aye, lad," the Chancellor bellows. "An' ye got it more right than ye can shake a hot iron at! I had a right fine talk with the Thane, just afore he ran off again. He said t' me, an' I'll tell ye true…he said he be the same one t' tell this tale for all those four hundred years! An' more, he was a young lad, younger than all me years in me own office, t' say nothin' of bein' on that throne durin' this time. There nay be any way I can think of for a dwarf t' live that long. Friends, brothers, I think the Thane be one of the foul lot that did this t' our people! The blastin' outside, the bricks, the men who nay ever did write even a wee note t' their pretties t' say they be alive an' well… It nay be point-ears, I say! I nay be a-knowin' their true name, but I'll be a-bettin' they bleed just as easily as any other!"

The crowd starts shouting violently, casting slurs and a call for war.

"Citizens," the Chancellor roars. "Send word down t' the forges! Tell them t' stop makin' bricks an' start makin' the true wares of war. There be a door in this room here. We nay be a-knowin' where it leads, but the hole we dug through the upper town took us t' the outside, an' this other door nay be a-goin' the same way!"

The crowd raises their arms and thunders a cry to take up arms and march on unknown enemies. They began stomping around the town square, stirring up their membership with even more vigor and fury for this injustice.

The Marshal stood back behind the gathering. He observed the riotous outbreak and moved away from the crowd. He glanced quickly around the nearby area before ducking behind a local shop into an alley, where he folded himself away.

He reappeared outside in the base, once again in front of the control booth. He turned and briskly made his way through the door and into the room.

"We have a serious problem here," he announces as he enters.

"What is the condition of the city?" Spook Kriv'tik asks.

"The dwarves have finally realized what has occurred here. They spoke of digging their way out into the open and discovering survivors out there, as unlikely as that may seem for the bombardment damage. They know the war is false, there was mention of discovering the mine out there, and they apparently also observed your staff retrieving the ingots at some moment. They have surmised their Thane is an imposter, based on a continual four centuries of storytelling…and in case you are not familiar with the relevance, this goes well outside their native lifespan."

"Oh no," Ayene moans. "That was not a very wise move to make. Ytani did not even think to change his presentation during this time?"

"It would appear that way. He apparently kept a youthful image in their eyes, and well longer than what might prove viable. And now, they are rioting in the streets, preparing to march on our position."

"What are your instructions?" Spook Kriv'tik wonders.

"We cannot allow them to discover our base here. If they move on us, they will do so in large numbers and overrun our position. At this moment, I do not see any value in quelling this uprising. To do so might destroy what is left of their race, and they could still be useful to us if we can recapture the situation at another time. For now, we must evacuate the base."

"Are we to dismantle the structures and remove them?"

The Marshal gazes at the Commander in consideration of the notion, glancing outside the window at the various buildings and facilities.

"No, I think we may not have time. We must destroy this base as we make our departure. You will set the reactor to overload as you make your exit. It will do the job for us."

"Understood. But now, as for Ytani, the Lieutenant here just now recalled something of importance she wanted to share."

"Oh? Very well, Lieutenant, what is it?"

Ayene now steps forward to play her role. She had to strain herself to remain calm and play this out like a theater act, which she had never done before.

"Marshal," she begins. "As Ytani was preparing to leave, I took notice of him loading up a number of large boxes into the cargo transport we used to retrieve the metal. This was just before he loaded up his work team and departed on his mission. I recognized these boxes as something I had previously tried to take inventory of in one of our storerooms. I found them once, some time ago hidden away in a corner, but they did not appear as anything I could recognize."

"Really! How did they appear? And did you look inside them?"

"Yes, I tried opening one to investigate the contents. The boxes were large, certainly large enough to fill one's arms, and they seemed heavy. They appeared to be made of a synthetic material, durable and all-weather, like from one of our industries. I also saw markings on the side, as if some form of writing, but not ours."

"What?" he shouts. "Where could he get something like that?"

"Unknown, Marshal," she shrugs. "So, I tried opening one of them. I originally thought they might be more of his entertainment devices. He was known to order those on occasion. But the crate I opened seemed to contain a large number of items, all the same, and at the time, I could only interpret them as some kind of children's toy gun, like you might find from some entertainment program. However, this seems irrational if they were packaged so professionally, and in his possession, then to load up on that transport. So, I am asking myself if they actually were toys, or something else, especially if you consider that alien writing."

"Alien…weapons?!" he barks.

"Yes, Marshal, I am forced to consider this. And the quantity in this one box, and then multiplied for the number of boxes he had in there, clearly represented enough for a small army."

The Marshal's eyes bulged, and he let out a boisterous roar at the implications. He glanced around the room, and then quickly outside, before returning to the conversation.

"What was that insipid fool doing here during my absence? Did you try questioning him about this, Lieutenant?"

"I did bring this to his attention as an inquiry for my inventory procedure, but he responded with insults and a threat to…um…well, I would prefer not to say."

"What?!" he demands.

"Well, it was a vulgar suggestion relating to my tail and bending over."

"Oh really!" he screeches. "He would behave this way to an official function?!"

"This was actually commonplace for his recent behavior."

Kaliya knew this was her moment. She was disguised as an Ensign for the occasion.

"Lieutenant," she interjects. "This was just after his return from his inspection of the processor, correct?"

"Yes, it was. He made that shortly before."

The Marshal passed his gaze between the two of them at the short interlude. The simple mention, at this point, was enough to make him nervous.

"What do you mean an inspection?" he blasts. "Why would HE, of all people, make an inspection of that place? Does he think he suddenly knows how to produce...eh..." he abruptly catches himself. "I mean, that he would know any of the technical details of that operation?"

"I would not normally expect it of him," Spook Kriv'tik offers. "It was my understanding his sole purpose was his interaction with the native population. Did you offer any additional training for this role?"

"No, I did not!" he grumbles. "Get them on the line. I want to see what he was doing over there."

The projected Kriv'tik motions to Petrith, who was disguised as another Ensign at the com-station to make the call.

"This is Morndindor Base to the Madzurki processor. Are you receiving?"

"This is intolerable," the Marshal groans. "And getting worse by the minute! Everything was going so well up until now...well, except for that little occasion on Therinë. But I'm sure that shouldn't be much of a bother," he sighs and glances around the room. "Yes, we should be well enough prepared if to continue as we are. Did you say the stores were at eighty-six percent?"

"Yes, Marshal," Spook Kriv'tik nods. "This was our last count. I believe this measured at over seventeen hundred units."

"Not bad...yes... I suppose we could work with this. After all, this stuff goes a long way. I'm sure we can find our way through with what we have…"

"Commander," Petrith interrupts. "There is no response from the processor."

The Marshal snaps around to him.

"What do you mean, no response?!" he shrieks.

"The com-link does not respond to my hail."

"In all Creation… Now what?!"

The Marshal steps up to the com-station to check the link.

"This is Marshal Darumon to the Madzurki processor, acknowledge!" he shouts.

The link was silent.

The Marshal turned sharply to the station where the conveyor controls were found. He punches up the selection menu to examine the destination indexes. The index for Madzurki appeared active.

"The conveyor is still available, so it couldn't be any sort of accident on the factory floor. Commander, do you have an explanation for this?"

"Negative. At last notice, the factory crew was on duty."

"When was that last notice, before or after his so-called inspection?"

"Admittedly, it was before."

"And how long did this…inspection…of his take?" he panted with an increasingly raspy voice.

Kaliya again steps forward for the reply.

"I recall seeing him departing early in the day in his shuttle. He spent most of the morning over there."

"Most of the morning!" he rages. "For an inspection of something he shouldn't know anything about?! Aargh!"

The Marshal was fuming by now. His breathing was heavy, and his voice was gravelly. He darted a stare at the conveyor outside.

"Stay here, I'll be back!"

He rushes outside to the road and pauses in contemplation.

Kaliya turns and points assertively at one of her teammates.

"Get over there and set up with your trans-com in video mode."

The agent flashes away quickly.

The Marshal again raised his hands to recall the image, and then pulled the fabric of space around him to fold away.

"I wonder how much more he can take before he bursts a vessel," Kaliya winces.

"Him?" Spook Kriv'tik jests. "What about us?"

"Can we actually burst a vessel in this condition?" Ayene wonders.

The Marshal appeared directly inside the factory control room. The facility was empty. The atomic device they left behind had also been moved out of sight.

He studied the room and peered out onto the factory floor to see it was shut down. He tried calling on the local intercom for anyone to respond, but there was no answer. Lastly, he turned reluctantly towards the console on the rear wall, where the com-system and conveyor controls were located. He stepped over to it and hesitantly examined the conveyor index control, pulling up the list of available indexes. He looked through them silently. The list showed one active link to Morndindor, and an inoperative link to Ooduan. He then let out a tumultuous roar which rattled the walls of the room and reverberated throughout the facility. He expended his breath, and then paused, leaning on the console.

"Four centuries of labor, and so close to our goal!" he grumbles. "We spent a world on it, and now it is lost to us. We cannot even continue our efforts without searching for some new species intelligent enough to harvest this material, and all due to an insolent little worm with delusions of godhood over an accidental mutation! If I should ever find that insect, he shall know what a true god is about!"

He pulls back from the console and browses the scene again. Except for a small drinking cup sitting in a corner of the forward console, the room appeared empty of anything interesting. And so, he stood there in deep reflection of his efforts.

"Maybe I should have taught the Suuden'kai how to do it themselves," he relents quietly. "Keep it local and better under our control. But this also implies several factors of learning they're not ready for. And yet..." he ponders distantly.

He sighs deeply as he gazes out the window onto the factory floor.

"It would be a curious study," he considers. "But no, it would need to be another carefully kept secret. They couldn't use this locally. And if any of their science factions were to hear of it, it would break just about everything they thought they understood about Creation. They are already a very mature society. More so than anything, um..." he trails off.

He stands there in reflection of his personal thoughts. He eventually shakes his head to cast them aside.

"No. In their present day, I need to keep them as they are. If I were to bring them in on this, and then if HE should ever see it..."

He halts his statement as his mind now returns to the factory. He scans the floor through the window as if trying to interpret the situation.

"Where did they go?" he muses silently.

He decides to check the flight bay, so he turns and leaves the room. And once he departs from view, the drinking cup, which strangely enough had a trans-com sitting inside with the video recording mode turned on, also vanished.

The projected spy was trying to record Darumon's movements. He flashed out of the factory control room, and into the upper corner of the hallway as a semi-circular wall sconce overlooking the hall, still with the trans-com in video record mode.

The Marshal strolled to the end until he passed through the door to the flight bay. The projected spy once again folds to a new location inside the bay to another corner where he can continue recording the Marshal's movements and dialog.

As the Marshal enters the room, he again studies the scene.

"The transport is gone, so whatever happened, they departed from here. And I suspect it was not through to Morndindor, not if the Commander is unaware of it. This leads to only one other destination."

The Marshal again sighs deeply and resigns himself to the obvious loss. He then folds himself away from the local space. After the Marshal was out of sight, the spy also vanished in a puff.

The Marshal once again reappeared outside the control booth. He lingered momentarily while he looked around the base, then strolled pensively back inside the room.

"What is the status of the processor?" Spook Kriv'tik asks.

"The facility is empty," the Marshal replies somberly. "The equipment was shut down, and what is worse, the conveyor link to Ooduan is showing inoperative, which is not a good sign."

"The facility is empty?" Ayene wonders. "This is irrational. Where could they be? They did not pass through here."

"Of course, Lieutenant, but I also took notice that the local transport was missing, which means they had to be somewhere. And for this point, there is only one other destination. Ooduan."

"But that would mean... Marshal, why would they go there? There is no other destination to travel to after that. And if the conveyor link is inoperative...in all the nether-space, does this mean..."

"Yes, Lieutenant, I think it does. If our little nuisance was behaving in such a way as to lose control of the city, and further to steal a ship, he might have left a little going away present for us. But there is nothing we can do about it here. When I return, I'll have our people send a scout to investigate. Perhaps it is something of a lesser concern, a simple malfunction of the conveyor, or some other innocent cause."

"Perhaps. But Marshal, my interpretation of that material is that it was highly volatile. What would that much quantity do if detonated, if I may ask?"

"It would create a substantial blast cloud. The material is classified, however, but I will say the blast cloud, for that quantity, would be enormous. I think...yes, I think I will need to treat this cautiously. There is no sense in losing ships to something as obvious as this. We will send a vessel equipped with beacon probes and a conveyor launch system. They can station themselves at a safe distance and launch the probes from there. This can help us build a situation report of the cloud and its expansion progress. We can go from there."

"This is reasonable."

"Meanwhile, prepare yourselves to abandon this post. Follow your instructions and report back to Azgarén."

"Acknowledged," Spook Kriv'tik affirms.

The Marshal leaves the building and strolls back across to his ship. He powers up and lifts off, then quickly departs through the conveyor.

The team inside the building watch as his shuttle vanishes, and then breathes a collected sigh of relief, followed by a soft applause.

"People," Kaliya admits. "If I had a real body, I'd be sweating."

"You're not alone, Lieutenant," Spook Kriv'tik agrees.

"I have a real body…back home," Ayene grins. "And I'm sure it must be sweating by now."

The room offers up a bold series of laughs.

"So," she continues. "Does this mean we can call this a successful operation?"

"Up to this point," Kaliya nods. "But we still need to play our role to finish the base. Meanwhile, I'm going below to let our friends off the hook."

"Lieutenant," ushers the teammate from the recent spy run. "Later on, when we return home, you might want to review the video I made of him at the processor."

"Oh? Does he do something interesting over there?"

"Yeah, it seems he talks to himself," he chuckles. "And I overheard some curious references along the way."

"All right, later for that. Let's finish this up first."

Kaliya now directs her attention to the city below, to the Thane's Hall and the square just outside, and folds herself away. She reshapes herself to her natural form and arrives on the steps to make her official presentation to the assembled people. She is greeted by the shouts and roars of an angry mob storming through the square as the Chancellor and Eiki continued their rant about the Thane and his ravings. But unfortunately, since this was her first time out in public, her sudden appearance out of thin air, compounded by her alien form of a Daanen'kai female, turned the shouts and hollers into shrieks and screams.

"Oops, I probably should've anticipated that," she mumbles.

The Chancellor and Eiki both turned suddenly to observe her, with the Chancellor also letting out a yelp at the sight of the stately young, blue-skinned woman.

"Chancellor," Eiki urges hurriedly. "Take ease now, she be a friend. One of the folk I told ye about from outside fightin' the true war."

"Great All-Father, that nay be any folk from outside!"

"'Tis true, but I did'na tell ye where she be a-comin' from yet, an' it nay be from our world."

"Aye t' that!"

"Good citizens!" Eiki shouts to get their attention. "Hear me now, this be right important. This here be a friend, one of the people fightin' the true war. I nay can tell ye why she made herself t' be a-showin' up here like this, but I'll be a-guessin' she has word for us of some kind from outside."

"What in the name of the All-Father be that there?" shouts one of the people in the square. "An' where did she come from, ay?"

"Allow me, Eiki," Kaliya offers.

Kaliya takes a small step forward to present herself on the platform overlooking the square. She makes ready with her form of Dwarvish that she learned as part of her studies in the academy.

"People of Glimmerheim, my name is Lieutenant Kaliya Nazég. I realize my appearance just now might seem frightening, and for this I am sorry. I just went through a very difficult challenge, and I'm a little bit weary from it. I am a member of a military force fighting a war that unfortunately passed across your world, if only to steal your adamantium."

"What kind of, eh…thing…be ye there, if ye'll pardon me words?"

"My people are called Daanen-Aryku, a renegade faction to the ones who were operating the base installed in the mountains above us. Those people are called Suuden-Aryku. Our world was once taken long ago by a being some might call a Titan, and his name is Sargeras."

The crowd begins rumbling in hushed murmurs at the mention of the mythical term.

"Yes, I am already aware you people tend to believe the Titans are old tales told to children at bedtime, or some similar notion. But they are real. They were once a race of beings called Primordials. Long ago, in times too old to remember by any other than the gods themselves, there was a war. We call it the Celestial War. The current gods we know today came upon the Primordials and found they were performing hideous acts of perversion, creating worlds and placing life on them, then to use that in a game of sport, competing with others to the death, all for the simple amusement of their masters."

"This be in times long ago?"

"Yes, long before any of us ever came into existence. The Primordials lost that war, and the survivors were cast into a kind of prison for all time, but apparently one got away. That was Sargeras. He went into hiding, hoping one day he could come back and free his brethren, and this is what he is trying to do now. His servant, one named Darumon, has made a lot of trouble for many people, and across many worlds. But now, his old enemies have become aware of him, and we are marching forward to finish him."

"But how d' ye fight a Titan, lass? By the old tellin', they be a yay powerful bunch. Ye may look t' be a right sturdy folk, if me eyes be a-seein' it right, but if the stories of the Titans be true, even by a wee bit, ye'll need a lot more than what ye be a-packin' t' d' it."

"Yes," she chuckles. "But we have a few clever tricks up our sleeves, and you can be sure I'm not alone. We have some strong friends behind us, so it is he who should be the one to be afraid. But this is another story. The reason I'm here now is to tell you we were successful in our play up there with his servant. With your help down here, he took the strong impression that he would not be getting any more of his metal. Instead, he gave orders to pack up and leave, which is what we were hoping for."

"But what be next for us? An' how does this fit with all the other wild tellin' by the Thane? Can ye tell us this now?"

"Eiki knows the full story, and I am sure she can do this for you. Now that we feel this time is past, you can all know the truth of what happened to your world, and where this brings us. Our people have already made a promise to Eiki and others to help rebuild what you lost, to the best of our ability. The trades we have been making are just one small part of it. There is also the dying land outside, and we are working to save what is still alive out there so we can restore it back one day."

"How d' ye d' that, if I may be askin'? The tales are there nay be anythin' left out there."

"We hold knowledge over many things, and some of this may be unknown to you in your modern day. But if you would join with us in a partnership, we can teach you how to help save the land outside. It will not be quick, nor will it be easy, but it must be done."

"An' what about the war? Where d' ye go next for it, if it nay be here by now?"

"We have already made a move to another world where we will continue our war. We have people there now scouting to learn where our enemy is so we can prepare our next move."

"An' the Thane? He be dead by now, ay?"

"Oh yes, very much so. I saw to this myself with several of my teammates. We took him down after the Chancellor had his last meeting. But our next move must be to help my people, the Suuden-Aryku. Darumon is using them as his servants, and apparently, they have no idea what he is doing out there."

"But lass, how can anyone serve up t' the likes of that an' nay be a-knowin' the better?"

"The answer to that is as unfortunate as it is sinister. Darumon has apparently become a master of lies. He tells them only enough to convince them they are following a noble cause, but without proper reason for it. It is shameful for me to call myself a part of that same society, as we always prided ourselves on our ability to reason and understand all that is around us. And he has thoroughly twisted that into such a convoluted maze that no one can see the exit by now."

"Oi, lass, I feel for ye. Me pardons, if ye please."

"Just look at your Thane, he learned from the best, although he didn't play it as successfully."

"Aye t' that!" he chortles.

"Such a foul thing, this be!" yells a female onlooker. "When d' we get back some of our honor for what he did t' us? An' what about the men sent out for the feast?"

"I know many men were lost to that," Kaliya admits. "We are no less angry than you, and not only this, but many others on other worlds who were also sacrificed. I was born in a city that numbered maybe a hundred thousand once. Then we were attacked and those of us who managed to escape barely number just ten thousand now. I have also learned from others that he ordered attacks on worlds that were blasted to oblivion, much like yours outside. I cannot even begin to imagine how many have been lost because of him, or what might have been lost if he was successful in his play."

"Unbelievable…it be truly amazin' that any single beast like this could be a-holdin' so much vileness inside."

"I know. It shocks all of us. But all things considered, it would not be wise for you to declare war on him as you are. Not when you have so few people and only one city to fight with. Instead, if you would join us, perhaps in support of our own efforts, together we are much stronger. Each of us holds power in the skills we offer to the whole. You do not need to be a warrior. You could be a shopkeeper, a smith, a miner…each and all of these are necessary for us to find our victory. And if you offer your finest to combine with the rest, we will take this fight straight to his throne!" she finishes boldly.

The crowd shouts a cry of accord, letting out yips and hollers resounding through the streets and avenues.

Kaliya gazes out onto the square at the sudden jubilation that the crisis was over and now they had the freedom to seek justice and rebuild their world.

"Kaliya," Eiki calls up to her. "Ye've got a good way with yer words. Mayhap ye have a few highborn bones in ye from somewhere?"

"Well Eiki, I don't want to make it sound like I'm bragging, but I suppose you could say that. My father is the leader of my people."

"Say now, be it true, lass? Oi, methinks ye did come from a right grand family, by the way of yer tellin'."

"Not only that, but I learned a lot from Thaelyn, also."

"Aye t' that!" she howls.

◆

"This is especially good news, Kaliya," Thaelyn sighs as he relaxes into his chair. "We listened in to the conversation from that one shard-com you had sitting there, and it sounded as though your play carried off in a well-planned sequence."

Kaliya was making a quick diversion to the WIC building to report to Thaelyn and the other officers. The timing was important, so as not to delay the apparent evacuation of the base. She still had to cover for the obvious loss of the base staff.

"Yeah, but it was nerve-wracking," she accedes. "So, um, does this still mean you're putting me down for that additional mark you mentioned?" she raises her brow tenderly.

Thaelyn grins and lets out a contented laugh, accompanied by the General and Kailen.

"I think this will require something a bit more noteworthy than a simple mark. I was paying attention to your wording during your conversation with Central Command. How you were informing them of the hidden details while at the same time conveying the warning to those who might talk too much. This is worthy of its own mention, and I think we can play on this in the future."

"Wow, and this just means things are getting even more complicated."

"They likely will, but our form of complicated is to combat his form of complicated. This may turn out to be as much a war of words as it is anything else."

"Right. But now, we need to finish with the base. This should be fairly simple, by comparison, and I don't anticipate any repercussions as Darumon already gave orders for the destruction of the base using the reactor. We're just going to make it sound a little more interesting. And for this, I'm calling in a number of mages, and a few of our own dwarves to assist."

"Very good, Lieutenant," Thaelyn asserts. "Be on your way and bring this to a final close for us. Then we can focus ourselves on other matters."

She salutes and fades from sight.

She came into view once more at the base. The area was teaming with mages and dwarves taking up stations outside the control booth. She made her way back inside to meet with her team for the final performance.

"I need a report from inside Central. Who is present right now?"

One of the teammates flashes away to investigate, again arriving inside the ventilation duct. She appears in insect form and briskly peeks through the grating, then returns back to the base.

"Lieutenant, it's the same crew as before, plus the Marshal who looks like he's waiting for something."

"Probably to hear the final outcome of the evac, for all the other troubles Ytani has caused today," she giggles softly. "Spook Kriv'tik, did you get those files sent?"

"Yes, Lieutenant, I sent those recordings of Ytani's ranting while you were meeting in Rolsklinde. We're all set here."

"Excellent. We need those on file since I suspect they might come in handy later on. All right, here we go. Does everyone out there have their ears plugged up tight? Remember, we'll be using a lot of flash-bangs on this occasion."

The people outside the window all nod and shout in affirmation.

"Good! Then, places everybody...and action!"

The dwarves start running in circles shouting war cries at the top of their lungs. The mages hold back for Kaliya's signal through the window.

"Spook Kriv'tik, call up Central," she instructs.

The projected teammate engages the com-system and calls in to Central Command.

"Commander Kriv'tik to Central Command… Urgent!"

"Central Command responding, what is the situation, Commander?"

"We are under attack. The local population has discovered our location, and they are now swarming the base."

Kaliya points to one of the mages through the window and he conjures up a flash-bang orb into the air, where it detonates a short distance away with a loud bang. The sound echoes through the building.

"Commander!" shouts the Captain. "What was that sound!"

"They are using explosives to demolish the buildings. Our escape route is cut off. They are everywhere out there!"

Kaliya signals to more mages for multiple rounds.

"Commander, do you need assistance? We can send a detachment to reinforce you."

"I do not think we have time. They have surrounded the building and are attempting to reach us."

Kaliya points at a group standing outside the door carrying large sheets of wood and axes. They start chopping to make sounds of hacking through the door, while others throw glassware to the ground to simulate the sounds of breaking windows.

"They are breaking through to us," Spook Kriv'tik urges. "We are unable to escape the building."

Commander Geilv was still present in the control center and listening to the unfolding disaster. And even though he was under the control of the chips, his body language revealed a developing sense of dread. He instantly lurched forward.

"Lajivi!" he shouts. "You must try to push your way through."

"Commander," shouts one of the teammates. "They are setting one of those canisters near the reactor. If it detonates…"

Kaliya points to another mage outside, who then throws up a large fireball into the air, detonating in a thunderous boom.

"In all the nether-space," Ayene shouts. "The reactor!"

"Commander!" shouts another team member. "The reactor is losing containment. Stabilizers are offline. The control links are cut."

"Lajivi!" Commander Geilv shouts again. "You must attempt to reach a transport. Jump out a window if nothing else."

"Impossible," Spook Kriv'tik relents feebly. "There must be hundreds of combatants outside, and the reactor is losing containment. Remember my words. This mission was…"

Before he finished his statement, he abruptly cut the link.

"All right, Petrith…" Kaliya commands. "Shut that thing down. Ayene, power down the conveyor!"

Petrith was still sitting at the com-station. He works vigorously to disable the communications system while Ayene, now sitting at the conveyor control panel, makes a full power-down of the unit, including the ping responder, so it will appear fully inoperative.

"Navina," Kaliya urges. "Get back over there and check on things."

"Right away," she responds, and then vanishes.

✦✦✦✦✦

In the control center at Central Command, all eyes were on the com-station after the signal cut out.

"Morndindor Base, respond," issues the Ensign at the com-station.

"Conveyor control," the Captain directs. "What is the status of the ping signal for the base?"

An operator at another station pulls up the indexing configurations for the base's primary conveyor, which held a master set for all the connections they linked to. He scrolls to the line entry for Morndindor.

"Captain," the operator replies morbidly. "The index for Morndindor is showing inoperative. There is no ping response."

Commander Geilv had pulled back by now from the com-station. He stood silently and stoic as he listened to the resulting reports, while his eyes stared blankly into space. The Captain studied him briefly, but had to divert away to give his final account of the situation.

"Marshal," he concedes. "It would appear we have lost the outpost at Morndindor."

"Yes, so it would seem," he ushers mildly. "And such a pity, those were some good officers, well worthy of keeping in service. But at least those worthless peons lost a few of their own in the process. Very well, we shall leave that world for now and see about recovering for our losses elsewhere. I will never again entrust such a delicate matter as this to such a lowly incompetent, no matter how simple it should have been."

The Marshal makes a passing glance at the officers around the room.

"We need to discover the fate of Ooduan," he emits distantly. "Send out a vessel with beacon probes and a conveyor launch system. Eh..."

He pauses in his thoughts, and then steps over to the rearward console, waving at the operator to leave his seat so the Marshal can take over. He pulled up a calculator app on the data terminal and began punching in some numbers.

The Commander remained motionless and still staring out the window into open space. The Captain again turned to examine him. He could see the elder officer's eyes glazing over, and a tear rolling down his cheek. He reached up and laid a hand on Geilv's arm, squeezing to draw his attention. This brought Geilv's eyes around to meet with his, but the Captain noticed Geilv's cheek was twitching repeatedly, and his lips had tightened, showing signs of high tension. Geilv then rolled his eyes in the direction of the Marshal.

The Captain took notice of this reaction, but he recalled Commander Kriv'tik's words from earlier in the report. He squeezed harder to regain the Commander's attention, causing him to roll his eyes back around. The Captain frowned silently to gesture restraint, but Geilv's eyes simply drifted back to the Marshal. So, the Captain applied a gentle shake on the arm, once again pulling Geilv's view back to his. He frowned deeper and shook his head slightly to reinforce the notion of restraint. This sent Geilv back into his distant thoughts staring into space.

The Marshal continued with his calculations on the data terminal.

"What was that formula again…" he mumbles to himself. "And we had seventeen hundred and…well, we'll just round it off. We might be missing half the spiral arm by now. Then, he supposedly did it sometime in the morning Morndindor time, so we'll stick in an approximation here…hmm…this isn't good. All right, Captain, get a ship out there and station it…oh, let's say around five thousand lightyears distance from the mark and have them start launching probes into the area at intervals to check the blast wave."

"Five thousand lightyears?" he wheezes.

"This is simply a, eh, safety precaution, for the radiation hazard. The blast wave travels at hyper-luminal velocity in this case, so we don't want anyone to get in trouble out there. When you find the outer edge, let me know. But I wouldn't advise sending any ships inside the cloud. They won't survive it. In fact, we may need to quarantine the entire area…indefinitely. Until then, I'll be in my office."

He jumps out of the chair and briskly leaves the room. The other officers glared at each other for the apparent implications.

"Five thousand lightyears," mumbles one of the Ensigns. "And what does he have in mind for THAT? Sir, with respect, regardless of who these insurgents of his are, this is enough firepower to blow up half a galaxy, if distributed around evenly. I thought we were supposed to help him recover his former holdings, not blow them up completely."

"I do not have an answer for you, Ensign," the Captain submits. "But it does raise a few troubling questions as to why he would want it, and why it was so heavily classified that we were not allowed to know what it is or why we were producing it. Especially as we ARE supposed to be assisting him in recovering something."

"I agree, Captain," the Commander ushers solemnly. "But for now, do as he says. And brief me when you have a result. I will return to my office as well."

"Commander, how do you feel?"

"Bad."

"Is there anything I can do?"

"Negative, this damage cannot be corrected."

The Commander turns and slowly exits the room. And once again, in the ventilation duct in the back of the room, a tiny visitor peers through at the scene. When it had seen enough, it disappears in a puff.

The spy returned to the control booth at the mining base to report in, but as she arrived, she held the appearance of deep melancholy.

"Navina?" Kaliya intones softly. "What is it? What happened over there? Did it work?"

"Yes, Kaliya," she advises delicately. "We have our result. The Marshal was thoroughly convinced by the display. He even made mention of the unfortunate loss of good officers, although I'm asking myself if he was saying that more for their value to serve him, or if he truly felt they were good officers by their own merit. I'm a little at a loss here, but by the tone of his voice, he may have actually held feeling for this point."

"Interesting, but then, I suppose even he might have a tender moment, if it's something he might see special value in. Even someone who plays with toys might have an occasional favorite. What about the rest, and why do you look like this?"

"Well, first, he followed this by spitting a curse at the dwarves, saying they got their own taste of it."

"Oh, how nice of him to show such sympathy for those who suffered so much. There go my feelings for HIS loss. I swear, I cannot imagine any creature to hold this level of antipathy for anything else around him."

"Yeah, although I suppose if we say he lost a favorite toy, this could amount to his fury of losing good soldiers to something unworthy in countermeasure."

"Well, maybe."

"After that, he started giving orders to send a scout to investigate Ooduan. He crunched a few numbers on one of the terminals and told them to station a ship at five thousand lightyears distance. Can you believe that number?"

"Wow, is that supposed to suggest the size of the blast cloud?"

"Well, I think he was covering for himself a bit, but he suggested the blast wave travels at hyper-luminal velocity, and this is to protect against a radiation hazard."

"Meaning to say, stay away from that side of the galaxy from now on. Wow."

"Yeah, even to put a permanent quarantine on it. He left after that with his orders to send out those beacon probes at intervals until they found their numbers. I'm curious as to what numbers they'll actually find since only one unit was actually detonated, not all seventeen hundred."

"Right, so we'll need to watch for that. It might prove educational. But now, what is it that makes you look so glum?"

"There was a bit of conversation following his departure. One Ensign commented on that number, and why have something that could blow up half the galaxy if their purpose is to recover something intact."

"Yeah, that would stand out a bit."

"But it's the Commander himself, Kaliya. I think we broke his heart. He just stood there, staring into nothingness, like a man who had lost his best friend. I popped across the room again to see his face. I thought I saw a tear rolling down his cheek, and even with his chips, he looked very distressed. He also looked like he was ready to take it out on the Marshal, but the Captain stopped him."

"Oops! How did he stop him?"

"Silently, of course, taking his arm and making faces to keep it under control…multiple times, by the way, as the Commander was seriously disturbed."

"Cu'Nar's pity," Spook Kriv'tik moans softly. "Lieutenant Ti'van, do you know if the two of them were close?"

"It's hard to tell when you don't have emotions," she considers. "But if they were on a first-name basis, it stands to reason they were. My Commander and I sometimes use this when we engage in something personal. Our military maintains a strict hierarchy of authority, but even at that, people are still people, and you might have occasions of relationships developing. And these two are old-timers from before the Arrival. So, they might have a history of some kind."

"Wonderful."

"All right," Kaliya relents. "We can't do anything about it where we are right now, and Geilv is simply too close to the Marshal to offer any consolation. That demon has brought harm to too many people during this time, and we're probably not done yet. We'll just have to repair this damage at a later time."

"And hope Geilv doesn't go haywire on us before then," Navina suggests.

Chapter 11

LANDFALL

"**M**arshal, I have a report."

Commander Geilv had been sitting in his office since the time of the events at the mining base, silently mulling over the broadcasts made by the base staff and the sounds of the attack outside. The twitching in his cheek had slowed by now, but he was no better for the loss of his friend, to say nothing of the rest of the crew and the report they gave about the illegitimacy of the operation.

He had been reviewing the recordings of Ytani's conversation with Kriv'tik during this time while he waited for the scouting report regarding Ooduan. The report came in some time ago, but he delayed turning it in due to a series of new concerns that suddenly plagued his mind.

In the meantime, the Marshal had been keeping to himself, in part sulking for the loss of the Arcanicium and his mining operations, and in part dwelling on the impertinent behavior described of Ytani. He slowly reached over to answer the link.

"Commander, it has been some time for you to file a report. I suspect this is concerning Ooduan, correct?"

"Affirmative…partially… My report begins with Ooduan and continues with Madzurki."

"Commander, when you put it into such terms as those, I feel the hair on the back of my neck starting to rise. What do you have?"

"First, with Ooduan… The scout vessel arrived at the designated station and began its operations. It launched a series of probes at midpoint intervals testing to find the outer extreme of the blast effect. The first location was at twenty-five hundred lightyears outward, and it survived. The next was at midpoint from there to Ooduan, and it also survived. The progression continued to narrow the numbers until they found the outer layer at roughly two-point-five lightyears from Ground Zero. Is this appropriate to your expectations?"

"What?!" he screeches. "In all Creation, NO, it is not! By the love of the Master, that number is… Wait one moment. I know this must be wrong. Are you absolutely sure of that number, Commander?"

"Affirmative, the vessel confirmed it is still receiving telemetry from that location."

"Blast! What is going on here! This does not make any sense at all! All right, wait, let me think. Eh, let me see, that formula again was…"

The Marshal made a series of mumbles as he apparently was making another calculation.

"Commander, given that we had at least seventeen hundred units in there, that number should be many orders of magnitude larger. Unless…oh no… One moment, let me try another one."

The Marshal makes another series of grumbles as he tries reformulating his equation, finally to come up with a new result.

"I don't like this at all. Ytani was over there for some kind of inspection, so they said, and he spent all morning at it. Why would that insipid fool want to make an inspection of a factory he knows nothing about? But if it wasn't the factory he was inspecting…and the factory itself was abandoned… Commander, I think we have a problem."

"I suspected as much. But can you explain? What would this number represent to you? As I suspect this would not represent your expectation of the full amount."

"You are very good, Commander, this cannot be the full amount.

In fact, according to my calculations, given the formula we would use to calculate blast areas for this material, this would approximate only one solitary unit, not seventeen hundred."

"One unit?" he furrows his brow slightly. "Then, Marshal, we must ask about the remainder of it, especially if Ytani was making an unplanned visit to a place he had no business visiting."

"Indeed, Commander! And further, that Lieutenant over there said something about him storing some crates of alien weapons he was apparently collecting. Then he loaded them onto the transport with his work crew. Commander, I think that insolent young man must have been in contact with someone recently. And if that someone was able to meet him at Ooduan with the factory crew to unload the materials onto a ship of some sort...but they left one unit behind... Aargh!" he screams. "This is clearly a message that he has it! In all Creation!!" he roars.

The Commander listened as he heard crashing sounds of things being tossed around the room and furniture being toppled. The raging continued for several moments until the Marshal returned to the com-link.

"Commander!" he pants. "If that impudent little miscreant has stolen my stockpiles, I can only hope he blows himself up somewhere. But if not, we could be in serious danger!"

"How serious, Marshal? I think I need to know if Azgarén is in jeopardy. If just one unit of that material can blow up an entire star system, we are not simply in danger, but rather, this amounts to a crisis of insurmountable proportions."

"I know! And what's worse, they stole one of OUR ships. No doubt that gives them easy access to find their way back here. Commander, even if we were to find them, it would be a suicide run to kill their ship. But we must consider Azgarén for this point. I want all ships on full alert. Send out patrols to all our local neighbors. Drop long-range sensor buoys to check for jump signatures. You must do everything in your power to protect this planet!"

"Yes, Marshal. But one other question comes to mind. What

would be the blast radius of that full quantity if it were to go off cumulatively?"

"Commander…" he sighs through his heavy breathing. "You honestly don't want to know. But if it were all combined into one lump, we are speaking of several thousand lightyears radius. And that's if it goes off in THIS universe. This means, he must be found and eliminated at great distance to us."

"In this universe, Marshal? Is there a difference to any other?"

"Yes, but it gets technical from here, so let's not go into it, as it's irrelevant to our needs."

"As you wish, Marshal… But now, as for Madzurki. When I received these results, I sent a scout to investigate that destination as well."

"Oh no…what now?"

"I ordered the scout vessel to investigate Madzurki using the same method. The star system appears intact. So, I gave orders to make a cautious approach. The moon with the processor appeared normal, but as they made a close approach, the processor was destroyed."

"WHAT!!" he shrieks.

"The scout made a scan of the surface and found traces of radioactivity consistent with a standard atomic weapon."

"Aargh!" he screams again.

The Commander heard more crashing sounds from the com-link, as the remainder of the Marshal's office was torn apart. Finally, the noises settled, and a beleaguered Marshal came back on the line.

"Commander, I think someone is toying with us, and likely watching us, and I can only imagine who it is right now. That city with the dwarves, the base, and now the processor… Someone is cleaning up their loose ends and leaving clues behind to tell us he is playing god now."

"Ytani?"

"Yes! And no doubt, based on what those people said about him, I suspect he might be making a few demands on US next. And if he has that weapon in his hands, he holds a very big chip to play with."

"Marshal, we need a solution to this."

"Yes, Commander, that much is clear. But I need time to think. Maybe, if we're lucky, we won't see anything in the immediate term. He'll probably need time to organize, maybe to decide his next move. But I wonder... Who did he find out there to make friends with?"

The link goes silent for a moment as the Marshal ponders this question. The Commander also pondered the question, but in his mind, there was only one likely answer, and yet the Marshal did not seem to be using it on this occasion. Instead, he was silent.

"Marshal," he redirects. "I also have a report on our expedition in abnormal space."

"Oh? Well, it's about time. What do we have? Maybe we can salvage something yet."

"Our ship has discovered a massive construct in abnormal space. We believe it is the designated target of our search. It represents a large toroidal structure, hollow but with no obvious entry points. Scans reveal a large number of lifeforms inside."

"I find it curious that it was so difficult to locate. I was under the impression it should be near to that rock they call The Spire. Very well, I suppose that should remind me not to rely on the rumors of ignorant fools. You must find a way into it, but do so cautiously. I am aware that it is governed by a very potent being, and likely she will not care for you cutting holes in her precious little city. Make a small entrance, sneak in, and find your way to the street level. You might be able to simply wander about without interference, but do take care of the locals. Some of them are said to be rather unpleasant."

◆◆◆◆◆

A couple of days passed, and Thaelyn was in his usual meeting at the WIC building. Kaliya and Ayene were both in attendance, and together they were reviewing some of the recent spy videos.

"In this one," Kaliya notes. "We have the Marshal's response to Ooduan and Madzurki, and he was apparently so boiling hot, he tore up his office, by the sound of it."

"Indeed, so is this to say he has a temper?" Thaelyn muses. "Hmm, I wonder if we could play into this sometime."

"So long as it doesn't involve any of the people."

"Absolutely, he is enough of a danger even without that."

"Also, it sounds like they found Sigil just recently. So, we can start to expect something out of that."

"Very well, we will need to send our own investigation out there and see what we can do about it."

"Maybe start another mutiny?" she grins innocently.

"I somehow suspect this is where it will ultimately lead, but let us feel around gently here, as the Marshal will not take kindly to a mutiny, or even the straight loss of another ship. He will more likely send replacements until he achieves what he wants."

"What if the Estelar get involved again, even if in theory, like we used here on Therinë?"

"This is also a possibility, and it could potentially deter him from making any new attempts, at least by these same means. He might then choose to lay low until a later moment, or perhaps try something new. In the absence of anything else occurring, he might even try producing another weapon. So, we must be sure to make our own move before he has a chance to make his."

"One thing is for sure," Ayene notes. "Both the Marshal and Commander Geilv are very upset with Ytani stealing the first weapon. My recent runs into Central have seen most of the base in an uproar over it. I don't think they've been so excited over anything since the Tav'ageen Scare, and maybe not even that."

"This will surely give them something to think about in the near term. Whether they describe it as more insurgents, or something else, it should keep them busy for now."

"In the meantime, I was speaking to several of the crewmembers of the Ghan'aju. The Commander has been working to settle them on Ruuki uy'Daan, but as I mentioned before, Captain Va'tyn was concerned over his family and any notes going home from Central about his loss. He asked me if I could pass a discreet message of some kind, but before I take any steps, I wanted to confer with you."

"I certainly do feel sympathy for them, as well as the base crew at this time. But if these messages should pass through Central Command, or otherwise filter back up to them, we could have a serious complication facing us later."

"I thought about that, but then I had an idea. If I work with Petrith on this, I think we could cover ourselves with a little of his hacking skills."

"Uh oh… And what devious plan do you have in mind for that innocent young man?" he grins.

"Innocent!" Kailen bellows a laugh. "That's not the word I would use based on that little prank he played on Ruuki uy'Daan."

"Indeed, Commander, but if channeled the right way, it could possibly serve a valuable role for us."

"My idea goes like this," Ayene smiles. "They all have vid-mail addresses, so if I collect these and write up a form letter, merge this with the mailing list, and send it off, we can get the word out. Then I could have Petrith simply erase all our evidence from their outbound mail system."

"Interesting, but then what sort of message would you send?"

"We would need to cover for ourselves. We're basically saying people who are being declared dead are not actually dead. So, I'm going to say we were all reassigned to a top-secret covert operation to investigate a series of suspected illegal activities within Central Command, and our participation is highly classified for some very obvious security reasons. After all, if Central is being described as conducting something illegal, who are you going to call about it to get information? There is no other organization above that except the Council, and they're probably missing completely."

"To say nothing of holding their own guilt," Kaliya adds. "In one form or another…"

"Yes," Thaelyn nods. "This is a curious one. Is there anything like an internal security agency within your government?"

"Not that anyone knows about…yet," Ayene grins mischievously.

"Right, I should have guessed," he smirks and glances around the table. "Good, and therefore you will tell them to keep it quiet as it is a top-level agency conducting its work as perhaps a new government program. This could prove interesting, actually. I wonder if we could establish an actual presence of some kind."

"That's a really interesting idea. But what would we call it?"

"Well, such a thing might sometimes be called a secret service, or some manner of intelligence agency. Maybe if to use such words as…hmm…"

Thaelyn mulls over several ideas in his head until one comes to mind with a pleasant ring to it.

"You are a united world body, so what about Azgarén Central Intelligence…how does that sound?"

"Ooh! I like it," Ayene smiles. "Now we just need an office and some people inside."

"I could allocate a few from our ranks for now," Kaliya muses. "But if we're going to operate an actual office, we'll need funding of some kind to pay for it."

"Not that I would normally wish to argue," Kailen considers. "But do we actually hold any real authority to create such a thing as this?"

"This is a good question," Thaelyn notes. "And so, to answer it, I would need to approach the suggestion like this."

The other officers at the table lean in to see what sort of extraordinary justification he has to offer on this occasion.

"First, if we say the Council is absent, we are saying Azgarén is currently without its own government, and I would hardly describe Darumon as a valid government entity, as he is technically an alien lifeform. The Azgarén military, being the only other form of authority you may have available, is similarly under his control, and unfortunately the citizens are oblivious of everything he has done to them. Therefore, we can say the world is under a hostile form of control."

"All right," Kailen admits. "I suppose I can't argue with this."

"You, Commander, represent the highest form of military authority we have available with legitimate cause to serve the people. Commander Kriv'tik is also a high-ranking officer, and well-recognized within their own military, and he is currently on our side. This gives us military authority. Your father and the Elder Council, even though you deem yourselves to be in exile, are still a government body, to some degree or another, and also with the best interests of your people in mind. Further, you are all technically Suuden-Aryku and therefore native to Azgarén. That world is your birthright."

"I like where this is going so far," Kaliya smiles.

"This leaves us with only one clear solution, and that is to give Darumon a real insurgency to worry about…a liberation force. You are essentially conducting a revolution, and installing your own government to replace the old one."

"Well," Kailen relents. "I guess I can't argue with that mentality, either. But it also brings up a curious question. Which is the more dangerous? Darumon, or a Celestial with a mind to get the job done using any means necessary?"

The group at the table all join in bold laughter at the suggestion.

Kailen continues, "This just leaves us with a matter of how to do it."

"Right," Ayene contends. "Petrith can hack into anything we set him to, and this is a legitimate need if we're trying to save our people. So, maybe the Council accounting office can be convinced of a new operation opening up."

"All right," Kaliya offers. "Check around the area for any available office space, and who we need to talk to about it. I'll pull in some additional people, and we'll dress them up like they have official business to attend."

"I think we should also bring in Commander Kriv'tik. We'll need a top-level command rank to enforce our position, and his would do very nicely. Besides, he looks a little lonely in that office of his."

"But how do you plan on doing that? He's on Ruuki uy'Daan, and this is on Azgarén."

"Well, then I guess it's time to teach an old bull a new trick," Ayene smirks.

"Oh, cu'Nar help us. But do you think he can actually do that?"

"An old bull?" Thaelyn raises his brow.

"Yeah," Kaliya smiles. "It's another of our cute expressions. It reflects on that term 'old-timer', which is anyone who is one hundred plus, and in this case a male. They tend to get a little stubborn after a while."

"Uh huh…" he rolls his eyes.

"And here I thought Petrith was bad," Kailen moans and shakes his head. "Now, my own baby sister, and her latest accomplice, are going to create a fake government security agency to incur a hidden insurgency of a world thought already to be under siege by insurgents."

"A part of me must agree," Thaelyn admits warily. "Between these two, to say nothing of the rest of her friends, I think we are in a lot of trouble. Or maybe it is Azgarén that is in trouble, I cannot be sure by now. Therefore, Kaliya, it becomes necessary to consider you for a higher level of privilege to provide you with the authority to carry it through."

"Whoa!" she screeches. "My Lord, what do you mean by that?"

"First of all, the General and I, as well as your brother here, have been discussing your recent performance with Morndindor, among other things, and it becomes clear that we need to expand your capacity somewhat. This is especially true as we move towards Azgarén and therefore have a greater need for greater coverage. Your suggestion for this agency could offer us an important venue to provide our services, as well as support, should we find any additional sympathizers. A local office would be highly advisable, with our only true shortfall being a full-time staff to operate it. Your team is still mostly in training, so we will need to juggle our schedules some more."

"Right, and here I was thinking they might have a chance to relax so they could get back to their original class schedules. Oh well…"

"Perhaps we can remedy this with some carefully chosen local agents. But the pressures we are under right now are great, and this is a new body that needs to be pressed into service with all due haste. And yet, it also needs leadership, and that naturally reflects back on you…Captain," he winks mischievously.

Kaliya stared blankly at him with her mouth agape. She could feel the blood rushing out of her face. Ayene turned to gaze at her in astonishment.

"Do you know how long I've been a Lieutenant waiting for MY promotion, you little tart!" she teases avidly. "And at only four centuries? Well done, Kaliya!"

"I, uh…" she croaks. "Dear cu'Nar, give me strength. I only got the Lieutenant's badge recently, and I'm still trying to settle into that one! But I suppose it was Fated. If I'm supposed to be leading the Stormhooves, I'll need a higher leadership rank. But cu'Nar's Pity, this is moving fast."

"We will help you, Kaliya," Thaelyn assures. "Perhaps I can sit down with you on a few occasions for some private tutoring, and we will ask some of our other officers, like the General here, to offer their advice. We will need you in full service as a proper leader if we are to take this to the next level. Meanwhile, we shall prepare ourselves for the formalities to observe the occasion. I am currently ordering the guild artisans to design a new merit award to commend your recent performance. Once this is ready, we will combine this into a special ceremony in the Great Hall."

Kaliya sighs hesitantly and gazes at Kailen. He returned a warm smile.

"Kailen, what are we building here?"

"A new future, it would seem."

"In the meantime," Thaelyn resumes. "We now have Morndindor to ourselves, and this opens the way for us to begin a more earnest approach to restoring that world. I am told Shescellaie is almost ready with some new seeds for us. So, we will attend to that, once they are ready, in order to begin the process. We will need to spend a considerable amount of time on this, and call a lot of people into the effort. We also need to educate the dwarves for their part."

"That should be fun to watch," Kaliya notes. "Dwarves aren't known for their love of hugging trees."

"This may be true, although we did manage to bring those we have on Tae'Eladar forward a few steps. But I think the desperate nature of Morndindor will provide enough incentive. And when they see it in action, it might change a few of their attitudes, especially after I perform the ritual to restore that portion of the land just outside their city. We will use that as our starting point."

"Your Lordship," Kailen wonders. "About this ritual of yours. Is it the same one you performed in the valley before settling Firstfall?"

"It is. This is a special ritual we call Shescellaie's Rebirth. It is a very difficult affair, and very draining on me, as well as those who participate. But in the end, it can immediately restore an area to full life, irrespective of what damage was caused to it prior to this, such as was the case when we first arrived and devastated the land with Mystra's Fury to remove the orcs."

"Your Lordship!" Ayene interjects. "In all the nether-space, I've seen that place out there, and it's as dry as a desert waste. And you're saying you can somehow restore it to life with some kind of ritual? Is this more of that magic of yours? I swear, I really want to learn more about this."

"You are welcome to join with us to observe it if you like. I am fairly sure we will have a number of witnesses to the occasion."

"Yes! I would like this very much."

"As would I," Kailen offers. "And would you allow us to bring a video recorder to document it?"

"Very well, Commander, why not," Thaelyn affirms. "Just keep in mind it brings about gale force winds, so you should secure any loose objects very tightly. You may wish to confer with Kaliya on this matter, as she has already been there once."

"Thank you."

Several days have passed and preparations were underway on Morndindor for the delivery of the new life-seed. Kaliya and Ayene were coordinating the dismantling of the base structures, and Captain Hagmaert was preparing to move his outpost closer to Glimmerheim so he could work as an intermediary and assist in developing the region, at least until a more official office was established with a proper ambassadorial representative.

By this time, the dwarves had been fully informed of the story of Sargeras and Darumon, along with Thaelyn and his efforts, and the march towards Azgarén. Word was spreading through the streets relating to the coming of the new Tree of Life, and many of the citizens were preparing to participate as witnesses. Tol and his people were slowly returning home, and the stories of their life on Therinë continued to stir up fascination for the kingdom and its prosperous attraction.

As a new week arrived, Thaelyn made his journey to Morndindor. He was joined by a full assembly of his officers, including the General, Commander Nazég, Lieutenant Lapäli, and Captain Hagmaert. Kaliya stood at his side to help coordinate the gathering of bystanders, since she had previous experience with this event.

Belrum and Tol also joined the scene, along with their wives, and many others who were now coming outside to witness the occasion. The Chancellor followed close behind as he consulted with Tol and Eiki, in hopes of spending a moment in conference with Thaelyn.

An assembly of druids was forming in a region of the valley at a distance from the outer city. This would be Ground Zero, to allow a broad range of coverage across the surrounding area. The effect would cover a wide radius, and it was important to reclaim as much land as possible in order for it to produce the necessary resources to provide for all the subsequent outposts and shrines that would eventually dot the land. But most of the spectators were keeping at a safe distance on recommendation for the disturbance caused by the druidic storm.

"Which one be he, Eiki?" the Chancellor mutters nervously.

"Over yon, Chancellor," she replies reassuringly. "The tall one with the right fancy armor an' cape..."

"They all look like a mighty tall folk, especially those Daanen-Aryku. Oi...be they the menfolk of their kin?" he points discreetly at the Commander and the Lieutenant.

"Aye t' that! An' that one be a fine commander of their army."

"Great All-Father! What be this war about, ay? A war of gods, titans, an' sturdy tall folk leapin' from one world t' another…"

As the two of them worked their way across the field, Thaelyn was finishing up a few last-minute details of organizing the spectators.

"Commander," he directs. "You and yours should take up to the side, so you can make a better record of the event. A broader view will be desired, and not only of my position, but of the general area. And remember to hold on tight, as we would not wish you to be carried away by it," he grins.

"Of course, Your Lordship," Kailen accedes. "And I have to admit, I'm a little nervous about this, based on Kaliya's depiction from her earlier experience. I still recall those first days where our long-range scouts reported those huge disturbances over the mountains resembling something like a heavy bomb blast, and then a fierce storm of some kind. But anyway, we have several people with video cameras, each with their assigned tasks to record different aspects of it."

"Excellent."

The Chancellor was fidgeting anxiously the closer he came to the gathering. Eiki was walking alongside him trying to comfort him along the way.

"Chancellor, what be ye about here? Ye're gettin' yer whiskers all tied up in knots!"

"Eiki, I'll tell ye true, me innards be a-twistin' up on me. He be a King. That yay be a fine highborn stand, t' be sure. An' look at me," he glances down at himself.

"Chancellor, he be a kind an' goodly soul, nay anythin' like the Thane used t' be, ye can be sure of that!"

"Aye, so ye say, but I nay can help me'self from twitchin'."

Eiki shakes her head humorously as they continue towards Thaelyn and his delegation.

Relissa, Haran, Marelle, and their Daanen'kai friends, as well as Ayene, were arriving through a portal onto the scene from the guildhall. The first thing Relissa noticed as she set foot on the ground was the high gravity.

"Buggers!" she yelps as she stumbles away from the portal exit. "Haran! Why did I let you talk me into this bit?"

"Oh, come now, Relissa," he retorts soothingly. "This shouldn't be anywhere near as bad as the first one."

"Aye, sure!" she perks up enthusiastically. "If it's so great, you go first!"

Relissa twists around and starts pushing, and taking shelter behind him.

"Hey!" he protests. "I beg your pardon…"

"Relissa," Marelle mentions. "Leave a little room for me, will you?"

"Wow," Sulíma moans. "I feel so heavy here."

"This is the first time for all of us, Suli," Túfula admits. "One thing is for sure; we're getting a lot of experience travelling to other worlds lately."

"Are the two of you alright?" Petrith asks. "I would offer to carry you, but under the circumstances, I think I could only lift one at a time here."

"I'll manage," Sulíma relents. "I really want to see what this is about, so I'll get through it somehow."

"For all I've seen so far of your magic," Ayene muses. "I'm still baffled at how someone can invoke such a torrent as what you described, Relissa."

"Stick around long enough," she snaps playfully, "and you'll be wondering why you wanted to see it at all."

The group worked their way across the field, taking notice of Kailen rejoining a group of Daanen-Aryku gathering on one side. He was relaying instructions and checking their condition, including his young bride who was also attending.

"Ankhia, are you sure you can handle this?"

"Kailen, there are a lot of things in this new life I want to experience, and this is one of them."

"I understand. Just stay close. How is little Sani?"

"He's fine. I have Tyanna watching over him while I'm out."

Eiki and the Chancellor finally made it out to Thaelyn's

delegation. The elder dwarf hunched low with his hands clasped together in expectation of his formal audience.

"Yer Kingship," Eiki announces. "Mayhap ye have a moment for a word afore ye go in t' yer work out there?"

Thaelyn turned to see the two dwarves presenting themselves forward.

"Ah, Eiki, of course... I think we can surely spend a moment in light conversation."

"That be a grand thing. This old frizzle-beard here," she teases to lighten the mood, "for all his twitchin', be our good Chancellor. He had a wish t' speak with ye, if ye have time t' give yer ear for it."

"Indeed, I was made aware of his desire. Dear Chancellor, please rise up. I have found myself saying this numerous times by now, but you do not need to bend so low before me."

"Thank ye, Yer Kingship," he responds timidly. "I be a humble old man who's seen many a day pass before me, an' a good few of those be with our old Thane, may he burn for all he did t' us."

"Yes, I am well aware of his treatment, and not only to you, but to all of your people, and even his own kind, so it would seem."

"Aye, an' now we find ourselves with nay a sturdy soul, with stout arms an' iron whiskers, t' pull himself up t' the task. There was once a good long history t' our people of great men who took up great deeds, an' we sung many a song t' their good name."

"This is the way of many dwarves, even those who make their homes on our world. Your people have a long tradition of this sort."

"Eiki an' many of the folk from outside tell the tales of yer good deeds. Her husband Tol, an' also Belrum from out yon, an' many of his kin who took up with ye durin' this hard time. I nay can be a-knowin' how ye can manage it all, but any a man who can d' all this, surely be one for many a long tale, an' much more than that."

"Chancellor, if I may, before we go any further, I wish to make it clear, as I know where this is leading. You should know it was not my intention to come here and perform such heroic deeds to convince your people to follow me over any other qualified leader native to your society. This war has driven me to make many turns that I might not have otherwise expected, and this includes taking many new people, as well as two new worlds into my keep. I will admit it is a bit surprising to see where I stand now."

"Mayhap, but ye can'na deny how ye came here t' a world ye knew nothin' about, an' helped a people who were a-dyin' that nay were yer own, givin' them food an' shelter, an' what more t' be a-goin' out in t' this dyin' land that nay be yer own, an' sendin' yer people t' save that which ye nay even need t' be a-botherin' with, an' for what? Ye give yer honest word that it nay be more than the kindness of yer soul? Yer Kingship, there nay be a man or woman alive that would turn away from this deed. For all the Thanes an' other great men we ever had, ye'd be the top of the mountain for it!"

As Thaelyn listened to the Chancellor, he felt a strong rush of emotion flowing through him for the lofty praise and commendation. He was speechless for an extended period after the Chancellor finished, and dropped his gaze in a moment of quiet contemplation.

"Chancellor, it is simply by my nature, and that of my Father and his kind. This is how we are taught, nothing more."

"Aye t' that, then!" he responds exuberantly. "An' if this be the way of it, I nay can call it any better. Yer Kingship, the people of Glimmerheim, for all that we have t' offer ye, would yay ask ye t' take us as yer new folk. They be good kin, an' will serve ye t' their dyin' days. Mayhap ye would consider this?"

"I would be most honored," he bows politely. "Some might even say this would be a natural conclusion, where we already have so many that we hold dear to us, that we now bring the rest into it. The stout folk are a welcome sight amongst us, as are all my Children," he scans the surrounding assembly. "I hold each of them in endearment for their special gifts, and surely you are no different. We have a special rite we make of new aspirants to my kingdom…an oath they should take to swear their allegiance. Perhaps we could attend to that later after we are finished with this ceremony."

"Aye then, that be a fine one, an' I'll be a-tellin' the folk t' make ready for it."

"There will be many details to work out, language being one, as my people speak a different common form than yours. We will offer your people lessons to help you get started, as well as an introduction to a rather lengthy list of other chores ahead of us, not the least of which is an idea I had not long ago as I look at the remains of this mountain and what we can do to rebuild your city."

"Oh?" he turns to glance at the landslide and pulverized remains of the mountainside. "If I may, what be this idea ye have?"

"Clearly, this rock is too loose to be of any proper service for us to build on…or under, for that matter. I was thinking we could clear it out completely to open up the side and reveal the sturdy bedrock again. Then we could build an elaborate terraced cityscape many stories high as it emerges back out here onto the land. You would have your space under the mountain, the return of your outer city, and reaching upwards with the mountain itself. The dwarves of Tae'Eladar have created some fabulous engineering designs in their day. We could borrow from that, and I could have my people draw up some concept designs to give you an idea of how it might look."

The Chancellor gazed at the mountainside and the rubble that had collapsed from the bombardment. He tried to envision a new city rising up from the ground and reaching out onto the land, as well as touching the existing city inside. The vision seemed surreal, but at the same time it would represent a marvel to bring back the glory of their former home.

"That would be right amazin', t' be sure…" he muses. "Aye! I'd like t' see what ye have in mind for it. But now, I think I should be on with me'self, an' let ye be on with yer work. Yer Kingship, I hope t' be offerin' ye a good service t' help me kinfolk. I may be gray in the beard, but I nay be ready for me bed just yet."

"This is good to hear, as I think we will be spending much time together to settle the needs of the city, and more outside."

The Chancellor bows politely and departs, along with Eiki, as they return back across the field to find Tol and others huddled together in a group.

Thaelyn conducted another survey of the area. Everyone seemed to be settling into position by now. He then turned and ambled out to the cluster of druids.

"Priestess Rumoren, are we ready?"

"Yes, my Lord, we are assembled and awaiting your company."

"Captain Hagmaert, see to it our friends are informed that we are ready to proceed."

"Right away, my Lord," he shouts and heads off to the Daanen-Aryku and other native guests.

"Kaliya..." Thaelyn calls out boldly.

Kaliya was overseeing the arrangement of the dwarven visitors when she heard her name echoing across the field. She turns promptly at the summons.

"Yes, my Lord!"

"Give the word we are about to begin, and remind them to keep low and secure any loose articles."

"Absolutely!" she returns eagerly.

Thaelyn enters the circle of druids and takes up his druidic staff of twisted vines from one of the members. He stands in the center of the circle and pulls out a small compass to orient himself northward. The circle adjusts to his new direction. He puts it away and waits for the druidic high priestess to make her approach.

The ritual followed in the same fashion as it did that first day, when Thaelyn made his initial appearance in the Badlands. He set the staff to the side, where it stood erect as if held in place by an unseen force, while the high priestess made her entrance with a small satchel closed by drawstrings.

"What's keeping that staff standing upright?" Ankhia hushes.

"Don't ask, probably more of their magic," Kailen responds.

"This looks like some sort of holy ritual," Túfula observes.

"Aye," Relissa admits. "Those are druids out there, like what I hear that girl Tana is studying now. And the seed and the tree are sacred objects to us, especially us elves."

"So..." Ayene ponders. "This is at least as much a holy ritual as it might be magic of some sort?"

"Aye, but priest magic and arcane magic are two different items."

Thaelyn formed a cup with his hands as the priestess opened the satchel and poured out a quantity of enchanted glowing dust. Once the pouch was empty, she backs away while Thaelyn lifts his hands to the sky for a moment of pause. The druids in the circle begin a murmuring chant as Thaelyn shifts the dust to one hand and swings his free hand in a wide semi-circle down on top of the mound, capping it and gently rubbing to cause the contents to trickle out. The flow follows a curious downward swirl around him into the ground at his feet, causing the soil to glow briefly. After that, he relaxes and the chanting stops.

By this time, Kaliya had returned from her interaction with the dwarves and took up next to Kailen.

"And now for the fun part," she mumbles expectantly.

"Aye," Relissa declares. "Hold on tight, folks. Here's where it gets rough."

Thaelyn snapped open his hand, allowing the staff to jump into it. The druid circle begins a determined song, swaying to the sides and moving their arms in small arcs. They continue this way for several moments, and the air seems to become charged. The sensation wafts outward among the assembled guests, tingling the hair on their arms and the back of their necks. He brings up the staff in front of him, holds it briefly, and thrusts it firmly to the ground. The impact sends a soft echo through the soil.

"Did I just hear something?" Sulíma wonders.

The druid circle now elevates their chants, calling out much louder. The simple swaying motion now turns to the jumping and hopping dance of the second phase of the ritual, with their arms swinging fully around. The air begins moving in a gentle breeze, and the sky above shows a haze forming.

Ankhia takes notice of the sudden shift in the air currents. She makes circles around her trying to understand where it was coming from, until she looks up and sees the once-clear sky now changing. She instinctively reaches to grab Kailen's arm and pulls herself in.

The voices of the druidic chant rise and fall, and their dance turns them around in slow circles. The breezes increase to a moderate wind, and the sky becomes cloudy, until it finally blots out the sun.

"Kailen," Ankhia shudders. "I think I'm having second thoughts on this."

"Great All-Father!" the Chancellor cries. "Look at that, will ye! He be a-callin' up the four winds an' the clouds above!"

"This is irrational," Ayene mumbles nervously. "Can this strange force actually alter the weather patterns so much?"

Thaelyn brings up his staff again. He turns it outward in his hand as he crouches low to the ground, preparing for a powerful jump. In order for him to make this maneuver here, it was necessary to enchant himself on arrival with additional strength to compensate for the high gravity. On his cue, he vaults upward above the heads of the circle, bringing his staff to bear again and pounding it firmly into the ground as he landed, sending a thundering reverberation through the land.

Sulíma jumps as she felt the wave rumble under her.

"Petrith, you said you could only hold one? Well, it's going to be me, because I'm climbing on your back soon."

"And that's only the second one," Relissa quips.

"There's more?"

"Aye, and when the third one hits, that's when we hit the dirt."

The druid circle now takes on its third stage of activity, which was boisterous and rambunctious. The level of energy elevated to a frenzy, with loud clamoring shrieks and vigorous swirls, twirls, jumps, and bows. Their arms now waved high and low in wide arcs and spins, and with this new level of dance came a new level of alteration to the weather. The winds magnified strongly, and the sky grew dark, and in the distance, lightning began to flash.

Ayene jerked around at the first rumbling sounds, trying to follow the spectacle from all angles.

"In all the nether-space!" she yips. "He's tearing the place up!"

"Blessed Mother," Eiki drones. "What be he a-callin' down on us here?"

"Kailen!" Ankhia flusters. "I don't like being out here! Not with all that going on over our heads."

"You asked for it, but we'll get through it. Just hold on tight."

The druidic dance carries them in arcs around the circle and back again, periodically throwing up their arms and hollering loudly as a spike in the vociferous wail.

The winds now blast the land at gale force, making the full assembly take shelter within each other's arms and huddling low to the ground. The sky was now menacingly black and streaked with countless webs of lightning, which was the primary source of illumination by this time. And above their heads they witnessed a swirling maelstrom.

"No!" Ankhia screeches as she buries herself in Kailen's shoulder. "I'm too young! I just became a mother! I can't go yet; I owe it to my parents!"

"Lads!" shouts Belrum. "It looks like we're getting set for a mighty pummlin'. Hold on t' yer pretties, or ye might lose them!"

"This is impossible!" Ayene shrieks at the sky above. "There is no power in existence that can generate this much energy, let alone contain it!"

The winds turn in a spiral to match the swirling vortex above, creating a funnel out of the dusty land around the circle.

"Cu'Nar's eyes!" Kailen yells. "He's creating a cyclone! Get down hard!"

The surges of lightning blanket the heavens, intensifying and coalescing as a never-ending spray of electrical fury. And then the display realigns itself, with the chaotic webbing now turning to directed bolts, masses of them, pouring into the vortex.

"In the name of the Soul Forger!" the Chancellor bellows. "It be a-comin'!"

"Petrith!" Sulíma screeches and buries herself under him.

"Leave room for me, you twit!" Túfula screeches back, and burrows under the other side.

Ayene screams as she angles her head up into the raging tempest.

"All right! I'm sorry! I believe!" she sobs. "Whatever's up there, please don't hurt me! I'm fragile!"

Relissa grabs her from one side, and Marelle climbs over to take the other side, and together they huddle close.

Thaelyn brings his staff around once more for his final strike. He raises it in front of him. The crowd watches intently as he holds himself steady, seemingly oblivious to the raucous activity of the winds and lightning, and the furor of the circle of druids. By now, the vortex is glowing with highly charged energy.

"If that comes down here," Ankhia screams into Kailen's ear. "We're all dead!"

The potent streams of lightning now change color to a yellowish green.

"What in all the nether-space is that?!" Petrith shouts. "That doesn't even look natural!"

Thaelyn readies himself, turning his staff to the side again and crouching for another leap. The circle of druids halts their movement and stretches their arms skyward, bellowing one final outpour. The cyclonic winds racing around the scene suddenly alter course, turning inward to the circle and lifting up, and with this, Thaelyn leaps into the updraft, allowing it to carry him aloft well above the land.

The eyes of the crowd follow him as he rockets vertically towards the eye of the storm, and as his momentum slows, the winds die and the lightning ceases. The scene goes eerily quiet.

"Is that it?" Ayene whimpers.

"Nope," Relissa replies assertively.

Ayene jerks her head around and shoots a hard stare at the dark elf.

"I hate you!" she blasts briskly.

"Lads!" Tol shouts to the group. "Grip yerselves hard! I have a bad feelin' about this!"

"May the Shield Brothers protect us all!" shouts another dwarf.

"Kaliya, what happens next?" Ankhia urges.

"Now comes the good part," she returns calmly.

"What's good about this?!" Ankhia shrieks.

Thaelyn's ascent comes to a halt, and now he makes his downward motion. The winds pick up in a powerfully accelerating downdraft. The vortex above releases its energy within fierce bolts directed into the bodies of the druids in the circle.

"People cannot survive that!" Ankhia yelps.

The vortex itself is next to move, following Thaelyn and descending towards the land. He makes impact and slams his staff into the earth, the force of the blow blasting dirt and rock outward in a wide spray, while sending a massive shockwave ripple through the land. The vortex strikes the ground and envelops the circle in a dense violent whirlwind that expands rapidly outward as more of the sky plunges down. High-velocity winds rush past the bodies of the spectators, pelting them with small particles of sand and rock. The ground reverberated, and waves of yellow-green energy flashed all around them within the murky cloud. But soon the eye of the storm opened up inside the circle and quickly expanded, causing the inner storm wall to move past the visitors and leaving clear sky over their heads again.

Ayene popped her head up promptly as she realized the winds had died off and light returned. She turned to observe the receding wall of clouds as it poured down onto the land in a wide circle, still flashing with energy and moving off in the distance.

"Now is it over?" she asks tentatively.

"Aye, that part is over," Relissa answers soothingly.

"Kailen," Ankhia murmurs gently in his ear. "Can we go home now?"

"Ankhia," Kaliya whispers. "Why would you want to go home? You haven't seen the grand finish yet."

"Please don't tell me there's more."

Tol and the other dwarves struggled desperately to pull themselves together, spitting out dirt and brushing themselves off. Ankhia surveys the circle of druids to see they're all lying motionless on the ground.

"You see? I told you, people can't survive that. Now what... Am I supposed to go out there and try resuscitating them?"

"They're not actually dead," Kaliya offers. "Just stunned."

"Stunned?" she returns audaciously. "Kaliya, I would bet that if I went out there with a scanner to measure the volume of energy coming down, it would go off the scale. And I'm talking about an industrial strength scanner here!"

"Yeah, maybe so, but this is a different sort. Druidic magic isn't the same as the arcane stuff I've been learning, and it's supposed to be compatible with living things."

"Yeah, sure... So, what's the next miracle we're supposed to see?"

"It should be popping up...right...about...now..."

Kaliya climbed to her feet, drawing up Ankhia and Kailen. She then casts her gaze downwards.

Ankhia followed her stare, wondering what she was supposed to be looking at, until it dawned on her how the composition of the soil had changed.

"Cu'Nar's grace..." she wheezes.

She kneels down to examine it just as something started to move. She jerks back.

"Kaliya, what's under there?" she asks urgently.

Sulíma and Túfula had pulled themselves out from under Petrith and were studying the scene when they also noticed something moving just in front of their faces on the ground. Sulíma shrieked and jumped on top of Petrith, followed shortly after by Túfula, and the two of them now fought over what little real estate was available on his back.

"Hey! What are you doing?" he grumbles as he tries to hold his head up. "Get off, you're smothering me!"

Ayene jumped nervously to her feet at the sight, while Relissa casually pulled herself up, and dusted herself off in the process. Marelle also hoisted herself upright briskly, not knowing for sure what to expect.

The dwarves all began to jump as they saw the beginnings of slender green tendrils shooting out of the soil and wriggling into the sunlight.

"Great All-Father, what be that now?" calls one of the members.

The scene began to transform as the barren land turned green with fresh grass sprouting out of the rejuvenated soil at an unnatural rate. At various locations, saplings began shooting up, also growing at breakneck speed. The air filled with the freshness of springtime. Flowering shrubs were blossoming, wooded groves thickened, and green meadows formed.

The gathering of onlookers gazed in awe of the spectacle. Ayene made a full survey of the land, trying to catch every aspect of it. Kailen and Ankhia were left speechless, and Marelle simply shook her head in disbelief.

"So, this is what happened in the Badlands that day."

Ayene felt weak in the knees. She was overwhelmed by the unparalleled forces she witnessed and their obvious result.

"Relissa…" she mutters timidly. "When we get back home, would you please help me to visit Lady Aerlie? I'm going to need some therapy after this."

She pauses a moment, glancing down at herself.

"And I also think I need to change my underwear," she peeks around abashedly.

"Ayene," Ankhia mentions. "Save a seat for me, as well. There's clearly something I'm missing here, and this would certainly rub a person's nose in it."

After several long moments, the Druids returned to life, and Thaelyn found his strength to stand up again. He repositioned himself in the circle and the high priestess came forward with the life-seed, cradling it in her hands and transferring it to his. As before, he holds it up to the sky and the circle begins another low murmuring chant. He kneels to the ground and digs out a small hole, setting the seed inside and covering it up carefully. He stands up again, takes his staff and waves it over the seed, sprinkling a shower of yellow-green sparkles onto it, and then steps back.

The crowd waits, and a short moment later the ground begins to stir, with a small shoot breaking through and growing into a young sapling. It extends upward until it reaches over Thaelyn's head before slowing to a stop. He moves in front and offers his respect by kneeling before it.

"An' that there be the tree, I reckon?" the Chancellor wonders.

"Aye t' that, Chancellor," replies Tol. "An' this nay be a tree ye'll ever take an axe t', if ye know what be good for ye. This one will make the land fertile an' the air sweet. An' when it grows up strong, it'll make the world a right fine place t' live for many a kinfolk."

"Nay in me life did I ever see soil like this afore," Belrum marvels. "I know he be a great leader an' a sturdy warrior, but how d' ye describe this here?"

"Be he a man, or a god, d' ye think?" Eiki wonders.

"Eiki, me love," Tol answers. "He be a wee bit of both."

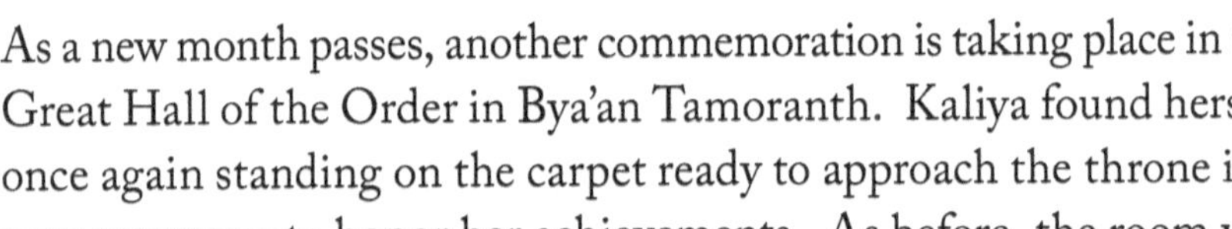

As a new month passes, another commemoration is taking place in the Great Hall of the Order in Bya'an Tamoranth. Kaliya found herself once again standing on the carpet ready to approach the throne in a new ceremony to honor her achievements. As before, the room was filled with friends, classmates, and her fellow teammates to oversee the event. Although, on this occasion, they could not invite Velen or the Elder Council, as the details leading up to this achievement were part of their military movements, to which the Council had to be kept unaware, due to their security issues with Darumon.

Thaelyn had positioned himself on his throne, and two attendants stood ready at his side. Once the audience had settled, he gave his announcement.

"Lieutenant Kaliya Nazég, approach and be recognized."

Kaliya made her approach in tune with the drumroll. The scene was once again being recorded by Padriyl on his camera for posterity. When she arrived at the steps, she offered her salute and knelt down.

"We have gathered here once again…so it would seem," Thaelyn chuckles lightly.

The room shares the moment of humor with soft laughs and quiet murmurs.

"Kaliya, you are setting a series of standards that are proving difficult to follow. But your inspirational leadership and enthusiasm is doing exactly that, driving others to the same level of excellence as what you have chosen for yourself. In addition, the Stormhooves are developing as a membership deserving of its own commemorative merits and honors. It is also becoming apparent that it will demand its own special training portfolio. Due to the unique nature of this body, I feel new trainees will need to participate in enhanced studies of politics, diplomacy, philosophy, and even a fair amount of theatrical study."

Kaliya felt a sudden rush of tension pass through her at the thought of so many additional courses being added into the mix.

"Fortunately for you," Thaelyn comforts. "You have the lifespans to afford it."

The room ushers up another round of laughter. This also eases Kaliya's stress a little as she joins the humorous moment.

"As we move forward in our pursuit of Darumon and Sargeras, we find ourselves in need to expand our limits and capacities. But along the way, we must give credit to those who have overcome challenges that travel outside the common realm of traditional military exercise. The Stormhooves is clearly a breed unto itself, and due to the recent successes you and yours have achieved on Morndindor, we must bestow upon you a new honor."

He motions for the first of the two attendants to step forward.

"And since you are also devoted as a paladin of Lord Oghma, we feel this would be appropriate to credit under his domain. We will call this one the Sight of Continuity, to commemorate the fulfillment of protecting those from themselves and their unknowing actions, while at the same time deterring the wrongful actions of others."

The attendant opens his box and presents the badge to Kaliya. She studies it alluringly as he pulls it out. It was oblong like her previous one, but with a starry background and an all-seeing eye in the upper left corner gazing down at an open scroll opposing it.

"Ooh," she croons. "That's a nice one."

He pins it to her jacket, and then steps away.

Thaelyn continues, "The duties that wait for us will demand many to serve in ways we can only imagine thus far. This will require enhanced leadership. Therefore, you must now rise to a new level of prestige. And even though it has been said by some…" he glares teasingly at Ayene in the audience, "…that you are…only… four centuries old…" he smirks.

The crowd now rises in a bold laugh at the suggestion, while Ayene blushes at being the brief center of attention. Kaliya also felt a relaxing moment to let go a little of her own.

"It becomes clear to me," Thaelyn resumes, "that you have a gift…and I know talent when I see it. And so, we must now bestow upon you the capacity to carry us to this new extreme, where you will hold greater regard, greater responsibility, and greater opportunity for troublemaking," he grins.

Now the audience gives up a loud cheer, as well as more laughter.

"And greater chance for more marks on your list too, I'll bet," she responds eagerly.

"Indeed! I think the General is planning on writing a book on you by now."

He now motions for the next attendant to step forward with his box. He approaches and opens it to reveal her new rank insignia. He then affixes it to her jacket, replacing the old one, which he hands back to her to keep as a memento. When he is done, he returns to his former post.

"From this moment forward," Thaelyn concludes. "You will command more of your troops into the field…may the Powers help us for whatever results this will bring," he chuckles again. "But by the looks of it, we will need them. Rise and present yourself, Captain Kaliya Nazég."

The audience now rises up in full applause and cheering. Kaliya turns to present herself. She is then greeted by pats and hugs from friends and classmates, kisses from Kailen and Tyanna, and playful jeers from Relissa and her friends.

✦✦✦✦✦✦✦

In the days that followed, Kaliya had arranged a new team consisting of a full company. This would represent her new command. She selected and briefed them on their mission objectives, which would now involve an official incursion of Azgarén. But before they could begin, they had to prepare themselves, and this involved sharing the memory image of their first landfall foothold.

Thaelyn was holding a special gathering in the WIC building for the occasion. Kaliya, Ayene, and Petrith were all present, as each of them was familiar with the initial landing site. The rest of the team had lined up for processing, forming up rows in front of the three founts, where they would sit in chairs and link telepathically to share the vision of their destination. As each of them took their turn, they retreated to another room where a large number of chairs had been positioned for them to relax and project themselves. Once the entire assembly was ready in projected form, they reassembled at attention for a final review. Thaelyn inspected the troops as they lined themselves up.

"On this day," he declares fervently. "Darumon shall feel the weight of our providence pressing down on him. We defeated him on our soil. We defeated him on foreign soil. And now, we shall defeat him on that soil he has taken as his own. He will learn his time was at an end an epoch ago. He should never have come back, and neither should he have made such mischief along the way. Now, he and his master will meet the same as the rest of their kind. Brothers and Sisters of the Order; launch forward and carry us to those far places. Set our feet on that world that was once your home and let us take it back unto ourselves. We shall educate those who are unaware of his true origins and liberate them from his grip. And he shall not know of it until we are ready to meet him on our terms, not his!"

The assembly lets out a holler and salutes proudly. Kaliya then turns to face them and gives the signal, and the full group vanishes in a puff.

On a darkened hillside, on a far distant world, a curious sight appears out of the night. Kaliya and her team arrive on a modest mesa overlooking the city of Capitol Prime in the distance. She immediately turns to assess her group.

"Welcome to Azgarén, everyone…we're back! First, I need a head count. Squad leaders; call up your groups and report forward."

The groups form up and the leaders take a roll call, reporting that the full assembly was present and accounted for.

"Good!" she asserts. "Now, everyone, make careful note of where we are. Burn it deep into your memories. We'll be making a lot of return trips here. And no doubt, we'll need to become familiar with a lot of other places we might visit."

They all examine the local terrain, refreshing their memory images, and taking notes of what is now a personal experience, rather than the borrowed memory. Kaliya waits as she studies the group until it recomposes itself.

"All right, how do we all feel about a nice little jaunt? Everyone, change to birds and take to the skies!"

The full assembly reimagines themselves as birds and takes off as a flock, moving away in formation for a brisk flight around the city and the surrounding area.

To anyone who might have been observing on the ground, the sight would be a most unusual one, for all the environmental and ecological damage the world has taken during the time Darumon has dominated the scene. It would be even more curious for the specific breed in play here, as it was clearly a non-native species. But to the benefit of Kaliya and her team, no one was present out here on the hillside. And even as they passed over the city, the general population was too centered on their personal activities to notice birds in the sky. Nothing that interesting has ever occurred in this world…not in living memory at least. And so, Kaliya and her troupe enjoyed a pleasant tour of their ancestral home without any special notice, as they prepared themselves for their grand homecoming.

TO BE CONTINUED